D0839955

THE DAWN OF FREEDOM

For a long time Mary sat looking out into the garden. She did not see the silver moon on the moving water of the Sound or hear the nightingale in the East Garden. The moon went slowly from sight behind the dark massed spire of pinewood that fringed the shore. She sat motionless for many hours until banners of red flamed across the eastern sky. The sun came up—another day. But it could never be the same. Brother had fought against brother on the soil of Carolina. A battle had been fought—the first battle of revolt against the King and the King's government. What would be the end? In her mind came a picture—lines of men marching; endless lines of men—young, old —marching to the beat of drums. . . .

Here lay the destiny of her country and her people.

Bantam Books by Inglis Fletcher
Ask your bookseller for the books you have missed

BENNETT'S WELCOME
LUSTY WIND FOR CAROLINA
MEN OF ALBEMARLE
RALEIGH'S EDEN
ROANOKE HUNDRED

Raleigh's Eden

by Inglis Fletcher

BANTAM BOOKS

TORONTO • NEW YORK • LONDON • SYDNEY • AUCKLAND

*This low-priced Bantam Book
has been completely reset in a type face
designed for easy reading, and was printed
from new plates. It contains the complete
text of the original hard-cover edition.*
NOT ONE WORD HAS BEEN OMITTED.

RALEIGH'S EDEN

*A Bantam Book / published by arrangement with
The Bobbs-Merrill Company*

PRINTING HISTORY

*Bobbs-Merrill edition published September 1940
7 printings through September 1947*

*Dollar Book Club edition published July 1941
2nd printing . . . . October 1941
3rd printing . . . . . . December 1941*

Bantam edition / March 1970

2nd printing . . February 1971	5th printing . . September 1974
3rd printing . November 1971	6th printing . . . . March 1976
4th printing . . . October 1972	7th printing . . November 1980
	8th printing . . . August 1986

*All rights reserved.
Copyright 1940 by The Bobbs-Merrill Company.
Copyright © renewed 1968, by The Bobbs-Merrill Company.
Cover art copyright © 1986 by Bantam Books, Inc.
This book may not be reproduced in whole or in part, by
mimeograph or any other means, without permission.
For information address: The Bobbs-Merrill Company,
A division of Macmillan Publishing Company,
866 Third Avenue, New York, NY 10022.*

ISBN 0-553-25950-4

Published simultaneously in the United States and Canada

*Bantam Books are published by Bantam Books, Inc. Its trade-
mark, consisting of the words "Bantam Books" and the por-
trayal of a rooster, is Registered in U.S. Patent and Trademark
Office and in other countries. Marca Registrada. Bantam
Books, Inc., 666 Fifth Avenue, New York, New York 10103.*

PRINTED IN THE UNITED STATES OF AMERICA

KR   17 16 15 14 13 12 11 10 9 8

TO
MY MOTHER FLORA CHAPMAN CLARK
AND HER PEOPLE THE CAROLINIANS

Contents

BOOK ONE

BOOK TWO

BOOK THREE

BOOK FOUR

Acknowledgment

FIRST, I wish to express my obligation to my Grandfather, Joseph Chapman, who died many years ago, for my first interest in the history of his native state, North Carolina. I can well remember him, tall, thin, judicial, sitting in his armchair by a roaring fire, his long sensitive hands resting on the carved mahogany dogs that formed the arms of the chair. He had a love of history—a genius for narrative and a sense of humor.

"I was born," he used to say, with a twinkle in his bright eyes, "in that valley of Humiliation, between two mountains of Conceit," which was his way of explaining the lack of knowledge the average person had of the Colonial and Revolutionary history of North Carolina, while Virginia and South Carolina basked in the sun.

The second thing that interested me was the variety of races and religions represented in the Royal Province: French Huguenots; Germans and Quakers; Highlanders and Lowland Scots; and the English gentlemen who came to the coastal regions with their slaves and household treasures and established themselves as they had lived in the English country. Then there were the sturdy English yeomen and husbandmen in the western counties; indentured men—and women—who had been young gentlemen, rebels to civil authority; and indentured men, the thieves and rascals of London. Even Arabs came to live and make their homes in Carolina. Pirates frequented the islands and inlets while honest men built villages and towns and cultivated the rich land and gained wealth from the great forests. Out of this rich and varied racial background the sturdy independent Province had its inception. From the time the Gentlemen Adventurers from England came to Raleigh's Eden under the Lords Proprietors to the time of the Revolution it maintained its independence, and has until this day.

In writing a historical novel the problem is not to turn fiction into fact but to make a fact appear to be fiction. Out of the rich storehouse of Provincial history it is difficult to select the incidents that best illustrate the character of the people and their lives.

One thing stands out prominently in the Colonial and Revolutionary history of North Carolina. That is the close association of the Royal Province with England and the West Indies in trade and in social intercourse.

The northern Colonies and cities, New York, Boston and Philadelphia, were little known to the Carolinians. They sent the products of their plantations direct to England, or to the West Indies. They traded with Portugal, Spain and the Barbary States, even with India. Before the Revolution the sons of the rich planters were sent to school in England or France rather than to the universities in the northern Colonies. But during the Revolution all this changed and the new unity came into being.

There has been no effort to treat the material as chronological history. My aim has been rather to accent the thought of the people, their way of living; particularly, to show the effect of the Revolution on the lives of the people of one district. I have tried, in all political discussions by historical characters, to use their own words taken from letters, memoirs and journals.

I made two journeys to North Carolina to familiarize myself with the background, to visit libraries and museums, and to talk with people who knew the early history. Everywhere I found great sympathy for my undertaking. I wish to thank the persons who helped me in my search for original material, and the members of the staffs of various libraries and museums where I visited.

Charlotte, North Carolina, Public Library
Cupola House Museum, Edenton, North Carolina
Congressional Library, Washington, D. C.
New York Public Library
Los Angeles Public Library
California State Library
Library of the United States Army, the Presidio of
    San Francisco
University of California, Bancroft Library
Vestry Records of St. Paul's Episcopal Church,
    Edenton, N. C.

I also wish to express my thanks to Miss Bruner, Librarian in the Sutro Branch of the State Library at San Francisco, for her interest and help over a period of months of research.

To Mr. Randolph Scott I am indebted for providing me with unusual facts about early Virginia and North Carolina families and their history, as well as historical data of Colonial North Carolina.

Balboa Beach, California　　　　　　　　　INGLIS FLETCHER
December, 1939

BOOK
ONE

THE HOUNDS
ARE RUNNING

A FAINT glow in the east caught the weather vane of Town Hall and gilded the spire of St. Paul's, rising above the leafless trees. The village below was silent, wrapped in the grey mists of early morning. An easterly wind was blowing off Albemarle Sound. It swung the wrought-iron sign of King's Arms Inn on its rusty hinges, and ruffled the feathers of the doves in the cote above the stables. It was September in the year of 1765. So far it had been a turbulent year in his Majesty's Province of North Carolina; what the winter and the new year would bring, no man could predict.

A troop of horse, riding out of the grey mists, splashed through the ford at Queen Anne's Creek and turned into the lane that led to Town Hall. A young officer gave a sharp command. Two sergeants dismounted and went up the steps. While one man held a torch, the other fastened a paper on the door. When he had almost finished he stood back, squaring it with his eye to the door panel, before he hammered the last tack with the butt of his pistol.

In a house that faced the Common's green a shutter opened cautiously. A head appeared, only to be quickly withdrawn. In the half-light, the red coats of the soldiers were black against the dawn-grey of the houses and trees, blending into a mosaic against the changing sky. Other shutters opened narrowly. At the far end of the Common's green a few herdsmen and boys from the farms crept out from their blankets and from under oxcarts. They had come to Edenton late the previous night to be ready for early Market. Now they stood in the shadows, watching sullenly.

The watchman, his aged body bent to meet the wind, made his way cautiously down the darkened street by the wharves. He tapped at the door of warehouses and shops, calling in a hoarse voice, "By the Mercy of God, five o'clock and all's well." He did not notice the shadowy moving figures of soldiers at the upper end of the Commons. His rheumy old eyes saw no farther than the rim of light cast by his ship's lantern.

Their task finished, the soldiers mounted again. The chang-

3

ing light shone on headpieces and cuirasses and touched the spearheads of fluttering pennants as the troops clattered down the lane. They passed the shadow of the church, riding swiftly, muskets slung over shoulders, each man holding in his bridle hand a bit of burning wood.

The villagers who had been watching saw the dragoons cut across the open fields to join the post road. A few miles away at Chowan Ferry the command waited. A bugle sounded. A moment later the rumble of heavy gun carriages began as cannon and culverins were dragged along the hard roads.

When the soldiers were far down the road, a few cloaked figures slipped out of their houses and moved like grey wraiths across the Commons, following the shelter of the deep shadows cast by trees and bushes. By the light of carefully shielded lanterns, they scanned the printed notice the redcoats had nailed on the paneled door.

The proclamation was signed by the Lieutenant-Governor. It concerned the billeting of soldiers. On December first, three hundred soldiers and officers, under the command of Colonel James Weavly, would be billeted in the village of Edenton and the precinct of Chowan. A special poll tax would be levied for the maintenance of said troops. Residents of the several villages in the district would pay the tax in coin. In lieu of cash farmers would be permitted to pay their due in provisions for soldiers and forage for horses and stock. Inhabitants of the precinct would treat his Majesty's soldiers with every consideration and courtesy. Below the signature of William Tryon was affixed the seal of the Royal Province of North Carolina.

The grey-cloaked men read the proclamation silently. Silently they crossed the square to their darkened homes. A sudden glow in the eastern sky splashed the floating clouds that hung along the horizon, turning them to crimson.

A new day had begun.

Market Fair and the Hunt crowded the courtyard of King's Arms Inn, overflowed the open field beyond Town Hall and filled the roads that converged at the Common's green.

The morning air vibrated with sound, the bustle and stir of the Market coming to life. Wagons were backed along the square to form booths where rosy-cheeked women sold their dairy products. Beyond the Inn, back of Town Hall, husbandmen were making ready for the horse and cattle auctions. Clouds of dust rose from the tramping hoofs and mingled with the acrid smell of closely packed cattle and damp wool.

Farm boys dressed in homespun shouted and kicked and cursed, driving cattle to the pegged rope lines for display to early buyers. Shepherds in faded blue smocks pulled their recalcitrant flocks with crooks while well-trained dogs nipped at the flanks and heels of bewildered sheep. Negro boys stood guard over fattened cattle and razorbacks. The creak of oxcarts rose shrilly above the neighing of horses and the shouts of men.

Adam Rutledge, planter, put his sorrel gelding over the footbridge that spanned the drain at the lower end of the green. He pulled up near a gaily striped carnival tent to watch the shifting spectacle of Market day.

Tall and lean, over six feet three in height, Adam had the broad shoulders, flat back and narrow waist of a man who has spent much of his life in the saddle. He sat his horse indolently, his long legs swinging free of the stirrups, as he watched the Market crowd. His coat of hunting "pink," his white cord breeches and his varnished boots were well seasoned, and by their cut showed their London make. Slung over one shoulder was a curved hunting horn of ancient design. Adam had been Master of the Albemarle Hunt ever since he had come down from Virginia, five years before, to take up his land on Albemarle Sound. He was an heir to John Archdale, one of the eight Lords Proprietors who held most of the Carolinas under the Great Charter.

Now he watched the activity at the wharves with lazy interest. Barques and fishing craft were close together, piled high with the morning's catch. Turtles and crabs and shellfish were strewn along the wharf, ready for customers. For Edenton housewives sent their slaves early to Market to get the choice cuts of meat and fresh fish from the fishing grounds off the Banks.

A moccasined hunter, dressed in fringed deerskins, hawked venison and smoked turkey in a voice pitched to carry great distances. Adam caught his eye. The man's bronzed face lightened in a smile that displayed his white teeth. He made his way with the litheness of a forest animal through crowds of farmers and fishermen mending nets. At Adam's stirrup he stood holding up a smoked wild turkey wrapped in grape leaves.

"Twenty-four pounds, sir. As fine a bird as ye'll ever see. Shall I drop it at the plantation on the way back?"

Adam said, "What are you asking for it?"

The hunter grinned, showing his strong white teeth.

"Top price to you, Mr. Rutledge. Though I'd be asking the

Governor more, and mayhap the King. But I don't mind saying that I'd rather see a prime bird like this on your table than on the Hanoverian's."

"Treason, Enos Dye." Adam's tone was light. "The military have long ears these days." The grin faded from the hunter's face, a sullen look took its place. He stepped closer, his hand on Adam's stirrup.

"They can hear plenty of treasonable words if they are of a mind to listen to the people up Hillsborough way, Mr. Rutledge."

Adam quieted his horse and leaned over as if to examine the fowl.

"More trouble with the farmers, Dye?"

"Aye. That thief, Edmund Fanning! Why doesn't the Governor appoint a new recorder? Surely the people have complained enough."

Adam said, "Dobbs is a sick man. He doesn't know or care what is happening in the Province."

The hunter's jaw stiffened. His eyes met Adam's with quick understanding.

"We'll get no help from Tryon when he gets to be Governor."

"I think you are wrong, Dye. The Lieutenant-Governor has been handicapped by the whims of a sick old man. When he gets the power you will see."

"I hope yo're right, Mr. Rutledge. If there's much more of this selling land over people's heads when they've paid good money for their deeds, there will be trouble. The people will rebel. The farmers in the northern counties aren't men to be put upon for long."

A crowd of laughing, shouting children ran down the Commons. They were headed for the Punch and Judy show which was opening near the carnival tent. Adam lifted the reins, preparing to ride on.

"Keep me informed of what is going on in Orange and the northern counties, Dye. If you can't reach me, talk with Dr. Armitage. He will send me the message or give you advice, if you need it," he said in a low tone.

Two men in the uniform of noncommissioned officers drew near. Enos raised his voice.

"Thank ye, Mr. Rutledge. I'll leave the bird at your North Plantation. Thank ye." Slinging his turkey over his shoulder, the woodsman moved off and was lost in the crowd.

Adam rode slowly from the wharves toward King's Arms Inn at the head of the Commons. The sun was up now, and the crowds increasing. Booths that had been set up along the green consisted of wagons and carts backed up to display farm produce. Women and girls were decorating them with sumac, bunches of bittersweet and festoons of wild grape. The booths overflowed with plenty: butter, golden and firm, marked in quaint forms; shining pans of clotted cream, round cheeses, pumpkins and squash and red Indian corn dried on the cob; hickory-smoked ham and bacon; jellies and conserves, purple and red and golden; bottles and glass jugs of wine made from elderberry and wild grape; brandy from peaches.

Thought Adam, "This should be a year for thanksgiving in Albemarle. A full harvest and an open season; just enough rain for spring planting. We can be sure of good crops for another year." For the land and the work of the land was Adam Rutledge's first interest. A deep, inherited feeling that had come to him from long generations. Since the early times in England, the Kentish Rutledges had held land and loved it above all, save one thing: freedom from unjust taxes. "Free men of Kent," they were called. They had won the title after years of struggle and they held it with pride. In this Adam Rutledge was no different from his fathers.

Now he approached King's Arms Inn at the head of the Commons. He wanted to see the hounds which had been sent over recently from the Pytchley pack to the Inn kennels. The Hunt usually met at the Inn but today it would start from the wood back of St. Paul's Church.

The Blessing of the Hunt would be held this morning. The rector insisted on carrying on the old custom in the same manner as it was done at his home in Ireland. Every year a few of the younger planters protested, only to be laughed down by the "hunting parson," as Daniel Earl was affectionately called by his widespread congregation. His answer to protests was always the same. "Indeed, it will do you no harm to get up a half-hour earlier one morning in the season, me lads! Besides, it pleases me to have you all out at chapel at once. It's a brave sight you are, in your hunting pink; and there isn't a chapel in the Province that can say the same." So the custom continued from year to year.

The courtyard at the Inn was bright with color and movement. Planters sat on their hunters or walked about the galleries of the Inn. In the yard they mingled with farmers and husbandmen, talking of crops and bargaining for cattle and horses. They greeted old friends or bellowed orders for ale and brandy. Harassed barmen, their homespun breeches cov-

7

ered with leather aprons, ran from horsemen to the men at tables, their trays filled with pewter mugs balanced precariously.

In the road, Negro slaves walked strings of rangy hunters up and down, scattering sheep and swine before them. Openmouthed herdboys and children gaped at the horsemen and hounds, as the servants strutted, aping the manners of the lesser gentry.

At the kennels Adam found his man Gilsen walking a pair of liver and white bitches. The pack, fifty or more couples, was in the lane pulling hard against the restraining leathers held by Negro boys. The dogs were giving voice to their impatience to be off after their ancient enemy, the red fox. Adam dismounted and ran his hand over the satin coat of the bitch Gilsen was holding on a leach. He pulled her long ears gently, then withdrew his hand from her too-ready pink tongue.

"Mrs. Warden says she's the best we've had from Northamptonshire, Mr. Rutledge. She says she'd like to buy her off you for breeding if you don't want her for the pack."

Adam smiled a little. Mary Warden was a great favorite of the old stableman. He always backed up his own opinion of a horse or a dog by saying "Mrs. Warden says." He considered Mary the best judge of horses in the country, and the best rider. Adam agreed with him, but he pretended always to take issue with Gilsen.

"Would she, indeed? You tell Mrs. Warden that we're going to use Crossie in the pack. And how did Mrs. Warden come to know she was so good?"

A sly smile came over the man's wrinkled face. He pretended to be busy with a collar buckle. Seeing Adam was waiting for an answer, he said, "Mrs. Warden, she worked 'em yesterday with a drag, down Mulberry Hill way. She says they went fine." He hesitated, a troubled look in his clear blue eyes. When Adam said nothing, Gilsen continued by way of a roundabout apology, "I knew you wouldn't mind, sir. You've been so busy with the plantation lately you've had no time for the pack or the jumpers. Mrs. Warden, she always has time for them."

Adam laughed. The man's troubled face cleared.

"Ye will have your little joke, Mr. Rutledge, but it's God's truth I'm saying. You don't give no proper time to the horses, you just shut yourself up in your counting room, or set yourself over to those Mecklenburg plantations. We don't see you out hunting with Mrs. Warden any more—". He paused, thinking he had said too much.

"You are right, Gilsen, I haven't hunted enough this year.

But it's time to go to the chapel. Take the hounds far enough away so that they don't break up the parson's service. By the way, how's Hoag?"

"Flat on the bed with a wrenched back, sir. I brought the indentured man, Marcy, in his stead."

"Does he understand about the pack?" Adam asked dubiously. He remembered vaguely the stocky, redheaded Irishman he had bought at an auction at Annapolis over a year ago.

"Aye, that he does. And he knows horses, too. I seen him taking a six-barred gate when he thought there wasn't anyone about."

"I must look into this," Adam said.

When Adam came around to the front of the Inn the riders had started for St. Paul's on the other side of the village. They were streaming down the lanes in pairs or threes, talking and laughing as they rode.

By the time he turned into the lane that led to the chapel the Hunt had arrived, the last of the riders going up the steps of the church. Adam dismounted and strode up the path. He paused a moment at the slab of stone that marked the grave of Sir Charles Eden. As he glanced down at the inscription, he wondered, as he had done before, whether the old Governor had really harbored Blackbeard and divided spoils with the pirate. Whether the old wives' tales were true or false, there were still plenty of places up the river and in the Great Swamp where a man could hide a boat and be safe from capture.

Every pew was taken, so Adam joined a group of men standing against the wall at the back of the church.

James Iredell, the barrister, and Samuel Johnstone from Hayes were seated in Adam's pew. Next to Iredell was Meredith Chapman, a distant relative of his own who had come down from Virginia the previous year and bought a plantation in Tyrell on the Scuppernong, called Black Ridge. Beyond Chapman, he saw the dark, handsome face of his cousin, Peyton Rutledge, whose plantation joined the Eden House land on Salmon Creek.

Adam was only a few months older than Peyton but he felt responsible for him. For one reason, Peyton belonged to a branch of the family that had little money. He had not inherited under the Archdale will. Adam knew that Peyton resented this, although the subject of the Rutledge Riding grant was never spoken of between them. Peyton's wife, Lavinia, spent most of her time in London. She said she was staying on so that their young son, Peyton II, could prepare to enter Eton, but Adam suspected the truth was that Lavinia was bored by plantation life. She preferred the gay life of the Court. She was welcome there because of her beauty, her gaiety and the position of her family. Adam liked Lavinia, but in the back of his mind he knew she should be at home. Peyton needed her. Left alone, he managed to get himself into any number of scrapes, from which Adam usually had to extricate him. After the last time, when he bought off the daughter of a fisherman at Nags Head, Adam vowed he would never interfere again. He tried to talk with Peyton, who either grew sullen and would not speak or was gay and would not be serious. "A man is all of his ancestors rolled into one," he would say to Adam. "The Rutledge men always had a way with women; they can't help it. It's in the blood." He would laugh and finish off with "You're the exception that proves the rule, Adam. Sometimes I think you're not a proper Rutledge."

Adam's eyes lingered on Peyton's strong handsome face. "The Black Rutledge," he was called, because of his dark skin and eyes, and his waving black hair, now without powder. While the other occupants of the pew repeated their prayer from their knees, Peyton's eyes were fixed on the innkeeper's girl, sitting among the humble folk in the gallery.

The rector walked to the chancel. Below his sweeping black cassock Adam saw his hunting boots. The choirmaster gave the pitch and the congregation rose. Voices, untrained but lusty, took up the first hymn.

Adam's thoughts wandered again. The gayness and color of the Hunt at its devotions pleased him. The chapel needed new windows before the rains set in, he decided, and as a member of the Vestry he must work with the parson more than he had. The parson had a rough time with a parish that extended over miles of uninhabited country without proper roads. The parishioners in the back country and in the fishing hamlets along the Shore were so wretchedly poor they had to pay their tithes in produce, a trial, surely, to the proud, aristocratic Irishman. Only his sense of humor saved him. It was fortunate that Earl had private means, for the money he was allowed by the parish would not feed his hunters, let alone his servants at Bandon, his house a few miles beyond the village. He had talked of starting a school for boys, but Adam had heard nothing of that for some time.

The people settled back into their seats. William and Mary Warden walked down the aisle to their pew near the chancel.

Mary's habit was Lincoln green and she carried the long skirt over her arm. Her brown hair was unpowdered and wound into a smooth knot at the nape of her neck. A long plume curled away from her small hat and fell over one shoulder. Adam's eyes continued to rest on her after she had taken her seat. From his vantage point he could watch her secretly, without fear of observation. He had come to the dangerous conclusion that he had missed Mary more than he should have.

In the past six months he had not seen Mary more than two or three times. There were several reasons for this. First, he had been working at his plantations in Mecklenburg district. Then he had been to Charles Town and had taken a voyage to St. Croix on one of his shallops. So the summer had slipped by. This was what he had told Mary when he met her by chance on the road to Eden House. The real reason was different. It was because of Sara. Suddenly, after all her years of complete invalidism, she had refused to see Mary Warden, Penelope Dawson or any of her friends from Edenton or the near-by plantations. This had been going on since Easter. He thought of the time Mary had turned her ankle when she jumped off the ferry at the Island and he had carried her up to the Manor House. Sara was looking out of the window when he stepped on the gallery and he saw her draw the curtain, a strange look on her face. When he had explained Mary's accident, Sara drew her lips together and asked petulantly, "Why should she jump off the ferry? Why didn't she wait to be handed off by the overlooker or one of the boatmen?" Adam puzzled over this but found no answer. It did not occur to him to think of Sara as jealous of Mary Warden, or of his friendship for her. Since Sara's illness, he had lived the life of a hermit, with little thought outside his deep concern for her and the work on his plantation. Now as he watched Mary, he knew that he had missed her more than he cared to admit even to himself. Into his mind entered an old saying he had heard his father repeat more than once, "When I find a woman who can turn my head, I let my heart be the judge of my conduct." Adam smiled to himself at the thought of his father. He might have been Peyton's father from their likeness and their easy philosophy of living.

Mary was looking toward the altar. How tranquil she seemed as the light from the window fell across her face. Adam drew a quick breath, his eyes softened. Almost as if she felt his eyes, she turned her head. Beyond her, he saw the angular, cadaverous face of her husband. A strong face, with

11

the deep burning eyes of a Savonarola. William was too old for Mary, Adam thought. Yet some of her sound judgment must have come from her association with his clear, judicial intelligence.

He was roused from his thoughts by the stir about him. People were moving forward to the chancel for communion.

Kneeling at the rail, he found himself beside Mary, his coat brushing her shoulder. As she glanced up from her prayer book, Adam had a warm feeling of nearness and quiet.

From where he knelt he could see diagonally to the altar. On it was the gleaming Moseley silver, half hidden by bunches of Michaelmas daisies and scarlet bittersweet. After a time the sights and sounds of the chapel grew hazy to him. The droned words as the parson passed the sacrament . . . the squeak of his heavy riding boots . . . the cuff of his red coat stretched out beyond the sleeve of his cassock, giving a bizarre look to his clericals . . . the straight stiff back of Colonel Weavly. With the wine acid on his lips, Adam thought vaguely that he must remember to send the parson a pipe of really good Madeira.

Adam walked quickly down the side aisle and went out of the door before the others had left their pews. He saw Gilsen and one of the grooms standing on the steps looking at a paper that had been fastened to the wall above the cornerstone. Gilsen's face was red, as it always was when he was angry. He looked up and, seeing Adam, his face cleared, although his mouth was grim.

"Shall I tear it up before the others leave the kirk?" he asked, indicating the offensive object with his thumb. Adam looked over his shoulder and saw a torn piece of paper crudely printed:

> A tumble-down church,
> A broken-down steeple,
> A herring-catching parson
> And a damn set of people.

Anger rose swiftly in Adam. He tore the lampoon from the wall. Hearing voices in the vestibule, he crumpled the paper and thrust it into the inner breast pocket of his coat.

"Say nothing about this," he said to the men. The groom spat contemptuously.

"A dirty trick I calls it, sir. The parson he shows the fishermen how to cast a proper net to get a bigger catch and what

12

do they do? Make up filthy lies like that." He walked off down the path toward the horses.

Gilsen fell into step with Adam. They crossed the grave-yard to the edge of the wood before the older man said anything.

"I saw the Quaker preacher, Husband, at the Market early this morning. He was standin' on a wagon tongue shoutin' his grievance to the crowd. He fetched some of his Orange County roughs with him. I'm a-thinkin' he ain't here for any good."

Adam nodded. The same thought had gone through his mind for he also had seen Husband. He hoped he wouldn't stir up trouble in the Albemarle district as he had in the western counties.

Riders were waiting, impatient to be off. The wood was alive with shouts and high, gay laughter as men and women quieted their horses. It would be a record run. Every plantation house was filled with visitors who had come from Orange and Mecklenburg; from Tyrell and beyond the Dismal Swamp across the Virginia line. All were eager for the Hunt. As Adam watched them congregate he hoped it would be a good run and that they would not draw blanks. The moment before he gave the signal to cast off he leaned over Saladin's neck for a word with Gilsen.

"Keep your eye on Colonel Weavly's Irish hunters," he said. Again Gilsen spat contemptuously.

"Those hunters won't stand up to the long run over the spinney or the river jumps, Mr. Rutledge. They haven't the bottom. You'll never be thinkin' of crossin' that strain with our mares?"

"I haven't made up my mind." Adam rode over to where Marcy stood amid the pack.

"Ready?" he asked. The indentured man touched the visor of his cap.

The horn sounded. The pack was cast off. Down the lane, between the leafless hawthorn hedges, the hounds swept, noses to the ground, the impatient horsemen following close, crowding the narrow lane.

The first field beyond the wood drew blank. When Adam jumped the hedge to the second plowed field he saw a fox beside a fringe of low bushes. He galloped ahead and got the bitches laid on. They caught the scent at once, giving full cry. An avalanche of sound followed. The fox left the bushes and ran along a log that crossed a small creek. Adam put his mount into the cold water of the creek. Other horsemen followed. Noses to the ground, the pack followed the red plume, passing over the log one at a time, Crossie in the lead. At the first oxer the riders spread out fanwise across the field; the horses pounded across rough ground and stubble, jumped over low stacks of Indian corn. A planter wearing a bright coat new from London slid from his horse at the second stream and landed in the bluish slime near the bank.

"Who's down?" Adam called to Peyton Rutledge, who was close to his horse's rump.

"Don't know. The going's too good to inquire," Peyton shouted back as he put his black horse ahead. He was laughing now, the excitement of the chase shining in his eyes.

Adam kept his eye on Colonel Weavly. At the beginning, the Irish hunters were up with the first of the field, but now they were dropping back. The Colonel used spurs frequently. Adam put his hand caressingly on the satin neck of Saladin.

"They haven't the bottom for this country; we can outstay them, my beauty. We'll beat them in the end. It's the end of the race that counts. Not the beginning," he thought.

They came to the five-barred gates flanked by a hedge separating the north end of his plantation, Rutledge Riding, from the open Crown lands. Weavly did not lessen his pace. He went at the fence, lying back, pulling heavily on the curb. His hunter, tired now from the forty minutes of stiff going, had not strength to regain its balance with its head in check. It crashed on the far side of the gate. Peyton, following close, swerved his horse in time to avoid disaster. He glanced back but did not pull up.

Adam dismounted and ran across the stubble to the fallen man. Weavly's aide, Captain Atwell, was there a moment later. Together they got the Colonel to his feet. He stood for a moment swaying, slightly dazed by the fall. Heavy men fall hard.

"Is the horse hurt?" was his first question.

"He's on his feet again, sir," Atwell answered.

"Then give me a leg up," commanded Weavly.

Adam felt a reluctant admiration. At least there was no lack of physical courage in the man. He ventured some advice.

"These gates are tricky. Try leaning a little forward on the take, Colonel . . ." he began.

Weavly interrupted him. "When I want advice on jumping a hunter I'll ask for it, Rutledge."

Adam swung into the saddle, cursing himself for a fool. After a time the exhilaration of the chase took hold of him.

The rhythmic strength of a swiftly moving horse between his knees, the cold wind whipping against his face, made him forget Weavly.

A green skirt flashed into view. He had a glimpse over his shoulder of Mary Warden's pale provocative face. There was a gay challenge in her voice.

"You're slow this morning, Adam. What's wrong? I'll lay you ten to one you won't be in at the death!"

Adam pressed his knees gently against Saladin's sides. The sensitive creature lengthened its stride. "Are you challenging Saladin or me?" he asked as he overtook her.

"Both! Since you are inseparable these days!"

They were riding hard, their horses side by side. Mary glanced at Adam. He was looking straight ahead, his blond head, his clear-cut profile, his lean strong jaw sharply outlined against the heavy green of the young pine thicket they were skirting.

"Breakfast at Queen's Gift after the Hunt," she called out. "You're coming, aren't you?"

"I don't think so, Mary. I want to see Armitage before I go back to Rutledge Riding."

A shadow crossed her face. Her jaw set a little.

"William wants to speak to you. He expects Maurice Moore and John Ashe up from Wilmington next week. They want to see you."

Adam spoke quickly, almost sharply. "I have made up my mind not to be drawn into politics, Mary. It's no use for me to talk with them."

She shrugged her shoulders.

"Well enough to say, Adam. But I don't see how you can avoid it. After all, you do live in the Province of North Carolina."

Adam did not answer. At the far side of the field the hounds were circling, closing in, baying excitedly. Mary spurred her horse, her eyes shining.

"Quick, Adam! We must be in at the death."

Adam glanced over his shoulder. The field was following close, spread out along the creek. He laughed aloud as his horse lengthened its stride.

Suddenly, without warning, ten or twelve roughly dressed men jumped the low stone wall and advanced down the field toward the riders. They were shouting and brandishing clubs. Some of them carried stones in their hands.

"Get off the field! Get off the field! The farmer'll have the law on ye for trespass. Get off!"

Adam held his breath waiting for the crash. The speed of the galloping horses was unbearable. He jerked on the reins, lifting Saladin off his front feet just in time to keep the horse from striking a man.

"Out of the way, you fools! You'll be killed. We can't stop! Out of the way!"

It was too late. There was a frightened scream from one of the women as men and horses crashed. The weight of the racing horses threw men to the ground. The impact of the horses against bodies was terrifying. A flock of crows, rising from corn stacks, circled, uttering shrill cries.

Adam heard a man's voice high with excitement and rage.

"Use your clubs, men! Drive the gentry from the field! Use your stones! Get up, you louts, and fight for your rights!"

Adam recognized him. It was the Quaker, Husband. He was standing on the stone wall, well out of danger. His long skinny arms waving, his black cloak flapping around his thin shanks, his red beard flaming, he needed only crows lighting on his shoulders to be a scarecrow.

"Go back to hell where you belong," Adam muttered.

Mary cried out, "Adam, the girth is slipping!"

Adam turned quickly. Her horse, frightened by the sliding saddle, reared. Before Adam got to her side, Mary had ripped herself free of her long skirt, which had caught on the pommel of the saddle, and jumped to the ground. Like a young boy in trousers and riding coat, she clung to the reins, trying to quiet the plunging, frightened horse. Adam leaned over and grasped the bridle, twisting it, forcing the horse's head to one side, and under control.

"Get out of the way of his hoofs, Mary. Let go the reins. I've got him now."

Mary jumped away as the horse whirled, half stumbling over the body of a man lying on the ground. His face was covered with blood. On one cheek was the mark of a horse's iron shoe. His eyes were closed, his face white. It was young Will Daventry, a boy of no wit, who lived near by. Mary knelt on the ground and raised his head against her knee. A groom ran to her aid.

"Get water from the creek," she said, wiping the blood from the man's mouth.

Peyton rode up in time to witness the scene.

"Got what he deserved! What right have those yokels to interfere with gentlemen's sport?"

The tall gaunt figure of Harmon Husband advanced threateningly. Pointing a bony finger at Peyton, he cried, "The

16

right of men to protect their land against vandals. Vandals, you are, for all you're the gentry!"

Peyton struck the Quaker's cheek with his open hand. Two riders caught Peyton's arms. He struggled, cursing, his face white with rage. Adam ran to him to stop him. There must be no trouble.

Husband stood for a moment, his eyes venomous with hate. Peyton broke from his captors. Husband threw up his hands to protect his face, stumbling back a few steps. Out of reach of Peyton's long arm, he turned and ran across the field. Passing his little group of followers, without looking at them or pausing to ascertain their injuries, he jumped the low stone wall and disappeared into the thicket. Peyton laughed aloud at the grotesque figure and other planters joined in the laughter. Adam did not laugh. He had a strange feeling that this was not the beginning nor the end of the incident.

Across the field a man was running, waving his pitchfork above his head. It was Wessels, the yeoman who owned the fifty acres along Bitter Creek. He came up to Adam, puffing, sweat running down his full red cheeks.

"I ordered that rabble off my land and they hid in the scrub. Gentlemen, I want that you should hunt my farm. It is overrun with foxes. Last night a vixen killed six of my buffs that I had ready for market. Gentlemen, please hunt down the foxes!" He turned about and, seeing the men near the wall, he brandished his pitchfork and charged at them like an angry bull. Their leader gone, they did not face the angry farmer. Jumping the fence, they ran, crouching low to avoid the clods the farmer picked up as he pursued them.

In the far end of the field the fox slid out of a hollow log and ran along a furrow behind a stack of maize. The new bitch, Crossie, lifted her head. When the pack got the wind a moment later, they followed down the furrow in full cry. The horsemen leaped to their saddles. Adam saw Mary Warden's green shirt fluttering, well in the lead. He lingered a moment to reassure Wessels and noticed that Daventry had been left behind by his companions. He was slumped against the wall, breathing heavily, the blood running over his face. Adam called Gilsen and two grooms who were riding over from the wood. Together they made a litter by putting poles through the sleeves of their leather jackets and carried Daventry to the farmer's cottage.

"The poor daft fella'," Gilsen muttered, "getting him into trouble. That shows the breed of Harmon Husband."

Adam waited long enough to arrange with the farmer to

17

hitch up his oxen to a cart and start the injured man to the doctor before he followed the hunt.

He met them crossing the post road. Mary had the brush stuck jauntily through the headpiece of her horse's bridle.

"Breakfast at my house," she reminded him as he came up.

He repeated his excuse. "I must stop at the village to see Armitage."

"Sara? Is she worse?"

Adam shook his head, then fell in between Mary and John Harvey. Mary was looking at him curiously, her small firm jaw set. She looked as if she would speak, then thought better of it. Adam knew what it was. Mary didn't understand why his wife no longer sent for her to come to the Island, or why he stayed away from her home. But there was no explanation he could give. Harvey spoke first.

"I don't like what happened there on the field, Adam. A small incident in itself, but a forerunner, I'm afraid. I wish they would keep Harmon Husband in his own county. We've a peaceful, contented lot of farmers here in Albemarle; we don't want that radical demagogue putting ideas into their simple heads."

Adam agreed. They talked for a moment about the near riots in Hillsborough recently.

"When Dobbs either dies or goes back to England, it will be different. Tryon is not a man to stand any nonsense. He will handle the situation," Adam said.

Harvey made no answer, his stern features expressed nothing. Mary looked at him anxiously. John Harvey of Perquimans was the foremost man of the Albemarle district in the matter of politics and affairs of the government. She waited for him to give his opinion.

After a moment he spoke. "You are sanguine, Rutledge. Tryon is already pledged to Edmund Fanning and all his works. I can see no hope for betterment in the matter of taxes or the land scandals." He glanced quickly at Mary Warden and said no more. She knew the reason. Her husband had come to the Province to represent the Granville Land Grant interests. He still did some of their work in the western districts.

She said, "What happened to Daventry? Did those men take him away?"

Adam answered grimly, "No. They deserted him on the field. What could you expect of men like Husband? He'll always save his own skin at the expense of his followers. We'll

18

have trouble, serious trouble, with that man before we're through, Harvey."

"I wish I could argue with you on that point, Rutledge. I believe as you. Something is happening all around us, and we can't quite put our finger on the danger."

They had come to the village. Adam left them at the Commons and rode down toward the Sound to Dr. Armitage's home, next door to Corbin's Cupola House.

It was mid-afternoon before Adam got away from the Doctor and started home to Rutledge Riding. After they had discussed Sara and her condition, he and the Doctor had talked about the disturbances of the morning. Adam took the crumpled paper from his pocket and smoothed it out before he gave it to Dr. Armitage.

The Doctor put his spectacles over his thin nose and read the verse. Adam felt his anger rising.

"I don't like it, I don't like it," he kept muttering. "Coupled with this business of the Hunt—" he paused to take snuff. Blowing his nose loudly in a great square of silk, he walked about the room. Adam watched him. The Doctor was thin almost to emaciation. Adam thought of the heavy roads, the long trips on rainy, blustering nights and wondered how he kept going. People didn't half appreciate him. He had a quick tongue and no patience with deceit or pretense. People had the flat truth from him. Sometimes they didn't like it. "It takes a strong man to stand the truth," the Doctor often told Adam. "But there's one thing I never do: speak the truth to a woman."

About Sara he was noncommittal. In his opinion she was no worse off than she had been from the first physically. He pursed up his lips and tugged a lock of grey hair which hung down over his forehead. Several times during Adam's recital he gave him a swift, quizzical glance. When Adam had finished, he said, "I'll talk to Sara. She should rouse herself, see people, have some life about the place."

The Doctor's eyes followed Adam's tall figure as he strode up and down the office. "He's too much alone," he thought. "Sara is jealous, but he'd never think of that." Aloud he said, "It must be deadly for you at Rutledge Riding. I remember Annandale, your father's place in Virginia. It was always gay, crowded with people. What's the good of having a great Manor House, as you have, and not a soul in it to laugh or dance or sing?"

Adam's mouth closed. "There's no use talking to him,"

thought the Doctor. "The man's not human. He's controlled his thoughts and desires until he no longer feels."

"I don't like it," he repeated.

"Nor I, Doctor. We must watch these men. We want our farmers happy and contented."

The Doctor had not been thinking of the events of the morning but he held his peace. You couldn't get beyond a certain point with Adam. Yet the vital, moving spirit of the man rose above his reserve.

"I'll drop over one day this week, Adam," the Doctor said, as he stood in the doorway of his office watching him swing onto his horse. Adam touched his cap with his riding crop and cantered down the street that led to the post road.

He rode along lost in deep thought. Peyton troubled him. He must make an effort to see more of him. Perhaps they could talk things out if he had patience. The cry of a waterfowl caught his attention. Ducks rising from the reeds along the river, wedging their way south. His eyes followed the curved shore. Brown fields, winter would soon be on the way —that meant months before time to plow and plant the fields to grain.

In spite of Armitage's reassuring words, Adam was more discouraged than he had ever been about his wife. For the first time since the sudden stroke that paralyzed her limbs Adam wondered if she would ever walk again.

He had come to Dreary Ford. The water splashed to his face, cold and invigorating. Saladin broke into a gallop as they reached the bank. He passed Pembroke and the road that led to Eden House. The crisp, bright air and the undiminished strength of the great horse stirred his blood. It was good to see the fields lying fallow, waiting for the plow. The *Bon Venture* would bring seed cotton from Egypt on her next voyage. He could plant it in the lowland near the patch of hard kernel rice he was testing. He would clear more land. A thousand acres . . . two thousand. To turn raw land into productive acres: there was something to put life into a man. His spirits rose to match the quickened hoof beats.

He came, after a mile through the pines, to his boat landing. From here the ferry took him to his red brick manor house on the Island. Two Negro slaves waited to pull the boat across.

The sun was low, the wind had died down. Adam quieted at the sight of the water, for the events of the day had disturbed him deeply. He was shaken by the things that had not happened rather than by those that had. The boat was drift-

ing downstream, the only sound the creak of the pulley sliding along the ropes. How tranquil it was! The fragrance of
pines in his nostrils, the quiet lapping of the water. Why
should he be troubled about things that had not happened?
Perhaps they never would happen. He thought of the Market
Fair, the booths piled high with produce. That was the
answer: a full granary, a cellar piled high with winter vegeta-
bles, a smokehouse hanging with hickory-smoked hams and
bacon, apples and potatoes in the bin, grapes pressed into
wine. With a good harvest and plenty of land to clear and
plant there would be no time for a man to think of unrest
and discontent with the government.

The thought heartened him. He was whistling as he walked
swiftly up the path to the Manor House. There was much to
interest Sara in the day's happenings.

He knocked lightly at the door of her room. Judith, Sara's
slave, opened the door an inch, her tall, gaunt body blocking
the room.

"Miss Sara, she sleep. Better you come tomorrow."

Adam turned away. The joy of home-coming faded from
his face. He crossed the hall and walked up the broad stairs,
encountering no one. The house slaves were at their evening
meal. Suddenly, he knew he was weary, bodily weary. He
went slowly to his room in the east wing and closed the door.

ORIFLAMME

THE Manor House at Rutledge Riding took on its early morning activities in the slave quarters and kitchen. When the sun had risen high enough to cast a line along the mark of eight on the sundial, the curtains of Adam's sleeping room were drawn and Cicero, his body servant, stood for a moment at the window. This was a signal to a pickaninny, watching in the garden, to run to the kitchen and let the cook know that the master was awake.

Black Malsey turned the hourglass. She put a rasher of bacon on an iron spider, set it over the glowing charcoal, and stood, hands on her broad hips, waiting for the sands to run to a certain depth before she put two eggs into cold water. She knew to the second when Adam would be in the breakfast room. When he came the fire in the fireplace would be burning brightly, the porridge and bacon would be standing in covered Sheffield dishes on the sideboard, and the hot corn pone, wrapped in a napkin, would be ready to serve. She stood by the stove giving orders while her helpers ran to do her bidding. Malsey was a Congo woman with broad flattened features and a bronze skin. She wore a white muslin coif and a white kerchief of the same material tied about her neck. The opening showed an amulet—a crescent of ivory dotted in red—which she wore on a braided thong.

Cicero boasted to the other servants that "a gentleman could dress heself and be shaved in ten minutes." Ten minutes later, when Adam went to the window, he saw a small procession of his house slaves, headed by Aaron the butler, hurrying along the passage that connected the kitchen with the main house. Aaron carried a tray containing the tea caddy, pot and hot-water jug, for tea making was a sacred rite trusted to no one but the cook and butler.

Adam Rutledge would have been surprised had he known the detail involved, the careful observance of his preferences which lay behind this daily service. He was a kind master and understood the Negro character and temperament, but he had never given a thought to his own position. Nor did he realize that his every movement was important to his slaves; that his small likes and dislikes were discussed among them, even to the degree of crispness of his breakfast bacon and the way he liked his morning eggs. Had he known he would have laughed, but he would have been a little touched.

Malsey stood near the door to inspect slaves and food.

"Don' you shake dos egg dish," she scolded. "How offen I tell yo he don' lak hissen eggs shook up an' riled? He lak dem whole, so he ken cut into dem heself wid he silber spoon."

A yellow girl, washing dishes, grumbled, "Don' I know dat, Malsey. Don' I have to polish dat spoon every mo'ning when hit get black wid de egg yoke. Sometimes I wish he eaten em whole lak we do. I don't lak to polish—"

"Keep yo hush, Liz, else I put you rubbin' all de knives on the brick," Malsey retorted. "Yo don' know when you well off; yo just a jungle wench, das what you are. You ain't fit to do house service."

The girl sloshed the silver in the dishpan, making a great clatter and muttering to herself.

"What you saying?" Malsey demanded.

"Polishing knifes and forks is men's work not women's."

Malsey stood off looking at the girl, a frown on her usually placid face.

"I don' know what's come over you, Liz, all time making a fuss."

Eph came in from the dining room in time to hear Malsey's remark.

"I ken tell you what's the matter wid Liz. She's a-grievin' for dat Zulu Herk what run away to the swamp."

Liz wheeled around, her wet hands clenched, her eyes blazing.

"You shut yo' big mouth, Eph, elsen I tell Cicero about you and dat swamp."

Malsey pricked up her ears.

"What dat you say?" she asked.

Eph only laughed and poked at the girl's rib with a long finger. He broke into a monotonous Bantu song set to a minor key.

> "Dula Nitima Ndi
> Iwe Namwali
> Kwucha Tontoza
> Ige Sauka Mtima."

"What dat you say?" demanded Malsey, now thoroughly aroused. She could not understand the talk of the Zambesi people. "Say what you got to say in de English talk, not dat jungle gibberish."

Aaron came into the kitchen from the pantry. He stood for a moment, disapproval on his face. "You git out of here, Eph, and git the floors clean and polished and quit tormentin' Liz. Git I tells you—"

Eph slid out of the door, out of reach of Aaron's strong arm. For a moment he put his hand back in, raising his voice again.

> "Dula Nitima Ndi
> Iwe Namwali,"

he sang.

The girl burst into tears. Throwing her apron over her head, she ran from the kitchen, out into the back garden. Malsey looked after her, her black face puzzled.

"What did that good for nothin' Eph sing that make she so mad?" she asked Aaron.

"Don' know why Liz get mad at dat little song. Hit just say: 'De girl is grievin'—come comfort her poor heart—de girl is grievin' . . .' Can you tell me why dat mak she to go off lak dat, Malsey?"

Malsey set her lips firmly. "I'll skin dat Eph effen he don' leave she alone." She was diverted by the arrival of a slave from the North Plantation with a haunch of venison a trapper had shot the day before, and a brace of wild ducks. Owen Tewilliger had sent for Adam's dinner. Malsey told one of her helpers to hang the venison in the cellar, and laid the canvasbacks on her work table. While she and Aaron were gossiping with the man, Judith came in carrying a copper ewer with hot water for her mistress's bath. Her eyes fell on the ducks. She set the jug down on the floor and went over to the table. Malsey turned quickly and grabbed at the ducks Judith had taken up.

"You drop they ducks," she said, her voice raised in swift anger. "Mr. Owen sent dem for de master's dinner."

Judith did not loosen her hold. The two black women faced each other, each hanging onto the birds.

"I think I'll take them for my lady," Judith said calmly. "She likes duck. You can cook a chicken for he."

"You can't have them," Malsey shouted, her voice showing her active dislike for Judith. "Let go, will you?"

Aaron turned. "Seems lak women always fitin' among they-self. Give the ducks to me. Why you fuss? Dey's two ducks, one for she and one for he." He handed one of the birds to Judith and one to Malsey. Without answering, Judith picked up the water jug and left the room walking swiftly, her head in the air.

"Why you get she mad with you, Malsey?" Aaron said, after Judith had gone. "It ain't safe to do dat. You know she can mak *Mankwala* on you ef she wan' too—she bad, she is."

Malsey sat down suddenly as if her knees had given way.

"I know, I know," she wailed. "But I jes' can't let her all time take everything good for she mistress and leave nothin' for master. No matter what I cook she come right into my kitchen and take what she want."

"Well, maybe she do, but you better stay on good side of she lessen you want to get in trouble."

Adam, unconscious of the disturbance in the kitchen, ate his breakfast deliberately, and went to his counting room to wait for Marcy. He had sent his indentured man across the Sound to Edenton the afternoon before to arrange that his shallop, the *Golden Orchid*, be dispatched at the same time that Hewes and Smith's barques sailed for Charlotte Amalie and St. Croix. He thought it was safer to send the shallop under convoy since ships sailing up from St. Croix and Charlotte Amalie had reported pirates lurking among the smaller islands and around Mono Passage. Two of the Hewes barques were sailing that afternoon, and they carried three-pounders for protection.

Marcy came in shortly. All arrangements had been made, he said, and the ships would sail late that day. Adam took the lists, and they began to check them against the manifest.

"We will be ready before long," he said to Marcy. "You can tell Captain Allen to loaf along so that Hewes's ships overtake him before he reaches the entrance. I think he should have a convoy until he sights one of Kreuger's ships somewhere near St. Thomas harbor. Will you tell him?"

"Yes, sir. I think he already understands, but I'll make sure. They're saying in the village that the pirates are making their headquarters in St. Thomas harbor."

Adam nodded. St. Thomas had been a safe harbor to free-booters and ships sailing the Jolly Roger for many years. Tripoli pirates had swarmed those waters in the early days as well as Blackbeard and others of his kind.

Adam was almost through checking the manifest when he

was aroused by an exclamation from Marcy, who was looking out of the window down the Sound.

"What's wrong?" Adam asked, turning in his chair.

"A full-rigged ship, sir. Looks as if she is headed straight for our landing. I can't make her out, but she is a big one."

Adam got up and went to the window. A great ship, all her canvas spread, was steering directly toward the Rutledge Riding float.

"She's probably putting into Queen Anne's Creek, but we can't take any chances with Barbary pirates around," Adam said. "Better have Aaron unlock the gun room so we'll not lose any time."

"I don't think it's a pirate, Mr. Rutledge," the indentured man said. "She is square rigged like the *Oriflamme*."

Adam opened the window to get a clearer view.

"It can't be time for LaTruchy to get his slaver here from Lobita Bay," he said, half to himself.

"He could, with fair winds," Marcy answered. "Must be more than a year since he brought those last slaves over—why it's a full year since they ran away!"

Adam grunted in agreement. He didn't want to think about those runaways, the first slaves that ever made a break from any of his plantations. "A poor lot they were," he said. "LaTruchy swore they were the best he had, but he's always swearing that. I should have known better than to trust the rascal."

"They were Zulus, Mr. Rutledge. I've noticed that Zulus don't take to field work. They're a fighting tribe in their own country," Marcy volunteered as he moved toward the door.

Adam called after him, "Marcy, bring the spyglass. I think you'll find it on the table in my book room."

Marcy left the room, Adam's Irish setter, Red Rowan, at his heels. Instead of thinking about possible danger from the approaching ship, Adam allowed his thoughts to dwell on the indentured man. How did he happen to know that Zulus were a fighting tribe? Adam remembered what Gilsen had told him about the Irishman's skill with horses. He had bought the fellow for a groom and stable boy, but he found he could trust him to do other things. Red Rowan was always at his heels these days. Up to now the setter had belonged to Adam alone. It occurred to him that the two were not unlike: Marcy's red-brown eyes, almost the color of the dog's, and his reddish hair like the dog's coat. He hoped the man had the faithful, loyal qualities of the dog. But that was a good deal to ask of a man who had been bought on the block for twenty guineas for five years' indenture. He was certainly not a yeoman, although he knew something about crops and land. Now he was showing knowledge of books and accounting. There was some mystery here, but Adam did not dwell on that aspect for long. Such things were not uncommon. For a hundred years past, gentlemen rebels to the Crown had been sold as indentured servants to the plantations along with petty thieves and other criminals.

Marcy returned with the telescope. The ship was still too far off to make out either the name or the figurehead. Adam glanced at the clock. It was almost eleven. He got up from his desk.

"Finish checking the list, Marcy. When it is done take it down to the shallop and give it to Captain Allen. I've given him all his instructions so that he can sail to twelve. Better keep a watch on that ship. If you make out what she is, let me know. I will be with Mrs. Rutledge."

The clock in the hall struck eleven as Adam crossed to the west wing where Sara had her rooms. He always went to her at eleven each morning. If she had had a good night, he would sit with her while she ate her breakfast. If she insisted, he would drink a second cup of tea. Sara drank green China tea, which Adam didn't like. If she was asleep, he would look in on her for a moment, and tiptoe from the room, careful not to waken her.

This morning he found her sitting in an armchair near the window. He stood for a moment looking at her. It was good to see her dressed, smiling a welcome to him. He pulled a chair close to hers and took her hand. It had been several days since he had found her well enough to see him; always the same words from her black woman Judith, "Mis' Sara, she rests now. She have a bad night—better she keep sheself quiet now."

Adam did not like Judith. He thought that Sara depended on her too much. But Judith was Sara's slave, given to her by her father long before they were married. The woman hated him. Many times he had noticed her watching him when he was with Sara, a malignant look in her bold black eyes. She moved silently, like a jungle animal. She was not far removed from the jungle and she had strange, untamed jungle ways. The other slaves were afraid of her. "She make *Mankwala,*" his body servant Cicero told him. "She bad, very bad." But Cicero did not tell him that the black folk believed it was Judith who kept her mistress from walking, that this was part of her dark jungle magic. He knew Adam would laugh at

27

him. Cicero did not want his master, whom he loved, to laugh at *Mankwala*. That would bring bad fortune to everyone in the house.

Adam thought the slaves were envious of Judith for her power. When she moved out of her mistress' rooms, it was to give orders to cook and housekeeper, butler and house slaves. She stood as a symbol of authority which she exercised to the fullest. She was the only black person on the plantation who could read or write, and that gave her power and authority. Sometimes, on a fine evening, she would stroll to the slaves' quarters. When she came, the dancing and singing ceased, the drums and banjos became silent. The black people were more than afraid—they were terrified of her. But they must treat her with respect, for if she were angry who could tell what would happen? Half the slaves on the plantation had been brought from Africa within the past five years. They had not forgotten the strange power of certain men, and even women, to bring evil to people they did not like. None of these things were known to Adam or to any white man on the plantation, but the black folk all knew.

Once, a year or two before, Adam had talked to Sara about sending Judith away and replacing her with one of the other house slaves. He had been appalled at the effect of his words on his wife. After he had quieted her, and kissed away her tears, he resolved never to speak of it again. It was far better not to disturb Sara. "Let her have her way as much as you can," Dr. Armitage had told him. "Keep her mind at peace—that's about all you can do for the present. Remember that small things assume great proportions to an invalid confined to a chair."

But Adam was not thinking of these things now. He was thinking how lovely Sara was and his heart overflowed with pity for her. Her great blue eyes were shadowed, making them even larger and deeper than usual. Ill health showed in the drooping lines at the corners of her mouth, in the transparent whiteness of her skin, and her thin, blue-veined hands. Even in her complete invalidism she managed to maintain the aura of a great lady. She was fastidious in her selection of gowns, which were sent to her from a London mantuamaker, and in the fashionable arrangement of her thick light brown hair. A blue satin quilt, tufted in rose, covered her useless limbs; her slim feet in buckled satin slippers showed beneath the robe. She wore a rose-colored wrapper of soft silk, with a froth of delicate Mechlin lace from neck to hem. Looking down at her, Adam felt his own vitality and strength must be

28

a constant reminder to her of her own ineffectual living. A wave of deep tenderness rushed over him. He lifted her hands and pressed them against his cheek.

"Darling," he said, his voice low, "darling, I wish I could give you strength and the will to be well again."

A shadow crossed her face. Her lips drooped at the corners as she turned away so he could not see her eyes. She was not pleased with what he had said. He was sorry. He had not meant to hurt her, only to express the depth of his pity, to let her know how dear she was to him.

He got up and moved aimlessly about the room, the black woman watching him from her chair on the opposite side of the bed. She arose and went across the room to a satinwood commode. Adam watched her take a pellet from a thin vial and pour some port from a decanter into a glass. She walked past Adam without glancing at him.

"Time for your mediceen, Mis' Sara. You be careful lessen yo tire yo'self." Her voice was harsh. Sara took the pill without comment. Adam walked to the window. He did not want to show the anger that had risen so swiftly at the slave's words and implication.

"There is a ship coming up the Sound, Sara. Marcy thinks it is LaTruchy's slaver. Don't you want your chair moved so that you can see better?"

Sara leaned forward. "That would be nice, Adam. I love to watch ships."

Adam felt pleased at her interest. He moved her chair and then sat down beside her and took her hand.

"Are you going to buy more slaves?" Sara asked the question idly. He knew she wasn't really interested in plantation affairs.

"I don't think so. But I intend to make LaTruchy live up to his contract and replace those runaways. That was part of the bargain."

Sara released her hand and picked up a tapestry that lay on a low table. Adam watched her as she pushed the blunt needle through the stiff backing, pulling the bright wool into place. As he watched her hands moving surely and expertly, he thought that her eternal stitching was a symbol of her ineffectual living. Her narrowed existence, the pattern of her drab life so sharply contrasted with the false gaiety of the pattern she wove with her delicate, clever fingers. The futility of her life bore down on him with sharp bitterness. What did it all mean?

Aware of his growing absorption, Sara broke into his

thoughts with the thin silver of her voice. "You must have close to three thousand slaves now, Adam," she said.

"Not quite that many. Haskins says about twenty-seven hundred," Adam answered, pleased at her display of interest. "I mean here and at the Mecklenburg plantation."

Sara glanced at Judith. "When will we need a woman to replace Lily?"

"Where is Lily?" Adam asked, not waiting for Judith to answer. Sara did not speak for a moment. She was holding the tapestry at arm's length, looking at it intently, her head bent to one side.

"I believe it needs a deeper green there in the trees, don't you think, Judith?" The slave laid a skein across the pattern. Sara took it in her hand. "That's exactly the right shade. Thank you, Judith." She leaned back against the pillows of her chair, and raised her eyes to Adam. "Lily is out of shape," she said delicately. "I have had her sent to the mainland. I can't have a slave around me who is out of shape."

For a moment Adam did not understand. Then he said, "You mean she's going to have a child?"

A slight flush came to Sara's cheeks.

"Must you be so blunt, Adam?" Sara lowered her voice. "She will have to stay on the mainland until she's through with it. I should have a new woman to take her place, but I don't want a raw native. It takes so long to train one. It is hard on Judith—" she paused, looking thoughtfully at Adam, her crewel needle tapping against her white teeth. "Still—"

Adam lifted his long body out of the chair and looked out to the docks. He had seen Marcy crossing the gallery, the spyglass in his hand. He opened the window.

"It is the *Oriflamme,* Mr. Rutledge, but she's changed her course. She'll put into Edenton before she comes here. If you like I can row out and tell Captain LaTruchy that you want to see him."

Adam thought a moment.

"No, don't bother. He's sure to come here by sundown. He'll want to save wharfage costs."

Marcy grinned. "He's a rare one at bargaining."

Adam closed the window. "I'm going down to the dock," he said to Sara. "I want to see Captain Allen before he sails. I see they are pulling up the loading plank."

He kissed her and started toward the door. Sara stopped him.

"Adam," she said, "when Lily's baby comes, I want you to sell it at once. I don't want her to have it. It's too distracting,

30

and if she nurses it, she won't get her figure back. You know I want my maids to be slim and straight and to look well in my livery. Will you have Haskins sell it?"

Adam turned slowly. For a moment he was silent, looking at her as if he had not heard aright. He tried to keep his voice even when he answered.

"I can't do that, Sara. I can't have Haskins sell a young baby. It would be too—" he stopped in time. He had meant to say too cruel, but it was no use to hurt Sara. She didn't understand what she was asking. "No one would buy such a small child," he finished lamely.

Sara's lips trembled; tears gathered in her wide blue eyes. Adam couldn't stand that. Women's tears unnerved him, especially Sara's.

"Don't cry, Sara darling," he said soothingly. "We will find some way. We can arrange for a foster mother—"

Sara picked up her tapestry. She pushed the needle through the cloth.

"I don't care what you do with it, only don't let me see it around," she said indifferently. "Perhaps it would be better for you to get me another woman. That is if LaTruchy has a good strong woman, but she must be young and personable and carry herself well. Don't get me one of those sooty black Negroes. A brown one looks better."

"I'll see what can be done when the *Oriflamme* comes, but I doubt if LaTruchy will have any women that answer your description." He closed the door quietly. What he wanted to do was to shut it with a bang. He was ashamed of the thought almost as soon as it came to him. He must be patient with Sara, patient and tender, but sometimes she made it very hard.

The *Oriflamme*, because of the wind, went first to Edenton. It was almost sundown when she anchored off the Island. Adam went to the landing as the longboat swept across the water. LaTruchy sat in the stern, a swarthy man, with black eyes and a thin nose that curved downward; a man to watch in a bargain. Four Negroes in tattered rags rowed the boat, muscles rippling under sooty skin as their backs bent to the burden of the oars. In the bottom of the boat two women were huddled, sitting on a bale of rugs, their faces hidden under bright scarves.

The Frenchman jumped ashore with the agility of a man whose body is made of steel springs. He bowed to Adam and swept his cocked hat, his white teeth gleaming behind his short curled beard.

"M'sieu Rutledge! I salute you. It is a pleasure to see you wear your excellent health as a banner. And Madame, how does she fare?"

A shadow came over Adam's face. "Not too well, La-Truchy. Some days I think I see improvement. Other days I know it is only my wish to see her well that makes me think so."

"Can the surgeons do nothing? Is she able to walk?"

Adam shook his head. "She has not walked for four years now."

LaTruchy shook his head. "A tragedy for one as young as Madame."

"Not yet twenty-three," Adam replied impulsively. "Why dammit, man, I've only turned twenty-three myself."

LaTruchy's eyes narrowed. "Not yet in your prime, not for twenty years."

Adam changed the subject. "What's the cargo today, Captain? You owe me for ten runaways."

"Ten runaways, mon Dieu! Surely not ten? That will destroy all my profits!"

"Yes, ten. And a bad lot they were. My overlooker said they needed the whip too often. You know I don't favor the whip."

LaTruchy laughed as he crushed some long leaves for his clay pipe.

" 'Spare the *Kiboka* and spoil the slave!' In Africa, we use the rhino whip."

He squatted down on the ground, balancing himself on his heels. Adam sat on a bench, his back against the brick wall of the boathouse. LaTruchy took a few puffs before he spoke.

"I didn't forget to bring you the seed rice from Madagascar that I promised you. I had trouble to get it . . . and some danger. Almost, I lost my little barque to pirates. Did you know, M'sieu Rutledge, that pirates still hold rendezvous at Madagascar? Somewhat like the old days, when your Captain Keed and Morgan sacked towns and held great cities for ransom. My countryman, François l'Olonnois, too, was a man of courage and spirit. He did not hesitate to carry a cutlass and head a boarding party, himself; or stand on the deck of a fire ship until it ran against his quarry and set fire to their vessels. But those women pirates—they were worse than men—more vicious—"

"Are you speaking of Ann Bonney and Marie Reed? They've been dead these many years," Adam commented.

32

"I know, but the story of them clings—just as people here talk of your Stede Bonnet and Teach—you call him Blackbeard—and it's been over forty years since he was captured."

Adam looked at the Frenchman in some surprise. He seemed to have an extraordinary interest in pirates and buccaneers.

"It must have been of an excitement here in Albemarle in those days, M'sieu Rutledge—pirate ships sailing in at night; your villages overrun with Malays and Lascars, in their gaudy colors, carrying their glittering cutlasses. Did you ever hear that Blackbeard's *Adventurer* sailed up to the head of the Sound, and that they buried treasure up Chowan River?"

Adam laughed. "Are you thinking of hunting for pirate goods, LaTruchy?"

The Frenchman did not meet Adam's eyes. "Puerto de Principe yielded up three hundred thousand pieces of eight to Morgan and a thousand head of cattle to l'Olonnois," he said thoughtfully. "He took the cattle to the island of St. Thomas where he had safe harbor." LaTruchy turned his head slowly, his sharp black eyes scanning the tree-lined shore. "You have yourself chosen a safe harbor, M'sieu Rutledge." He took a small silver box from his pocket and extracted a betel nut, rolling it in a spiced leaf before he put it into his lips. He chewed for a moment, then spat the crimson juice from his mouth.

The Frenchman had the trading habits of the Near East. Up to now he had not mentioned his cargo. He said, "I have Zanzibar slaves this time, M'sieu. I went to the Island of Zanzibar, seat of all slave trading. There is an island—beautiful as a dream! Fragrance of spices float out to sea to meet you." He spat red juice of the betel on the ground. "It's a sight to see the people who bring their ships to Zanzibar—Barbary pirates; Persians; men from Muscat; Arabs from the Red Desert and Yemen; black Somali robed in white; Indians wearing turbans of every color." The Frenchman leaned forward. "I bought slaves there. I almost lost them in a fight with an Arab dhow. But I got my slaves to the mainland, then walked them across the whole of Africa."

"You walked your slaves across Africa?" Adam was incredulous.

"Yes, M'sieu Rutledge, we walked the Great Slave Road. A thing of fright it was! Bleached bones piled high by the side of the road. A broad track, beaten smooth by the bare feet of niggers." He was silent a moment, then went on, "Vultures followed us, waiting for death. Every night black

33

men lay down for vultures to feast on. I lost fifty men and half that number of women. I tell you, M'sieu, when I first saw the blue water of Lobita Bay I was wild with joy. I can still feel the heat, the heavy stifling heat of the jungle and the Great Slave Road! Dieu, it was horrible!"

Adam said nothing, thinking of LaTruchy's words.

"Slaves of all the world go on the block at Zanzibar," La-Truchy continued, rubbing his hands together. "No slave market like it. Such women!" He ran his tongue along his full lips. "Women, standing on the block, moving their sinuous bodies. Women well trained to be the delight of their masters! The Sultan takes first choice for his harem, but sometimes his eunuchs overlook a prize." He stopped, glancing at Adam, then looking quickly away. "A man must have a stout control of himself when he sees those houris. The women of Zanzibar know how to stir the depths of men." His eyes narrowed, his face showed too plainly where his thoughts ran. "All day long the young ones practice a dance they call the Duc-Duc. When they reach perfection—muscular perfection —they are ready for sale. Old crones teach their young ones arts unknown to the women of Europe, movements of the body that make moments an eternity of delight for their masters."

Adam rose abruptly; his voice was harsh. "I don't want your women, LaTruchy. I want replacement of those runaways . . . men for the fields, to drain swampland and cut timber. I want blacks with strength who do not need the lash to drive them to a day's work."

"I've got that kind, too, M'sieu, but the women . . ."

"I don't want women, I tell you. We've got enough breeders now."

LaTruchy got to his feet. He beckoned a man in the boat. "Bring the girl Azizi," he called.

"What the devil are you up to, LaTruchy?" Adam demanded, angered by the Frenchman's insistence. "I told you I don't want more women."

"Wait until you have seen this one, M'sieu. I swear by Our Lady, she is the finest flesh I've brought to America since I've been trading in black ivory."

"LaTruchy, I don't want your black women. Talk to Marcy about field hands. Make your bargain with him."

A sly look crept into the trader's bold eyes. "The girl is not black. She is amber. She is gold and ivory. Look, M'sieu. See how she walks; see the movement of her hips."

Adam stopped and glanced over his shoulder. The two women had stepped from the boat and stood on the landing. At LaTruchy's command they moved forward. In spite of the veils that covered the lower part of their faces, he saw that one was young. The other, an old woman, walked a few steps behind, as a slave would walk. She carried a large bundle wrapped in a square of faded calico against her sagging breasts.

Adam turned to watch their approach. LaTruchy was right. The girl's skin was amber, almost ivory. She moved slowly, her back straight. Her head, wrapped in a turban of green silk, was held high. She met his glance once, then her dark eyes looked beyond him as if there were some inanimate object in her path. As she moved there was a faint tinkling sound of silver anklets and bangles. Strings of colored beads, amber, lapis and cinnabar, circled her throat and fell to her waist. She came as far as the boathouse and stopped.

"Come here," Adam said.

The girl did not stir. She pulled her veil higher across her face until only her long dark eyes were visible.

Adam turned to LaTruchy. "Is she dumb?" he asked.

LaTruchy shook his head. "No. She understand well enough when she wants to, English or French. The old woman is dumb. She had her tongue cut out by desert Arabs." He took a step forward and laid his hand on the girl's shoulder. She shook it off, her eyes blazing resentment.

"Come here, Azizi," he said harshly. "This is your new master. Strip down your calico so he can see your back and feel the muscles of your legs and arms. I want him to see that you are strong and worth the buying."

The girl's eyes blazed again, then went dull and lifeless.

"No need of that, LaTruchy," Adam said. "I don't want her." But his eyes followed the soft curves of her slim body. "I don't want the girl," he repeated. "I have no use for her. I need men, field hands."

LaTruchy, sensing his indecision, took a step forward.

"Take off your calico," he said. "Let the master lay hands on your body." He jerked at the cotton sari with his stubby fingers. The cloth fell from the girl's shoulder, baring the curve of her arm and her firm rounded breasts. She caught up the sari quickly and hugged it closely about her.

Adam felt the blood rise in him, but her look of contempt shamed him. There was no hint of submission in her eyes, only scorn and defiance. This was strange in a slave. Strange

35

too was the color of her skin and its texture. He turned to LaTruchy, who was watching him, a curious gleam in his beady black eyes.

"The woman's not a Negro. What is she?" Adam asked.

LaTruchy shrugged his shoulders. "I don't know, M'sieu Rutledge. We don't inquire too much about women who go on the slave block in Zanzibar. Perhaps she belonged to the Sultan's harem, or to one of the rich Zanzibar merchants. She could be Arab, Persian or Ethiopian. The Somali are sometimes light colored when they breed with East Indians. Who knows? She's a slave—" he gave Adam a sly glance. "As I said, M'sieu, the dancing women of Zanzibar—"

Adam interrupted him. He was angered by the Frenchman's implication.

"Take the woman back to the ship." Adam's voice was harsh. The old woman picked up the bundle she had put on the steps of the boathouse and limped away. LaTruchy caught at the slave girl's wrist when she started to follow.

"Wait, M'sieu, wait. Do not make a decision now. I'm going to Edenton again. Keep the girl until I come back; you may find use for her."

Marcy came down the path from the house. He did not look at the girl.

"Mrs. Rutledge asks you not to forget that she wants a woman house slave, Mr. Rutledge," he said to Adam.

LaTruchy, quick to see his advantage, shoved the girl forward. She stumbled against Adam. Her body was soft against him; the heavy odor of sandalwood struck his nostrils. Words tumbled from LaTruchy's lips: "Take her, M'sieu Rutledge. She is strong. She has crossed the Great Slave Road through the heart of Africa. Take her and check off the ten runaways."

Adam hesitated. A sense of foreboding gripped him. Marcy looked at the girl.

"Mrs. Rutledge says the woman must be young and not ill favored. She would like one that is strong, but comely. Perhaps this girl will answer if she is as strong as LaTruchy says she is."

"She has strength. Pay no attention to her slight body. She is wiry. She can work and she is stronger than she seems." LaTruchy was insistent.

Adam said to Marcy, "Take her to Mrs. Rutledge. If she approves, we can talk terms." He turned to LaTruchy. "Your price is outrageous, and you know it. One slave is not worth the price of ten field hands!"

The trader laughed, his sharp pointed teeth showing through his black beard. He knew his bargain was made.

"I throw in the Old One for good measure. She will wait on the girl and protect her." He laughed again. "The other slaves fear her. She protects the girl with teeth and claws. Why she even made them carry her mistress in a machella when she got tired!"

After his lonely dinner, Adam went to Sara's room to find out what she had decided about the slave. Sara was in bed, propped up by pillows, a tray on a table within reach of her hand, and her Bible open beside her. When Adam came into the room, she picked up her tapestry and began stitching.

"Do you want me to buy the slave?" Adam asked, after he had kissed her cheek. "Do you think she is strong enough for housework?"

Sara looked surprised. "I thought you had already bought her, Adam. I had Judith take her to the seamstress to have a livery made. I can't have her going about the house half naked in front of men slaves."

"I haven't bought her yet," Adam said, controlling his annoyance. "LaTruchy is holding her for the price of those runaways. That's too much money for any slave, even if she should turn out to be a good breeder."

Sara's thin hand touched Adam's strong brown fingers lightly. "Not too much if I want the girl, is it, Adam?"

Adam made one more protest. "But you said you wanted a strong girl, Sara. This one doesn't look strong to me. She seems fragile, almost delicate."

"But I do want her, please, Adam, I want her—please."

Adam turned to the window. He wondered why he was so reluctant to buy the woman. The price was exorbitant, but he had paid exorbitant prices for slaves before this. Was it because Sara was so set on the girl? Somehow, of late, he found himself combating her in his thoughts. He must not allow himself to fall into a habit of separateness from her. He must not shut her out of his inner life. She was looking up at him with wide blue eyes, round and inquiring as a child's.

"Please, Adam, I want the girl. She will look so well in my plum-colored livery with a coif and kerchief of white mull. What does one more slave mean to you, Adam? I ask so little . . . so very little." She paused, her eyes clouding, ready for tears.

He was lost. He knew it. Yet some perverse thing in him

37

made him hold off. She caught his hand and held it for a moment lightly against her cheek.

"You love me, Adam, you do love me," she murmured.

He knew he would give way to her tenacious will as he had always given way before. She did not need the girl, but he could not steel his heart against her and she was taking advantage of it. In relation to her he had no confidence in himself; he lost that masculine sureness that was so much a part of the real Adam. She clung to his hand, her pale face lifted to his, her lips quivering.

"Of course, I will buy the girl," he said quickly. "But I'm damned if one house slave is worth ten field hands."

She dropped his hand and said primly, "Thank you, Adam, but I wish you would not use such words. Mr. Whitefield preaches that it is very sinful to curse or use oaths."

Adam did not speak. He was on the point of saying something about Whitefield and his preaching, but he held his tongue.

He went directly to the counting room from his talk with Sara and worked until almost midnight. The stillness of the night bore in on him. Within his counting room his world was his own. Working on his ledgers he broke the barrier and went beyond the garden and the blue Sound into the great world of ships. Ships bore his cargoes to England and Portugal. Shallops plied between his wharf at Rutledge Riding and Port o'Spain, St. Croix and Charlotte Amalie. They carried cargoes of wheat, tar, turpentine and pitch in exchange for coffee and spices. Sometimes he let himself dream far into the night of cargoes he would send to Spain and to the East Indies. In those still watches he broke the confines of his daily existence and set his course for the future.

The clock striking twelve brought him back to reality. He took up a candle and went across the gallery to Sara's room. He opened the door, moving softly, his hand shielding the candle. The sinister figure of the slave woman rose from a couch near Sara's bed, the whites of her eyes gleaming in the darkness as she barred the way. Adam pushed her aside and moved past her to the bed. Sara was asleep. Her eyes, deeply circled, were closed; dark lashes lay against her white cheeks. How frail she was! How small in the vast white expanse of the great canopied bed, so small that the outlines of her body seemed to make no unevenness in the smoothness of the counterpane. The woman stood by his side as if to shield her mistress. The same words came to her lips that she seemed to

38

speak as a formula: "Better you go now, better she rest to-night."

Adam left the room silently. A young Negro boy was sitting on a mahogany chest outside the drawing-room door, his back against the wall, his head falling forward on his chest.

"What are you doing here?" Adam asked.

The slave sprang to his feet at the sound of Adam's voice, rubbing his eyes with the back of his hand.

"Aaron he say, 'Keep the fire bright, lessen the master come.'"

"You can go to bed, now. I don't want the fire kept up tonight." Adam stood at the door and gazed thoughtfully at the pools of light made by the glow of the fire on the dark polished floors of the long drawing room. The heavy crimson damask curtains had been drawn across the windows and candles cast wavering shadows on the white paneled walls. The room was warm, inviting. It lacked only laughter and gay voices to give it life and beauty. He saw that the slave had not gone.

"Bank the fire and snuff the candles, Castor," he said kindly; "then run to bed. Tell Aaron you needn't work until noon tomorrow."

"Thank you, master."

Adam walked slowly through the dark hallway. Why should the empty rooms depress him tonight? He did not know. This was no different from other nights. It was always the same, day after day, month after month. He moved wearily up the stairs, the sound of his footsteps echoing sharply through the still rooms. In his bedroom he crossed to the window and drew the heavy curtains. The *Oriflamme* had sailed at sunset. Now the waters of the Sound glinted in the moonlight with scarcely a ripple to break the moon path that lay on it. He paced the room, his hands behind his back, his head bent, an unaccountable restlessness upon him.

A packet of letters lay on his desk. Marcy must have brought them from Edenton and forgotten to tell him, he thought. One was from Marsden, his London agent. He opened it first. It contained the usual items of business—tobacco and hides sold, orders for next season's crop. Marsden always saved his personal comments for the last.

"I thought you would like to know that Henry McCulloh has introduced a new bill into Parliament; one that we must watch. He wants taxes in the Colonies to be increased by a Stamp Tax. Adam, this is a vicious measure. I'm sure our people will rebel against it. The Virginia agent, James Ogle-thorpe, and I went direct to McCulloh and protested. We told him that such a tax would bring hardship to our people. The Province is very poor. We haven't had time to recover from the burden of the money we advanced for the wars they have been fighting in India.

"The committee was not even civil to us. One man said, 'Your antagonism is based on an inclination to break with England, not on the proposed plan of taxation.' He banged the table with his fist. 'That is the real issue. You want to break; any excuse will do!' McCulloh argued. He was violent about it.

" 'If trouble does arise over taxation, it will be handled with an iron hand,' McCulloh shouted. We both had a hard time keeping within bounds at their insolence. There is a party in power now that wants to work the Colonies for all they are worth. 'Bleed them white,' is their motto. I don't know what is going to happen. I'm sending the official report home as soon as I get the list of articles and transactions to be taxed. The bill comes up for reading soon. It's bad, very bad, Adam. I feel that we are on the verge of serious trouble. Political preferment is at the root of the whole trouble. This bill is not all to be blamed on McCulloh; it is along the pol-icy of Grenville's ministry."

Adam laid the letter on the table. He shared Marsden's anxiety for he was certain that the Province would not stand for more taxes. When he picked up the last *Weekly Post-Boy* to see if there was any comment on the new Stamp Tax, he found the item inconspicuously tucked away, sunk deep be-tween the parliamentary procedures and announcements from the Court Calendar.

He would take the letter to Edenton next week. The meet-ing of the Edenton committee and the Wilmington delega-tion, which had twice been postponed, was now set for the following Thursday. Both Judge Moore and John Ashe were in close touch with all the bills introduced in Parliament that had any bearing on the Colonies. They would surely know about the Act.

After he had gone to bed, Adam's thoughts turned to Mary Warden. He must talk to her about this, show her the letter. He wished he could share her interest in the politics of the Province. But he did not have the time. He hadn't seen Mary since the Hunt. But what was he to do? If he suggested to Sara that she ask Mary over to the Manor House, she said she felt too ill to see anyone. Every time he went to the village Sara would ask, "I suppose you had tea with Mary?" And if he said that he had, she was unhappy. He did not want to lie to Sara, so he stayed away. When he chanced to meet Mary, he had no answer to the questioning in her eyes. In the rare times he allowed himself to think about it, he knew Mary was necessary to him. He counted on her quick sure sympathy and her understanding; more than anything on her understanding. He wondered how happy her life was with William. Mary, always so lovely and serene, was she really happy? But, after all, happiness was merely a vague term, he told himself. It was enough to have a few high moments . . . let the rest be work, hard work. The thought of Mary faded. As he neared sleep the swaying body of a woman floated before him. Dark eyes looked at him obliquely, scornful and defiant. Firm rounded breasts, a body of amber . . . La-Truchy's sly smile, his insinuating voice . . . "in Zanzibar, women are trained to the arts of love . . . smooth rounded bodies that bring an eternity of delight—"

Chapter 3

QUEEN'S
GIFT

MARY WARDEN turned Black Douglas into the magnolia-lined drive that led to Queen's Gift. The great stallion quickened his trot without urging. He was at home and he knew that a dozen ears of dried corn were waiting in the manger.

It was mid-afternoon. The autumn sun lay in bright patches on the lawn that sloped gently away from the house to the shores of Albemarle Sound. The old house, bathed in sunlight, stood out boldly against the deep green of the forest. Turpentine pines spired to the sky beyond orchards and vineyards. Deer roamed at will through the deep woods, and the sharp bark of a red fox broke in on the low moaning of doves, or the frightened burr of a swift rising pheasant.

The broad façade of the house was inviting, the two low wings extending arms of welcome. Mary loved the old house. During the years she had lived in England with her grandmother she had dreamed child's dreams of going home to play on the broad galleries, to romp in the box bordered garden with her dogs, or to sail with her father across the Sound and down along the south shore until they reached the surging Atlantic. Mary was born in the west wing of Queen's Gift in a room that overlooked the stables and rolling pastures. A few hours later her young mother died in the same room.

Her grandfather, Roger Mainwairing, had built Queen's Gift. It was patterned after his family home in the Midlands and he had given it the same name. Only the new house was built of lumber cut from his own timber-land instead of buff Cotswold stone. He began the house soon after he came to Albemarle but it was two years later before it was finished.

Mary loved the story of her grandfather Roger. He was a rebel and walked his own way. A rebel he had been since the day he ran away from Magdalen College to ride with the Duke. It was a fatal ride for twelve young Oxford students for it led him straight into Monmouth's Rebellion. It led also to death for five on Sedgemoor Field and imprisonment for the others. Because he was only sixteen Roger was convicted of High Treason and sentenced by Lord Jeffreys to be sold to a planter in the West Indies in lieu of imprisonment in a dungeon.

One cold December morning, when the fog lay heavy on the Thames, Roger stepped aboard the *West Wind,* George Gibbs, master, at Tilbury dock along with one hundred and forty convicts whose crimes ranged from debt and petty thievery to murder. They were outbound for St. Kitts and seven years of slavery.

Three months on the stormy Atlantic gave the young rebel time to think. To be bunked in the stinking hold of the *West Wind* with unwashed, foul-spoken men, the scum of lower London, was a poor return for youthful ardor to right the wrongs of the people and set the Duke on the throne. High adventure languished in the stench of rank flesh and bilge. Vermin and slimy, creeping things, that belong to unclean bodies and filthy ships, dampened high hopes. Roger lost his enthusiasm to right the peoples' wrongs when he came in close contact with them. But he made no complaint. He stood his watches and manned the sails and waited on the drunken captain. He ate wormy, rotten food until his stomach rebelled. His pride and breeding gave him strength to drive his weary body. The crew scoffed and reviled him but he fought his way to their respect with bare knuckles. "The Duke," they called him, and he carried the name to his death. The long voyage put iron into his soul and gave him the strength for the years that followed.

Captain Haimes was reckoned a hard master. Roger never saw him until he had been on the plantation for two years. One day the Captain, dressed in fresh white linen and carried in a hammock by eight slaves, inspected the sisal field where Roger was working with half a hundred blacks. The pale shrewd eyes of the master appraised men and crops. Roger did not look up or give the servile salute as the other field workers did. His hoe fell rhythmically, turning the fertile soil. Haimes stopped his carriers.

"Come here," he shouted.

Roger knew he was calling to him but he did not stop. Haimes raised his great voice, "You with the yellow hair, come here!"

Roger looked up, his steady blue eyes met those of his owner without fear.

"Your name?" Haimes demanded.

Roger told him.

"Your crime?"

A faint smile rimmed Roger's wide, firm mouth, but he made no answer.

"Speak up, man, have you no English?"

The half-caste overlooker hurried up, followed by a slave carrying a many-lashed whip.

"The blacksnake will give the fellow tongue," he said eagerly.

Haimes's gorge rose.

"Get to Hell out of here!" he shouted angrily. "I'll deal with this man."

He turned to Roger. "Go to my office and wait for me."

He gave a quick order and the black carriers moved off at a steady swinging lope. Roger's eyes followed the heavy figure of the master, swaying in the hammock, as the runners carried him along the rows of stiff, bayoneted sisal.

Roger waited an hour in the shade of a great mango tree that overshadowed the plantation house. When Haimes appeared he was on foot. He motioned Roger to follow him into the office where he sat down at his desk while a slave changed the position of the jalousies, to give more light in the darkened room. Roger felt Haimes's keen eyes follow the lines of his hard sinewy figure from his sunburned yellow hair to his bare calloused feet. He stood at ease and met the Captain's gaze without flinching. Haimes was not used to that. It puzzled him. He lifted a decanter from a table at his elbow and poured a stiff drink of plantation rum.

"What crime?" he said, wiping his mouth with a large India silk handkerchief.

"No crime," Roger said shortly.

Haimes laughed and helped himself to another drink.

"Don't hesitate to confess. On this plantation we have thieves and murderers, and men who have beaten their wives, or committed crimes against nature. What was yours?"

Roger had no stomach for explanations. The past was done with. He had no wish to revive it, so he did not answer.

"We have a whipping post and a dungeon on the plantation." Haimes's words fell smoothly. "Or we might turn the savages loose to run after a man with bows and arrows."

As an afterthought, he added, "Poisoned arrows."

Still Roger did not speak. He saw that the man was not angry. After a moment, Haimes heaved himself out of the rush chair and crossed to a desk on the far side of the room. He lifted a great morocco-bound book from a shelf and turned the pages slowly until he found the item he was seeking.

"Roger Mainwairing, Market Harborough," he read aloud, "Rebel to the Crown in the army of the Pretender, James Duke of Monmouth. Oxford, Magdelen College. Orphan. Age 16."

He closed the book slowly.

"You have been here two years," he said. "In the name of Christ, why did that ass Thompson put you to work in the fields with the blacks when we needed overlookers?"

He frowned at Roger as if he were to blame for Thompson's misdeeds.

"Go to the store and draw some decent whites, Mainwairing. Report here in the morning."

He wrote something on a slip of paper. "Give that to Thompson. He will assign you a room in the bachelor mess."

"Thank you, sir," Roger choked on the words. He was steeled against abuse or brutality but he was ill prepared for kindness. Haimes leaned back in his chair and looked at Roger speculatively.

"So you rode with Monmouth. A fool. A silly young fool. Can't you look out for yourself instead of hitching your chariot to some other man's wild dream?"

Roger laughed suddenly. "I loathed Latin, and I despised my tutor. It was more fun to ride with the Duke."

Haimes's great laugh filled the room. He got to his feet and clapped a heavy hand on Roger's shoulder.

"I'm with you there, Mainwairing. I never could build the bridge across the Aquitania. A sorry time I had down at Cambridge, so I cut out and came to St. Kitts to be a planter." He filled his glass again, drinking slowly, his mind turned to some past living. He had forgotten Roger, who waited to be dismissed.

Suddenly he said, "Now get out of here. Don't let me see you again until you are fumigated and into clean clothes. If you are smart and do as I tell you, I'll make a planter out of you. That's more than Monmouth could have done for you, me lad."

Captain Haimes kept his word. For three years Roger went from plantation to plantation, from Island to Island, learning about land and crops. Then for two years he captained cargo ships to London, Lisbon and the Barbary States. One morning Haimes sent for him. Roger stood at the door for a moment waiting for his eyes to adjust themselves to the darkened room. The jalousies were tipped to soften the white glare of the midday sun. Haimes was at his desk, his broad back bent over the ledger. Roger advanced into the room and waited for his master to speak. The room was cool and quiet, with no sound but the scratching of the quill on the heavy paper. After a time Haimes looked up.

"Oh, it's you, Mainwairing. I didn't hear you come in. These damn invoices of Thompson's are the devil to decipher." Haimes poured a drink and pushed the decanter toward Roger. "Sit down, there's something I've been wanting to talk over with you. I'm sending the *Kentish Maid* to the Port of Roanoke in the Carolinas with a cargo of sugar and rum. You will go, but you will not be in command of the ship. Grimes will captain her."

A sinking feeling hit the pit of Roger's stomach. Something must have displeased Haimes. He watched the man lean back in the rush chair and make a tent of his short stubby fingers. Roger waited.

"How old are you, Roger?" Haimes asked abruptly.

"Twenty-three, sir."

Haimes nodded. "Just the right age. The first call will be the village at Queen Anne's Creek. It lies on the north shore of Albemarle Sound, almost at the head. Get off the ship there and look about for good acreage. They tell me that there are thousands of acres of virgin land to be had. Look first at the soil and drainage, then for timber and water. You may have to get some of the Granville Grant, but don't pay too much for it."

Haimes pushed a leather sack across the desk toward Roger. It was heavy with gold doubloons.

"You want me to buy land for you, sir?"

"God's death, no! Haven't I enough trouble with land without wanting more? It's for you, Roger. You have earned the gold."

Roger's surprise was complete. He stammered his thanks, smiling. Haimes was not listening. He had turned to his ledger. Roger took up the moneybag and crossed the room.

"Mind you, get yourself a plantation as good as this one or I'll come up with my blacksnake and lay on with a will."

46

Roger laughed explosively.

Haimes smiled, rubbing his hands together, pleased with himself at his witticism. "Before you go, Mainwairing, I want your name to a contract for pine poles for my masts. At a decent figure, mind you! No trying to skin your old master on price! Now get down to the ship, and the next time you want to reform the world, follow your own star, not some rattlebrain Duke's."

The *Kentish Maid* sailed up Albemarle Sound at the Ave Maria hour a month later. On the northern shore lay the village of Queen Anne's Creek, turned to gold by the low sun. Roger stood on the bridge looking with eager eyes on the fair land, its blue water, green pines, and dark, rich earth.

The ship tacked slowly across the Sound and came to anchor opposite the village. While the blacks unloaded sacks of Island sugar and hemp into barges, Roger was rowed ashore to the crude wharf. The evening was warm, a light breeze blowing off the Sound. Flowers blossomed in trim gardens behind hedges. Girls in light gowns sat on pillared galleries behind swaying vines of scarlet trumpet and yellow honeysuckle. Gentlemen on the backs of fine bred horses nodded to Roger, or touched their hats with their riding crops as they passed the stranger. Perfume of honeysuckle and jasmine floated out from the hedged gardens; gay, high laughter of unseen women mingled with the heavier voices of men. Suddenly Roger was very lonely. For the first time the thought of a home for himself came to him.

At the edge of the village Roger saw a white-haired Negro working a small patch of cotton. The bushes were heavy with white bolls, the largest he had ever seen. Roger knew cotton. That was part of Haimes's training. He stopped and leaned against the whitewashed gate, watching the rhythmic movement of the hoe.

"The land is very fertile," he said.

The old Negro straightened himself, mopping his forehead with the back of his gnarled, black hand. "Sir, it is 'The Garden of Eden.'"

"Is there vacant land near by?" Roger asked.

The Negro shook his head. "No cleared land, sir."

Roger looked around. The deep forest was close, he could hear the call of night birds. Herons stood in the stream that bounded the garden.

The Negro stared at him curiously. After a time he said, "Be you rich in gold, Master?"

Roger shook his head, smiling.

The black man's face fell. "Too bad. If you had gold you could buy cleared land close by. Old Master Blount he die last year. He land bound to come for sale, 'causewise Master James, he don' want no more land 'longside Mulberry Hill."

"Where is this land?" Roger asked.

The old man waved his hand vaguely to the east and south. "Hit goes that way from the woods right down to the Sound. A pretty piece of land, Master, put out to fields and orchards. This crick she run right through hit, and there's a sight of good standing timber. But if you hain't got gold—" The old man bent his back to the hoe. The subject was closed.

Early the following morning Roger Mainwairing went to a land sale, the notice of which he had seen posted on the walls of the Inn. By nightfall he was the owner of nine hundred acres of Blount land, "leaning against the village land on the west, bounded on the north and east by primeval forests, and on the south by Albemarle Sound."

The next few years Roger spent in developing the plantation. Then he began trading the products of his land with his old master, Haimes, at St. Kitts. By the time he was thirty Roger Mainwairing was a rich man in land and slaves and ships. When he was thirty-three he went to London for furnishings for the new house he was building. When he came back he brought a bride with him to live in Queen's Gift. The Lords Proprietors still held title to North Carolina but Roger hoped their arbitrary rule would soon give way to a different government. The day had passed when a King could give away an empire in land to some dissolute favorite!

Rhoda Chapman was co-heir with her brother Thomas to the great Chapman and Ainsworth collieries in the Midlands. She tolerated life in the Albemarle country in her casual, erratic way, for she loved Roger, but she had little to do with the village. She missed her old life until Roger had her hunters brought over; then she was quite happy. The Blount brothers, who hunted and had a proper stable, were among her few friends. She liked to boast that an ancestor of hers was among those officers of the King who hunted in the Northamptonshire country while they waited for the battle of Naseby. The parson, Dr. Blair, she asked to tea and supper so that she could argue with him against converting the Indians.

48

Because there was no public building to house the Assembly the meetings were held at the homes of planters in the different districts. The ballroom at Queen's Gift was used when the sessions were held in the Chowan District. Rhoda enjoyed the Assembly. She attended each session, sitting in an elbow chair of red damask near the speaker's table. She entered the discussion when she felt like it and interrupted speakers at will. The whole Province buzzed with excitement the time she struck Tom Gooch, the member from New Bern, with her riding crop when he hinted in the Assembly that Governor Eden was in league with Edward Teach, the pirate; or Blackbeard, as he was better known. That was in 1718, shortly before Captain Maynard captured Blackbeard. She made an impassioned speech before the Assembly meeting in her ballroom, saying that things had come to a pretty pass when a commoner could accuse a Governor of piracy because Blackbeard had once gone to Eden House to plead the King's Proclamation which offered pardon to those who would abandon their buccaneering ways. The Assembly, being in a measure guests under her roof, listened in silence. There were many members who privately believed with the member from New Bern that Sir Charles Eden was not above taking his share of the loot that Blackbeard was supposed to have hidden in his secret retreats in the Chowan River.

This plain speaking of his wife did not embarrass Roger. He reveled in it. As for Sir Charles, he gave a splendid dinner at Eden House in her honor, saying that he was glad there was one voice in the Province raised in his defense.

Rhoda bore Roger one son, Hesketh, a quiet, sickly child, whom she took over to England and put in Eton the day he was nine. She saw her child only twice from that time until he was twenty, a grown man. But he was being well schooled, and she was proud of that.

When Roger Mainwairing was drowned bringing his ship through Mono Passage in a hurricane Rhoda went back to England to her old home in the Midlands. But she sent Hesketh to Edenton to manage Queen's Gift. A few years later he married Ann Blount, who lived just long enough to give birth to a daughter. This was a great blow to Hesketh. It drove him to a hermit's life on the plantation, with only his books and his slaves for company. The infant child he gave over to the care of the slave Cissie. It was Dr. Armitage who finally persuaded Hesketh to let him take the child to her grandmother in England. Mary was eight then and she wept bitterly when she left her father. He promised her that she could come back in two years' time. But she was seventeen, and Hesketh a dying man, before she came to Queen's Gift.

Rhoda had married again. This time to Sir Nigel Carstairs, for no particular reason save that he was a pleasant, agreeable gentleman, and he hunted with the Quorn.

The day Mary arrived her grandmother took her to the stables and set her on the back of a great Irish hunter with the admonition to sit tight and if she did take a spill, not to cry. She ordered the old groom O'Leary to put the child over the low jumps to see how she behaved.

"Teach her how to sit a horse properly, O'Leary. If she's got the Chapman blood you won't have to teach her how to handle a horse. The Chapmans are born with a light hand on the bridle."

Mary proved her right to the Chapman name. From that time on she could be seen trailing the Hunt, a lonely little figure mounted on a great bay hunter.

"Isn't Mary rather small to be riding a sixteen-hand hunter?" Sir Nigel asked his wife one evening after a stiff run in the driving rain. "I was thinking of having a little mare sent down from the Shetland Islands for her for a birthday gift."

Rhoda choked over her brandy. She laughed until the tears came.

"You are too amusin', Nigel! Fancy giving her one of those wee animals. You know I've told you that the Chapman women can always take care of themselves where a horse is concerned."

So Mary went on riding sixteen and seventeen-hand hunters. She seemed quite content and happy in a world of grown people.

The April Mary was seventeen Rhoda suddenly bethought herself that she should see something of Society. She called Mary in one morning and looked her over as if she were a filly she was thinking of purchasing. She wasn't too pleased. She said frankly, "Your eyes are your best feature. They are dark blue, the kind that won't fade, and your lashes are incredibly long and black. Your hair is a good thick chestnut. Some people like a widow's peak, but I don't—" She turned Mary from side to side. "Legs too long, body too thin, face too thin, mouth too wide, nose too straight. I like a nose that turns up; it gives a provocative look to a face. And you haven't a scrap of color. No, Mary, you're not a beauty, so you will have to make yourself pleasant and agreeable to people."

Sir Nigel had come in during his wife's recital. He adjusted his glass to his eye and said, "My dear, if I may be permitted a word of advice?"

"Go ahead, Nigel," Rhoda said. "No doubt you men have a different idea of beauty."

"I wasn't thinking of beauty, Rhoda," her husband said. "Mary will do well enough as looks go." He turned to Mary. "Don't mind what anyone says, Mary, just be natural. Let your heart tell you what to do, not your head." He cleared his throat, somewhat embarrassed that he had allowed himself to be serious even for a moment.

Rhoda opened the town house in Audley Street and the family moved up to London for the Season.

"It's all very boring, Nigel," Rhoda complained to her husband. "But in spite of what you say about being natural, the child must have some of the training of a lady of fashion. I don't want an awkward young woman on my hands. She must go to balls and suppers and appear at the theaters on gala nights. But I am sure it will be a failure. The young men will run the other way. Mary is a nice child, but she is too quiet, and she hasn't enough money to interest a proper match."

But much to her grandmother's surprise the young gallants liked Mary. Invitations poured in on her to ride in the park or to coach to Virginia Water, and she never lacked partners for a minuet or contra-dance.

"I don't understand it," confessed Rhoda to her husband one morning after a ball at Dorchester House. "Mary hasn't a grain of coquetry in her, but the young and the old like her. Did you notice that Banastre Tarleton danced with her twice? What they see in her, I don't know. She's too reserved. Now, in my day, a girl had to have dash and a few tricks to attract a male."

Sir Nigel smiled a little as he adjusted his peruke before a gilt Florentine mirror. "Mary is an excellent listener," he said.

"Nonsense, Nigel, a girl won't be popular if she sits like a stick listening to men talk."

Sir Nigel did not argue. It would have done no good. Mary was a prime favorite with him. He liked her steady, blue eyes, her quiet humor and her way of turning a deft phrase. He had put her down in his will for a sum of money large enough to give her independence the rest of her life. He knew that Mary must have independence. He had no faith in Hesketh, whom he considered too much of a dreamer. Mary would inherit Queen's Gift plantation in the Carolinas, but suppose she wanted to marry and live in England? She would need a suitable dowry. As for her grandmother, his wife, she had long since gone through her fortune with the same high-handedness that characterized all her living. Stables, hunters and impecunious followers got most of it, although thousands of pounds had been put into the South Sea Company.

When Lady Carstairs met her death jumping a stiff oxer, Sir Nigel signed over the fund to Mary. He wanted her to have the money while he was still alive, to prevent any claims against it.

A few days after her grandmother's funeral Mary sailed on the *Bright Star* for the Carolinas. A letter had arrived, written by Dr. Armitage, asking her to come home. Her father, Hesketh Mainwairing, was a sick man. He would not live out the year.

Mary married William Warden, her father's friend, the day before Hesketh died. During his long illness Hesketh had worried about her future. Then the thought of William Warden presented itself. William had come from London, five or six years before, to untangle the Granville Land Grant affairs. Hesketh liked him and had put the plantation law business into his hands. From that, friendship had grown. William had already gained a high position in England as a barrister. A man of distinction and means, he was in every way a suitable husband for Mary. The fact that he was twenty years her senior was no obstacle to Hesketh, or to Mary. When her father spoke to her of the marriage she made no objection.

"Armitage tells me I have only a short time, Mary. I would be happy to know that you were well married before I die."

The Doctor and the slaves made up the small group around the bedside when Parson Daniel Earl of St. Paul's read the marriage lines.

Hesketh's voice was thin and very tired. He told her, "I hope you will live at Queen's Gift, Mary. Perhaps you can make it the place my father dreamed of. I had not the strength or will to accomplish it." Those were Hesketh Mainwairing's last words.

Mary accepted her life without question. Marriages arranged by parents were the custom. There was no other man with whom she had been in love, so the word meant nothing to her. That was before Adam Rutledge came to Edenton and built the great house at Rutledge Riding.

Something of all this was in Mary Warden's mind as she rode up the driveway of Queen's Gift on this sunny autumn afternoon. But she dismissed the thought when she saw the saddle horses tied to the rail at the side of the house. She had forgotten the meeting that was to take place today. William had told her but the day at Eden House had put the matter out of her mind. The Wilmington men would be there by now and she had not given cook last orders for supper, nor had she found out from William the number of guests he expected. She dismounted at the carriage block and gave the reins over to the waiting Negro groom.

"Blanket him and walk him around the track before you feed him," she told the boy.

"Yes'm. Look lak he fret heself to a lather," the boy answered, rubbing his hand over the shining satin neck.

"He pulled all the way in from Edenton, wanting to gallop. I think he needs more exercise."

"Yes'm, he do. He need more jumping to take the tuck out of he."

Mary patted the horse's arched neck. "Tell Lugu to set up the gates in the south paddock. I'll work him in the morning," she said.

"Yes'm, Lugu, he make some fine new oxers for jumpin'. They wide and high. Tain't many hoss' ken jump 'em, but Black Douglas, he ken. He got wings, jes lak a debbil. He mak' *Mankwala* on heself, and ris' right up in the air."

Mary laughed. "I've never seen his wings, Ches, but I think he does have the Old Nick in him at times."

She hooked up her green velvet riding skirt to walking length and went across the gallery to the side door. As she passed the dining-room window she saw two of the women slaves laying the long mahogany table. She must hurry. Cook would be in a proper rage. She wondered how many men were on the Edenton committee. She would call her husband to find out after she had pacified Chaney.

Mary crossed the covered brick passageway that led from the main house to the kitchen and buttery. There was great activity in the low, whitewashed room. The cook was an old slave of her father's and spoke to her with freedom. She stopped her work and stood looking at Mary, her hands on her ample hips.

"Why fo' you go skitterin' round the countryside on that black debbil when you outer be at home seein' that you' gentlemen guests get theyselves fed? You ride off early this mornin' no time tellin' I what fo' to fix fo' supper."

Mary took her plumed hat from her head and ruffled her hair.

"I knew you would think of something delicious, Chaney," she said with a quick smile. "What are you going to have?"

The black woman was not pacified. She went right on with her monologue. The slaves stopped their work. The moment Chaney's attention was removed they took advantage.

"Look lak you druther spend time with a hoss than see to you' house duties. Howfer' yo' think we goin' to get supper for they Wilmington gentry ef yo' don't tell what you want I to cook?"

Mary crossed the kitchen to the brick stove and lifted the lid of a steaming kettle. Chaney grabbed the lid from her hand.

"Want to mak you'self a steam burn?" she grumbled. She threw a handful of cloves and allspice into the liquid and turned on her idle helpers.

"Get to work ef you don't want blacksnake on you' triflin' shoulders! Zettie, give me those slabs of bacon, then run tell Ebon to give I some sherry wine. Tell he not to send any that no account Province wine he makes. I wants the best Madeira. I aims to have cookin' mak' those Wilmington gentlemen remember Queen's Gift."

She put the slabs of bacon into the liquid and threw in sticks of cinnamon bark. Then she drew a key from her pocket and unlocked the spice cupboard and took one nutmeg from a tin box.

" 'Tain't many No'th Carolina families got nutmeg to season they cooters," she announced with satisfaction.

"Oh," said Mary, as if she did not already know, "you are going to make terrapin soup?"

The old woman waved her hand. Outside the kitchen door, two Negro boys were sitting by the meat block, picking over cooters and opening the shells with a sharp knife.

"And I won't give I soup rule to nobody," the old woman mumbled as she waddled back to her stool.

"What else are you going to have?" Mary inquired, seeing that Chaney was still in a black mood.

The woman smoothed her white apron over her knees. She reached over to a table and dipped a small stick into a tin snuffbox, then laid the stick carefully along her gums, the end protruding beyond her teeth. A loud sneeze followed.

"This mornin' I tak I down to the smokehouse. I unhook one of those hams we had put away seven years ago. It a prime ham, Miss Mary. Course you wouldn't know, brang up lak you is in Englan'. But your paw, he know. He send Ebon all the way to the north end of the country to get the right kind of hickory wood to mak the smoke. Your paw he know good eatin' and jes the right wine for a gentleman's dinner."

She turned her full black eyes on Mary accusingly. "What they teach you over there in Englan'? Nothin' about food. Just how to put on a red coat and a long skirt and fly around the country on a big horse. Chasing a little red fox," she said as an afterthought.

"You shut you' big mouth, Chaney." Cissie, the housekeeper, stood in the doorway. She was as broad as Chaney and a good six inches taller. There was eternal enmity between the two. "Shut you' big mouth," she repeated.

Chaney turned her back and began to slice an onion into the kettle without a word. Cissie ruled the house slaves with a heavy hand and a sharp tongue.

Mary laughed. "Chaney is all right, Cissie. She likes to grumble but what does it matter when she cooks such delicious dinners?"

Chaney looked up from her work. "Miss Mary, you tell dat woman to open she cupboard and fetch that guava jelly paste from St. Kitts, and I wants sugar, aplenty sugar. We got to show dose Wilmington gentlemens dat de Edenton gentry know sompin' 'bout cookin'."

Cissie was in agreement with this. She hurried off to the storeroom, her black silk skirts rustling. Mary started for the door.

Chaney took another dip of snuff. "I ain't goin' to make a move, Miss Mary, lessen I know how many gentlemens goin' to sit at table."

"I'll ask Mr. Warden. Cissie will let you know," Mary said.

As she crossed the board hall that divided the lower floor she saw the butler, Ebon, standing in front of the library door. He had a tray with decanters and glasses in his hand. William Warden motioned Ebon in. About to close the door, he saw Mary and crossed the hall to meet her at the foot of the stairs.

"Did you have a good day?" he asked as he kissed her cheek. The question was perfunctory. Mary saw that his

55

mind was on other things. He looked tired and there were deep lines around his eyes. She heard the rumble of voices behind the heavy mahogany doors. "Will you have Cissie see that the three bedrooms are ready. I have asked the Wilmington men to stay here instead of at the Inn."

"Who came up?" Mary asked.

"Judge Moore, Richard Caswell and John Ashe." He smiled a wry smile. "They have sent up the heavy artillery to battle the Edenton committee. They say they bear the olive branch and want to make peace with the Albemarle men. But I don't know." He passed his thin hand over his forehead. "John Harvey won't give way an inch on the numbers of our representation in the coming Assembly." He paused, touching her cheek lightly with his fingers. "But political discussion doesn't interest women."

Mary drew back a little. It pleased William to say that. He liked to assume that Mary had no interests other than the plantation and her horses. He turned to go back.

Mary said, "Chaney wants to know how many at the table."

"Parson Earl, Iredell and John Harvey are here. Sam Johnstone is coming, and Phelps to represent Tyrell district. I expect Jo Hewes and the Doctor any moment. They will all stay." He hesitated a moment. "Perhaps it would be as well if you did not dine with us, Mary. It will bore you. Nothing but political discussion."

"Whatever you say, William." Mary was disappointed but she did not show it.

"Politics boring to Mary?" John Harvey came out of the library in time to hear William's words. "Of course she must dine with us. As chairman of the Edenton committee, I insist. To tell the truth, Mary, I am so dead weary of wrangling about quitrents and taxes that your presence will be a diversion."

Mary laughed. "Very well, John, I will dine with you. I hope I may be diverting, but please don't ban politics because of me."

Harvey glanced over his shoulder and lowered his voice. "Impossible to get off that subject with Maurice Moore here. He is like a dog with a bone in his teeth. He won't stop a moment." He put his hand on William's arm. "Come on, William; I need your keen legal mind. Moore is disputing the tax revision with me again."

At the door William turned. "I forgot to mention Rutledge, Mary. I sent a slave over to Rutledge Riding early this morning to ask him to come to the meeting. I haven't heard from him yet but he may be here later." Mary's hand tightened on the bannister but the expression of her face did not change. She had long since learned to conceal her thoughts and emotions. When she reached the landing, she heard a loud knock at the front door. She looked over the rail and saw Dr. Armitage unwinding a woolen scarf from his throat. Joseph Hewes was with him. Ebon took their coats and showed them to the library. Mary went on up the stairs to her room in the west wing. She was suddenly very weary. Dinner would not be ready before six, so there would still be time to rest and bathe. Cissie was waiting for her in her room where a cheerful fire was burning in the fireplace. A tea tray stood on the piecrust table.

"Thank you, Cissie," Mary said, sinking into the low slipper chair by the table. "That will be all. Send one of the girls to lay a bath and tell Chaney if Mr. Rutledge comes there will be twelve for dinner."

Chapter 4

IRON MEN
OF ALBEMARLE

THE dinner was going well and not a word of political import had been spoken. Mary Warden leaned against the high back of the Queen Anne chair quietly watching her guests. Judge Maurice Moore at her left was talking with Dr. Armitage about the dangers of swamp fever. John Ashe was occupied with Parson Earl and John Harvey. Horses and jumpers were their subject. Ashe was a vigorous, florid man, with a simple, direct manner in contrast to the dry, slightly sardonic Moore whose sharp biting tongue made him unpopular with the people. Mary liked Maurice Moore and respected his judgment. His temper was quick and he was a fighter. "A good enemy," people called him, straightforward and forceful.

Caswell, she knew only slightly. He was a man of distinction. As tall as his nephew, Adam Rutledge, Caswell had cultivated manners but he sometimes did inexplicable things. He was an advocate of moderation and held the Greek "golden mean" as a solution of the difficulties between the Colonies and the Mother Country. He had been a surveyor in his youth but later took up the practice of law. His interest in building up a strong militia for home defense led him into Provincial politics. Maurice Moore strongly opposed this measure and there were many heated debates between them on the subject. Caswell was complex and subtle. But he was a strong man, hard to move when once he was convinced of his duty and responsibility. Adam was like him in this, but he was not so outspoken.

The trouble between the men of Albermarle and the southern districts was an old one that had its origin in the dispute over the seat of the Provincial capital. Wilmington was chosen and the capital was moved from Edenton. Although this had happened some years earlier the antagonism had not died. The Albemarle men remained a solid bloc in the Assembly when it came to issues which concerned their district.

Mary Warden was a little proud as she looked down the long table. The Iron Men of Albemarle, as they had been called, made a good showing. Distinguished men of many interests, men of breeding and wealth, men of intelligence, but above everything, men of decision and proved integrity.

It was almost a scene on a stage. The brilliant Moore pitted against William Warden, or the keen witted James Iredell. A newcomer in Edenton, Iredell had already made a place for himself as a barrister. He was more liberal than William, quicker to take up the new and discard the old.

William was talking now to John Harvey. Harvey was the most distinguished man of the group. He had been speaker of the Assembly and held other offices. Mary looked at him affectionately. He was an old friend of her family. His father, also John Harvey, had been a comrade of her grandfather, Roger Mainwairing. Together they had fought many battles for the county and for their own advancement. John Harvey was a mild man, but there was no weakness in his mildness. Mary often relied on his wisdom as she did on that of Dr. Armitage and Joseph Hewes, the merchant.

"A stiff-necked lot," Maurice Moore said, following her glance. "You'd think they were Scots. The kind who stick to their ancient privileges of wearing their hats in the presence of kings."

She laughed, a teasing lilt in her voice. "I think they must be getting the best of you, Maurice."

Maurice shrugged his sloping shoulders. He leaned toward her. "They have won every point so far, Mary. I think we will have to send south for reinforcements," he said wryly.

"The Iron Men of Albemarle," she murmured.

"They are living up to their name, but it's time to forget old grudges," he said more seriously. "We have to preach unity now." His eyes wandered aimlessly about the company, then he leaned forward, looking past Armitage and John Harvey toward the end of the long table.

"Who is that blond giant down there talking to Caswell? I don't seem to recognize him."

Mary did not turn her head. "Adam Rutledge, of Rutledge Riding plantation," she told him.

"Ah! Caswell's nephew! So that is Rutledge. He is younger than I thought."

She lifted the crystal goblet to her mouth, then touched her lips delicately with her serviette. She wanted to ask a question, but she hesitated. John Ashe turned from Dr. Armitage to Moore.

"Has Caswell sounded out Rutledge?" he asked.

The Judge shook his powdered head. "No, not yet. He wanted me to talk with him first. Do you think he is too young, John?"

Ashe turned his fine brown eyes toward Adam. After a brief examination his face cleared as if he were pleased with what he saw.

"He looks a reliable fellow, rather serious for twenty-three."

The Doctor turned in his chair. His thin, alert face expressed his interest. "If you can persuade Adam Rutledge to take Sam Johnstone's place in the Assembly you'll be getting a good man. But I don't think you can, eh, Mary?"

"I don't know, Doctor. Adam has never shown any interest in politics."

Armitage gave a dry chuckle. "Adam's wedded to the land like all the Rutledges. Give them an acre of land and the first thing you know they've got a hundred. I've known the family since I was a boy, and they are all alike, all land crazy."

Moore twisted the slender stem of his wineglass in his fingers before he tasted the wine.

"Perhaps Mr. Rutledge may realize that it is an honor to be appointed by the Governor to the Provincial Assembly."

Armitage threw back his head and laughed until his queue bobbed.

"Not Adam! He won't be caught like a fly with molasses. Adam Rutledge is no green provincial. He's been down to Cambridge and had enough of life at Court to know his way about—"

"I still maintain it is an honor." Moore assumed a judicial air. "A great honor for a young man."

"Stuff and nonsense, Maurice. You want Adam, and you know it."

John Ashe turned in his chair to join the discussion. His smooth even tone was a balance for the peppery Moore, although Ashe could be fiery and eloquent when the occasion demanded.

"We had better let Caswell talk with Rutledge, since he is in the family. The Doctor is right. We need Rutledge. He's the largest landholder in the Province. . . ."

The Doctor screwed up his thin lined face as he always did when he was thinking. He addressed Ashe. "You might interest Adam, but it won't be by flattery or pretending it is an honor to sit with a crowd of wrangling politicians down at Wilmington."

Moore drew himself up; he didn't like the Doctor's casual words. But John Ashe forestalled the Judge's answer.

"Perhaps you will tell us—" He paused, waiting for Armitage to go on. The Doctor glanced at Mary. The raillery was gone. Instead, there was a serious, questioning look in his eyes.

"What do you saȳ, my dear—shall we tell them?"

Mary put her hand out as if to stop him, then withdrew it. She knew the situation at Wilmington. She went down each year with William when he attended the Assembly. She understood the bickerings, the intrigues among opposing cliques; she knew that backstairs gossip was bought at a price by unscrupulous politicians; that there were men whose ambition to stand well with the Governor outweighed their honesty. What would happen to Adam there? How would a man of the soil, for that is what Adam was at heart, fit into that world of falseness and violent partisanship?

The men were watching her, waiting for her answer. Seeing her uncertainty, Armitage saved her. He looked at Ashe not Moore when he spoke.

"If you are able to convince Adam that he has certain duties and responsibilities to the Province that only he can fulfill, you may succeed."

Moore opened his mouth to reply. A gesture from Ashe stopped him. A lump rose in Mary's throat. Had she and the Doctor betrayed Adam? She met Armitage's inquiring gaze, a troubled look in her candid blue eyes. She had the feeling that he already regretted his words. It was almost as if he had given help to an enemy. A person, or event, that took Adam Rutledge from his land, was an enemy; a bitter, bitter enemy. For Adam personified a force, the hard, driving force of men whose natural fight is against nature and the elements, not against their fellow men.

Ebon had come in and was waiting to speak to her. "Miss Mary, Cissie say she bring coffee to de drawing room, 'cause hits too windy on de terrace. De wind blow mighty hard," he whispered.

Mary glanced out the window. She could see the dark mass of the trees bending to the wind. Rain splashed against the panes.

"Light the logs and have the candles in the chandeliers and wall sconces lighted. I want the room cheerful and bright." The slave bowed and went away.

William was looking at her from the far end of the table.

61

She nodded to him and rose. Chairs scraped as the men got to their feet. She turned at the threshold, smiling at the company.

"Don't linger too long over your port," she admonished them. "We will have coffee in the drawing room."

William bowed as he held the door open. "We will join you in a little while, my dear. I assure you we won't say a word about politics." Mary smiled, touching his arm briefly with her slim fingers.

She walked slowly across the wide hall, her full blue silk skirt rustling faintly as she moved. William looked worn, his face pale. Or was it his black coat that gave him that appearance? She wished William would wear colors. Plum color, or dark blue, such as Iredell and John Harvey wore tonight. Even the Doctor had on slate-colored brocade. Only Willian and Parson Earl wore black. It wasn't so mournful looking in the case of the Parson; his red face, his bright blue eyes, his white wig and jabot relieved the funereal appearance.

The great double doors of polished mahogany to the drawing room had been opened. The odor of burning resinous wood in the fireplace permeated the hall. Mary paused for a moment in the doorway. It was a pleasant room, a room that bore the mellow imprint of age and constant use. There had been little change since Roger Mainwairing built Queen's Gift nearly fifty years before. The furniture was the same; sturdy Queen Anne chairs and tables; a few stuffed elbow chairs of French make; two small, pillowed double chairs on either side the fireplace, flanked by gate tables. Pine logs, laid on the tall brass andirons, burned brightly, casting yellow pools of wavering light on the broad puncheon floor boards. The floors were mahogany. Roger had brought the wood from the Indies and it was hand-polished by the house slaves. The long room was paneled almost to the high ceiling and painted white. Every large panel carried a candle sconce with crystal drops matching the two great chandeliers. The space above the paneling was covered with a soft yellow brocade. Long, heavy curtains at the leaded bow window were made of the same brocade. The French windows and doors, opening on the garden terrace, were shaded by jalousies. Roger had brought them from his plantation in St. Kitts, for he had carried the tropical Indies, as well as London, into his house on Albemarle Sound.

Mary crossed the room and opened the glass door that led to the bricked terrace. It blew shut with a great clatter. Powerless against the wind, she stood looking through the rain into the darkness. Flickering lights showed on fishing craft anchored at the mouth of the creek. It was a wild night of wind and rain. She was glad she had ordered Cissie to open all the bedrooms and have fires lighted in every fireplace so none of the men would have to venture out into the storm. Certainly the Parson would not want to ride to Bandon Hall miles away. As for Dr. Amitage, she would not permit him to go. She noticed his cough had returned. The man had no notion of caring for himself. He was too busy with the health of others.

She moved about the room, rearranging scarlet bittersweet in a silver bowl, changing the position of the candlesticks on a Queen Anne side-table. Roger had bought the table at an auction. It had come from some great house in Sussex.

Mary had her grandfather's journals, written in his large bold hand, every expenditure itemized. He had haunted auctions and was a frequenter at Tattersall's near Hyde Park turnpike. There he had purchased many a hunter as well as berlins and coaches. He liked bidding against another man and carrying off the prize. Mary had Roger's blood. She liked the excitement of London auction rooms, filled with gay, laughing people intent on outmaneuvering friend or stranger.

Her mind on the past, she pulled a Chippendale tea table out from the wall and tilted it to show the fine design of black and gold enamel. The table reminded her of her friend Patience Wright and the day they had gone to the auction rooms to buy some Staffordshire china Patience wanted for her little house in Story Gate. All fashionable London was there, for the sale—so the catalogue said—included the furnishing of young Lord X's flat in Mount Street. Everyone knew who Lord X was in spite of the effort at anonymity. The scandal about him and one of the 'indelicates,' called Dally the Tall, was common gossip. The *Morning Post* had printed a story the day before telling how a certain young gentleman of the nobility had sold his inamorata to his best friend because he was temporarily short of cash.

Mary turned the table a little more, to reflect the candlelight on its polished surface. She wondered whether the famous, or infamous, Dally had taken tea from this table. The idea amused her. Her thoughts returned to Patience Wright from whom she had not heard for months. Mary counted on her to keep her informed of things that went on in London. Patience was a sculptor who had become famous in fashionable society for her portraits in wax. Mary had often sat for her in London and the miniature on the mantelboard was one Patience had made. Patience came from Philadelphia. She was an intelligent woman as well as a talented one. Mary wondered again why she had had no letters recently. Perhaps she had come back to America by now.

Ebon came into the room carrying a large Sheffield tray with coffee cups and put them on a table in front of one of the little love seats which flanked the fireplace. Mary looked to see if there were plenty of long sugar in the silver box and if the cream jug were filled with rich yellow cream. She told Ebon to use the large coffee pot and bring it in as soon as the gentlemen were ready to leave the dining room.

She went once more to the window to see if the storm had abated. On the contrary, the wind was blowing harder, lashing the limbs of trees against the walls of the house. Far down the road which skirted the Sound she saw lights. She thought it might be a coach escorted by several outriders with swaying torches. If it were a traveling coach it would be having a sorry time with the wind and the rain and the ruts of the Shore road.

Presently Adam came into the room. He was alone. The men were lingering over their port talking about Wilmington affairs and the state of Governor Dobbs's health, he told her. He was bored so he came away. "Do you mind?" he asked. Mary did not tell him that his presence always made her heart beat faster, but silently motioned him to a seat near her. When Ebon came in again with the great coffee pot she quickly sent him away. She wanted these few minutes alone with Adam. It didn't matter what they talked about; it was enough that she was with him.

He was saying, "It is very attractive here." Though the room was not so stately nor so elegant as the red and white drawing room of the Manor House at Rutledge Riding he found it more inviting.

They were silent for a moment, the crackling of the fire the only sound. Suddenly he said, "Roger must have been a jolly old fellow who believed in doing himself very well indeed."

Mary laughed. "You have only to read his journals to know he was jolly. I have always loved all the stories about him. There must have been something so robust and warm about his hearty voice and big laugh. You see, I've thought of him so often that he seems very alive and real to me." She smiled wistfully at Adam.

"He was always a rebel at heart," she said after a moment. "He liked his own way—" Adam smiled. He leaned over and placed his firm, strong fingers over her hand.

64

"I think you have a good deal of Roger in you, Mary. I sometimes wonder why you are so quiet and self-possessed, having the blood of the rebel Roger and that major-general of a grandmother."

Mary filled his cup and lifted out a strip of sugar with a pair of silver tongs. "Perhaps I am my quiet mother, or my bookish father."

Adam stirred the sugar absently. "I had a letter from my agent, Marsden," he told her. "He writes that there is a great deal of talk in London about a new tax bill to be introduced soon. It will provide for stamps to be set on commodities and transactions. A Stamp Act, he calls it, and says it will work a great hardship on the Colonies."

Mary put her cup down. Her great blue eyes were filled with apprehension.

"He can't mean there is to be another tax? Why, Adam, our people won't stand it, you know that!"

Adam shrugged his shoulders. "If it is voted in Parliament, they will have to accept it; there is nothing else to do."

Mary dropped her voice. "They can rebel," she said.

Her face had a serious expression, almost hopeless. Adam smiled at her, lifting her chin with his fingers.

"Don't take it so to heart, Mary. We will never rebel against the Crown. A way will be found. Come, smile! I hear the men coming."

"You must tell the news to John Harvey and the others. I am sure they have not heard of this new tax."

As the men entered the room, Richard Caswell was saying, "The opinion of Albemarle is never an index of what the Province thinks, Harvey. You have only two classes here, the English aristocrats and the sturdy English yeomen. Now in other districts we have a Joseph's coat of nationalities: German Moravians, Quakers, Scotch-Irish Highlanders, French Huguenots, and Spaniards from Florida, even a few Moors. You see our problems are more complex. I don't think you will have any real trouble here," he said as they moved to the fire.

William Warden passed the coffee to the group at the fire. He answered Caswell. "Unless trouble seeps in from Orange County. If we have serious trouble it will come from the farmers around Hillsborough."

Mary looked up, surprised at her husband's words. Whenever she had spoken to him he had laughed at her fears.

"Did you say 'if or when,' William?" Iredell's crisp, acid

voice broke in. The room had suddenly grown quiet. Everyone was listening.

"I said 'if,' Iredell, not 'when.' I do not believe that rebellion is inevitable unless people make it so by their fears." William's tone was as sharp as Iredell's. The two men did not like each other. More than once they had clashed over Granville Grant litigation.

Mary broke the silence that followed. "Adam has had a letter from his agent in London. He says that a new bill is coming up before Parliament imposing a special stamp duty on goods sold or bought in the Colony. He calls it the Stamp Act."

"Stamp Act," Moore almost shouted. "What the devil is the Stamp Act?" He glowered at Adam as if he were responsible.

"Have you the letter, Rutledge?" Harvey asked.

"Yes, I have it in my dispatch case."

John Ashe and the Doctor came across the room. "May we see it?" Ashe asked. "This must be the bill I saw mentioned in the *Weekly Post-Boy*. Maurice, you know you wondered what it meant."

Adam left the room. He returned in a few minutes with the letter which he handed to Harvey, who read it aloud.

Mary walked to the bow window and looked out. The rain was coming down heavily, the strong wind blowing the trees, whipping the shrubbery. Voices came to her.

"We can't put up with it." . . . "What can they be thinking about?" . . . "It will never get a second reading. . . ." She looked at the group around the fire. Faces were flushed and angry voices raised.

Lights in the driveway caught her attention. A coach rocked from side to side. It was flanked by outriders carrying torches, their cocked hats dripping with rain and their sodden cloaks flapping about their shanks. Ahead of the coach a dark figure, carrying a ship's lantern, was leaning against the wind, struggling to reach the front steps. Mary called hurriedly to William, interrupting the violent flow of conversation.

"There is a carriage coming up the drive, William."

"Nonsense, no one would be out in such a storm." But he left the group and started toward the door. "Who can it be?" he asked.

There was a short imperative knock at the door followed quickly by another. Then they heard the shouts of men urg-

66

ing tired horses, the cracking of a whip, the clanking of harness chains and the grinding of brakes.

Mary saw Ebon crossing the hall. When he opened the door the wind blew out the hall candles. William moved swiftly to catch the door as the wind forced it from Ebon's rheumatic old fingers.

A woman's voice rose above the cries and shouts of slaves and house servants who had run from the back of the house.

"God's death! Is there no one to answer the door?"

Mary crossed the room and stood at the door of the drawing room. Flunkies were holding flares, the footman was off the box, opening the door. He lifted a woman from inside the coach, staggered across the open space and deposited her at the top of the steps in the shelter of the gallery. The second footman carried another woman out. William was at the step, the wind flapping the tails of his long black coat and twisting his wig to one side of his head.

The first woman pushed the footman back. Standing erect, she was as tall as William, who followed her into the hall. Mary could see little of her but a firm cleft chin under the folds of a soggy bonnet.

"If you will help me with the string," the woman's clear voice commanded. "My maid is utterly useless."

Mary glanced over her shoulder. The eyes of every man in the room were focused on the storm-bound traveler.

"There, that's better." She flung the offending head-covering at the footman who caught it deftly. Ebon closed the door and the slaves lighted the candles. The maid stood dumbly near the door, water dripping from her garments. The mistress, Mary saw now, was a handsome woman with clear-cut features and a mass of auburn curls tumbling over her forehead and down the firm column of her throat. Her eyes looked dark under her curved brows.

Her red lips parted in a flashing smile as she looked over William's shoulder to where Mary Warden stood in the doorway.

"I was told by some fisherman I met on the road that I would find shelter at Queen's Gift, so I came. I am embarrassed to find it is a private dwelling, not a public inn." Mary thought in spite of her words the traveler was not in the least embarrassed.

"You are more than welcome, Madam. We hope no traveler would pass our house on such a night. I am Mary Warden. This is my husband, William Warden."

By a quick look from one to the other and a slight lifting of arched brows the stranger showed that she noticed the difference in years.

Mary called to Cissie, who was at the dining-room door.

The traveler threw her long sable cape carelessly over her maid's arm. "Stop your smiling, you fool. Go with this woman and get my bed prepared." She kicked off her furred carriage boots without assistance, displaying bronze shoes with square buckles. With her long white fingers she smoothed the full folds of her russet skirt. She then moved easily toward the drawing room, her head held high, not troubling to pause before the Florentine mirror.

"I have not had the pleasure of meeting your guests, Mrs. Warden." She laughed, a full-throated, husky laugh, as she moved across the hall.

"A laugh to stir the senses," thought Adam, watching the little scene as he leaned against the mantel. "An impressive person, accustomed to a great deal of homage," he decided. The woman stopped in the doorway and summed up the room with a quick inclusive glance. Her eyes lingered on Adam a moment, and passed on to John Harvey and the Doctor, who were nearest the door.

Mary mentioned names quickly, then turned to her guest with lifted brows.

The woman laughed again. Her wide mouth showed dazzling teeth. "you must pardon me, Mrs. Warden. Your rough roads have rattled my poor brain." She made a slight movement, spreading her silken skirt. Something of her vitality, her assumed power, seemed to fill the room.

"I have come from Wilmington." She paused a moment, looking at the men gathered around the fire. "I have letters to some of you, I presume, from his Excellency, the Lieutenant-Governor." She waited just the suspicion of a second, then made a gracious inclination of her head. "Permit me to introduce myself. I am Lady Caroline Mathilde. I am on my way to the Carbarrus plantation, Pembroke, which I have taken for a year." She turned to Mary with a charming smile.

"Now, my dear, the amenities are taken care of. If I may have a cup of coffee or a sip of port, I will retire."

Half the men in the room sprang forward. A chair was placed by the warm fire, and a cup of coffee, a decanter of port and another of sherry at her elbow. Mary left the room to see that Cissie had opened the great bedroom in the east wing that was reserved for their most distinguished guests. Everything was in order.

She went down the stairs and crossed the broad hall, walking slowly. She could hear bursts of laughter and the rumble of gay voices. In her drawing room a strange woman, driven in by the storm, was holding court.

Adam alone made no move. He kept his place, leaning against the mantel watching, a slight smile in the corners of his firm, wide mouth. He was thinking that the woman was beautiful. She had the poise and assurance of a person familiar with Society and Courts. What could she want in the quiet backwaters of Raleigh's Eden?

Chapter 5

RALEIGH'S EDEN

IN THE months that followed her arrival Lady Caroline continued to be the storm center of excitement. The seven day wonder of having a great lady of fashion living at Pembroke was not permitted to die down. Lady Caroline herself kept the ember glowing with an occasional burst of flame.

She seemingly was unaware of the interest she created. As she mentioned casually, she lived the same every place she went—London, or in her home in Mecklenburg, or in the West Indies. Whatever she wore, whatever she did, had a touch of the flamboyant. She was like the great flaming hibiscus flower she cultivated in the Pembroke gardens.

She had a red morocco sedan chair sent up from the capital. It was lined with stamped velvet picked out in gold threads. In this, carried by four large Madagascari wearing baggy breeches and red turbans, she took the air in the gardens of Pembroke. No one had ever seen her put foot to the ground although she declared she was ravished by the garden.

Adam, on hearing this, made a dry comment to the effect that his conception of ravishment was quite a different thing. Peyton, obviously annoyed with the remark, got up and left the room. Adam had no idea why he behaved in such an extraordinary manner until he heard some time later that Peyton was almost a daily visitor at Pembroke.

Accepted as such by the Governor, the Lieutenant-Governor and other officials, Lady Caroline's stay in Albemarle took on the aspect of a visit of Royalty. In truth, the rumor was soon noised about that Lady Caroline was a sister of Queen Charlotte. She herself never made any allusion to the rumor, either to affirm or deny it. She was tired of the bickerings and intrigues of London and the Court, she wanted to rest, "to get back to natural things," she told Mary Warden. But certainly she had the manner of Royalty, so Joseph Hewes said. The little bachelor had better opportunity than anyone to know, for he had constant dealings with her. It was his ships that carried her household from Wilmington to Edenton. "Only a few little things to make me comfortable while I am at Pembroke," she told him, but the bills of lading contradicted that. When the Assembly met the following year she would go back to Wilmington where Guernsey House was being remodeled and made ready for her.

Guernsey House, which had once been the residence of a Royal Governor, was a great estate on the river a few miles from the city. She must have a fabulous fortune, people said, if she redecorated every house in which she lived even for a few months. It was commonly known that she had a house in the Indies also, and one on the island of St. Croix. "I like living in the tropics, excepting for the hurricanes, but Raleigh's Eden is more delightful," she told everyone. "I must always be on the water, you know. It helps my migraines to get the sea air. London fogs are deadly," she said in her husky voice with its slight accent. Just the right accent for one born in Mecklenburg—Strelitz. Above all, she insisted repeatedly, she loved her garden at Pembroke. "Mary, you must give me some of your daphne plants to send to London. Sophia, you know, loves gardens, too." She spoke of the Queen simply as Sophia, not Charlotte, just as a member of a family might use a name unknown to the public.

The men all fell victims to her charm. The women had little opportunity. She was frank in her opinion of the "run of the mill" women. Mary she liked, and Jean Corbin, and a few others. But men rallied to her, and in a little time the whole of Albemarle district talked of her salon. Conversation was brilliant and her suppers epicurean. Her Madeira came from Funchal, her sherry from Spain, and her casks of rum from distilleries at Charlotte Amalie.

Mary wondered whether all the men were as fascinated as they appeared, or whether the hope for patronage did not enter in. She put the thought out of her mind as unworthy. But how would it be in Wilmington? For in the capital there were always so many more politicians seeking favor and buying their way into the good will of people in high places.

Cissie was outspoken against her. "She call herself a Lady. Why do she talk to her slave so familiar and let men talk back to she?"

William, as Lord Granville's agent, had to be politic, but he had little to say about her. Adam was never at her "routs," but Adam went nowhere. Mary knew from the Doctor that he had been at his Mecklenburg plantation for months now.

Edenton was prospering. Many ships from the Indies came into the Sound. They brought trade goods from far countries. A new shop opened on the wharves where the women went to buy brass from Persia and silks and jewels from India. It was run by a Levantine named Nicholas, but it was La-Truchy who brought in most of the goods. He had given up trading in black ivory, he told Marcy. "It is easier to trade with the Island or with the southern mainland," he said. Other ships came besides LaTruchy's, bearing cargoes of spices and sugar, silver dishes from the Spanish countries, shawls and mantillas and laces, leather from Morocco, and jewels from no one knew where. The women did not question; they thronged the shop of the sly-eyed Levantine, with his olive skin and his long smooth fingers, and made it the fashion.

Mary Warden galloped down the post road toward Pembroke. Early that morning, while she was still in bed, one of Lady Caroline's slaves had brought her a note. In it the newcomer bewailed a cold that confined her to her house, to complete and utter boredom. "Please come for tea and a gossip and save me from drowning myself in the Cypress Swamp." Mary laughed over the words and wondered at the strong, bold writing. She hurried through the letters she was writing to catch the English packet the next morning, and ordered Cissie to bring her warmest habit.

Cissie took the brush from Mary's hand and with the long braids of chestnut hair wound about her fingers, she was ready to inform her mistress of the gossip on the plantation and in the village. Mary let her talk, paying no heed to her rambling until she said, "And Mr. Peyton Rutledge, he always hang around Minch's tavern. Some say he gamble and let heself in for a mighty lot of money to old Minch, who everybody know is crookeder than a ram's horn . . . but it's Minch daughter that brings he to the tavern. That girl she no good, she done already have one bush baby, maybe two, nobody knows. Mr. Peyton he get heself into trouble one dese day, he will fo' shur, with that gal, or maybe that woman at Pembroke."

Mary jerked the braid out of Cissie's hand. "I told you I didn't want to hear village gossip, Cissie. Now go downstairs and tell the groom to saddle Black Douglas." Cissie went off grumbling. Mary dressed hurriedly and ran down the broad stairs.

She met William as she was crossing the hall. "I'm going to

Pembroke," she said. "If you are bringing anyone home for supper, have Ebon tell cook."

"A party?"

"I don't think so. Why do you ask?"

"Lady Caroline Mathilde gives a great many parties. Sometimes one wonders where the money comes from."

Mary interrupted. "But you asked me to entertain her, William. You told me that Tryon had written to you to show her every attention."

William nodded. "That is true, but do not make an intimate of her." He looked at Mary searchingly. "How is it that you never go to Rutledge Riding to call on Sara any more? Have you had trouble with her?" Mary said she had not. Sara had been rather more wretched than usual and was not seeing people lately. As she made this feeble excuse she knew that William did not believe her. What he was thinking she did not know, for he seldom admitted her to his thoughts. They would sit in the same room for hours at a time not speaking, she with some needlework in her hands, he with a book or some legal papers. She had an uneasy feeling that he was questioning her now to some purpose, and she got away as quickly as she could.

A cold wind was blowing off the Sound. Black Douglas whirled and danced and pulled at the reins. She had trouble quieting him down to a steady trot. At the river ford she saw Peyton Rutledge through the woods. He was taking a short cut from his plantation which was a few miles up the river from Pembroke. Mary had heard from others than Cissie that Peyton was spending a great deal of time with the fascinating Lady Caroline. But so, she told herself, did half the prominent men of Edenton, some because they were amused by her gaiety and others because of her secret history which had somehow become public knowledge.

Mary thought of William's words. Were they a veiled warning? She herself had reservations about the lady which she had not voiced. When she was with her she was amused. Who could not be? The woman had wit and was a master of double entendre. She was outspoken to the point of being Rabelaisian. But that was London fashion. Her barbed tongue made people laugh. Perhaps they were afraid not to laugh. She might after all be the Queen's sister!

Mary laughed with the others when, for example, Lady Caroline made an adjective out of the family name of Colonel Buncombe. The Colonel, who had come up from St. Kitts, was building a mansion on the Sound and his love of display and grandeur offered opportunity for her nimble wit. It became the fashion after that to speak of Buncombe as synonymous with bombast.

Mary's thoughts were interrupted by Peyton, who rode up and saluted her with his riding crop. He looked disappointed when she said she was going to Pembroke to see Lady Caroline.

"She is ill and bored," Mary said.

"She wrote me the same thing," he told her. "I wonder how many more notes she sent out."

Mary smiled. "Enough to make two or three tables of whist, I suspect."

"She'd die without her gambling games," Peyton said. "We're alike in that respect." Mary started to speak, but Peyton stopped her. "If you are going to scold me, Mary, don't, please. I just had a proper wigging from Adam. I'm not in the mood for another harangue."

"Adam doesn't harangue," Mary found herself saying with more heat than the occasion called for.

"Of course you would defend Adam . . . but damn it all, Mary, Adam would never understand a man like me."

Mary thought he was easy to understand but she did not say so. They rode in silence. Across an arm of the swamp they were skirting a vulture rose suddenly from a black log with a sharp upward sweep of strong wings. Perching on a grotesque cypress knee that rose blackly from the brackish water, it uttered weird cries. It was an eerie spot, dark under the overhung banks. The cypress trees with their long streamers of old moss and tangled vines made it seem a place of evil. Mary shuddered as the vulture swooped on the floating log when they had passed. Over her shoulder she saw suddenly that it was not a log after all but the floating body of a black man. . . . She put spur to her horse.

Peyton laughed grimly. "Not a pretty sight," he admitted. "A ship can go a long way up into the swamp, though you wouldn't think so from here. They say Blackbeard used to take his pirate ships up there to divide his loot and hide it."

"I don't believe the tale," Mary said.

Peyton shrugged his shoulders. "But we do know that he used to anchor at Pembroke, so why not a more concealed anchorage in the deep swamp?" They were riding through the pine woods now. The smell of pine in Mary's nostrils cleansed away the evil of swamp vapors. Peyton spoke abruptly. Mary realized he was still thinking of Adam.

"I don't want you to think I am ungrateful to Adam. He

has done so much for me, but he is of a different temperament. I don't think he ever gave a thought to any woman but Sara."

A slow flush went from Mary's throat to her cheeks. "Adam has self-control, if that is what you mean."

Peyton laughed shortly. "Abnormal living is what I call it." They rode along for some time in complete silence. Peyton rode in a slumped posture, his head low, both hands on the pommel of his saddle. She would have liked to say something comforting, but she found no words. Presently he turned to her. "When I am at home, alone on the plantation, I think about what will happen to us, until it seems to me I shall go mad."

"Peyton! What are you saying?" Mary turned in her saddle facing him. He looked so gloomy that she was alarmed. She felt that he had reached some crisis; a few minutes ago he was gay, now he was sunk deep in the doldrums. This wasn't like Peyton. He wanted cheering. "I can't think what you are talking about," she said.

"About the little group of people here in Raleigh's Eden." He turned his brooding eyes on her. "If it is Eden, Mary, it's the garden after Eve ate the apple." He slowed his horse down to a walk. "Take Adam—a strong, handsome fellow, the biggest landholder in the Province. How does he live? He works, I can tell you, like a galley slave on his plantation! And tied for life to an invalid wife who can't walk!"

"Peyton, how cruel you are!"

"It's the truth and you know it. And there's more to it than that. Sara will sap the very lifeblood out of him before she is through."

"Oh, Peyton, why does he allow it?" Mary found herself speaking what was in her heart.

"God knows. Some misgotten idea of duty, I suppose. Adam is strong for loyalties." He dismissed Adam and moved on to his own case. Mary knew that was the seat of his misery.

"There's Lavinia and me. What a mess we have made of things! She must live in London. She must have the boy at Eton. But I stay here on the plantation because I haven't enough money to live anywhere else, and I refuse to live on hers."

"You want young Peyton to go to Eton, don't you? That is the family tradition."

Peyton turned on her then. "I'm surprised to hear that from you, Mary. What did we come to America for? To

75

carry on old traditions? We might as well have stayed in England. . . . Lavinia is bored when she is here." He dropped his voice. "I bore her, too, Mary. I'm no match for Lavinia. I'm a dull fellow, moody. She is gay. She should be married to a great man, a Royal Governor perhaps, or a statesman." There was no reproach in his voice, only sadness. "Lavinia can run from what she doesn't like, but I can't. I'm stuck here. I tell you, Mary, I'm damn well going to move heaven and earth to get out of here. I'll go to London, fair means or foul! Don't laugh, Mary. I may even turn pirate and scuttle a ship."

Mary did not feel like laughing when she looked at the glittering intensity of his dark eyes in his handsome, somber face. "You are low today, Peyton. Tomorrow everything will be different. Don't you think we should ride on?"

He detained her. "Just a moment. I'm not through yet. I know you think Adam has all he wants: land, land, raw land to cultivate and plant. That won't always be enough to satisfy him, Mary. Working every day until he's exhausted; riding that devil Saladin until man and horse are worn out . . . one day Adam Rutledge will find out that he's missed most of life, and what then?"

She was grateful that he did not expect her to answer.

Suddenly he turned to her. "You and William are no more suited to each other than—" he paused, finding no suitable comparison. She started to speak in order to stop him, but he would not let her. "Don't interrupt me now, Mary. I know you are loyal to William. I've seen you interpreting him so subtly that people think he has warmth and friendliness. I know William. He has ice water in his veins instead of blood. He would betray you, or anyone, if it would benefit him."

"Peyton! I will not listen!"

He closed his fingers over her bridle hand. "Oh, but you will. I want to know if you can stand the truth, Mary Warden. You are in love with Adam Rutledge. And he's a fool if he doesn't see it and take you away from William Warden."

Mary snatched her hand from his grasp. Her cheeks were crimson, her eyes blazing in anger.

"Gad, but you're beautiful, Mary. For a tuppence I'd make love to you myself and let Adam go hang."

She leaned forward, her eyes still afire. "Peyton, if you say another word, I'll never speak to you again." Her lips trembled. She struggled to keep back the tears of anger and mortification.

"Truth-telling always gets one into trouble. I'm sorry to

hurt you, my dear." Mary knew by the look in his eyes that he was not contrite. He had meant what he said. That terrified her. If Peyton had noticed, why not others . . . William?

She touched Black Douglas with her heel and the horse broke into a gallop. She was angry with Peyton, but more angry with herself. She felt that some impending tragedy had overtaken her. The beauty of a hidden, secret thing had been disclosed. For a few moments she gave herself over to despair. But as she galloped along the wooded road, her normal assurance returned to her. She must stop Peyton from talking.

Peyton overtook her at the gates to Pembroke. She took heart at his penitent face.

"I'm sorry, Mary. You know I wouldn't say anything to hurt you. But I wish you and Adam would look at these things as I do."

"You must never mention it again, Peyton. Promise me! If Adam—" She could not say that if Adam realized it would make an impossible situation, for if she admitted that it would mean that she tacitly admitted that Peyton had spoken the truth.

"Believe me, Mary, I will not mention it again." They rode up the drive in silence. As he helped her from her horse he kissed her cheek lightly. "You don't know how beautiful you are when you are angry, Mary. If Adam were half a man he'd carry you off and be damned to William and the rest of the world!"

Two of Lady Caroline's slaves were at the carriage block to take the horses to the stables. Mary hooked up her velvet riding skirt and they went into the house. Lady Caroline came out of the drawing room to greet them, her playing cards in her ringed hand. She wore a peignoir of satin, flounced to the waist with heavy lace. Lace outlined the square-cut neck and half sleeves. A double rope of pearls hung almost to her waist. Her auburn hair was looped in a chignon held in place by a russet net.

She brushed Mary's cheek with her lips and extended her hand to Peyton to kiss. "My dears, how delightful of you to come to see me and save me from absolute boredom. You've no idea how this weather depresses me."

The little blackamoor she called Beelzebub held the door open. He was dressed like the Grand Turk in velvet satin trousers and a braided jacket of crimson.

"You know everybody," she said as they entered the room. Mary nodded to Meredith Chapman and Joseph Hewes. With

Virginia Jarvis they made up the table where Lady Caroline had been seated. Nearer the box window was a second table around which were grouped Colonel Weavly, Jean Corbin and a man Mary did not know.

"Will you make a fourth at Jean's table, Peyton? Mary, take my cards. I'm having wretched luck."

Mary said, "I'd rather not play unless you need me."

Lady Caroline sat down at once and put her cards into the deck.

"Amuse yourself, my dear. You'll find the London *Morning Post* in the library. Dr. Armitage is there reading the last number of the *Gentleman's Magazine.*" She took up the deck and shuffled the cards expertly. "I don't see how anyone reads the *Gentleman's.* I find it too dull. But you'll find some delightful bits of scandal in the *Post,* Mary."

"Are you playing, partner?" she asked.

Mary escaped to the library. She found Dr. Armitage in a wing chair by the fire, his feet on a stool, a decanter of brandy on a table at his elbow. He glanced up. When he saw Mary, he was visibly pleased.

"Come in, come in, my dear! I've been wanting someone to read this to. It seems that it is the fashion in London to speak of the ladies of a pleasant hour as the *Impures.* Egad, it's amazing that such a thing could be printed. Listen to his, Mary, 'It is a rather remarkable circumstance that a certain young gentleman has never seen the prolific Dally since her present enlarged state. She was loaned to the R—— D—— by her old love, Lord C——, and the result of one short-lived hour is now but too visible.' Can you imagine this, squeezed in between the notice of a levee at St. James and another interesting item? Shall I read it? Are you shocked at such frankness?"

Mary laughed. "Please go on. I had forgotten the way London lives."

"This is also about an *Impure.*" The Doctor adjusted his spectacles again. " 'P—— sports a new carriage, which will astonish the wondering town, and like the Chariot of Phaethon, kindle a conflagration. It is Parisian built, the body mounted with inlaid devices and foliage of mock pearls and other jewelry, upon a pale crimson ground called *Daphne's Blush.* The harness is yellow leather, edged with red, double gilt buckles of various shapes, and short plumes in the horses' heads. The hammer-cloth and lining are white velvet.' " The Doctor's face changed. A dull, angry red showed in his thin cheeks. He banged the magazine on the table, almost upsetting his brandy glass. "God's death!" he muttered. "This isn't amusing. It's tragic. The people starving, struggling to pay heavy taxes, and a *High Personage* spends three hundred guineas to buy a courtesan a carriage. What is the matter with Englishmen? We used to be vigorous, strong as lions." He picked up the *Morning Post* and turned the pages until he found an item.

"This in the morning paper, mind you: 'There certainly must be some extraordinary event soon to take place in this country for the men of Fashion are dwindling into females, and the ladies have put on the breeches.'" He looked up over the paper, voicing his agitation by muttering, "We're decadent, we're a decadent nation."

He got up and marched back and forth in front of the fire, his hands behind him, his coattails flapping. "It's an outrage to print such stuff for decent people to read." He stopped in front of a shelf of books. Attracted by a title, he drew the volume from its place. As he did so, a leather pouch, which had been hidden behind the books, slid out, scattering its contents.

The Doctor stood stock still, looking at the floor. "God bless me! What is this?"

Mary looked. A handful of jewels lay on the Turkey carpet, pearls, sapphires and emeralds. The Doctor's eyes remained transfixed on the glittering stones. Mary stooped. She had gathered them up when the door opened and Lady Caroline came in. Her quick glance focused on the sparkling stones in Mary's hand.

For a moment it seemed to Mary that she was pale with fright. But this momentary impression vanished as Lady Caroline stepped boldly inside and closed the door. Ignoring the Doctor, she walked across the room to Mary holding out her hand.

"Thank you for finding my poor little gems. It was so good of you. I had quite given them up for lost." Her hands closed down upon the jewels firmly. Her red mouth smiled but her green eyes were hard with suspicion.

Chapter 6

WILDERNESS
CABIN

IT WAS the hottest summer the Province had ever known. The crops without rain burned and withered in the blazing sun. Wheat and corn lay lifeless on the parched earth.

Adam's North Plantation, watered from Chowan River, had a fair yield, but far inland there was such scarcity of food that on many of the small plantations the slaves fed on cattle and apples. Potatoes were a failure. A law was hurriedly passed making it a criminal offense for vessels to buy or carry foodstuffs from the Province other than the least possible amount to sustain the life of the crews. Yellow fever broke out. Seasonal fever of the most virulent type raged in the swamp districts near Albemarle Sound and the great Dismal Swamp. Bloody flux caused terror among the poor people. Added to all this Dr. Armitage discovered the dread *mal de Siam* among the slaves on one of the coast plantations.

Adam did what he could to help. He sent apples from his Mecklenburg plantations and rice from his new fields to the stricken farmers who had taken up their grants of fifty acres under the old Lords Proprietors Act.

Late in August he and his indentured man, Marcy, started home from the Mecklenburg plantation. They were riding and had a Negro stable boy with them to care for the horses. Only the second day of their journey they were caught in a sudden torrential storm, a freak storm of thunder and lightning and high wind which forced them to seek refuge under jutting rock until its fury subsided. When the rains passed, Adam found that a slide of earth and boulders had shut them off from the road which led to the valley. The only thing to do was to go around, cutting their way through the dense bush. He sent the horses back by the Negro boy while he and Marcy set out on foot, following an old half-obliterated Indian trail to Catawba Springs. At the Inn they would be able to get horses or a stage to the post road.

They made slow progress. Interlaced vines of wild grape, whitethorn and blackberry tore at their leather breeches and scratched all exposed skin. They spent half the morning struggling up the shoulder of the mountain, their saddlebags slung over their backs. When the sun was at the meridian they reached the false summit. Instead of seeing the cluster of buildings that marked the Springs they found themselves looking across ridge after ridge of mountains covered with heavy growth, pine and spruce and darker, leafy trees.

"It must be that point," Adam said to Marcy and they started on up toward a jagged pile of rocks. In the afternoon when they reached the real summit they realized that they were lost. From the knifelike ridge of the hogback they had climbed, they discovered only a higher ridge. Adam threw himself on his stomach to rest. With the glasses he carried strapped around his neck he tried to discover an opening or pass through the hills, but he saw only a wilderness of trees and the deep-red gashes that marked the path of earth slides. He mopped his perspiring face and rolled over on his back while Marcy worked his way along the ridge. Presently Marcy signaled to Adam, pointing down the valley along the eastern slope. Adam focused his glasses. He saw a sight familiar in these days of famine: a small parched field, maize falling to the baked earth, a dried-up stream. He looked for the cabin. There should be razorbacks and children playing. But there was no sign of life. He closed the glasses and got to his feet.

"It will do for the night," he said to Marcy. "I've no intention of struggling through this forest after sundown."

"As you say, master." Marcy took up the rifles and started down the hill in the direction of the cabin.

The shadows were long in the ravine when they came to the edge of the clearing. A silver vapor seemed to be rising from the earth and through it fell long shafts of pale sunlight touching the trees and the waving curtain of vines.

When they crossed the field Adam saw a man sitting on the ground, leaning against the side of the cabin. He was motionless, unaware of their approach. The cabin was more like a crude stockade than a house. Upright sapling stakes driven into the ground were laced together with stripped palmetto thongs. It had no roof. In front was an oven of homemade bricks with two iron pots swinging over a bed of ashes.

The man turned a little, watching them with lackluster eyes. He made no effort to rise, nor did his dull, hopeless expression change. The low sun, slanting down the mountain, touched the treetops, leaving the cabin in shadow. A shiver passed over Adam. He looked around, but not a leaf stirred. The heavy dead air was hot as from a furnace.

"We have lost our way," Adam said. "May we have shelter for the night?"

The man's cracked lips moved. Adam had to bend down to catch the words. "There is no food." The voice was flat, without vibration.

Adam turned to Marcy. "Give him a nip of brandy from the flask." He saw the man was very weak. "Roll that blanket into a pillow to ease his back, Marcy. We must get some food down him."

The man's lips moved again. "The cabin," he whispered, "the cabin . . ."

The door was so low that Adam had to stoop to enter the room. A sense of foreboding came over him as he stood at the threshold. A strange quiet pervaded the room. The shadows of the trees formed the roof. There were no furnishings, only a rough table and two stumps for chairs. Hard-baked earth made the floor. His eyes, growing accustomed to the gloom, focused on one corner. A young woman with a child at her breast lay on a bed of boughs. Disturbed by his presence, the woman moaned and moved her arm. The child whimpered weakly, fumbling at the milkless breast with clawlike hands. Marcy brought in a candle. In the moving light Adam saw that the woman's skin was drawn tightly over her cheekbones, as if all the fluids of her body had been dried up. He bent over her. Her eyes were glittering with fever. He saw there was a second bed of boughs in the far corner. On it lay a small girl of ten or twelve. Her tangled brown curls lay across her pallid face. The shadows were thick in that corner of the room. Adam beckoned to Marcy. By the light of the candle they saw the wide-open eyes staring at nothing. The child was dead.

Drawing a quilt over the body, they went outside. The man looked up without moving. "Just a little while ago," he said, "I tried to bring her into the light, but the weakness caught up with me." His voice trailed off. Two tears furrowed down his leathern cheeks. Sobs, futile soundless sobs, wracked his emaciated frame. Adam could not bear the silent, hopeless grief. He wished the man would curse . . . anything but this despairing acceptance. He called to Marcy.

"Let me have more brandy. . . . There must be some biscuits in my saddlebag. We must do something for the woman . . . and the child."

"I saw a pick by the side of the cabin," Marcy said.

Adam nodded. "The living first, Marcy. I noticed dogwood

growing along the dry stream. It will answer instead of Peru bark. We have to break the fever, and the babe must be fed somehow."

When the draught was steeped Adam lifted the woman's head while Marcy forced the liquid through her clenched teeth. The baby cried and nuzzled against its mother's breast, whimpering like some animal, but there was no milk there, and no response from the woman except the ceaseless movement of her fingers picking at a tattered quilt.

Marcy searched the cabin. A few cobs of maize were all he found.

"I've some dried venison in my bags," Adam said. "Soften it in boiling water for the man and woman. We can make a soft mush of the maize for the baby."

While Adam was feeding the woman, he heard the sound of the pick against the hard-baked earth. He wrapped the dead child in a quilt and lifted her in his arms. When he stopped beside the sick man there was something in the soundless farewell that almost overcame him. Adam wanted him to cry out his grief . . . to raise his voice in protest to the God of his fathers. But there was nothing, no sound, only his thin hand touching the child's pallid cheek.

Marcy, working by the light of a pine knot, had hollowed a grave under a giant sycamore. Pine needles and ferns hid the hard earth. "Pine needles have a clean, sweet smell," he said as he laid the body in the shallow grave. The child looked very small and alone in her bed of green ferns. The small pointed face was waxen, but it had a look of peace. Adam tried to remember a prayer. He could think of nothing. . . . It was Marcy who said, "Unto the least of these, O Lord!"

Adam turned away before the first shovel of earth fell.

The man was quiet. The woman moaned restlessly. The infant slept. Adam touched its tiny wrist. The pulse was faint but steady.

In the ravine the dusk had deepened into night, but on the hilltop the sun still shone. Adam leaned against the door of the cabin, looking up to the hills. He felt a sense of complete exhaustion. The day's journey had been hard but it was not physical exhaustion that weighed upon him now. If these people were to be saved he must get them out of the dark valley.

A shadow disentangled itself from the background. Marcy moved into the circle of light cast by the fire.

"Do you think this dry stream runs into another below the

shoulder of the mountain?" Adam asked when Marcy came within speaking distance.

"It may. Suppose I walk downstream when the moon rises to see if we can get out that way?"

Adam nodded. "We must start by sunrise. They will all have to be carried."

"I wonder if the moon ever shows her face in this Godforsaken spot?" Marcy's tone expressed his doubt. "I think I won't wait for moonrise. I can find my way with the help of a pine knot."

Adam watched the indentured man move into the gloom of the forest and down a narrow path that led to the dry stream.

Water was boiling in the sooty kettle that swung over the embers. He mixed another drink of dogwood for the woman. As he gave it to her, the baby cried out feebly. Adam looked at the child helplessly. He had never seen so young a child before. What was he to do with it?

The baby whimpered again. Adam lifted it from its mother's side. He wrapped it in a bit of blanket, for the night was cool now with the chill that comes in the mountains after the sun goes down. He folded a quilt and spread it on the rough table top. On this he placed the child.

The woman would soon have enough of the dogwood drink to make her sweat. If she could get up a good sweat, the fever would break. She would be weak, but she might be rational. He piled all the blankets and quilts he could find on the bark bed and covered her up to the chin. This stopped her restless hands from picking at the quilt.

The child, now he must look to the child. He wished he had kept Marcy. The man was resourceful. Perhaps he would have known how to go about taking care of the infant. He took the tallow dip and searched about the cabin. In a small horsehair trunk he found a few clothes which he carried to the table. Each time he passed he patted the child to keep it from whimpering. He found himself wondering just how he should go about bathing it. The child looked so tiny, so very frail. His own hands seemed so large and clumsy. But the babe quieted under his touch.

He rummaged through his saddlebags, cursing softly. Cicero should have packed linen handkerchiefs. He dumped the contents of the bags on one end of the table and found them, as well as soap and a Turkish towel. That was all he needed. He brought a small basin of warm water and put it beside the soap and towel on the table. Now he had to have more light which meant another precious candle. With everything in readiness he sat down on a stump beside the table and gazed at the baby and the little heap of clothes.

After a moment he rolled up the sleeve of his linen shirt and tested the water with his elbow. It was just right. How heavy his hands seemed! He became acutely aware of his strength.

As he lifted the child, well formed in spite of its thinness, something deep within him stirred, responding to its helplessness. It had ceased to whimper now and opened its eyes, staring unblinkingly. Blue veins on its forehead stood out boldly like the veins of the very aged. A soft spot under the fuzz of dark hair on the top of its head throbbed. The little pulse at the temples throbbed also. Life . . . the small indication of life. He must work fast. The maize was cooking to a soft porridge over the fire and he went out to stir it. By the time he had finished with the bath, the food would be ready.

Marcy came into the cabin.

"It's the feeding that worries me, Marcy," Adam said, without looking up from his task of wrapping a strip of flannel about the child's middle. "If we only had a little milk . . ."

"The porridge will do. It will put something warm into the child's belly. Shall I bring it in now, sir?"

Adam nodded, too engrossed with the unfamiliar task of putting on a baby's shirt to speak.

"It's soft—a regular pap." Marcy held the pannikin of cooked maize out for Adam to inspect. Adam had come to a stopping place. The child, in fresh clothes, lay flat on the table looking up at him, its body relaxed.

"How are we going to feed him, Marcy?" he asked.

"Leave that to me, sir. Many a time I've watched the peasants on our estate feed the children with a false tit." Tearing off a small piece of handkerchief, Marcy put a few spoonfuls of mush into the clean linen. He knotted it at one end and held the bag to the baby's blue lips. There was an automatic movement, but it soon stopped.

"He won't take it." Adam's voice showed his discouragement.

"He'll take it if there is any life left in his body. Just be patient, sir. Come, you hold on to the tit. We don't want him to choke on it once he gets started."

The two men bent anxiously over the table, waiting. Was there enough life in the frail body to respond to the natural sucking instinct? After a time the blue lips curled inward, drew again more strongly. The men hung breathlessly over the babe. Would it go on? Did it have the strength . . . ?

Marcy stood up. "It will work now sure. Nature is a grand lady. She makes us cling to life from the very beginning."

Adam held on to a corner of the cloth while the baby worked its mouth automatically. After a time, when it ceased to pull at the tit, Adam glanced up at Marcy apprehensively. The man came quickly to the opposite side of the table.

"It's quite all right, sir. He's taken the whole thing." The servant held up the flattened cloth.

"Shall we give him more?"

"Indeed not, unless we want to have him yelling with a bellyache. Let's see how this sets on his stomach first. Look, he's going to sleep."

Adam drew the quilt over the child and followed Marcy to the door.

"There is a stream not far from here," Marcy said. "And I found a dugout canoe pulled up on the bank."

"Enough water to float it?"

"I think so, if the water is smooth."

"If we find it is crowded we can take turns at the paddle while one of us walks along the bank. Make everything ready for a start at daybreak. We will have to carry them to the boat, the man as well as the woman and baby."

Marcy nodded. "The way is rough, sir, full of wash-boulders and small rocks, but I think we can make it."

Adam did not answer. He was looking toward the fire where the man lay inert on the ground.

"He looks pretty sick to me. Keep giving him brandy, Marcy. That is the only way to hold up his strength. Then lie down by the fire and get some sleep. I will sit up until I give the woman one more drink of dogwood tea."

Marcy took a candle and went to look at the woman. "She's quieter now. Her forehead is a little moist. Did you notice, sir, the fine texture of her skin and how shapely her hands are? They are not hands that have seen much hard work." He was silent for a moment, a deep frown between his eyes. "Damn this talk about finding Eden in this Province, and damn the men who send such people out here!" He turned abruptly and strode out to the fire.

Adam sat down on a stump facing the cabin door and stared into the dark, quiet, almost soundless night. He saw Marcy put a cover over the sleeping man and lie down on the ground on the opposite side of the fire. Trees rose in dark magnificence against the sky, lightened now to a pale blue by the rising moon. A wolf howled in the distance and was answered from a thicket not far away. This was followed by the sounds of twigs snapping in the forest. He had a glimpse of emerald eyes gleaming beyond the circle of firelight. Unseen life was awakening about him, yet there was little sound.

The child stirred but did not wake. He lifted it in his arms and went out. Sitting with his back to a pine tree, the child cradled in his arms, Adam watched the moonlight creep slowly down the mountainside. The green canopy of trees spread above him, latticing the pale blue of the night sky. A star gleamed through the interlaced boughs. A gentle wind, with a soft moaning sound, swayed the treetops above him. The faint smell of balsam, the acrid odor of burning pitch were in the air. He glanced down at the small bundle in his arms—the little face a blur of white in the darkness. Adam touched the child's hand. The tiny fingers curled over his, holding closely, holding to life and warmth. He realized suddenly his great weariness. Shifting his position to ease his cramped legs, he lay down, the full length of his body against the warm earth, the child pillowed against his side in the hollow of his arm.

Pressed close to the earth, a new sound came to his ear—or was it to the inner ear? Was he feeling the pulsebeat, the strength of the warm earth? The steady beat seemed to be part of his body. It entered his body, as it entered his conscious mind. He realized that he had never felt the full meaning of the earth until now.

He was without sense of bodily discomfort as he lay on the sun-baked earth, his face pressed against the carpet of pine. It was as if he were detached from the outer shell of his body. Was the secret of the earth's power the secret of sublime fulfillment? Or was it only the seasonal routine, the cycle played out year after year into infinity, which gave strength and the ever-renewing vitality that swayed the world?

The babe at his side stirred against his strongly beating heart. It was seeking warmth, as he sought warmth. . . . The eternal silent voices of the night closed in on him. . . . He felt the dark mystery of its throbbing power.

Adam awoke to half consciousness when the false dawn came. He felt movement about him, but he kept his eyes closed to the light. The child was warm and living within the curve of his arm. Presently he was aware of Marcy standing near, looking down at him. He opened his eyes slowly, reluctant to shatter the unreality of a dream for the reality of day.

87

"The farmer is dead," the indentured man said.

Adam shifted the child to the ground and rose to his feet. Near the fire the stiff body of the man lay with wide-open, staring eyes. In the early morning light the distorted face with the mouth half open, the lantern jaw dropped, gave the semblance of a sardonic grin, ghastly in its significance. The man's silent acceptance of his tragedy was broken now. His unspoken curses rose to the heavens out of the granite of his dead face.

Marcy took the pick and walked across the clearing to the sycamore tree. Adam went into the cabin. The woman was awake but there was no light of reason in her staring blue eyes. When Adam held the cup to her lips she swallowed the bitter draught obediently. But when he laid the infant beside her on the rough bed she made no movement to reach her child.

Under the sycamore, by the dry stream, Adam found Marcy digging the second grave, a shallow one for a nameless man.

They started at sunrise. Marcy rigged a stretcher by slipping two poles through the arms of their leather jerkins. On this they laid the woman and her child. She was awake, but she still gave no sign of being rational. Adam did not know whether this was the result of the fever or of some shock. Now that daylight had come, he saw that she was young. Her skin was white, her dark hair lay in ripples along her temples. Marcy was looking at the woman, his jaw set. They were thinking the same thoughts. They must get her to Edenton, to Dr. Armitage. Neither she nor her dead husband was of pioneer breed. They had been physically unsuited to undergo the hardships of clearing land. But one thing was evident: they had had courage.

The sun beat down as the day advanced. Adam's skin blistered under his linen shirt. Nettles whipped against them and deer-flies tormented them. Adam's arms ached so from carrying the litter that he wished he had not sent his Negro boy back to the Mecklenburg plantation.

Marcy's voice broke in, "There is the boat, sir."

At a turn in the dry stream, down which they were still traveling, Adam saw another stream wide enough to be called a river. On a shelving sandspit was a boat made from a hollowed log.

Doubling his leather jerkin into a pillow, Adam tried to

make a comfortable rest in the boat for the sick woman. Marcy arranged a shelter of boughs and leafy branches to protect her from the blazing sun and then crouched near her, waving a branch of alder to keep the flies away from her face. Adam took the paddle.

They traveled eastward, downstream. Wherever the river went, it must eventually lead to the sound. Presently, they came to high banks of gashed red earth. The river was narrow here, the way tortuous with granite boulders and rocks pushing their way through the earth. The paddling became difficult. If he had been alone Adam would have shot the rapids, but always conscious of his burden, he proceeded cautiously. Now it seemed advisable to make a long portage across a neck of land to avoid the rushing white water. This took time. Marcy made two trips—one to help Adam carry the woman and child, the second to drag the boat.

The sun, reflected from the water, beat against their faces and blazed into their eyes, blistering and searing. All day they traveled without the sight of a human being. A few grouse, startled by the boat, rose with a rush from bushes by the riverbank, but Adam and Marcy could not reach their rifles in time. Adam did not think it wise to leave the boat to hunt, for time meant too much to them. On and on they traveled past miles of unbroken forest on both sides of the river. An eagle soared overhead and vultures followed them, planing in the blue sky.

Adam saw a cabin at the end of the stream. It was deserted. Again there was the familiar burned maize patch with the remains of fires showing where tar had been burned. As Adam walked to the edge of the small clearing his foot hit against something half buried in the dry earth. Looking down, he saw a pile of bleached bones, picked clean to shimmering, naked whiteness. A rusted rifle lay beside the skeleton. Two wild hogs ran into the woods and, though Adam raised his rifle quickly, disappeared before he could shoot. Even for meat he knew that he must not follow, that he dare not leave the stream, for it would be easy to stray in the deep forest. Their only hope for food lay in reaching a plantation along the river. As he walked back toward the boat, he came upon a pole stuck into the ground. On it was a paper, the notice of quitrent due in coin of the realm . . . over the signature of Edmund Fanning.

The woman scarcely stirred all day. Once or twice Adam thought he saw a gleam of recognition in her wide blue eyes, but it did not last. Toward evening, a red spot appeared on each cheekbone. The fever was rising again. They must take time to brew another dose of dogwood bark.

Once again in the boat, Marcy paddling, they came to a fork in the river below a beaver dam. "Take the upper turning, Marcy. I believe we have the best chance that way."

The man turned the boat into a narrow gorge and in a moment they were in a series of rapids. Whirling and turning from side to side, the boat swept along, bumping against boulders and throwing water over them. Both men were on their knees, trying to hold a course. It was impossible; Adam shouted to let the boat go with the current. Marcy bailed with his cap. After what seemed to Adam an eternity of anxiety, the boat swept through the gorge into quiet water.

The banks were greener now. The land was good, the soil rich and unbroken. Adam could tell that it was good because of the size of the trees and the heavy underwood. Deer came to the river to drink, raising startled heads and dashing into the underbrush at their approach. The tall, swaying canebrake cut off the west bank and as they journeyed anxiously on they saw rocks to be avoided, cool green hills, lowlands with cypress and great blue mountains that hung like clouds in the hot, shimmering air.

Adam took rude reckoning by the Great Dipper and the North Star when they camped by the river that night. They took turns sleeping with one always on guard. When wolves came close to the very edge of the firelight, snarling and snapping, Adam tried shooting, but his powder was wet. Marcy had lost his powder horn when the boat struck against a boulder as they came through the rapids. He threw a stone and the wolves retreated.

At daybreak they were off again. After another day without food Marcy's stroke lagged. They changed places frequently. Adam knew that if they did not reach a settlement by nightfall they must waste precious time trying to kill game. Late in the afternoon he noticed the evidence of tidewater in the river. At the same moment Marcy called out, "Plantation ahead, sir!"

A lean man was standing at the bank, a rifle in his hand. Adam hailed him. The farmer put the rifle down and called to a woman at the door of the cabin, "It's white folks, Mirandy."

A spry, little woman with bright blue eyes came running to the landing. She picked up the child and started for the cabin. In no time there was milk for the baby and some soft cooked hominy for the mother. Adam wrote a chit for payment. The farmer looked at the paper, then at Adam.

"So you are Adam Rutledge. There's been talk along the river that you will represent the Edenton district in the Assembly next fall."

Adam was in no mood for a discussion of the rights of the farmers or questions of government. His mind was too full of the events of the two days past. He answered the man's question absently, scarcely knowing what he said. It was the old question rising up again—why should he represent these people? He knew nothing about them, nothing.

The woman spoke up. "Don't pester Mr. Rutledge, Hiram. Can't you see he be plumb wore out?"

Adam turned at the sound of the woman's voice. Her wrinkled face was brown as leather. Her hand was knotted at the joints, but her voice was gentle. How kind her eyes were! Adam said, "Thank you. We are tired. We have come a long way."

The man did not heed. "How do you stand on the quitrents, Mr. Rutledge?"

"I haven't given them much thought. Such things seem to me to be a matter for lawyers."

The farmers's lean face was working, his eyes blazed. "We've had too much of lawyers and soldiers in North Carolina. It's men like you we need to make our laws—men who know the land, who understand our hardships. The farmers along the river were glad when they heard about your going to Wilmington. 'There's the man for us,' they said."

"What is your name?" Adam asked, without comment on the man's words.

"Hiram Whitlock, a Yorkshire man, sir."

The woman interrupted. "Leave him be, Hiram, can't you see Mr. Rutledge is beat?" She turned to Adam diffidently. "Will you rest with us the night, sir?"

"If you are not put to trouble, mistress."

"We will be honored." The woman made a half curtsy.

"Come, come, Mirandy! No need to curtsy to the Squire. We be free people now."

Marcy came up the incline from the river carrying the empty milkpail. "The woman has opened her eyes, Master."

Adam spoke to Miranda Whitlock. "Look after the woman, will you, Mrs. Whitlock? Make the child comfortable, if you can."

"You want that I should keep the woman and baby here with us until they are both strong?"

Adam glanced around the cabin, a one-room log house. He remembered the burned maize fields, the two cows—racks of bones—and the lean razorback hogs.

Whitlock caught his glance. "We can manage, Squire. We ain't so bad off that we can't share what we got with a sick woman and a waif."

"You are very kind, but I think we had better get her down to Dr. Armitage."

Miranda wanted to share what she had with those more unfortunate. Her eyes were alight with eagerness. "We've got cow milk in plenty, Squire. That's more than most of the people along the river have. Milk will get the red back into her purty cheeks, the poor creature."

How kind, how very kind these humble people were, sharing their crust of bread. Suddenly Adam felt near to them.

"You are very good, Mistress Whitlock. I am sure you are an excellent nurse, but it is a doctor that we need now."

Miranda opened a drawer in an old maple chest. She took out a bundle of clothes and a plaid shawl. "Watch the oven bread, Pap. See that it doesn't burn on the bottom. I'm going to wash the child and put one of Johnnie's dresses on him."

"I tried to bathe the baby last night." Adam laughed a little. "I had the very devil of a time. I was afraid it would break in two."

"Tha' dan't break so easy as that, Square," the woman said, slipping into the north-country dialect. "They hang to life for all tha' are wee ones." She went into an outbuilding, cradling the baby against her flat breast.

The farmer watched her, a sad far-off look in his eyes. "Ma's lonely for children," he said. He got up, walked across the room, and took a printed sheet of paper from the rough board shelf above the fireplace. "Have you seen the last paper the Association printed, Mr. Rutledge?"

"Association?"

"The County Association." Whitlock studied Adam with his shrewd eyes. "You're a King's man, are ye not?" he asked abruptly.

"Yes, I am, Whitlock."

"But if you be representing the district in the Assembly, 'twould be well for you to know what we are thinkin' and what our needs be."

Adam said nothing. He wanted no arguments now. He was too tired. The farmer put the printed broadside into his hand. "This is what our Royal Governor sends us in answer to our just complaints about quitrents being paid in coin," he said.

Adam glanced quickly through the printing. Then he read it again, this time more carefully. He had not seen the broadside before, nor the Governor's edict from which this was a reprint. The wording was undoubtedly Tryon's.

"Let us hope, Gentlemen, that laying aside all passion and privileges, you will calmly and with one accord pursue such line of conduct in these points of general concern to America as may be most likely to heal the unhappy differences now existing between Great Britain and the colonies. Consider how great an opportunity you now have to serve your country . . . manifest loyalty to the best of kings and demonstrate your attachment to the British constitution, the most free, the most glorious and happiest political system in the whole world."

Adam glanced up from the paper. Whitlock was looking steadily at him, his face as hard and dour as his Yorkshire moors. "It is the Stamp Act," Adam thought. "Tryon's aim is to pacify the old grievance of the people before the knowledge of the Act becomes general." He started to lay the paper on the table.

"Finish the piece, Mr. Rutledge," the farmer said.

Adam glanced at him. His face was grim, his jaw set. Adam thought, "Whitlock is in deadly earnest. These are the men we must deal with and satisfy. They are the ones that count, not the demagogues or the crackpots. It is the real farmer we must protect from misery and injustice if we want to have peace in the Province." He took up the paper again.

"Be it to your glory, Gentlemen, to record to the last posterity that, at the time when sedition was about to raise its impious head in America, the people of North Carolina, inspired by a sense of duty to King and country . . . stood amongst the foremost of his Majesty's subjects to resist secret invaders, who seek to break down good government, and strike at our sacred institutions."

Adam realized now that the Governor was not talking about the Stamp Act but of the trouble in the northern districts. "Where did you get this broadside?" he asked Whitlock.

The farmer hesitated a few moments. "I suppose I shouldn't say, but I will take the risk. We had a meeting at Maddock's Mills, Deep River. Husband, the Quaker minister of Orange, led the talk. Every man had a chance to say his grievance. There were aplenty about Fanning and his men, the quitrents, and the new 'thorough taxes.'" There was a moment's silence. Then Whitlock finished. "I've said too much, Mr. Rutledge. You will forget it? I've no wish to say aught to betray secrets of the Regulators, but my tongue ran off."

All weariness was gone now. Adam was alert, his mind on what Whitlock was saying. The Regulators were a group of radical malcontents. "I shall say nothing, Whitlock," he answered.

Whitlock leaned forward. "You rich planters along the Sound have no notion of how these quitrents bear down on us. Fanning's agents won't let us pay in produce. It is the King's shilling they want. We have no money. The land will sustain us if the government will let it. We have no slaves, no helpers. We work by the sweat of our brows, as the Bible says, but we have rights the same as you. We are not slaves, we are free men."

Whitlock . . . was it Whitlock who stood before him? His burning eyes were set deep in a thin, lined face. He might have been Isaiah the prophet, instead of Whitlock, lately indentured to servitude.

"I'm an ignorant man," the farmer said slowly. "But I know what me and my neighbors came to America for. We came here to be free, and to own land. Land is the way to freedom, Mr. Rutledge."

When they left the farm at sunrise Whitlock came down to the river with them. Miranda followed, carrying the baby. She laid it gently beside the woman, her face working. Adam saw tears gathering under her red-rimmed eyelids.

"It's the empty arms that kills us, not hard work or loneliness," she explained sadly.

Adam pressed her hard calloused hands in both of his.

Whitlock waded deep into the water to push off the heavily loaded boat. "I hope you will come to our help, Mr. Rutledge," he said at the last. "We know you will stand for us and our rights."

Again Adam felt himself being drawn into the torrent. How could he answer this man whose faith in him was so strong?

"I'll come back, Whitlock," he said. "Then you can have your neighbors come in, and they can tell me what they think should be done to help them and ease their burden."

The man grasped his hand and wrung it. "Thank you, thank you. I knew you was the friend we waited for. Poor folk as well as the rich have the right to be free."

He gave the heavy boat a shove and it slipped into the current. Whitlock stood on the bank, his wife beside him, watching them until they turned the bend. Adam waved his hand as the boat reached the main stream that flowed onward toward the sea.

Toward evening, when the boat entered the river, Adam recognized their position. They were not far above Rutledge Riding and the North Plantation. By sunset, they were bordering his own land. Women and children sat on the banks watching. A dozen slaves, with shouts of welcome, waded out to drag the boat up on the sandspit. Adam jumped to the bank. He called to the waiting slaves:

"Have the woman carried to the plantation house. Send a boy on horseback for Dr. Armitage. Tell him it is a matter of life and death."

"Shall I go to the Island with you, sir?" Marcy paused, looking down on the pale woman who lay motionless in the boat.

"Stay here with the woman, Marcy. Mrs. Tewilliger will know what to do for her until the Doctor comes. Let me know how things go."

A Negro woman, her bosoms full to overflowing with milk, sat on the bank, her child at her breast. Adam lifted the baby from the side of the sick woman and, crossing the sandspit, put it in the arms of the slave. Without a word she put her child on the sand, where it lay full-bellied and content, brown legs and arms waving. She laid the weak, exhausted child against her breast. The baby's thin, clawlike fingers pressed feebly against the full brown breast. Adam watched them for a moment. There was something of the warm earth-strength in the slave woman; something of the mystery and strength of the brown earth-mother . . . warm and life-giving.

Chapter 7

ADAM MAKES
A DECISION

WHITLOCK'S energetic defense of his own position and that of his neighbors won Adam Rutledge's respect. More than that, it set him thinking. His recent contact with Death had shocked him profoundly. The tragedy at the wilderness cabin was sordid, and unnecessary. It was Death without dignity.

The existence of those wretched people, under the blazing sun on the parched and waterless earth, was cruel enough. But to be living under the constant fear of dispossession from the land they had snatched from the forest and wilderness by heavy, backbreaking labor, was tragic.

Adam could not forget it. He kept coming back again and again to the same thought. The obligation of the government was to aid, not to oppress its people. Whitlock saw more clearly than he, for he had the shrewd wisdom of the simple man close to the soil who has always fought for his existence. He was a lionhearted man, whose honesty was compelling. Adam felt a growing respect for those who, like Whitlock, had taken a stand. It was a perilous position and one that demanded undiminished courage.

"Every man has a right to freedom." Whitlock had used the words prophetically. Freedom wasn't to be had for a price. It was won by work and sacrifice, and perhaps death. He didn't want to think so far . . . he wanted to close his eyes and his ears, but he couldn't. The words pounded in his brain. How long could he isolate himself? How long could he evade responsibility? A picture of the distorted face of the dead farmer; the penetrating, questioning eyes of Whitlock . . . Could he escape responsibility?

The sun was low on the horizon when he crossed the ferry to the Island. He felt a sudden desire to talk with Sara, to tell her about the sick woman and her starving baby, about the farmer and the lonely cabin. He remembered now, with a feeling of contrition, that he had not thought of her at all these past days. He walked swiftly from the boat landing to the house. Crossing the central hall to the west wing he knocked lightly at the door of Sara's suite.

Judith opened the door a few inches. Seeing Adam, she opened it wider to let him pass. "She would rather have closed it in my face," thought Adam. How he disliked the woman!

Sara was in her chair by the window. She was dressed in a thin robe of pale blue muslin with fluted ruffles around the bottom of the full skirt. Her hair was bound with a wide blue ribbon, and she wore the pearls he had given her as a marriage gift. Adam crossed the room quickly and took her hand.

"Adam, what have you been doing? Look at your face, and your hair!"

Adam caught sight of himself in a mirror. His hair was disheveled, a lock straggling over his forehead. Across his cheek was a long red scratch where the blood had caked.

"You should take time to freshen up before you come to me." Sara's tone was hurt.

"I'm sorry, Sara," he said. He wanted to speak of the courage of the woman who had borne a child without doctor or midwife to help her. He wanted to share with her the thought that came to him in the dark stretches of the night when he held the child against his body. But when he looked at her now, surrounded by the luxuries of her prolonged invalidism, he knew that he was a fool. He could tell her nothing. The story was too ugly, too brutal in its grim reality. He could not break through the barriers he had himself erected for her protection. He must go on as he had begun. A wave of passionate loneliness swept over him. "I'm so sorry, dear," he repeated. "I wanted to know that you were well, to assure myself of your security."

Sara opened her eyes wide, a puzzled expression on her delicate features. "Secure? Of course, I am secure, with Judith to care for me! You do say the most extraordinary things, Adam." He caught the gleam of triumph in the black woman's eyes.

The slave girl Azizi appeared from somewhere to open the door for him, but Sara kept him a moment. "Did you bring the wool for me from Charlottetown, Adam?"

"The wool?"

Sara's voice dropped plaintively. "Of course, you wouldn't remember my little wants, but I told you to ask Elizabeth Alexander to match the wool for my tapestry. I am almost out of wool for the background of green trees."

As she spoke, his mind flashed to a background of green sycamore trees near a dry stream casting a pattern over two unmarked graves. "I am sorry, Sara," he repeated wearily. "Very sorry."

Sara spoke sharply to the young slave girl. "Go upstairs and help your master take off his boots, Azizi. See that he has clean linen." She turned back to Adam. "Cicero went to the mainland to get the green wool, Adam. A ship has come into Edenton, and Mr. Hewes has some worsteds at his shop."

Adam's eyes narrowed. She had sent to Edenton for wool. She could get it there. She knew that, and still she took occasion to make him feel he had neglected her by not attending to her commission in Charlottetown. He wanted, more than anything in the world, to make her happy—if she would let him. But she was constantly combating him; her pettiness made him feel helpless.

As he swam in the sparkling waters of the cove at the end of the East Garden he wondered why Sara showed no interest in what he had been doing. She had not asked him why his clothes were torn, nor why he was scratched and bruised. Her one thought was to protest against the intrusion of ugliness into the cool orderliness of her room.

Bathed and dressed in fresh clothes, he went again to that room. He found the woman Judith seated in front of the door on guard, a position she often assumed when her mistress slept. "Damn her!" he muttered and strode away.

Seated at the end of the long table he ate his lonely dinner, served by Aaron and half a dozen slaves. As he looked about, he thought now, as often before, that the room should be filled with people . . . women in London frocks . . . officers in scarlet coats and uniforms . . . planters in their more sober blue or plum color.

Over the mantel, standing out from the dark wainscot as if it were the living man, was the Kneller portrait of his father. Adam glanced at the mirror opposite him. He saw reflected the same blond hair, high-bridged nose, long hazel eyes, the same strong firm mouth.

Aaron took away dish after dish untasted. His hands trembled as he placed the last plate on the table, a look of perplexity on his face.

Adam noticed his distress. "Nothing wrong, Aaron. I'm not hungry, that is all. Bring cold meats and ale to the library. I may want to eat later." He pushed his chair back and rose from the table before Aaron served the port. The sight of such abundance had choked him. Too lately he had seen the other thing. He wondered why Marcy did not come. He hoped he had been able to get the Doctor.

It was well after eleven when the indentured man knocked at the door of the book room. His face was worn.

"Sit down and have something to eat, Marcy," Adam said. "There's meat and cheese."

Marcy glanced at him quickly. But he sat down at a small table and attacked the meat and ale as if he were starving. "They will both live," he said between mouthfuls. "Dr. Armitage says the woman must have had a bad shock. It would take more than starvation or fever to put her in the state she is in now."

"I wonder what the story is," Adam said.

Marcy took a bundle of papers from the pocket of his leather jerkin. "The man was indentured and had worked out his seven-year bond. He took up land. Then he sent to England for his wife and child. He could not go back for he was a rebel to the Crown. Dr. Armitage found the papers in the woman's clothes. He sent them over to you. Her name is Lucy Williams. She was governess in a country family in Yorkshire when she met the farmer, Joel Williams."

Adam examined the letters. An official-looking paper attracted his attention. It was a dispossession notice, signed across the bottom in red ink: Edmund Fanning. His lips tightened. "Damnation to Fanning and his notices of dispossession!"

Marcy was watching him closely. A smile of satisfaction came over his face which made Adam aware that he had spoken aloud.

"And damnation to anyone who tries to enforce unjust taxation!" he completed the thought.

"Spoken like a Kentish man, sir," Marcy's smile was broader now. Adam realized that there had been a subtle change in their relationship in the last few days—a gradual change. They had been living, speaking, as men on an equal footing.

"How much longer have you to go on your bond, Marcy?"

The Irishman set down his mug and wiped his lips. He hesitated, then said, "Three years and five days, master."

"Give me the five days and I will give you the three years." Adam's tone was light. "Is that a bargain?"

Marcy pushed the pewter mug across the table. His face hardened. "Bargain? How can an indentured man bargain with his master?"

"There'll be no more master and man between us. You can have Lawyer Warden draw up the papers in the morning."

Marcy got to his feet slowly. His hands were clutching the heavy oak table, his voice was tense. "You are very generous, Mr. Rutledge."

"Let's not call it generosity, Marcy. I don't like the idea. There's something vitally wrong in the system that allows a man such as you to serve me or any other man of your class."

Marcy said, "I make no complaint. I got myself into the mess. Seven lawbooks! Seven years of bondage for books that were rightfully mine."

"Was that your crime?" Adam asked.

"That was my crime . . . but it happened that the magistrate who sentenced me wanted my little estate on the Shannon."

Adam clapped his hand on Marcy's shoulder. "You will forget injustice when you are free. It's the future we must think about now."

Marcy looked up quickly. "You mean I must leave Rutledge Riding?"

"You wish to stay?"

"I have no desire to live elsewhere. If you . . ."

"There is no reason why you should not go on looking after the accounting and the ships' cargoes. We will talk about wages later." Marcy was struggling to keep his composure. Adam did not want him to break. "I suppose there will be numerous papers but William Warden will arrange it," he said matter-of-factly. "Better go to bed now and get some rest."

The Irishman smiled. "It's not sleep I'll want on my first night of freedom, Mr. Rutledge. I'll be walking the woods until dawn comes."

It was Sara's idea that Adam should read a chapter from the Bible each Sunday evening. She was deeply religious. Her mother, a Scotch woman, had brought her up in the tenets of John Knox. The easygoing, fox-hunting parson of St. Paul's shocked her. A rector who would drink a glass of ale or enjoy his after-dinner port she could not understand. When the new religion of Mr. Whitefield began to take hold in the Province, Sara leaned heavily on its teachings for support. This worried Adam. He was freer in his beliefs but he tried to assure himself that Sara's constant recourse to her Bible gave her strength. He fell into the habit of Sunday prayers

100

readily enough since it was the traditional thing. His father had done the same at Annandale. He accepted it as he did other traditions, automatically, without any great reflection. The half-hour reading brought to a pleasant close an otherwise lifeless day.

The slaves were seated on benches in the counting room when he came in. A table had been placed at one end of the room with the closed Bible and a branched candelabrum of copper holding seven lighted candles upon it. Adam drew up a chair and sat down. He had no plan for reading but liked to open the book at random. He smiled at Sara, who sat near the window. How lovely she looked, fragile, elegant! Her billowing silk skirt gave the dominant note of color to the room. Judith stood behind her, her lean frame erect, her starched apron and fluted cap immaculate.

Half a dozen young slaves, born on the plantation, sat quietly near their elders. Even the old pagans out of the jungles seemed to have respect for Christianity. Adam sometimes wondered how deep it went . . . how far the religion of the white man had penetrated into the inherent paganism of the black. He questioned Cicero now and then, but the old slave was reluctant to answer. He did not want to talk of the pagan beliefs that were his when he lived in Africa. Instead he was eager to talk of the ways of the Lord. Cicero was deeply spiritual and held preachings on Sunday mornings for the field slaves. At times, he had visions and was inspired to speak with the gift of tongues.

Aaron was different. He was an old pagan, and he did not mind in the least Adam knowing. When he drank his allowance of rum he grew talkative. Once he told Adam that black Judith knew strange things, that she had the power to "fly right out of she body" into the body of an animal. She made charms for the young people so that their lovers would be true to them. She did other things, more wicked . . . made charms against people. But Cicero was afraid to talk about Judith. "Leave she alone," he would cry. "She's a debbil."

As Adam watched them sitting quietly with dark upturned faces, he wondered whether he had the right to lead them away from their deep-rooted old beliefs. He had owned slaves long enough to distinguish the differences in tribes and in tribal characteristics. In this he was helped by the intricate caste-marks tattooed on forehead, cheeks and lips; on chest and back or thighs. He had learned to mix tribes in order to get more work through competition. There were subtle differences in features, in color; in the way women draped their calicos, or knotted their gay Madras turbans. This knowledge had come slowly by observation, and by discreet questions.

Unmixed natives of the Gold Coast, fierce fighting warriors of the Negroes and Fawds, snake worshiping Congoes, Angolese and ebony black Mandingoes from the Gambia River, and bronzed men from the Zambezi country looked up at him now, waiting for him to speak. It did not occur to Adam Rutledge that hundreds of slavers like LaTruchy were violating all Africa to bring wealth and comfort to planters like him.

Adam opened the Bible to "The Song of Songs" and hesitated a moment, debating whether he should read the most passionate of love songs to his slaves. His eyes fell on the words:

> "I am black, but comely,
> O ye daughters of Jerusalem,
> as the tents of Kedar,
> as the curtains of Solomon.

> "Look not upon me,
> because I am black,
> because the sun
> hath looked upon me ..."

As he turned the page he saw Azizi. She stood at the back of the room leaning against a fluted pilaster which broke the flat surface of the paneled wall and supported the heavily carved cornice. The slaves were quiet. They could not understand the words, but they felt their rhythm:

> "The fig tree putteth forth her green figs ...
> Arise, my love, my fair one,
> and come away ...
> Behold thou art fair, my love ...
> Thy lips are like a thread of scarlet."

Adam raised his eyes. He knew then he was talking to the girl who leaned against the white pillar, her slim round throat bound with a golden chain. He had an overpowering sensation of a void, of rushing forward into the blackness of some nebulous world. The sound of his voice held him back. Her eyes, looking obliquely as in the past, were fixed on him, not veiled now, but alive, deeply glowing.

"Behold, thou art fair, my beloved;
our bed is green.
The beams of our house are cedar,
and our rafters of fir,—
How fair and how pleasant art thou,
O love, for delights . . ."

How long his eyes held the girl's he did not know. Conscious of the rustling of stiff silks, he saw that Sara was watching the slave girl, a curious, twisted smile on her lips. He closed the book abruptly. When he raised his eyes again the slaves were filing out silently and the girl had left the room. He saw her walking slowly down the terrace toward the East Garden.

Sara waited for him to carry her back to her room, the curious, twisted smile still on her lips. She was light in his arms, so light that it made him acutely conscious of his own strength. He laid her on the smooth white bed with its fresh linen sheets which gave off the crisp, clear scent of lavender.

"I think it will storm tonight, Adam," Sara said as Judith bent to loosen her dress. He opened the window. The air was heavy; a great cloud like a mare's tail swept the sky, almost obscuring the moon. Suddenly a flash of light came along the length of the horizon.

"Only summer lightning, dear. Shall I pull the blind?"

"If you will. I loathe lightning. I must sleep tonight."

Adam glanced at Sara's woman. The Negress nodded slightly. He knew that she would mix a sleeping potion for her mistress.

Sara lay quietly for a moment without speaking. Then she looked up at Adam.

"I saw you looking at my slave Azizi when you were reading from the Bible. Do you like the color I have selected for her livery? Judith tried plum color but I did not like it. I had the woman dye some cloth a dull yellow. I think she looks more attractive now, don't you, Adam?" A little secret smile showed in the corners of her lips.

Adam said nothing. He wondered why Sara wanted to discuss the color of a house servant's livery. She had never talked to him of such matters before.

"I want her to look well," she said after a time. "Lavinia writes me that bright liveries are the fashion in London among the great ladies of the Court, and they have blackamoors, too—dressed up like Turks. Judith said she heard in the village that Lady Caroline had a blackamoor—have you seen it?"

"No," Adam said, "I haven't seen Lady Caroline Mathilde's blackamoor."

"Then you've never been to Pembroke?" Sara asked, not looking at him directly.

Adam knew, now, why she had asked the question.

"No, I've not been to Pembroke," he answered with a touch of annoyance. He had no intention of discussing Lady Caroline Mathilde or her affairs.

Sara sighed, a long tremulous sigh. "If only I had enough strength, we would ask her to the Manor House—"

Adam crossed to the bed and took her hand for a moment. "Rest well, my dear."

"I hope so, Adam. I have not slept for several nights. It tires me so not to get my sleep." Sara put her cool fingers on his cheek for a second. "I have ordered your bed made up in the east gallery overlooking the garden. It will be cooler there and more comfortable."

Adam bent to kiss her. "You think of everything, Sara. What a dear little wife you are!"

"Thank you, Adam. I do try to make you happy. I want to think of everything."

"Everything, my dear, everything." Sara lay back, a smile of satisfaction on her face. Adam kissed her tenderly.

When he had gone out of the room and shut the door quietly behind him, Sara turned to Judith. "Did you tell the girl Azizi to make up the master's bed on the gallery?" she asked.

"Yes, Mis' Sara, I told she."

"Then hand me my Bible and light more candles. I think I will read a little."

"Want I should read to you, Mis' Sara?"

"No, Judith. Rub my poor feet and limbs; they ache so."

The slave got down on her knees to rub Sara's feet, using a slow revolving motion that began at Sara's ankles and moved slowly upward. Sara lay with closed eyes. "You begin to read the Book all over again," Judith said, without stopping the round movement of her strong fingers. Sara turned slightly so that Judith could reach her back.

"Yes, I began last night."

"What part you read now, Miss Sara?"

"Genesis. The fifteenth and sixteenth chapters."

The woman glanced at the open book, then turned back to her work, hiding a sly smile.

Cicero was waiting for Adam when he got to his room. The body servant dragged out his work, putting the room to rights, laying out Adam's clothes for the morning, folding lace ruffles with his deft black hands. He carried a quilt out to the veranda.

"You might catch cold if hit rain, master."

Adam knew the ways of the old man. Cicero had something on his mind so Adam helped him by a question. "Well, what is it? Is Mandy going to have another baby, or do you want a room added to your cabin?"

"No, sah, Mandy ain't goin' to have no baby, lessen she commit a miracle."

"Well, is it your good-for-nothing son, Zeke? Is he in trouble again?"

"Ain't heard from Zeke for a long time, master; not since that last batch of Zulu niggers run away."

"If you do hear from him, tell him I don't want him around here annoying you."

"Yassuh."

"Well, what is it?"

"That girl Azizi . . ."

"What of the girl?" Adam asked after a moment.

"She workin' up round here all de time now."

Adam said nothing. Invariably when the girl's name was spoken he remained silent. Why? He did not know.

"Yes, Mas' Adam, she cleans the rooms upstairs and sometimes I find she here. Tonight she makin' up you' bed out there. 'For why you make my master's bed?' I say to she.

" 'Judith tell me to make the master's bed on the gallery.' " Cicero mimicked the girl's accented words. "Dat what she say. I send she down the stairs. . . ."

"Well?" Adam found himself saying irritably. "Well?"

"Mas' Adam I take care you' father an' I take care of you when you was jes' so high . . ." The slave's voice broke. There was a mist in his eyes. One slow tear furrowed its way down the wrinkled black cheek.

Adam laid his hand on the broad shoulder of the old man. He smiled, but his voice was very gentle. "So you think the girl is infringing on your rights? Don't worry. You will have to take care of me as long as you live! Unless I die first, you old rascal."

"Thank you, master. I don' want no witch girl doing for you." Cicero picked up the blue coat Adam had taken off and flung carelessly on the bed.

"Witch girl? What do you mean?" Adam's voice was sharp.

Cicero spoke quickly, avoiding the flashing eyes of his master. "This old tongue ran away with hisself, master."

Adam was thinking rapidly. He remembered that Azizi was never with the other slaves, always by herself. Her work at the house for Sara might account for that, but he knew Cicero's words had a deeper significance.

"Answer me. Do the Negroes say the girl is a witch? Answer me at once, or I'll have Haskins give you ten of the finest . . ."

Cicero never had felt the touch of the whip. He saw Adam was angry, but he was reluctant as always to speak on subjects that dealt with witchcraft.

Adam took a step forward. Cicero opened his mouth, the words tumbled out. "They don't like she. They say she make med'cine agin' them. Last week Martha she baby die. Azizi she walking that way, with flowers in she hand, singing song to sheself."

"Martha's baby had a weak heart. The Doctor told her to keep the child in bed." Adam was impatient with this nonsense, but he knew that with the black people this sort of thing could not be talked down.

" 'Tain't nothin' about a bad heart, Mas' Adam. That chile die 'cause a spell bin put on she."

Adam saw that it would do no good to argue. He tried another tack. "You are an old fool, Cicero. You certainly don't believe such nonsense. You, a good Christian, preaching every Sunday morning to the field hands."

The old man shook his white head. Adam saw that he was torn between his pagan beliefs and his new religion. "I dunno, master. I dunno. . . . Sometimes people make *Mankwala.* I seed it in the villages many times, before I come to this land."

"Look here, Cicero," Adam said firmly. "The next time the Negroes say that Azizi is making witchcraft, you ask them whether anyone ever had *Mankwala* made against them before she came on the place. Just ask them that."

A smile came over Cicero's black face. "Shore they was. 'Member how that woman Judith usen to mak sheself into a cat and scare the children. . . . Ceph, he saw she. . . . Yassuh, folks make charms before that girl come here, that's the Lord's truth, Mas' Adam."

Cicero moved toward the door, his mind at rest.

Adam stopped him. "What's this strange drumming Haskins tells me is going on among the Negroes on the lower plantation?"

Cicero's eyes shifted quickly. "I don' know nothin' about no strange drummin', master."

Adam did not press. He knew this was the time to dismiss the subject as of no importance. He said carelessly, "I suppose the field hands are dancing because the harvest is over. It doesn't matter."

A look of relief passed over Cicero's face. "No, master, hit don' matter; hit don' matter at all."

Adam knew it did matter. There was some connection between the drum talk and witchcraft. He hoped it had nothing to do with the slave girl Azizi.

In the night the drums woke him. The sound seemed to come from the direction of the swamp. He sat up but the drumming soon stopped. He lay down again, wondering whether it had really been drums that he heard.

It was more than two weeks after Adam had come home from the western plantation before he went to Edenton. He had meant to go at once to talk with Mary Warden about Lucy Williams and her sick child but when he got back to Rutledge Riding the plantation harvest was on and he was too busy to leave. They had let the woman and baby stay on at the North Plantation where the child was doing well with its Negro foster-mother. Lucy had also improved bodily but she still remembered nothing of what had happened before Adam and Marcy had found her. The Doctor was dubious about a complete recovery. She might, he said, never remember the past, but it was possible that she would recover sufficiently to be aware of the present. After he had settled her and the baby in a small cabin near Stone House on North Plantation, Adam had let Marcy continue to be responsible for the two. It was now early in September. The Parson had called a vestry meeting at Cupola house on Tuesday. Adam thought he would go to the meeting and ride out to Queen's Gift later, in time for tea.

Monday night after he had had dinner he suddenly decided to sail over to the North Plantation. It was a warm night, the moon was at the full and there was a good stiff breeze blowing down the Sound. He would try out the new sloop which had recently been delivered to him from the shipyards at Elizabeth where it had been built to his designs. Sara was sleeping, so he left word that he would not be back before the next evening. Marcy would take the horses around by the post road, so he would have Saladin to ride to Edenton in the morning. He would stay the night at North Plantation, where

107

his rooms were always in readiness. It would give him a chance to talk with Owen Tewilliger, the Welsh manager of his plantations, who lived at Stone House with his wife Gwennie. He hadn't seen Owen since he came back, and there were things to settle about the tobacco shipment to London.

Cicero packed his saddlebags and Adam went down to the landing where his new boat was moored. He set sail and tacked until he was out from under the lee of the Island. Then he caught a stiff wind blowing down the Sound from the east. He set a diagonal course toward the light across the point which marked the North Plantation landing, and made himself comfortable, his knee thrown over the tiller.

Adam liked the quiet of the night. The sky was bright with stars, the dipper swinging low and the North Star shining steadily. A fish leaped from the water and a night bird flew low along the shore, uttering a mournful cry. Far in the distance, Negroes were singing, the work of the day over.

Adam looked forward to a talk with Owen. They would get through the plantation business, then they would go to Owen's book room, make themselves comfortable with pipes and jugs of Gwennie's ale, and talk. Owen was the man to whom Adam opened his mind and his heart. There was something about his detached, scholarly wisdom that held Adam's interest and his admiration. It had been more than three years since Owen had taken over the management of all of Adam's plantations. The arrangement had been more than satisfactory to Adam. Gradually, detail that had been a weight to Adam, was taken over by Owen.

Having him at North Plantation had been Mary Warden's idea. The Welsh schoolmaster had come to the Province five years earlier at the insistence of Daniel Earl to take charge of a parish school he was organizing. The plan fell through and Owen opened a small school for boys in Edenton. While he was cramming the minds of the lads with Latin and Greek roots and mathematics, his round-bodied, rosy-cheeked wife, Gwennie, was filling their stomachs with her delectable meat pasties and shepherd pies topped off by trifles and saffron cake. She settled their squabbles, mended their clothes, mothered them, and tucked them into bed at night after prayers.

The school flourished until Owen took sick with pleurisy one winter. Armitage had a hard time saving his life. He ordered him to give up the school and sedentary life and to stay outdoors if he wanted to continue to live.

Dr. Armitage took the Tewilliger problem to Mary and she

suggested the North Plantation. Adam, who was looking for a man who could take over the management of all the plantations, fell into the plan. In a week, Owen and Gwennie were established in the Stone House, the old Manor House on Adam's mainland plantation.

Adam, sailing in the still night, noticed that a heavy bank of clouds had gathered along the horizon. Mists were creeping in, lying low on the water. The light at North Plantation was dim, almost invisible. If the wind held, he could make it readily enough by not changing his course. Suddenly a great dark mass seemed to rise above the mists. The hull of a slow-moving ship made its ghostlike appearance.

There wasn't a minute to lose. He swung the tiller hard to the left and let the sail run. The sloop heeled over, preventing a collision, scraping the side of the ship as she passed.

"Port your helm! Swing clear," a voice cried from above him. There was the sound of bare feet racing across the decks, black figures silhouetted above him.

Safely out of the ship's lane, Adam stood up and shouted, "Ahoy there! Who are you?"

There was no answer. Adam heard shouts and the sound of hurried movement, a woman's voice high, excited, instantly suppressed . . . a man cursing . . . the scraping of a boat against the opposite side of the ship . . . and the rattle of oarlocks.

"Ahoy there!" he called again, putting his hands to the side of his mouth. "What ship is this?"

After a moment, a harsh voice with a foreign accent answered.

"The *Rajah,* Femandez, Master, ninety days out of Bombay, bound for the port of Roanoke."

Adam laughed. The man was using the old name by which Edenton had been known in early days. It flashed through his mind that the ship must be sailing by an old chart.

"You've oversailed your destination," he shouted. "Swing half and bear NNE."

A gust of wind filled his sails. He grabbed the ropes and the sloop moved swiftly out from the lee of the ship. The rattle of oarlocks and the dip of oars came clearly. He saw the shadow moving on the water, heading west in the direction of Pembroke landing. This puzzled Adam. Why should they be sending a boat out from the ship, and why should an India merchantman be sailing up Albemarle Sound?

Adam listened a moment, peering into the gloom. The dip of oars grew faint. Then he saw a light glowing in the blackness. It moved slowly in a small circle, as a man might swing a lantern. Someone signaling from Pembroke. Why should any member of Lady Caroline's household be signaling to an India merchantman? It crossed his mind that it was quite possible that Lady Caroline had ordered luxuries direct from India, as she did from the West Indies and London.

He had no time to think much about the incident. A sudden squall lifted the sail. He caught at the tiller as the boom swung around. For the next half-hour his mind was intent on sailing his boat.

Adam found Owen at the dock. It was late, almost midnight. He followed Owen into his library, filled from floor to ceiling with books and papers. Gwennie had set a tray with a decanter of Irish whisky and some meat and bread on a table. A fire was blazing in the stone fireplace, for it was cool now. The men sat down. Owen took down a great leather-covered ledger.

The clock struck two before they finished. Adam poured himself a glass of whisky and got up to stretch his legs. He stood with his back to the fire, glass in hand. He was pleased with the figures Owen had shown him. Things had gone well that year in spite of the drought. There was a good profit from all the plantations.

Owen sat drinking his whisky, looking at Adam contemplatively. "You are a young man, Adam, to be engrossed in land to the extent you are. How do you account for it?"

"I don't know. I suppose it's inherited. All of us want to own land." He lighted a long clay pipe, puffed for a minute before he continued. "Land is a heritage, isn't it? I often think about it when I'm riding through the fields and walking through the timber. We don't really own the earth. It belongs to the rain, the wind and the sun."

Owen looked at him for a moment, smiling slightly, his thin, esthetic face alight with interest. "That's a poetic conception, Adam. I've never thought of you as poetic. Romantic, yes, as all men who have the seeking pioneer spirit are romantic, but poetic—"

Adam shook his head. "I've no wish to be a poet. I've no knack for words, Owen, but I've some ideas of my own about land." He knocked out the pipe and moved about the room. His thoughts came easier when he was moving about. "We have the land to use as long as we take care of it," he said after a moment.

Owen did not answer. Adam was trying to express something he had thought of but had never put into words. Like most solitary men, he was not articulate when his deeper emotions were concerned. Owen did not press him.

Adam said, "We have the land as long as we care for it. If we give up, Nature takes it back. Jungles grow swiftly, and lands unwatered go back to desert. Desert sand creeps slowly but obliterates everything. If we do not keep the land as rich as we found it, we lose our heritage."

Owen leaned forward. "That is a fundamental truth, Adam. We must not starve the soil or wear it out. Land is a heritage we hold in trust."

Adam smiled, clasping his long fingers together behind his head. "There is more to land than planting wheat or rice or tobacco, Owen. We must guard it carefully."

Owen got up and went to his desk. In a moment he was back with a book in his hand. "Here is something to interest you," he said, leafing through the pages. He found the place. Before he began to read, he said, "A man I know—I was in Oxford with him—has done some writing on land. He has theories concerning the distribution of the wealth of nations." He adjusted his glasses and read: " 'Have you ever thought how thin is the layer of soil that covers the Earth? Yet it supports us all, and sustains life. Every man, even animals, birds, and plants depend on a thin crust.' "

Adam nodded his head.

" 'We know nothing of the force of this mysterious Earth on which we live. We do not know what for us pulsates in its center. It may be a revolving, seething mass of gas; or the core of it may be dead—and the crust which sustains us slowly dying—' "

Adam watched him holding the pages close to his near-sighted eyes to get the light from the candles. It was strange that Owen should think so much about land. Owen did not love land as he loved it. He did not know the intensity of such a feeling. His thoughts about land were abstract.

"I love the feel of land under my feet." Adam spoke aloud as a continuation of his thoughts.

Owen glanced up. " 'The heel of the conqueror,' " he said absently. " 'Primitive emotion—' I am looking for something else that will interest you. Here it is: 'We spring from the soil; back to the soil we go in the end to make up its richness. Trees, plants, animals, birds and man . . . There is a nice finality about this. A completed ever-renewing cycle, as inevitable as the phases of the moon—' "

Adam said nothing. Owen turned pages. "One thing more,"

111

he said. "This is the key to the book. I want you to remember it, Adam."

Adam thought, "It is the schoolmaster speaking."

Owen continued:

" 'The soil locks within its embrace the beginnings of all life and receives at the last their discarded forms.

It will outlive all the works of man; transcend all human thought.

It traces the progress of history and shelters its ignoble end.

It speaks eloquently and is dumb.

It is the imperishable storehouse of eternity.' "

He closed the book.

Adam saw Mary Warden riding along King Street, headed in the direction of Queen's Gift, when he came out from the Vestry Meeting at Cupola House. He swung on to his horse and tossed a coin to the small Negro who had been walking Saladin up and down the street. By taking a short cut along the Commons he caught up with Mary near Queen Anne's Creek.

Her eyes brightened with pleasure as he came up. She had been at Eden House, she said. Everyone was excited about the India merchantman which was lying off the town. It had brought in a cargo of spices and silks, and a great quantity of tea. Soon the women would be flocking to the Levantine's shop to look at the silks.

Adam did not speak about his encounter with the *Rajah* though he thought it strange that a ship of such size should come into the Sound. He had intended to talk to John Hewes about it, but Hewes had not come to the meeting.

He waited in the yellow drawing room while Mary changed, and Cissie brought in tea. Ebon came in and put a log on the fire, for the mist of the night before still hung over the Sound. Adam looked about the room. It was like Mary. It had a certain tranquillity that was her chief characteristic. It had comfort, too. He thought vaguely, as he had done often before, that the drawing room at Rutledge Riding was more elegant, but it lacked life.

In the hall the clock chimed five. Mary came in wearing a flowing house gown of some soft, rosy material, which swept the floor behind her. A faint perfume followed her as she moved to the lacquered tea table. Adam thought, "I am a fool not to come more often." He loved his wife and saw himself only as a husband. But he was too much of a man of the world not to know that he could not go on forever without some interest outside his plantation. Poor Sara! She had

112

the worst of it. The only thing he could do was to give her his continued loyalty. But surely he coud come to Mary's home more frequently than he did. She was a friend, a fine, true friend.

Mary handed him a cup, her deep blue eyes smiling at him. "Your thoughts are deep, Adam," she said. "I asked you twice about Sara, and you haven't heard me."

Adam grinned. "I'm sorry. It is a wretched habit. I suppose it comes from being so much alone."

Mary said, "That is your own fault, Adam. Why do you shut yourself off from people?"

He looked at her. The expression in her eyes was serious, almost sad. His eyes wandered past hers to the window. In the garden slaves were working, pruning a rose vine that covered a trellis.

"I think it will be different now," he said with sudden resolution. "I'll come here often, if I may."

Mary's face lighted, her red lips parted in a smile. She said impulsively, "Do come, Adam . . . I've missed you terribly. . . ." Then, because she had spoken so impetuously, she said in her usual even voice, "Let me fill your cup, and tell me about the woman and baby. Dr. Armitage talked to me about them. How sad it is, Adam, and how like you to bring them here where they can be looked after."

Adam smiled. "What else could I do? This was the only way. I knew Gwennie would take care of them. She's a heart as big as all outdoors."

"It's a pity she hasn't had children," Mary said.

Adam moved about the room restlessly, his fingers playing with the seals dangling from his watch fob.

"It makes my blood boil when I think that this kind of thing is happening all around us. Fanning and his crew snatching land from decent hard-working folk. Snatching land on technicalities. Have you heard that any number of farmers in Mecklenburg have lost their rightfully owned land because their old transfers and deeds were signed 'Hillsborough by his agent' instead of *'The Right Honorable Earl of Hillsborough?'*"

"It seems incredible," Mary answered. "I must ask William about it."

Adam stopped in front of her. His expression was serious, stern, his voice indignant. It warmed her heart to see him stirred by some cause outside his usual interests. If he could only see the whole instead of a part. But she must be patient. It would come.

"William had to straighten out enough of Corbin's blunders with the Granville Grant. He should know about this trouble."

"William doesn't talk to me about his affairs, Adam. He thinks women have no place in politics." She laughed a little, but Adam saw that William's attitude hurt her.

Adam sat down on the settee beside her.

"I want you to help me with Lucy. Gwennie will do what she can, but there are other things. I talked with Armitage this morning. He doesn't offer much hope. He says if she does get her senses back, she probably won't remember anything of the past at all."

"That would be a blessing, wouldn't it, Adam? I can't help thinking that the big shock was probably caused by that dispossession notice of Fanning's you found tacked on the fence post."

Adam nodded. "Yes, I feel that way too." He was silent, thinking of the wretched cabin, the terrible expression on the face of the dead man. After a time he was aware of the silence. He glanced at Mary. She was sitting quietly, her face averted. He leaned forward.

"No matter how I feel, how confused my thoughts are, when I come here to you, everything changes. I seem to see things clearly. I don't know what I would do without you, Mary."

She lifted her eyes and Adam was startled by their expression. A slow flush mounted from her throat to her cheeks. For a moment she was silent. When she answered there was something in her voice that stirred him deeply.

"I don't want you to do without me—ever. I want you always to come to me. Will you promise me that?"

He took her hand and lifted it to his lips.

"You don't need to ask me that, my dear." He stopped abruptly, afraid of saying too much.

"Don't let anyone keep you away from me," she whispered passionately, "no one—no matter who it is—"

Adam's grasp on her hand tightened until her rings pressed into her fingers.

"You must know what I cannot put into words, Mary, how dear you are to me—" He leaned forward and lifted her hand to his lips once more. "Why do you ask for a promise, my dear? You know I cannot stay away from you."

There was a sound of footsteps in the hall. Ebon came into the room carrying a candelabrum with tall white candles. He

114

put it on the table and thrust a twist of paper into the fire for a light.

"Don't light them yet, Ebon," Mary said.

"Yes, ma'am," he answered. He put a log on the fire and brushed the hearth clean of ashes.

To break the silence, Mary said: "You spoke of Lucy constantly moving her hands. Why not give her something to do? Suppose I take her some yarn and needles. She may know how to knit. If she doesn't, Gwennie and I can teach her."

Adam nodded. "Yes, of course, the very thing." She saw his mind was not on his words. He was looking out the window. The sun was low. The light fell in long shafts, breaking into a golden mist among the pines.

"The 'Ave Maria Hour,'" Mary said, half to herself.

She got up and crossed the room to the spinet. Adam's eyes followed her as she lifted the lid. She pushed the music aside and sat for a moment, her long sensitive fingers resting on the keys. Then she struck a soft chord or two before she began to play.

Adam sat with closed eyes, his head resting against the high back of the settee. His long body was relaxed, but his mind was struggling with confused thoughts concerning the events of the past months. The wilderness cabin; Whitlock's thin white face and burning eyes; his harsh disturbing words; Owen standing at the plantation gates as he quieted his restive horse. His words: "You will find you have a responsibility to land greater than planting and cultivating your own acres. . . ."

He was quiet, seeking the inner voice that sometimes spoke to him when he rode in the deep forest; or when he sailed alone, setting his boat in the teeth of a gale with a star to steer by, and the open sea ahead. The music grew stronger, sweeping him forward. Great chords crashed, noble, inspiring. What was the music urging—or was it Mary speaking to him through her music.

After a long time, his thoughts became clear. He saw the last gleams of the setting sun shining through the branches of the magnolia tree.

"I have decided to accept the appointment and take Johnstone's seat in the Assembly," he said suddenly, breaking into the flow of the music.

Mary's hands dropped on the keys. She turned slowly, her eyes on his.

"I knew you would not fail us," she said softly. "You could not—not when we need you so."

Chapter 8

DRUMS AND
THE SLAVE GIRL

THE night was sultry, the air heavy and stifling. Adam, awakened from a restless sleep by a vaguely familiar sound, sat up in bed. The flare of summer lightning broke along the horizon with clocklike regularity. The heavy scent of garden stock and star jasmine rose from the East Garden. Fireflies, tiny pinpoints of flame, glowed in the heavy dark. Perhaps the drought would break tonight. The air seemed charged with electric vibration.

Adam's thoughts returned to the emotions of the night before. The slave girl Azizi, bathing in the dark garden pool . . . all day he had struggled to put the image of her away from him. He had felled a great turpentine pine and plowed the long furrows in the north field. The warm overturned earth gave under his feet but the pull of the reins was heavy against his shoulders. The hard smooth handles of the plow under his hands steadied him. But now, lying on his bed in the throbbing dark, the image of the slave girl filled his mind.

He had seen her from the window of his bedroom. It was full moon and the garden was flooded with silver. She was moving slowly, with the swaying rhythm of women who walk in heelless sandals. The silvery tinkle of her anklets and the click of many bracelets came to him faintly. She was singing a strange, wordless, minor song full of loneliness and intense sadness. The dark tones of her voice stirred him unaccountably. He watched her kneel beside the garden pool, her slender body swathed in some dark cloth that left her shoulders and arms bare as she reached for a lotus bloom that floated on the water. The cotton clung closely to her soft, curving body, and accented the flatness of her back. She broke off a white bud and thrust it into the folds of the green turban that bound her small head. The bud lay caressingly against the slim column of her throat. Kneeling on the white marble that bound the pool, she lifted her dripping arms high above her head, as if she were beseeching the moon, prostrating herself to its pale cold beauty. The water slipped down her arms, crystal drops falling on her bare shoulders. Was she pouring libations? Making some pagan odylic plea to the moon-goddess?

She rose to her feet and waded knee-deep into the pool. Suddenly with a swift movement she removed the green turban from her head. A mass of dark hair cascaded down over her shoulders; a moment of hesitation and the sarong that bound her body was unwound. Her body curved like the crescent moon as she leaned forward to touch the moon reflected in the pool. A laugh floated out, a soft laugh that sent the blood pounding in his veins. Then the water took her. He could see only the ivory of the lotus flowers floating on the widening circles of black water.

He had walked quickly through the dark halls on his way to the garden. As he crossed the lower gallery, he saw a light burning in Sara's room. He stood still. The conjuring circle of the moon spread a magic spell over the garden. In the mystic stillness the small pointed light of the candle wavered. He moved across the intervening space until he stood by the open window. Sara lay asleep. The moonlight, full on her face, touched it with an unearthly calm. His heart flooded with tenderness for her. Her arms were straight at her side, one hand on the page of an open Bible. A shadow fell across the bed and blotted out the moonlight. Judith moved toward the window and drew the curtains.

Adam went to his room, walking slowly. The night was long. The crescent body of the slave girl came between him and the oblivion of sleep. Her low laugh, deep and smooth, strangely exciting . . . he had never heard her laugh before. Why should she laugh . . . a slave far from her people and her country? But the other slaves on the plantation laughed. They were gay with the careless gaiety of children.

He got out of bed and looked into the shadow of the East Garden. It was quiet, no sounds of night birds. The black pool reflected the seven stars of the Great Dipper and the failing moon.

Now the sound that had awakened him entered his consciousness: a steady pounding beat as of the surf on rocks. But it was not the surf. It was a menacing sound, sinister and persistent. The sighing winds in the pines echoed the sound, the garden rocked with it. It was an earth sound that came through the air surrounding him, beating down on him. Drums! It was the drums! Haskins had told him that the slaves were dancing after nightfall . . . but this was not the sound of dancing drums. It bore the black, heavy menace of dark jungles . . . of secret pagan rituals. Now he knew what

Haskins feared: a return of the slaves to their jungle rites and sacrifices. It must be the influence of those runaway Negroes, the shipment LaTruchy had brought from Lobita Bay. Adam thought they had gone into Virginia through the dark secret ways of the Dismal Swamp. But Haskins had spoken of warehouses in Edenton being rifled of food. Fishermen had complained that their catches had been taken at night. Strange that he had not thought of this before. Such things sometimes led to slave rebellion. And a rebellion at present was not altogether improbable, what with all the smouldering discontent of the farmers and the men of the mountain counties.

He got up but by the time he was dressed the sound of drumming had ceased. He threw himself, fully dressed, upon the bed and fell into a troubled sleep. Here Cicero found him, lying inert, the moonlight streaming upon his face. The old slave tiptoed around to the side of the bed and hung a counterpane across the balustrade. He knew that moonlight falling across the face of a sleeping man allows evil spirits to enter and have their way.

At the foot of the stairs Cicero suddenly saw Judith. A candle in one hand, a jug of steaming water in the other, she was moving stealthily across the hall toward Adam's workroom. She set the jug down on the steps, and tried the door of Adam's office, turning the knob softly. Cicero stepped out of the shadow. Judith, startled, turned abruptly. The woman had no right to be there, Cicero thought, but he would not speak of that. There was no need to make Judith angry. She was a mean woman when she was angry.

"Miss Sara, she sick again?" he asked cautiously.

"No sicker than she be exceptin' she don' sleep."

Cicero came forward and leaned against the newel post. He asked a question that had been troubling him for some time. "Why-for she don' sleep? She worrin' about he?" He jerked his thumb over his shoulder toward Adam's bedroom.

Judith scowled. "Why-for she worry about he?"

Cicero's smile broadened. " 'Cause he ride away to Edenton all the while and all the fine ladies there they make tea for him and ask him to eat at their table . . ."

Judith laughed. "She worry about dat?"

"Maybe he find some fine lady he like . . ." Cicero stopped suddenly. Protruding from the pocket of Judith's apron he saw something that brought fear to his eyes and to his stout heart—a clay image, stuck through the heart with thorns. The woman was making magic against his master.

118

Frightened as he was for himself, Cicero was more frightened for Adam. With a sudden lunge forward he caught the image from its hiding place. Tearing the thorns from the body, he threw the clay figure far out through the open door. It fell on the flagstones by the pool and broke into fragments.

"Don' you dare, don' you dare trouble he with your *Mankwala,* yo debbil . . . elsen I kill you."

The woman shrank back. For a moment she showed she was afraid. Then she turned around, walked majestically across the hall and disappeared into the shadows. Cicero leaned against the bannister wiping the sweat from his face. He ran quickly up the stairs and looked into Adam's room. Adam was sleeping peacefully. He tiptoed out of the room and went to his quarters below-stairs.

About two o'clock the drumming started again. This time its menace wakened Adam to full consciousness. The rush of garden perfume rose like a thin veil, tuberose and jasmine, stock and border petunia. Adam got up, intending to walk in the garden until he grew sleepy. Then he noticed a light burning in the window of the cottage where the slave Azizi lived with the old woman. Why was there a light at this hour? He walked through the lower garden and stopped to lean against a stone bench in the deep shadows. The pinpoint of light held him. It glowed and hung in the air like St. Elmo's fire drawing men to destruction. At the hawthorn hedge he paused once more, then turned to go back to the Manor House. But before he had taken a step the drums sounded again, a deep note of warning. For a moment he thought it might be distant thunder. But a second beat followed, then another and another at regular intervals. A signal! It seemed to come from the swamp on the mainland, close to the lower end of the Island, where a tree had been felled to make a rough bridge from the Island to the mainland. His senses alert, he heard a twig snap and thought he saw shadows moving near the cottage. He stood still, but there was no other movement. He would go back to the house, he decided again, and try to get some sleep. But at the door he turned back and, drawn by some strange fear, he broke into a run down the path to the brick cottage where the slave girl lived. The door was wide open. A sputtering candle stood on a low table. The girl was not there but on the floor lay the old woman, trussed up, a gag in her mouth. Adam snatched the cloth away and unbound her wrists. "Where is she? Where is the girl?" he shouted as if the woman were deaf. But she was not deaf; she was dumb. She tried to speak, uttering horrible, guttural sounds.

"Which way?" Adam said. "Which way did they take her?" The drum sound . . . the swamp . . . the runaway slaves. He ran down the path. In the East Garden he met Cicero. He too was running, a lantern in his shaking hand.

"Master, master . . . you are not hurt?"

Adam did not give him time for more. "Quick, go to the house. Send someone for Marcy. Tell Haskins to get the dogs ready. If I don't come back in fifteen minutes, tell them to come to the swamp with the dogs."

Cicero ran toward the house, Adam to the bridge. Even in the dark he knew the path. Lightning flashed intermittently. Dark clouds massed across the horizon. A sharp flash of forked lightning and the far roll of thunder mingled with the drum vibration. The humid air was swept by a swift fresh wind. The storm was closing in.

He crossed the log bridge, moving cautiously now. Obscure shadows were about him, vines swaying, moss-covered trees and grotesque knees of cypress forcing their way up through the brackish water. Once he stepped into a quagmire. Feeling his way, he pulled himself up by grasping a bush and got back on firm earth. He knew the place, an island where the charcoal burners had a hut. Then he heard voices in low ryhthmic chant, voices that came weirdly through the shadows of the moss-hung trees.

> "Yes, we are going to white man's land,
> To white man's land, to white man's land,
> With yokes on our backs.
> But we'll have no yokes in death,
> No yokes in death—in death."

What did it mean? Some pagan sacrifice? He turned cold at the thought. The Negroes believed Azizi was a witch. Were they going to test her power over life and death? He had heard of things the natives had done when they meted out their own terrible punishment—hacked off hands or feet . . . gouged out eyes . . . skinned off layers of flesh from a human body.

A vista opened through the cypress trees. He could see shadows moving by a fire. The chanting stopped; the drums started. He saw a woman, her face covered by a goat mask, her body wrapped in black. She swayed back and forth, her

120

thin arms waving. Dark figures knelt at her feet. Beside her were two giant Negroes with burning torches in their hands. Then he saw the girl Azizi. They had bound her to a tree and piled fagots at her feet.

For a moment Adam could not move. Then he plunged forward, his long, lithe body catapulting out of the dark into the glow of the fire. There was a sudden suspended silence. One of the guards dropped his torch and stepped backward, falling over a crouched worshiper. It was Zeke, Cicero's son. He cried out in fright. Adam stood in front of the girl, between her and the witch woman and her two guards. There was only one chance for him. Caught by surprise, the Negroes were momentarily confused. He must press his advantage, show no fear. He let his eyes go slowly around the fire. They rested on the giant Negro clutching the burning brand whom he recognized as one of LaTruchy's cargo. He had no doubt the other nine runaway Negroes were among the thirty or forty figures about the fire. The big fellow was the leader, a tall man of great breadth of shoulder, his body oiled, a loincloth about his middle with a knife thrust through the folds; tribal tattoo marks running from temples to neck, as if they had been gashed by a twisting knife.

It ran quickly through Adam's mind that he was dealing with savage Africa now. Whatever he did must be quick and sure. Suddenly he struck. Wrenching the brand from the Negro's hand he brought it down with full force over his extended forearm. The arm dropped to the man's side. He crouched by the fire, his body bent double with pain. Adam called out sharply to Zeke to untie the ropes. Accustomed to obeying, Zeke did as he was told. Adam called others by name, among them Eph. "Go home," he shouted, "you and you and you! What do you mean by coming here to make sacrifice?"

The big man was getting on his knees. Adam saw him reach for the knife with his left hand. The man was quick, but Adam was quicker. He caught the Negro's wrist, bending back his fingers until the knife dropped from his hand to the ground. Adam put his foot on it. He had no time to look at the girl. But as he moved back a few steps to the tree, he felt her body press against his, as if she were falling. The big Negro shouted some order. Two men near the fire caught up burning brands, a dozen others leaped forward. The drum began again—quick staccato beats. Adam kicked savagely at the drum, crashing through the drumhead. Suddenly the plantation bell began to ring with swift insistence. At the same moment came the bay of hounds. There was a moment's silence, then like shadows, they were gone, all—the old woman, the giant Negro and the crouching figures about the fire. The swamp had swallowed them up in its intense darkness.

It seemed like a nightmare without reality. There was the noise of men crashing through the bushes and the barking of dogs. Marcy and Haskins came out of the shadows, followed by a dozen men from the plantation. The bloodhounds pulled on their leashes.

Adam shouted to Marcy. "Take the dogs to the canal. They took the north path through the swamp."

Marcy and the men disappeared into the blackness. He felt the weight of the girl's body sag against him and, turning quickly, caught her in his arms.

The rushing of wind in the trees and the heavy roll of thunder warned Adam that the storm was coming. He hurried along the path, the girl a light burden in his strong arms. With a rush the rain came, a solid sheet of water driven along the Sound from the ocean. He realized it was a storm of hurricane proportions. Rain beat against them; long splinters of rain obscured his vision. He struggled against the rising wind, bending to protect the girl. The roar of the wind came like heavy breakers against the rocks. A great pine fell across his path. A branch of the tree, rasping along his forehead, cut a gash. Blood dripped into his eyes. Cut off from the cottage, he hurried to the shelter of the giant fig at the end of the East Garden, stumbling heavily through the bed of black marigolds. They gave off an acrid scent. Under the fig tree's thick-spreading crown of heavy leaves the earth was soft and dry. The girl slid from his arms to the ground. In the instant of lightning flash he saw that her dark eyes were filled with fear, her slim body trembling.

"Are you hurt?" he asked between thunder claps.

"I am not hurt, master."

Her voice was low. As he stooped to catch her words, his cheek brushed hers. He felt the smoothness of her skin, the fragrance of her body. A flame rose in him, driving him. He felt her body stiffen as his arms closed about her. The clasp of his arms about her body was strong. The want of her beat through him. How long had he coveted her! The want of her was a sharp sword. The strength of her opposing will was swept aside by the rush of his passion.

122

When the storm had passed he carried the slave girl to her cottage. Then he walked swiftly through the East Garden to the house. Under his roof all was tranquil, silent with the stillness of early morning. The rain had stopped. The sudden tempest had passed. All was quiet except the tumult within him.

Chapter 9

PRINCESS STREET

MARCY came back from Wilmington late in October. He had been south for a few weeks, arranging for a transshipment of pine poles, tar and turpentine. He was in the counting room one rainy morning, sorting over a great pile of correspondence that had accumulated in his month's absence, when Adam came in. Adam stood with his back to the fire, Red Rowan rubbing against his muddy gaiters. He had been out early shooting ducks, with the professional assistance of the dog.

He spoke with Marcy about one of the London letters that dealt with a shipment of tobacco sent from the Edenton warehouse. The tobacco wasn't up to the standard set by Rutledge Riding plantation. "We have named a smoking blend *Rutledge Riding* and we must keep up the high standard you have set, for we have the finest custom in London to satisfy," his agents wrote.

Marcy read the letter and laid it on the pile. Adam opened a ledger. Marcy sat looking out of the window for a moment, then spoke abruptly. "My mind is too much on something else this morning. Can you spare a few moments?"

Adam laid an ivory ruler on the page as a marker and closed the book. "What is it, Marcy? I saw that you were absent-minded when you weren't properly enthusiastic over Robinson and Robinson naming a blend *Rutledge Riding*."

"I'm sorry, Mr. Rutledge. It's the truth. My mind is whirling around, full of what happened at Wilmington about the stamps. I was thinking I would wait until the day's work was over before I did my talking, but it's no use." He grinned. "I'm like that. I haven't the brain to think on more than one thing at a time."

"What happened in Wilmington?" Adam asked, settling himself back comfortably in the leather chair. "I heard from Dr. Armitage yesterday. He mentioned that there was a rumor in Edenton that there had been a little trouble in the capital."

Marcy took a couple of steps up the room and backed to

the fire. "A little trouble—well, that depends on how a man views it, Mr. Rutledge. None were killed, but it is what didn't happen that bothers me. Sometimes blood-lettin' is a cure, as the Doctor will tell you." He walked to the window.

Adam said, "Sit down, Marcy, and quit prowling around the room."

Marcy laughed a little sheepishly. "It's a black mood I'm in, Mr. Rutledge, and a man's likely to prowl when his thoughts are black." He sat down by the hearth. Red Rowan got up and laid her long head on Marcy's knee, looking at him with great sad eyes. The Irishman pulled the long silken ears gently. He took a folded paper from the outside pocket of his jacket and handed it to Adam.

"I nearly forgot. It's the list of duty-bearing items. Mr. Caswell sent it to you."

Adam laid the paper on the desk without looking at it. "Get on with the story, Marcy," he said dryly.

"I'm sorry; I was thinkin' of a way to get it straight. The ship was still loading at Brunswick. It was late when I got through with Evans and Esterbrook, so I stayed all night at an inn in Wilmington. My room faced on the square. I noticed that there was a lot of movement in the street, but I didn't pay much attention. I was busy straightening out that cargo invoice. About nine o'clock, my candle began to flicker and I got up to hunt for another. When I stopped to look out the window, I saw that the square was black with men standing as close as sardines packed in a keg. The street lights were all lighted, and some of the men on the edge of the crowd had flares and lanterns. On the courthouse steps a number of the men were standing in a group. Behind them, under the portico, were a number of others sitting in chairs. There was a table with a jug of water on it and a number of lanterns and torches to make it light. I saw then that the crowd was waiting for a speaker. I knew what it meant. I'd been hearing rumors all day. People, particularly the merchants and lawyers, were fair put out about the stamps. There was a piece in the *Weekly Post-Boy*, but I hadn't had time to read it. I pulled up a chair by the window and tied the curtains in a knot so I could see, and perhaps hear. Almost at once a man came out. The people clapped a moment. I couldn't see who the man was, but he had a booming voice. He opened the sheaf of papers and started to read the articles that were set down as taxable and would have to have stamps."

Marcy indicated the list he had given Adam. "It's all there;

you can read it. It's devilish thorough. You will see that it hits every man in the Province, rich or poor. But the poor will be the ones to suffer most, for they haven't any cash to pay for stamps." Adam watched him moving about the room again. He seemed not to be able to sit for more than a few moments. "The people were silent, too silent, Mr. Rutledge. When I saw the man was on the last page, I ran out of my room and down the flight of stairs. It couldn't have taken me over three minutes. When I got out on the street the crowd was rioting. It came that quick!"

Marcy tried to keep his voice quiet and steady. "Men were shouting and cursing and waving clubs. Someone lighted a bonfire in the street. Four masked men jumped out of the blackness. They were carrying an effigy of the King tied to a long pole. The figure was straw, dressed in a red coat. Straw stuffing bulged out between buttons of the coat and the white breeches that covered the protruding potbelly. A brass crown was sitting on the head over one eye." He paused. "There's something bestial about a mob. It turned me sick at the pit of my stomach. This wasn't spontaneous emotion. It was cold and hard. It had been planned long enough for an artist to paint the likeness of the King, a horrible, obscene likeness."

He was silent a moment, then went on more quietly. "Men and women shouted and jeered. The Tories had a hard time. Some of the well-known Loyalists, who had voiced their sentiments in favor of the stamps, were dragged to the square to watch the King burn in effigy. Then they were obliged to drink a toast *'Liberty—Property and No Stamp Duty—and Confusion to Lord Bute and His Adherents.'* The crowd took up the cry and shouted over and over, *'Confusion to Lord Bute.'*"

Adam said thoughtfully, "Curious that they would burn the King in effigy, yet they did not drink to his confusion. Instead, they vented their anger on his advisor."

"I think the people know that George III owes his stubborn belief in the *divine right of kings* to Bute. He got hold of him while he was still a young prince and drilled that thought into him. But I'm thinking George will be the last king that will believe in his divine right to oppress the people."

"What happened then?"

"Nothing much. They had run themselves out in burning the straw effigy." He laughed suddenly.

"It was a bitter draught those Loyalist merchants had to drink! One old fellow had been pulled out of bed. A couple

126

of ruffians carried him to the square on their shoulders, his long skinny legs hanging down out of his woolen nightshirt and his nightcap askew, showing his shaven poll. He was frightened, and kept shouting, 'I'll drink, I'll drink. I'm against the stamps . . .'"

Adam was thinking of what lay behind this demonstration. Danger—the temper of the people was coming to the surface. The western counties had more than once showed their feeling in rioting. They were more to be feared than the coast people. The farmers were more serious. Their rioting was more deadly. They would not have made a silly, childish demonstration like the one Marcy was describing. Adam knew the western Carolinians. They were a rugged, insubordinate race of hunters and farmers, as intractable as the Albemarle men had been in the time of Seth Sothel and the earlier uprisings. The thought occurred to him that the Assembly was in the same mood of insubordination. They had fought the last governor steadily, and Tryon had inherited some of the animosity that the lawmakers had felt toward Dobbs.

He asked Marcy a question. "Do you think the Regulators had anything to do with the Wilmington demonstration?"

Marcy thought not. "There is a new society which holds secret meetings in the basement of a church. They call themselves the Sons of Liberty. The sailors at the docks say that there are such societies at all the ports where their ships touch: Boston, New York and as far south as the Chesapeake."

Adam meditated for some minutes. Coupled with the disturbances in the western counties, this unnamed menace began to assume unit, a great undercurrent of unrest emerging to the surface in a dozen places. He took up the list Caswell had sent. Stamps would be necessary on real and personal property, newspapers, advertisements, pamphlets and paper. Legal forms that required stamps included declarations and subpoenas. Twenty shillings was a high tax to put on legal paper. It was true, as Marcy had said, the tax would lay a burden on the whole Province.

Marcy went to his desk and climbed on his high stool. For a time the scratching of his pen was the only sound in the room. Adam smoked his long pipe and gazed out the window. After a time, he dismissed the disquieting thoughts and remembered he had not asked Marcy about the house he had leased in Wilmington for the duration of the Assembly. Dr. Armitage had talked him into taking Sara down for the winter. "It will give her new interest," he had told Adam. Much to his surprise, Sara had agreed. She began to take interest and made plans for entertaining their friends.

"Did you get me the lease from Dr. Cobham?" Adam asked.

"I'm sorry, I forgot to give it to you." Marcy slid off the stool and, looking through some papers, found the lease and laid it on the table. "The Doctor told me to tell you that the house is ready. It is completely staffed, and rooms prepared for your personal servants."

"How did you like the place, Marcy? Is it well located?"

"On Princess Street, and the neighborhood is most exclusive. I am sure Mrs. Rutledge will be delighted with it. It is almost as large as Guernsey House, and more conveniently located."

The mention of Guernsey House brought Lady Caroline to Adam's mind.

"I heard in Edenton that Lady Caroline had chartered one of Hewes's ships to take her household and her belongings to Wilmington. She herself went by coach."

Marcy grinned. "She already has Wilmington by the ears!" he told Adam. "When she goes down the street in that red morocco chair, half the populace follows her. They have never seen anything like the chair or her Madagascari with their red breeches and turbans. The woman knows how to create a sensation. A flamboyant creature, surely."

Adam said, "Do you believe she is a sister of the Queen?"

Marcy shrugged his shoulders. "The Mecklenburg-Strelitz is a large family, and one could believe almost anything about the Lady Caroline Mathilde. She is a shrewd woman underneath that studied artificiality. I think the lady knows what she wants."

"What does she want?" Adam asked.

"God knows! I've often wondered why she came to Pembroke, but I'll wager she was here for something more than enjoying the view of Albemarle Sound from her window."

Adam smiled. "She says she can't live any place but on the water."

Marcy ran his hand through his wiry, red hair. He fell serious. "I've thought about Lady Caroline more than once, Mr. Rutledge. Asked myself these questions: 'Did Tryon send her here to spy on Albemarle leaders? Is she actually what she claims, a bored woman wanting to get away from the Court life? Or has she been sent here by Bute or some of the ministers to swing influential men over to the Royalist side?' I haven't found an answer yet, but whatever she is up to, she isn't wasting her time." He turned back to his work.

Adam looked at his watch. It was almost eleven, and time to see his wife. Lady Caroline was an absorbing topic, but they would have to continue their speculations about her at another time.

A few days later Adam rode over to the North Plantation to see that Haskins had a cargo ready to go to London by the following week. Marcy's suggestion had been: "If we get the bulk of the tobacco off next week, we'll escape buying stamps."

The sound of excited voices reached Adam's ears when he turned into he drive. He saw a crowd of Negroes standing in front of a tobacco shed and Marcy walking across the open space between the sheds and the brick office, a musket in the crook of his arm. In front of him was the giant Zulu whose arm Adam had broken in the swamp.

The Negro was ready to drop with exhaustion. His black skin, caked with swamp mud, was scratched and gashed by brambles and thorns. His arm was in a rough sling made of palmetto fiber. Haskins followed, guarding four or five runaways. He was armed with a pistol, the second of the brace through his heavy leather belt.

Adam dismounted and walked across the intervening space to meet them near the steps leading to the office gallery.

Marcy set his musket against the steps and wiped the dust from his face. "Haskins found them," he told Adam. "They have been living in the Dismal Swamp, above the Virginia line. Two days ago they came out for food. Haskins got wind of it. I followed yesterday. We got Herk, the ringleader, first. He gave up without much trouble." Marcy lowered his voice. "The man is ready to drop."

Adam pulled up a hickory chair near the gallery rail. The prisoners were below him, a wretched lot, hungry and gaunt, fetid with swamp mud and slime, their few clothes in rags.

Haskins prodded one of the men in the back with the butt of his pistol to make him move out of his way. He then thrust the pistol into his belt and took a black-snake whip with a loaded handle from one of the plantation boys. His face was grim, his jaw set, and there was a peculiar, fanatical light in his china blue eyes.

Adam thought, "The man will take pleasure in whipping these Negroes; a sensual, voluptuous pleasure. I must stop this!" He said aloud, "What punishment have you planned, Haskins?"

The overlooker came forward eagerly. Adam felt a slight nausea at the look in his eyes and the expression of his heavy lips. "Five hundred lashes for the leader—three hundred for the others. Then I'll put them in slave sticks and feed them bread and water for a week."

Marcy took a quick step forward, his eyes blazing, his fists clenched. Adam motioned to him, and he sat down on the steps without speaking.

Adam said, "Take the men to the cabins and have them fed and bathed. Then lock them in the old smokehouse. Put a guard over them, but no punishment until I give the word. I'll talk to Herk."

Haskins opened his mouth to protest, but thought better of it. He left reluctantly with one or two backward glances at the group that remained.

Adam sent the plantation boys away and said to Marcy, "Now I will talk to Herk."

Marcy hesitated a second, looking at Adam with troubled eyes. "The Zulu isn't an ordinary slave, Mr. Rutledge."

Adam nodded. "Let him come up to the gallery." When he saw that the Negro wore iron leg chains he swore. "Have those shackles struck off! Haskins knows I've given orders never to use slave sticks or gyves. Come here," he said to the Zulu.

The giant Negro moved stiffly toward the steps and stood at the bottom waiting for Adam to speak.

"Does he speak English?" Adam asked Marcy.

"Yes, if he will talk."

"I'll speak to him alone. Take your musket and go after Haskins. See that he doesn't disobey my orders about those runaways."

"Do you want my pistol? You're not armed, Mr. Rutledge."

"Neither is Herk," Adam said shortly.

Marcy walked away toward the tobacco sheds, leaving master and slave alone. For some seconds, Adam looked Herk steadily in the eyes. The Negro returned the look without fear, his body erect, his head thrown back. The muscles of his neck moved under his bronze skin. Otherwise, he was motionless. There was something in the bearing of the Negro that Adam had never before seen in a slave. He had a certain dignity, even pride in his carriage.

130

Adam put his question abruptly. "In your own country are you a ruler of your people?"

The Zulu inclined his head slightly.

"Do you own slaves?"

"Many slaves, won in battle."

Adam waited a moment. "What punishment do you deal out to slaves that run?"

A look of fear came into the man's eyes, gone in an instant. He understood. He was caught. He would pronounce his own sentence. But he did not hesitate.

"Death," he answered.

Adam leaned forward, looking down. "Always death?"

"If the slave is a boy, his life may be spared, but a hand is chopped off at the wrist."

Adam did not speak. He had broken the Negro's arm in fair fight. Perhaps the punishment had been given.

"You are a king in your tribe?" he asked.

"The son of a great king."

"Do you punish by the whip?"

"The whip is the weapon of a coward," he said with contempt.

Haskins came across from the sheds, walking rapidly. His face was red, his light blue eyes hard. He had the black-snake whip in his hand.

"Two of them got away, Mr. Rutledge. They'll go back to the Swamp. Where's your hiding place?" he shouted to Herk.

The Zulu didn't answer.

Haskins, beside himself, snapped the whip around the Zulu's ankles before Adam could speak. Adam sprang down the steps, two at a time, and caught Haskins' arm before the whip came down on the Zulu's shoulders. His voice was quiet.

"We don't use the lash on this plantation!"

Haskins turned white and walked quickly away.

Marcy came around the corner of the house. He had not been far away.

Adam said to him, "I am going to let Herk go free. He has had sufficient punishment. When his arm is healed, send him to the Manor House. I think I will make him my body servant to go with me when I make journeys to Mecklenburg."

He looked at the Zulu.

"You are free," he said.

The Negro met his gaze. He said one word, "Master." Then he turned and walked away.

Marcy watched the light leopard tread of the jungle man as he crossed the open space to the fields. He turned to Adam.

"You have set him free, but I think you have made a slave for life."

Adam did not speak. He got on his horse and rode toward the post road. He wondered if he had been wise. He did not know. Only one thing was certain—one didn't punish a king or a king's son by the lash, even if he were a black man. As for Haskins—perhaps he would leave of his own accord. If not, that matter would adjust itself later.

When Sara told Adam that she was going to take Azizi to Wilmington his face did not change, but his pulse quickened. Sara was watching him. What did she know? Then he laughed to himself. She could know nothing . . . nothing at all. It was only his fears that made him suspect her of watching him.

"I want her dressed differently down there—in gay clothes, such as she wears in her cabin. Judith has seen her there at night with the dumb woman waiting on her as if she were a princess of the Orient." She laughed. "I should like a princess to wait on me. Dressed in gay satins and colored veils. Lady Caroline Mathilde would envy me and perhaps try to get her away."

Sara looked at him, her eyes cold, almost calculating. "You won't sell her, will you, Adam?"

He was on guard now. "Why should we sell her if she pleases you?" he asked soothingly.

"I don't like Lady Caroline," Sara said, after a moment. "I don't think she is quite a lady. She is too loud, too forward."

"But you have never seen Lady Caroline," Adam said, astonished at the turn of the conversation. "You wouldn't allow her to come to the Island."

Sara dropped back on her pillow. "I'm tired now, Adam. Will you please call Judith?" She looked up, her misty blue eyes childlike, without guile. "Darling Adam, you don't mind my taking Azizi with me, do you?"

Warned by what went before, Adam's expression did not change. "How can you ask, Sara? You know my first thought is always for your happiness."

Adam had seen little of Azizi since the night of the storm. The girl went about her work in her usual silent way, avoiding him, he was sure, except when she was in his wife's room and could not get away. He was constantly aware of her. Fearing Sara would notice his heightened emotional state, he forced himself to an assumption of indifference.

He was shamed by Azizi's power over him and felt contempt for his own conduct. Yet he asked himself, why should he? The story of white planters and slave women had existed since the earliest days, causing little or no comment; and white blood ran in many an African slave.

His disloyalty to Sara caused him deep distress. For the first time since her illness he gave many hours of thought to the situation. He had never been frank with her about his emotions. Their life together had been based on her desires, not his. She had been so young, so unprepared for marriage. She had loved him in a tender, childish way, but there had been times when her fear of him outweighed her love. Those few times when the rush of his natural passion got control of him, he had learned to subdue his stronger, vehement desires. The warm, living emotion he had had in the first year of their marriage had changed, even before her illness. Now it had turned to loyalty based on her condition, her pitiful weakness. There never were moments of passion that should exist between a man and woman in love with each other.

She wanted him to be calm, gentle, thoughtful of her every wish; a devitalized Adam of her own imagination. She could not face the reality of the natural man, strengthened by love and desire, with a passionate devotion to her body. After the illness this was impossible, but Adam knew it would have been the same, whether she were ill or in health. Sara would always have escaped reality.

The Assembly was to open the first week in November. A few days before they sailed on his shallop, the *West Wind*, for Wilmington, Adam walked across to Azizi's cottage. He had sent a brickmason to repair the cottage and he wanted to see whether the work had been done properly. He went about five, at the time when Azizi usually sat with Sara while Judith was preparing her supper.

He tied the horse to a rack and went inside. The girl had managed to give an exotic flavor to the simple room. Pushed against the wall, opposite the door, was a divan covered with a gaily colored India print. On the floor in front of the divan, a small rug lay like a jewel. At the side, on a low table, was a carved wooden box. It was about twelve inches long, made of ebony, with inlays of ivory.

Adam picked up the box to examine its curiously wrought

hinges of silver. It was not locked. He opened the lid. The box was filled with glowing colors: beads of lapis, great chunks of amber and dull green chrysophrase bracelets set with silver. In a separate tray were perhaps a dozen large pearls. He lifted them out of the case. They lay heavy and luminous in his palm.

Azizi's voice broke the stillness. She had approached so silently, he had not heard her. "The master does honor to his slave when he steps across her dooorway." Her voice, with the slight accent, was tinged with derision.

He turned quickly. The pearls dropped from his hand to the divan. Azizi stood in the doorway looking at him. The stiff uniform of her servitude to Sara did not hide the litheness of her body. The green turban she always wore gave a strange, exotic beauty to her golden skin.

Adam set the box on the table without speaking. Crossing the room, he laid his hand heavily on her shoulder. "You belong to me," he said, his voice harsh. He felt the pulse in his throat beating swiftly. The scent of amber filled his nostrils. He was painfully aware of his diminishing control. "You belong to me," he repeated.

The girl said nothing. She faced him, points of flame in her dark, liquid eyes. She was subtly intact in her scornful defiance. His hand dropped to his side. She moved into the room, standing near the divan, her back against the wall.

The thought came to him: "I can break her will by the whip as other rebellious slaves have been broken." But the thought died out in shame. He knew he had not the will to see the lash curve around her firm young shoulders. He moved toward her. She backed away, her body pressed closer against the wall. She would submit to his strength, but he knew he could not tame her or break through her contemptuous insolence. He turned swiftly and left the room.

When he had mounted his horse, he glanced back. Azizi was walking out of the cottage, followed by Fatima, whom he had not seen inside. The old slave spread a rug on the grass and Azizi knelt, touching her head to the ground. For a moment he watched her, puzzled. Then he understood. She was a Mohammedan, saying her obligatory prayers at sunset. The knowledge seemed to carry the girl even farther away from him into an unknown world.

The *West Wind* carried Adam and his household to Wilmington. The weather was warm for that season, and the sea quiet. Sara sat during the day on the afterdeck under a striped canopy. Marcy had rigged it to protect her from the sun. She grew more animated every day, talking of Wilmington, the new house, and the entertaining to be done. "I am now the wife of a Member of the Assembly," she told Adam. "I must take my place in society and do my part to help my distinguished husband."

At first, Adam thought this was badinage, but he soon saw that Sara was quite serious. He had no illusion about the position he was to take in Wilmington. If Sara derived pleasure in anticipation, he would not spoil it by the truth.

He saw Azizi only once or twice during the voyage down. She was busy in Sara's cabin and did not come on deck.

They rounded the Capes at sunrise and entered Cape Fear River, passing Fort Johnstone at full sail. They passed so close they could see the sentry on the parapet, and the defense guns pointing out of the square openings. His Majesty's sloop-of-war *Cruizer*, anchored inside the river, fired the sunrise gun as they sailed by.

It was just dusk when they sighted Brunswick, so Adam ordered the captain to proceed up the river rather than anchor for the night. After supper, he took the wheel. It was good to watch the stars through the sails. The moon, appearing behind a forest of pines, glittered in the fan-shaped wake of the slow-moving ship.

Adam thought of a meeting he had gone to the week before he left Rutledge Riding. Enos Dye had come down the river to bring Whitlock's invitation. Adam was glad to go. He wanted to talk to the farmers in order to be sure he understood just what their needs were. He considered a thorough understanding of their wrongs vitally important. Whitlock had acted as spokesman, enumerating the long list of grievances. One thing he said gave Adam pause: "We don't want to join with the Orange Regulators, Mr. Rutledge, unless we are forced to. But, if we can't have redress by legislature, then we must do what they are planning to do—fall back on force and rioting to get our rights."

Adam spoke strongly against this. "Wait; let us see what can be done by law," he told them. They had agreed but without any show of confidence. Adam realized then, as never before, the strength these men could gain by uniting with the western farmers. He hoped this would not happen. He was sure that the farmers, led by the erratic Husband, would get into trouble.

The Wharf at Wilmington was alive with activity and the

stir of ships loading and discharging cargo. While they lay in stream, Adam saw Marcy waiting at the dock. He came out in a boat and they lowered Sara in a chair swinging from the derrick on the forward deck. She was laughing and excited at the experience, not afraid as Adam had anticipated. It augured well for the new venture. "At least a mental cure," as Dr. Armitage had told him.

She was delighted with the waiting coach bearing the Rutledge arms, and the new, plum-colored liveries for the coachman and footman. The house on Princess Street also pleased her enormously. She had Adam wheel her from room to room, clapping her hands with ecstasy at the drawing room, at the view of the river and the famous garden and, finally, at the suite of rooms on the lower floor, off the terraced garden, that had been set aside for her. She lifted her lips to Adam. "I shall be happy, here, Adam. Very, very happy. You won't have the horrid old plantation to think of. You can spend every moment with me."

A chill went over Adam. That was exactly what Dr. Armitage had warned him against. He put his cheek to hers. "Dr. Cobham will call on you this afternoon, dear. He is a very good surgeon."

"And a good Royalist, too." She laughed, her eyes shining.

The door opened and Judith came in carrying a tray with hot milk and some food. She put it on a table and drew the curtains to shut out the sunlight.

"Better you rest, honey. You're tired," she said, without looking at Adam.

The joy went out of Sara's face. Her shoulders drooped. "I am tired, very tired, Adam. I must rest now. I'll have to send you away."

Adam kissed her forehead and left the room. A feeling of bitter disappointment dampened the hope that had risen in him. He had wanted it to be different in the new surroundings. Now he wondered. But he would try to interest her, he decided. The capital would be gay; the Governor and his Lady would give a State Ball, and the townspeople would entertain lavishly this winter, for as soon as Tryon's Palace at New Bern was built the capital would be moved.

Mary and William Warden were coming down by the end of the week. Adam wanted to see Mary; to talk to her about the meeting at Whitlock's mill, and—just to see her, he admitted to himself honestly.

A dozen notes were on the desk in his sitting room, invitations to early balls and dinner parties. One larger than the rest caught his attention. It was of heavy, cream parchment paper, folded square, sealed with purple wax under a large crest. He knew, without looking, that it was from Lady Caroline, who was already settled at Guernsey House.

"Mon cher Adam:

"Let us hope that since there is no plantation work to use as an excuse, we may have the pleasure of seeing more of you at Guernsey House than we did at Pembroke. Will you have supper with me, informally, on the 6th, at ten? Only a few guests. The Governor agrees with me that a supper, to be successful, should have no more in number than the Muses, or less than the Graces! May I count on you?

C. M.

"I would include poor, dear Mrs. Rutledge, for I am sorry not to have had the pleasure of meeting her when I was at Pembroke, but I know she is invalided, and stays constantly in her room. That must be devastating for you, dear Adam. You are so alive and vital. We must try to make it gay for you here in Wilmington to offset boredom!"

Adam smiled as he wrote an answer declining the invitation. Something the Doctor had said came to him. "You must let Sara know you enjoy going about in Wilmington. It won't hurt her to be a little jealous of your attentions to other women—in fact, it may help my cure along!"

He pulled the bell cord. When Cicero came he gave him the packet of invitations, with instructions to carry them at once to Mrs. Rutledge. He slipped the letter from Lady Caroline in with the others, and allowed himself a malicious smile.

He took his time bathing and put on a new coat he had ordered direct from London, a brown brocade with tan small-clothes. He tied his lace cravat carefully, while Cicero stood by holding a mirror at the proper angle.

Cicero gave him his cocked hat and threw the long cape over his broad shoulders. He went out through the garden, stopping an instant to wave to Sara as he passed her window.

Chapter 10

THE TEA
TABLE

MARY left her suite at the Inn and walked down to Broad Street. She had an appointment at the manteaumakers at four. After that she would go to Adam's house and ask for Sara. She was determined to change the situation that had existed at Rutledge Riding.

In front of the lapidary's shop she saw Lady Caroline's red morocco chair sitting on the bricked walk, her bearers standing on guard, their arms folded over their chests, their eyes staring straight ahead. Mary laughed to herself at the display, and at the young officers and men of fashion who were lazing about, waiting for Lady Caroline to step into her chair.

Guernsey House had already become the headquarters of gay young gentlemen who played for high stakes . . . some of them losing more than they could afford. Lady Caroline said politics were not to be discussed under her roof. But the Royalists were there in force, as the Whigs gathered in Mary Warden's suite at Bradford Inn.

She heard rapid footsteps behind her and Peyton's voice saying, "Mary, Mary Warden, why are you walking so fast?" Mary turned. Peyton fell in step, his dark, handsome face eager and smiling.

"What luck, Mary! I've been wanting to see you. Can't we have tea at the little shop on the square?"

Mary hesitated. "I'm due at the manteaumakers; after that, I'd planned to stop in to see Sara."

Peyton said he wanted to go with her for he hadn't seen Sara since she came down. It was arranged that he meet her at the manteaumakers in half an hour, and they would go to Princess Street together.

Mary turned as she went up the steps. Lady Caroline had come out of the lapidary shop and was seated in her sedan chair. She leaned out the window when she saw Peyton and beckoned to him. He went swiftly, eagerly, Mary thought. Lady Caroline withdrew her arm and Mary heard her say, "I shall expect you in an hour, Peyton."

Peyton didn't keep his appointment with Mary, who waited

fifteen minutes, then went on. She was prepared to have word that Mrs. Rutledge was not receiving but, on the contrary, Sara received her in the drawing room at once. She was seated at the tea table talking with Dr. Cobham and two men Mary did not know. Sara was animated, gay. She turned up her cheek for Mary to kiss, and greeted her cordially, mentioning the names of the two young naval officers. Dr. Cobham drew up a chair, and they fell to talking about the arrival of the new sloop-of-war *Cruizer* to which the officers were attached, and of the opening of the Assembly on Monday.

"I think Governor Tryon will have a difficult time at first," Dr. Cobham said to Sara. "He will have to break down the bad feeling left by Dobbs."

"He will," Sara said quickly. "He is so charming, so aristocratic, he knows exactly how to win the good will of the people, don't you think so, Mary?"

Mary didn't think so, but she didn't catch at the hook. "It always takes a little time to rectify a predecessor's mistakes," she said lightly. "The Governor is a man of pleasing personality and he will be greatly helped by his lovely wife."

Dr. Cobham brightened. "Charming, charming woman." He turned to Mary. "What do you hear about the palace the Governor is going to build? I heard he has brought an architect from London, a Moor named John Hawks."

Mary said, "So I've heard. How will the Wilmington people like it, having the capital moved to New Bern?"

The Doctor shrugged his shoulders and shook his head. He took out his snuffbox before he answered.

"I doubt if it is wise, Mrs. Warden. Some of our merchants are very bitter."

Sara broke in. "How insolent! Fancy people in trade having an opinion."

Dr. Cobham said, "Dear lady, you are quite right. The Governor should listen to no one. He understands the situation here perfectly."

Mary thought, "A city doctor, with his fastidious dress and his subtle flattering manner." Sara would like him. She noticed nothing was said about the taxes the people of the Province would have to pay if the Governor carried out his idea of building the finest palace in America as his residence.

Adam came in then. His face lightened when he saw Mary. He came to her, kissing her hand, holding it for an instant. "How nice to see you, Mary," he exclaimed. Then he greeted the men and lifted Sara's hand to his lips. "My dear, will you give me tea?"

Sara smiled up at him. "The Doctor says I'm to have tea every afternoon so that he has an excuse to drop in. Fancy needing an excuse to come to his own house!"

The Doctor's prominent eyes swept the room. "Dear lady," he said in his smooth voice, "you have already made it completely yours. Your taste in flowers and bibelots is exquisite. You grace my poor drawing room with your presence."

Sara's pleased smile showed Mary how she blossomed under the most obvious flatteries. "How delightfully you phrase your words, Dr. Cobham," Sara said. "No wonder you have the reputation of being a gallant!"

It came to Mary that Sara would enjoy Wilmington. She would get new life from Cobham's gallantry, a contrast to Dr. Armitage's blunt honesty.

The door opened. Aaron announced Lady Caroline Mathilde and Mr. Peyton Rutledge. Lady Caroline came in on the heels of the announcement, her mahogany satin skirts rustling. She flung her fur cape on a chair and advanced across the room with a regal air. She seemed to fill the room with the fragrance of rare perfumes, laces, silks and satins. Nodding carelessly to the company, she went directly to Sara.

"Dear Mrs. Rutledge," she said, "we've come to you to beg a cup of tea. I'm sure you will pardon the informality of such a visit, but I'm perishing for my tea, and the tea shops are too impossible." She sank into a chair near the tea table, extending her hand for Adam to kiss. "Ah! Adam! how nice to find you here!" She included the others in her smile. "Dear Mary, you must come to dine at Guernsey House. Dr. Cobham, how very pleasant to see you, but I might have known you always discover beautiful women." She held her hand to one of the officers, nodding to the other. "You are dining with me tonight, Gregory—at ten—promptly."

Sara said, "I am quite happy that Peyton brought you, Lady Caroline. Adam darling, ring for fresh tea, please. Peyton, my dear, sit here beside me. Where have you been? . . ." She turned to Lady Caroline, "Peyton is my favorite person. I am counting on him to help me keep amused while I am in Wilmington this winter."

"Peyton is an antidote for boredom," Lady Caroline said indifferently, and then—to Mary—"My dear you must see my garden at Guernsey House. My gardener at St. Croix has sent up dozens of plants, and they are all growing beautifully in my glass house." She included the group. "You know Mary Warden and I are both garden lovers, even though our political opinions differ."

140

For a moment no one spoke. Then Dr. Cobham said, "But Lady Caroline, I thought political subjects were taboo at Guernsey House!"

Lady Caroline laughed. "So they are! My drawing room is for gaiety—not for serious talk." She looked at Adam who stood in his favorite position, his elbow against the mantelboard, his back to the fire.

"You must come, Adam. I have a quantity of amusing new books from London, and some Rawlinson prints that are delightful." To Sara she said, "A little wicked, my dear, but very, very amusing. One can overlook wickedness, don't you think?—but not boredom."

Sara did not answer. She was busy arranging cups.

Mary wondered, "What is Lady Caroline up to now? . . ."

Dr. Cobham laughed. "My dear Lady Caroline, no one would think of being bored if he had the honor of your company!"

Aaron came into the room carrying two silver jugs of steaming water. Directly behind him was Azizi with a small tray containing a silver tea caddy and a box of long sugar. Adam looked at her once, then looked away. Sara had her dressed in bright silk trousers, covered by a long coat of gold and silver embroidery. She wore soft, flat sandals of morocco leather, and silver anklets and bracelets that clicked as she moved. Her head was bound, as always, with a green turban; but now she wore jeweled rings in her ears, and strings of beads about her throat.

She knelt near Sara and prepared the tea at a low table. The conversation languished. All eyes were focused on the brilliant figure. Mary glanced at Adam but he was looking down at Sara, a heavy frown between his eyes. Lady Caroline was frankly interested.

When Azizi had finished her work, Lady Caroline called her over. "Come here, girl, let me see those anklets. They look as if they were Madagascar work. Are they?"

Azizi answered slowly, "They are from Zanzibar, madam."

"That will be all, Azizi," Sara said. "You may go."

The girl left the room, followed by the faint tinkling of her anklets and the click of her bracelets. The eyes of all the men followed her lithe, smoothly moving figure.

Lady Caroline said to Adam, "I'll give you five hundred guineas for her!"

Adam shook his head, a peculiar smile on his face.

Sara was smiling, too. Mary thought she was enjoying the attention the girl had attracted.

"The slave is mine," she said before Adam could speak. "She is not for sale."

Lady Caroline's cold eyes rested on Sara for a moment. "You must be very sure of your husband, Mrs. Rutledge." She rose immediately, without waiting for Sara's answer.

"Come, Peyton, we must go now. Thank you so much for your hospitality, Mrs. Rutledge. Good afternoon, gentlemen. Mary, are you going? Let us walk to the door together."

Adam said, "I will go to the Inn with you, Mary. It is almost dark."

Sara interrupted. The angry flush which followed Lady Caroline's insinuating words had not faded. "No, Adam, you must stay. I am expecting other guests, invited guests."

Dr. Cobham sprang to his feet. "Dear Mrs. Warden, my coach is at the door, and at your disposal. May I have the pleasure of dropping you at the Inn?"

In the hall Peyton caught Mary's arm. She thought he looked harassed and remembered he had scarcely spoken. "Mary, may I come to see you tomorrow? I want to explain —it was impossible—" he stopped, embarrassed for words. Mary knew why he had not kept the appointment.

She said, "Do come, Peyton. As for the other thing, don't think of it again. I understand perfectly."

He kissed her fingers. "Dear Mary, one can always count on you."

Adam put her into Dr. Cobham's coach. The Doctor was talking with Lady Caroline, making his farewells.

"I shall see you soon, Mary," Adam said as he tucked a robe about her feet. "I have so much to talk about, and I need your advice."

Dr. Cobham got in and gave directions to his man to stop at the Inn. The coach rattled off down the cobbled streets.

Mary had a glimpse of Adam standing by Lady Caroline's chair, while Peyton quieted his horse, waiting for the gaily dressed chairbearers to move off. She heard Lady Caroline Mathilde's carrying voice saying, "You know I always get my way, Adam." Mary leaned back in the coach. Dr. Cobham was talking about the Governor's new coach and the races but she did not listen. Her mind was in the room she had just quitted, the people in it, and what had happened at the tea table. Little had been said, but she had been aware of the strain—that some tension existed, an undercurrent of distrust, or was it menace?

142

The night before the Assembly convened Richard Caswell called a meeting in his rooms at Bradford Inn. Adam had heard the rumor ever since he arrived the week before that Caswell would be the next Speaker. He thought his uncle was the logical man. He was moderate in his views and, with the Governor and the Assembly at loggerheads, he would be the natural selection.

When Adam arrived, he found Moore and one or two others already there. They introduced Hooper, whom he had not met. One of the Alexanders from Mecklenburg came in, followed by Iredell; also, John Harvey and Joseph Hewes. Caswell's body servant had put a tray of glasses with decanters of rum and whisky on a table.

Caswell said, "Now that the 'Iron Men of Albemarle' are here, we can get down to work. But perhaps you will have a drink first?"

While the men were pouring the drinks, Caswell stood talking to Adam, a little removed from the group around the table. "You will see how we do these things, Adam. You know I told you before, when we talked in Edenton, that the majority never rules. It is the organized minority that holds political power." He indicated the company at the table with his head. "They think it is all settled that I will accept the nomination for Speaker. I am not going to do it. I'm going to suggest John Ashe. Before they leave they will think it is their own plan." He laughed silently.

"It won't be a popular choice," Adam said.

"Then we will make it popular." He looked across the room. The men had found chairs. Glasses in hand, they were talking about the steeplechase the Governor was sponsoring the following week. "I must start the meeting," Caswell said. Leaving Adam, he went across the room and took a chair at a table covered with papers and books.

Adam sat down at the back of the room to listen. Silence fell when Caswell stated his plan to them. Then they all began talking at once. For two hours, they argued, but in the end Caswell won.

"Tryon will rage," chuckled Hooper. He was a big man with a pleasing manner and a sense of humor.

"He has had his plans set to put De Rosset in the chair, so Farquhar Campbell told me. I hope he doesn't take out his spleen on John Ashe," Maurice Moore said. He was still dubious about the plan.

Caswell laughed. "He won't know until it is too late. We

143

don't want De Rosset, and John is the best man. He won't be influenced by the Governor."

Moore spoke thoughtfully, "I wasn't thinking of tomorrow. I was thinking of the future. Tryon is a bitter enemy. John's skin is thin. The Governor may find the Achilles heel!"

Caswell did not smile. "We must have a man in the chair who will be fair yet hold the factions together on one issue. The stand of the Assembly must be firm; we must claim the exclusive privilege of imposing taxes on this Province."

The next day Adam went to the Assembly and took his seat early. He had never before been to an opening, and the feeling was general that the session would be a memorable one. "History will be made this session," Caswell had said the night before. "We must be cautious. We must take no position we cannot hold—no backward steps—from now on, everything must be forward."

The old members straggled in and stood around talking to friends. The new members, like Adam, were in their seats early watching the others. Presently, he heard the sharp tap of the gavel. Two wide doors, leading into a hall, were thrown open by men in uniform. The Governor's secretary, Edgecombe, came in. He walked slowly across the room and stood before the bar. Glancing at a paper in his hand, he read a few words in a high, monotonous voice:

"His Excellency, the Governor of the Royal Province of North Carolina, requires the immediate presence of the burgesses at the Residence."

There was a scraping of feet as the members rose. Two by two, they filed from the room. Adam found himself beside his uncle whose face was grave but calm. Adam wondered how Caswell was feeling. He was about to manipulate a political *tour de force* that would surprise and anger the Governor, whose temper was violent and vindictive. He noticed most of the men were silent as they went down the hall.

They were received in the State room of the Residence. The Governor was seated in an elbow chair, high backed, and covered with red damask. He was a large man of imposing presence, his eyes prominent and penetrating under heavy brows, his jaw strong and heavy. He wore the full uniform of a Colonel of His Majesty's Guards. Edgecombe was standing at his right hand; at his left were two members of his Council and back of them, in a semicircle, the members of his staff in full dress uniforms. Behind them, long thick curtains of red damask hung from the walls. Flags in standards were set on either side.

The medals and orders on the Governor's broad chest made a brave display. Adam thought, "He is an aristocrat, distinguished, intelligent." People said he was too fond of pomp. Some called him arrogant, but they might be wrong. Certainly he was a man who would uphold the dignity of his office.

The burgesses moved in single file around the edge of the room. As they passed him, the Governor inclined his head in acknowledgment of each salute.

Caswell bent his head, whispering to Adam. "The Governor will probably say a word to you, since you are a new member. It is not necessary to reply other than bow, unless he asks you a direct question."

As they moved slowly around the room Adam thought he heard the rustle of silks and the low murmur of a woman's voice. He looked up. Lady Tryon was in the musician's balcony with a tall, uniformed aide. The Governor's lady smiled at him, bowing her head graciously. She turned and spoke to the young officer. He looked down at Adam, then nodded to Lady Tryon and left the balcony.

The queue was nearing the Governor, the men ahead of him moving in. Caswell went by, bowing courteously, but he did not speak.

Tryon detained Adam, while he held a conversation with the young officer Adam had seen with Lady Tryon. His face wore a smile when he greeted him. "We welcome you to the House of Burgesses with pleasure, Mr. Rutledge. In Colonial affairs, his Majesty is very favorable to young men of your ability, with a knowledge of England and life at Court."

Adam thanked him with a gesture and took a step forward, but the Governor again detained him. "One moment. Lady Tryon has sent word to me that I must secure you for supper tonight—nine o'clock, she says, without fail."

Adam bowed with a word of acceptance, and moved on. He joined the circle of men on the far side of the room.

When every man had passed the Governor arose. In a loud voice that echoed against the walls of the room he authorized the members to go to the Assembly Hall and, when they had selected a Speaker, to return and inform him of their choice.

When the Assembly Hall had quieted down, and all the members were in their seats, Caswell got to his feet. His voice was not loud but it carried throughout the great room. When he placed the name of John Ashe in nomination for Speaker of the Assembly the dropping of a pin could have been heard. McKelvie, the burly Scot, got to his feet. A member from Mecklenburg County, he was spokesman for the western districts.

"I do not know why Mr. Caswell will not accept the nomination himself—but he says he has other plans. I, for one, will abide by his decision. I wish to second Mr. Richard Caswell's motion to nominate Mr. Ashe as permanent Speaker for this session of the Assembly."

There was a moment's hesitation. Then a dozen voices called for the vote by acclamation. No dissenting voice was heard, but Adam saw a number of men leave the hall before the roll was called, William Warden and Farquhar Campbell among them.

The roll call finished, a herald announced: "Mr. Richard Caswell has proposed and set up Mr. John Ashe of Hanover for Speaker of the Assembly. Mr. Ashe is unanimously chosen and placed in the chair accordingly. Mr. John Harvey and Mr. Adam Rutledge have been selected to inform his Excellency of the Assembly's choice."

On their way to the Governor, John Harvey said, "His Excellency will not be pleased with this. He wanted either a Cape Fear man or Campbell in the chair."

"John Ashe is a strong man," Adam said.

Harvey smiled quietly. "Too strong to suit Tryon, Adam. Ashe can't be influenced by promises of political preferment. Nor is he to be taken in by the 'petticoat government.' "

Adam thought of the invitation from Mrs. Tryon, or Lady Tryon as she liked to be called, to supper that night. He was a new member. They would try to sound him out no doubt. The Governor would have to work to increase the members favorable to him, for the division would be close and he stood to lose his control over the Assembly.

The footmen in red and gold livery opened the door. A messenger announced the arrival of "two gentlemen from the Assembly, with a message of importance for your Excellency!"

John Harvey did the talking. He repeated the words used on such occasions. At the mention of John Ashe's name for Speaker, the perfunctory smile faded from Tryon's lips. His prominent eyes glazed, his lips drew back showing his long, yellowish teeth. He looked like the "Great Wolf," the name the Indians gave him when he first came to the Province.

"John Ashe?" he cried, his voice harsh with anger. "John Ashe?" He caught at the arms of the chair, half rising. Then he sat back and gave the prescribed reply in a muffled voice.

"We will inform you of the acceptance by messenger, at the bar of the Assembly."

Adam and Harvey left the room. On the way back to the Hall, Harvey said, "There will be a division between the Whigs and Tories this session. I am sorry, but it is sure to come. Every man will be obliged to take his stand, Whig or Tory-Royalist."

Adam said nothing. He was determined to remain clear of parties. He wanted only to be of help to the farmers.

It was more than an hour before the messenger came from the Governor to inform the Assembly that the Governor was waiting to receive them at the Residence. In the name of the burgesses, the new Speaker made the announcement to the Governor, "We are now assembled to confirm the rights and privileges of the Assembly, and to state that no mistake or error of the Governor will be attributed to the Assembly." This was the ancient custom but today the words carried a special significance.

The Governor's answer was perfunctory. He promised to "support the Assembly in all its rights and privileges." Adam wondered how the words would be stretched to meet the situation, which was sure to arise.

Chapter 11

THE STAMP MASTER
AND THE PEOPLE

WHEN Adam reached the Residence he was shown into a small drawing room done in the French manner. Although he arrived on the moment, he found Farquhar Campbell and William Houston, the new Stamp Master, ahead of him. Lady Tryon, dressed elegantly in peach satin and Brussels lace, held out her hand for Adam to kiss, welcoming him with great cordiality.

"I am so sorry Mrs. Rutledge isn't able to venture out. Perhaps she will be stronger as the season advances," she said.

Lady Caroline was announced. She entered with the effect of excitement that she always managed to produce and gave Adam a flashing smile as she greeted her hostess. Lady Tryon seemed to shrink in stature beside the imposing figure of the London woman. Even her clothes seemed provincial in comparison with Lady Caroline's more sophisticated gown and furs.

A moment later, the scarlet-coated lackeys flung open the double doors to announce his Excellency. Everyone rose when the Governor entered the room. He greeted each guest individually. To Adam he was especially cordial, inquiring after Mrs. Rutledge's health and whether they were comfortably settled in Princess Street. Adam wondered why the Governor concerned himself with such a small matter as his renting Dr. Cobham's house.

The butler announced supper.

Lady Tryon smiled at Adam. "Will you give me your arm, Mr. Rutledge?"

They followed the Governor and Lady Caroline from the room. Supper was laid in one of the small rooms off the State dining room. Adam, sitting next to the Governor's wife, faced the French windows that opened onto a brick terrace. The Governor sat with his back to the window, Lady Caroline at his right. Campbell was opposite Adam. He was a thin sandy-haired man with pale blue eyes who wore his hair elaborately curled and powdered. Houston, Adam had not seen before, but he had heard enough about him and his precious stamps. Adam smiled to himself. He was in the Royalist bailiwick. He must be cautious if controversial topics came up.

Lady Caroline took over the conversation. She might have been the hostess and Lady Tryon a quiet, timid guest from the Provinces. She told of London and Court life, amusing anecdotes of gay young men of fashion and their well-known preferences in mistresses—how Lady X had taken a new lover. "A pity she did not wait until her late husband was decently buried—a young man, at that. It is said she furnishes him with his whisky and champagne, and all his dinners."

The Governor said little and drank heavily of Rhenish wine. Occasionally he laid a familiar hand on Lady Caroline's arm.

Campbell spoke of the great number of men who were leaving the colony to go to the Illinois country by the Wilderness Trail.

Tryon, suddenly angered, turned to Campbell.

"We must stop this! We have plenty of open land that can be had in the Province."

Campbell answered, "It would be difficult, your Excellency. You know our western men, how independent they are. Where we have thousands of acres of open land, there are hundreds of thousands of acres of raw land to be had along the Ohio and the Mississippi. And there is the post of St. Louis where furs can be sold or traded."

Adam caught Campbell's words: thousands of acres of raw land. They blotted out Lady Tryon's voice so that she had to tap his arm with her lace fan to attract his wandering attention.

"The Governor is very pleased to have you in the Assembly, Mr. Rutledge. My poor husband has many troubled hours over provincial problems. You have no idea how tiresome it is to deal with some of the men in the Assembly, and to govern a backward Province."

Tryon turned his head and fixed his heavy eyes upon his wife.

"My dear," he said, "you will remember what I told you —" Lady Tryon bit her lip and leaned back in her chair.

To Adam, he said, "I've been wondering, Mr. Rutledge, whether you have your land under Royal Grant, or did you purchase your acreage?"

"My land was inherited, sir, part of the original Royal Grant held under the Lords Proprietors."

"Uhm—that is interesting. I've been meaning to look up

the disposition of the original grant, but I've had too many immediate problems on my hands. Did you inherit through the Rutledge family?"

"No, the land came from John Archdale, one of the Lords Proprietors."

Lady Caroline leaned forward eagerly.

"Archdale, the Quaker governor? Then you must be related to Wexbrough. He belongs to that family."

"He is my father's cousin."

Lady Caroline clapped her hands together softly.

"La—la, Adam! You never told me that you were related to Wexbrough. You may have his title some day. I know Pippy very well. He's likely to pop off any time."

Adam shook his head.

"I'm sorry to disappoint you, Lady Caroline. There are too many people between Wexbrough and me to make that even a remote possibility. Besides, I belong to the Colonies, not to the Mother Country."

There was a silence. Adam saw he had gone too far. His answer was *gauche,* as if he had publicly made a declaration of political affiliation. Tryon leaned back, a frown between his heavy overhanging brows. No one spoke. The butler placed a decanter of port in front of him. He poured a glass and set the bottle in front of Lady Caroline. The silence continued as the decanter went the rounds. Almost as an answer to Adam's words, the Governor stood up and raised his glass. The company rose, also.

"His Majesty, the King," he said as he drank the toast.

Adam looked beyond Tryon's bulky figure. Through the French windows he saw a half-dozen men standing on the terrace, their faces pressed against the window.

"William! William! Look behind you!" Lady Tryon cried.

Tryon turned quickly. Instinctively his hand went to his sword belt. Adam and Farquhar Campbell moved toward the windows. There was a sound of shattering glass as the windows were pushed violently open. Adam saw the men were armed with stout clubs and pick handles. They were roughly dressed and had bands of white cloth, with the word *Liberty* printed in black tied around their hats.

Tryon was white with rage. His eyes were blazing, but he controlled his voice.

"What does this intrusion mean?" he demanded.

A heavy-set man with steady, fearless eyes and a jutting chin, took a step in advance of the others. Adam recognized Pugh, one of Husband's leaders, a man who had been daring in his criticism of Edmund Fanning's irregularities. He took off his hat deferentially when he spoke to the Governor.

"We want nothing of your Excellency. It is the Stamp Master we want. He refused us admittance to his office and would not speak with us, so we have followed him here."

Tryon's face was red now, almost purple. He banged his clenched fist on the table.

"Get out of here, you blackguards! How dare you force your way under his Majesty's roof!"

Adam glanced at Houston. His hands were clutching the table for support. He was shaking with fright, his eyes fixed on something beyond the Governor's shoulder. Adam looked in that direction. He saw that the men in the room were not the only ones who had come for the Stamp Master. The terrace was crowded—shadowy figures moved silently on the lawn below.

Adam's eyes swept the room. Lady Caroline was not in sight. She had slipped quietly away at the first alarm.

The Governor had himself in hand now.

"I'm going to the balcony to disperse this mob," he said, his voice harsh.

Looking at the faces of the men in the room, and the firm, protruding chin of Pugh, their leader, Adam thought this unwise. These men could not be ordered about.

Campbell said, "If it is the Stamp Master they want, let him talk with the leaders at his office."

Tryon's face cleared. This suggestion suited him. Adam knew the Governor had no fear, but he did not relish the idea of treating with a mob at their insistence.

"Come, my dear," he said to the trembling Lady Tryon. "We will retire to allow these gentlemen to make their own settlement."

He walked out of the room with dignified calm, his wife following, almost running to keep up with his long stride. The crowd began to shout for Houston.

Campbell turned to Pugh. "Go out and speak to them. Tell them to go home and we will settle this later."

Pugh hesitated a moment. "I don't think it will do any good, Mr. Campbell. The men won't listen to me now. They want to talk to the Stamp Master." He looked around the room. "Maybe, Mr. Rutledge could say something—"

"Go on out, Rutledge," Campbell said. "Get them away before the Governor decides to send for troops."

Adam stepped out on the low balcony. He could see now, by the light from the courtyard lamps, that there were several hundred men in the garden. He stood for a moment while his eyes adjusted themselves to the darkness; then raised his voice slightly, so that it carried across the garden.

"Mr. Houston will meet your delegation leaders at the Courthouse in half an hour. The rest of you disperse and go home."

"Where's the Governor," someone shouted.

A voice answered, "Keep quiet, fool! We don't want Tryon. We want the Stamp Master."

"I told you he would be at the Courthouse in half an hour," Adam said.

Several voices shouted at once. "How do we know Houston will come? Don't move, men, it's a trick. Tryon'll have his soldiers there to meet us—not Houston."

A voice from deep in the garden called out, "Who are you? How do we know you're not lying to us? It's a trick to get us out—stay where you are, men!"

Adam went quickly down the steps until he stood close to the crowd. He was angry now, but he held himself in check.

"My name is Adam Rutledge. I'm not afraid to tell my name or show my face."

A quick laugh followed from the man who had done the talking and who kept well back in the shadow of the hedge. Someone shouted, an older man by his voice, "That's right. We know Mr. Rutledge, one of the Iron Men. What have you to say?"

"Nothing more than what I've already said. Go home quietly. Let your leaders talk to Mr. Houston."

"You'll promise to deliver him?" A laugh followed.

Adam said, "Mr. Houston will be at his office at the time I told you."

An old man, with a white beard, slipped forward from back in the crowd. "We will go if you give us your word. We don't trust Houston or Campbell, or any of the rest of the Royalists. But you are a farmer like some of us, and we trust you."

"I give my word," Adam said. He turned and went up the steps, leaving the crowd to go of their own will. In the dining room he found Campbell forcing a glass of whisky into Houston's shaking fingers.

"Man, man, pull yourself together! You can't let these fellows see you like this. Pull yourself together! You won't have trouble if you use diplomacy. Didn't you see how Rutledge put them off with a few words?" Campbell urged him.

Adam looked at the Stamp Master's white face and his

152

loose, trembling lips. He was not as sanguine as Campbell. He had felt the temper of the mob at close range. It was not diplomacy they wanted but honesty and the truth. He knew they could not get that from the Stamp Master.

That same night, the so-called "Secret Committee" was dining with Mary Warden in her suite at Bradford Inn. William had gone to Georgia on land affairs and had not returned. Caswell and Iredell left early, but John Harvey, Judge Moore and Hooper stayed on. Earlier in the evening, Mary had sent a messenger to Adam Rutledge to ask him to join them, but the messenger returned with word that Adam was at the Residence.

"How long have you known young Rutledge?" Moore asked John Harvey when Mary repeated the message.

"Five years or so. Ever since he came to North Carolina."

"Do you think we can count on him?"

Harvey considered a moment.

"I don't believe Rutledge has given political affairs much thought. His interest is his plantation. He is a man of sound judgment and integrity." He smiled at Mary. "Mary knows him much better than I do."

The Judge turned to Mary. "What do you think, Mary? Just how far is Rutledge to be taken into the secret councils?"

Mary put her knitting on the table.

"Not too far, yet. Adam is just becoming aware of the wrongs of the Colony. His life, so far, has been very personal —his plantation and his invalid wife. He is aristocratic by training. His wife is a Royalist." She hesitated, weighing her words. "But Adam believes a man can keep a middle way in political affairs. We know that won't be possible for very long."

"Why do we bother with him?" Moore asked. "It seems to me he's more likely to stick on the side of the King than to come over to the Province. I don't trust men who evade a definite stand."

Harvey interrupted. "There are a great many men who are still taking a middle course—Caswell, for one, believes in conciliation. I, too, favor using every method in our power to smooth out difficulties before we go wild and commit some irrevocable act. We don't know yet how the other Colonies will stand."

"Damn the other Colonies!" Moore cried. "We are North Carolina. We don't need the leadership of any other Colony."

"Tush, tush, Moore," Hooper interjected. "You are too violent . . . too radical. You'll have us in hot water. Let's be frank. We're not in a position to fight Britain now, or ten years from now, unless we have some trained fighters!"

Mary took up her knitting again. After a moment she broke the silence which followed Hooper's words.

"I think Adam Rutledge will throw his weight with the Colonies when the time comes. He loathes injustice. The moment he is convinced that the mass of people have had real injustice from Parliament he will take a stand."

Moore turned to her. "But he dines with the Governor."

John Harvey said, "So have you, Maurice, and all the rest of us."

"I may have in the past, but I don't intend to in the future."

There was a sharp tap, and the door opened suddenly. Iredell came hurriedly into the room. He was breathing fast, as if he had been running.

"There's trouble at the Residence," he cried. "A mob has gone to the Governor. The sentries tried to hold them back, but they bound the sentries and forced their way to the garden, breaking windows and throwing stones. We had better get to the square at once. We don't want a riot this time. It might be a bloody one."

John Harvey said, "Take your time, James. Why did the mob storm the Residence?"

"I'm not sure. They say they wanted Houston, who is dining there. I don't know the details. They told me that it is a mob of farmers bent on trouble, but Rutledge managed to put them off. Caswell and Ashe were with me when I heard this. They went directly to the Courthouse."

"Rutledge stopped them?" Moore asked, incredulously.

"Yes, Rutledge. He got them out of the Residence grounds by promising to have Houston meet their leaders at the Courthouse. They're on their way now."

Maurice Moore was already out in the hall, slipping into his greatcoat. The others followed quickly.

Mary said to John Harvey, "Wait until I get a wrap. I'm going with you."

"It's no place for you, Mary."

"I will go up to William's office. I can see the square from there." She caught up an Indian shawl from the back of a chair. "Come, let's hurry," she cried.

Mary paced back and forth in William's darkened office. Below in the square she could see the surging mob. There

154

were masked men and men unafraid to show their faces. Many were armed with pick handles and clubs and occasionally she caught the gleam of a musket barrel. A bonfire had been lighted, casting macabre shadows. There was no noise but the silence was more ominous. Mary knew these were determined men who would demand their rights and not be put off by words. Lights were burning in the Courthouse where men were talking, arguing, standing on their rights. Was this the way revolutions began?

The crowd was densest near the Courthouse steps. By the light of the torches Mary saw three men come out onto an upper balcony. A shout went up. One of the men stepped forward, grasping the rail for support. It was the Stamp Master.

"Men, men, I want to tell you—" Houston's voice was shrill. He struggled to go on but could not speak. Richard Caswell made himself heard above the angry shouting of the crowd.

Men, I beg you to be quiet. Mr. Houston wants to tell you that he has resigned as Stamp Master. We now have no Stamp Master in the Province of North Carolina."

"Hooray! Hooray! Hooray! Liberty and not stamps! Destruction to Parliament! Liberty and not stamps! What do you say to that, Stamp Master?"

"Go to your homes quietly," Caswell went on. "You have no complaints now. Go to your homes and forget about tonight."

"Right you are!" The crowd applauded Caswell, shouting and laughing. Then some of the men started to move out of the square.

Mary groped for a chair. Her knees would no longer hold her. She lighted a candle, her hand shaking.

After a time, she heard footsteps coming down the hall. John Harvey and Adam came in, followed by Caswell and Moore with Colonel Waddell of the militia.

"We've had a close call, Mary. If we hadn't persuaded Houston to resign, it would have been a bloody riot," John Harvey said as he pulled up a chair.

The men sat down around a table, talking together.

Mary said, "I'm sure William must have some brandy here, probably in that cupboard." She indicated with her hand.

Adam opened the door of the closet. A decanter and glasses were on a shelf.

"We will all welcome a drink," Caswell said, pulling his chair closer to the table.

Adam poured the brandy. Moore lifted his glass.

"To a Royal Province without a Stamp Master!" he said.

"They all lifted their glasses.

"Did Mr. Houston resign without trouble?" Mary asked.

Everyone laughed. Harvey's tone was scornful.

"The man was so frightened he could scarcely hold the pen to sign the paper. As contemptible an exhibition of cowardice as I ever saw."

"He hadn't the voice to swear not to execute his duties as Stamp Master. He could only mumble words," Iredell said.

Adam, seated near the window, got up. He spoke to Iredell. "I don't know the law, but what about an oath given under duress?"

Iredell smiled acidly. "I don't believe the legality of the oath will ever be questioned, Rutledge."

"What will Governor Tryon do? Do you think he will have the leaders arrested?" Mary asked.

Iredell and Harvey looked at each other. The question had been asked at the Courthouse.

Adam said, "I don't think so. He didn't make any effort to help Houston tonight. He said nothing about soldiers. I believe he will keep out of this affair."

Iredell's thin, solemn face bore a faint smile. "He will keep out of it if he doesn't want real trouble."

Moore said thoughtfully, "I wonder if it wouldn't have been better if we'd let things take their course. I'm not sure but what we had our chance and missed it.

"I doubt the wisdom of overt acts now, Maurice. We are not prepared to fight Britain." Caswell continued, "We haven't the soldiers or leaders. Ask Waddell, he can tell you that."

Waddell spoke for the first time. "How can we fight without trained soldiers or leaders who have any military knowledge? Will you tell me why you oppose Caswell's bill for State militia. Moore? The way things stand, it will take ten years to train enough men to defend this Province."

Moore didn't answer. He was hotheaded, impulsive, but no one doubted his loyalty. He had fought hard against the organization of militia, but he had not foreseen the outcome.

Caswell said quietly, "We can't fight battles without troops. We must wait. Whether you like it or not, you must admit that Tryon is a soldier well versed in the strategy of war. He knows he has the power in his hands as long as he has troops. He may try to enforce the Stamp Act. But I agree with Adam in that he will wait—let things take their course. The Act may be repealed."

"But the law was passed by Parliament at the King's request," Moore said.

"I know, but laws that can't be enforced have been repealed. The Province has friends in England who will take up our fight."

"Who? In god's name, who?" Moore shouted excitedly.

"William Pitt," Caswell answered.

Moore sneered. "Pitt is out of power now. How can he help us?"

Caswell smiled quietly. "I don't know, Maurice, but I have a hope, a very strong hope, that Pitt will find a way. He may help us because he likes Americans, or because he wants to fight the government. In either event, we will be the gainers."

Adam walked home with Mary. It was long past midnight. The streets were quiet. The air was crisp; the sky bright with stars. Adam wrapped his cape about her when he saw that she had only a light shawl over her shoulders.

"Were you afraid the mob would get out of hand tonight, Adam?" she asked, after they had left the square.

"For a few minutes," he answered. "It came out all right this time, but these men wouldn't have been satisfied with anything less than Houston's resignation."

"You think there is still danger?" she asked.

"I don't know, Mary. These things are indications—the little blow-off that comes before an eruption. It was no mob of young, half-grown, reckless boys. These were resolute men who were aware of what they were doing. For myself, I think Tryon was wise to keep away from it. If there had been any show of force by the guards or the troops from the Fort, we'd have had a real riot tonight."

They had come into Princess Street. At the entrance to the Inn lights were shining from the windows. People were moving about in the hall and the ordinary. Mary detained him a moment.

"Adam, there is something I have been wanting to tell you. Do you know how often Peyton is at Guernsey House these days?"

"I haven't seen Peyton more than once or twice since I came to Wilmington, Mary. He told me he was going back to the plantation."

She looked at his stern, unyielding face. "If I were you, Adam, I would talk to him—"

Adam interrupted, his voice cold. "The last time I gave Peyton advice I swore to myself that I'd never do it again."

157

Mary laid a conciliatory hand on his sleeve. "I know how Peyton is. He doesn't like interference, but I think you should do something about this. There's too much gambling at Guernsey House. It would be an open scandal if it weren't that the Governor and Lady Tryon are so friendly with Lady Caroline."

Adam said, "You think——?"

Mary broke in, "I don't think! I know a dozen young officers and Wilmington men who can't afford it who are losing money out there, a great deal of money. There are other things—I won't go into that, it is too unpleasant. I like Peyton. He is too fine a person to get involved with that woman."

"You liked Lady Caroline well enough when she was in Edenton. You were often at her house."

"Lady Caroline was different when she was at Pembroke. I think she is showing her true colors now." She held out her hand. "Good night, Adam. Iredell told us about the way you handled the mob at the Residence——" She hesitated a moment, "I was proud, Adam, very proud." She went up the steps quickly.

Adam walked down the two blocks to his house. Cicero was asleep in a chair outside his door. He sent the man to bed. Tired as he was, he went to his desk and wrote a long letter to Lavinia. He suggested that she come home by the first ship sailing for Cape Fear. She was not to use young Peyton as an excuse to keep her in England. He could go to school at Annapolis, or Owen Tewilliger could tutor him. No matter what her wishes, she was to come home at once.

Adam waited in his library for the architect Hawks. The Moor of Malta, as he was called, had already gained fame in the Colony for his plans for Tryon's Palace. Somehow, in spite of the feeling against the extravagance of Tryon in building a palace in these times, Hawks had managed to keep the respect of the people. The building was going to be beautiful; no one who had seen the plans could deny that. The Moor himself was liked by everyone who came in contact with him. Sara had expressed a desire to have alterations made on the Manor House: the west wing enlarged and a new ballroom built. She wanted Hawks to draw the plans.

Aaron announced the Moor. Adam greeted him warmly. He liked the man, his dignity and reserve, and his pride of race. He had the calm and assurance bred into the Arab for

158

a thousand years. Hawks unrolled the plans and spread them on the table. He and Adam were soon deep in talk of materials and costs. A slave brought in the tea tray.

A moment later Azizi, dressed in the colorful silks Sara had chosen for her livery, came into the room.

"The mistress sent me to serve tea for the master and his guest." She spoke in her slow, inflected tone. Then she saw John Hawks. With a swift, deft movement she drew a veil across her face, leaving only her dark eyes visible. To Adam it was as if she had made the same movement a thousand times until it had become habitual. She took her place, standing by the tea table. John Hawks watched her as she poured the tea. With a murmured word of explanation, she left the room for sugar which she had forgotten.

Hawks turned to Adam. "Do you mind telling me the name of the slave girl, Mr. Rutledge?"

The question angered Adam. For a moment he thought he would not answer—but why not?

"Azizi is her name," he said.

"Azizi," Hawks said meditatively. "Azizi. that is an Arabic word. It means someone beloved."

"Someone beloved," Adam repeated. He saw that John Hawks was watching him closely. He must be careful or he would betray himself.

"May I ask where you got the girl?"

"LaTruchy brought her from Zanzibar."

"A mulatto, I presume, from her color?"

"LaTruchy told me that many of the natives of the East Coast are light in color and have clear unnegroid features."

"That is right. The Queen of Sheba, for instance."

"But she was Caucasian."

"Yes, so the legend says. But beautiful! Solomon gave no heed to the color of her skin. This girl is very light in color —I wonder—"

The Moor paused. Azizi came into the room with a faint tinkling of silver anklets and bangles. As she passed the silver box of long sugar to Hawks he spoke to her rapidly in some language unknown to Adam. The girl shook her head. But Adam saw that her hand trembled when she put the silver box on the table.

Adam felt annoyed at Hawks's interest.

"That will be all, Azizi. You may tell your mistress that I will be here for supper," he said, dismissing her.

When she had gone, Adam turned to the Moor. "What language did you speak?"

"My own—Arabic. I asked her where she came from, what she was doing in this country."

"Did she understand?"

The Moor smiled a little. "She pretended not to. But I think she did. You noticed she has made the Pilgrimage."

"The Pilgrimage?" he asked.

The Moor explained: "She wears the green turban. To a Mohammedan that is the sign by which we know those who have been to Mecca."

"You are of the same religion? I beg your pardon—I should not have asked you that, Hawks."

"It is quite all right, Mr. Rutledge. I am a Mohammedan. Inside my own home I practice my religion. In your world I try not to be conspicuously different from the people with whom I dwell. Do I make myself clear?"

"Yes, of course. Why did you think the girl would understand Arabic?"

"Because I had a feeling . . . But she did not wish to speak to me."

"You say you think she understood?" Adam insisted.

A blank look passed over the Moor's face.

"Who can say?" he said, spreading his hands in a primitive Oriental gesture.

Adam had a strong feeling that the girl had understood Hawks. He thought of the time he had seen her in front of the cabin kneeling on a rug facing the east. The swift movement with which she veiled herself when she saw the man. John Hawks was looking at him. Adam asked a question about the plans of the house, and the awkward moment passed.

Adam, worn out by a long session in committee, left the wrangling men and walked home. He went at once to Sara's room. She was propped up by small pillows, the bed covered with skeins and balls of varicolored woolens. He started to sit down on the edge of the bed, but she stopped him.

"Not here, Adam. you'll get my colors mixed. I've spent hours sorting them out. Judith will bring you a chair."

The Negress slid a tapestry-covered chair across the room and placed it near the bed. She did not look at Adam directly but out of the corners of her eyes. Her antagonism was apparent even to Sara.

"Stand on the other side of the room, Judith," she ordered sharply.

The woman obeyed sullenly.

160

Adam felt ashamed of his active dislike of Judith. The woman was so necessary to Sara but she always had the appearance of being on guard with a drawn sword. She looked at him now across the room, her veiled eyes holding the age-old wisdom of primitive people. Sara lay back, her tapestry frame dropping from her limp hand to the counterpane. Judith came back to the bed, took the frame, gathered up the woolens and bent to smooth the pillows.

"Honey, you is weary." The slave's voice was soft and soothing, as if she were talking to a child. She straightened up, looking at Adam across the whiteness of the bed. "Better you go. Miss Sara, she don't sleep so good last night. Better she sleep now."

"Damn the woman!" he thought. Always the same words; always the same scene. What was she trying to do? . . . protect Sara from his passion? He laughed grimly to himself.

"Better she rest now," the woman repeated monotonously.

"Shall I go?" he whispered, bending over Sara. He hoped she would ask him to stay a moment more, but she closed her eyes wearily. "Do you want me to go?"

"Judith thinks I must sleep."

He kissed her cheek. "Have a good rest, my dear. Perhaps you will have dinner with me tomorrow."

"Perhaps."

Adam made a signal to the slave to follow him from the room. She came with visible reluctance.

"The girl Azizi is not to do the men's work. A few days ago I saw her in the halls doing Aaron's work. See that it doesn't happen again."

The woman looked at him slyly.

"Miss Sara, she say take Azizi away from the lower floor work and keep her upstairs. She move she clothes down to the end of the east wing to sleep."

Adam felt the implication of her words. "Remember what I have said. If the girl is given men's work again, someone will go out to the overlooker," he said harshly.

Judith turned back to the room and closed the door. He heard the lock click. So Sara had put Azizi in the east wing to sleep. That was near his own room, too near. He walked slowly down the hall, thinking of what the woman had said. As he crossed the terrace, he glanced into Sara's room through the window. She was sitting up again, the tapestry in her hand, looking at Judith with a smile on her lips. The slave woman's voice drifted through the window.

"I don' wan ma child all wore out with foolish talkin'

161

about politics and things that happen on the plantation. Better you forget that now, honey. Just have youself a good time restin'. Judith she rub you' legs and body. You like that, honey? Make you feel good . . . make you rest quiet."

Adam turned away. He felt suddenly weary, his feet dragging. A dull rage burned in him. Damn the black woman and her devotion to Sara. And why would Sara—he checked his thoughts and entered the house. In his room he rang for Aaron and ordered some food.

After a time, Azizi came carrying a heavy tray.

"What the devil do you mean by this?" he said to Aaron, who followed her. "Why do you let this girl carry the tray?"

"It wasn't me, master. Judith she say that Azizi fetch hit." He hurried to take the tray. Azizi was silent, her eyes cast down. Adam was angry, but he kept his temper. His voice was quiet.

"You wait outside, Aaron." The man shuffled out of the room.

"Sit down," he said abruptly to Azizi. She hesitated a moment, then took her place on a stool by the hearth. Adam poured a cup of tea. "Drink this." The girl took the cup. There was something particularly elusive about her. Her small body, wrapped in the gay silk clothes, gave her the look of a bright tropic bird. For the first time Adam thought of her . . . of the girl herself. How alone she was. How strange their world must be to her. Alone among alien folk. Zanzibar —what was it like?—strangely exotic as its name? He remembered a picture he had seen of great carved doorways, gardens of tropical verdure and fountains splashing in marble pools in which blue lotus floated.

Azizi lifted the teacup to her lips and drank the tea slowly. Adam waited until she put the cup on the table, hoping she would speak or look at him with her dark brooding eyes. When she raised her eyes, he thought he detected a mocking light in them.

"May I leave, master?" she said. He didn't want her to go. He wanted to talk to her; to have her talk to him. He wanted to get past her calm exterior—to know what she was thinking —but how could he? She repeated her question; her low-pitched, husky voice stirred him unaccountably.

"No, do not go, yet. I want to talk to you. There are questions I want to ask—" He paused. He was not sure how to proceed.

"A master may ask of his slave," she said. He felt the irony in her tone. But he went on, not concerned with what he said, hoping to get past the barrier she had raised against him.

"What did the Moor say to you the other day?" he asked abruptly.

The girl made a startled movement, turning her head away.

"What did Hawks ask you? You understood him, didn't you?"

She nodded affirmatively. "Yes, master."

"Then, why did you pretend not to understand? What difference did it make?" Adam asked.

"I do not desire to answer what he asks," she said.

Adam leaned forward.

"I wish you would tell me, Azizi. Don't you think you can tell me?"

She waited a moment, then she said, "He asks from where I come, and of my father and his people, and the place where they now live. I do not answer him. . . . I have a great fear." She sat immovable, but he saw that her slim ivory-tinted hands were clasped tightly under her long veils.

Adam put his hand on hers. "You need have no fear of Hawks or anyone, Azizi," he said quietly. "He is very kind."

"He of the long beard says he will buy me. He will take me away from here—from you, master."

Conflicting emotions raced through Adam's blood. First, anger—then another emotion became dominant. She did not want to go even to one of her own people! She wanted to stay. Could it be possible that she loved him? He lifted her chin so that her eyes must meet his.

"You must not be afraid, Azizi. No one is going to buy you—Hawks or any other man—if you want to stay." Soundless sobs shook her. "You want to stay?" Adam asked. "You must tell me."

She turned slightly and put her hand on his for a moment. "I want to stay, master. Among my people it is always so. Kindness is not forgotten. It becomes a debt one pays in return."

Adam was touched by her words, but he did not want her gratitude or her thanks. The thought that she wanted to stay, that she trusted him, made his heart beat faster.

She looked up at him, her eyes large and deep circled. She hesitated, searching for the right words. There was no need for words, Adam thought. The sound of her voice alone stirred him profoundly.

"Even a slave may give," she said. "May Allah prolong life

163

and bring male children." She bowed her turbaned head, her arms crossed over her breast.

Adam looked at her, startled by her words. Her face was again impassive, her eyes devoid of expression. He knew she had used a familiar proverb of her people.

He held the door open as she went through, her silver anklets and bangles clinking musically, her veils giving off the fragrance of verbena and sandal. He watched her go, his heart warm toward her. He had gone past the barrier she had raised against him.

He was closing the door when he saw Judith standing near the door to Sara's rooms. She was watching Azizi as she walked down the long hall toward the stairway.

Chapter 12

LAVINIA
COMES HOME

WEEKS and months passed swiftly. The division in the Assembly widened. Debates were prolonged and violent. Talk was open now that a break with the Mother Country might come over the Stamp Act or over trade restrictions. An attempt to levy taxes to pay for increased civil and military establishments in the Colonies, or to make up the deficit caused by the French war, would meet with resistance. America did not want the status of a Colonial possession. The Colonies wanted to be taxed by representatives of their own choosing.

Tryon had made enemies. At first his regime was mild, but as time went on, things changed. His quick, vengeful temper did not help to heal the widened breach. He was the symbol of Royal power, and he was hated for that. It was hard to distinguish between personal quarrels and the deeper antagonisms based on principles. The western districts had many yeomen and hunters who did not relish the display of pomp. The Palace became an issue. Malcontents were quick to use any cause that could be turned to keep the people enraged against the Governor. The Quaker, Husband, caught at the Palace as a means to incite rebellion. "Tryon's Palace" became fighting words. Husband stood on the steps of schoolhouses and churches shouting against Tryon, his extravagances and his love of power.

"Tax every man, woman and child in the Province, so Tryon and his Lady can live like Royalty," was Husband's climax. "A red carpet so that his feet will not touch the common soil; elbow chairs of gold under a canopy of velvet for him to receive selected people of a free Province—that is Tryon. Shall we pay taxes to maintain our Governor in regal splendor?"

The answer to this ringing question was always the same . . . and so the torrent gathered momentum.

Adam Rutledge did not join in the criticisms. He believed that the Governor of the Province should have a residence in keeping with his position. But he knew that the Stamp Act as it stood would cause trouble more serious than anything that

165

had happened so far. Sending away a ship that carried stamps, forcing the Stamp Master to resign, would not solve the difficulty. The King, because of a mental malady from which he suffered, had not signed the Act. The Royalists used this as a point for argument that the Act would soon be repealed. But Adam's London correspondents thought differently.

It had passed in the House of Commons by a majority of five to one. Every member of the Lords had voted for it. The only hope for repeal lay in a change of government, with Grenville out, and someone friendly to the Colonies in his place; or from the people of England, from the merchants and manufacturers, because of the losses in trade with the Colonies. They might bring pressure on the King and the ministry.

So the months went on, each day bringing closer the rift dreaded by thoughtful leaders of the Province.

Adam's letter to Lavinia had the effect for which he had hoped. Early in the year he had word that she was coming back, bringing her son with her. It was not until March that Peyton had a letter giving the date of sailing, and the day of her arrival in America. She would come on the *Flamingo*, arriving at Annapolis early in May.

Adam was not sure whether Peyton was pleased that she was coming home or not. He had been very quiet the evening he brought the letter to him.

"She is tired of London," he said when Adam finished reading. "But she will not like it here. She thinks young Peyton should go to Eton—the only school that turns out gentlemen."

Adam laughed. "Lavinia's a strong Etonian. She is like her father in that."

Peyton nodded morosely. They were seated in the library of the house in Princess Street. Adam had tried several times to speak to Peyton about Guernsey House after Mary had called the matter to his attention, but Peyton managed always to turn the conversation. Tonight he was restless, pacing the floor, running nervous fingers through his dark hair.

Suddenly he said, "Adam, I want to borrow a thousand guineas."

Adam set his brandy glass on the table before he answered. "That is impossible, Peyton."

Peyton stopped his pacing. Adam saw by his white, stricken face how disappointed he was.

166

"I tell you, Adam, I must have it! Do you understand—I must—"

Adam thought, "He has lost money at Guernsey House, just as Mary said he would. It is my fault, partially. I should have found out what was going on instead of spending all my time with committees, and talking to men about political affairs."

"I haven't such a large sum in cash, Peyton," he said aloud." My money is tied up with cargoes and shipments. It will be six months or more before I have any returns from the last West India cargoes. You know that the West India trade has fallen to almost nothing since the Importation Act was passed. I couldn't possibly get my hands on such a sum in less than ninety days—if then."

Peyton sat down heavily and covered his face with his hands.

Adam spoke cautiously, knowing his violent temper. He did not want to antagonize him now, for he saw that Peyton was really in trouble. "There might be another way to extricate you without cash from your difficulty."

Peyton sat up, a look of hopeless anguish in his dark eyes. He shook his head violently. "No, no—there is no other way."

Adam said, "If you will explain, perhaps I can see a way—"

Peyton jumped to his feet. He faced Adam, his eyes blazing, his face white.

"I won't have you prying into my affairs! I thought I could rely on you, but I see I can't. You're too interested in running other people's affairs to think about your own family." He snatched up his hat and went out of the room, banging the door after him. Adam called him but he did not answer.

That was over a month ago. He had seen Peyton twice since then. The subject of money was not spoken of—not even mentioned. Adam thought he must have found the money in some other way, selling land or some of the property in Wilmington he had inherited from his mother.

Then one afternoon he came in to tell Adam and Sara that Lavinia and the boy were coming home.

Adam went with Peyton to Annapolis to meet them. They traveled north on one of Adam's shallops carrying a cargo of tobacco and indigo that had been warehoused on the plantation since the collapse of the British markets. When they arrived at Annapolis they went at once to Brice House to wait for the *Flamingo*, which had not yet been spoken at the mouth of the Severn.

That night at supper they met Charles Carroll and Thomas Stone, men of affairs in Maryland. The talk of rebellion grew hot around the table. Their host was for conciliation. He thought that the King would give way before the strengthened will of the people. The Maryland men told Adam that the proprietary Governor, Sharpe, had alienated many men who were not opposed to the government, but to the administration of it.

In the morning Adam and Peyton went to King William's School. Peyton was pleased with it. The list of the governing board comprised the principal men of the Colony, men of culture and learning. The students came from the best families of Virginia and Maryland. Many of their masters had been educated at Oxford or Cambridge. Adam and Peyton, both, liked what the headmaster had to say about the object of the school; to train boys so that they would be ready to take their places in Colonial life and governmental affairs.

The tuition was high. When he heard the amount, Peyton said it was out of the question. He took up his hat, and was about to leave the room, when Adam spoke up. "I have always intended to take over the education of young Peyton so why not begin now?" The documents were signed, the gold paid over. Peyton Rutledge II was enrolled in King William's School.

Peyton was nervous. "What if Lavinia does not approve? What if she refuses to have the lad sent to a provincial school?"

"Then we must convince Lavinia that it is for the good of the boy," Adam said promptly. "If he is to live here, it is better to have him educated here, so that he can take his place in the Colonies when he grows up." Adam was half laughing but Peyton took the words seriously.

"Take his place in the affairs of the Colonies? What nonsense! The boy's only seven years old. Besides, he'll not live in the Colonies. We'll be back in London before the year is over—" He stopped abruptly.

"In London? When are you going to London, Peyton?" Adam asked, surprised that his cousin should display such intensity of feeling on the subject.

Peyton's face darkened.

"I said too much. Please forget it."

They walked in silence down the street toward the Severn.

"I may as well tell you," Peyton burst out. "I have been

promised a position at Court, a splendid one that will pay me three thousand pounds per annum, and a house . . . no mean house, either . . . one of consequence. Lavinia will be proud of me. She won't have to say any longer that my income isn't large enough to buy her gowns and shoes." His voice was bitter.

Adam waited a while before he spoke.

"Who is getting this appointment for you?" he asked.

"I'm not at liberty to say. I am honor-bound to keep the secret until my appointment comes." He laughed suddenly. "Wouldn't it be splendid if my papers came on the *Flamingo*? Then we could all go back to England by the same ship."

Adam said nothing. Disturbing thoughts were in his mind. Whom did Peyton know that had the power to give out such appointments? It occurred to him that Peyton no longer talked against Tryon. Could that be the answer to the puzzle?

He looked at his cousin. His face was alive and smiling. This was the old Peyton he had not seen for months. How handsome he was with his clear, dark olive skin, his sparkling, dark eyes! He would cut quite a figure at Court with his easy grace and rare charm. His Irish mother had given him that. It was an ever-bubbling spring. There were times when Adam despised Peyton for his foolish ways, his sullen temper. But when he was like this, he was irresistible.

"That's the reason I didn't want you to lay down your money for the boy's tuition, Adam. I should have told you before," Peyton said.

"It's of no importance. If your appointment comes, I'll get the money back. If it doesn't . . ."

Peyton stopped him.

"Don't say it. Let's have no 'if's' this day. Look! A full-rigged ship sailing up the Severn! It must be the *Flamingo*. Come, Adam, I'll race you to the wharf!"

Lavinia dominated the situation. Cool, assured and beautiful, she sat in the lovely drawing room of Brice House, her arm thrown about the shoulders of her son. Peyton was sitting across the room. His gaiety had gone out like a snuffed candle. Adam didn't need to be told that the papers for his appointment had not come on the *Flamingo*.

Lavinia's welcome was tempered by restraint when she greeted her husband. Peyton, sensitive to moods, was silent. Adam could understand his disappointment at not getting the coveted Court position but not his indifference to his son. He should be proud of him. The child was ready to throw himself into his father's arms but Peyton had only given his hand a swift grip.

The lad stood by his mother's side, held by her soft arm, but he never took his eyes from his father's face. He was like Peyton in looks and coloring. There was a shy eagerness in his eyes when he looked at his father. He was tall for his seven years, with a sturdy independence and poise unusual in so young a boy. The oval face above his round, white collar was thoughtful, the mouth sensitive, but not weak. Lavinia was arguing: what was the good of taking the boy to England only to have all the polish rubbed off by a rough provincial school? She would prefer getting a tutor out from England.

Peyton suggested that Owen Tewilliger was a learned man. He could teach the boy. Lavinia scoffed at the idea.

"You men think it is only a matter of mathematics and Latin. It is much more. It is the conduct and manners and culture a boy gets at a Public School that makes the gentleman."

Peyton did not reply.

"I thought a gentleman was born, not made," Adam said lightly to break into their seriousness. "Suppose you let young Peyton go over to the school and look about. You go, too, Lavinia. Dr. Martin is an Oxford man. He had his turn at Eton. I think you'll find that the boys there are not the crude provincials you imagine."

Young Peyton looked at Adam. There was a little smile at the corners of his mouth. He said to Lavinia, "Come, Mama, I'd like to see the headmaster and the boys at King William's School." He turned to Peyton. "Can you come with us, Father?"

From the door Adam watched the three as they walked along the path to the school, the boy between his parents. Adam thought he had unusual sensitiveness and wisdom.

Before nightfall everything was arranged. The lad had said firmly, "I like the school. I want to stay. With your permission, Father," he added.

Lavinia wept. "You must come home to the plantation first, Peyton."

"I want to stay now, Mama. Why should I go to the plantation? Already these boys are ahead of me. Will you tell her that I'm to stay, Father?"

Peyton shook his head. "Your mother knows best, child."

The boy ran to Adam. He put his small hand in Adam's great one, clasping his fingers closely. "You'll persuade Mama, Cousin Adam. I like the master. I talked to Carroll

170

and Key and the Curtis boys. Some of them have been to school in England." He turned to his mother. "They're not country bumpkins. They are like the boys at Eton, and they play the same games. I want to stay."

"The boy's right, Lavinia," Adam said. "Why not try it until the summer? It's such a short time. If it does not please you then you can send for a tutor."

Lavinia turned her deep eyes on Adam. "You, too, Adam?"

"Why not, Lavinia?"

Young Peyton looked from one to the other. He walked slowly toward his father. "I'll do whatever you say, Father."

A look of pleasure came over Peyton's face. "What do you want to do, son?" he asked.

"I want to please you."

Peyton put his arm around the boy. "Then stay at King William's School, and I will come to see you often."

"Thank you, Father," he said slowly, struggling to hold his voice steady. "Thank you!"

Adam glanced at Lavinia. She was looking at the man and the boy, her straight, black brows drawn together. It came to Adam that Lavinia, at that moment, had lost control of her son. From now on it would not be Lavinia and her boy, it would be father and son. Somehow in his heart Adam knew that this was right.

Lavinia met her defeat gracefully. By the time they were ready to go it seemed to them all that it was her idea that young Peyton should be left at King William's School. Adam watched the good-bys from the coach that was to drive them to the wharves. Lavinia with her arms about the boy, kissing him, weeping; the lad comforting her; the smile he gave his father, full of love and reverence; Peyton, his hand on the boy's shoulder, bending for a last word, pride in his face; the boy's companions waiting for him to join the game; the lad waving good-by and turning to run to join his comrades before the coach was out of sight; Peyton comforting Lavinia . . .

Lavinia and Peyton came to stay at the house in Princess Street. It was Sara who suggested it. "It will be gay having them with us," she said to Adam. It was Sara, also, who asked Mary and William Warden for dinner the night after Adam and the others came down from Annapolis.

She told him at tea about her plans. "Mary is such an old friend, almost one of the family," she said. "And William is

Lavinia's counselor. I am sure that he will want to see her."

Adam made no comment. He accepted her arrangements as if he thought them natural. It was like Sara to do things this way, to reverse her attitude completely and make no explanations. After refusing to have Mary Warden at the plantation for a year, she spoke of her now as "almost one of the family."

Sara liked Lavinia. She wanted Mary Warden to see the beautiful gowns Lavinia had brought her from London. She imagined Mary would be envious—Mary who gave only the most cursory thought to clothes, who wore, without question, any gowns her London manteaumaker sent out to her.

Adam had no inkling of the thoughts that went through Sara's head. He laid the change to her improved health and to Lavinia's influence. For Lavinia was gay, and she brought gaiety with her. At times Adam knew that her laughter was forced. That was when she was unsure of Peyton. For she was too wise, too intuitive, not to know when he was straying. She was also too wise to let him know what she knew or suspected. She allowed him to think he was hiding his little adventures from her. It was easier that way. Better to avoid explanations and not put Peyton on the defensive.

Mary Warden knew what went on inside Lavinia's mind and heart. She wondered what the situation would be with Lady Caroline, now that Lavinia was home. Lavinia was more worldly than when she left the Province; she had more poise. And she was very lovely.

William brought up the subject of the Stamp Act. He asked Lavinia what the London people were saying about it and its effect on the Colonies. Lavinia's blue eyes opened wide with surprise.

"But the Stamp Act is repealed," she exclaimed. "Didn't you know? Haven't you heard about Pitt's great speech in defense of the Colonies?"

"We have heard nothing," William said.

Lavinia looked from one to the other. "And to think you know nothing about the exciting speech Pitt gave! Why, Adam, never if I live to be a thousand, can I forget the excitement of hearing his magnificent voice rolling through the great hall. He was fighting for us, and I was proud of being an American. For the first time, I knew what we stood for." She turned to William. "You know what it means, William, for you are one of the men who has had the courage to stand against the King and his unjust laws. But I didn't realize what it meant. In London I was having a good time dancing, gam-

172

ing and hunting; wasting my days and nights. I know better now." There was silence in the room. Lavinia put her hand in Peyton's. "I cried when Pitt spoke. I couldn't help it. Tears ran down my cheeks. I'm sure I looked a terrible sight, but I didn't care. Colonel Barre got seats for Patience Wright and myself in the ladies' gallery. I was crying when I came down. Colonel Barre had to wipe my cheeks with his handkerchief."

William said, "It's strange that the *Gazette* has not published this news."

"I believe there was a special messenger on the *Flamingo* with dispatches for the government," Lavinia said.

Mary turned to her husband. "Will this do away with all the quarreling and unrest?"

William Warden said decisively, "I am sure it will, Mary."

Adam spoke thoughtfully. "I wish I could agree with you, William, but I can't. There are other wrongs besides the Stamp Act, although it has held the center of attention."

Peyton laughed. "You haven't always been so gloomy, Adam. The King can't be so black as you and your friends paint him. He surely has no intention of draining the life blood out of the Colonies."

Mary glanced quickly at Peyton. He was the one who had changed. A few months ago he was damning the King and the military and all the government. She wondered, had Lady Caroline and her satellites something to do with his changed attitude?

Aloud she said, "I wish you could tell us more about the speech, Lavinia. What did Pitt say? How was the speech received?"

"With hurrahs and with jeers," Lavinia told them.

"I can't imagine William Pitt defending the Colonies," Sara's cool voice broke in. "He couldn't have been serious."

Lavinia turned. The color rose to her cheeks, but she held her voice steady. "Indeed he was serious. Sara, you should have seen him—his vivid face, his burning eyes, and his splendid voice! You've no idea how moving he can be. Did you know that he had been ill? Very, very ill? He got up from a sickbed to make the speech. People thought he might die on the floor of the House!"

William's smile was thin. "What an excitable little person you are, Lavinia! But we must use our brains about this matter. William Pitt is a politician, first of all. He defended us, but a defense of the Colonies could be an excuse to confound the government. Pitt is the opposition—and Pitt is always exigent."

Lavinia's blue eyes flashed. "William Warden! how can you say such cruel things? No one could talk as he talked and not mean it. Wait! I have the newspaper. I'll run and get it." She left the room hastily.

Sara took up her needlework. Her brittle voice broke the prolonged silence. "I can't think how a born aristocrat like Mr. Pitt could defend the low-class people of the Colonies. Still, if you think of it, the Stanhopes were always rather queer.

No one answered. In a few moments Lavinia came back into the room with a bundle of papers which she gave to Adam.

Sara said to Judith, "Bring more candles. Put them on the table so that Mr. Rutledge can see to read." The slave left her position behind her mistress' chair and, taking a great candelabrum from the spinet, placed it on a table at Adam's elbow.

The newspaper account, he saw, was more than a report. The words gave a picture of Pitt at his greatest, as he hurled the torrent of defense for the Colonies he had never seen. Adam's voice broke the silence.

"It was an exciting moment," Adam read from the paper. "The greatest orator of our time speaks on a matter of vital importance to the Colonies. What would Pitt say? How would the great statesman put forward his argument to break down the opposition against repealing the iniquitous Stamp Act? There are plenty of people, political opponents, who say that Pitt is a mountebank. If so, he is a great mountebank. He may not be the greatest debater in Parliament but he is the greatest orator. His words deal with great events, great characters and empires.

"Pitt rose from one of the front benches, and looked about him, alert, at ease, with a brilliant smile on his handsome face. Here were his enemies, political and personal; a few friends. But not many had the courage to be on the side of the Colonies. Pitt's figure is slender but commanding. It must be evident to any observer that he has at his command all the arts of dramatic action. In motion his body is the epitome of grace. His grey eyes seem black. He can put terror into his glance.

"Pitt has extraordinary powers of persuasion. I remember hearing Lord Cobden, his great opponent, say: 'Give Pitt a short quarter of an hour and he can persuade anyone of anything.'

"He bowed before the Speaker: 'Sir.' He turned to the

174

benches: 'Gentlemen.' He launched his opening sentence: 'I have been charged with giving birth to sedition in America . . .' The House settled back. Pitt was in form. He would carry the war directly into the camp of the enemy. He would spike their guns and drive his weapons straight into the heart of the government.

" 'The men of our Colonies have spoken their sentiments freely against this unhappy Act, and that freedom you term a crime. Sorry I am to hear liberty of speech in this house imputed a crime . . . The gentleman tells us America is obstinate; America is almost in open rebellion.

" 'I rejoice that America has resisted. I have said that before. I repeat: Three millions of freemen, so dead to all the feelings of liberty, as voluntarily to submit to be slaves, would be fit instruments to make slaves of the rest.'

"Pitt paused, his long fingers busy with the dangling seals of his black ribbon fob. His head was thrown back. No veiled sarcasm, now. Open irony.

" 'I come not here armed at all points, with law cases and Acts of Parliament, with the Statute Book doubled down in dogs' ears to defend the cause of liberty. If I had, I myself would have cited the two cases of Chester and Durham. I would have cited them to show that, even under former arbitrary reigns, Parliaments were ashamed to tax a people without their consent and not to allow them representatives . . . The gentleman tells us of many who are taxed, and are not represented—the India Company, merchants, stockholders, manufacturers. Many of these are represented in other capacities. They are all inhabitants, and as such are they not virtually represented? Many have it in their option to be actually represented. They have connection with those who elect, and they have influence over them.'

"Pitt's voice was level, calm with a note of insinuation running through the calm. The ministerial bench was alarmed. When would the thunderbolt fall? What lightning shaft would bring into the full glare of light some hidden secret diplomacy, some secret treaty? They knew Pitt's solemn opening, his calm demeanor, was only momentary. He was reaching out to his audience, gathering it close. The vibrant voice rose and fell, it sank to a whisper, full of menace.

" 'The gentleman boasts of his bounties to America. Are not these bounties intended finally for the benefit of this kingdom? I am no courtier of America. I stand for this kingdom. I admit that Parliament has the right to bind, to restrain America. But legislative power over the Colonies is sovereign

175

and supreme. I would advise every gentleman to sell his lands, if he can, and embark for that country. When two countries are connected together, like England and the Colonies, without being incorporated, one must necessarily govern. The greater must rule the lesser.'

"Pitt wheeled suddenly, pointing his finger at the leader of the opposition, seated on a front bench.

" 'The gentleman asks, When were the Colonies emancipated? I desire to know when they were made slaves.' . . .

"There was a long silence. But no voice answered. Pitt, the defender, dropped back to a conversational tone.

" 'When I had the honor of serving his Majesty, I availed myself of the means of information which I derived from my office. I speak, therefore, from knowledge. I will be so bold as to affirm that the profits to Great Britain from trade with the Colonies, in all its branches, is two millions a year.

" 'This is the fund that carried you triumphantly through the last war . . . this is the price America pays for her protection . . . You have prohibited where you ought to have encouraged, and encouraged where you ought to have prohibited. . . .

" 'A great deal has been said without doors of the power, of the strength, of America . . . In a good cause, on a sound bottom, the force of this country can crush America to atoms . . . But on this ground, on the Stamp Act . . . when so many here will think it a crying injustice, I am one who will lift my hands against it!

" 'Is this your boasted peace? Not to sheathe the sword in its scabbard, but to sheathe it in the bowels of your countrymen?'

"He sat down. The House was silent. Then the tension snapped. The applause broke. I had the feeling that I had heard history made at that moment."

Adam put the paper down. Something of the fire of the great orator carried over into the quiet drawing room. No one spoke for a moment.

Then Lavinia said, "The Act was repealed the eighteenth of March. Pitt's speech was the turning point, although his enemies said it was because the merchants of London had brought great pressure on the government. London rejoiced for a month. Suddenly, we had many friends!" Lavinia laughed. "Fair weather friends."

William carried the paper to the table where the light was stronger and began to read the article. Adam glanced at Mary. She was very still, her hands folded. He saw her eyes were wet—she was deeply moved. He looked beyond Mary to Sara. She was holding her tapestry at arms' length, matching a bit of wool.

Peyton's face was unusually grave.

He said to Adam, "I don't understand. Lady Caroline told the Governor that Pitt had retired to the countryside—his health completely broken."

Lavinia turned slowly, a strange smile on her lips. "Lady Caroline? I seem to have heard of such a person quite frequently since I came back. Is she a woman of consequence?" Lavinia did not wait for an answer. "But she has been away from England for some time, has she not? I fear that her information is not recent."

There was an undercurrent of tension at Lavinia's words. Sara looked up and Mary gave Lavinia a quick glance. Peyton frowned as he moved away toward the fireplace. But Lavinia was calm.

"Lady Caroline seems to know everyone in Court circles, Lavinia. They say she is high-born," Mary said in an even voice. Adam looked at Mary. He noticed that when she spoke in that tone she was after information.

Lavinia straightened the ruffles on her bodice. "I am curious to see this Lady Caroline," she said smoothly. "Perhaps you will take me to call on her, Mary?"

Peyton interrupted. "I'm afraid you will have to defer your visit for a time, Lavinia. Lady Caroline plans to leave for Charlotte Amalie on the next Jamaica packet."

For a moment there was silence in the room.

Then Mary said. "It is just as well, Lavinia. I am not on calling terms with Lady Caroline these days. I'm an avowed Whig and she is a Royalist. She has made it plain lately that she doesn't want Whigs at Guernsey House."

Adam knew this was not altogether true. Lady Caroline had written him several letters asking him to come to see her. He had not gone. In the back of his mind he had reservations about her. Perhaps he did not mean to allow her to add him to her list of victims. For, in spite of his reservations, the woman had a subtle fascination that he knew would be hard for him to resist.

As Adam opened the door for William and Mary to leave, Marcy was just entering the hall. He was breathing heavily from running.

"What is it?"

"Pirates," Marcy said. "We just got news from the captain of a shallop that escaped them off the Capes!"

Adam thought fast. His ship, the *Golden Orchid,* would be in that vicinity.

Marcy answered his unspoken question: "The *Golden Orchid* was boarded, the cargo taken, and the crew made prisoners."

"What of the ship?"

"Burned," Marcy said, "burned to the waterline after it had been raked with gunfire."

Adam was silent. This was a blow. Beside the valuable cargo, the *Golden Orchid* carried five thousand pounds in cash to pay his account with Kreuger Brothers at Charlotte Amalie.

"Adam," Sara said when he returned to the drawing room, "Why do you look like that? The captain and the crew are safe, aren't they? Just prisoners."

"Yes, I know . . . just prisoners."

The following day the people knew that the Stamp Act had been repealed. The steady resistance of all the Colonies had had its effect, not only in influencing the repeal, but in uniting the Colonies.

Bonfires were built in the square. Speeches were made, church bells rung, the Royal salute of twenty-one guns was fired; patriotic citizens opened pipes of Madeira in front of their houses and invited everyone to drink. The Sons of Liberty held their celebration in the square where they had forced the Stamp Master to resign not so long before, and where they had burned George III in effigy. All that was forgotten now. Tonight another toast was drunk.

"To his most Gracious Majesty, George III, Mr. Pitt and Liberty!"

A new element entered into the controversy. Great Britain had made new conquests in the Far East. Delhi had fallen; Bengal, Orissa and the Circaras were under her protection. Indian merchantmen were sailing around the Cape of Good Hope with full cargoes, spilling the riches of India into the lap of Great Britain. The question of the disposal of these cargoes troubled the East India Company, Parliament and the Ministers. "Perhaps the American Colonies would buy the cargoes of Indian merchandise and pay a liberal duty for the privilege!"

The Ministers planned for the future: "Give them a little time to forget the Stamp Act, then impose a new duty that will fill the treasury to overflowing—a tax on tea."

178

BOOK
TWO

Chapter 13

BORN
IN FREEDOM

ADAM's work in Wilmington was over but he was asked by Caswell to go to Charles Town on a secret mission. This meant that he would not return to the plantation until too late for spring planting. The task of moving the household from Wilmington fell upon Marcy. Lavinia and Peyton and the Wardens were going north at the same time, so the journey would not be too hard for Sara. Adam was seriously disturbed now about Peyton. He had seen little of him all winter and less since Lavinia's return, although they had stayed on with Sara and Adam in Princess Street. When he did see him, Peyton avoided any serious conversation. The few times they had dined together he was always in haste to go on somewhere—to a ball or for cards. Lavinia was not happy. Although she tried to be gay, Adam saw it was an effort. One thing pleased him—Lady Caroline was out of the way for the time. She had gone back to the West Indies.

The trouble with Peyton was that he was always the hunter. Some other woman could so easily interest him and engage his errant fancy. "Affairs of the moment," he called them. Adam knew that, for all of Lavinia's apparent worldliness, these wandering adventures made her unhappy. Once she had said to him, "You think I stayed in England because of the boy. That was not the only reason, Adam. When I am here, I die a thousand deaths. You see, I love Peyton." Adam had no answer for that. He could not even speak to Peyton. Since the time he had taken the slave girl he had been in no position to act as mentor to his cousin, even if he had the inclination.

In Charles Town Adam found the leaders were not so sanguine as the people of North Carolina. They did not think that the repeal of the Stamp Act would settle all differences. Word had come from Mr. Laurens, who was in London, that the King flew into a rage when he heard Parliament had repealed the Act against his wishes. He vowed he would lay a new tax that would strike every colonist.

His mission finished, Adam sailed for Edenton on one of Joseph Hewes's vessels. Marcy met him at the wharf and went with him to Durant's yard where Adam left an order for a new ship to take the place of the *Golden Orchid*. This vessel would be twice the size and tonnage, and carry more spread of canvas. In addition there would be mountings and swivels for four cannon. He had no intention of allowing pirates to take another vessel for want of speed or defense. He and Marcy then went to King's Arms for breakfast. While they ate ham and hominy and one of Hurd's omelettes, Marcy gave him news of the plantation. It was none too good. They had lost hogs and cattle by cholera; heavy rains and high water had torn out the dam on the Blue Creek; and the rice beds had been flooded, carrying away the young plants.

"I wish I could have brought better news, Mr. Rutledge," Marcy said. "Added to the loss of the ship, it makes us on the wrong side of the ledger this season."

Adam nodded without speaking. It was always so. The plantation without him was always ill-fortuned. Some force seemed to work against him, to his detriment. Careless as he was of money, he wanted the plantation to carry itself and furnish him the means to go farther into untilled lands. But when he was away from the land, things happened to hold him back. It was as if the land said, "It is your fight to conquer me, yours alone."

Back at the wharves Adam commented on the new store. "It seems to be thriving," he said to Marcy.

"Yes, this Levantine—he calls himself Nicholas—carries a vast stock of merchandise, from silks to jewels, and from cutlery and plate to firearms. The ladies are quite delighted," Marcy told him.

Adam laughed. "And the husbands pay the accounts! We must look into this one day soon."

The sailboat was tied up at Hewes's dock. Marcy got in while Adam was talking to two men who had hailed him. When he got rid of them, he stepped into the boat and Marcy shoved off. There was a good breeze. Adam sat in the stern and took the tiller. When they were well out into the Sound on their way to the Island, Marcy said, "I wouldn't trust that Levantine so far as I could throw a horse, nor his two helpers. They look proper cutthroats to me, for all their smooth oily ways."

Adam listened to what Marcy had to say without much interest. Years later he had reason to wish that he had followed Marcy's hint and made some investigation, but then it was too late. Now his mind was on something else, something to do with his tax-free land. He had slowly come to a realization that he could no longer hold his land free. On every side of him men were struggling and working and paying. He could no longer face the fact that he was evading rightful responsibilities. He must find some way to get the money.

Sara was sitting on the gallery near the East Garden. He paused for a moment to watch her. At her feet was Rowan playing with three small puppies. Sara was laughing at their antics. He moved forward slowly not to startle her. But Red Rowan caught scent of him and uttered sharp, excited barks. Sara's hand went to her heart and remained there.

"Adam, how you frightened me!" she whispered.

"I'm sorry, Sara. I thought I'd surprise you!"

Sara lifted her cheek for him to kiss. "I'm not sure I like surprises, Adam. One's nerves suffer, even from small shocks."

Again she had succeeded in making him feel selfish, thoughtless of her well-being. Then he saw Lavinia coming across the garden. She wore a white muslin gown without hoops, and a wide white sun hat with blue ribbons. Her arms were full of apple blossoms and dogwood. When she saw Adam, she dropped the flowers and ran swiftly across the lawn.

"Adam, Adam, what a delightful surprise!" She threw her arms about his neck, kissing his cheek. "Sara, why didn't you tell me Adam was coming? It's too wonderful having you home." She flung her hat on the grass, and sank down on the steps. "Sit down and tell us everything. All the Charles Town gossip. Did you see Esther Pinckney and the Laurens?"

"I have a gift for you from Esther. Some woman's folderol. Mr. Laurens is in England, but John was at home."

"As handsome as ever?"

Adam laughed. "The girls seem to think so. I never saw a man so much in demand. But he is quite indifferent. He is interested only in politics and the affairs of the Colonies. He vows there will be war."

"John Laurens?" Lavinia said, horrified. "Why, John is only a child."

"A tall child who thinks quite like a man, Lavinia. There is something nowadays that makes boys turn suddenly to man's estate."

"Don't speak of it," Lavinia said, putting her hand over his mouth. "You shall not speak of war. I'll not let you."

Sara looked up from her tapestry.

"You are foolish, Lavinia; there will be no war. A few crude discontented farmers, that's all. It is laughable, their thinking they can stand up to the King's soldiers. I've had letters from my father in London. It is the gayest season in years. Nobody takes this little rebellion seriously."

"That's strange," Lavinia said. "I hear quite the contrary from Patience Wright. She says the King is worried, but stubborn."

Sara drew her lips to a thin line. "Oh, if you take her word —I can't imagine an *artist* knowing anything about the Court."

Lavinia's face flushed. She was annoyed by Sara's air of superiority. "Patience may be just an artist, but his Majesty comes to her studio every week—yes, and Mr. Franklin, too, and other men of note."

Adam looked from one to the other. He disliked senseless argument and spoke rather sharply. "It doesn't really make any difference what they think or say in England, Sara. It is what we do here that really counts."

Sara picked up her work. Her jaw was set, her lips tight.

Lavinia's gaiety was gone. She got up. "I must be going before the sun gets low and Peyton gets home," she said and bade Sara good-by.

Sara said, "Good-by, Lavinia," without looking up from her tapestry.

Adam walked to the landing where Lavinia's coach was waiting. She spoke of young Peyton, his good marks and his high spirits. "He likes the school so much. I'm glad I brought him over here. I've never thanked you properly, Adam, but you were a dear to write for me to come home. This is where I should be, even though it breaks my heart."

She got into the coach. Adam could not ask her questions with the servants near. He stood watching her as the coach drove onto the ferry, a vague fear in his heart.

Adam put Sara on the bed and covered her with a silk quilt. Through the open window came the cheerful chirping of crickets, the fragrance of clove pinks and jasmine. Sara lay with her eyes closed.

"Get Judith," she whispered. "I can't think where she is."

"I'll call Azizi," he heard himself saying.

Sara opened her eyes and looked at him. "The girl is no

184

longer here. Please close the window, Adam. I don't like the sound of crickets at night, it is too lonely."

"Where is the girl?" Adam asked—casually, he hoped.

Sara looked away. "I sent her to the mainland when Lily came back. I could not have the girl around. She was big with child. Didn't you notice her in Wilmington?"

"With child?" The words were torn from him.

"She was growing ugly. She moved so heavily I could not bear to look at her."

With child . . . Azizi was with child . . . his blood turned to ice in his veins. Cold sweat broke out on his forehead. He wiped it away quickly. Sara was looking at him strangely.

"I don't know who the father is," she was saying. "Not one of the slaves—they are all afraid of her. Perhaps one of the overlookers, or a soldier. We had some soldiers quartered here late last summer, don't you remember?"

Adam remembered many things. What was she saying? Words to torture him—every word was a red-hot iron burning into him.

"At first I suspected Marcy, but it's the daft woman Lucy who interests him. Who do you think it could be, Adam?"

Adam thought, "Will she never be done? Will the cool tinkling voice never stop?" He could not answer. His lips were stiff, his throat dry. Sara went on talking.

"I think it silly of Marcy. He can do better for himself than marry that woman Lucy. He told me once that she seemed to grow quiet when he was near her. That's no reason to marry. Imagine his wanting to saddle himself with a daft woman and a child . . ." Her soft voice trailed off. "Do you think one of those rough mountain men—the soldiers, I mean—might be accountable for Azizi's condition? She wouldn't tell me. She is very sullen, Adam, and I have been so kind to her."

"Where is she now?" His voice was harsh.

"I don't know. Judith took her away. I think she is at the North Plantation."

The black woman came in carrying some steaming liquid in a silver jug.

Adam said: "Put that down and come into the hall. I want to talk with you."

The black woman gave him a malignant glance but she followed him into the hall.

"Where did you send Azizi?" he asked.

The woman hesitated. Adam took a step forward. The

woman shrank back against the wall as if she thought he was going to strike her.

"I sent she to North Plantation to have she baby. Mis' Sara she say treat her like we treat Lily. She wants overlooker to sell the baby when hit come."

For a moment Adam did not speak, trying to control his anger. Then he said quietly, "You will do nothing about Azizi—now or in the future."

The woman's eyes met his for a moment, then shifted, but not before he saw the fear that had been there give way to a sly look of understanding. Suppose she did know—what of it? He didn't care now.

For an hour Adam walked up and down the paths of the East Garden. Thoughts raced through his mind with panoramic clarity, scenes in which the slave girl was the dominant figure. He thought of the first time he had laid eyes on her when LaTruchy's ship had sailed up the Sound; his reluctance to buy the girl; the Frenchman's leering smile when he spoke of the slave markets of Zanzibar and of women trained to dance the Duc-Duc. He should have been warned then. What a fool he had been! It was not the moral side that bothered him now, but his own lack of control and the attitude of the girl. Her first resentment had never given way. He did not want to acknowledge even to himself how completely she possessed him. The months had not changed his feelings for her or his desire. He could not put her out of his secret thoughts. Well, he would stop trying.

The night air was soft. The garden flowers sent off mingled perfumes into the warm darkness. Summer was coming on, the feeling of warmth, of earth and sun that led to autumn harvest. Adam came to the dark pool. As often before, the picture of the crescent body of the slave girl intruded itself in his mind. In the morning he would go to the North Plantation . . . he would go now, tonight. He went rapidly toward the house, walking in the dark like a man whose path was plainly visible.

He met a slave from the North Plantation when he got off the ferry on the mainland side. The man had a note from Owen Tewilliger. Adam read it by the light of a torch held by the ferryman.

"Dear Adam:
"It is near her time and the slave girl asks for you. Will you come?"

He drove his spurs into the horse's flanks. A dozen miles to travel. What if he were too late? What if she were to die before he saw her again? He must speak to her. What did it matter . . . master or slave . . . what did it matter to him now? Why had she not told him that she was to have a child? But if she had spoken, what could he have done? Was that what she had meant when she quoted the Arab proverb that time in his room? How stupid he had been! Suddenly poignant pity for Sara swept through his mind. Sara. She must not know. He must keep this from her. It would hurt her too much to know that another woman had borne his child.

A light rain had begun to fall, drenching the hedgerows of hawthorn that lined the drive to the North Plantation. Adam tossed the reins to a pickaninny and went up the steps two at a time. He strode across the hall into the library where Owen sat reading.

"How is she?" he asked quickly, without preamble.

Owen looked up from his book, his short-sighted eyes focusing on the tall figure blocking the doorway. "That you, Adam? Everything is all right. Gwennie is there and the Doctor."

"You reached Armitage? Thank you, Owen," Adam said. "I will go to her now."

"Wait, Adam, wait a moment. The Doctor will be in presently." Owen's eyes ran up and down the impatient man standing at the door. "I'll call a pickaninny to clean your boots. And your cloak—isn't it wet?"

Adam threw the coat on a chair. "Tell me, Owen, she is not . . . she is . . . ?" He could not say the words.

Owen smiled a little. "This is a natural event, Adam. But she asked to see you before the child came. I told Armitage, so he understands. You will find the girl's English much improved. She has worked hard—reading, studying the language—since she has been at North Plantation."

Gwennie came into the room. She curtsied to Adam, her face calm. Behind her was Armitage.

"I'll see the girl now," Adam said. He spoke harshly in his endeavor not to betray himself. The Doctor raised his eyebrows a little, but nodded affirmation.

"Come along, Adam. This way—there's no hurry."

Adam followed him down the long corridor to the north wing of the house. A strange uneasiness came over him, yet his mind was calm, clear, taking in impressions of his surroundings. He noticed a rain-soaked spot above a window, making a stain on the landscape paper he had brought from

France two years before. At the door, Armitage detained him.

"The woman is resting quietly for the moment, Adam. She has had some pain, but she'll have more before the end."

"The end . . ." Adam whispered.

Armitage looked at him inquiringly. "Before the child is born, I mean. But she wants to speak to you. Her mind is uneasy about something. I don't want her troubled now. Go in—I will tell you when to leave."

Adam advanced into the dim room, lighted by the reflection of a small fire on the hearth and two candles that stood on a table near the bed. The girl lay in the great mahogany bed.

Adam moved quickly across the room, and stood looking down at her dark eyes. She had sent for him, called him to her, but her eyes had the same look of scorn in their depths. Was there no difference in her feeling toward him?

The counterpane was pulled to her chin. Her small face was drawn, her eyes shadowed deeply. He dropped on his knees beside the bed.

"Azizi," he whispered. "Azizi."

"Call Fatima," she said weakly.

The old woman came from the shadows with a box. Adam recognized the box as the one he had held in his hands the day he had gone to her cottage.

Azizi reached out her hand. In the flickering light of the candles, it was transparent, almost like alabaster. She said a word in her own tongue to the old woman. Fatima set the box on the table by the bed, turning over the bangles and bright colored beads.

She was searching for something—a square of silk the size of a small handkerchief. She untied the double knots with her gnarled clawlike hand and spread the contents before him. Adam leaned forward—the pearls he had seen in her cabin lay on the dark cloth, catching the soft reflection of the candlelight.

He turned toward the bed. Azizi had lifted herself to her elbow, and was looking at him anxiously.

"They are my inheritance," she said slowly, searching for words. "They come from Bahrein. My father gave them to me for my protection when I made the Pilgrimage . . . Fatima hid them, so they were not found."

She reached for the pearls, and laid them in his hand. "They are for you," she whispered, her voice flat, without warmth or vibration.

188

"For me?" Adam asked. "Why do you give me your pearls? They are yours."

"I want to buy freedom," she whispered. "Write the papers that make me free. Go quickly, my lord." She closed his fingers over the pearls and sank back on the pillow.

"Go? Where?" Adam did not grasp her meaning. The girl closed her eyes wearily.

Armitage came into the room. He put his fingers on her wrist, feeling for her pulse.

"Please, master, make me free, make me free."

Adam put the pearls carefully into the box. A look of defeat, of utter weariness, came over the girl's face. Her eyes seemed to sink into her head.

"Do you want so much to be free, Azizi?" Adam asked.

She nodded. "The papers, quick!"

Armitage looked at the pearls, then at Adam, but he said nothing. He moved to the fire, and stood with his back to the blaze, his hands under the tails of his long coat.

Adam leaned down. "You are already free, Azizi. You have been ever since—ever since the night of the storm. The papers are at the Manor House on the Island."

The girl's voice changed. It was warm, vibrant. "Free, master? I'm free?" She closed her eyes. Tears flowed from them. He leaned over, searching under the coverlet for her thin hand.

"Do you hate me so much, Azizi, that you want to buy your freedom with these pearls—your father's gift to you?"

She opened her eyes slowly. "It is not for myself, my lord. It is for him . . . your son."

"My son?"

"He must be born free—not the child of a slave. It is for him that I wish freedom. My father's children must be free not slaves."

Adam was shaken by her words. He knelt beside the bed. These were the thoughts of a slave girl, her deep thoughts unspoken through long months of waiting, asking nothing but that her child should be born free.

She turned restlessly. In the dim light her skin was ivory white. Her eyes were closed, her face contorted. What if she were dying?

Adam spoke sharply, in quick alarm. "Armitage. Quick."

The Doctor moved deliberately to the bed.

"Another pain coming on. You had better go outside now," he said. "Steady, Adam, steady! Don't lose your head.

There's nothing alarming in a woman having a child. Get on out of here. We don't need you."

Azizi moaned once. Her face was drawn, her body moved convulsively. Adam caught her hand. Her fingers closed over his, clinging to him.

"If she would scream, it would help her," the Doctor muttered. "Go outside, Adam, I tell you. You're no good here. The old woman and I will take care of this."

Adam paced the hall for what seemed to him hours. Then he went to the gallery and out into the garden. It was raining, a slow, misty rain. Up and down the garden near her window he strode, waiting . . . waiting. A son—what if it should be a son?

Toward morning he could stand the strain no longer. He went into the room again. The girl's face was distorted. Tears streamed down her cheeks. She was clutching the hand of the old woman.

The Doctor's back was toward the door. He had taken off his coat and rolled his sleeves above his elbows. He was bending over a table. Adam caught the glint of steel.

Dr. Armitage noticed Adam. "Go outside. Everything is all right," he said crossly.

Adam did not answer. He went quickly across the room to the bed. Pushing the old woman aside, he took Azizi's hands in his. She opened her eyes for a moment; again her fingers tightened on his. Then she lay as still as death. He noticed nothing but her waxen face. Blue veins stood out on her temples; under her eyes were deep purple shadows.

Armitage touched his shoulder. Adam rose and stumbled from the room.

After a time, Gwennie found him in the garden. Her round face was wreathed in smiles. "A boy, Squire! A grand wee lad."

Adam hurried to the room. When he came to the bed, Azizi opened her heavy eyelids slowly. "Lord, I have borne a man-child for the delight of your youth and the comfort of your old age," she whispered. He knew that she was repeating age-old words, symbolic of some ancient way of living.

"Come, Adam. The woman must rest, the woman must rest," Armitage said testily. "Do I have to drive you out?"

But Adam did not hear. There was no hatred for him who had been master of her body without her will, no hatred in her voice when she whispered the words, "Lord, I have borne you a man-child. David, son of Adam. . . ."

He walked blindly from the room and went to the library.

Owen looked at him, then went to a cupboard and got a decanter.

"Better take a drink, Adam," he said kindly.

Adam shook his head. "No. I must get back to the Island. Armitage says that everything is as it should be with Azizi and the child. I'll come back."

"But you haven't had a wink of sleep all night!"

Adam shook his head impatiently. A new thought had entered his mind. "I do not know who she is or which of the Arabian lands she comes from. Yet she bears me a son. . . . Does that seem strange to you, Owen?"

"Strange, aye, very strange. Have you no wish to know?"

Adam shook his head slowly. "She will tell me some day."

Owen looked at him a moment. "John Hawks speaks a language native to them both, although she comes of the East and he of the Far West, of the Moorish countries," he suggested.

"I'll not ask John Hawks," Adam said. "She must tell me herself."

"Choose your own way, Adam."

"There is nothing I can do about it," Adam burst out. "It is intolerable, but I can do nothing."

The exultation he had felt when he first held his son in his arms had passed. A dull anger possessed him. He was bound, held in a vise—pushed away from the thing he wanted. First the land, now the woman who had given him the son he had so long desired. What was happening to him? Was he caught in a torrent? Was he being swept out beyond his will to some unknown destruction?

After a long silence, he said, "Owen, I want you and Gwennie to take care of Azizi and the boy. They must stay here with you until I'm able to make plans."

"Azizi is welcome here; already she is soft around Gwennie's heart. Now, with the child to care for, my woman will be happy."

Adam took his riding coat off the chair back and went outside to the long veranda. Herk was holding Saladin's reins while the horse nibbled the young tender grass. Before mounting he stood for a moment looking over the broad sweep of fields and trees down to the Sound. Turning toward the cleared rolling lands, he said slowly to Owen, who had followed him out, "It is good to see the plowed fields . . . to see the first grain sprouting, the fields lying fallow, waiting. It is all good because it is the natural cycle of life and the promise of the future."

191

Owen looked up at the powerful man now seated on the powerful horse. He was thinking, "He is young to have lived so fast. Young to have reached out for unknown horizons. They are all young, these men of the Province, too young to be swept with the torrent into a raging sea of revolution. Too young, too ardent, too filled with life . . ." But he knew it was inevitable.

Adam looked at Owen. How thin he was, how worn. "You are overtired, Owen. Why don't you rest? Go over to England or to the Indies on one of my ships."

Owen shook his head. "I think there'll be no rest for any of us these coming days, Adam."

Adam did not answer. He did not want to think of what might come. The present was enough. He rode down the lane between the hawthorn hedges. The rain had stopped. He glanced over his shoulder toward the wing of the house covered by scarlet trumpet and star jasmine, his thoughts on the woman and her child.

A rush of sharp wind against his face gave him an outward sense of cleanness. Memories of the dark mystery of the night held him in a void of self-detachment. A sense of exhaustion came over him, not of the body, but of his inner self. The wind on his face was good. It went deep into his lungs with each sharp intaken breath, rushing like a clear cold flame. He closed his eyes, conscious only of the swift motion of the galloping horse. Why should he fight against the torrent?

He recalled a conversation with Hawks. "The movement of a man's destiny has no beginning and no end," the Moor had said. The sweep of his destiny was unimpaired by outward things. An inner force drove a man forward. He must not seek. He must close his mind against the force that held him. The task at hand would take all he had to give. Perhaps that was the way his destiny worked. What was it the Moor Hawks had said to him? "A star never rises or falls save at its own hour." That was a belief of Azizi and her people—a good thought.

It was borne upon his consciousness that he was moving forward swiftly, away from old moorings, breaking through into new living. A momentary terror seized him. What was to happen to him if he were torn away from his work on the land? Driven away from the soil and the cultivation of the earth? Would he be following St. Elmo's fires . . . to no end?

He brushed aside the dark thoughts. They had no relation to the Adam Rutledge he must be. He would make a more determined effort, he told himself. And then because of his great need for someone who understood he rode straight to Mary Warden in Edenton.

He found Mary in her garden cutting roses. She wore a soft green cotton dress and a hat with a brim that shaded her face. Her eyes were very deep and gentle when she looked at him. Whatever she thought, she would listen. They sat down on the garden bench. Stumbling through the beginning, unable to speak without showing emotion, Adam told her the story. Mary listened. She was quiet, so quiet it seemed to Adam she did not breathe. Once he lifted his head and looked at her. She was gazing toward Edenton where the spire of St. Paul's rose above the green trees. How still she was, how very still. Her face was without expression. She made no move toward him; she did not touch his hand, nor did her eyes meet his. Yet he knew she was his friend. He knew his life in some vague way rested with hers. It seemed to him for the moment that he was looking ahead, outside of themselves. What had Mary to do with his life? It was only a flashing thought. Then his mind went back to Azizi and the child.

Mary's voice was steady when she spoke. "Does Sara know?"

"I don't think so."

"Will you tell her?"

"I don't know, Mary. I can't decide. That is why I have come to you."

"No one can show you the way, Adam. You must find it for yourself," she answered. She spoke dispassionately. She was turning from him. He could not have that. He could not lose her friendship.

He said, taking her hand, "What you think means a great deal to me."

She turned her eyes to him. The clear look of friendship was gone. She did not answer.

"I think Sara knows," she said after a moment.

He was disquieted. He had not thought of this contingency. Sara was so remote—so uninterested in what went on about her.

"What makes you think she knows?"

Mary smiled a quiet enigmatic smile. This was a Mary he did not know—so withdrawn, so judicial. He got up.

"I'm sorry. I should not have troubled you, Mary."

She stopped him with a gesture. "Please sit down. I want to help you, Adam. I'm trying to think of the right way.

There is nothing to be done about the girl or the baby now. Gwennie will see to them. When must you go back to Wilmington?"

"In a few days—Thursday or Friday at the latest."

"Then let things take their course. Say nothing to Sara for the present. I think she knows already, but I may be wrong."

"Thank you, Mary."

She reached out her hand. The uneasy thoughts and worries seemed to pass away with her touch. Mary watched him ride down the magnolia-lined driveway. She wondered how Adam could be so blind as to think Sara did not know. Sara knew everything that happened on the plantation, through that black woman of hers. Yes, and everything that went on in Edenton, too.

Adam rode homeward, a feeling of peace in his heart. He remembered other times he had gone to Mary when he was troubled or worried. She was always able to make things clear and give him peace. Those were her attributes. She reached past externals and touched his soul, leaving him at ease and with some of her quietness in his heart.

In the late afternoon, Marcy came to the counting room with a sheaf of papers in his hand. Two slaves followed, carrying ledgers and accounting books. Adam made a grimace when he saw the books. Marcy shrugged his shoulders.

"I'm sorry, Mr. Rutledge, but Mr. Hewes's vessel sails Wednesday. You said you wanted to check the invoices. We have a heavy cargo this trip."

Adam took off his coat and called to Cicero to bring him his dressing gown.

"Sit down, Marcy. I suppose we will have time to finish before supper."

He picked up a list. "Tar and pitch pine, lumber and short boards, turpentine, a few sheep, twenty sows and a dozen boars," Marcy read aloud. Adam checked.

Suddenly Adam said, "Does Matthew Caswell still want the land against that parcel Spruill owns, Marcy?"

"Yes, sir! I'm sure he does, or at least he said he wanted it when I saw him last week. I told him I didn't think you would sell. He wants Addison's Island, also. He's determined to buy it. I told him you had promised the Island to Parson Earl for his flax experiment."

"So I have, but we can sell him Briffet's Island. It's just as good land and it's an acre or two larger. Or the parcel of woodland near the swamp. Drive as good a bargain as you can, Marcy. I want cash or no sale."

The Irishman opened his eyes in surprise. "But—"

"I know. I said I wouldn't sell, but I've changed my mind. There's something else for you to do. I want you to figure up what the taxes on this plantation come to. Use the money you get from the land sale to pay back taxes on Rutledge Riding."

Marcy did not answer for a moment. A look of understanding and admiration came over his rugged features. "It will take a large sum, Mr. Rutledge."

"No matter. We must pay. I'm not going to have the small farmers bent double to pay taxes while I get off free. But we must have cash."

"I'll get cash, no fear, Mr. Rutledge. Old Matthew has plenty," Marcy answered. "I'll have it next week."

Adam said, "It might do no harm to tell Matthew that Meredith Chapman has been after the land and stands ready to buy, but since he asked first, he has first choice. You may get the price up. If he doesn't want it, sell to Chapman, but sell right away. I want this whole thing cleared up."

"I will sail over to see Caswell tomorrow." Marcy folded up the lists.

Adam got up. At the door he paused. "Armitage tells me that you think Lucy is improving."

"Yes, I'm sure that she knows the boy, and I think she knows me, sometimes."

"My wife tells me you are thinking of marrying Lucy."

"Yes. I intended to speak to you about it before now."

Adam stood silent a moment. "She will always be an invalid, Marcy. Have you thought of that?"

Marcy got down from his stool and walked across the room. He started to speak, but the words did not come readily. A slow flush crept over his cheeks from his neck to his forehead. His voice wasn't quite steady when he answered.

"It is not the body of the woman I want, Mr. Rutledge. There are plenty of women to be had in the village. She seems to lean on me. If I can help her, if I can bring the light of reason to her eyes . . ." He stopped, unable to go on.

Adam looked out the window to the garden, his long fingers busy with the seals on his fob. "You are a man of honor, Marcy," he said after a pause, "but a wife who is not a wife can bring sadness beyond your realization. But have it your own way. The child is fine and healthy and will want a man's care as he grows up. For Lucy's marriage portion I'll give her the land beyond the wood lot, fronting on the river—one hundred acres."

He turned quickly and left the room before Marcy could speak. He didn't want his thanks, or to hear his expressions of gratitude.

Once in his library, he lost his air of casual assurance. He sat down heavily, his head resting on his hands. His mind was on the order he had given Marcy, to sell his land to Matthew Caswell. Old Matthew would snap at it as a terrapin snatches at mangrove root. Acres and acres of land would then pass from his hands. A thought that had been in his mind often of late came to him now. Land got so easily, would go easily. He would not be able to hold it. If he lost his land, what would he have to leave to his new born son?

Chapter 14

THE
REGULATORS

THE Stamp Act repealed, the people of the eastern littoral of the Province fell back into their accustomed easy living, lulled into mistaken security by the assurance that no future extraordinary taxes would be laid on the Colonies by Parliament. The majority of the people of the Albemarle district were satisfied. They had no wish to rebel against the Crown or to make a serious break with the Mother Country. The immediate danger was past.

They did not take the newly organized Regulators seriously: "Country yokels" for the most part, men who could neither read nor write. Who were they to set themselves up to regulate laws made by their betters?

Adam Rutledge did not share this view. He had made too many journeys through the disaffected areas not to know the temper of the farmers, the men who now called themselves Regulators. He knew them to be honest, sturdy folk; yeomen and husbandmen, and indentured men who had served out their bonds and taken up the fifty acres allowed by the Crown. The Stamp Act was only one of a long list of grievances and wrongs imposed by the Hanoverian Parliament. The organization of the Sons of Liberty had not been the act of the farmers, but of the merchants and professional men of the coast whose trade was shattered by the heavy taxes imposed by the Stamp Act. The wrongs of the farmers lay deeper. Their very existence was involved. The ownership of the land they had cleared and planted was endangered by taxes, by the dishonesty of collectors and by the favoritism of courts.

If only Edmund Fanning could be removed as recorder of deeds and collector of taxes in Orange, Adam thought the other troubles could be smoothed over. But Fanning was too close to Tryon to allow any hope for that.

Fanning's insistence that taxes be paid in cash instead of in produce and commodities worked great hardship on the small farmer who saw no money from one year's end to the other. But Fanning had been accused of a more criminal wrong.

There were many stories that he and his men were selling land from the Granville Grant to the farmers, then reselling the same parcel over and over, dispossessing the buyers by falling back on some legal technicality or irregularity in the deed. A wave of fear lay over the country. No man knew whether the land he had labored over and snatched from the wilderness by daily backbreaking work was his own even though he had bought it and held the deed. At any time Fanning's men could come and serve a dispossession notice, saying the transaction was illegal. Recourse to the courts brought no help. The Justices were Tryon's men and they made their rulings according to his wishes. Time after time, claims were made against Fanning and his illegal methods. The claims were dismissed. Only once was he adjudged guilty; then the fine was set at one shilling. Fanning, secure in his protection by the Governor, was growing rich and arrogant. But he was hated by a thousand men who were waiting for the time to come to avenge their wrongs.

Adam had heard of many cases of wrongdoing from Marcy and from the yeoman, Whitlock. The Yorkshireman was now heart and soul with the Regulators. He himself would have lost his farm to Fanning's men if he had not driven them off at the point of his musket, nicking their heels as they fled. He had treated the officers who sought his arrest in the same manner, so he was left alone, although a warrant for his arrest lay in the sheriff's office in Hillsborough. Both Marcy and Whitlock were certain that serious trouble was only a matter of time. They had convinced Adam that they were right.

Still Adam continued to hope that internal trouble would not arise when unity was needed to strengthen the claims of the Province. He had often pleaded the case of the farmer on the floor of the Assembly, and once he had talked to the Governor about the situation, hoping to make him understand what was happening. The opportunity came during a garden party at Government House. They were alone in the drawing room and Tryon was in a gracious mood. He opened the way by inquiring whether Adam thought there was any serious undercurrent of discontent in the Province. Adam answered truthfully that he did. Tryon was not pleased. Adam soon saw it was useless to try to make Tryon understand the views of the farmers. Then Adam spoke his mind. For once the Governor would hear the truth. He spoke with some heat.

"Your Excellency has a wide understanding of the military, the merchant and the professional man, but not of the farmer. The others will submit to discipline more readily than your man of the soil. They have ways to get what they want: the merchant with his money, the lawyer with words, the soldier with his guns, but the farmer must stand alone. He has one great love—his land. For that he will fight, not subtly, but savagely, with all the weapons at his command—axes, pick handles and pitchforks. Crude weapons, but effective when wielded by strong, muscular arms."

Tryon looked at Adam attentively. For a moment Adam though he would burst into one of his fits of rage. Then suddenly he laughed.

"You are a very convincing young man, Rutledge. It's a pity you waste eloquence on so futile a cause. I don't understand why a man of your position here and in England should be interested in these despicable farmers, these grubbers in the earth."

"I am a farmer, your Excellency. Perhaps there is an affinity between people who love land—or grubbers in the earth, as you put it."

The Governor laughed at Adam's retort. "Come, come, Adam. Save your argument for the Assembly chamber. I'll look into the grievances of your farmer if you promise to get rid of Husband. The man sickens me with his long, pasty face, and his red beard waving like a goat's. I don't trust the fellow."

"Nor I, your Excellency. But please do not neglect your loyal subjects, the farmers, because they have a poor spokesman. Most of them wouldn't presume to address your Excellency. They do not want to be rebellious, they only want to be able to raise their crops and have a little to tide them through the winter." Adam leaned forward in his earnestness. "Your Excellency must know that the men who raise the food to feed us are an integral and important part of our life. They deserve recognition."

But Tryon was not interested. His eyes fell on Lady Caroline who had recently returned to the Province and was now entering from the garden and making her stately way across the room. Her blackamoor followed, carrying her small belongings.

"La, your Excellency. What are you and Adam Rutledge talking about that you both look so serious?"

The Governor indicated a chair at his side. She sank into it with a rustle of silks and laces and a faint rising of perfumes.

"Adam is talking about farmers. A dull subject that would not interest you, Lady Caroline."

"I'm not so sure, your Excellency. It depends on which farmer. Now if you are talking about Adam, I am interested, very much interested." Her tone was light.

Tryon smiled indulgently. "He is an unpredictable fellow, this Adam Rutledge. I think I shall turn him over to you. Perhaps you can find out why he is so interested in the wrongs of the farmers. I want to talk with Hawks about the decorations of the Palace."

He got to his feet with the aid of a cane and walked stiffly across the room. The wound in his leg from the Indian wars bothered him when the weather changed.

When the Governor was out of hearing, Lady Caroline turned to Adam. "Is there news about the Regulators? Are they up to more mischief?"

"Not that I know of. I was trying to convince the Governor that he should give some of the leaders an audience and find out for himself what their grievances are."

"But he wouldn't listen? Tryon is a fool. I have it authoritatively that unless he is able to check the growing strength of the Regulators he will be transferred." She leaned forward, her face close to his. Adam felt her nearness, the warm fragrance of her hair against his cheek. She had dropped her casual, indifferent manner and her face had lost its masklike quality. Instead, her eyes were alive with some secret bitterness.

"Tryon is worse than a fool. He is criminal. Can't he see that these wretched men who are bearing the brunt of unjust taxation will make an outcry that will be heard from here to England if he doesn't do something? But no! He is too smug, too vainglorious. He wants to go from one part of the Province to another, attended by bards and a band of music—unrolling the red carpet, aping Royalty. Royalty, bah! If he could only look behind the scenes! A King who gets vicarious thrills mating his dogs in his bedroom, pursuing the Queen's maids into dark halls and behind hedgerows. Tryon has no thought for the suffering of his people. His one thought is to live in luxury and grandeur. He deserves what is coming. He is pulling down the pillars of his house about his head."

She dropped her long white fingers on Adam's hand. Her eyes were clouded with some hidden grief. Adam, watching the play of emotion on her face, realized that he was seeing another woman—the real woman.

"Tryon hasn't the intelligence to read the handwriting on the wall," she said after a moment. "Most of your great men

200

are too stupid or too shortsighted. But human beings, even dumb, inarticulate peasants will stand just so much."

She sat looking at the floor, scarcely conscious of Adam's presence. After a time she looked up, forcing a smile to her wide, mobile mouth. "I'm sorry, Adam. I must not let my emotions ride me. But I have seen the poor in London. A hungry mob is not a pleasant sight to contemplate. One doesn't soon forget hunger."

Adam was aware of incongruity. The fashionable dress—the long strand of pearls swinging from her white throat the matchless emerald on her finger. What was going on in her mind he did not know. But all pretense was gone from her. She moved slightly, leaning back against the brocade chair.

"Hunger forces men to great lengths. There is nothing so horrible as poverty and nothing so degrading. I have seen the degraded poor and their servility to the unworthy rich. It turns the stomach." She looked at Adam with her large, serious eyes. "That is why I like America. All men have the sense of freedom, even though they have not quite reached it. But they will, Adam. They will! It may come from humble people like your Regulators."

"Don't call them mine," Adam said, unwilling to answer her more serious words.

"Don't be ashamed of emotions, Adam. You, of all people in your class, have an understanding of the wrongs of these men. For that, I respect you."

She rose slowly. Gathering up her long skirts, she moved away, her small servitor following. Adam stood watching her, puzzled by this glimpse behind the mask. Her scathing words about Tryon and her contempt for him were hard to understand. He wondered if he had not been altogether wrong in his estimate of Lady Caroline Mathilde. Here was a woman he had not known or even suspected. Up until now he had not taken her seriously. He did now. She had suddenly become a woman of impenetrable depths and baffling mystery.

A week or so later the subject of the Regulators came to Adam's attention again. At Hillsborough, where he had been on some matters concerning land deeds, he had had a sharp difference of opinion with Edmund Fanning over the title to property belonging to Enos Dye who had found refuge on his Mecklenburg plantation after he was dispossessed. Adam went to the recorder to see for himself the status of Enos' claim on a small farm on the Yadkin. He had gone through the records thoroughly before Fanning discovered he was in the Courthouse. Fanning was annoyed and not a little disturbed when Adam laid the notes he had made on his desk. He not only asked Fanning to rectify his mistake in reselling Enos' acreage but he demanded restoration and return of money taken in excess taxation. Fanning tried to bluster but when he saw it was no use, he mumbled an apology for poor help in the office which resulted in inaccuracies. Adam made no comment. He waited until the deed for the farm was in his hands. Then he left with a curt nod to Fanning and his clerk. Fanning said nothing, but Adam knew he had made an implacable enemy.

On his way home Adam stopped at the river farm where Whitlock welcomed him with quiet pleasure. They talked of crops and the coming harvest. After a time they got around to the subject that was uppermost in Adam's mind—the Regulators.

Adam said, "I am in sympathy with the farmers, Whitlock. I think they have real grievances, but I don't like your leadership. I think Husband is an ambitious demagogue. He will betray anyone, or any cause, if it will benefit him. He is the kind of man who takes advantage of a situation like this and uses it for his own selfish ends."

Whitlock gave Adam a shrewd look, but he did not reply at once. Adam had the impression that he was hesitating, wondering if it were wise to speak his mind. He had the shrewd wisdom of men whose perceptions are sharpened by close contact with Nature and solitary living. Added to this, he had the caution of the Yorkshiremen talking with men outside their own class.

"Husband has had a little power, and it tastes fine to him," he said after a time. He watched Adam's expression. It seemed to satisfy him. He pulled his hickory chair across the uneven floor of the gallery and dropped his harsh voice to a confidential pitch. "If there were other leaders fit to hold Husband in check, it would be well. But who can do it?"

"James Hunter?"

The yeoman shook his head. "James is honest, but he is slow and has no confidence in himself. He is half daft. He thinks he has a mission to save the Province and put us all on the side of the angels. Pugh is the best man, but he is too young. The greybeards won't allow him to sit at the councils. Old men won't listen to youth, Mr. Rutledge."

"I heard that Pugh was the ringleader of the 'Black Boys.'

If that is so, he wouldn't be the one to keep the Regulators from overstepping."

Whitlock's face went blank, his light blue eyes expressionless. Adam knew that he had hit the truth.

He said, "Something must be done to keep the people calm and steady if they are to have redress from their wrongs."

Whitlock answered instantly. "If there was some way to get the Governor to let us pay taxes in produce as we used to, it would help, Mr. Rutledge; but it can't be done by the Regulators. It must come from the rich planters on the coast so that Fanning won't oppose it. It can't come from Orange County men."

All the long ride down the river to the coast Adam thought of Whitlock's words. He had thought the same thing for some time. Now the germ of an idea came to his mind. His proposed solution must be arrived at in some roundabout way, he knew, or the political opposition would kill it. He turned the idea over in his mind as he rode through the pine forest that skirted the shore of the Sound. Tobacco was the answer —inspection of tobacco by the government in government warehouses. The farmers could bring in their crop, get tobacco paper when the crop was inspected. The paper could be made legal tender for payment of taxes. That was the answer! He was a fool not to have thought of it before. For a long time he had argued with the Albemarle planters on raising the standard of their leaf by grading. They were too indifferent to do the work, but they were full of complaints because the Rutledge Riding tobacco brought more at the London auctions. But if they had a warehouse in Edenton and universal inspection, they might support the idea. He would see Jo Hewes first. Hewes would like the plan. It would mean more cargo for his ships. Harvey would get the Perquimans planters in line. He knew Mary Warden would inaugurate the idea at Queen's Gift. He would have to do some trading with the politicians in the south, but he was adept at that now. If the plan worked with tobacco, it could be extended to other commodities—tar, pitch, tallow, indigo, wax and turpentine. Lumber and poles, also. He was sure it could be done. All the farmers would benefit, as well as the towns where the warehouses would be built. He touched his heel to his horse and set it to a gallop.

The moon came up and shafts of light fell through the great trees. Adam rode swiftly toward Rutledge Riding. He slept the rest of the night secure in the thought that tobacco paper would solve one of the most bitter controversies that had raged between the government and the Regulators.

Adam went as often as he could find the time to North Plantation to see his son and Azizi. A subtle change had come over the girl. The defiance was gone, but it was not replaced by any show of warmth or affection. She simply accepted the arrangements that he made for her without comment, as if they were her due. Adam was conscious of his old feeling of defeat, but somehow the pain of it was not so sharp. Fortunately, Gwennie had taken a liking to Azizi from the beginning. She petted her and hovered over the child as if it were her own. This pleased Adam. He had Hawks remodel the old wing of the house and landscape a garden which was planted with rare tropical plants he ordered through Peyton from the Indies. He wanted Azizi to be surrounded by things that pleased her, things of her own selection. The change in her he attributed to her motherhood. She was devoted to the child, who took up her thoughts and her waking hours. Watching them in the garden, Adam wondered sometimes at the strange trick Fate had played on him.

Early in the spring of 1769 Adam started on a two-year tour that included Virginia, Maryland, New York and New England. Ostensibly on his own affairs, he was in reality a secret emissary of the Council. These journeys opened his eyes to outside feeling and gave him an understanding of the necessity of the union of the Colonies. The smaller Colonies in the North were against it. They feared they would be swallowed by the more powerful Provinces.

Subtle changes were taking place in all the Colonies. Up to now, London was closer to the Carolinas in trade than New York or Boston. The West Indies and the Carolinas were in even closer contact. The life of the Carolina coast districts was the life of the English countryside and the great country families. New England with its more provincial Puritanism, New York with its predominating Dutch influence, were far afield temperamentally and geographically. But now this was gradually changing. Common fear was slowly binding America.

Adam did not like these long journeys. It meant time away from the plantation and the land. But his Uncle Caswell and John Harvey persuaded him. He had great respect for the opinion of Harvey, who was wise, moderate, but firm in his convictions. Owen Tewilliger stayed on and managed the plantation with the help of Marcy while Sara and Lavinia went north, Sara to be with her father in Virginia, Lavinia to Annapolis to visit with her connections, the Hammonds, so she could be near young Peyton. For some time now Peyton had been in charge of Adam's export business. He had developed a great interest in the West India trade, and made frequent journeys to St. Kitts and to Charlotte Amalie to trade with the Danes.

Lady Caroline had disappeared from the Colony. Her departure was secret. She managed even in that to shroud herself in mystery. Some said she had gone to England; others, that she was living in one of the great houses on St. Croix, in the Leeward Islands.

The winter of 1769-1770, while Adam was visiting Colony after Colony in the North and in the South, finding bitterness and hatred growing daily, Mary and William Warden were in England. Mary was seeing the other side—the complete indifference of the great world of London to the fate of the Colonies. No one took the idea of revolution seriously. Men that she met at dances and levees called her "little rebel" and laughed away any serious talk. More sober minds were turned to continental affairs, to France and Spain and the Peninsula Wars. The fashionable London world was extravagantly gay. Profligate times and profligate people set the standard of living. Young bloods spent enormous amounts on their horses and on their mistresses. Vast sums were spent daily at Tattersall's. Every man was betting on races, riding in steeplechases, gambling on every possible event. Fashionable men, married or unmarried, flaunted their mistresses in public. Actresses, sponsored by the nobility, rode in the Mall, their gowns and their coaches the subject of newspaper comment mixed with the happenings of the Court and the King's levees. The wretched poor stood in lines in the rain or bitter cold waiting to see some great lord ride by, or to get a glimpse of a prostitute raised to fame by the patronage of some man of fashion. Famous writers curried favor with George III by writing articles on the divine right of kings. Even the great Johnson turned his pen to writing a pamphlet titled *Taxation No Tyranny.*

All this made Mary Warden heartsick. She begged William to take her home to Carolina, but his work with the Granville Grant leases took more time than he expected. He would have to stay until it was finished. The only person she could talk with was her friend Patience Wright to whose studio she went often. The Philadelphia artist was modeling a wax bust of the King, who came almost daily to sit for her. For years she had been a great favorite of his. He liked to talk with her, for she was one of the few people about him who spoke out.

Mary, whose thoughts were so deeply impregnated with the new idea of liberty and freedom, could bear it no longer. She told William that she was going home. When he saw that it was no use to argue he hurried through his work to sail with her.

At home Mary found no such indifference as in England. A dozen people came to see her the first day she arrived in Edenton. The people were talking now about the Regulators and their continued opposition to the Governor. The Black Boys, the Tories called them, because at first they had disguised themselves as Negroes when they meted out punishment to politicians responsible for what they considered wrongs against freedom and personal liberty. Tryon made a public announcement that his patience was at an end and that he intended to resort to severe measures. That statement angered the people of Orange and Granville. They refused to pay taxes and violence was rife. No one knew what was going to happen, but the situation was considered to be the gravest since the Stamp Act.

Tryon ruled now with an iron hand. The date for the completion of the Palace had been postponed again and again. First there had been an announcement that the Palace would be formally opened and the government moved to New Bern in the summer of 1770. Plans were discussed: it was said that there would be barbecues and open-air dancing in the square for the common people and a great ball at the Palace for the gentry. Now, for lack of funds to complete the building—as had happened too often before—the date for the opening was once more set forward, to the following spring. Each time he ran out of money Tryon managed, in spite of bitter protest, to squeeze thousands of pounds more out of an unwilling Assembly. Some people thought the Palace would never be finished. Twice fires had been put out; once gunpowder exploded, wrecking one of the rooms. The Governor set a guard over the workmen. This caused dissatisfaction. Lampoons were written and posted on buildings. Crude drawings in chalk on the walls showed Tryon, dressed as a Pharaoh with whip in hand, driving slaves and building the pyramids.

William rarely talked to Mary about the conditions of the Colony. Time after time she tried to open the subject, but he put her off. John Harvey and Samuel Johnstone were in Wilmington, James Iredell in Philadelphia, Adam Rutledge away, no one knew where. She must talk with someone who knew. She ordered her horse saddled early one morning after her return, and rode to Dr. Armitage's house. From him she would find out the truth. But she knew in her heart that another motive prompted the visit. She wanted news of Adam. Where was he? It had been over a year since she had seen him or had direct word from him. The Manor House was open she knew. Sara Rutledge had come home, and Lavinia was there too, but no one had spoken of Adam. She did not ask for fear of betraying herself. The long months had not lessened her thought of him nor her love.

She walked into the Doctor's office, old Crit leading the way, bowing and smiling.

"Mis' Mary here, Doctor," he called, opening the door of the dispensary. "Mis' Mary Warden jus' arrived from London," he announced with a flourish.

Armitage looked up from a book. He rose to his feet with alacrity at the sight of her.

"Mary, Mary Warden, why wasn't I told you were home?"

Mary kissed his cheek. She held his thin hand in both of hers.

"I don't know, Doctor. I should have thought my homecoming so important that everyone in Edenton would know about it." She was laughing. Suddenly she knew how good it was to be with her own people.

She sat down near him. Almost at once they were talking in low confidential tones. Before her eyes Armitage unrolled the great drama of revolt that lay so close to the surface.

"It will come, Mary, as sure as God made little apples," he told her in his characteristic speech. "You'll find people saying otherwise, but that is because they won't face facts. Revolution is on the way. It is so near, I cannot sleep nights. When it does come, it will mean that we will fight until we win or are wiped from the earth."

Mary could not take her eyes from his thin, ascetic face.

"Are the other Colonies ready?" she asked.

Armitage shook his head.

"They are lagging behind us, Mary. They are still talking conciliation, just as some of our own leaders are, but most of the people in North Carolina are primed to fight. Tryon knows it, though he won't admit it."

"How long will it be?" the question trembled on her lips.

"That I can't answer, but soon, far too soon, there will be bloodshed in the Carolinas."

Mary knew he spoke the truth. Whenever it came, it would be too soon. Before she left, she mentioned Adam's name. Armitage did not know much. He had heard that Adam would be home from the North before long. He had done much good work, Armitage said, seeking to unite the North and South in a common cause. The summer before he had gone to Fort Pitt and from there as far west as the Mississippi. This journey was at the instigation of Patrick Henry who had great dreams of pushing the boundaries of Virginia far to the West.

As she was leaving, Armitage said, "I'm expecting Maurice Moore tomorrow or the next day. He'll be holding court here. I'm sure he will want to see you and hear what you have to say about conditions in England." He followed her to the carriage block, talking with her while she mounted.

As she rode down the drive she turned. The Doctor still stood at the door, his thin, white hair blowing in the wind.

Penelope Dawson sent for Mary to come over for tea at Eden House. There she met Maurice Moore. John Harvey was there also, looking aged from a recent illness. She and Moore found a seat on a small settee at the far end of the drawing room, away from the gay group at the tea table.

"I've been wanting to see you, Mary, ever since I heard you were home. I have just come over from the western counties. Things are deplorable there—I can't tell you the seriousness of their situation. The Hillsborough trouble has gone deep, Mary. We can't pass it over lightly. The men from Orange are fighters. You will be surprised, but I have come to the belief that it is necessary for us to be cautious now." Moore dropped his eyes to the floor, lost in thought. He looked old and very tired. Mary felt discouragement was weighing him down.

"Caswell and John Harvey think Husband and his kind are a menace," he said, suddenly attentive again. "Caswell thinks Husband should be banished from the Colony. Hunter, their other leader, is deranged, I grant you that, but many ignorant folks believe he has divine guidance. What are we to do about it, Mary? These men can't think things out for themselves. They are swayed by what their leaders say. What's going to happen?"

He seemed to Mary to be talking to himself rather than speaking to her; a lawyer and judge asking and answering questions.

"Am I overly disturbed? I hope I am. But unless some

208

honest settlement is made—unless the Governor removes Fanning and his men—we won't be able to hold these Regulators in check much longer is my opinion."

"Is it indeed as serious as that?"

"Yes, Mary. You have come home just at the moment when we are in the greatest danger we have ever faced. We all want peace, peace under the law, not rebellion. The law should stand higher than any man or any government or group of men who govern. But today, in our Province, law is only a tool in the hands of a few. Justice has become a travesty. Yet we don't want to see the law in the hands of impetuous radicals who will rebel without looking ahead. It will be a long fight when it comes and we must be prepared if we hope to win."

Mary gathered up her small belongings and said good-by to Penelope. Moore walked to the door with her. Her groom was waiting at the carriage block with her horse. Moore held her hand closely for a moment.

"I saw William today. He looks worried and ill. Take good care of him, Mary. We need William Warden."

Mary took up the reins.

"I'll do my best, you may be sure."

On Friday Lavinia and Peyton came over for a few days' visit. Lavinia came direct to Queen's Gift. Peyton stopped in Edenton. Mary went with Lavinia to her room and sat by the fire while she changed from her habit to a house gown. Lavinia's voice ran smoothly, relating family gossip. Young Peyton would be home in June. He was growing tall, getting on well at school. Sara went every day to Adam's office and made a pretense of managing the plantation. It would be amusing if it weren't pitiful. She had noticed that Sara's health was always better when Adam was away.

"She dramatizes her illness when Adam is home," she said. "I know you'll think it beastly of me to say that, Mary, but it's true." Mary did not speak. She had thought the same thing many times, but she could not say it to Lavinia. "Sara says Adam is coming home soon," Lavinia continued as she brushed her hair. Mary, aware that she was watching her covertly, turned away, straightening some papers that lay on the table. "I don't think Sara knows really. Peyton thinks it may be some time before he gets back."

Mary made a pretense of reading one of the papers. She didn't want Lavinia to see her disappointment.

Suddenly Lavinia said, "Why doesn't Adam realize he is in

love with you, Mary? You love Adam and Adam loves you, even if he won't admit it to himself. What would be wrong in that? He has a helpless wife, and surely you don't love William Warden."

"I respect William," Mary found herself saying.

Lavinia laughed. "You love Adam. He loves you. I've seen the look in his eyes when he was watching you, Mary. I know. I may not be so intelligent as you, but there are some things I know."

"I think he loves Azizi," Mary said slowly.

Lavinia shrugged her shoulders. "You don't really believe that unless you are as naïve as an eighteen-year-old girl. Sara managed that. She is the one who put the girl under Adam's feet day and night. She wanted him to take the girl. She thought she could keep him from you. I've seen her reading her Bible: the story of Abraham and Sara, and the slave girl Hagar—"

For a moment Mary was stunned by Lavinia's perception. "Lavinia!" she said. "You can't believe that!"

Lavinia whirled around on the stool, her long, dark hair flung back from her face. "I tell you it's true. Sara hates you. She knows that Adam likes you better than any other woman, so she tries to keep him from you. I think it natural for a woman to fight for the man she loves. But Sara doesn't really love Adam. He is her possession and she will scheme and plot to hold him because she basks in his adoration and his protection. She's a selfish woman and hard as nails, and she uses her helplessness to bind him hand and foot."

Mary knew this was true. She remembered that long ago, Peyton told her the same thing. Only Adam was blind.

She said, "You are quite wrong, Lavinia. Adam doesn't love me. We are friends, nothing more." Her words had no conviction behind them.

Lavinia brushed her hair vigorously; then she jumped to another subject.

"David's a lovely child," she said. "But he is so like Adam that everyone will know."

"Do people talk?"

Lavinia nodded. She looked out of her eyes obliquely. "Perhaps I should not tell you, but some of your dear friends hint that David is your child."

A wave of anger flowed through Mary's body, leaving her cold. "How could they?" she cried.

Lavinia shrugged her white shoulders. "God protect you from your friends if your back is turned," she said.

Mary got up and walked about the room. Lavinia came over to her by the window and put her arms about her. "I shouldn't have told you that, darling. Please forget it."

"I'd like to know who said it," Mary was calmer now, her voice steady.

"I won't tell you. It would do no good. You know there are always envious women in the world who can't believe in a real friendship between a man and a woman." Mary did not speak. Lavinia hastened on, trying to repair the hurt. "You are always open to attack, Mary. So is every woman whom men like."

Mary still said nothing. She did not trust herself. Lavinia could not know how deeply she loved Adam Rutledge. She could imagine just how Lavinia had thought the whole situation out. To her it would be the natural thing.

Lavinia took up the brush again. She counted the strokes.

"Sixty-seven, sixty-eight, sixty-nine, seventy. There, that is enough to get all the powder out. I'm almost of a mind to follow your example, Mary, and quit powdering my hair. I have a fancy not to follow the dictates of London any longer."

Mary laughed. "You think it more—let us say, Colonial not to follow the London fashion?"

Lavinia raised her long slim arms above her head. The shining mass of her hair fell over her bare shoulders and covered her rounded breasts. "Yes, I'll go even further tonight. William is going to turn the force of his arguments on me to keep me from selling my London shares. But I am determined to do it, even if I lose money by it. Mary, I don't know what has happened to your Lavinia, but she is quite patriotic these days!"

Mary laughed aloud. Lavinia was slipping a gown of dull rose taffeta over her head. When Lavinia came one always laughed.

"I stayed a week last winter with Lady Tryon," Lavinia said as they walked down the broad stair to the drawing room. "She is sad, very sad. I think the Governor is sad also, and not a little bewildered. Why should it all be so confused like this, Mary? I think he wants to know how the people feel, but how can he? The men around him conspire to keep him from knowing. He is as far away from the people as a king from his subjects. He is suspicious of everyone now; he believes in no one. One night the Governor said to me: 'If Adam Rutledge were here he would tell me the truth.' I told him to get the truth from Judge Moore, but he shook his head. 'Moore hates me so much that he could not help being prejudiced. He's so carried away by the fancied wrong of the people that he no longer is able to be dispassionate. Rutledge could be. He can stand away and look at things. Why in God's name isn't he here?' "

"There is something in what you say," Mary said thoughtfully. "Tryon is too far away from the people, and he listens to the wrong men."

"I felt really sorry for him that night," Lavinia went on. "He drank enough brandy to speak what was in his mind. I know he was almost beside himself about those riots in Hillsborough that took place while you were gone."

Mary thought of what Maurice Moore had told her.

"There must be some way out," she said.

William could not change Lavinia's mind about her shares. Though he argued and pleaded she was determined to transfer them to North Carolina land. Mary suggested that she always followed William's advice in matters of money, but Lavinia was determined. She was in good humor and wheedled a confession from William that he had no real reason for disapproval, except that London shares seemed more secure than any Colonial investment. "Prejudice," she called it, and in the end she not only had her way, but turned the subject to Peyton's visit to St. Kitts.

Peyton talked of the growing trade with the Indies, of the cargoes of sugar and rum that he had brought back, and of the bags of coffee from Martinique. He was building up a trade with the other islands equal in volume to the trade to Port au Prince, Kingstown, and Charlotte Amalie. Mary watched Peyton. He had changed in the past few years. He seemed steadier—to have more poise.

The evening passed without a discussion of political events. Peyton had no thought beyond his business, that was plain. And William would not bring up the question of Colonial affairs Mary was certain. He did not approve of her outspoken comments on the way things were going. It was as if he were a stranger who lived under the same roof but had nothing to do with her life or her thoughts.

She and Lavinia went out on the gallery while the men had brandy. Lavinia wanted to see the new moon over her left shoulder and insisted on William giving her a sixpence so she could hold money in her hand for good fortune. The night was lovely, with a feeling of spring.

"How quiet it is!" Lavinia exclaimed. "Everything is so

212

quiet and peaceful. Surely, Mary, we have dreamed these thoughts of revolt. They can't be real. Nothing is real but this beautiful night."

Peyton came to the window.

"Lavinia! Lavinia!" he called. "Come play a game of chess."

She answered and went swiftly toward the house.

Mary, drawing her light scarf about her shoulders, walked in the deep shadows of the garden. It was quiet. She felt the soft wind against her face. She stopped by a bush, attracted by the clean, compelling scent. Her fingers touched the opening flowers. They made her think of Adam and the time they had planted the daphne bush he had brought her. She brushed the tears from her eyes with an impatient movement of her hand. It would not do to dwell on the past. She must work—and think of the future. She could keep herself occupied with the management of Queen's Gift. William was far too busy to pay any attention to the plantation when he was at home. But he was traveling almost continually on land affairs—long journeys to the Cape Fear districts, South Carolina and Georgia. In their infrequent talks about politics William tried to reassure Mary, telling her peace would last, that all difficulties could be adjusted as they arose. But Mary thought differently. The little fires had been lighted throughout the Colonies. One day they would spread. . . .

Chapter 15

WE WILL
BUILD SHIPS

MARY read the Governor's proclamation in the *Weekly Post-boy* that the Palace would be formally opened on the sixteenth of April, 1771. Because it was one of those rare warm March mornings Cissie had set the breakfast table under a magnolia tree in the garden, and hurried back and forth between the summer kitchen and the garden, carrying food: a pot of tea, hot corn pone, a bowl of Bow china heaped with deep red strawberries, and a silver jug of clotted cream. She placed the tray in front of Mary, her massive arms akimbo.

"How do you like dose stra'berries?" she inquired when Mary had eaten the last berry.

"They are delicious, Cissie. I didn't know we had such fine berries so early in the season."

"No more we have. Dese are spec'l berries. Dey come from Rutledge Riding. Dey rais' 'em in de glasshouse—" She paused and leaned forward to give her words emphasis. "Mr. Adam, he done bring 'em heself."

Mary's hands dropped to her lap. She sat very still. Adam was back. She had not known.

"Heself bring they. He say, don' distu'b your mistress if she sleeping. Tell her I'll come back—one hour, two hour—" Cissie was enjoying the effect of her news.

Mary cried, "Cissie, why didn't you tell me before? I've a good notion to beat you!"

The Negress was not disturbed by the threat. "Whyfo' I tell befo' you eat yo' breakfast? If I tell yo' you got a flutter in yo' stomack and yo' don' eat."

Mary laughed. Cissie was quite right. Already she felt the "flutter." She tried to think how long it had been since she had seen Adam. So much had happened in that time—so much and so little—

Cissie said, "I rec'on hit most time he come back."

Mary put up her hands to smooth her hair. Cissie's heavy body shook with silent laughter.

"Yo' look good dis mornin', Missie. I lays out dat blue

muslin wid little lace ruffles 'cause I know Mr. Adam he lak blue."

Mary stood up and threw her arms around the black woman. "Oh, Cissie, I'm so happy."

Cissie patted her shoulder. "Cissie know. Now you put on yo' hat, 'cause hit look awf'l nice." She picked up the broad leghorn hat from the chair and tied the blue ribbons under Mary's chestnut hair. "Yes, better keep on yo' hat. A'ready you got a nest of freckles on yo' little nose." She stood off to survey the effect. "I don' think dose London ladies half so fine as yo'," she said with satisfaction. "Now sit down and don' twis' yo' kerchief lak yo' was a little girl."

Mary laughed. "Cissie, you're an old fraud! Clear the table and bring some fresh tea. You know the kind Mr. Adam likes."

Cissie shook her head doubtfully. "We got precious little dat good tea, Mis' Mary. Last time yo' said we only use hit on grand occasion."

"Well, this is a grand occasion. Hurry! I hear a horse coming up the drive."

Across the lilac hedge, Mary saw Adam dismount and throw the reins to a pickaninny. Her throat tightened and the hot blood rose to her cheeks. She sat down at the table, watching him come toward her. In a moment he would be beside her. She hoped he would not know the swift beating of her heart, or notice her trembling hands.

Adam made no effort to hide his delight. He put his arms about her, lifting her from the chair. He kissed her smooth forehead, then her mouth, his lips pressing hard against hers. Mary could not speak. Only her heart said over and over, "Adam . . . Adam . . . Adam . . ." He sat down beside her, his eyes warm and deep.

"You don't know how I've missed you, Mary. I believe I've thought of you every day since I've been gone!" He laughed a little. "I thought I'd never get here once I had started. I got up this morning at six to ride over to see you, even before I went to the North Plantation, and you, my little Mary, were asleep!"

"I didn't know you were coming, Adam. Why didn't you have Cissie call me?"

"I came very near throwing pebbles through your window," he grinned. "But I thought better of it. I rode off down the old wood road to the charcoal-burner's hut instead. Time never went so slowly."

"But now you're here," she said softly. "Dear Adam, I have missed you so much."

He leaned toward her, inclosing her clasped hands with his strong fingers.

"Nothing in the world can equal a friendship like ours, Mary. Nothing. A man learns something in two years." He looked up toward the house, then dropped her hands and leaned back in his chair. The warm look was gone. Mary followed his eyes. William was walking slowly across the lawn, reading a paper as he came. She filled Adam's cup and handed it to him silently. The beauty, the warm intimacy of the moment was lost.

William was genuinely pleased to see Adam. He shouted for a servant and sent Negro boys to find John Harvey and James Iredell to ask them for breakfast. A sudden fear came to Mary. The men would all come presently. They would besiege Adam with questions about the conditions in all the Colonies he had visited. They would talk about affairs in the Province. There would be no more time for them alone, no time for her to say the thousand little things that she had wanted to say through the long months of separation.

In half an hour they came. She sat quietly, pouring tea, giving low orders to the servants about food and drinks. Once or twice Adam's eyes sought hers for a moment before he turned to answer a question. It seemed to Mary that a pattern of revolt and revolution was woven before her eyes. Names of men in the North and in Virginia were mentioned, men who were to guide the destiny of a new country about to be born. The northern Colonies had been lulled into false security after the repeal of the Stamp Act, as had the Carolinas. She heard Adam saying, "The people of Boston are now roused. Newspapers are printed with skull and crossbones at the masthead. Americans are being drawn into a unified body. Liberty in danger holds them together."

"But the new taxes? How do the Northerners like them?" Iredell asked.

Adam shook his head. He told them something about the meeting at Old South Church to protest against the new taxes.

"The excise taxes will be the King's downfall in America," John Harvey said prophetically. "It was an ill day when he listened to the stupid counsel of Lord North and Bute. They know nothing of the minds and thoughts of our people and care less. They do not realize that it is not the taxes that we oppose, but Parliament's right to tax us."

216

Mary saw Joseph Hewes coming across from the house. With him was a lean, awkward, young man, who carried his three-cornered hat in his hand. He bowed jerkily to Mary when Hewes presented him as Mr. John Paul. Mary had heard of him. He had come from Scotland to stay with his brother in Virginia. Caught by the young man's love of ships and his knowledge of sailing, Joseph Hewes had become interested in him.

Mary made a place for him at her side, smiling at him as she did so to put him at ease. While the others talked of New York and Boston and the situation in Philadelphia, she spoke to him about Virginia and his journey down. Soon he was talking easily. He had forgotten himself and his embarrassment. He spoke of the thing that lay nearest his heart: ships for the defense of the Colonies. That was the first time Mary had heard the words, although she was to hear them many times in the coming years.

"I can't make anyone see the necessity of building ships to defend these shores," he said to her earnestly. "Sometimes, I think Mr. Hewes believes as I do—again, I realize that he does not. They are all thinking of their wrongs. They talk about the defense of the land, of soldiers to defend their homes. They don't realize that it is the sea that they must watch, that the war will be won from the sea . . . not the land."

Mary watched John Paul's eyes light up with an inner fire. She realized that the others had stopped talking to listen to his words. "If there is a war, England will attack from the sea . . . Boston, New York, Charles Town, the Chesapeake and the Albemarle. Don't you see, Mrs. Warden?" He began drawing lines on the white cloth with a fork. "Here is our long coast line, exposed to attack. Here are the islands of the West Indies, an absolutely impregnable base for the English Navy. Sloops of war here and there and here. They will protect the transport of troops. Under the powerful guns of sloops-of-war, regiments and brigades will land here and here and here. So we are conquered before we start, if we have no ships. But no one will listen to what I say, Mrs. Warden. I can't make anyone see as I see." There was acute despair in the young man's voice.

Adam came over and sat down near them. "Would it encourage you, Mr. Paul, if I told you I had placed an order for six large schooners . . . the staunchest, the swiftest that can be built . . . and they will have emplacements to carry cannon?"

John Paul's face lighted. Mary thought he was almost handsome when he smiled. "I pray to God that I stand on the bridge of one of your ships, Mr. Rutledge."

Adam laughed. "I hope you will. The ships are built to use for the India trade but, when the time comes, they will be at your service."

Paul leaned forward and grasped his hand. "At last I've met a man who sees the importance of ships," he said. "There's wisdom in doing that. We'll want privateers to defend our shores, Mr. Rutledge. I hope we can find other men to see as you do. There will be some hope for us then."

"But the troubles between us and Great Britain are smoothed out," Mary found herself saying.

John Paul looked at her pityingly. His Scotch burr was thick on his tongue as he spoke. "It is only a matter of a few years before war comes. We must build ships and more ships. We must train sailors to sail ships and to fight." There was a fanatical light in his eyes that made the blood chill in her veins.

"It is unthinkable that Briton should fight against Briton," Mary exclaimed.

"We will fight the Hanoverian king before many years are past," John Paul said harshly. "A short while—little enough for us to prepare in, madam."

No one spoke. They felt the import of the Scot's words. Only William and James Iredell had not drawn near. They had moved a little way beyond the lilac hedge. Mary heard Iredell say, "I wouldn't trust Tom Jefferson so far as I could throw a horse. Always exigent . . . looking out for Tom, grasping other men's ideas and using them without acknowledging credit. That's Tom. Oily Tom, we call him."

"Aren't you a little too hard on Jefferson?" William asked.

"Not hard enough," Iredell replied. "The man is a politician of the meanest kind. Seeking aggrandizement and self-glory, sucking ideas from the brains of better men. Bah! The thought of him sickens me."

Mary looked to see if the others had heard. They had not. Adam was still talking with John Paul. Harvey was listening. Hewes leaned back in his chair, smiling a little at John Paul and Adam. He was proud of his young protégé.

The weight of impending revolution bore down on Mary. It was easy to talk of wrongs done, of standing on ancient rights, of Liberty and Freedom. Vague talk, abstract words. But here was talk of men and guns and ships, of transports laden with troops, of regiments and brigades. That was war.

The Scot's words were heavy with tragic portent. The Colonies were being pushed into the future—not the far-off future, but the immediate, pregnant future of tomorrow and the next day and the next. "Build for defense," Paul was insisting. "If we must take the offensive, then God help us if we are not ready."

John Harvey's even voice broke the quivering silence that followed. "You have spoken the truth, John Paul. God help us if we are not ready. Let's pray that some miracle will happen to keep peace, for if we have war, there will be no giving up until the last free man is dead."

Adam lingered after the others had gone. Mary walked with him to the carriage block where the groom held his horse.

Mary said, "Surely you don't believe things to be so serious as John Paul says they are?"

The smile left Adam's face and his eyes. "Nothing can keep us from revolution, Mary. A few months . . . or a few years. I have traveled from Maine to Florida and as far west as the Mississippi—everywhere I have been, that is the opinion of sober, serious thinking men. Not hotheads . . . but men who want to think differently and cannot. Paul is wiser. Most of us dread war so much that we are trying to fool ourselves into thinking what we want to think. John Paul is the most farsighted of us all. He has given up hope of conciliation, and is bending all his thoughts to plans for defense."

Mary said stubbornly, "I don't think the situation irrevocable."

Adam mounted. She remembered then to ask about Sara. She had stood the trips well, Adam told her, although she would have preferred to remain in New York where she had gone from Virginia. It was gay there. There were many Royalists who were her friends in the city. She would have remained north much longer if she had known he would be unable to return to Rutledge Riding until this spring.

"Sara remains loyal to her King. It is very unfashionable to be rebellious. Only common people are Whigs," Adam said, smiling a little. Mary smiled, but did not speak. Adam continued: "She shuts her eyes to what is happening and to impending danger. Perhaps it is as well. Sara can never face reality."

By sheer force of will Mary brought herself then to speak of Azizi and of David, for she felt that it would be unnatural not to mention Adam's son. She was not prepared for Adam's response to her simple question. His face softened. He seemed very young, very proud, when he said the words, "My son."

"I am going to North Plantation to see them now," he said. His voice grew tender when he spoke of Azizi. "She has given me a son, Mary. No matter what happens, I cannot forget that."

Adam seemed reluctant to leave and their conversation drifted to casual comments about people in the village. Finally he mentioned the subject uppermost in everyone's mind, Tryon's Palace and the coming celebration.

"People in the back country are outspoken in their disapproval of the extra taxes that Tryon has levied for the building. They think it is too splendid—too extravagant for a new Province to support."

"What do you think, Adam?" Mary asked.

He shrugged his shoulders. "I think we can support it well enough. It isn't really the Palace itself. It's the symbol of Tryon's pretension which annoys them. Maybe it is just as well that the Palace wasn't completed by the date Tryon originally set for the opening. People will have time to cool off."

Mary agreed. A moment later Adam spoke of Lady Caroline. "Hawks tells me he has sold some of Lady Caroline's furniture to the Governor for the new Palace."

Mary looked up quickly. "Isn't she coming back to the Province?" she asked impulsively.

"Oh, yes, she's already back. I believe she is planning large entertainments in the place she has taken in New Bern for the opening ball. She had a great many fine pieces of French and English furniture sent up from the Indies—more than she could use."

Mary's tongue ran away with her. "Lady Caroline is always taking another house—at Edenton—at Wilmington—now at New Bern—"

Adam turned on his horse to face her.

"You don't like Lady Caroline, do you?" he asked.

"I wouldn't say that I dislike her. I'm quite indifferent concerning her."

"Why?" Adam persisted.

He could see that Mary for some reason resented the inquiry.

"Because Cissie doesn't like her. She says she 'ain't quality.' I always go by what Cissie says," she answered evasively.

"You're being flippant, Mary. I really want to know the

220

reason why you don't like her—if you have a reason," he added.

"She doesn't like me," she said. "I'm too unimportant for her fine parties."

"Don't answer if you don't want to," Adam said. "But I'm sure you have a reason—a good one. She must have offended you. You were quite friendly at first."

"That was because William asked me to be pleasant to her. She had an introduction to him from some client at St. Kitts."

"Oh," Adam said, and dropped the subject.

Mary felt his impatience with her answer, but she had no intention of telling him why she instinctively disliked Lady Caroline. She had known from the first that Lady Caroline liked Adam. Lady Caroline made no secret of it. Mary remembered with distaste the time, over four years ago, when Lady Caroline had asked her outright whether she and Adam were lovers. Mary had been furious, but she managed to control herself. Lady Caroline had laughed. "You needn't get into a rage, Mary, or be shocked. That is too provincial. Why not? He's the most attractive man in Albemarle—and William is—" she shrugged her shoulders expressively.

From that time on Mary had seen as little of her as possible. And Lady Caroline had pointedly ignored her. She had little use for the society of women.

But Mary could not tell Adam this. The very thought of the conversation upset her even now. Mary didn't like to be upset.

After Adam had disappeared down the drive, Mary thought over their conversation. The disturbing thoughts about Azizi and Lady Caroline receded when she remembered what he had said about Sara. It was the first time she had ever heard Adam speak critically of his wife. She realized how his interests had widened. She thought, "He has gone far beyond me in his interest in the Colonies. He has knowledge of the condition of the country and the people, and the danger that lies ahead." Perhaps she was like Sara. She did not want to look too far ahead—she was afraid. She had not the courage to face what she knew was coming.

Mary ran into Lavinia a few days later at the Levantine's shop. She had stopped to get a silver pot that had been left to be soldered. Lavinia was looking at a necklace of rubies and emeralds set with pearls. She held the glittering bauble against her throat, glancing at a mirror to see the effect. She was obviously pleased by the reflection, but she shook her head and laid the jewels in the Damascene box.

The man ran his brown fingers over the stones. "It is a beautiful piece of India work," he said in his oily voice. "Madam should have the necklace. Madam may pay when she pleases. Madam should wear the necklace to the Governor's ball. It will set off any costume."

Lavinia fingered the necklace, examining the exquisite workmanship of the setting. She turned then and saw Mary. She called, "Come, look at the necklace. Isn't it lovely?"

Mary gave the necklace a casual glance. "Very nice, if the stones are real. But I never cared for red and green combinations."

The enthusiasm faded from Lavinia's face. She pushed the jewels across the counter. "No. I won't take it," she said firmly.

The Levantine locked the necklace in the Damascene box, and took it away. A few moments later he came back carrying Mary's tea pot. There was nothing in his inscrutable face to show that he resented the intrusion of Mary Warden, but his beady, black eyes were hard as he watched her leaving the shop with Lavinia.

At the curb Mary said, "Come home with me, Lavinia, and I'll give you tea. I have a little real tea left."

Lavinia hesitated, looking down Broad Street toward the commons. "I don't know—I promised to meet Peyton at five at King's Arms Inn. He said we were going to sail home tonight."

Mary answered, "We'll leave word at the Inn for Peyton. He can come for you at my house. I've only to stop for a moment at Joseph Hewes's store. The seamstress wants some thread and a yard of satin to finish lining a gown."

Lavinia got into the carriage. "I may as well go with you, Mary, if you're going to the shop. I want to see if the gloves I ordered came on the ship from London."

At Hewes's store they found half the women of Edenton. They had not waited for the merchandise to be unpacked before they descended like a flock of twittering sparrows, filled with curiosity to see what had come on the ship from London. Counters and tables were piled with silks and brocades from India and China, cotton prints from Manchester and woolens from Perth. Clerks were running from one group to another, pulling at the pieces of silks; at the same time they were trying to unpack the new goods and put the bolts on the shelves. But the women gave them no time. Their white hands dipped into boxes and bales. Pulling and tugging, they brought to light fans and feathers and laces. Yards of white linen, thin as a cobweb, trailed on the floor, to be trampled by buckled shoes and entangled with straw packings from barrels of Chelsea and Bow china.

Mary stood looking at the confusion, a slightly derisive smile on her lips. Lavinia's eyes were glistening. She walked swiftly across the room to where Jean Corbin stood examining a length of pearl grey satin shot with silver that a youthful clerk was holding at arm's length.

"Do you think it will be too old?" she asked Lavinia doubtfully. "I love grey, but I'm afraid . . ."

"Use it with coral pink trimmings," Lavinia suggested briskly, "over a pink satin petticoat quilted in grey. It will be beautiful, Mrs. Corbin, not too old at all."

The clerk laid a strip of coral beside the grey. Lavinia pleated the colors together with swift, sensitive fingers.

"The Levantine has some wonderful rosy corals at his shop," she told Jean, "earrings, carved pendants and string after string of beads rolled together. You must have them to wear with this. I'm sure you'll be the loveliest woman at the ball."

Jean Corbin's hearty laugh filled the shop. "Go along, child! It would take more than a string of corals to do that." But she was pleased.

A chorus of voices arose as other women came to look at the silks:

"Lavinia, shall I get this blue?"

"Do you think yellow will dull my hair?"

"Lavinia darling, you have such good taste. Do help me decide."

Lavinia went from one to another. Mary smiled fondly at Lavinia's exuberance.

"And how can we be of service to Mary Warden?" said a voice behind her. Mary turned to face Joseph Hewes, smiling and bland, with a little twinkle in his blue eyes.

"Nothing, thank you, Joseph. I have made my small purchase. You are very busy here today," she said.

"Yes, a little more than the usual excitement when a ship docks. It is on account of the ball. Every woman must have a new gown for the Palace ball."

Mary was serious. "Joseph, I wonder whether the Governor isn't going a little too far with this display of pomp and red carpets."

Hewes glanced over his shoulder to be sure no one overheard. "They're saying Tryon is worried. Threatening letters are coming in, lampoons—and the like."

"But what do the people have to say about the wording of his proclamation? The gentry invited to dance at the new Palace, the common people to dance in the streets. Certainly that shows too much class distinction for us."

Hewes glanced toward the counter where Jean Corbin was sitting with Lavinia, their heads together over a pile of gay silks. "The common people have been forced to pay their share toward the Palace against their wills," Mary continued. "Are they to be allowed to view it only from the streets?"

Hewes moved closer. Always cautious, he did not want his customers to know his real opinions. "I wouldn't say too much about that, Mary. It is dangerous, very dangerous, to put such thoughts into words. But I must see to my customers. They'll be exhausted if I don't serve them from my last remnant of China tea." He smiled again and moved away.

Mary called to Lavinia, and they walked from the store to the waiting carriage.

"I'm exhausted by the noise," Mary said. "What is it that makes women's voices get higher and higher when they are in a crowd?"

Lavinia did not answer. She had sunk back against the seat, her eyes fixed on the moving crowd that lined the street leading to the docks. Beyond the low building, the great ship loomed large and impressive. The tarnished figurehead rose above the building. Masts and spars and furled canvas were dark against the blue sky.

"I think you have a knack for selecting colors and styles, Lavinia. You must love clothes," Mary said after they had crossed the bridge.

"Certainly, I like clothes. They are part of my equipment as a woman—an important part," she said, half to herself, her eyes on the floor of the coach. The brightness faded from her face; she seemed tired, under a strain. As they neared the house she looked up. Mary was shocked by the despair reflected in her eyes. "I need that equipment more than I ever needed it in my life, Mary. Lady Caroline has come back. She has taken a great house in New Bern for the Governor's ball. Oh, Mary, I don't think I can stand it!" She put her hands before her face, her shoulders shaking. Then she pulled herself together. They were at Queen's Gift.

Mary took Lavinia directly to her sitting room, pausing only long enough to order tea brought upstairs. They talked of inconsequential things until the slave had left the room. Lavinia put down her cup without having tasted the tea.

"I've said either too much or too little, Mary. Too little I think. I'm the most unhappy woman in the world." She came over to Mary and knelt beside her. Mary was moved by the tragic look in her beautiful eyes. "I know I was wrong, but I made Peyton tell me. You see I found letters, peremptory letters telling—no, ordering—Peyton to do certain things."

Mary waited, stroking the bowed head. "Perhaps it would ease you if you told me from the beginning, dear."

Lavinia lifted her tear-drenched face. "You wouldn't understand, Mary. You see, I love Peyton. Sometimes I think your way is best. A woman makes a better wife if she doesn't love the man she's married to. Then she can be a complete wife. Her emotions play no part. But what would you do if you loved a man and you knew he was unfaithful to you? Not once, but many times. And no matter what promises he makes, you know in your heart that he will go on doing the same thing as long as he lives. You can never trust him. You are always watching . . . always watching."

Mary touched Lavinia's soft hair with comforting fingers, but did not speak. Lavinia must talk to ease her soul and her heart.

Lavinia repeated, "It is terrible to love a man and not be able to trust him. Then it becomes passion alone—a matter of night and the bed."

Mary said, "I thought Peyton had changed. You seemed so happy the last time you were here."

"For a little while. Then it all began again. I don't know what I would have done without Adam. He paid off the Minch girl. I don't know how many others. Mary, sometimes I wish Peyton were dead. Then I'd have peace." She lowered her voice. "Then he would be mine."

Mary tried not to show her alarm at Lavinia's words. She said, "Peyton's trouble is that he is too charming. Women swarm around like bees. He can't resist flattery and adoration. It pleases his vanity . . . makes him feel more of a man."

"I know all that, Mary. Don't think I haven't gone over it a thousand times. This woman coming here again is terrifying!" There was a note of despair in her voice.

"Many men have fallen in love with Lady Caroline," Mary said. "I never thought Peyton cared for her particularly." Yet

225

as she spoke she seemed to see a series of pictures of the two together which belied the comforting words she had spoken.

"You don't know, Mary. I do. He had been seeing her secretly for the past two years, here and in the Indies. When he went to Charlotte Amalie she was there too, living in one of the great houses on the Island. He stayed in her home for weeks at a time."

"Lavinia! How do you know that?"

Lavinia lifted her head from her hands. "Ah, now you are shocked! I found letters. I forced him to tell me. I took an evil delight in making myself suffer. I thought I could cure myself of loving him—but I can't, I can't! Oh, Mary, what am I to do?" She got to her feet and paced the floor, her hands clasped in front of her. "I know I shouldn't have forced him to tell. I hated myself for doing it. I should have gone on not knowing really, only suspecting . . . but I couldn't. I made him confess. First he lied—that was bad. Not so bad though as when he broke down. Truth is horrible. We should never force truth." Tears streamed down her cheeks. She made no effort to dry them. "You must not think me a jealous woman. I am not that. I am a woman in love, fighting for my home—for my happiness." Her voice broke. "More than anything I want our son to love and respect his father." She dropped into a chair. Her slender body was shaken with emotion. Mary was aghast. She prayed for the right words for there was no wisdom in offering banal encouragement. Lavinia was too far gone in emotion for that.

"Have you talked with Adam?" Mary asked.

After a muffled "No," Lavinia sat up and wiped her eyes. "How can I? Adam has told me on several such occasions that he would never help Peyton again. The last time I know he meant it. He said he was only weakening Peyton by assuming his debts and his responsibilities. He was right, Mary. I know he was right, but Adam can be hard—hard and unforgiving."

Mary did not agree, but she did not say so. "Perhaps this time he might help."

Lavinia stiffened her body, set her small jaw. "No, I won't tell Adam. Don't ask me. It isn't money now. Peyton always seems to have plenty of money. But Mary, how can I live with him when he defiles his body with that woman and then comes to me?"

There was the sound of a door opening and Peyton's voice below. Mary was glad not to answer the question.

Lavinia sat up suddenly. "I must bathe my eyes." By an effort she controlled her voice. "Call down to him, Mary.

Make some excuse—give me a little time." Her smile was pathetic. "We must observe the amenities." She crossed the room and put her arms about Mary, kissing her cheek. "Dear Mary, it has helped me to talk with you. Please don't worry. There must be some solution—some easy way for a woman to hold the man she loves—if only she can find it."

Before they went downstairs Lavinia said, "There is something else that worries me, Mary. I spoke about David to Sara. I didn't mean to make trouble for Adam, but sometimes my tongue runs away."

Mary stared at Lavinia in astonishment.

"We were talking. She mentioned Azizi of her own accord. That situation doesn't seem to bother her in the least, Mary. She accepts it as a masculine prerogative. She was so sensible, so calm, that I thought it was a good time to speak about David. I asked her why she didn't bring the child to the Manor House sometime. Adam is so fond of him."

"She was angry?"

"Angry? She was raging! Her face grew scarlet. I really thought she would have another fit. I was frightened, Mary. I tried to smooth it over, but she wouldn't listen. She began to cry. She said I had designs against her, wanting her to bring a bondwoman's child born out of wedlock, under her roof; that it was disgraceful, humiliating. I tried to quiet her—'

"What could you say, Lavinia?"

"Not much, I assure you. I mentioned that General Burgoyne was a natural child—you know she has spoken of him with admiration, but I couldn't calm her. She began to cry harder, and to laugh. Then Judith came running in and I escaped. Do you think I ought to tell Adam?"

Mary thought a moment. "I'd wait to see if Sara mentions it again. If she doesn't, don't worry Adam. He has enough on his mind and heart—'"

Lavinia's face cleared. Mary saw she was relieved.

"I'll not say a word. I'm sure Sara won't speak of it again. You know how she is. She ignores things that don't please her. She pretends they don't exist."

"Perhaps it's the best way, Lavinia. We must always remember that Sara is sick and has a sick woman's fancies."

Lavinia knew Mary was referring to Sara's treatment of her. "I've told you she's jealous of you, Mary," she said.

Mary's face did not change. She met Lavinia's eyes frankly.

"There's no reason for that, Lavinia. I wish she could understand. It hurts me to know that I cause her worry even though it is without foundation. But there is nothing I can do about it."

Mary gave no promise of silence to Lavinia concerning Peyton. She had determined to talk with Adam at the first opportunity. It came a day or two later when she was riding along the wood road that led to the abandoned hut of the charcoal-burner's. A Negro groom was with her. She dismounted from Black Douglas and sent the boy along the banks to gather dogwood for the altar at St. Paul's. It was late afternoon with the sun slanting through the pines. A jay planed his bright blue body across the river, uttering harsh, discordant cries. Squirrels ran across the mossy bank, and bees droned in the wild plum blossoms. She sat down on a bench and leaned against the rough hewn logs of the hut. After some time, she heard the sound of branches snapping and the dull pounding of a horse's hoofs. Through the aisle of trees a horseman was riding along the river bank. When he came closer, she recognized Adam. He was riding slowly with lowered rein, his tall body bent, his shoulders slouching forward. When he saw her, he waved his hand, urging his horse into a canter.

On their way home through the sunset, she told him of Lavinia's unhappiness. She tried to be casual about it because it always angered Adam when she talked about Peyton.

"Peyton is a fool," he said briefly. "A damned fool!"

Mary did not argue that point. "Is there anything to be done?" she asked as they crossed the ford. Adam did not seem to hear her. The splashing water under the horses' feet and the mournful cry of a blue heron flying low across the swamp were the only sounds. They were at the turn of the road, near the edge of the village, before he spoke.

"I'm going to New Bern on Monday. I think I shall call on Lady Caroline."

A strange feeling of anxiety came over Mary. "I think the idea is good," she said, making an effort to be natural.

They stopped at the North Plantation on the way home and Mary went to Lucy's cabin while Adam walked toward Stone House. She knew he was going to see Azizi and the boy. That was only natural, she reasoned with herself, but she could not reason away the thrust of pain that the thought of Adam with the Arab girl and his child always caused her.

Lucy was sitting in her little garden, knitting stockings. When she saw Mary, her face brightened. She drew up a chair and brought her a glass of water from the spring.

"I have knitted more than fifty pairs of socks this winter," she said diffidently. "Would you like to see them?" She went quickly across the lawn and came back after a moment carrying a great rush basket with a cover. "Marcy had an Indian make the basket for me, Mrs. Warden. He is very kind and so thoughtful." Her blue eyes filled with quick tears. "He is so gentle, so patient, trying to teach me—to make me remember, but I cannot—nothing that is past, just what is now." Her face lost its life. She sat very still, her eyes gazing into the distance.

Mary laid her hand on Lucy's arm. "My dear," she said, "you must not worry. Perhaps it is better as it is. You have Marcy, your boy is healthy, and you are getting stronger every day. It is far better now than it was before—" Mary stopped. She didn't want to talk of the cabin in the wilderness.

Lucy's thin hands were busy folding and unfolding the neat packages of socks she had knitted—bundles of white, grey and brown.

"He says the same, Mrs. Warden. Marcy says we must think of the future. He always speaks of the future—what we must do—"

A thought came to Mary: I believe Marcy loves her. It is her helplessness, but she is lovely too, with her fine, delicate skin and wide childlike eyes.

Lucy said, "In a little while Azizi will be here. She comes every afternoon and brings her boy to play with mine. Sometimes I think one child is not enough to fill the heart—" She sat for a moment looking across the lawn, a frown between her brows as if she were trying to remember. "One is not enough—" she repeated.

Mary got up. She felt as if she could not see Azizi or Adam's son today. She spoke again of the socks and said she would like a dozen pair for William if Lucy would let her pay for them. Perhaps Mr. Hewes could sell some at the shop. Lucy smiled happily. She was pleased at Mary's words of praise about her work.

"I want to be busy," she said. "Every moment—then I am happy."

The boy called her from the house, a broken toy in his hands. "Mama, Mama," he cried in distress.

"You'll excuse me, Mrs. Warden? My boy wants me now." Lucy walked swiftly across the lawn. Mary saw her lift the child in her arms and bury her face against his cheek.

Chapter 16

QUEEN'S
SISTER

ADAM'S coach drove up at Swan Inn at New Bern late in the afternoon. The landlord, Peate, took him to the west wing where rooms had been reserved for the week of the ball: rooms for Sara; a drawing room, dining room and another bedroom for himself. Lavinia and Peyton were across a small hall, the servants close by. His bedroom faced the new Palace. The drawing room looked on the river. It was gay and bright, with printed red and white tulle for curtains and chair covers.

Adam had come to New Bern ahead of the family. There was a Provincial Council meeting to attend, and he had been asked by the Governor to serve on a committee of hospitality. The men from Virginia and Maryland and South Carolina who had been invited to attend the dedication of the new Palace must be looked after and entertained according to their rank and position.

While Herk was unpacking his boxes, Adam stepped out to the balcony to look at the new building. The Palace was a three-story building of red brick, the gallery rails and the fluted Doric columns of white. The central building was flanked by crescent colonnades ending in two smaller wings of the same design. The chaste façade gave classic dignity to the building. Adam had never seen a more perfect example of the period. The Moor had surpassed Mansion House in London, which did not have the perfect setting of massed trees and the glimpses of the broad river through the colonnades. Any reservations that Adam had had about the cost disappeared. It was suitable for the Province to have such a building—a symbol of the wealth and abundance of the land itself. It might be a burden in taxes for a few years, but people would soon forget. They would always be proud of their Palace.

A hundred men were working on the lawns; great trees and shrubs, balled, stood ready to be planted on the terrace; full-leafed magnolias of great height bordered the curving drive; tulip trees bloomed in the lower garden; box hedges and

230

privet outlined the formal gardens, the maze, and the long marble pool; yellow plumes of mimosa shadowed the brick walls that enclosed the grounds. Nothing had been forgotten that would enhance the beauty of the building. Adam went into the room well satisfied with what he had seen. As the years went on people would forget the burden of taxes.

After he had bathed and dined, he went down to the Ordinary and inquired of Peate where Lady Caroline lived. The landlord gave him directions. He said Lady Caroline had come back from the Indies with a larger retinue of slaves, and had taken the dwelling that had housed the Governor before he moved to the Palace.

"It's mighty gay at that house now," Peate said slyly. "The gentlemen and ladies have a merry time, so they say."

Adam cut him short. "Please order my carriage," he said.

Peate went away toward the back of the house. In a few minutes Cicero drove up to the front door of the Inn, Herk on the box beside him. Loungers about the Inn yard came to see the smart blue coach and to gape at the mammoth Zulu on the box. The name Rutledge ran from lip to lip, a name well known in the Province. Heads were turned as Adam came out of the Inn. A beggar whined, craving alms. Herk tossed a coin and ordered the fellow out of the way of the prancing horses. The coach drove off, turning past the square to the broad road that followed the bank of the river.

As the coach drew near the entrance of Lady Caroline's Adam heard the sound of music and gay laughter coming through the open windows. He gave his name to the servant and sat down in the great hall. The slave returned at once. "Will Mr. Rutledge please step up to Lady Caroline's sitting room? She will receive him there immediately."

Adam glanced into the drawing room as he went up the wide stairs. Red-coated army men were talking with officers from the *Daphne* which was anchored beyond the bar. He recognized planters from the Wilmington district and from Charlottetown. Moore was standing near the carved marble mantel talking with Captain Stephens of the *Daphine*. Someone was playing the piano. A deep bass voice roared out a sailor's song about the coast of High Barbary. Farquhar Campbell and Fanning were seated at a small table, tall, thin glasses in front of them. Fanning, with his saturnine face, his insolent black eyes, faced the door. He glanced up as Adam passed and nodded briefly.

The footman opened the door at the head of the stair. Lady Caroline was sitting on a green satin sofa, a small table

231

with a decanter and glasses in front of her. John Hawks was near the window talking to a young naval officer. Adam had never seen Lady Caroline look more beautiful. Her heavy, white satin gown flowed in widening folds, revealing in some subtle way her long limbs and graceful body. A necklace of square-cut emeralds set with hundreds of small brilliants clasped her strong, white throat. A coronet to match held her elaborately curled wig in place. A provocative patch near the corner of her wide red mouth emphasized its generous curves.

"Adam!" she said as she extended her hand to be kissed. "You are very welcome." As he bowed, she added in an undertone, "I will send these men away presently." Aloud she made a casual introduction, "Mr. Adam Rutledge, this is Lieutenant Grafton from the *Daphne*."

Adam bowed and then shook hands with the Moor. "I saw your new building today for the first time. It is everything it should be."

The Moor smiled, pleased at Adam's words.

Lady Caroline said the officer, "Mr. Rutledge has a plantation near Edenton. He is one of the famous Iron Men of Albemarle."

Adam shook his head. "I can't claim that distinction. I did not come to Carolina until after that title had been earned by the real Iron Men."

"But you are one now," she said, "as stubborn as all the others."

The officer listened without comment. He had heavy black brows and a quick, bold glance. After a moment, he addressed Hawks: "The Palace is a copy of Mansion House, is it not?"

The Moor shrugged his shoulders expressively. "Both might be said to be adaptations of the earlier and more beautiful form used by the Greeks."

The retort made Adam smile inwardly. The officer drew his brows together, visibly annoyed. "We've heard in England that there is much dissatisfaction over the excessive taxes for the building," he said with a touch of acid in his tone.

Lady Caroline's throaty voice interrupted. "How silly to make a fuss about cost over anything so beautiful. Beauty should always be its own excuse." Adam felt a subtle, almost sensual implication in her words. She turned to him. "You don't think a suitable Palace for the Royal Governor a great extravagance, do you, Mr. Rutledge?"

232

"No, I don't. I think such a building justifies even what this gentleman calls excessive taxes."

Hawks fixed his somber eyes on Adam. "I assure you, Mr. Rutledge, I have no desire to start a revolution over the cost of the building."

"A revolution!" The officer's voice expressed some surprise. "I didn't know it had gone that far."

"The northwestern counties have already sent written protests. They say they'll burn the Palace to the ground rather than bear any more taxation," Lady Caroline said to Grafton. "But we don't take them too seriously."

"By God, these Colonials are insolent! Why don't you clap them into the gaol and be done with it?" Grafton exclaimed.

Adam said, "You heard what they did about the stamps and the Stamp Master, Grafton. The people here in the Carolinas are independent folk jealous of their rights."

Grafton gave Adam a swift, appraising glance, then said with stiff superiority, "Better turn them over to us. We'll deal with them—"

Lady Caroline raised her fan. "La, la, Grafton, you don't know these strong free men of the Colonies." Her tone was light, mocking. "They are not easy to deal with. I give you my word, you don't know what you're talking about."

Grafton's tone changed when he spoke to Lady Caroline. It was suave, almost deferential. "My father is a friend of Rockingham. I know something of the government's plans. Britain will send ships and troops over here in a flash, Lady Caroline, if there is any sign of revolt."

Adam found himself glaring at the young Irishman. What did the young puppy know of Colonial affairs? "Will that be soon?" he asked, hiding his anger under a slight veil of irony. "The army seems to be very much engaged at the moment."

The Irishman's face reddened. "They've had a bit of hard luck—but it won't be long before all our troops are home again. Then we must have another war to keep them from getting out of hand."

"I see. And you think we Colonists will be the ones to quarter rebellious troops?"

"That is my opinion." The officer's face was flushed. He poured himself a glass of brandy. "We've got to settle things over here. What makes you think you can set your own taxes? Parliament sets the taxes, not Colonial Assemblies."

Adam raised his brows slightly. Though he did not like the fellow's insolence and air of superiority he remained casual.

233

There was no irony in his voice now but his words held a challenge.

"You have not been here long enough to understand our people, Mr. Grafton. In the matter of setting taxes England is the head, but she is not the members too. We are a separate people. We cannot be dealt with as uncultured country folk accustomed to follow the will of a few, like sheep. Taxes that originate in the antechamber of some of the noble Lords will not be imposed without strong argument from this Province." There was a pregnant silence in the room at his words.

Lady Caroline held out her slim, white hand. "Gentlemen! Please! You remember that I will not have political discussion under my roof."

Adam bowed. "I'm sorry, Lady Caroline. I let my tongue run away with me. Shall we talk of something more agreeable?"

The Irishman was not so easily mollified. He stood in a belligerent attitude, his feet apart, his hand on the hilt of his sword. "The whole thing is a delusion, this business of wanting representation. You have no right to it until you prove your ability to govern. So far you are a long way from that, Rutledge."

Adam looked back at him with level eyes. There were many things he could say, but he did not speak. Lady Caroline laid her hand on the young officer's arm. "Have you forgotten that you are to play escarte with Colonel Fanning? I'm sure he is waiting for you. Will you show Lieutenant Grafton the way down to the card room, Mr. Hawks?"

A faint gleam of understanding, tinged with amusement, crossed the Moor's dark face. Adam knew that he saw through Lady Caroline's subterfuge.

"Good night, Mr. Rutledge. Your servant, Lady Caroline. This way, Lieutenant." He led the way toward the door.

The Irishman clicked his heels together and bowed to Lady Caroline. At the door he turned to Adam. "Parliament is likely to lay you new and heavier taxes if you are disobedient," he said.

"Who is this Lieutenant Grafton?" Adam asked of Lady Caroline.

"A cousin of William Pitt on the distaff side."

"That accounts for his arrogance. All the Pitts are arrogant."

"Excepting Pitt himself."

"Excepting the Great Commoner himself," Adam agreed. "He is very simple and very kind."

234

"When he pleases. It seems that no one can afford to be simple but the great." The bitterness in Lady Caroline's voice made Adam look at her attentively. "Simple and insolent—and inordinately cruel," she added. It seemed to Adam that a mask had dropped from her. The hint of laughter that usually indented the corners of her mouth was gone, leaving a look of discontent. For a moment her expression was hard, almost vindictive. Then the smile returned and an upward turn of her chin effaced the momentary mood. She had assumed the smiling mask again, the studied gaiety.

The sound of laughter, the low rumble of voices and snatches of song came from the lower floor. They were far away, as if they belonged to another world. What the woman had been thinking of, what bitter experiences she had passed through, were unknown to Adam. Of one thing he was certain, life had not always been kind to her. Just what truth there was in the rumor that she was born Royal, he did not know; but she had all the attributes of Royalty.

"You want something of me?" she said. The suddenness of her question startled Adam. He had intended to lead up to the subject of Peyton gradually in some diplomatic way. Her question changed that. He answered frankly.

"Yes, Lady Caroline."

"Is it about Peyton Rutledge?" she asked, her lip curling back over her strong teeth.

"Yes."

"I knew you would not come to see me unless you had a good reason." There was no anger in her voice, only a little sadness. "Why do you never come on your own account, Adam?"

"I have been very busy and we've both been away," he said briefly. Dismissing the personal, he continued: "Since you have been frank, I will be the same. I do want to talk about Peyton. I am worried about him—have been for some time." He paused, wondering how he could put the question without giving offense. He didn't want to anger her. He wanted her help and if Peyton was in her debt he wanted to know it. Peyton had not spoken to him of personal matters since the time he refused to let him have the thousand guineas. He avoided Adam, only seeing him with other people—never talking to him except about business. But Adam had observed that Peyton was unnaturally quiet—the lines between his nose and chin had deepened. And he knew from what Mary Warden had told him how worried Lavinia was about him. It was not only his unfaithfulness, but the fact that he was drinking heavily night after night that worried her.

Adam was sure that Lady Caroline held the key to Peyton's trouble. Watching her now, he knew that his best chance lay in being very open with her.

He said, "Yes, I'm here to talk about Peyton. Some time ago he came to me asking for money, a very large amount of cash. I didn't have it, nor could I get it. You know we do most of our business by trade, not by coin. You know Peyton's temper. He flew out of the room in a rage. . . . Since then he has avoided me. I thought—perhaps—" Adam stopped. He didn't want to make accusations at this stage. Lady Caroline was watching him, a curious, unreadable expression in her long, green eyes. Adam hesitated, then went on, "Why did you allow Peyton to come to your house so often at Pembroke, at Guernsey House—will it be the same here at New Bern?"

A slow smile came to her red lips. She leaned forward a little. The lace at her square-cut bodice fell away from the full curve of her white breasts.

"You would not believe me if I spoke the truth."

"You might try me," Adam said.

"I have wanted Peyton for one thing. He brought me closer to you."

Though he passed her words off with a laugh, a feeling that she was speaking the truth came over him. He knew he must keep the conversation casual.

"Well, here I am," he said.

"Are you prepared to bargain with me?" she asked.

"No. I will not bargain. But I think you will send Peyton about his business. It will be better that way." His words had purpose behind them.

Lady Caroline leaned back, watching him lazily, her eyes following the length of his body. "I could have served you better than the Arab girl," she said abruptly.

Adam kept his composure by an effort. "I'm not here to discuss myself or my affairs."

"You are not angry, Adam! I want to make you angry. I know that under your indifference you are a strong man, with strong passionate emotions."

Adam kept silent. The woman was trying to bait him, but he would not let her. "It will be more pleasant for everyone if you send Peyton about his business," he said.

Her tone changed. "I have need of Peyton. I have no intention of letting him go." She shrugged her shapely shoulders. "He is too deeply involved now," she said, as an after-thought.

"Peyton is not in love with you. He loves his wife." Adam regretted the words as soon as they were out.

She seemed not to have heard. She repeated her words: "He is too deeply involved. Not with me, Adam, but with other people. He dare not desert them, even if he wanted to." She dropped her voice. "They would kill him. . . ."

Adam's apprehension rose at her words. If some unknown danger threatened Peyton he must move cautiously until he found out what it was. He must play with this woman at her own game. He leaned back. He, too, was watching.

"If it's gambling debts," he said, "I might now be able to pay."

She shook her head. "Nothing so simple. Don't ask me, for I shall not tell you." She got up and moved about the room. Her slow, almost feline movements stirred him. He made an effort to keep his mind on the business at hand. "Why do you think only of Peyton? My word! He isn't worth it. He has no strength, no character, bad or good. He is vain and weak." She paused, measuring him with an appraising glance. "But you could never understand weakness in a man, Adam."

Adam felt his pulse rising. It was hard to keep from thinking of the woman in front of him.

There was the sound of horses' hoofs on the hard drive, and the sharp imperative rap of the knocker at the door. Lady Caroline's words died away. She went to the window, drawing the heavy shades to look down at the entrance of the house. A Negro serving woman appeared at the door. She had been running.

"His Excellency has arrived, madam. He asked to be shown up."

"Shut the door, fool." Lady Caroline's voice was sharp, her eyes darted about the room. "He mustn't find you here, Adam." She took his cloak and hat from a chair and thrust them into his arms. "Quick, go in there.

Adam protested. "I will stay here. Why should I not see Tryon?"

"Please! You don't understand. Wait in there until he goes. He won't be here long. I want to talk with you. If you really are interested and want to help Peyton—stay!"

Adam said, "I don't like furtiveness. I will leave the way I came."

"You can't! You can't! Please! For Peyton's sake, you must trust me." She pushed him across the threshold and closed the door softly. Adam heard the turn of the key in the lock, followed immediately by a loud knock at the door and the footman's voice announcing "His Excellency, the Governor."

The room he had entered was in darkness. A faint light outlined an open window. He looked out. The room was on the third floor above the ground. He caught hold of the ivy that grew to the brick walls of the house. It tore away from his hand. Damn the woman! Why hadn't she let him out through the door? What harm if he had met the Governor coming up the stair as he went down? He was in an intolerable situation, hiding in a woman's bedroom.

He sat down on a chair trying to accustom his eyes to darkness. The faint illumination from the half-moon came in through the shutters. He made out the dressing table by the highlights of silver stoppers and glass bottles. On it were perfumes, powders and women's trinkets, and in the center of the room stood a broad bed with a silken flounced coverlid. Was he to sit like a rat in the dark until Tryon left the place? He felt along the walls. One door, a closet, and the one window. There was no way out. Tryon's voice became audible.

"Will you have the information before the *Daphne* sails, Caroline?"

"Without fail, your Excellency. It is on the way now."

"You think Lord North will continue to dominate? It was rumored that his position is unstable."

"I am positive, William. I have it from confidential but most reliable sources that the Rockingham ministry won't last out the year." Lady Caroline's voice was not raised but it came through distinctly.

"Then a new ministry will be formed?"

"Undoubtedly, your Excellency. I told you yesterday the names of the men. Lord George Germain, for one, is mentioned."

"Damn it, damn it! Such a ministry would be doomed from the beginning. What will happen here? North would be too lenient or too indifferent to think of the Colonies. Pitt is a sick man. His little clique in London with Temple at the head isn't strong enough to carry through any plans."

"I'm positive that my information is correct, your Excellency. There is a cousin of Mr. Pitt's here in New Bern, a naval man, detached from his ship on some special mission. He is downstairs now."

"Why didn't you tell me! Send for him at once."

"He has been here only a few days. He came as a passenger on the *Daphne*. Wouldn't you rather talk to him in the library?"

Adam heard the rustle of silk as Lady Caroline moved about the room.

"No. I'll see him here. It is quieter—less danger of being overheard. Where does the door lead?"

"To my bedroom, my Lord!"

Tryon laughed. "Therefore inviolate, madam?"

"I trust so, your Excellency."

Adam sat very still. He would have liked to open the door and confront the Governor, but he knew he was trapped. He must remain where he was, trusting to her wit.

She laughed. "The library is perfectly safe and the chairs more comfortable."

"Tut, tut, I prefer to stay where I am. Send for the man. By the way, what is his name?"

A silk gown rustled. A door opened. Adam heard the tap of Tryon's heels on the hard wood floor as he paced back and forth. His sword hit against the fender. Adam could imagine the Governor standing before the fire. Adam heard Lady Caroline saying, "I've sent for Grafton."

"Thank you, Caroline." There was a moment's silence. Adam could hear the ticking of a small clock on the dressing table. "I've been thinking over what you told me about the new ministry. Perhaps it won't be too bad. Germain is a soldier," Tryon continued.

"A discredited one, your Excellency."

"You mean his conduct at the battle of Munden?" The Governor's voice was impatient. "Senseless talk! There was some excuse—he was young—"

"Most people are not so lenient—they call him a coward." There was scorn in her voice.

The Governor said, "How hard you are, Caroline. You never forgive or forget a man's mistakes."

"Not if a man is weak—or a coward."

After a brief pause, the Governor went back to the original theme. "All this is in the future, this new ministry. Many things may happen in the meantime."

"The change may come in a few years—or tomorrow; but when open rebellion comes in America, it will be put down with arms. If you want approval from high places, William, you must use determination and crush any sign of revolt in North Carolina. You want to be Governor of New York. The way to accomplish that is to handle any sign of rebellion by strong measures."

"You should have been a general, Caroline," he said, "or an admiral commanding Sail of the Line."

"That would be glorious!" Lady Caroline exclaimed. "Nothing could be more thrilling than to command a ship!"

There was admiration in the Governor's voice. "Again, I repeat—you should have been a man."

Adam heard her laugh ripple out. "Really, your Excellency, really. . . . You say that to me?"

Tryon laughed. "Words, my dear, words. You know I prefer you as you are with all your feminine allure and charm. Tell me—what kind of men do you prefer?"

There was a short silence.

Then she said, "Like the Virgin Queen, I prefer strong men, men who have courage—decisive men, bold in action. Otherwise, why should I like your Excellency?"

"Caroline, no one knows so well as you how to draw a man on—yet hold him off. How long am I to wait?" His voice dropped. Adam could not hear the next words, nor her answer.

In a moment he heard her say, "I had your word we would not talk of these things until later. After all, I believe we will go downstairs. Wait for me in the small room off the drawing room. I don't want Grafton to think his information is important enough for a secret audience with your Excellency."

"You are quite right. You think of everything. My dear, you are superb tonight." Adam heard Tryon moving about the room. The door knob turned. "Did you say this was your bedroom?"

"Yes, your Excellency. But come! You must go downstairs at once or Grafton will be here. Don't go in there, I beg you. Think of what might be said in the Province if someone should see you coming out of my bedchamber."

"No one will see. I will set a guard. After all I *am* the Governor."

Her voice was smooth. "An adorable Governor! But we must be discreet. Come! Well, just one! Do not disarrange my coiffure. There are twenty women downstairs who would tear my reputation into tatters if they saw me with a disarranged coiffure."

There was a swish of skirts and the click of a sword hitting against a chair. The door banged. Adam heard the clatter of boots on the stairs.

He waited a moment, then tried the door cautiously. While his hand was still on the knob, the key clicked. Lady Caroline

240

opened the door. Her cheeks were flushed, her eyes shone, the lace on her breast rose and fell with her quick breathing.

"I'm sorry," she said, her hand against her heart, "but what could I do? I had forgotten that the Governor was coming. You make me forget everything, Adam." She spread out her hands in a hopeless gesture.

Adam moved to the outer door.

"Don't, don't!" She caught his arm. "We haven't finished about Peyton. Adam, wait. . . ."

Adam's voice was harsh. He was still annoyed by the way she had maneuvered him into an awkward position. "If Peyton has got himself into any more trouble, he will have to get himself out of it. It is not my affair."

"You can be very hard, Adam hard as all strong men are." She stood near him. He felt the closeness of her soft body, the perfume in her hair; the soft huskiness of her voice held a challenge. She laid her hand on his arm. "Let's talk no more about Peyton. It is better for him to learn to stand on his own feet. Why do we waste time talking of him? He will find a way out—he always manages. Let us think about ourselves. We are alive, we two. . . ."

Still holding his arm, she drew back a little, her face upturned, her red mouth half opened. Her eyes were filled with a strange light that made his blood race. The intoxication of her fragrant body had a fascination, full-flavored in its complete wantonness. Her hand fell from his arm.

"I have waited a long time for you, Adam." Her voice was very low.

Adam did not move. His eyes followed the long outline of her offered body. Here was no woman of innocence and virginity. Here was a woman who had had many men—who had grown in understanding. What did it matter? He had no love for her. She did not ask love. The passion of the moment was enough for her. She put her arms about him. Her inviting body—warm and living—against him, her lips warm with slow passionate kisses. She would live each moment with intense awareness. Adam had a momentary sense of the outside world. She answered his thought:

"No one will come—no one. Forget the world for a little time, Adam. The adventure of living is enough for the moment."

They moved forward into the shadows of the room he had just left. Her nearness, the fragrance of her pulsating body was an intoxication bringing him swiftly alive. Her arms were about him, the strength of her body against his. A strong masculine sureness possessed him. He would match this woman in strength and power. She was laughing. He closed her mouth with the swift hard passion of his lips.

. The night air against his face was strong and cleansing as he leaned out of the open window of his coach. When he arrived at the Inn, he remembered that Lady Caroline had given him no explanation about Peyton; nor had he once thought to ask what danger threatened him. He cursed aloud —well, it was too late now. After all, why should he worry about Peyton? It was, as she had said, better to let him stand on his own feet.

Chapter 17

TRYON'S PALACE

IT WAS almost five when Adam came into his bedroom at Swan Inn, after a meeting of the Provincial Committee, and saw the clothes Cicero had laid out for him to wear to the ball that night. It was so long since he had worn Court clothes that he looked with distaste at the blue embroidered satin coat, the flowered brocade waistcoat and white satin smallclothes. There was too much contrast between this suggestion of elegance and gaiety and the matters the Committee had been discussing. He sat down by the window, his mind reviewing the happenings of the day.

Adam had not known until he had arrived in the capital that the Governor had arrested Harmon Husband and had him in gaol in New Bern. The news filled him with apprehension, although no one else seemed to share his fears excepting Maurice Moore. The fact was mentioned casually after they had heard the report on the new tax of 2s 6d imposed for three years to finish paying for the Palace, and had discussed plans for the public warehouses for tobacco, following the success of Adam's plan at Edenton, to be established at various points throughout the Province.

The Governor, looking worried and abstracted, stepped into the committee room for a few moments. He came to talk about a petition to the King for leave to issue 100,000 pounds in paper currency for use in the Province. Maurice Moore at once raised objection and the argument became violent. The Governor got angry, and hot words passed between him and Moore, Caswell trying to make peace between them. Tryon would not listen. He pushed back his chair and banged the table with his clenched fist.

"If you don't pass these currency measures, the Province will be bankrupt."

Moore glanced out of the window toward the Palace where a hundred men were working on the gardens and the lawn, preparing for the ball that night.

The Governor's face grew crimson although he appeared to take no notice. He got to his feet.

"I've had word from the Earl of Hillsborough either to adjourn or dissolve the Assembly, unless certain measures are passed," he said hotly.

There was a complete silence for a few moments, broken by Richard Caswell's quiet, even voice. "Your Excellency, will you give us a little time to discuss this measure with the other members? This Committee hasn't the power to force a measure through the Assembly. We can only suggest—"

Tryon did not hide his displeasure but, after a moment's thought, he agreed and left the room.

The men looked at one another.

"His Excellency's in a bad humor. I wonder what's wrong?" John Ashe asked.

"He has much on his mind with the ball and all the entertainment for the populace," William Warden said quietly. "We must think of these things and not be too critical."

"I've a mind it's Harmon Husband that is worrying him," MacLeish, the member from Orange, said.

"Are you having more riots among your radicals in Hillsborough?" Caswell asked.

"Nothing much," the Scot answered. "Some of the farmers got tired of waiting. They've been promised much and given nothing. Last month the sheriff of Orange distrained a horse for a levy. The people took this for a just cause to resist. A hundred men marched into Hillsborough. They tied the sheriff up and took the horse." The Scot settled back in his chair.

Moore leaned forward. "Why don't you tell the rest, about their other activities?"

A grim look came upon the Scot's face. "I had no intention of bringing up our county affairs with a Provincial Committee, but since you ask—yes, there was some shooting, and a few houses were burned. Someone shot a few bullets through Colonel Fanning's house but, unfortunately, he was not there."

No one spoke for a moment. Then Ashe said, "We hadn't heard this, MacLeish. That's the reason Tryon wants the captains of militia to raise their companies to full strength."

"Aye, that's it. Fanning's got to him with his tale," MacLeish said bitterly. "And that's not all. The Governor sent his secretary with dispatches and warrants for the arrest of Harmon Husband and William Butler. Fanning took his men and made the arrests. Before the farmers in the district knew anything about it, Fanning had Husband—"

"And he's in gaol here now?" Adam asked.

"Yes, and when our people get word where he is, there's likely to be trouble."

Maurice Moore spoke. To the astonishment of everyone in the room, he was on the side of Tryon. "The Governor was right in arresting these men. We can't overlook law-breaking. They must be punished. We want liberty and redress for wrongs and grievances, but we want it within the law, not outside. I'm against all such action. It does the Province great harm."

Most of the men present agreed with him. MacLeish made no comment, though he had a dour look on his rocklike features.

But Adam did not want to give assent to Moore's words by silence. "Perhaps you don't understand the grievances these farmers have, gentlemen. I know, for I have been through the counties in the north and west many times these last few years. I know many of these people personally. I know how much they have been promised—and how little they've received."

Moore turned around in his chair and looked at Adam. Adam knew that Moore had never liked him. "I suppose you believe in putting Harmon Husband in the Assembly."

Adam felt his anger rise at the implication.

Moore continued: "I don't blame them for attacking Fanning. His treatment has been abominable, but they can't attack the whole judiciary. That's going too far." His keen eyes were boring into Adam's. "But perhaps Mr. Rutledge believes that is right, also, and that Husband is a wise leader for these radicals."

Much as he hated an argument, Adam felt he must answer. "I don't like Husband any better than you do, Judge Moore. Perhaps less, for I know more about him. I think he will play either side if it suits him and he can gain by it. It's the people I'm thinking about—the farmers. They are honest, hard-working folk. . . . They suffer from bad leadership."

"But you don't believe the Governor should have put Husband in gaol?" Moore's words had the impact of bullets.

"No, I don't," Adam snapped back, for once out of control, "not unless he wants to give Husband more power by making a martyr out of him."

Caswell adjourned the meeting in a few moments. Adam was the first out of the room, followed by MacLeish.

"I'm glad you spoke up, Rutledge. These coast men don't half understand what's going on in the Province."

Adam nodded. He wasn't happy over it. He disliked losing

his temper. MacLeish fell into step as they crossed the Public Parade.

"There's another thing. Did you hear that young Hilary from Orange shot himself in Lady Caroline's garden last night?"

Adam turned quickly. "No, I hadn't heard. What was wrong?"

The Scot shrugged his shoulders. "Heavy losses at cards, they say. It's not the first time this sort of thing has happened."

Adam said nothing though he considered the incident unfortunate. He had heard other criticisms about Lady Caroline. And he was sorry for he had the feeling that she was being maligned. He could not help remembering the times he had seen her when she had dropped her artificiality, when her genuineness had aroused his admiration.

"Our people liked young Hilary and his father. I'm afraid they won't overlook this."

MacLeish left Adam at the door of the Inn, but his words stayed in his mind. The whole session had been a disturbing one.

Adam's thoughts were interrupted by the entrance of Cicero carrying a well-varnished pair of paste-buckled shoes and a lace cravat and sleeve ruffles, freshly pressed. "You bath ready, master. Hit all laid in de ante-room, nice and hot."

Adam glanced at the clock. It was later than he thought. He undressed hastily and bathed. When Cicero had almost finished shaving him, there was a knock at the door, and a small Negro boy came in carrying a bowl of flour. Adam turned his head.

"What's that for?" he asked sharply.

Cicero's voice was conciliatory. "Mis' Sara she say all the gentlemen in London powder dey hair. Mister Peyton he powder hisself."

"Well, I sha'n't powder mine. Take the stuff away."

Cicero tried another tack. "Maybe yo' wear a wig den? Mis' Sara she fetch a nice white one from Mr. Hewes's shop."

Adam interrupted. "I don't want a wig. Get me a black ribband, Cicero, and don't stand there arguing. Get back to the kitchen," he said sharply to the boy.

The pickaninny, who was balancing the bowl of flour in the palm of his hand, jumped at Adam's command, trembling with fright.

246

"Watch yo' hand!" Cicero cried. But it was too late. The bowl crashed to the floor. Flour rose like a cloud, settling on the child. Cicero snatched Adam's embroidered coat out of the dust, shouting to the boy to get out. Adam leaned back, laughing. Cicero muttered to himself as he brushed the coat.

Judith knocked at the door to say that her mistress was waiting in the drawing room. Would Mr. Rutledge please come at once?

Adam slipped on his flowered brocade waistcoat, while Cicero held the blue satin coat. He adjusted the sleeve ruffles carefully, and took some time to wind and tie the lace cravat.

"Hurry, Cicero. That will do," Adam said, impatient at the delay.

Cicero backed away to see the effect. "You looks like a royal prince, Mr. Adam. Why don't you wear dese clothes all de while, like de Governor?"

Adam laughed. "Now wouldn't I look nice plowing the fields in white satin breeches?"

"A Rutledge otten to plow no fiel's," the old man grumbled, as he held the door open for Adam to pass through.

Adam found Peyton and Sara waiting in the drawing room. Sara was dressed in a powder-blue gown and looked fragile and lovely. Adam leaned over to kiss her, but Sara drew back and put out her hand instead.

"Don't touch my lips, Adam. I have made them red with rose petals," she said.

"Sara will be the loveliest woman at the ball, won't she, Peyton?" He turned to his cousin, who was standing in front of a long mirror.

"Sara is always lovely," Peyton answered, busy with his cravat. "She is like a fragile flower."

Sara blushed a delicate pink. "How charming of you to say that, Peyton, almost as if you meant it."

"I do mean it," he answered. He came over to her side and kissed her on the lips. Sara drew back with a little cry of dismay.

"Peyton! Didn't you hear me tell Adam that I had just put crushed rose petals on my lips to make them red?"

Peyton laughed gaily. "Of course, I heard you, Sara. Damned if I paid any attention. There are plenty more rose petals but only one moment like this."

Sara laughed too. "I declare, you are irresistible, Peyton."

Adam looked at his cousin. How ready with a word he was. Sara liked it. She didn't mind the trouble of more rose petals. Adam felt that he was clumsy—he took women at their word. He wondered what would happen if he tried to be more dominating with Sara. How lovely she was tonight! The blue shadows of long invalidism about her eyes added to their depth.

Herk came to the door with Adam's sword and sword belt.

"Not that one, Herk," Adam said. "I want the light Toledo blade with the gold hilt."

Herk turned the sword in his great hands. "Master does not want his stabbing spear tonight?"

Sara smothered a scream. Adam and Peyton laughed.

"Stabbing spear!" Sara cried. "How frightful! Send that savage away, Adam. The idea of allowing him to come to my drawing room! Stabbing spear, indeed!"

Adam refrained from smiling at the bewilderment in his slave's face. "No, Herk. I shall not need the stabbing spear. Tonight is for dancing. The light blade will do."

Herk smiled then, showing his strong, white teeth. "I know. The drums will beat, and the people will dance and make laughter." He left the room quickly.

Sara's thin lifeless voice rose. "I can't see how you keep that great savage Zulu near you, Adam. He frightens me to death. How do you know he won't kill you one day?"

At that Adam laughed indulgently and patted her arm. "He won't kill me, or anyone else. Herk is the most faithful slave I own. I trust him with my life."

Peyton broke in, "You must admit, Sara, that Adam has a way of handling men. They love him and they do anything he says. They don't do that for me. But I had rather have women love me than have men follow me."

"You have your wish," Adam told him, ruffled by his tone.

"Why are you so rude, Adam?" Sara spoke sharply. "Peyton is not serious. He was being amusing." She looked at him more closely, disapproval growing in her face. "Didn't Cicero tell you that I wanted you to powder your hair or wear a wig?"

"Yes, he told me," Adam said shortly.

"Adam likes the idea of being the only man in the Colonies to go with unpowdered hair," Peyton said lightly. "I must admit it has a certain distinction." He took out his watch. The gold seal made a faint tinkling sound. "It's past eight. What can be keeping Lavinia? She was ready when I left off dressing."

Lavinia's languid, carefully cultivated voice broke in. "How little you know what constitutes a lady's dressing, my dear!"

248

They all turned toward the door at the sound of her voice. "By Jove, you do me proud, madam." Peyton made a sweeping bow and walked to her side.

Lavinia curtsied in a billow of pearl satin draperies, her powdered head drooping on her graceful white neck. Adam thought of a white swan settling in the mirrored surface of a glistening pool. Sara looked at her grimly. She smoothed the panniers of her gown with thin nervous fingers, a look of discontent on her face.

"I never saw that gown before, Lavinia," she said petulantly.

"I've never worn it before. I have been saving it. It is my war gown. Well, Squire Rutledge, why are you so silent? Don't you approve of your cousin Lavinia? Come, you may kiss my fingers." Lavinia extended her hand with studied grace.

"Peyton says I have no manners with women," Adam said. "He thinks I'm more at home with horses and dogs and men in coonskin caps. But I know a beautiful woman when I see one. My homage, madam!" He bowed with exaggerated dignity.

Lavinia smiled.

Sara interrupted the little scene. "I think you need color, Lavinia. Your costume lacks emphasis," she said.

Peyton crossed the room and took up a shagreen case from the table. Opening it he took out a necklace and lifted it up near the candelabrum. A shower of pale blue sapphires reflected a hundred lights on their many facets.

Lavinia caught her hands to her breasts. Her lips parted. "How beautiful—how beautiful!" she whispered. "Is it for me?"

Peyton smiled back at her. "For you, my darling—for whom else?"

Sara's crisp voice showed her disapproval. "A royal gift, Peyton, but was it not very expensive?"

Peyton laughed, a little disagreeably. "Let's not talk of expense tonight, Sara. Let's be gay, very, very gay."

Adam thought there was a challenge in his voice. He could not help thinking of the situation between Peyton and Lavinia, and of Lady Caroline's words hinting of danger. Perhaps Peyton's challenge was not to Sara or Lavinia, but to Fate. Adam looked at him closely. There was nothing to show fear, nothing. Perhaps the whole mystery in which his cousin was supposed to be involved was the product of the too imaginative minds of women.

Peyton asked for the honor of riding in the coach with Sara. She was pleased at his attention. It had been arranged for Sara to be taken to the small balcony overlooking the ballroom. Dr. Armitage would meet her there and see that she was comfortable. The Governor himself had made the suggestion.

Lavinia and Adam went in the second coach. Adam sat on the opposite seat for Lavinia's flowing skirts and hoop took more than half the space. At the last moment Sara delayed them, protesting that she had not the strength to go. Lavinia motioned the coachman to drive on while Sara was still debating.

They drove for a time in silence.

"I wonder if this excitement won't be too much for Sara," Adam said dubiously.

"Don't be stupid, Adam," Lavinia answered. "Sara thrives on excitement. She was piqued because she thought my gown handsomer than hers. And she didn't like Peyton giving me this necklace. I don't know why. He gives me little enough." Her slim finger toyed with the glittering stones as she raised troubled eyes to Adam. "I wonder myself, Adam. When he put it around my neck I had the most horrible presentiment of evil."

Adam laughed at her then. "It's you who are silly," he said teasingly. "You have too much imagination. It is a superb jewel. Why not enjoy its beauty?" But he wondered a little himself. The stones must have cost a great deal of money.

They drove in silence. When they neared the Palace, they saw that great fires were burning in the square where crowds of gay, laughing people had gathered around barbecue pits and beer barrels. Dozens of link boys, carrying flaming pine knots, stood along the curved driveway from the garden walls to the broad entrance of the Palace, lighting the way for coaches and chairs.

Lavinia caught Adam's hand. "Stay near me tonight, Adam," she whispered. Her hands were as cold as ice. He felt that she was trembling.

"Of course, I shall be near you, my little cousin, but you have Peyton," he answered, wondering what had suddenly disturbed the usually gay, poised Lavinia.

"I can't trust Peyton. I want you near me. Oh, Adam! I need your strength."

Adam patted her hand as he would a child's. "What! Not nervous at the thought of all the formality?"

"You know it is not that." With an effort she regained her

composure. "I will walk between you and Peyton tonight when I make my bow before the Governor and Lady Tryon. My entrance will be worth seeing, for I shall have the two handsomest men in the Colony by my side!"

Adam's fingers closed on her hand strongly. He wanted her to know that, whatever it was that worried her, he was there to support her.

"I told you this is my war dress, Adam. I meant it. I fight a battle tonight, not with rapiers, but with woman's wits."

"Lavinia, you are not—"

She stopped him. Her hand buried itself closer in his.

"Don't worry, Adam. I shall not make a scene. But I must fight with what weapons I have at hand. I understand Lady Caroline will be there. Wish me good fortune, my cousin."

By the light of the fagots outside the carriage door Adam saw her eyes were clouded with tears.

"Oh, Adam! I love him so much . . . so very much," she whispered.

Armitage was with Sara when they reached the balcony. He gave them the latest gossip which he had from Farquhar Campbell and Edmund Fanning. A Great Personage had arrived unexpectedly that afternoon on the gunboat H. M. S. *Jupiter,* now anchored in the river. The Great Personage was traveling under the name of Baron Cotswold. Under no circumstances was he to be addressed as the Duke. He would not hold special levees but would be one of the Governor's party. It was his desire to meet the people of the Colony informally.

Adam looked down to the floor below. The State ballroom was crowded. At the far end of the room a raised dais had been placed, above it a canopy of red velvet decorated with the crown and the coat-of-arms of the Province. Dozens of crossed flags and banners hung from the walls, and the great crystal chandeliers held myriads of lighted candles. On the dais were two large armchairs. A step below was a smaller chair. A smile of amusement hovered over Adam's lips. Tryon had made it as much like a throne-room as it was possible without using the Royal Arms.

Women in gay flowered silks and satins sat in gold chairs along three sides of the room. Groups of men, in richly embroidered coats, satin smallclothes and flowered waistcoats, exchanged snuff and small talk. Buckled shoes moved across the floor or tapped nervously to the strains of music from an orchestra concealed behind a screen of magnolia blossoms opposite the throne chairs.

Excitement pervaded the room; powdered heads were close, voices lowered, quick glances cast over white shoulders toward the door from which the Governor and his party would enter. In spite of the effort at secrecy, the presence of the Great Personage had been noised about. Adam, looking down on the gay scene, felt aloof from the excitement. He could not get his mind off Harmon Husband in the gaol at the far end of the Public Parade.

A maid, dressed in Government House livery, gave Mary Warden her supper seating when she entered the powder room at the Palace. She slipped the card into her small pearl-studded reticule without glancing at it. The powder room was filled with women arranging their hair and gowns, changing shoes and drawing on their long gloves. A dozen of them at once called to her when she came in.

Mary took off her silk cape and gave it to a slave. She stood for a moment smoothing the shining sheath of her bodice, arranging the heavy fulness of her satin skirt. The long mirror reflected her somber figure against the gay background of the other women's varicolored frocks. Her gown, a heavy black satin, was made without hoop or crinoline. The weight of the material held it in undulating ripples that caught the light in their shimmering folds. The thick mass of her unpowdered dark chestnut hair was caught low on the nape of her neck and held by a net of braided silver threaded in seed pearls. She wore no jewels. The simplicity of her gown had a distinction that the rich, heavily trimmed brocades of the other women did not attain. Mary did not notice the envious glances as she left the room. Her mind was on other things. That afternoon she had gone into William's room at the Inn to get the latest paper from Wilmington. On the table was a half-completed letter. Her eyes fell on the name John Paul. Scribbled on the margin in William's handwriting were the words, "This man bears watching." William came into the room before she had read any further. He looked worried and abstracted as he quickly covered the letter with the papers he had in his hand.

Mary said, "Are you feeling quite well, William?"

He made an obvious effort to smile. "Quite. Why do you ask that, my dear?"

"I don't know, William. It seems to me that you must have something on your mind lately—something that worries you very much."

He laughed. Tilting her chin, he kissed her cheek lightly.

"Nonsense. You are imagining things. There is nothing unusual, my dear, only other people's troubles that a barrister must assume."

She persisted. "Are you sure there's nothing wrong—nothing disquieting going on in the Province?"

"Nothing serious, my dear. The usual reports from the northern border, that is all."

"You mean they are angered over the display and extravagance of the Governor and the new Palace?"

William protruded his lower lip a little. After a moment's hesitation he said, "I don't think it is cause for worry, but the farmers have been meeting again. No one seems to know just what is brewing. But don't think of it. There's no need to worry your little head. You must learn not to take things too seriously, Mary."

Annoyed because he was putting her off, she left the room then. This conversation was on her mind as she walked down the long corridor between rows of soldiers to the entrance of the ballroom where William was waiting for her. He was talking to John Harvey and James Iredell. She saw Samuel Johnstone and Willie Davenport from Tyrell talking earnestly to Parson Earl. They fell silent as she drew near. William came forward to meet her.

"Let us go in," he said quickly, giving her only time to nod a greeting to the group. "The chairs will all be taken if we don't hurry."

At the wide doors to the ballroom, lackeys in powdered wigs and plum-colored livery bowed as they passed, while a major-domo indicated their seats. They had been seated only a moment when a bugle sounded. Two rows of soldiers entered the ballroom and stood at attention, forming an aisle from the throne chairs to the Governor's study. The door of the study opened. Two men stood for a moment on the threshold, the tall soldierly figure of the Governor, dressed in full regimentals of the Guards, and a short, fat man with a very red face and bold, searching eyes.

Women curtsied and men bowed low as the Great Personage and the Governor of the Royal Province of North Carolina passed to take their places on the dais where Lady Tryon was waiting, standing at the lower steps.

Adam joined Sara and Lavinia to watch the pageant. The Great Personage was fat, as all his family were fat, with heavy jowls and overlying chin. His great stomach was covered with a broad expanse of silvered waistcoat. His purple coat was embroidered in gold and silver threads and set with pearls. He wore the Order of the Bath slung from a red ribbon. A dozen more glittering Orders hung from his silvered waistcoat. Adam recognized the Garter, the Russian St. Andrew, the Golden Fleece of Austria, St. James of the Sword and St. Maurice and Lazarus of Italy. There were other decorations as well, diamond and jewel-studded. For a simple Baron of the Empire, he displayed a gallant array of honors bestowed, Adam thought.

The stream of Colonial officials, clothed for the best part in somber black, moved slowly by the dais. Deep bows, hand on sword hilt, by the men; curtsies to the floor by the women and young misses. Moving slowly on the dark polished floor, slippered feet with shining buckles approached, paused and passed by; silk and satin skirts billowed like a gay garden of multicolored flowers swept by a light breeze.

The end of the line was in sight in the outer hall. Adam turned to Lavinia. "Shall we go down now?" he asked.

She looked suddenly alarmed. "Where is Peyton?"

"He was in the lounge a few moments ago," Adam told her. "He said he would wait for us at the door of the ballroom."

Peyton was not in the lounge. Adam sent a page-boy to look for him but the boy did not come back. Lavinia was nervous and worried.

"You had better look for him, Adam," she said. "Wherever the punch bowl is, I should think."

Adam went to a small antechamber off the lounge. He saw Peyton with Lady Caroline. She had her hand on his arm and was talking earnestly. As Adam stood in the doorway, he overheard her say:

"But you must, Peyton. I want two escorts, one on either side of me. You must walk with Captain Atwill and me. It will show that you have now taken your stand on the side of the Royalists."

Peyton shook his head. Adam could not hear all she said, but he caught the words, "Do as I say. I will not have insolence from you, Peyton."

Adam hesitated. He did not relish interrupting or making a scene, but there was Lavinia to be considered. Before he had quite decided on his course of action, the Governor's A. D. C. came to the opposite door, a list in his hand. Lady Caroline motioned to him imperiously.

"I shall be escorted by Captain Atwill and Mr. Peyton Rutledge," she said to the harassed man. "We are ready to be presented to his Excellency now."

Adam took a step forward to remonstrate, when he saw that Lavinia had followed him into the room.

"There must be some mistake, Colonel MacLeod," Lavinia's clear voice broke in. "This person has been misinformed. Mr. Peyton Rutledge will escort his wife." Slipping her hand through Peyton's arm, Lavinia moved slowly across the room without a backward glance. Lady Caroline was on the point of protesting, but Captain Atwill's hand on her arm restrained her.

A murmur of approval went through the room as Lavinia advanced toward the dais a step or two ahead of her escorts. The Baron leaned forward, fumbling for his eyeglass.

"Upon my word," he boomed out, "they grow lovely women here in the Colonies." He put his glass to his eyes. Then he recognized her. "God's death," he said, "if it isn't la Belle Lavinia! What are you doing here, madam? We have missed you in London for a long time." He rose from his chair and took a step forward. "And who are these tall gentlemen?"

Lavinia curtsied, her pearl satin sweeping the floor. "My husband, Mr. Peyton Rutledge, your Highness, and our cousin, Mr. Adam Rutledge of Rutledge Riding."

The Baron looked fixedly at the men. "Ah, Adam Rutledge! One of the Iron Men of Albemarle," he said, raising his voice slightly. "You see I've heard of the Iron Men."

Adam bowed, but did not speak. The Baron turned to Lavinia. "Come, stay beside me, my dear Lavinia. Already I find myself becoming bored." He glanced at the Governor. "This lady had a reputation for a pretty wit at the Court. Can we not have a chair for her?"

Peyton stood for a moment, a puzzled look on his face, as a lackey brought a small gilt chair for Lavinia. The Baron had him place it close to his side, which necessitated Lady Tryon moving back. She gave Lavinia an ill-humored look, quickly erased. Adam moved away. After a moment, Peyton followed him.

Adam went over to speak to Mary Warden, who was standing at the far end of the room. As he bent over her hand, holding it closely, Mary glanced up and saw that Sara was watching them from her seat in the balcony. While they were talking, Lady Caroline came into the room, her hand on Captain Atwill's arm. When she saw Adam, she motioned to him, saying something in a low tone that Mary could not hear. Whatever it was did not please Adam. He shook his head and returned at once to Mary's side.

Mary watched Lady Caroline move down the room and thought, "Her carriage is regal, her gown and jewels superb." Suddenly Lady Caroline stopped. Her hand went to her throat, half covering the square-cut emerald necklace that she wore. Mary saw her sway a little and catch at Captain Atwill's arm for support. She heard the captain say, "What's wrong? Are you ill, Lady Caroline?"

"The room is suffocating," she whispered hoarsely. "Step out of the line. I must get some fresh air."

"Over here by the window," Captain Atwill urged.

"No, no, let us leave the room—out on the terrace."

They passed near enough to Mary for Lady Caroline's sweeping skirts to touch her. But Lady Caroline did not appear to see her, or Adam. Her face was white as chalk under her rouged cheeks. She looked over her shoulder toward the throne chairs as she went through the French doors that led to the terrace—a quick, furtive look, as if she were frightened.

"What was wrong with Lady Caroline?" Adam asked. Mary turned. He was watching the two figures moving swiftly down the terrace toward the garden.

"I don't know," Mary said. "The heat, perhaps. I feel it myself. There isn't a breath of air stirring."

"It is humid," Adam said, still watching the retreating figures. "I noticed the barometer was falling. I hope there won't be a storm tonight."

There was a stir in the ballroom. The Baron had risen from his chair. His gutteral accent could be heard plainly as he spoke to the Governor.

"I'm going to walk in the garden. You and your Lady can finish the audience. Come, Madam Lavinia, I have a feeling that it will be cooler outdoors."

Tyron glanced at his wife. She was watching the pair as they walked across the room toward the door leading to the terrace. Disturbed by the break in the procedure, she looked hopelessly at her husband. He said something to her, and she turned at once, smiling at the couple advancing toward them.

Mary had no time to speculate on the little scene she had just witnessed. She was sure it held some special significance for Lady Caroline to shock her out of her usual studied indifference. Ann Blount and Jemmie Davenport came up just then, their eyes shining with excitement. Jean Corbin followed them, her cheeks as bright as her quilted coral petticoat. She caught at Mary's arm, pulling her to the window enclosure. The girls hurried after them, skirts swaying and rustling.

"Have you heard the news?" Jean whispered, looking over her shoulder to see that she was not overheard. "Lady Caroline's chair was halted on her way to the Palace tonight. A crowd of roughs frightened her bearers so, they set down her chair on the road and ran away. The crowd hissed and booed, and called her a scarlet woman."

"Yes, and she shouted at them, and they say cursed like any pirate!" Jemmie Davenport broke in.

"But why—why?" Mary asked, turning from one to another.

"Haven't you heard that that Hilary boy from Orange shot himself last night in her garden? The whole town is buzzing about it," Jean Corbin said, her voice rising. "I thought every one had heard."

"No, I hadn't heard, had you?" Mary turned to Adam, who had joined them.

His face was grave. He hesitated a moment, for he had no desire to add to the gossip, but Mary was insistent.

"Had you heard? Is it true?"

"Yes, I'm afraid it is true. It was very unfortunate. He could have got the money from any one of a dozen men, if he had asked."

Mary looked at Adam significantly. "Oh, it was gambling," she said. She was going to say more, but caught herself in time. Like Adam, she had no wish to have her words repeated. But the women had already gone on to another group, whispering, hoping to carry the news to someone who had not already heard it.

"I'm sorry for her," Mary said impulsively. "I had the feeling a moment ago that she is in some sort of trouble—deep trouble."

Adam glanced down at her, his eyes softened. "You have a great heart, Mary," he said, his voice low. "You never hold a grudge."

She made no answer.

"I hope it doesn't storm," she said a little later, as they moved with the crowd toward the dining hall. "Lady Tryon told me she planned to have dancing in the pavilion by the river after supper. Come, let's find our places at the table." She took the card from her bag. "No. 2 table," she read. "Where are you, Adam?"

"At the high table," he said indifferently. "But I must first

257

take Sara to her carriage. She wants to go home before supper." He leaned toward her. "Save some dances for me, Mary, the second, third and fourth. We need not dance; we can walk in the garden instead. I have something that I want to discuss with you."

Adam passed Lavinia on his way to the gallery. The Baron had not let her move from his side but when she saw Adam, she hurried over to him.

"Adam, please try to find Peyton. I haven't seen him for some time. Don't let him out of your sight," she whispered.

Adam nodded. He knew that Lavinia was troubled about Peyton and Lady Caroline. "Don't worry, Lavinia," he said to her. "I'll find him."

The Baron called to Lavinia. He wanted her to sit at his right. In the dining hall his eyes wandered about the crowd. Then he saw Mary Warden. "Who is that woman who looks like a Florentine painting?" he asked Lavinia. "Where does she come from?"

Lavinia turned her head. "That is Mary Warden, the wife of William Warden, a London barrister. Mary is a friend of mine. She owns an old plantation called Queen's Gift, a few miles up the Sound from Edenton."

Lady Tryon leaned forward. "Mrs. Warden is one of the great Whig hostesses. I'm a little surprised to see her at the Palace tonight. She doesn't like Royalists."

The Baron had found his glass, and put it in his eye. "I like her looks," he announced. "She has individuality. You can see by her clothes that she isn't like the other women here—Colonials, aping London fashions. Ask her to come and sit by me, Mrs. Tryon. I would like to have a chat with this charming Whig."

Lavinia smiled inwardly. Lady Tryon's carefully laid plans were going awry. She had noticed Lady Caroline's name on the card where she was now sitting, next to the Baron. Now Mary Warden would have the place Lady Tryon, as the Governor's wife, had reserved for herself.

Lady Tryon hesitated a moment. The Baron scowled. His temper was notoriously short, his tongue scathing. Lady Tryon hurriedly called a flunkey and sent for Mary Warden. Her manner was cool when she made the presentation. Mary bowed slightly, instantly aware that something was wrong. There was a little secret smile on her lips and in her eyes as she obeyed the Baron's request and took the seat at his left. He leaned back in his chair, spreading his napkin across his protruding stomach.

"Now I have the handsomest women in the room to entertain me. I'm quite content."

The amused smile lingered about Mary's lips. "I suppose your Highness is aware that you have honored two Whigs instead of two Loyalists?" she said.

"Ha! I thought as much from Lady Tryon's look of disapproval."

"A hostess doesn't like her plans to be upset," Lavinia said, smiling demurely. "One can't blame her."

"God's life! Now she is angry." The Baron's laugh rolled out. "It's too amusing. I don't like the woman. She is overly pretentious. . . ." He turned his protruding eyes to Mary. They were cold, calculating eyes, but not unintelligent. "Now tell me why you don't like us," he said abruptly.

She turned the question lightly. "I do not like thee, Doctor Fell—the reason why I cannot tell," she said, quoting the old rhyme.

"Come, come. I'm serious. I didn't come out to the Plantations to meet our Royalists and receive their homage. I came to find out what the devil is wrong with you Whigs that you are stirring up such a tempest."

The smile left Mary's face. "Perhaps it would be better if you would ask yourself the same question," she said quietly.

The Baron raised his overhanging brows. "Wrong with us?" he repeated. Then he laughed. "By Gad! I thought you were different when I first saw you. Now I know it. Come, madam, a truce. I swear to listen to all complaints you have to make!" He settled back in his chair. Mary studied him a moment.

"Agreed," she said with an engaging laugh. "I will tell you the truth, and God help me afterward!"

The Baron put his hand on her arm for a moment. His voice was uexpectedly friendly. "Whatever you tell me tonight will go no further. You can trust me, Mrs. Warden."

Mary turned the stem of her wineglass in her slim, white fingers. Then she leaned forward a little and began to talk. After a few minutes Lavinia's attention wandered. Her eyes were searching the tables for a sight of Peyton, but she saw neither him nor Lady Caroline. The room was unbearably warm. She slipped off the lace scarf that she had been wearing over her shoulders and laid it on the back of the chair.

The Baron stopped in the middle of a sentence, his eyes fixed on her neck.

He said abruptly, "I have seldom seen a finer necklace of sapphires, my dear Lavinia, never but once. Such a splendid example of the lapidary's art!" He was still staring at the stones. "The necklace I speak of had a secret mark on the clasp—a crown with the monogram C. R. below it." He looked up suddenly, meeting her eyes. Lavinia's heart contracted. The necklace burned into her skin. There was such a mark on the clasp! She had noticed it in the cloakroom where she reclasped the necklace after she removed her wrap. "There was an interesting story about the necklace I'm speaking of," the Baron continued. "It disappeared under mysterious circumstances. Some other jewels were lost at the same time an emerald necklace and one of rubies and emeralds combined. They all came from India, and had the same ornate settings."

Lavinia glanced at Mary. "The necklace at the Levantine's shop," she thought. "It was set the same way."

The Baron's voice was sharp, imperative. The pleasant affable tone was gone. "Do you mind telling me where you got your necklace, Mrs. Rutledge?"

Lavinia prayed that her voice would not betray her anxiety. "My husband gave it to me. I believe the stones were part of his mother's collection," she smiled naturally, she hoped.

The Baron did not smile. "Have you had them long?" he asked.

"Quite a time," Lavinia said evenly. "Aren't they beautiful?"

The Baron continued to stare at the jewels without answering her. Mary, realizing that something was wrong, came to Lavinia's aid.

"If you are interested in jewels, you should see Lady Caroline's collection," she said. "But perhaps you have already seen them?" She did not wait for him to reply, but went on to tell him of the time she and Dr. Armitage had found the bag of unset stones in the library at Pembroke. The Baron listened attentively. When she had finished, he asked:

"Who is this woman you speak of? Lady Caroline who?"

Mary smiled. "Now you are teasing, Baron!"

"I assure you I was never more serious, Mrs. Warden." He called a footman. "Have Lieutenant Grafton come here at once," he said. Then he turned to Mary. "You look an intelligent person. Why don't you answer a direct question? Who is this woman who collects unset jewels and hides them behind books?"

"She calls herself Lady Caroline Mathilde. It has been rumored here in the Province that she is a sister of the Queen, although I never heard her say so," Mary replied.

"Sister of the Queen?" The Baron's voice rose, then he broke off suddenly. "Well, perhaps she is—the old Duke had a way with him." He laughed coarsely. "I'd like to see Lady Caroline Mathilde. Where is she?" He turned to Lavinia. "Do you know her?"

Lavinia shook her head. "I've never met Lady Caroline Mathilde, your Highness."

The Baron turned his head, looking over his shoulder toward the door. "God's death! Where is Grafton? I want to see him at once."

Mary looked at Lavinia. She was white, a fixed smile on her lips. Mary didn't understand what was behind the Baron's interest, but she knew it was something that frightened Lavinia.

"Do you mind if I examine the necklace, Mrs. Rutledge?" the Baron asked.

Lavinia unclasped the necklace and dropped it into his fat, pudgy hand. He looked at the clasp, and put the necklace into his waistcoat pocket.

"I haven't my glass at the moment," he said. "Where is that Grafton? Why doesn't he come? I think he's been looking for these stones for some time." Lavinia gave Mary a terrified look. Fortunately the Governor came over to them then. He leaned over the Baron and spoke deferentially:

"Your Highness, I'm sorry to interrupt, but it is the hour set for your appearance on the balcony, so that the people of the Province may see you and pay you homage."

The Baron put a hand on each arm of the chair and raised himself slowly. "We must not keep the commonalty waiting, Governor Tryon." He turned to Lavinia. "Don't go, dear Mrs. Rutledge. I want to talk further with you and your husband. If Lieutenant Grafton comes, keep him until I return." His words were casual, but they were a command. As soon as he had gone Lavinia caught Mary's arm. Her face was working pitifully; she was shaking with fear.

"I'm so frightened, Mary. The necklace has a mark just as he said. I saw it on the clasp—a crown with a C. R. underneath."

"Where is Peyton?" Mary asked sharply.

"I don't know. I haven't seen him for hours. I suppose he's with that terrible woman. Oh, Mary—how could he have got it?" She sank down in the chair by the table, her hands over her face.

Mary's hand gripped her bare shoulder. "Hold your head up. Do you want all of New Bern to see you like this?"

Lavinia drew herself up at the shock of Mary's words. "Find Peyton," she whispered, "please, Mary."

Mary looked at her drooping figure, her frightened eyes. "I'll find Peyton," she said more kindly. "He'll have some simple explanation to clear this up. Rutledge men aren't jewel thieves. Don't wait here for the Baron or Lieutenant Grafton, and don't talk to them until you have seen Peyton." Without waiting for Lavinia's answer she walked swiftly across the hall toward the ballroom. She would not waste time looking for Peyton. It was Adam she must find.

When she passed the open windows she noticed the wind was rising, the air heavy. The ballroom was empty; the dancers had gone to the front windows and the terrace where they could see the Baron and his Excellency the Governor, greeting the commonalty from the balcony.

Chapter 18

MARS RISING

ESCAPING the crowds around the supper tables, Adam walked through the almost deserted ballroom on his way to the entrance of the Palace. He was curious to see how the populace would receive the Governor's speech, and how they would welcome the Baron.

He heard the shouts of the crowd and the cheering. A cannon roared—a salute for the Great Personage—and a bugle blew to announce the arrival of the Royal Governor.

Adam found a place at the side of the Palace where he could see the length of the Public Parade and the balcony as well. The square was solidly packed with people—men in butternut clothes, trappers and woodsmen in buckskin, women in gay calicoes and freshly starched mob caps and kerchiefs of white. They were quiet now, their faces turned toward the Palace. A gust of wind whipped the awnings and the smoke of the barbecue pits filled the air.

"A mess of strangers here tonight." Adam turned to find Dr. Armitage and Joseph Hewes behind him. "Look at that crowd there on the edge of the Parade. They look a proper crowd of cutthroats to me," the Doctor continued.

Joseph Hewes laughed, his long nose almost meeting his chin. "If you could see the crew off some of my ships, you would see ruffians. But they're not so bad as they look. These men are farmers and small tradesmen. Don't you think so, Adam?"

Adam nodded. "Yes, from the Ready Creek districts and a scattering of northern county men. I seem to recognize some of their faces."

"They don't look very pleased at the Governor's words. Look at them now."

Adam thought the same. Strong-faced men, hardened by the vicissitudes of the frontier country. "If only Tryon would be diplomatic in his speeches," he said. "But no, he must use the high hand. Even now he is criticizing the resistance to crown officers in the upper counties."

Armitage muttered. "Why shouldn't they complain when a

farmer can't get more than five shillings a bushel for his wheat and only a shilling out of five in money? Why shouldn't they complain?"

A man standing near turned at the Doctor's words. "You're right, mister. That's what we get—a bushel of wheat for a bushel of salt. That's what they offered me today, and they levy double taxes. We'll do more than complain before long if Tryon won't listen to reason. Ask Rednap Howell or Malachy Tyke. They'll tell you some pretty stories. Yes, and James Few, poor soul, half daft since that beast Fanning outraged the girl he was going to marry. You don't hear about these things down here in the big cities, but you will."

The man's voice rose. People turned to stare. "Sh! sh!" someone said. A guard stepped forward and the man melted into the crowd.

Adam and the Doctor looked at each other. Hewes said, "It's a crime, that's what it is—"

Adam thought now of the strangers he had seen that morning when he went to the wharf to talk with Marcy. The inns and dramshops were crowded, the streets along the river front swarming with men. Marcy had called his attention to them when they went on board the shallop which lay in the river waiting for the loading to be finished.

"The Governor can feed them beef and give them beer and whisky, but it won't do any good," Marcy had said. "They're in a bad mood, Mr. Rutledge, there's no denying that."

William Warden joined them and drew Adam to one side. "I'm worried about Peyton. He's been drinking brandy straight. You know how quarrelsome he gets."

"Where is he?" Adam asked, remembering suddenly that he had promised Lavinia to look after him.

"I don't know. When I saw him last he was with two officers from the *Jupiter*. They talked of driving down the Wilmington road to Hewes's plantation. I tried to persuade him not to go—we're going to have a storm before long if the barometer is to be trusted."

Adam glanced at the sky. There were a few stars visible, but the smell of wind was in the air. "I'll go hunt for him. I don't want him to get into trouble tonight. It's too hard on Lavinia."

When Adam saw that it was no use to try to push his way through the crowd, he went down in the garden near the outer wall where he had ordered Cicero to keep the coach in readiness for Lavinia. By the time he got there, the speeches were over. Hurrahs for the King, the Baron and the Governor had quieted. The people were back on the Parade at beer barrels and barbecue tables. Inside the Palace dancing had begun. He saw the Governor and Baron Cotswold enter a card room. The Baron seated himself at a table with officers from his ship and two other men.

Everything was calm. The Governor's plans had gone off perfectly. The people were gay, almost too gay. Somehow, Adam felt uneasy. He had noticed, without comment, that the men in the square were mostly Loyalists, farmers of the coast districts, workmen and tradesmen of the town. Where were all the others, the ones who opposed the Governor—the men who had protested violently against the extravagance of Tryon and the heavy taxes levied to build his Palace? At home in bed? Sleeping peacefully while the Royalists danced and feasted? Adam wondered.

He stood in the dark garden looking toward the ballroom. Silk-clad women with powdered heads moved slowly through the stately figures of the minuet, bowing to their partners—brilliantly uniformed officers from ships lying in the rivers, red-coated officers of the Guard and militia, a sprinkling of kilted Highlanders. Sentries were walking back and forth near the Palace gates—the line beyond which the common people were forbidden to pass.

Adam was aware now of the stillness—the heavy, somber stillness that precedes a tropical storm. In the distance, blue lightning flashed intermittently along the horizon. His ears were attuned to the silence now. Suddenly, he heard a sound from the river below, the sliding sweep of muffled oars, a faint rattle of oarlocks. He went out the gate to the bank of the river. Black shadows were moving on the breast of the stream—longboats, canoes.

Trained to the ways of woodsmen, Adam followed along the bank in the shadow of trees and bushes. The flare of distant lightning gave him a clearer vision. There were dozens of boats, each one filled. He caught the light on pikes and musket barrels. Two hundred men, perhaps more. His mind raced. What did they intend to do? They would not attack the Palace alone. He knew that there were not enough for that. More likely, they would mingle with the crowd in the Public Parade, incite the half-drunken men to violence.

He turned back and ran through the garden. He must warn the Governor as quietly as possible. Caswell and Hewes also; they were quick-thinking men, accustomed to dealing with emergencies. He had no idea how far-reaching this protest might be, but he could imagine.

Suddenly, he knew the meaning of the invasion. They were coming for their leader Harmon Husband whom Tryon had thrown into gaol without just cause or fair trial.

On the upper reaches of the Neuse, down the length of the river, boats were gliding—canoes, barges, shallops. For days through the deep forest to the west, far into the mountains, grim-faced, determined men, hardened by poverty and the daily fight against wind and flood, draught and burning sun, had been marching. They had heard of the great Palace the Royal Governor had built. They had heard of throne chairs for Tryon and his lady. They had heard of jewels and satins and lavish living introduced into the Province by Lady Tryon. They had heard of Lady Caroline Mathilde and her extravagance, of the wild gambling at her house, of young officers drowned in the river, of duels fought in her gardens. They had heard of money squandered like water, luxuries brought from overseas, from the Indies, from France and Spain. They had heard of prodigal living, of mad, inordinate waste, while the people starved.

They had come to the end of their silent endurance, these rough men, dressed in homespun. Armed men, carrying pikes and pick handles and long rifles and muskets, had embarked in canoes, home-made rowboats and crowded lumber rafts. Grim-faced, resolute, they had rowed downstream, and walked through the great forest, bent on protesting against the extravagance of a Royal Governor who had impoverished the Province and the people to build a Royal Palace.

Adam made his way through the gay, laughing crowds that filled the corridor and went into the lounge. There he found Colonel Weavly and some officers seated at a table, a bottle of Irish whisky in front of them. He saw that it was almost useless to speak to Weavly, but he would try to make him understand the danger that threatened. He leaned over and said:

"There is a mob of armed men coming down the river. I think they intend to make some kind of demonstration in front of the Palace."

Weavly looked at him through blurred eyes. "What's you say, Rutledge, armed men?—Damn it, that's a lie. Every man in the Province is happy tonight. You're drunk, Rutledge. You're seeing things. Have a drink!" He pushed the bottle toward Adam, and turned away.

Adam gave up, and started for the ballroom. One of the young officers followed him—a clean-cut young man in kilts, with a strong Scot's burr. Adam recognized him as David Moray, who had come out with the last regiment of Highlanders.

"What can I do, sir?" he asked, his face grave and troubled. "It will be bad if anything happens tonight with the Du—I mean the Baron—here."

"Do you know Richard Caswell or Joseph Hewes—or Samuel Johnstone from Edenton?" Adam asked.

The officer nodded. "By sight, sir."

"Find them. Tell them quietly what is happening. Ask them to go to the ante-room behind the ballroom, near the Governor's offices. I'm going to find the Governor. Don't lose any time. Every minute counts, if we're going to prevent a riot."

The officer hurried off. Adam went into the ballroom, his eyes sweeping the room. After a moment, he saw the Governor dancing with Mary Warden. He made his way along the side of the room until he stood near the spot where the Governor would meet his vis-à-vis in a figure of the dance.

"Your Excellency," he said, "a messenger has come with important news. He's in the ante-room near your office."

Tryon glanced at him, scowling. "Let the messenger wait," he said sharply.

"This is important," Adam insisted. He leaned forward. "An armed mob is coming down the river. There is no time to lose."

Tryon was instantly alert. He motioned a couple who were watching to take his and Mary's place in the dance.

Mary leaned toward Adam as they moved off the floor. "Is it the Regulators?" she whispered in a low voice.

"I don't know. It may be. Don't say anything now; we may be able to handle this," he said as they walked across the room. "Where's Lavinia?" he asked, thinking suddenly of Peyton.

"I don't know. I couldn't find her. She may have gone home while I was searching for Peyton. She's awfully worried, Adam. The Baron—" Mary paused. Adam was not listening. He was looking across the room. Mary's eyes followed his glance. She saw Richard Caswell and Dr. Armitage going through the door of the corridor which led to the Governor's offices. A moment later, Joseph Hewes followed, and Colonel Waddell of the militia. There was no use to speak of Lavinia and the necklace now.

Adam stopped. "You'd better wait here, Mary," he said. "If there's trouble, try to keep the women quiet."

The Governor was seated at a table when Adam entered the ante-room. Caswell, Hewes, Armitage and Waddell were standing.

Tryon demanded, "Didn't you say a messenger had come?"

"Yes, your Excellency," Adam answered. "I didn't want anyone to overhear. I thought this might be handled quietly."

As Adam told what he had seen, Tryon's anger rose visibly. He could not believe that there was any danger of a hostile demonstration before the Palace with the cheers of the people still ringing in his ears.

"I don't believe it," he said sharply. "Your imagination is getting the best of you, Rutledge. I have men in the Public Parade and at the wharves. They will report at once." He turned his cold, penetrating eyes on Caswell. "Do you believe his tale, Caswell?" he asked.

"I wish I could say that I didn't. But whatever you believe, I think we must investigate. We don't want to be taken unawares."

Hewes spoke. "Your Excellency, we all know that there is a great deal of discontent among the people in the northern counties and along Ready Creek over the heavy taxation for the Palace. Don't you think it likely that they would choose this time to make their protest, even though they may not intend to resort to violence?"

Tryon got up and walked to the window, his back to the room. Adam thought he was trying to control his anger. He turned suddenly to Hewes.

"I think insolence should be met with firmness. Violence with violence. Hewes, if you give these people an inch, they'll demand more. I have made up my mind to call out the troops with orders to shoot at the first display of violence."

No one spoke for a moment. Then the Governor said: "Mr. Rutledge, will you call my aide? I want Colonel Weavly here at once."

Adam hesitated. Caswell held out a protesting hand. "Your Excellency, don't call out the militia. See the leaders—find out what they demand."

Adam spoke then. "I know what they want. They want Harmon Husband. They want him released from gaol."

Tryon took a step forward. The blood rushed to his face. "By God! They can't have Husband. I've got the rascal in gaol, and I intend to keep him there!" He glowered at Adam as if he were personally responsible for the situation, then crossed the room and jerked at the bell cord. A flunky came into the room. Tryon said, "Call my aide, Captain McCleod.

268

Ask him to come, then find Colonel Weavly. Say that I want to see him at once."

Hewes and Caswell spoke at the same time. Hewes gave way to the older man. Caswell's face was grave. "Your Excellency, this is very serious. I beg you to reconsider. Even if you have to release Husband, it would be better than violence. You know what happened in the North."

Tryon silenced him. His long jaw was thrust forward, his eyes gleamed with anger. "I'm the Governor of the Province, Caswell."

A light knock at the door and the Governor's aide, Captain McCleod, came in. With him was the young officer, David Moray.

"Why didn't you advise me that an armed mob was advancing on the Palace?" Tryon shouted angrily. "A fine set of officers I have, when I have to get information from civilians."

McCleod looked genuinely bewildered. He stammered, "There is no mob, your Excellency. I've just been to the entrance of the Palace. Only the loyal subjects of the King dancing and feasting—shouting their good will toward your Excellency for your generosity."

Adam glanced at Joseph Hewes. He looked grim and determined. Caswell's face was like a rock. The Governor's anger subsided. He turned to Adam.

"There is no mob, Mr. Rutledge. You must have been misinformed."

Lieutenant Moray stepped forward and saluted. "Your pardon, sir, may I make a report?"

Tryon turned around quickly. He had given no heed to the young officer when he entered. "Who are you?" he asked sharply.

"Moray, sir, acting officer of the day," he said, after a moment's hesitation.

Tryon said, "Where's Colonel Weavly? I sent for him five minutes ago."

"Colonel Weavly is—" Moray's face reddened.

"Never mind, don't answer," Tryon said angrily. "Weavly's drunk—that's what you were going to say?"

Adam thought the young Scot tactful and loyal.

"Your Excellency," Moray said steadily, "I was about to report that there are a number of strangers on the Public Parade. They are neither eating nor drinking. They are standing in groups apart, at different places on the Parade and on the streets leading to the river."

"What sort of men?" the Governor snapped.

Moray hesitated, then said, "Some might be up-country farmers from their dress. Others are sailors from the ships at anchor in the river. They are rough-looking fellows—Lascars and Levantines, some of them, but they are mingling with the others."

The Governor was silent. Adam thought he was disturbed, but he was too stubborn and too arrogant to admit defeat. "Very good, sir," he said. "Find your Colonel and ask him to come here."

"One thing more, your Excellency. My men reported just a moment ago that boatloads of men were seen on the river. Some of them were landing below the town near the old wharves."

"Well, what have you done about this, Lieutenant?" Tryon demanded.

"I've set a double guard around the gaol, under a sergeant, sir, and given orders to the men not to use arms without orders from an officer."

The Governor dismissed him. "Very good. Report directly to me whenever there is anything to report. But get Weavly here if he can stand on his feet."

As Moray left the room, Farquhar Campbell, John Hawks and Colonel Fanning came in. Fanning's face was white and his hands were trembling.

"Your Excellency, we're in great danger," he said. "I've had word that a thousand men from Halifax and Orange are marching on the capitol—another five hundred are coming down the river. This is Rebellion, sir, Rebellion! You must order out the troops."

Tryon looked at him contemptuously. "Keep quiet, Fanning. There's no cause for alarm. You'll manage to save your skin—"

Fanning stepped closer to Tryon. His voice shook. "Your Excellency, this is Rebellion, armed Rebellion and treason to the Crown!"

Adam heard a sound and turned. Baron Cotswold stood in the doorway, a man in livery at each elbow holding him erect. "What's this about armed Rebellion, Tryon?" he demanded in his heavy, gutteral voice. "Don't try to keep it from me. Haven't I eyes—and ears? You haven't fooled me with your big demonstrations. We have the same kind in London, whenever his Majesty feeds a mob." He turned to Caswell. "Speak up, Caswell. What's happened?"

For a man who could not stand without aid the Baron's mind was remarkably clear, Adam thought.

"Your Highness," Tryon started to speak.

The Baron waved his hand. "No, no, Baron is the title." He motioned to the lackeys who helped him to a chair. "Now, Caswell—" he began, looking ludicrously pontifical.

Adam moved quietly to the door. He couldn't stay any longer while they argued about what should be done. He must see for himself what the situation was in the town. He escaped through a side door without encountering anyone. Halfway down the Parade, he overtook Lieutenant Moray, who was sauntering along slowly as if he were enjoying the gaiety and the dancing.

He turned when Adam called his name, a look of quick relief passing over his face. As he fell in step, he spoke in a worried voice. "I'm glad you came, Mr. Rutledge. I'm bewildered. A little while ago, I would have sworn something was about to happen here on the Parade, but look at it now. Everything's natural."

Adam glanced about. It did look natural on the surface. The crowds were dense around the barbecue pits and beer kegs. People were shouting and laughing. At the far end a half-dozen Negro slaves were playing violins and banjos. Another group had bones and a big drum. Many couples were dancing on the grass.

Adam saw Enos Dye pushing his way through the crowd. He motioned to him and a few moments later the trapper joined them.

"I was looking for you, Mr. Rutledge," he said, dropping his voice. "I saw farmer Whitlock down by the old docks. He said to find you and give you this message: 'One o'clock.' "

"Is that all?" Adam asked, somewhat mystified.

"That's all he told me. He said you'd understand—that you'd know he opposed a break, but he was outvoted. They're determined," Dye added significantly.

A light began to dawn on Adam. One o'clock—that must be the hour set to get Husband out of the gaol. He understood now. Whitlock would be against violence. He had managed to send Adam a warning.

"What's going on, Enos?" Adam said.

Enos glanced at Moray, then shrugged his shoulders. "They're having a wild time—like they always do if you give them enough to drink. Seems like city men can be put off mighty easy."

Adam glanced at his watch. It was ten minutes past twelve. Almost an hour, if he had interpreted Whitlock's message correctly.

"How many strangers are there in town, Enos?"

The trapper shifted his feet and cast a wary eye on the Lieutenant. "Oh, round two thousand—maybe, three thousand, far as I know."

Adam nodded. That was the information he needed.

"I think I'll go back to the Palace for a few minutes, Moray. Where can I find you later?"

"Down near the gaol," the officer answered. "I have to be there when they change the guard—at one."

Adam saw that Moray understood. He turned to Enos. "Find Whitlock if you can, Enos. Tell him I'll be near the gaol at one. You be there, too. Bring any stout fellows you can trust—"

Enos grinned. "I'll be there, sir. There are plenty of back-country men in town who're against violence." He laughed, then disappeared into the crowd.

Adam went swiftly to the side entrance of the Palace. The door to the ante-room was ajar. He saw that Weavly had come in with two officers from the *Jupiter*. Tryon was talking to John Hawks. He heard the Moor say: "—through the secret entrance to the river. I'll have a boat ready to take him to the *Jupiter*."

Adam stepped forward. "Your Excellency, I've been down on the Parade. One o'clock is the time set to deliver Husband from the gaol."

Tryon wheeled about. "You sure of this, Rutledge?"

"Yes," Adam answered. "I have it from a man I trust."

Tryon turned to Weavly. "Order your men to be ready to clear the Parade the instant there is any sign of trouble."

Both Caswell and Farquhar Campbell protested.

"Wait, your Excellency, wait," Caswell said earnestly. "Why not have the Regulators brought here, to see what they have to say—James Hunter, or Pugh? They are the leaders now. We may be able to make a trade of some kind—conciliate them."

Tryon exploded. "Trade? Conciliate? Do you think the King's Governor would trade with the rabble?"

Suddenly the sound of shouting reached the room. Every man, except the Governor, and the Baron, who slept, rushed to the window. The merrymakers were silent, huddled in frightened groups at the edge of the Parade. They had been forced back by the line of marching men carrying pikes and

272

pick handles. A few had muskets. They were moving toward the Palace, eight abreast, shouting the name of Harmon Husband as they marched: *"Free Harmon Husband. Free Harmon Husband."* A sentry on the wall fired his pistol. A cry was raised, "Call out the Guard! Call out the Guard!"

Soldiers came running out of the guard house and sentry boxes.

"It's come," Caswell said. "It's too late now."

Tryon hastened to the door. "Call the Guard. Order out the troops," he called to Weavly, who had gone into the hall.

"You can't do that," Iredell's dry, crisp voice cut in. "See that mob? Three thousand men at least."

"Come out on the balcony, your Excellency. Talk to them. Suppose you do free Husband. What does it matter?" Caswell pleaded.

"By Heaven! I won't let them intimidate me," Tryon shouted. "I won't open the gaol doors and let that rascal out. I'll see them in Hell first!"

His voice roused the Baron, who lifted his chin from his chest and opened his heavy eyes. "Gaol?" he repeated. "Gaol?" Then his face lighted. He sat up, the golden Orders on his chest jingling. "That's what I forgot to tell you, Tryon. Open gaol doors. Always order all political prisoners freed when I visit a Colony. Kind, generous, Royal gesture, makes good impression." His head dropped on his chest, his eyes closed. His two officers went to his side.

"We've got to get him to the ship," Adam heard one of them say. "The secret way is best."

Tryon stood looking at the Baron, disgust on his face. He had a strong man's contempt for weakness. Suddenly the expression on his face changed.

"A Royal gesture," Adam heard him mutter. He stood a moment in deep thought. Then he turned to Caswell. "Get those men here—Pugh and Hunter—any of the leaders. You can talk to them. It's your idea—we'll see what comes of it—" His eyes swept the room. "I must say, I myself am not in favor of giving an inch to the ruffians."

Adam smiled to himself. The Governor did not fool him. The Baron's words had opened the way—Tryon could release Husband and still save face. He was almost at the door when angry shouts, followed by more shots, filled the air.

"It's too late," Caswell repeated.

Adam wrenched the door open and ran into the hall. From a window he could see the Parade. The sentries were trying to shut the iron gates. A bugle sounded. Soldiers came double-quick from the barracks. In the ballroom, the music stopped with a sudden crash on the drum; a woman shrieked, shrill, staccato. Officers, drawing their swords as they ran, dashed through the doors into the corridor. Adam saw Lady Tryon running across the hall toward the Governor's study. She met her husband at the door. He pushed her aside impatiently. Caswell and Campbell followed him, expostulating. The Governor drew his sword from the scabbard.

"Let me go, your Excellency," Caswell pleaded. "Don't use force yet. It may not be too late."

Adam did not wait. He ran down the corridor to the carriage entrance. If he only could get to the gaol in time to prevent an attack! As he ran, he glanced into the ballroom. The women were huddled near the wall. Men with drawn swords ran about from windows to doors. The utmost confusion reigned. A few men, assisted by red-coated flunkies, tried to calm the shrieking women. All the officers had gone. No one knew what was happening.

Adam was at the door when he heard a crash, followed by hysterical screams. He looked over his shoulder. A well-aimed stone had shattered the high fan window, scattering glass over the ballroom floor.

He heard his name called. Turning he saw Lady Caroline. She had a dark coat over her ball dress, and she carried a small leather dressing case in her hand.

"Adam, get me out of this! Where's my chair? I want to get to my house."

Adam pulled her back into the hall. "You can't go that way," he said shortly. "Run to the ante-room. They're taking the Baron out by the secret passage to the river. You'll be in time if you hurry—"

She broke his hold on her arm. "No," she said violently; "no, I won't go that way."

"Don't be a fool," he said. "You won't be safe here, if the mob gets in, but you will be safe on the *Jupiter* with the Duke."

"No, no, not the Duke!" she cried.

Adams saw fear, deadly fear in her eyes. What could it mean? She seemed suddenly aware of his questioning look.

"He hates me," she muttered. "He hates my family—" She looked about her desperately, her whole body shaking with emotion. "I don't want to go on the *Jupiter*," she cried hysterically. "No, no—" her voice broke suddenly. "Adam, hide me—somewhere—anywhere."

He caught her shoulder to steady her. "Listen, this isn't the time for hysterics—" he looked hopelessly around. "Go into the ante-room. Wait there, but keep away from the windows." He pushed her toward the room. "I'll come back," he said, softened by her white, stricken face.

Adam ran silently along the path outside the Parade. He heard the angry shouts of the approaching mob. The gates were closed. By the light of flambeaux and pine torches he could see the gleam of rifle barrels at the portholes of the sentry boxes. The shouting swelled into words: "Husband. Husband. Give us Harmon Husband." Over and over, rising and falling.

When he reached the foot of the Parade, near the gaol, he saw that Whitlock and Enos Dye were waiting with ten or twelve men wearing trapper's buckskins. A half-drunken man, in the leather apron of a blacksmith, pushed his way out of the crowd. His eyes fell on Adam. He leaned over, catching Adam's shoulder.

"What you doing here, fine gentleman?" he shouted.

Adam pushed him aside, but the fellow hung on. Dye started forward but Adam wrenched himself free. Putting out his foot, he tripped the blacksmith who fell over on the ground and lay there. Adam hesitated, looking down on the motionless man. Dye turned him over.

"He's not hurt," he said. "Come on, we'd better get to the gaol. Marcy is there—Whitlock's got something to tell you. Better hurry, Mr. Rutledge. There's no time to lose."

Mary tried for some time to prevail on Lavinia to go home. Their search for Peyton had been fruitless. No one had seen him since before supper. Lady Caroline, too, was missing. Mary wondered vaguely why she had not gone to make her bow to the Governor. There was something about her sudden illness that she could not fathom, something to do with the Baron, Mary was sure, from the strange expression that had come over Lady Caroline's face when she saw him beside the Governor, but Mary put the thought from her mind in her anxiety over Lavinia.

She had found Lavinia sitting in the deserted powder room in a low chair near the window. Her eyes were red, as if she had been weeping. Her slim body drooped, the picture of woe. Mary's heart softened.

"Come, I'll take you to the coach," she said. "Wait up for me. I'll be at the Inn in a little while. I want to find Adam to see what he knows before I give up. But you must go. If the Baron should ask for you, you would have to submit to his questioning, and that wouldn't be pleasant for you. Besides, you might say something to endanger Peyton without meaning to."

Lavinia finally consented. She was terrified of encountering the Baron. Luckily, Adam had told them he was having Cicero stand at the garden gate near the river instead of at the main entrance.

On their way to the garden they saw no one except servants clearing up the supper tables. Mary waited at the gate until Lavinia was in the coach.

"Drive the back way to the Swan," Mary told Cicero. "You'll never get through the crowd otherwise."

Cicero took up the reins and turned the horses away from the Public Parade to a lane that ran along the rear of the Palace. Mary walked slowly through the gardens. When she turned into the long path, a heavy gust of wind from the south caught her full on, swirling her skirts, almost throwing her against the arbor. She caught at the balustrade to steady herself. As she stood clinging to the rail, she heard a commotion in front of the Palace—shouting and yelling—voices raised in anger. She leaned forward, listening. The sound was wordless, a horrible angry roar.

It had come. The protest of the people against Tryon's taxes—against the Palace—against everything he stood for. She caught up her long skirts and ran toward the terrace that led to the ballroom, the angry sweep of the wind carrying her forward.

Whitlock stepped away from the others, Adam following him. The old farmer's face was grey in the flickering light from the bonfires in the square.

"They're mad," he said, his voice dropping to a hoarse whisper, "but we could not hold them. They'll have Husband, or they'll fire the Palace!"

"What?" Adam cried.

"That's the plan, Mr. Rutledge. There's three thousand of them come down from the north and more from the Ready Creek district. They won't be put off. Tryon can make his choice."

Adam stood still, thinking of what Whitlock had just said. "Where are the others, the real leaders?" he asked, after a moment.

Whitlock nodded vaguely toward the river.

"How long will it take them to get here?"

"Ten minutes—maybe five, when they hear that noise. I

got them to promise to send a committee to the Governor with their demands. I convinced them that if it were done orderly and not by violence, no one would be punished." He stopped suddenly, his eyes turned in the direction of the Palace. "What's that?"

Adam turned around. At the same moment, Enos Dye ran to them.

"Look—back of the Palace—"

They saw flickering lights—a dozen or more, moving along the wall at the back of the gardens near the kitchen.

"By God! They're not going to wait," Whitlock said, breaking into a run. "We've got to stop them. Come on, Dye, bring your men. We'll need men."

Adam followed, cutting along the narrow lane between stores and houses. As he ran, he looked down a street that led to the river. Lights were moving, coming up the long hill. He knew what that meant. Men marching, determined men—farmers, woodsmen, yeomen and husbandmen. He drew a quick breath. If they could only keep them from an overt act until Caswell informed them of the Governor's decision. The crowd on the Parade had moved to the Palace. They were still outside the closed gates, stopped for a moment by gun muzzles pointed through the loopholes. Every sentry box on the wall was filled with soldiers.

It seemed to Adam that they would never cover the ground in time. If they were too late—if the buildings were set on fire, Tryon would order the soldiers to shoot. What would happen then, with thousands of men marching?

Whitlock, followed by Enos and his trappers, ran on ahead. "Don't come," he called to Adam. "Let us take care of this. Go to the Governor."

Adam hesitated a moment. Then he realized the wisdom of the old farmer's words. The Governor must be held in check. He crossed the corner of the garden. On the terrace, he saw Mary struggling to open a door which had been closed by the wind. Her skirts were whipping around her, her hair blown across her face.

"Oh, Adam, don't let him send soldiers to shoot the people!" she cried, catching his arm.

He did not answer. He wrenched open the door and pulled her inside the corridor.

"Go in there," he said. Not stopping to explain, he ran down the hall toward the front of the house. As he crossed in front of a window he saw flames leaping up from the roof of the kitchen wing. Dozens of men, carrying torches, were silhouetted against the blackness of the pine trees and the high wall. He took the steps two at a time to the entrance of the small room opening onto the balcony above the front portico. Two flunkies stood by the closed door. Adam entered in spite of their feeble protests. Iredell was just inside the door. He held up his hand in warning. Adam saw Tryon sitting at a table, his face covered with his hands; Farquhar Campbell and his aide stood behind him. They were looking out toward the balcony.

Adam's gaze followed theirs to the balcony where Caswell was standing with James Hunter and Pugh, the Regulator leaders. Caswell was saying: "—and now the Governor has given free pardon to all political prisoners in the gaols to commemorate the completion of your Palace, built by you as a symbol of the greatness of your Province." Caswell turned to the men beside him, motioning them forward.

James Hunter stepped to the rail—a rough, solid figure of a man contrasted with the soldierly elegance of Richard Caswell. He spoke a few words Adam could not hear. Then he raised his voice so that it carried to the far end of the Parade. "Harmon is free," he shouted. "The Governor wants that ye shall eat and drink now." A thousand men shouted the name of their leader—hurrahs that filled the small room.

The Governor sat up. His face was stern and set. Anger had given way to something else—fear and resentment. Tryon had been forced to give way. Adam could imagine the means. He could hear Hunter's rough voice saying, "Give up Husband or we'll burn your Palace to the ground!" He glanced out the window and saw the flames rising to the roof of the kitchen. Tryon too had seen the flames. He had realized these men were not to be put off. He would never forgive them this humiliation. He would hold resentment—bide his time.

These thoughts ran through Adam's mind as he ran down the steps and out through the hall to the garden. He must let Whitlock know that Husband was free. Keep the men from setting the Palace itself afire. The flames from the burning building lighted the way. He saw Whitlock on the low roof of the smokehouse trying to beat out the flames with his coat. Slaves were running with buckets of water.

A man ran around the corner of the house, waving his arms, shouting, "Husband is free. The Governor's given in. Put out the blaze—we don't need it now."

The men stood dumbfounded for a moment. Then their leader caught a bucket from the hands of a slave and ran toward the building. Whitlock, Enos and his men and the house

278

slaves fought on while men responsible for the blaze ran to join their fellows in front of the Palace. Adam worked with Enos until the danger of the fire's spreading was past. Then he went back to the house to repair the damage to his clothes. He washed the smudges from his face and ripped out the scorched ruffles from the sleeves of his coat. Out in the corridor he saw Mary standing at the entrance of the ballroom. She beckoned with her fan.

"I've been searching for you everywhere," she said when he joined her. "The Governor wants us to dance. Everyone is to dance and be very, very gay."

Adam looked at her as if he had not heard aright. She dropped her voice. "Didn't you know? They are allowing the people to go through the Palace. They are permitted to walk down the corridor and look about. We must dance and be gay as if nothing has happened—as if everything were a part of his plan."

Adam moved with Mary toward the ballroom. Tryon was shrewd, Adam thought. He saw him standing near the entrance, a fine soldierly figure of a man, bowing with gracious dignity to the people as they entered the Palace door.

Richard Caswell's voice came to them as they entered the ballroom. "Two by two, men. Don't crowd," he was saying. "You have plenty of time to look at the Palace."

The music started. Women, still a little frightened, took their places, bowed low to their partners, pointed their slippered feet and smiled coquettishly over their fans. They must be gay. They must give only quick side glances at the rows of silent, rough-clad men, walking through the corridors, looking with frank curiosity at the slow-moving dancers.

Adam was near the door, bowing to his vis-à-vis. He heard a subdued laugh—a man's voice saying, "It's a bitter pill Tryon swallowed for all his smiling airs."

Another voice answered, "If we only had Lady Caroline on the ducking stool it would suit me well."

Adam glanced at Mary. There was a stiff, unnatural smile on her lips. She had heard and realized, as he did, that this was the lull before the storm. He looked around. Tryon was astute in some things. His guests were laughing, and gay. He wondered how many of them knew how near the edge they stood—how close they had been to disaster.

Armitage was waiting for them when the minuet was over. "I'm going to take you to the Inn, Mary, on my way home. You look dead on your feet."

Mary put her hand on his arm and smiled up at him. "I won't argue. I'm quite ready to go. I don't think I can stand much more."

While she went for her wrap, Armitage said, "Tryon's luck held tonight. By God! I thought we were in for it. Did you see the way he caught up the Baron's drunken words, and used them to his advantage?"

Adam nodded. "But he did free Husband. If he hadn't, we'd have been done."

Armitage said, "I'm not so sure. I think it was a bluff. They wouldn't have dared fire the Palace."

Adam said nothing. Not even Armitage seemed to realize the seriousness of the Regulators.

After they had gone, Adam remembered Lady Caroline and wondered if she was still in the ante-room. He opened the door but the room was empty. Most of the candles had gutted with only a few sputtering stumps left burning. He noticed a litter of glass on the floor; a rock the size of an orange had rolled onto the hearth, leaving a scar on the waxed floor.

A clock on the mantel struck three, a thin tinkling sound. The music had stopped and voices were saying good night—bidding farewell to friends and neighbors. He went out through the garden to the entrance where Cicero was waiting. Marcy was on the back seat of the coach, sound asleep. When Adam opened the door, he sat up, rubbing his eyes and laughing a little sheepishly.

"I knew I'd find you if I waited long enough," he said in explanation. "I came to tell you that the ship's loaded, ready to sail at daylight, sir. You said you wanted to see the captain before he sailed."

Adam thought a moment. "I'll have to go to the Inn and change first. You'd better go on down to the wharf and wait for me at the boat landing. I'll be down within an hour." Marcy went off down the street toward the docks and Adam got into the coach.

Cicero whipped the horses. When they turned the corner on Duke of Gloucester Street, Adam heard shouting. He put his head out the window. Armitage's coach had been stopped by a crowd of half-drunken men. The Doctor was remonstrating with them. Adam could hear his voice, high-pitched with annoyance and anger.

"Lady Caroline isn't here, I tell you. I haven't seen her. Look in the coach if you don't believe me." He threw open the door. A man Adam recognized as the owner of a ship's chandlery thrust his head inside.

280

"Nobody here," he shouted to his companions. "She's given us the slip. Let's go down the street—she can't be far off."

Before Adam drove up, they had gone off down the street and the Doctor had driven on.

Adam got out of the coach at the Swan and went into the Ordinary. The barman was asleep, his head on the counter. Adam woke him and gave an order. The barman poured out a double portion of whisky. Adam swallowed it, too tired to gain warmth from the liquor.

He walked up the stairs and opened the door to the little sitting room. A woman rose from the wing chair and came toward him.

"Lady Caroline!" he exclaimed.

She stood before him, her face white, her hair awry, the skirt of her satin gown torn and soiled.

"Those horrible men are after me!" she exclaimed. "One of them saw me. Then they threw a great rock that shattered the window." She held up her arm. Adam saw a long cut which she had half-covered with a lace handkerchief. "I came here when they tried to enter the room . . . I don't know where to go."

She sat down suddenly as if her knees would no longer support her. Adam reached for a decanter and poured a glass of port.

"Drink this while I think of what can be done." Even as he said it, he remembered the scene he had just witnessed. The mob with drunken tenacity was still searching for her. How was he to get her out of the Inn, and if he could get her out, where could he take her? Where was there any safety?

Chapter 19

SIROCCO

THE shutter banged. Adam got up to latch it. He noticed then that the wind had changed. It was blowing steadily now from the southeast. That would certainly bring the storm.

"I should never have come," Lady Caroline's voice broke into his thoughts. "But I had nowhere to go—" She leaned forward suddenly. "All of my friends have fallen away. Rats desert a sinking ship," she said bitterly. "Now, ruffians overturn my chair, call me vile names, throw stones through a window at the sight of my face." She got up and went to the mirror above the mantel, wiping a tiny trickle of blood from her cheek. "I felt sure I could depend on you, Adam," she said, going back to her chair. "You can see, I must get away."

Adam scarcely heard her. He was searching in his mind for a way to save her from her pursuers. Suddenly, he knew —the *Saucy Susan* lying in the river ready to sail at sunrise —Marcy waiting for him now at the wharf.

But how could he get her to the boat?

He glanced at her haggard face, her despairing eyes.

"I'm frightened, Adam. Once before a mob—" she covered her face with her hands, her bare shoulders shaking.

He tried to think of a way to get her out of the Inn without attracting the attention of the mob. Opening the shutter of the window cautiously, he looked down into the courtyard below. It was filled with men, shouting and singing, carrying lanterns and torches. The whole town was awake. He drew the curtain when he saw a man glance upward.

"I'll go," Lady Carolina said. "I should never have come here."

"Sit down," Adam said sharply. "Do you think I'd turn you over to those drunken men? I must think of a way. Clothes for one thing. You can't go like that—you'd be recognized instantly."

There was a light tap at the door. Crossing the room, Adam opened the door a few inches. It was Mary Warden.

She was still in her ball gown and she had a lighted candle in her hand.

"I saw your light and hoped you were here," she said. "I want you to come to Lavinia. She's hysterical—I can't do anything with her—" she stopped suddenly when she saw Lady Caroline.

Adam caught her arm as she turned away. "Come in, Mary," he said briefly. "We need you here."

Mary came into the room, nodding stiffly to Lady Caroline, who had risen from her chair.

"I'll go, Adam. There's nothing you can do now."

"Sit down," Adam said impatiently. "Wait, both of you." He turned to Mary. "I'll send Cicero for Dr. Armitage. I know he is in his rooms. I saw him drive home a few minutes ago." He went into the bedroom, closing the door.

Mary sat down. After her brief acknowledgment, Lady Caroline settled herself in the chair, her eyes closed. Mary looked at her curiously. What had happened to make the proud, almost arrogant woman change so suddenly?

Adam came in. "I've sent Cicero to get the Doctor for Lavinia."

Mary got up. "I must go to her," she said, without meeting his eyes.

"No, don't. I need you here. We must think of a way to get Lady Caroline down to the docks and out on the *Saucy Susan* without running into—without anyone recognizing her," he finished lamely.

Mary stared at him. "I don't understand," she said quietly.

Lady Caroline opened her eyes. "Tell her, Adam, tell her the whole sordid story. What does it matter now, who knows that I am being hunted by the rabble?"

Instantly, Mary was all quick sympathy. "How dreadful! Adam, we must find a way to protect her. Can we take her to Edenton, to Queen's Gift?"

Lady Caroline looked at Mary searchingly. "I believe you mean it," she said, her eyes filled with wonder. "But that won't do. I must go to Wilmington where I can get a ship for the Indies." She turned to Adam. "I have a house on St. Thomas—a stone house, strong as a fortress. I will be safe there."

Adam glanced at Mary. She was sitting quietly, her elbow on the table, one finger making a little dent in her chin—a trick she had when she was puzzled. Then her face cleared.

"I will order my coach and drive to the wharf, as if I were

going on the ship—" She looked at Lady Caroline. "What will we do about your clothes?" she said, a little line coming between her eyes. "You can't wear mine."

Lady Caroline laughed shortly.

Adam said, "I'll give her one of my riding capes. It will cover her. But you can't do this, Mary, without telling William."

Mary interrupted. "William left for Charles Town at twelve o'clock. I found a note when I got back to my room." She said to Lady Caroline: "I'll bring you a scarf for your head. You can wrap it like a turban to cover your hair. No one must see your hair."

She went out of the room, but she was back in a few minutes wearing a dark cloak over her satin dress and carrying a long black scarf and a dressing case.

"I hope the Doctor gets here soon," she said to Adam, when he came in with a dark cape over his arm. "I'm a little worried about leaving Lavinia, but I've instructed her maid to sit by her." She went to the window and pulled the curtain. "Ebon is there, now. I see him driving up to the side entrance. The courtyard is full of men, but we'll have to go anyway. We will walk boldly through the lounge." She turned to Lady Caroline. "I've brought my dressing case. You can carry it as if you were my maid."

Lady Caroline nodded. She was wrapping the scarf about her head, leaving the long end ready to draw over her face. She took up Mary's case in one hand. From the floor by the chair she had been sitting in, she lifted a leather-bound satchel of similar size and slid it under her arm.

Adam put the cape over her shoulders. Mary looked at her critically. "We have to pin your skirts so they won't show. Adam, will you cut the buckles off her shoes? They would give her away instantly."

When he had finished the task, Adam went to the window. The shutter slammed shut, driven by the wind.

"We'll have to hurry. I'm afraid the storm will break before we get to the wharf."

"That might be better," Mary said, sensibly. "A storm would distract their attention."

They walked through the hall and down the stairs, Lady Caroline a few steps behind. The men drinking buttered rum in the Ordinary glanced up as they passed the open door but showed no curiosity. In the lounge they encountered only a few men, most of them strangers. Ebon had the coach ready.

284

Adam helped Mary in and got in after her, leaving Lady Caroline to follow with the luggage.

"To Hewes's and Smith's dock," he said, in a clear voice. In case anyone overheard, he wanted to give the impression that they were going on one of the regular ships sailing north.

When they turned the corner, Adam put his head out the window and told Ebon to drive to the lower wharf with all speed, choosing the quietest streets.

There were no quiet streets. The Palace was dark, but every inn, tavern and dramshop was filled. Men and women, coming and going, pushed through the crowds that filled the streets. Music sounded along the quay. The wind was blowing strongly, whistling around the corner of the buildings, bending trees and bushes.

Intermittent lightning flashed along the horizon at lessening intervals. When they got to the lower town, they saw shopkeepers putting up storm shutters while their slaves held lanterns. They were preparing for a blow. With the wind from that direction, it was sure to come. Once or twice the coach was halted by street crowds blocking the way, or a drunken man getting in front of the nervous, restive horses.

At the wharf, Adam got out of the coach. "If anyone questions you, tell him you are going aboard the *Saucy Susan*," he told Mary.

He went as rapidly as he could down the long wharf to the place where he hoped Marcy would be waiting. At the end, he saw the outline of a boat. He called, "Marcy!" At the second call there was an answer.

A few moments later, Marcy climbed out of the boat and stood beside him. "The boat's ready, Mr. Rutledge, but I've sent the crew to the tavern to get the ship's grog. They should be back any time now."

"I can't wait for them. Lady Caroline is in the coach. I must get her aboard the shallop at once."

Marcy said: "I know, I heard them talking up there. They're still searching for her. They want a victim tonight—man or woman, they don't care which."

Adam thought a moment. "I'll take this boat. You get one from the wharfinger."

"Where are you going to send the woman?" Marcy asked, as they walked up the wharf to the coach.

"She wants to go to Wilmington. I thought the captain could put her ashore there."

"She'll fare worse in Wilmington," Marcy said, shortly.

"What do you mean?" Adam exclaimed.

"The Provincial Committee had Guernsey House searched two days ago. They found papers—a lot of incriminating evidence—enough to hang the wench if we ever take over the government. It's too complicated to go into now."

Adam thought rapidly. "Then we'll have to send the shallop to Virginia first."

Marcy made no comment. Adam knew he would like to turn the woman over to the Committee and be done with it.

"Marcy, I know what you're thinking, but I'm duty bound to get her out of the country." Even though they were out of earshot of the coach, he kept his voice low.

"They're wild because they didn't get the real lists," Marcy said.

"What lists do you mean?"

"They say she had a book with a list of the men who had paid her for patronage—paid high, for promise of positions in the army, and at Court."

Adam listened, disturbed by Marcy's words. "We've got to get her away! If this involves any Whig leaders, it will be a pretty scandal. Tryon would be quick to take advantage of it."

"I wish the woman was in Gehenna," Marcy muttered. "She's caused enough trouble."

Adam heard voices—men walking along the loose floor boards of the long wharf, followed by a rumbling sound.

Marcy said, "That's our crew. I can hear them rolling the rum kegs."

"Go up and meet them, Marcy," Adam said quickly. "Get them into the boat and off to the ship. I think, after all, it would be better for you to start first. You can notify the captain so that he will be ready to weigh anchor."

Marcy hesitated. "Hadn't I better go with you, sir? The boat's heavy; there'll be a blow—listen to the wind down the river."

"I'll manage," Adam said. "Be off now, before the men get down here."

Marcy walked quickly away. Adam waited until he had time to reach the wharfinger's house, before he went up the side street where the coach was waiting.

"Thank God!" Lady Caroline exclaimed, when she saw Adam. She was not frightened now. Her voice was firm. "Where's the boat? Can I charter a boat to Wilmington from here?"

286

"You can't go to Wilmington now, Lady Caroline," Adam said. "You'll have to go north to Virginia."

"I don't want to go to Virginia, Rutledge." Lady Caroline's voice was impatient. "I must go to Wilmington. I can get a ship for St. Thomas from there."

Adam thought he might as well tell her the truth. "It's too late, now," he said. "The Committee has searched Guernsey House—" he stopped. He did not need to finish the sentence.

There was an acute silence. Even through the dark the vibration of her fear was manifest. When she answered, her voice had lost its vitality. She was beaten, and she knew it.

"As you say, Adam. Let it be Virginia," she said wearily.

They got out of the coach and walked to the end of the wharf without speaking.

The storm broke when they were a short distance from shore. A great roar and rush of wind churned the dark water. Adam shipped his oars, ready to turn back. On the bank, the dark mass of trees was swaying, bent to the ground. A limb snapped with a sharp crackling sound like a rifle shot. The wind hurled it into the river; it struck near the boat, the splashing water drenching them to the skin.

"Get down into the bottom of the boat," Adam shouted. "Get down. Cover yourself with your coat, Mary." He could not hear her answer.

"Give me an oar," Lady Caroline shrieked above the wind. "I'll help now."

"No, no! Stay where you are," Adam shouted back.

But she had already dragged an oar from the bottom of the boat and, by an overwhelming effort, got it into the locks. Moving slowly so as not to disturb the balance of the boat, she got into the seat behind Adam and, after a moment, caught the rhythm of his stroke. She rowed strongly, like a person accustomed to the use of oars. It was all he could do to keep the boat headed downstream, but the second oar helped. The woman had courage and strength—an Atlantean strength. Adam's back ached. His thin linen shirt clung damply to his body. Mary was a dark heap in the bottom of the boat. She had not spoken since they had left the wharf.

A flash of lightning showed Lady Caroline bending over the oars, dark strands of hair whipping against her cheek and neck, her gown clinging close to the curve of her long limbs and her full breasts, and her bare arms shining with rain as she pulled at the oars.

Adam gave up the struggle. It was no use. They would have to drift—let the wind drive them down the river. They might, with luck, be able to see the ship in time and pull over into the lee.

After a time, the fury of the storm spent itself. The rain stopped. It was growing lighter. Adam saw a dark shadow loom up before him. Before he could swing the boat around, they had grazed the piling of the long wharf.

"Pull aft," he called to Lady Caroline, "aft—we've been blown in a circle."

Overhead, he heard running feet. A voice called out. "Ahoy there, who are you?"

Adam did not answer. With his oar against the barnacle-covered piles, he pushed the boat out into the current.

"Seen anything of a boat with a woman in it?" the voice called out.

Adam heard the sides of a boat grating against the piers, followed by the splash of oars. Lady Caroline heard, also. She redoubled her effort, quickening her stroke. Spurred on by the sound of the men in the boat shouting for them to stop, they rowed frantically until the voices grew dim.

After what seemed to Adam hours, the hull of a ship loomed high above them. In the half-light, Adam recognized the figurehead of the *Saucy Susan*. He put his cupped hands to his mouth, shouting, "Ahoy—ahoy there!" In a moment, Marcy answered.

"I'll throw you a ladder," he called. A rope ladder slid down the side of the shallop. Adam caught it, holding it taut; Lady Caroline laid her hand on Adam's arm.

"I'll never forget, Adam, never," she said. "Or you, Mary Warden, I won't forget you, either. I hated you once, and everything you've stood for. But I know, now, I was wrong. Will you forgive me?"

"There's nothing to forgive," Mary started to say, but she was interrupted.

Marcy's voice came over the side. "Hurry, hurry! I can see boats, hurry!"

Lady Caroline climbed the swaying ladder, her wet skirts dripping from seam and hem.

"Now, Mary," Adam said, standing at the stern, steadying the boat.

"No, I'll stay with you. Perhaps I can help—"

Adam had no time to remonstrate. A rough, heavy voice came from the river. "There they are! I see a woman in the boat. Hurrah! We've got her; we've caught up with Lady Caroline at last."

Mary drew her coat closer about her and sat up. Adam looked anxiously at the side of the shallop and was relieved to find that the rope ladder had been hauled in. A few moments later, a boat carrying eight or ten men came alongside. Rough hands grasped the side of the boat.

"Here they are! Here's the woman. We've got Lady Caroline."

Before Adam could think of an answer, he heard Mary's clear, calm voice saying, "You are mistaken, gentlemen. Lady Caroline is not here. I'm Mrs. Warden of Edenton. I'm going north on this ship."

Marcy, leaning over the rail, heard her. He responded instantly to her cue. "Is that you, Mr. Rutledge?" he called out. "Just a moment, we'll throw a ladder for Mrs. Warden. Hope the storm didn't do too much damage."

"Couldn't be wetter," Adam answered. "Down with the ladder, Marcy. Mrs. Warden will be glad to get dried out."

The rain had stopped and the wind had died down. It was light enough now to make out faces. The man holding the side of the boat hesitated; he leaned forward to scan Mary's face.

"It's Mrs. Warden all right," he shouted to the others. "I've seen her before in Albermarle. Come on, fellows—let's try the next ship down below."

They let go the side of the boat and, after a brief consultation among themselves, rowed away, steering down river.

When they were out of hearing distance, Adam said, "I'm afraid you'll have to go aboard now, Mary. They'll be watching when I return to the wharf. If you're in the boat, they may suspect—"

"Yes, I know. I don't mind going as far as Edenton. Will you have Cissie pack my clothes and send her up in the coach?"

Adam agreed but on the shallop Marcy and the captain suggested another plan. The ship would stop again at Hurd's plantation on the way down the river. Marcy could engage a conveyance there and drive Mrs. Warden back to New Bern. They should be at the Inn in the afternoon at the latest. This seemed a good way out of the difficulty.

Adam followed Lady Caroline and Mary below. At the last, Lady Caroline held his hand in a strong grip. "I'll not forget," she repeated, quickly, "either you or Mary Warden.

She saved me. They'd have searched the shallop if it hadn't been for her quick wit. Good-by, Adam Rutledge. One day, I may be able to repay."

"A good journey and safe haven at St. Thomas," he said, kissing her hand.

She dropped her voice. "Don't forget me entirely, Adam."

"How can I?" he answered quickly. "I can't forget a woman of rare courage. Good-by, Lady Caroline."

Mary went on the deck with him. "I feel sad for her, Adam," she said, as they stood at the rail. "I'm so glad you found a way to help, now that everyone has turned against her."

After he had gone over the side and rowed away, Mary remembered she had not told him about Lavinia and Peyton, and the affair of the necklace.

When Adam woke late that morning, Cicero told him that Mrs. Peyton Rutledge was waiting in the sitting room.

"She waiting since most of de mornin'," he said, "cryin' into her little kerchief."

Adam got out of bed and dressed hastily, cursing at Cicero for not calling him earlier. In spite of his sympathy for Lavinia, his annoyance at Peyton grew. "Why couldn't he behave himself?" he thought, as he twisted his white scarf around his throat and got into the coat that Cicero held out. His annoyance turned to anxiety when Lavinia told him of the occurrence of the night before. This was something more serious than gambling and a night of drinking.

"Don't you think that you should ask Peyton where he got the necklace?" he asked, after she had told him about the mark on the clasp—the initials C. R. intertwined beneath a crown.

"I don't know where he is, Adam! He didn't come home last night. I haven't seen him since before supper at the Palace." She looked at him, her eyes tragic. "He was with Lady Caroline then," she said, beginning to weep. "Oh, Adam, could C. R. mean Caroline—not Charlotte? Do you think he would give me a necklace that had been hers? Oh, Adam, what shall I do? I can't talk to the Baron—I can't ask him not to do anything to Peyton. He can have the necklace. I never want to see it again!" She leaned forward, her head on the table, her body wracked with sobs.

Adam laid a comforting hand on her shoulder. He was glad she was not looking at him; the expression on his face might have confirmed her fears. How was he to approach the Baron without betraying Peyton? Just what was Peyton's part in the affair? He walked up and down the room, his eyes on the floor, trying to think it through. Lavinia sat up and dried her eyes, watching him.

"Curious," Adam was thinking: "Last night I helped Lady Caroline get away—the one person most likely to know the truth about this." He had not the slightest doubt but that she had given the necklace to Peyton. Everything pointed that way. He thought of other things—Lady Caroline's extravagant display of jewels on every occasion; Mary Warden and the Doctor finding the unset stones in her library at Pembroke; Peyton's curious dependence on the woman. He remembered something Lady Caroline had said to him that evening he had called on her—what were the words she had used? "Peyton cannot get away. He's in too deep—they would kill him." Who would kill him? Peyton had been drinking and philandering, it was true, but he had seemed to have no money troubles of late. Adam saw no reason to be disturbed by that fact for Peyton had done remarkably well with the West Indies business. He had made many trips to the Islands in the last four years. Adam was suddenly aware that Lavinia was looking at him, her eyes filled with anxiety.

"I'll find Peyton, don't worry, Lavinia," he said. "There'll be some simple explanation for all of this. Does anyone know about it? Did anyone overhear the Baron?"

Lavinia shook her head. "Only Mary. She was there when the Baron spoke of the disappearance of the jewels. Oh, Adam! I was so terrified. I'm still terrified. What if Peyton has gone off with that woman!"

Adam laughed shortly. "I can assure you on that point, Lavinia. I put Lady Caroline on a ship bound for Virginia—one of my own ships."

Lavinia gave a gasp of relief and sat erect. A tremulous smile came to her lips. "I can stand anything, Adam," she said, her voice firm. "It wasn't the necklace—it was Peyton. I thought I was losing him." Her white hands went up to her mouth to keep Adam from seeing her trembling lips.

"Don't worry, little cousin," he said gently. "We will get this straightened out."

After she had gone, Adam went downstairs to the Ordinary. The room was crowded with officers from the ships and important men of the Province eating and drinking. Adam asked one or two discreet friends if they had seen Peyton. No one had. He was about to leave the room when he saw Lieutenant Grafton with two officers from the *Jupiter*. Adam nodded to him briefly.

Grafton stopped him. "Won't you have a drink with us, Mr. Rutledge?"

Adam was about to refuse, then thought better of it. This man was close to the Baron. Perhaps he could get some information from him without betraying his purpose. He sat down and ordered a brandy.

The officers were talking about the happenings of the night before.

"The Baron and the Governor are on the *Jupiter* now," Grafton said. "We got the Baron away through the secret passage. It is fortunate that the Governor had the forethought to include a means of escape when he had the plans of the Palace drawn.

Adam nodded absently. His mind was occupied with Lavinia and her problem.

"The Governor should profit by this and use a firm hand," Grafton continued. "He's been too damn lenient with these people. If I'd been in his place, I'd have called out the troops and shot the ringleaders.

Captain Eastwood interrupted. "That would have been madness, Grafton. You must remember you are dealing with a different class of people here. These men have had a taste of freedom and they don't intend to give it up." He turned to Adam for confirmation. It crossed Adam's mind that Grafton was trying to get information about the country—that this talk was planned. He would be wary. He didn't want to enter into an argument. That would close one avenue for obtaining information. He said:

"Governor Tryon is wise. He knows the people and has made a careful study of the situation here."

Grafton's face darkened. He was disappointed in the answer. Adam saw a quick glance pass between the officers. He finished his drink and pushed back his chair.

"If you'll excuse me, gentlemen," he said, "I have a meeting at the Palace in a few minutes." Before Grafton could protest, he had walked away.

He found Herk waiting for him outside in the courtyard with news of Peyton.

"Mas' Peyton, he follow two officers off the ship. One of de slaves say dey all gallop down de Wilmington road last night, but de officers, dey come back."

Adam thought for a moment, then said, "Get the horses, Herk. We'll ride down that way."

292

"De road hit washed out just past Hurd plantation. Mister Marcy told me when I see him while ago," Herk said.

So Marcy had returned. That meant he had brought Mary back from the shallop. Perhaps he should speak to her before he started to find Peyton. She knew about the necklace. She might have some plan. . . .

"Get the horses saddled and wait for me at the side entrance," he said to Herk. He walked swiftly through the hall, upstairs to the second floor, and tapped on the door of Mary's suite.

In a moment, Cissie opened the door. Her face was glum. "I done got she a mustard foot bath. Look lak she old enough to keep sheself out de rain," she grumbled, as she opened the door wider for Adam to enter.

Mary was sitting before the fire wrapped in a blanket, her feet in a foot bath, drinking a cup of steaming tea. When she saw him she pulled the blanket over her feet. Then she laughed.

"Come in, Adam," she said. "Cissie thinks I'm going to die because my clothes got wet in last night's storm."

Adam sat down in a chair Cissie pushed forward. He went to the point at once. What did Mary know about the jewels? What did she think the Baron intended doing about it, and in the name of God, where did Peyton get the necklace?

"I don't believe he got it from Lady Caroline," she said, answering his thought instead of his words. "Peyton is impulsive—but he wouldn't do anything as contemptible as that!"

Adam said nothing. The whole thing was too involved.

Suddenly Mary thought of something. "I know—the Levantine's!" she exclaimed. "Do you suppose Peyton bought it at his shop in Edenton?"

Adam knew little about the Levantine and his merchandise. "It's possible," he said, after she had explained. "Peyton might have bought it there. You say the necklace Lavinia was looking at at the Levantine's had the same type of setting?"

"Yes. Very ornate—quite different from the usual Amsterdam settings. Lady Caroline's emeralds have a similar setting, very Oriental." She stopped suddenly. Then she said, almost as if she were speaking to herself, "Why didn't I think of it? Lady Caroline's emeralds . . . that would make the third necklace. The Baron spoke of three necklaces." She caught Adam's arm, alarm in her eyes. "Adam, you'll have to see the Baron. You can't allow Lavinia to be mixed up in a scandal about stolen jewels."

Adam got up. "I wish I had something to go on," he said,

wearily. "I can't very well approach the Baron with an explanation unless I know the truth."

"There's only one thing to do, Adam. You must find Peyton first."

Adam nodded. He left the room, closing the door quietly behind him. Herk was waiting at the carriage entrance with the horses. Adam vaulted into the saddle and they started down the road in the direction of Wilmington.

Mary dressed and went to find Lavinia. She was in her room directing her packing. She sent the slave away. Peyton had not come back, she said. While they were talking, Judith came to the door to tell Lavinia that her mistress wished to speak to her. When Lavinia came back, Mary saw she had been crying.

"Sara is starting for Rutledge Riding at once," she told Mary. "Dr. Armitage and the Blounts are going at the same time. She is furious about the riots and the attempt of those men to burn the Palace last night. 'A Whig plot,' is what she called it, 'a dastardly Whig plot, in which you all are involved.' She is angry with Adam because he is not here to see her off. I explained that he had gone to find Peyton—" She stopped abruptly, pressing her lips together to keep from speaking her mind.

Mary did not want to make any comment about Sara. She said, "If there is nothing I can do here, Lavinia, I'll go back to see that Cissie starts packing. I'll be in my room if you want me."

ADAM FIGHTS
A DUEL

ABOUT three o'clock one of the Inn slaves knocked at Mary's door and gave her a large square envelope sealed with red wax and carrying a crest. It was from Baron Cotswold.

"Dear Mrs. Warden:

"Will you do me the honor to dine with me at six o'clock this afternoon on the *Jupiter?* The Governor and Lady Tryon will be the only other guests.

"I got the impression last night that you were an intelligent woman, therefore discreet. I prefer that your visit to the *Jupiter* remain as secret as possible.

"Will you please send an answer by the messenger?

"COTSWOLD"

Mary read the note a second time before she sat down at the desk to pen an affirmative answer. She was apprehensive. What did the Baron want? Was he going to question her further about the necklace, or did he wish to continue the conversation they had begun concerning the grievances of the people of the Province? In either case, she didn't want to talk. What was she to do? This was not an invitation but a command. If only William had not left for Wilmington with Judge Moore, or if Adam were here to consult! She glanced at her little traveling clock on the dressing table; almost three hours before she would have to leave. She got some comfort from the thought that Adam might return before then.

At a quarter of six Cicero told her that Adam had not returned. She dared not wait any longer so she ordered her coach and drove to the wharf. At the dock a seaman from the *Jupiter* stepped up, touching his cap.

"The Admiral has sent his barge for you, Mrs. Warden. Will you please come this way?"

She followed him along the dock and stepped into a barge manned by eight rowers. The *Jupiter* was anchored in stream, a half-mile down the river. She sat back, shielded by the folding canopy, watching the steady, rhythmic sweep of the long oars.

Her apprehension increased as she neared the vessel. She must be very cautious in speaking of affairs in the Colony; if the subject of the necklace were mentioned, she would know nothing at all.

The barge reached the ship. The companionway had been hung over the side and two sailors stood at the bottom step to assist her aboard. A smile crossed her lips when she thought how she and Lady Caroline had crawled up the swaying rope ladder in the wind and driving rain last night. Last night—was it only last night? It seemed an eternity.

The sun was low, the air, after the storm, balmy and soft. She found the Baron seated on deck under an awning. Lady Tryon was drinking tea; the Governor had a decanter of whisky on the table in front of him. The men got up when Mary crossed the deck. The Baron indicated a chair near him.

"You are very kind to come, Mrs. Warden," he said, after he had ordered tea for her. "We are beginning to be bored with our own company."

A fleeting, rather tired smile crossed Lady Tryon's lips.

"She's worried," thought Mary, instantly sympathetic. She looked at the Governor. He was smiling blandly. There was no trace of the anger or terror she had seen on his face the night before.

"I did not include your husband in my invitation, Mrs. Warden, for the Governor told me he had left for Wilmington with Judge Moore last night."

Mary wondered how Tryon could have known that. She saw the Governor glance at his wife, raising his bushy eyebrows.

"Shall we take a stroll about the deck, my dear?" he suggested.

Lady Tryon got up at once. The Baron settled back in his chair, his glass in his hand, and signaled the steward for more whisky. Behind the Baron's heavy body, Mary saw the setting sun reflected in the smooth river. She looked at her host and wondered what was behind that impassive face.

As he turned she caught a swift appraising glance from his pale blue eyes. He raised his glass to his lips, drank deeply, and put the empty glass on the silver tray, wiping his lips on the lace ruffles of his cuff.

"I wasn't quite fair last night, Mrs. Warden," he said, breaking the silence. "I let them think I happened to be pleased by your appearance. I had heard of you before. You are exactly as your friend Patience Wright described you."

296

"You know Patience?" Mary exclaimed, her surprise showing on her face and in her voice.

"Very well, indeed!" the Baron answered. "I'm an admirer of hers. She is very talented—and something more: a discreet woman. I suppose you know that she is one of the few women that his Majesty talks to in confidence?"

"I have met the King at her studio," Mary said guardedly.

The Baron laughed. "I see you, also, are discreet. I thought last night when you talked about our responsibility to the Colonies that you resembled Patience. She always says what she thinks. Do you know that you are the only one here who has been frank enough to give me a true picture of what is happening? And I have talked with half a hundred of your leading men."

Mary smiled. "Perhaps our leaders have learned diplomacy by past experience."

The Baron turned his heavy body around in the chair so that he could face her directly. "I'm not going to talk politics now. I learned all I needed to know last night. There is another matter—what do you know of the necklace Mrs. Rutledge wore last night?"

Mary opened her lips to deny all knowledge of it but he stopped her.

"I know Lavinia lied when she said it came from her husband's family. She was protecting her husband. If he is what I think he is, he doesn't deserve protection." His voice was harsh, quite different from a moment before.

Mary said, her steady, blue eyes holding his: "I don't know what you are trying to say, Baron, but Peyton Rutledge is not a thief."

The Baron pursed his thick lips. "No—? Well, will you tell me how he happens to be in possession of jewels that belong to the Queen?"

"The Queen?" Mary pretended astonishment.

"Yes, they belonged to the Queen. They are part of a collection that was stolen some years ago."

Mary tried not to show alarm. This was even more serious than she had thought. She felt the Baron watching her with his pale shrewd eyes.

After a moment, he continued, "There is an officer on the *Jupiter* who has been searching for the jewels ever since we've had a clue that they were in the Colonies. He had some success last month. He found some of the stones in the hands of a Dutch lapidary at Charlotte Amalie. They had been taken from their settings, but he had no difficulty identifying them from the description he had."

Mary said nothing. She sat quietly, not moving, but her heart was beating violently.

"The Dutchman swore he had never seen the three necklaces." The Baron paused a moment while a lackey filled his glass. "They were valuable, very valuable. It happens they had been presented to her Majesty as an official gift of the newly acquired Provinces of India."

Mary listened, her fear growing. The Baron's eyes were boring into hers. She was glad she could speak the truth. "I never saw the necklace until last night," she said slowly.

It flashed across her mind then that she should tell him of the ruby and emerald necklace she had seen at the Levantine's shop in Edenton. But she held her tongue. There might be some connection which would involve Peyton.

The Baron leaned forward. "Tell me about this Lady Caroline you spoke of last night—the woman who keeps bags of loose jewels lying around her house."

Mary thought fast. She must be very cautious. It would be so easy to say the wrong thing—something that would turn the Baron's mind toward Peyton again.

"Speak up, Mrs. Warden," the Baron said impatiently. "You may as well tell me what you know. It would be easy enough for me to find out from some other source. But just now the fewer people who know about the jewels the better."

Mary knew she must answer something. If she could only tell a little—just enough to turn his suspicions away from Peyton and Lavinia. "I really know nothing of importance about Lady Caroline," she said. "She came to Edenton and leased Pembroke, an estate at the head of the Sound. She said she liked it there so she stayed some months—perhaps a year, I'm not sure of the time. She entertained very lavishly."

"Are you a friend of hers that you are afraid to speak out?" he asked, looking at her shrewdly.

Mary smiled. "No, Baron, we could scarcely be called friends—acquaintances would be a better word."

"Why is that? What have you against the woman?"

"Nothing," Mary answered evasively. "Lady Caroline doesn't care for Whigs and, as you know, I'm a Whig."

There was no answering smile from the Baron. His small, light blue eyes did not leave her face. "You said she claimed to be a sister of the Queen?"

"That was the rumor. She never, at any time, mentioned such a thing to me. But she is a woman of distinction with an

298

intimate knowledge of the Court—and of Palace politics," she replied. "But why do you ask me this? Surely you know Lady Caroline?"

The Baron thrust out his heavy pendulous lip. "The Queen has a score of relatives I've never seen or heard of. . . . I've been away from London for some time, visiting Colonies—out to India. . . ."

There was a slight suggestion of embarrassment in his manner. In the back of her head Mary seemed to remember that the Great Personage was not in favor with the King—that he was sent out on various missions that would keep him away from London.

"So you don't visit Lady Caroline?" he said, after a long silence.

"No, Baron, not now. I saw her occasionally in Edenton, but I've never been to Guernsey House."

"Guernsey House!"

"The place she took at Wilmington one season when the Assembly was in session—that was before the capitol was moved to New Bern—a beautiful old house on the river."

At the word "river" the Baron looked up from his contemplation of the deck. "On the Sound—on the river," he said, half to himself. "This Lady Caroline seems to like the water."

"She says she can't live away from it—or from the sight of ships," Mary answered, glad that he showed so much interest in these small unimportant things. "The water, it seems, cures her migraines."

He sat up. Mary saw behind the dilatory questioning that there was a purpose.

"I'll speak to the Governor about her. I must meet the woman. You have made her a very interesting person, Mrs. Warden—but I trust you will say nothing about this.

"I have sent for Rutledge," he said abruptly. "I won't talk to Lavinia—I like the woman, but not enough to let her husband off unless I have a satisfactory explanation as to how the stones came into his hands."

Mary spoke quickly, "I'm sure she knows nothing, Baron Cotswold."

"That may be—it will come out in Grafton's examination. He is determined to get to the bottom of this. There is more involved than stolen jewels, Mrs. Warden." He straightened back in his chair when he saw the Governor and Lady Tryon approaching. A moment later, a steward announced dinner and they went below to the wardroom where the Admiral and Lieutenant Grafton were waiting.

Mary ate little of the elaborate meal. She was watching Grafton. He had a thin, tight-lipped mouth, at once cruel and determined. Tryon and the Baron carried the burden of the conversation. The Baron asked questions, purposely embarrassing to the Governor, which Tryon tried to answer casually. But Mary saw he was worried.

"You will have to exert more discipline if you don't want your people out of control, Tryon," the Baron said insinuatingly. "If the King should hear of last night's exhibition, it might interfere with his plans." He choked over a huge mouthful of fowl. The steward handed him a goblet of water which he drank at a gulp. He wiped his lips with the corner of the napkin that was spread, like a child's bib, over his large stomach.

"The King was speaking of New York," he went on. "You'd like New York, wouldn't you, Tryon?" The Governor's face brightened, but the Baron gave him no chance to answer. "I'd advise strict discipline here, then. If you want New York, hold the people in check. Don't let them get out of hand again. Quell riots with soldiers and guns—" he paused, looking at Mary. "You wouldn't agree with that, would you, Mrs. Warden?"

"No, Baron, I would not," she said with spirit.

"Mrs. Warden is a professed Whig," Lady Tryon said dully.

The Baron turned to her. "At least she has the honesty to say so. I admire you for that, madam. Don't you, Admiral, and you, Lieutenant?" he said, turning to the officers.

They had no opportunity to voice their sentiments for just then a young officer came into the room. Saluting the Baron smartly, he said: "A gentleman is waiting at the companionway for permission to call upon your Grace. Rutledge is the name he gave."

The Baron glanced at Mary. She went on eating quietly as if she were not in the least disturbed, but her heart was pounding. It was Adam! She wished now that she had not told him to talk with the Baron.

"Let him come aboard. Take him to my sitting room," the Baron said to the officer. "I'll see him later."

He turned back to his heaping plate. Mary sat very still. She answered his questions, she smiled, she even laughed at some quip he made. He grew more gracious with each glass of wine. After a little time, Lieutenant Grafton leaned over and spoke to him, and then got up from the table. Mary watched him as he left the room. She felt certain that he was going to question Adam.

If there were only a way to let Adam know what the situation was before he talked to the Baron. But she could think of no way. She could only wait, hoping that nothing would happen to cause trouble for Lavinia or Peyton.

Course after course was set before them; the Baron ate of everything—the thick soup, the joint, the suet pudding. Mary thought he would never finish eating, or relating court scandal. She and Lady Tryon escaped when the port was brought and went on deck.

It was quite dark. The lights from New Bern shown dimly, making little ladders from the landing toward the town, marking the streets that led to the Palace.

Mary and Lady Tryon stood at the rail looking out over the darkness of the river. Officers and sailors in white uniforms walked about the deck or stood at their stations. A light shown in the cabin at the forward end of the sloop. Mary wondered if it were the Baron's quarters, and if he and Grafton were there. She could hear the murmur of men's voices, but she was too far away to distinguish words.

Lady Tryon sat down near the rail. She looked tired and pale. She had dropped her arrogant manner and was sitting very still, apparently brooding over some unpleasant thought. Mary glanced at her once or twice, but made no effort to break the silence. She thought: "Lady Tryon is a worried, nervous woman, submerged by her dominating husband."

"Don't you think there is something very mysterious about the way Lady Caroline disappeared last night?" Lady Tryon asked suddenly. She seemed to have forgotten her annoyance with Mary for being a Whig.

Her words took Mary by surprise; she was instantly on guard. "Has she disappeared?" she asked cautiously, moving a little so that the direct rays from the lantern did not fall on her face.

"I thought everybody knew," Lady Tryon said. "She was at the ball early in the evening, but she did not come to kiss hands, or be received by the Duke—I mean the Baron. Captain McCleod told me that her coach had been stopped on the way over. The people were shouting and cursing her, and calling her the Scarlet Woman—they were roused about a young man killing himself in her garden. Hadn't you heard?"

Mary said, "I heard something of the kind."

Lady Tryon moved a little closer. "I never liked the woman," she said, fiercely. "I loathe her, but—" She stopped suddenly, realizing what she was saying. But she had said too much not to clear her mind of the thoughts she had suppressed so long. "I loathe her superior ways. There's something sinister about her. I told William that in the beginning but he couldn't see it."

She got up and walked a little way along the rail and back. "Grafton isn't an officer on the *Jupiter,* really. He belongs to the Household. He came out on the *Daphne* to the West Indies to search for some jewels that were stolen from the Queen by one of her ladies-in-waiting—" She stopped in front of Mary and bent down, her face a white blur in the darkness. "Did you ever notice Lady Caroline's emeralds?" she whispered.

A heavy step put an end to the strange conversation. The Governor walked across the deck and sat down in a chair next to Mary without speaking. His wife moved nervously. Mary wondered what he had heard.

"Where's the Baron, William?" Lady Tryon asked. "Don't you think we can make our adieus now?"

"He asked us to wait," Tryon answered gloomily. "He is talking to Rutledge. I wonder why he called on the Baron?" He leaned close to Mary. The fumes from the wine he had drunk made her draw back. "I suppose you wouldn't tell me if you knew, Mrs. Warden." He was silent for a moment. Then he said, "It's a pity you and Rutledge have drifted over to the rebels. You should be with us, not with Moore and Caswell and those radical provincials. I can't understand you." He sank back in the chair.

Mary thought: "He is confused by the events that are taking place. He doesn't understand—he's bewildered and unhappy." She felt very sorry for Tryon.

In the silence that followed, Mary heard the continued mumble of voices from the cabin. Sometimes a word or two; the Baron's voice raised; then Grafton's; but never Adam's voice. She glanced at Tryon. He had not moved; his wife, after one brief outburst, dropped back into silence.

As time went on, Mary's anxiety increased. Peyton must be in serious trouble. What could Adam do about it? She sensed that the Baron, behind his affability, was deliberately cruel.

The voices were raised again. It was the Baron speaking now.

"I suppose you are denying all knowledge, Mr. Rutledge—" the rest of the sentence was a meaningless rumble.

The Governor leaned forward, straining his ears to listen. His wife had moved to a chair quite out of earshot.

Suddenly, Mary heard chairs scraping on the floor, followed by a crash, as if one had overturned.

"By God! This is more than enough——" Grafton's voice, high and excited. There was a confusion of sounds. The Baron's gutteral Germanic utterance, followed by silence.

Then Adam's voice, cool and clear, came to her ears. "I will dispense with seconds. . . ." he said.

Tryon got to his feet and walked swiftly across the deck. Lady Tryon came over to Mary.

"Did you hear that?" she asked, her voice shrill with excitement. "They can't be going to fight a duel—there's a death sentence against dueling, ever since Judge Berry——" she broke off suddenly.

Figures were moving silently along the decks toward the lighted cabin.

"The afterdeck will do very well," Mary heard the Baron say. "There is no need of going ashore."

Mary thought there was exultant excitement in his heavy tones. Lady Tryon's words were in her ears . . . the death sentence for dueling . . . Why should Adam be fighting Grafton? It must be Grafton, since it could not possibly be the Baron. She got out of her chair, and stood uncertainly, wondering what she could do. Tryon came back; he was breathing heavily.

"The fools, the damned fools!" he said. He turned to Mary. "What's got into Rutledge to challenge the Baron's aide? Has he lost his mind?"

"Are you sure that Adam challenged?" Mary asked, quick to defend him.

Tryon did not answer. He stormed at her as if she were responsible for the affront to his dignity. "They can't fight under my nose. I won't allow it. Have they no respect for the law?"

Mary took a few steps toward the afterdeck. Tryon caught up with her. "You can't go there, Mrs. Warden," he said decisively.

Mary shook off his hand from her arm and sped down the deck. She stopped abruptly outside the wardroom and leaned against the wall, out of breath.

On the wide afterdeck a dozen sailors were drawn up, holding lanterns above their heads so that the light would fall on an open space before them. The door of the wardroom opened. Mary sank back in the shadows. She need not have troubled to conceal herself, for no one looked her way. Grafton and the Baron, followed by two officers, walked out and into the lighted circle. Grafton had his coat off and was rolling up the sleeves of his white linen shirt. A moment later, Adam came out of the door. He, too, was coatless, his sleeves rolled back. A young officer followed him, carrying swords. Adam and Grafton stood in the circle of light. Mary thought she had never seen Adam so angry, his face so grim and determined. They stood silently for a moment while the selection was made. Then they measured swords and stepped into the ring.

Mary crouched against the wall, her heart beating violently. She was trembling so that she managed to keep her feet only by grasping the door frame. Adam's voice came distinctly:

"On guard," he said, his voice strong and unhurried; "on guard, sir."

Her impulse to cry out was checked by Tryon's hand on her shoulder. "We're leaving now, Mrs. Warden. You must come with us," he said. His back was to the afterdeck. "Hurry! Lady Tryon has your wrap. I must go—I can't stay here and be witness to a duel!"

He hurried her along the deck, his hand under her elbow, guiding her so that she would avoid the ropes and chains that lay in their way. Mary wanted to resist—to hold back—to go to Adam, but she knew she could not. She knew how adept Adam was with the sword—but suppose the other man had even greater skill?

Lady Tryon was waiting at the head of the companionway. In spite of the abrupt departure of the Governor, a guard of sailors was drawn up to pipe him over the side.

In the boat eight sailors were at their stations, oars uplifted. Ceremony must be observed, thought Mary bitterly, even if men were dying. Above the rattle of oars in the locks she could hear the terrifying clash of steel on steel. She put her hand over her mouth to keep from screaming.

Sudden anger at Peyton, at Lavinia, came over her. Why should Adam shoulder their burdens? They were adult. Why shouldn't they assume their own responsibilities? It was always Adam they called on. Her anger died slowly; despair filled her heart. What if Adam should be injured—killed? She forced herself to answer Lady Tryon's trivial questions. The Governor came out of his brooding silence.

"Why should Rutledge fight Grafton? He knows I shall be

forced to pronounce sentence upon him. He knows the dueling laws."

Mary did not reply. His words sounded like a doom to her. No matter what happened, the Governor could not neglect enforcement of the law.

When Mary got back to the Swan she found Lavinia waiting in her sitting room. Her eyes were red, her hair disarranged. When she saw Mary, she burst into tears.

"He's back, but he won't talk, Mary. I can't make him talk. He won't tell me where he got the necklace." She stopped short. "Peyton came home drunk," she said in a flat voice, "so drunk he had to be carried to the room by inn servants. He's asleep now." She sat down on the sofa, covering her pale face with her hands.

Mary tossed her cloak onto a chair. She sat down beside Lavinia, and put her arms about her shaking body. But she could think of nothing comforting to say, for she didn't care what happened to Peyton Rutledge. He wasn't worth Lavinia's tears or her poignant grief.

She got up after a little while and walked to the window. Adam—what was happening to Adam? She could see the lights from the ships lying in the stream. One of them was the *Jupiter*. On the afterdeck, surrounded by a group of hostile sailors and officers, Adam was fighting a duel—a duel that might cost him his life—for a man who lay on his bed in a drunken sleep.

She turned from the window and touched Lavinia's shoulder. "Go lie down, Lavinia. You need rest. We will see what can be done."

Lavinia made an effort to control herself. "You always know what is best. Thank you, Mary."

Mary watched her walk down the hall to her room before she closed the door. Then she blew out the candles on the mantel and the table. Drawing a chair to the window, she sat down where she could see the lights of the *Jupiter*—to wait.

Her anxiety built dreaded images. To wait—that was the woman's part. Wars would come, and women would wait for their men. Words entered her mind: "Return with your shield, or on it." Spartan women told their warrior sons, their husbands and their lovers: "With your shield, or upon it—" Die to uphold their honor. What if Adam Rutledge should die to uphold the honor of the man lying inert on a bed in his room?

Near midnight, a slight knock at the door roused Mary from her dark thoughts. She lighted a candle and went to see who was there. Lavinia stood in the hall. The light from the candle she held in her hand cast strange shadows on her livid face.

"Come quickly, Mary! Adam—" she stopped, catching Mary's arm, and began to cry hysterically. Mary grasped her shoulder, giving her a shake.

"Stop that, Lavinia," she said sternly. "Tell me what's wrong."

Steadied by Mary's voice, Lavinia said, "Dr. Armitage says Adam's badly hurt. There was a duel on the *Jupiter*. Oh, Mary! Do you think he'll die?"

Mary stood very quiet, her pulse pounding, her throat dry and constricted.

"Where is he?" she asked, when she could speak. "Where is he?"

"He's lying on the sofa in his sitting room. Dr. Armitage is with him and a doctor from the *Jupiter*. Dr. Armitage said—"

Mary did not wait. She ran down the hall to the head of the stairs and into the west wing. At the threshold she stopped for a moment to regain her composure; then she opened the door quietly and went into the room.

Adam was lying full-length on the sofa, his eyes closed, his face very white. His linen shirt had a great splotch of red on the shoulder, and blood was running from a long gash across his cheekbone. An officer was holding a bowl of water while Dr. Armitage tried to staunch the wound on his shoulder. Armitage looked up when Mary entered the room.

"Ah, Mary! Just the person we need. Hold the bowl, will you, so that Captain Orrick can help me? It'll take two to draw the cheek together properly. I'm afraid there'll be a bad scar," he muttered, half under his breath.

"A bad scar?" Mary breathed more normally at his words. If Adam were desperately hurt—if he were dying—the Doctor wouldn't be concerned with scars. She knew she must have turned white for Armitage looked at her keenly with his bright, searching eyes. His thin, old fingers closed reassuringly on her shoulder. He spoke in broken sentences while he worked.

"He's all right—bleeding like a stuck pig—it's the other fellow . . ."

Captain Orrick spoke in answer to Mary's look of inquiry. "Lieutenant Grafton slipped on the deck and managed to impale himself on Mr. Rutledge's sword."

306

A feeling of terror seized her. What if Adam had killed him?

"Is he—" she could not pronounce the word.

"No, he's alive, but it's a bad wound. We don't know yet . . ." Armitage stopped his explanation. Adam's eyes were opening slowly. He tried to sit up, but Armitage pushed him back. His voice unexpectedly gentle. "Not so fast, Adam, not so fast. Give me time to do my sewing."

"What happened to Grafton?" Adam asked in a strangely weak and unnatural voice.

"You ran him through neatly," the Doctor said. Then seeing the effect of his words, he added hastily, "But you aren't responsible. He slipped and fell on your sword. You're not to worry about it."

Adam sank back against the pillows. "I'm glad. I didn't want to injure Grafton. I could have had him a dozen times," he said weakly.

"That's right," Captain Orrick said, stepping into range of Adam's vision. "I witnessed the duel, sir. You were very forebearing, Mr. Rutledge. Grafton has no defense at all against your sword, although he's constantly boasting of his skill." He was silent a moment, then said, "I know I shouldn't say this, but all the officers on the *Jupiter* despise Grafton. He is a braggart, but he has a deal of influence. Through his connection with Rockingham he always gets choice assignments. He's a member of the Royal Household; now the Duke—I mean the Baron—has taken him up."

He glanced at Dr. Armitage. Mary saw the Doctor make an almost imperceptible movement with his head. He wanted to stop Captain Orrick. Why? Was Grafton hurt more seriously than they admitted to Adam? She tried to think what the penalty for dueling was when the opponent was only injured. Then she remembered—imprisonment, the length of time at the discretion of the Governor. But if the duel were fatal then the punishment was death. Mary felt her knees giving way when she thought of that contingency. She put the basin of water on the table and sat down. She heard Orrick say:

"I'm afraid I'll have to go now, Dr. Armitage. I left Grafton in charge of my assistant on the *Jupiter,* but the Baron is so disturbed that I think I'd better take charge myself."

"I'll report to you in an hour or so, Captain," the Doctor answered. "I don't believe there is any cause for alarm here; the wounds are clean." They walked to the door.

The Captain said, "Lieutenant Duval will wait in the Ordinary for your report. There is no need for him to come up here."

"Thank you, Orrick. I'll be responsible."

Be responsible! What did Dr. Armitage mean? In a moment, Mary realized—Adam was already under arrest.

Armitage came back in the room, followed by Herk with a pail of steaming water.

"Now we'll wash the shoulder wound properly. Stand here, Mary—the swabs are on the table. Herk, raise your master a little—turn him on his right side—easy there—that's better."

Adam's face was white, his mouth drawn. While they worked, the door opened softly and Lavinia came in. At the sight of the blood-saturated towels she put her hand over her lips and went quickly to the window. After a time, the long, gaping wound on Adam's shoulder was cleansed and stitched together.

The Doctor searched among his medicines and took out a bottle. He gave Adam a pellet, motioning to Mary to hold a glass of water to his lips.

"This will deaden the pain and put him to sleep," he said to Mary. "He needs quiet and rest—he has lost a lot of blood."

Adam swallowed automatically. Then he opened his eyes slowly. "I'm all right, Doctor," he said. "Just a little dizzy, that's all. I'll get up now."

"Oh, no, you won't," Armitage said, sharply. "Lie still. Sleep is what you need. I'll be in the next room. Lord! I'm sleepy." The Doctor stifled a yawn with the back of his hand and began stuffing bandages into a satchel.

Lavinia crossed the room and put her hand on the Doctor's arm, looking up at him with her tired eyes. "Is he all right—will he get well?" she asked, her voice low.

Armitage laughed. "Of course. Just a scratch—a mere scratch. It will mean nothing to a man with Adam's vitality."

"Why did he fight?" she whispered. "Why?"

"I don't know—something about a necklace the Baron accused him of stealing. I don't know much, only what Orrick told me."

Lavinia caught at the edge of the table. "A necklace?" she whispered. "He fought over a necklace?"

The Doctor looked at her searchingly. He reached across the table and caught her by the arm. "Quick, Mary! She's going to faint."

Mary pushed a chair forward in time to keep Lavinia from

falling. Armitage got out smelling salts and thrust the bottle under her nose, muttering, "Women—women, you never know what they will do.

"What is the meaning of all this, anyway?" he asked, his querulous voice filling the room. Lavinia began to laugh and cry at the same time. Armitage shook her. "Stop that, Lavinia! I'll not have a woman with the vapors getting my patient upset!"

Lavinia quieted down at his words. Mary glanced over her shoulder. Adam was sitting up, his back against the sofa. Herk was stuffing pillows behind him.

"Make a sling out of a scarf, Herk," the Doctor said, looking up. "I'll show you how to tie it to ease his shoulder. Mary, give Lavinia a sip of brandy from that bottle."

Mary, pouring brandy from the decanter, did not hear the door open. When she turned, Peyton was standing in the open doorway. His clothes were rumpled, as if he had slept in them; his handsome face was bloated, his wavy black hair disheveled, stray locks hanging shaggily over his forehead. He was holding the doorknob for support, his eyes had focused on Lavinia, as if he did not see anyone else.

"So here you are, madam," he muttered, his voice thick, sullen and angry. "Will you tell me what you are doing in a gentleman's room at night?"

"Oh, Peyton, please—" Lavinia whispered. "Please, Peyton." He turned around and faced the others.

"So you're all here, talking it over, talking over my affairs —me—the prodigal Peyton! Well, stop it! I won't have you talking about me. I'll attend to my own affairs, and my wife's, do you hear?"

No one spoke. Mary saw Armitage draw his lips together to repress the words on his tongue. Lavinia was looking at Peyton with frightened eyes, unable to speak. With a sudden revival of energy, Adam got to his feet. He spoke distinctly, looking directly at Peyton:

"No one has been discussing your affairs, Peyton. Sit down; I want to talk to you."

Peyton turned on him. "You think you can tell me what to do! You can't talk to me about morals—you with your bastard child and your mistresses—you—"

Armitage moved forward. He caught Peyton's arm and pushed him into a chair.

Adam walked unsteadily across the room. His long fingers were shaking as he fumbled in his waistcoat pocket. In a moment, he came back and laid the sapphire necklace on the table. Peyton fixed his eyes on the stones as they lay in a pool of light on the dark wood.

Armitage glanced at Mary but she looked away. A great fear descended upon her. It seemed to her that this was not the time for words or recriminations. Too much had happened; nerves were drawn too taut—but she knew she could not stop these overwrought people.

Adam spoke slowly; speech seemed an effort to him. "There is no need for us to discuss your affairs, Peyton. The duel has been fought with the man you challenged. The Baron has promised to ask no further questions concerning your possession of this necklace that belonged to her Majesty until Grafton has completed his investigation."

Mary looked at Petyon. His face was livid; his mouth had fallen open loosely; his hands were shaking. He had not taken his eyes from the stones.

"I didn't know," he muttered. "I didn't know it belonged to the Queen until Grafton told—you must believe me—"

"I think that it would be well for you to take Lavinia and retire to your plantation until this—this unpleasant affair blows over," Adam said sternly.

Peyton's face lost its sullen, defiant look. He looked very young and pitiful, Mary thought.

"I'm sorry, Adam," he said in an unsteady voice. "I was beside myself. Grafton goaded me into the quarrel." Great beads of perspiration broke out on his forehead. "They said I challenged Grafton—I don't remember," he looked up in a bewildered way. "I . . ."

Adam didn't look at him. He spoke to Herk: "Take the master to his room and put him to bed, Herk."

Armitage got up and poured a glass of brandy. He put it into Peyton's shaking hand. "Here, take this first. You need it."

Lavinia had not spoken. She got up now, without looking at anyone, and followed Peyton from the room.

Armitage spoke first. "Get back on that couch, Adam," he said. He sat down and poured a stiff drink of brandy for himself. "God's death!" he cried irritably, "for a moment, I thought I was going to have everyone stretched out—everyone but Mary." He lifted his glass to her. "Thank God, I can always count on you keeping your head, Mary."

Adam smiled at Mary. "Yes, one can always count on Mary," he said. He leaned back against the sofa and closed his eyes for a moment.

Mary saw that Armitage was watching him closely. He got up and put his long, old fingers on Adam's wrist. After a moment, his face cleared; the worried look left his eyes. He said energetically, "I'll have Herk put you to bed when he comes back. You must get some sleep. I'd like to ask you some questions about this duel and those stones." He nodded his head toward the table where the necklace still lay. "What are you going to do with that bauble, Adam?"

Adam didn't look at the necklace. "Will you give them to Lavinia in the morning, Mary?"

Mary had a feeling of revulsion when she picked up the sapphires. It all seemed so futile as she thought of it—a few colored stones of no importance, yet they might be the instrument of destruction to half a dozen people.

The Doctor started toward the door. "Come on, Mary. I don't think Adam will need you—he's drowsy already."

Adam caught her hand and raised it to his lips. "Thank you, Mary," he said, dropping his voice. "I haven't thanked you yet for helping Lady Caroline."

Mary stood looking down at him. Something deep in her stirred at the sight of him lying helpless. A swift change came over her; her eyes softened, her fingers tightened on his.

"I didn't do it to help Lady Caroline," she said huskily. "It was for you. I'd do anything for you." She leaned over and kissed him impulsively. Then she ran from the room before he could speak.

Armitage was waiting for her in the hall. His face had lost its casual, easy smile. A heavy frown lined his wrinkled forehead. "I don't know the truth of this whole affair, Mary, but there will be real trouble for Adam if Grafton dies."

Mary caught his arm. "What will Tryon do? Arrest Adam for fighting?"

"He'll have no alternative," the Doctor said.

"From what he said, Peyton must have quarreled with Grafton, but what could have happened on the *Jupiter* to make Adam fight instead of Peyton? Do you know, Doctor?"

"No, but neither do I know about that pile of stones—or Lady Caroline's disappearance—or what Grafton is after—or any one of the rumors that are flying about New Bern." He touched her cheek with his fingers. "Go to bed, Mary, and don't worry about this. Whatever it is, Adam will find a solution. Good night, my dear child. It is late and you need sleep."

Mary moved about her room quietly, trying not to disturb Cissie, who slept on a trundle in the dressing room. She wondered why she had had the sudden impulse to speak to Adam as she had done. Adam didn't like emotional display—but she had felt so warm toward him, so tender. Then she thought of the Doctor's words: "Adam will find a solution." That was what she resented; too many people were leaning on Adam, looking to him to find a way out of their troubles and difficulties. She drew the curtain and opened the window. The dawn was streaking the east with long glowing lines of gold.

Mary, attired in her riding habit, went down to the court-yard of the Inn where a groom was waiting with her horse. It was almost four in the afternoon and Adam was still sleeping. A slave had brought a hastily scribbled note from Lavinia, shortly after breakfast, saying that they were leaving immediately for the plantation. Mary sent Cissie to Lavinia with the necklace and a note of explanation. She was glad to be rid of it.

Mary mounted and trotted out of the side entrance of the Swan, taking a short cut that led to the river-road. The town seemed to be in a normal state after the flare-up of two nights ago, although a number of yeomen were still lounging about the courtyard of the Inn and in the streets. It was Market day and the farmers' wagons and booths were set up in the square north of the Palace.

Mary was glad to be alone. Riding along through the pines she had her thoughts to herself. They were disturbing thoughts. She could, with her vivid imagination, build up a picture of what had happened, but was it the true one? Why hadn't Adam asked Peyton where he got the necklace? He had tossed it on the table with a gesture of distaste and final-ity, as if he were done with it forever.

In her preoccupation, she did not notice the approaching horsemen until the Governor spoke her name. She looked up to find that Tryon and two of his officers had drawn rein and were waiting for her. At a word from the Governor, the officers rode on ahead.

"Have you heard anything of Rutledge's condition today?" the Governor asked, as they trotted along.

Mary shook her head. "Adam's body servant said he was sleeping and I couldn't find the Doctor. Crit said he had gone down to the *Jupiter*."

Tryon frowned. Mary thought he looked harassed and worried. He glanced at her an instant, as if reflecting on the advisability of speaking frankly. Finally, he said, "I don't like this situation, Mrs. Warden. I can't imagine what could have happened on the *Jupiter* to lead to a duel. The Baron sent for me this morning. I found him in an ugly mood. Grafton is a favorite of his. If he is seriously injured, it will go hard with Adam Rutledge—" he paused, looking at Mary to see if she understood the implication. She understood only too well.

Tryon pulled at his gauntlets, a frown between his eyes. "I like Rutledge," he said, after a moment. "I'm sorry that he is involved in a situation like this. We may as well be frank—if Grafton dies, the Baron will insist that Rutledge be turned over to him. You know what that means, Mrs. Warden? It means that, as an official of the Province, Adam Rutledge must stand trial in England."

Mary's heart contracted. She had not thought of that aspect of the situation before. How could she have forgotten? It was one of the grievances listed when the King was memorialized by the provincial leaders. The Whigs had been bitterly opposed to trial of provincial officials in England instead of in the Province.

"But if Grafton should get well?" she asked hopefully.

The Governor's face cleared a little. "Then the sentence is at my discretion. There must be a sentence—the Baron will insist on that, for the law against dueling is clear."

Mary's voice was low. "I can only hope that the sentence will be pronounced by your Excellency and not by an English court."

Tryon was suddenly stern. "But there will be a sentence, Mrs. Warden." He drew himself up to his accustomed attitude of remote dignity. "You must remember I am the Law. I stand in lieu of King and Parliament."

"I remember," she said slowly. She turned in her saddle to watch him canter down the road to overtake his officers. "He is afraid of any generous impulse," she thought.

When she got back to the Inn, she found Armitage waiting for her in the hall. Marcy and Enos Dye were with him. She knew at once that something was wrong.

"We will come up with you, Mary," Armitage said. "There's no place here to talk."

By the time they got to her sitting room, Mary had steadied herself. She hoped she was prepared for whatever came. She could think only of the worst—Grafton had died!

Inside the room, she caught the Doctor's arm. The sudden strain on her nerves made her voice husky and unnatural. Somewhere in the distance Negroes were singing. Below, in the courtyard, men were calling to one another, laughing, speaking gaily of inconsequential things.

"Has Grafton . . . died?" she began.

313

Armitage answered quickly to relieve her anxiety. "No, Grafton is no worse. I just saw him. It is not that."

"What is it then?" she cried, turning from one to the other.

Marcy answered, "The Baron's gone over the Governor's head and had Mr. Rutledge arrested. He sent a patrol ashore with an officer and took Mr. Rutledge on board the *Jupiter*. He will keep him there until they see how Grafton gets on. May God damn him!" he muttered fiercely.

Mary looked at them hopelessly. "But the *Jupiter* has sailed," she cried. "I saw her while I was riding down by the river—just after she had fired the sunset gun."

"Yes, the *Jupiter* has sailed—with Adam Rutledge aboard," Armitage said. "That is what we came to tell you. They have sailed for the Indies."

Mary raised her head. A strand of dark hair had loosened and lay across her cheek. Her eyes were veiled. Something that lay behind them made Armitage move between her and the other men. He said, speaking in a tone of forced casualness:

"He will be well cared for—Orrick assured me of that. He has charge of both Adam and Grafton until their wounds are healed. He told me privately that there is much sympathy for Adam among the officers on the *Jupiter*." He stopped. Mary was not listening. She was looking accusingly at Marcy, then at Enos Dye.

"And you let them take him?" she said scornfully. "You let them take him back to England to be tried for fighting a duel that Grafton deliberately provoked."

Marcy didn't speak. Enos Dye answered:

"Don't be too quick, Mrs. Warden. I didn't know nothin' of this dueling business—nor did Marcy. I heard down the street what had happened. We came up here all fixed to tie up that young sprig that was aguarding him. We aimed to carry Mr. Rutledge off to Mecklenburg and hide him until the whole thing blew over. We could've done it easy, Marcy and me. There was a dozen other men, farmer Whitlock among them, who'd hev' come arunnin' to help us if there was a fight. But Mr. Adam, he wouldn't let us. It was him, Mrs. Warden. He's just as stubborn as a mule. He said he'd have to take the punishment—whatever it was."

Marcy interrupted Enos. "Mr. Rutledge said he must be prepared to stand trial, if necessary. He knew what the penalties were when he fought the duel, and he'd have to stand the consequences. He talked to Mr. Iredell, and he said the same

314

thing. You can understand that's just what he'd do, can't you, Mrs. Warden?"

A silence pervaded the room. Chairs creaked as the men stirred uneasily. On the wall above the hearth a big clock ticked. Mary's voice was muffled when she answered. "Yes, Marcy, I understand."

Marcy and Enos got up and left the room. Armitage lingered after they had gone. "I think Grafton will get well," he said. "Don't worry too much, Mary."

Mary smiled faintly. "He must get well," she whispered. "It wouldn't be fair—"

Armitage took a note from the tail of his coat and laid it on the table in front of Mary. "Adam told me to give it to you," he said. Then he too walked softly from the room.

Mary sat looking at the square of paper for a long time before she broke the seal.

"Mary dear:

"Our destination seems to be the Indies. Write me a line at Charlotte Amalie, in care of Kreuger Brothers.

"Do not blame Peyton too much. My anger against him has burned itself out. He swears he knew nothing about the stones being stolen. He says he bought them from the Dutch lapidary at Charlotte Amalie. Perhaps, I'll be able to verify that—or, again, I may not take the trouble. It might be better not to know the truth.

"Until the very last, after the duel, the Baron thought I was Peyton. He was furious when I continued to deny all knowledge of the necklace. He was so infuriated at what he called my 'Whig defiance and insolence,' he could not get over it when he found I was Adam, not Peyton Rutledge. But Grafton knew all the time. It seems he held some grudge for something I said when I met him at Lady Caroline's house not long ago. What it was, I have no idea—it must have been something political.

"I need not ask you to be gentle with Lavinia since you know the situation so well. Write to me of the plantation affairs, and of yourself.

"As always,
"ADAM"

"The words you spoke when you left me today have given me a warm memory to carry with me."

Mary sat for a long time, the letter in her hand. Then she called Cissie. The slave came hurriedly from the ante-room where she had been waiting.

"Get the rest of my clothes packed, Cissie. And tell Ebon to have the coach ready. We're starting for Edenton tomorrow morning at sunup."

Chapter 21

FIRST
BATTLE

THE MORNING H. M. S. *Jupiter* entered the river below Wilmington, Captain Orrick knocked on the door of Adam's cabin and entered. He seated himself astride the one chair, a quizzical smile on his lips.

"You'd better get up and dress yourself, Rutledge," he said. "A steward will be here in ten minutes to pack you up."

"Pack me up?" Adam repeated, mystified. "I don't understand."

Orrick shrugged his shoulders. "Neither do I but those were the orders I've just received. You are free, Mr. Rutledge, free to go ashore, and go home to your plantation."

Adam slung himself out of the berth and began to put on his clothes. "What happened?" he asked.

"I'm not sure. A messenger from the Governor came aboard the ship while we were lying off the fort before daybreak. The order came to release you a few minutes ago. There may be some connection."

Adam was struggling with his boots. "Who signed the release?" he asked.

"The Duke himself. Don't ask me why. Perhaps it was because Grafton is getting well—perhaps the Governor made a plea for you. One thing is sure—if I were you, I'd get off the ship as quickly as I could, before Cotswold changes his mind again. He's been known to do that. He's erratic as the devil —that's the reason they don't want him at home. They keep him moving here and there on these quasi-diplomatic missions. India next, I think."

Adam wasn't listening. He tied his cravat and got into his coat with Orrick's assistance.

The steward knocked at the door, and the two men went out on deck. The *Jupiter* had anchored and a number of small boats from the town, piled high with ship's stores and fresh green goods, lay alongside. A young officer came up and saluted Captain Orrick. "The Admiral's compliments, sir. Mr. Rutledge's boat is waiting. The Admiral regrets that his

316

duties prevent his seeing Mr. Rutledge before his departure. He trusts Mr. Rutledge will have a pleasant journey home."

Adam glanced at Orrick. The Doctor was smiling. When the officer had gone, he said, "Mr. Rutledge, every officer on the ship regrets this incident, from the Admiral down. But what could they do?"

Adam grasped Orrick's hand. "I appreciate your position, Captain. Thank you for your care of me—and thank the other officers, will you? I think I'll take your advice and get away before the Baron changes his mind again." He went over the side and into the waiting boat.

In Wilmington he went at once to see Maurice Moore. He found John Ashe with him, and Colonel Waddell. He felt them looking at the scar on his face, but no one mentioned it, or the duel.

"Everyone feared you would be carried to London to stand trial," John Ashe said as he shook Adam's hand warmly. They attributed his release to Tryon's influence.

"He probably sent word to the Duke that you were called for military duty."

"Military duty?" Adam was astounded.

"Of course, you couldn't have heard," Moore said, "but the Governor has come to Wilmington to consult with Waddell and other militia officers. He has issued orders for the militia to assemble and is calling for volunteers and drafting men from every county."

"But why does the Governor want so many men?" Adam turned to Waddell.

"He has given out that it is for a maneuver of some sort. Actually, he intends to march to Hillsborough and subdue the Regulator insurrection."

"A very good idea, I think," Moore said. "It's the only good idea Tryon has produced for some time."

Adam looked at Moore to see if he were in earnest—or whether he had dropped back on his strongest weapon, irony. John Ashe answered Adam's look of inquiry. "One of the Regulator leaders, James Hunter, published a slanderous letter in the New Bern *Gazette* last week addressed to Maurice Moore."

Moore turned quickly, his black eyes flashing. "You needn't imply that my attitude in this is personal. I believe the Governor is right to use force to quell insurrections. You can't have a group of men—any group—deliver an ultimatum to the King's Governor, as the Regulators have just done in protesting against Fanning's election to the Assembly.

Why, they propose to use force to prevent him taking his seat! They sent a letter to Tryon filled with threats! Damned impudence, I call it!"

"I'm glad someone had the courage to protest against Fanning. We all know he's a thoroughgoing scoundrel," Adam said, with some heat.

Moore looked at him a moment, a thin, dry smile on his lips. "I've heard that you were getting pretty radical in your views, Rutledge."

Adam did not answer. He had no intention of arguing with Moore. Instead he questioned Colonel Waddell. "This means that the maneuvers of the militia are just a cover. Tryon will try a surprise attack on the farmers? Has he any legal authority for such a move?"

Waddell turned to Moore. "The Governor has the authority, Rutledge—the Riot Act."

Adam felt his anger getting the better of him, but he tried to keep his voice steady. "So he'll use Johnstone's 'Bloody Bill' as a legal basis to shoot down these wretched people."

Ashe nodded. His strong, kindly face was grave. "I've always thought it a bad law," he said.

Moore interrupted. "It's a good law to invoke in rioting," he said sharply. "You can't have people meeting together, defying law, disturbing the public peace, after they have been warned to disperse by the sheriff and other lawful peace officers."

"The punishment is too severe," Ashe continued without heat. "Death, banishment, loss of property, public whippings —all too severe. Maurice. Why shouldn't ten men meet to talk over wrongs and grievances? Does that constitute felony? Death punishment?"

Adam got up and walked to the window. He wanted a moment to think. From where he stood he could see the *Jupiter* lying in the stream. So this was why he was released—to serve in the militia; to make a show of force before unarmed men; to feed the vanity of Tryon. He knew the Governor would never forgive the Regulators for forcing his hand, for making him release Husband from gaol. It was a blow to his prestige. "He will have his vengeance," Adam thought bitterly. "He will sacrifice innocent people for the sake of stubborn pride."

He became conscious of the silence and turned slowly. They were all looking at him, waiting for him to speak—to hear his opinion. Well, he would speak his mind for once. He had been silent too long.

"I'm not in favor of this show of force by the Governor," he said. "I think there is another way to quiet them."

"And that is to give them a free hand to rule the Province —any way they see fit—without law?" Moore's tone was edged with sarcasm.

Adam overlooked the implication. He must not lose his temper or his words would lose force. "No, Judge Moore, I'm not in favor of anyone ruling the Province without law, but I am in favor of every man's rights within the law."

"And what would you suggest, Mr. Rutledge?" Moore asked ironically. "What is your remedy?"

"Get rid of Fanning first. If the Governor could be made to see that that is necessary before any other adjustments can be talked over—"

Ashe nodded. "I would have agreed with you once, Adam, but I think that time has passed. The wounds are too deep. They will be righted only by stronger means now."

"You mean bloodletting?" Adam asked.

Ashe did not answer. Colonel Waddell said, "Whatever your beliefs are about this Regulator business, Rutledge, you are on call. You had better go to Edenton at once. We must draft up there."

"You won't find much sympathy with that idea in Albemarle, Colonel," Adam told him. "Our people are too far away for all this quarrel to arouse interest—and what interest there is, is likely to favor the Regulators."

Ashe joined Adam and they walked down the street to the Inn where Adam was going to make arrangements for horses for his journey home.

"I don't understand you men down here," Adam said, still incensed at what he had heard. "You fight tooth and nail against Tryon's oppression—then suddenly, you are on his side against a lot of God-fearing farmers who only want their rights."

John Ashe shook his head. "We're not on the side of Tryon, Adam. We are on the side of the law. These matters must be adjusted by law—not by taking up arms. We can't afford a clash at this time—we're not ready. Caswell says the same. You'd better talk with him before you go home. He'll explain our position in this matter."

"Would the Governor be satisfied if the Regulators got rid of Harmon Husband?" Adam asked.

Ashe shook his head again. "Not now, Adam. It's gone too far. All our leaders have volunteered—John Harvey, Caswell —you must realize that for once the Governor is right. You can't let any faction hold itself higher than the government and the law."

Before he left for Edenton, Adam had a talk with Caswell whose opinion coincided with Ashe's.

"We had a hard time convincing Moore on this, Adam, but he finally came around. So must you." He handed him a paper. "Here are your orders. You will ride north as swiftly as possible and join the Edenton leaders in putting through the draft."

Adam left Caswell's office much disturbed in mind. Caswell had convinced him that these leaders—these thoughtful, liberty loving men—must be right; that a display of force was necessary in order to prevent bloodshed. The Governor would go no further than a display—he had promised that.

Adam rode north with all speed. The highways were alive with men, some in uniform. Many who were going to join the Regulators were riding west. They crossed his route again and again. Adam's apprehension increased with every mile. When he crossed into Tyrell County, he met Enos Dye. He was on his way to Hunter's plantation on Sandy Creek, he told Adam, but he would say no more. There was a curious reticence about Enos that Adam did not like.

"I can't talk as free as I like," Enos said, as he was ready to move on. "After all, you be a gentleman and a rich planter, Mr. Rutledge. You have helped us many a time, but you can't be expected to understand us now—that's what Whitlock says." He shouldered his long rifle and slipped away into the woods.

Adam rode on. He felt there was some truth in Enos' words, but he resented them. Why couldn't he understand? The needs of the farmer—poor or rich—were the same. That was the common ground where they could all meet: love of land—the right to ownership—to defend what they held. . . .

He rode direct to Edenton. There he found the village had already been informed of the Governor's proposed march to Hillsborough. He heard from the Doctor that the Regulators were assembling in force between the Haw and the Deep River. Alarmed at the thought of violence from these men, Adam set to work at once. Caswell and Ashe must be right —a display of strength would make it unnecessary to fight.

He met William Warden as he went up the steps to the Courthouse where Armitage told him the Committee was in session. William was disturbed by the situation, he said. He expressed surprise that Adam was home.

"Do you think calling out the militia will cause more trouble, Mr. Warden?" Adam asked, after he had briefly explained his return.

"It is the only solution, Rutledge," William said emphatically.

Adam followed him into the room where the Committee was already in session. As he took his seat he glanced out the window and saw a long queue of men waiting to move up to a table where the draft officers were seated.

Adam rode out to Queen's Gift at William's invitation. When Cissie told them that Mary was down at the stables, William turned to Adam.

"Why don't you go down? I remember Mary told me at breakfast that she was going to work some of the young jumpers this afternoon."

"Won't you come along, Mr. Warden?" Adam asked.

"No, Rutledge, I've some office work waiting for me that I must finish before evening. Go on down—Mary will be delighted to see you . . ." He paused for a moment. "She thinks you're on your way to the Indies."

Mary was jumping a green hunter over a four-barred gate when Adam rode up. She was so intent on the performance of the gelding that she did not see him. Adam dismounted, gave the reins to a pickaninny and walked over to the white-washed fence where the trainers and grooms were watching the action of the jumper.

It was after she had made the jump that Mary first saw Adam. For a moment she stared at him, not believing her eyes. She lifted her whip in brief salute, but she did not ride over to speak to him. Her conduct seemed unaccountable even to herself but for some perverse reason she continued to put her horse over the gate until his performance was perfect. Then she dismounted and joined Adam, climbing up beside him on the fence. For a moment, she did not speak. Adam noticed that her hand was trembling when he raised it to his lips. A twinge of pain passed through him as he saw her shrink back suddenly at the sight of the scar on his face.

"Is it so repulsive?" he asked bitterly.

"How can you say that?" she cried. "It shocked me a little at first; that was all."

Adam was silent. Dark thoughts, which had been his constant companion for the past weeks, rose again.

Mary touched his arm lightly to bring him back. "Adam," she said, her voice a little husky, "I thought you were—"

"On my way to the Indies?" he interrupted. "I was released at Wilmington."

"The whole thing was too unjust," she answered fiercely. "I don't want to think of it again, ever!"

Adam looked at her expressive face. He made an effort to speak lightly. "You have a real temper, haven't you, Mary?"

"I loathe injustice," she answered. "Oh, Adam, have you heard what the Governor is going to do now?"

He nodded. He didn't want to talk about it—he wanted to forget for a few moments. It was such a pleasure just to see her—to be near her. Instead of answering her question he said, "That black is a beauty—just like his sire. What do you call him?"

"He's Black Douglas, too," she said absently.

They talked of horses then and of the possibility of a good hunt early in the fall. Mary was making conversation—something Adam regretted. There had always been such freedom and understanding between them. Now she seemed to be tense, abstracted, although he saw she was making a determined effort to be natural. She spoke of Azizi and David and said she had seen them recently at North Plantation.

"David is growing so fast," she said. "I notice the difference every time I see him. He will be tall, like you—he looks so much like you now."

"I hope he inherits something from his mother," Adam said impulsively, "—her gentleness—her dignity." His mind flashed to the day of David's birth. "And her intense love of freedom," he added.

Mary looked at him. A shadow crossed her face. "That was a nice thing to say, Adam," she said in a low voice. He did not answer. There was a moment's silence, then she said, abruptly: "Did you hear anything of Lady Caroline in Wilmington?"

"Nothing in Wilmington," he said, "but I found a letter from my agent in Norfolk when I got home. He had been able to secure a passage for her on a ship sailing to St. Kitts the day the shallop put into Norfolk." He did not say that the letter contained the bill for Lady Caroline's passage. But that was natural. She had had no time to get money. Neither did he tell her that he had heard from Caswell that Guernsey House was closed and that the furniture was to be auctioned to satisfy Lady Caroline's creditors. He could not bring himself to accept the general opinion of Lady Caroline, for he remembered the courage with which she accepted defeat.

"Samuel Johnstone was here yesterday, and John Harvey rode in from his plantation. They are alarmed," Mary said.

"What do they think about Tryon ordering out the militia?"

Mary hesitated. "We didn't agree on that. I don't know why it is, Adam, but we can't get past our class distinction. I've come to think that our Whig leaders resent the actions of the Regulators. Is it because they are not afraid to come out against Tryon's injustices while we are hesitating? But perhaps our leaders are wise in waiting," she said thoughtfully.

Adam got off the fence and helped Mary down. For an instant her slim body was in his arms. He caught his breath, his pulse pounding. He glanced at her, thinking she must have noticed his sudden, quick emotion. But she gave no sign.

"Why should they think that they are the only ones to lead a revolt against Britain?" she asked suddenly. "Must the lawyers and rich merchants and owners of the great plantations always take the lead? Why can't a yeoman or a freeholder voice his wrongs without being called a rebel—will you tell me?"

Adam answered reluctantly. He didn't want to go over the whole thing again. He was convinced now, he told her, that they must stop an insurrection of the Regulators at any cost though his reasons were not the same as those of Caswell and Ashe. He simply didn't want these farmers to get into trouble through Husband's leadership.

She turned on him, her eyes flashing. "You're like all the rest, Adam! I had hoped you would understand, but you don't. I expected William to agree with Tryon, but not you, Adam! I'd hoped you would see it as I do."

"This is very serious, Mary—much more so than I thought at the beginning. We must preserve the idea of Law, We can't let that break down now."

She caught her breath sharply. "Does this mean that you will go, Adam?" she asked, her voice quiet—too quiet, Adam thought miserably.

"I'm an officer of the militia, Mary, sworn to defend the government."

"You can resign from the militia!"

Adam stared at her, unbelieving. "Now? When men are marching? Resign?"

"Yes, now."

He shook his head. What had come over Mary Warden? He had never seen her like this. Her jaw was set, her lips firm and unsmiling. They were walking through the small copse of birches that cut off the stables from the house. The sun was low, slanting through the trees. A chipmunk scurried across the path, rustling the leaves. The only other sound was that of Negroes' voices far away.

Mary walked ahead. Her blue habit was hooked up, giving her freedom to move swiftly. She turned suddenly and faced him. "Would you give me the order to fire on farmer Whitlock or Enos Dye?"

Adam stopped also. For a moment he could not answer, startled as he was by her question. "God! I don't know, I—"

Mary did not meet his troubled eyes. She was looking at the thin red scar that crossed his cheek. Drawing her breath sharply, she repeated: "Whitlock and Enos Dye—could you shoot them down in cold blood? Think about that, Adam, think hard before you kill men whose only wish is to be free." She turned and walked on rapidly along the path.

Adam overtook her. He caught her arm, pulling her around to face him. He saw she was white with anger and disappointment. "We're not quarreling, are we, Mary?" he asked softly, still holding her arm.

"I don't know—perhaps we are." Her voice was strained.

"We can't do that, my dear," he said gently. "We're too close—we have been friends too long to allow anything to stand between us."

She did not soften. "There'll be many rifts in friendships —even old friendships—before these disagreements are settled," she said.

He drew her toward him, lifting her chin with one hand. "Mary, this is not like you. Don't take it so hard. This trouble cannot affect us—it'll soon be over. Look at me, Mary."

She turned her face away and drew back, her body stiffening against his arm. He looked at her steadily, but her eyes did not meet his. There was no yielding in her attitude.

"I'm sorry, Mary," he said, releasing her. "A man must do what seems right to him."

She did not answer. "She is afraid to trust herself to speak," he thought. Turning swiftly, she walked on swiftly as if she were running away from him.

Adam followed in silence, profoundly depressed by her action. He realized that he needed her now as he had never needed her before. He wanted her understanding—he could not let her go. Yet something within him prevented him from making an effort to hold her. Their friendship had been so secure, so strong. Now some intangible thing had come between them.

She said good-by at the steps, gravely, quietly—almost irrevocably, Adam thought. He held her hand a moment before he raised it to his lips. Once he turned to look back. Other times she had been waiting to wave farewell—now she was walking swiftly across the gallery without a backward glance. He rode on down the driveway—a bewildered, desolate feeling in his heart.

Days went by without any definite word of the Governor's action against the Regulators. Mary attended to her duties on the plantation with a queer feeling of emptiness and futility. Why had she quarreled with Adam? Why? She tried to forget the bewildered, hurt look in his eyes when he left her. Why had she been so hard? Yet she knew if he had come back she would not have changed. She could not help but show her disappointment, her bitter, overwhelming disappointment in him. She tried to occupy her mind with other things, but she could not. William had gone to New Bern to meet the Governor and she was alone. For the first time that she could remember she felt alone. Always before she had had a secret inner life of which Adam Rutledge was the center—the very core. Now that solace failed her.

Mary decided she would ride over to Rutledge Riding and accept Lavinia's invitation to stay overnight. Lavinia might have had some news. Edenton was a dead village as she rode through the tree-lined streets. The men she knew had gone to New Bern at the first call from the Governor. She stopped for a moment at St. Paul's and spoke to Parson Earl who was in the garden tying up his rose vines. He got up from his knees when he saw Mary and drew off his damp gloves. He had heard nothing, he told her, although wild rumors were flying about in the village.

"The Regulators have three thousand men, they say, while the Governor's forces number only a little over a thousand."

Mary quieted her horse and looked down at the Rector's troubled face.

"It isn't possible that they will fight," he said. "They can't —it would be too horrible."

She thought he looked a broken man. His color had gone, his lips trembled when he spoke the words, almost to himself, "brother against brother." Mary rode slowly down the lane past the churchyard. She looked back once. The Rector had not moved. He was looking down at the ground, lost in his dark thoughts. She thought of what she had heard. The villagers called him a Royalist now, and small boys threw stones at the chapel windows because he would not give up his belief that there could be no break in the church, no matter what the stand of the Colony.

Lavinia, pruning shears in hand, was cutting early daffodils in the East Garden when Mary arrived. The two women sat down on a bench. Lavinia slipped off her long gloves and threw them down near the basket of flowers.

"You must stay a few days, Mary. I've been very lonely. Peyton has been gone for weeks now. And Sara keeps to her room, since Adam went away."

"Is there any news?" Mary asked.

"Nothing of any importance. Peyton wrote me from Wilmington that he thinks the trouble with the Regulators will soon blow over. He doesn't believe there is any special danger of an uprising now."

Mary shook her head. "I don't agree. Maurice Moore thinks the contrary and he has a better idea of what is going on in the Province than all the others put together."

Lavinia occupied herself with rubbing some soil off her arm.

"You and Maurice are great friends, aren't you?"

"If you mean he talks politics to me, yes. I enjoy talking with him. We have always seen eye to eye on affairs of the Colony, Lavinia. Until now," she added to herself.

"I know. He thinks you are the only woman in the Province that knows anything about politics. He told me so the last time I saw him." Lavinia laughed. "I'll tell you a secret, Mary. I'm trying to get Peyton interested in Colonial matters. The way I rouse his interest is to ask him questions about things as if I knew nothing. He has to keep up with what is going on for fear I may ask something that he cannot answer." Lavinia's eyes were merry. "It's a game, but I suppose you would think it a stupid way to rouse a man's interest."

"Indeed, I would not. I wish I had a little more of your—"

"Guile, Mary? Guile or feminine trickery. Give it its proper name."

Mary looked at her, and they both laughed.

"Men are such stupids," Lavinia said.

They walked across the lawn to the water's edge where a tea table was set. The water was red from the last strong rays of the sun. The air was still, so quiet that a fish leaping from the water made them both turn nervously.

"This waiting is beyond human endurance," Mary said suddenly. "Something must happen; nerves do not stretch to snapping point and stay that way."

Lavinia poured the tea. Mary watched her jeweled fingers moving gracefully among the delicate china. Each movement was assured, finished. Lavinia seemed happy and contented now. The trouble about the necklace seemed to have gone completely from her mind. Mary wondered if life for Lavinia were always to be like that—a mirrored reflection without depth. She was not prepared for Lavinia's words:

"Peyton told me he never really cared for Lady Caroline. He had some business dealings with her—that's all."

Mary looked at her. She wondered how Lavinia could be so sure—so complacent.

"I wonder where she went," Lavinia continued. "Sara says to the Indies. I don't know how Sara knows. Perhaps Adam told her."

"Haven't you talked to Adam?" Mary asked, somehow glad of the chance to speak his name aloud.

"No, not since I gave him the necklace to send to the Governor. I didn't want to talk about it—he didn't either. Sometimes it is better not to know everything, Mary. Sometimes it is wiser to let a man think you believe what he says."

Mary smiled a little. Lavinia occasionally surprised her with a flash of wisdom.

They sat for a time, each intent on her thoughts.

Mary raised her eyes and looked down the Sound. A shallop, with spreading sails, was coming from the east. "Look, Lavinia!" she exclaimed, getting to her feet. "A ship!"

Several slaves ran out of the boathouse, shouting that a ship was coming. Old Cicero limped down the path from the house carrying a telescope. "It looks like Mr. Adam's shallop, the one Mr. Peyton went to Wilmington on," he said, handing the telescope to Lavinia.

Lavinia took the glass. "It is, Cicero. I think it's Peyton on deck, Mary. There is another man with him—I can't see his face," she said, still looking through the telescope.

The shallop came in slowly, for there was little wind. After a time Lavinia said: "It's William, Mary. How fortunate that you are here. Won't he be pleased to see you! Come, let's run down to the landing. We can get there by the time the shallop docks."

Peyton did not wait to get ashore. "There's been a battle

—the Regulators and the King's men fought at Alamance on the seventeenth," he called out.

Mary did not move. She could not speak or ask the questions that came surging to her lips. She waited until they came ashore.

"What happened, William?" she said, falling into his stride as they walked up the path.

"You mean who won the battle?" he asked. "The Governor's men, of course. The militiamen conducted themselves very creditably for raw troops. Only about one thousand of them, and more than three thousand Regulators. The Governor himself took command."

"Was anyone hurt?" She did not say "killed." She was afraid.

"It was a battle," he answered impatiently. "Battles aren't fought without casualties, my dear wife. The Governor was exceedingly brave. He shot an escaping prisoner with his own hand. The fellow turned out to be a renegade—better dead than alive." They walked along silently. After a time, he said, "Eight or nine militiamen were killed and sixty or seventy wounded. The Governor gave the Regulators fair warning. He sent word to them that if they did not lay down their arms he would order the troops to fire. But they defied his Excellency. 'Fire and be damned,' they shouted to Tryon. Then he gave the order. The first line of militia fired. Husband ran from the field at the first volley and took to the woods. A number of fine fellows followed him but some stood up to fight."

Mary felt her knees shaking. She knew now that William was making light of something of far-reaching importance. A battle had been fought between men of the Province, a battle in which men had been killed. She didn't dare ask about Adam for fear her voice would betray her.

"Were many Regulators killed?"

"Twenty or so, and some prisoners taken." Mary saw that he did not want to discuss the battle. "The Governor ordered one man hanged as an example to people not to take up arms against the King. The rest of the leaders will be banished from the Province."

Mary moved on mechanically. She was alarmed, but she must not show her feelings before William. They overtook Lavinia and Peyton. Mary heard Lavinia say:

"A surprise, Peyton? When will you give it to me?" She hung on Peyton's arm, looking into his face with bright, eager eyes. She had not made a comment on the news the men brought, or asked a single question.

"You'll get your surprise at dinner, not before, madam." Peyton was teasing her.

"That is hours away. I can't wait that long. Please, please." Lavinia was on tiptoe, her lips against her tall husband's cheek. "Please."

"Not an instant before dinner, my dear. It may be even a little later, when we are having coffee in the drawing room."

"Peyton, how can you be so cruel! Have you brought me a new fur piece, or a jewel?"

"Madam, none of your blandishments," Peyton said. "I shall not tell you or let you see the surprise before the proper moment, so don't try to tease me."

Lavinia pouted. "I shall punish you for this, Peyton. I shall think of some especially cruel way to punish you."

How gay they are! Mary marveled. How far removed from thought of battle and discord. They did not seem to realize what was happening—that tremendous forces had been let loose.

In her room Mary found that one of Lavinia's slaves had unpacked her saddlebags. Her flowered silk dress was laid out on the bed, freshly pressed. She threw herself onto a couch by the window to rest a short time before dinner. The door into the adjoining room was open. William was moving about, old Cicero busy with his boxes. She dozed off.

A knock on the door roused her. She sat up, her hands going to her disheveled hair. She saw William standing in the doorway, a slight smile on his lips.

"May I come in, Mary?" he said.

"Please do. Sit down here by the window." She got up from the couch and went to the dressing table to rearrange her hair. "I must have fallen asleep," she added.

William was looking at the array of brushes and crystal bottles in her dressing case. He said absently, "I came to the door once or twice. You were sleeping so soundly I hadn't the heart to waken you."

Mary wound the long dark braids into place. In the mirror she saw that her husband's eyes were on her.

"I have a letter for you from Maurice Moore," he said, after a silence. "Moore's a queer fellow. After being on the side of the Governor, he changed around after the battle and turned on the Governor for ordering the men to fire." He got up and moved about the room. Mary followed him with her eyes, wondering what the cause of his perturbation could be. "Caswell thinks as I do. So does John Harvey. This lawlessness has to be checked, and it has gone so far that it can be stopped only by force. Moore has probably given you his version." He laid a thick package on the dressing table and stood for a moment watching her. He surprised her by saying: "Maurice has great respect for your judgment, Mary. I sometimes think I should have talked more freely to you—but often the things that trouble me are matters that concern other people." He stopped abruptly.

Mary felt his embarrassment. It was hard for William to admit that he had been wrong. She crossed the room and kissed his cheek.

"I understand, William," she said.

"Thank you, Mary," he spoke brusquely. There was a look of pain on his thin face. "Thank you, my dear," he repeated. "Now, I'll leave so that you may dress. We must not be late for dinner tonight. Remember, Lavinia is to have her surprise at dinner."

When Mary finished dressing, there was still a little time before dinner. She opened the package. It contained a short note from Moore and several pages cut from the *North Carolina Gazette.*

"Dear Mary:

"Inclosed is a copy of the *Gazette* with a comment on Tryon and the battle of Alamance. You can guess who the author is. The piece has created much comment, as it should. You understand that I do not condone the ill-advised actions of the Regulators. They were acting outside the law; but I do despise Tryon for his attitude and the severe measures he took after his victory. A man who has won can afford to be generous; a man who is right can go more than half way. Tryon did neither. But read the paper I'm sending you.

"People here think this blood-letting at Alamance will quiet everything. It will not. We are headed straight for disaster. It may be a few months, or it may be a few years, but the time is approaching when we will defend our rights as free men. I say too much always when I talk to you. You lend a sympathetic ear and a real understanding.

                                        "M. M."

Mary looked through the paper. Several passages in an open letter to his Excellency, William Tryon, Esq., signed Atticus, were marked in red ink:

"—last September the Regulators forcibly obstructed the proceedings of the Hillsborough Superior Court, obliged the officers to leave it, and looted the records. You wrote an insolent letter to the judges and the attorney-general commanding them to attend to it. Why did you not protect the court at this time?

"Now your Exellency says that *you arm to protect a court!* Had you said, to *revenge an insult,* it would be more generally credited. Some of these people were fined and imprisoned. On this occasion, sir, you were alike successful in diffusing a military spirit through the Colony and a warlike exhibition.

"Then the Riot Act. The Regulators refused to surrender themselves by the time set by the Riot Act and your Excellency opened your third campaign. These indictments charged the crimes to have been committed in Orange County, in a district distant from that in which the courts were held. The Superior Court law prohibits prosecution for capital offences in any other district than that in which they were committed.

"What distinction the gentlemen of the long robes might make I do not know, but it appears to me that the indictments might as well have been found in your Excellency's kitchen.

"These men who have been charged have been illegally indicted. I mean to expose your blunders, not to defend the conduct of the Regulators. I'm willing to give you full credit for every service you have rendered to this country—your active and gallant behavior in extinguishing the flame you yourself have kindled does you great honor. For once, your military talents were useful to the Province. You bravely met in field and vanquished a host of scoundrels, whom you made intrepid by abuse.

"It is difficult to determine, sir, whether your Excellency is to be admired for your skill in creating cause, or your bravery in suppressing effect. This single action would have blotted out forever the ills of your administration, but the conduct of the general after victory was disgraceful. Why did you stain your good actions with the blood of a prisoner who was in a state of insanity? The execution of James Few was inhuman! That miserable wretch was entitled to life until nature, or the laws of his country, deprived him of it. The battle of Alamance was over. The soldiers, Governor, crowned with success. The peace of the Province restored.

"There was no necessity for the infamous example of arbitrary execution, without judge or jury. I can freely forgive you for your conduct at the beginning of the battle, for killing Robert Thompson, your prisoner, who was making his escape to fight against you; but the execution of James Few—the sacrifice under its criminal circumstances could neither atone for his crime nor abate your rage. . . ."

She was interrupted by the dinner gong. William came to the door, ready to go down to the dining room. The Atticus letter would have to wait.

Lavinia and Peyton were in the drawing room when they got downstairs. Sara was not able to join them. Lavinia, dressed in a peach silk gown covered with flounces of lace, was openly coquetting with her husband, trying to induce him to give her the "surprise" before dinner. Peyton shook his head, laughing at her efforts. It had been a long time since Mary had seen them so happy. How could they laugh, when men lay dead? She resolutely turned her thoughts away from Alamance. She must enter into their gaiety.

Peyton offered his arm. "Mary, will you allow me? William, will you escort my wife?"

William was smiling, looking down at Lavinia. When they were seated at the table, Peyton said, "Shut your eyes, my dear. You must give me your word not to peep." His voice was gay, his face unclouded. He was handsome, this tall, dark Rutledge. How could he be so carefree? Had he forgotten what had happened only a few months ago? Had he forgotten that Adam had fought his fight—leaving him free?

Peyton lived only for the excitement, the personal interests of the moment. He and Lavinia were alike—charming people, wihout capacity for deep feeling.

Lavinia said, "Hurry, please. You know I was never good at waiting."

There was a muffled sound of doors opening and closing. Mary glanced over Lavinia's shoulder. Young Peyton was tiptoeing across the room back of his mother's chair. How tall he was, how like his father! The lad clasped his hands over Lavinia's eyes.

"Guess!" he cried, "guess who, Mother, guess who?"

The blood drained from Lavinia's face, leaving it white as chalk.

"Peyton," she whispered. "Peyton." She sprang to her feet and threw her arms about his neck, her face against his shoulder. "My son, my tall son," she said, pushing him off to look at him. "How you have grown, my dear boy."

Mary turned away; her eyes filled with quick tears. She was ashamed to have sat in judgment on Lavinia.

It was a gay dinner. Mary thought she had never seen Lavinia so lovely. Time after time Lavinia looked proudly from father to son. She had young Peyton stand by his father to see how near they were in height. Peyton was proud too.

"He is a Rutledge in size," he said to William. "I believe he's taller than I was at his age."

"Just how old are you, Peyton?" William asked.

"Twelve in October, sir. Father, do you think I may leave school now and help you on the plantation?"

Lavinia said, "Of course not. You must go to school for years and years and years."

Young Peyton turned quickly. "I don't need to, Mother, I can add and spell. Why should I have any more Latin declensions? They are so dull. How can I need dead languages?"

"What do you intend to do with yourself, young man?" William asked.

Young Peyton looked surprised at the question. "I'm going to be a planter, sir. All the Rutledge men love land and they fight for it, too."

Mary gazed at the boy's wide, clear eyes. There it was: "Unto the third and fourth generations—" All the Rutledge men loved the land.

Lavinia threw her arm over his shoulder. "Just the same, you must go back to King William's school in the autumn."

Peyton broke in, "But you can take your first lesson in managing an estate this summer, my boy. Marcy will take you in hand."

The boy's eyes brightened. "When am I to begin? In the morning, Father?"

All evening there was not a word said about Alamance, or Adam Rutledge. Twice Mary questioned William, but he put her off. Then she spoke to Petyon. He had not been at Alamance Creek but at a camp on the Haw and had seen nothing of the fighting.

At ten she got up and excused herself. She wanted to go to her room to read the rest of the newspaper, and to question William further. When they were alone, perhaps he would talk more freely.

She found William strangely reluctant to go into detail. "The Governor led the charge," he said, when she pressed him. "It is not true that he ordered his soldiers to fire the woods where the scattered remnants of the Regulators sought refuge."

He stood beside the table as he talked. Suddenly, he said, "I think Adam got himself into trouble. When his Excellency was about to order the soldiers to fire on the Regulators, Adam rode up to the Governor and remonstrated with him, begging him not to fire on the farmers. 'They are the King's loyal subjects, your Excellency. It would be criminal to slaughter them. Look at the militia—they don't want to fire. Do not ask them to shoot down their neighbors.' The Governor was in a rage. I didn't hear what his words were, but I heard Adam. He spoke loud enough for anyone to hear: 'I thank you for the suggestion, sir. I'll take my place, but not with the King's men.' Then he spurred his horse and galloped across the field to the edge of the wood. I saw him take his place beside Whitlock and that crackpot James Few." William stopped, his voice trembling with indignation. "What could have got into him to do such a thing—a Rutledge rubbing elbows with yeomen and tradesmen—led by lying renegades like Harmon Husband?"

Mary sat very still, too overcome by what William had told her to speak. A feeling of exultation came over her. Adam had not failed! It took strength and courage to do what he had done—to defy Tryon—to take his stand before the men he knew, the leaders of the Province. How proud she was of him! Adam, dear, dear Adam.

Suddenly the swift exultation died. She had not seen Adam since she had quarreled with him, since she had deliberately hurt him. She turned away to hide the rising tears.

After William had gone to his room, she took up the Atticus letter. It seemed to her that everyone must know it had been written by Maurice Moore. Who else had the caustic, sardonic turn of phrase, the mastery of the written word? Not another man in the Province—not even James Iredell. She read the last paragraph a second time:

"Your Excellency, your actions contradict your words. Out of twelve Regulators condemned to death you spared the lives of six. Do you know, sir, that your leniency on this occasion was less than that of Bloody Jeffreys in 1685? He condemned to death five hundred but saved the lives of two hundred and seventy-five."

For a long time Mary sat looking out into the garden, the paper in her hand. She did not see the silver moon on the moving water of the Sound or hear the nightingale in the East Garden. The moon went slowly from sight behind the dark massed spire of pinewood that fringed the shore. She sat motionless for many hours until banners of red flamed across the eastern sky. The sun came up—another day. But it could never be the same. Brother had fought against brother on the soil of Carolina. A battle had been fought—the first battle of revolt against the King and the King's government. What would be the end? In her mind came a picture—lines of men marching; endless lines of men—young, old—marching to the beat of drums.

When Mary and William rode into Broad Street the following morning, they found the village alive with excitement. Crowds of men stood in the commons, in the courtyard of the Inn and on the Courthouse steps. As they turned into the street, they were overtaken by Joseph Hewes. He drew rein, his lathered horse panting from the gallop.

"Have you heard?" he cried. "The Governor has sent soldiers, and an officer is to read a proclamation from the steps of St. Paul's. Better ride over now so you can find a place—" He did not finish the sentence. Wheeling his horse, he galloped down the street toward his warehouse.

William looked doubtfully at Mary. "Do you want to go, my dear? There'll be a crowd—it's Market day, you know, and a lot of rough farm workers and fishermen are in town. They may be boisterous and unruly."

Mary had already turned her horse. "Certainly, I'm going," she called over her shoulder. William followed, his face showing his disapproval. "I wonder what *this* proclamation is about?" she said, as they dismounted.

William raised his eyebrows. "Something concerning Alamance Creek, I presume." He tossed a coin to a Negro boy who led their horses to the rack south of the church.

The crowd was approaching from all directions. Every road and lane that led to St. Paul's was crowded with people. They were not boisterous, but apprehensive, talking in low voices, their faces grave and anxious as they hurried toward the church.

Mary thought, "The people know by now that Alamance was not a riot as the earlier troubles in Orange and Mecklenburg had been. This was something more serious. This was a battle—the first battle of the Revolution."

Mary and William went into the churchyard, taking their place near the stone slab that covered the grave of the Royal Governor whose name the village bore. The churchyard was thick with people, many of whom she knew—villagers, farmers, soldiers from the garrison, fishermen from the lower village. She saw Parson Earl in his black cassock coming across from the north gate. With him walked James Iredell and Joseph Hewes. They were talking earnestly, their faces grave and serious.

An officer in a red coat, whom she had never seen, mounted the steps. In his hand he held a parchment. He unrolled the paper slowly and stood for a moment, his eyes sweeping the crowd. After a fanfare of trumpets, he began to read:

"On the authority provided for in the Riot Act the death sentence is passed on six leaders of the insurrection.

"The sentence of five hundred lashes on the bare back of the man who spoke disrespectfully to the Governor's Lady.

"A reward of one thousand acres of land and one hundred pounds in money for Harmon Husband and other leaders of the Regulators who escaped.

The officer paused a moment, then spoke again—words that burned like fire into Mary's brain:

"The following Regulator leaders to be outlawed from the Province, their property confiscated under conditions specified in the Riot Act:

"Harmon Husband
James Hunter
James Pugh
Andrew Bullit
Adam Rutledge."

Mary caught at William's arm. He turned to her, his face showing surprise and growing concern. "It can't be," he whispered. "Tryon wouldn't—" But the voice of the officer was loud enough for everyone in the churchyard to hear.

The officer repeated the name:

"Adam Rutledge, planter, late member of the Assembly."

There was a movement in the crowd. People looked from one to the other in consternation. A rough voice shouted: "Down with Tryon! Down with the Governor!" A soldier clapped his hand on the man's shoulder. Soldiers who had been standing idly came forward into the churchyard.

William was moving slowly, making his way out of the crowd toward the gate. Mary followed, too stunned to speak. She might have known that it was not in Tryon's nature to

336

forget animosities. Adam had been too frank in his support of the farmers. He had moved outside his class. Tryon would never understand or forgive that.

They gained the wall that enclosed the churchyard. Mary stopped at the gate, turning to hear what the officer was saying:

"—to lesser rebellious spirits, imprisonment and stripes on their naked backs to the number of three hundred."

A roar, angry, muffled, went up from the crowd. It died quickly. A platoon of soldiers moved out from behind the church and brought *arms rest* on either side of the steps below where the officer stood. Mary was conscious of the straight, disciplined line of red-coated men, standing close to the huddled, unwieldy mass of yeomen and fishermen. "Without leadership," she thought sadly, as she followed William to the horses.

Other thoughts filled her mind as they trotted along the quiet forest road that led to Queen's Gift. Something strange was happening. She was suddenly freed from old personal relationships. She had a feeling of detachment, as if she stood far-off from people and their confused lives. Only yesterday, she had been concerned for Peyton, for Lavinia; she had felt anxiety over Adam and his problem with Azizi and his young son; over Sara; over Lady Caroline and her strange living, her jewels, her unholy influence in the lives of men, her mysterious comings and goings; and she had been deeply discontented with her own unsatisfactory life.

Now all of these things lost importance—dwindled into nothing. She was caught up, enveloped in some great force that was rushing upon them. What did all their small lives matter? Nothing mattered except a scarlet line of soldiers drawn in stiff formation, facing grim, determined men dressed in walnut-dyed homespun, faded blue smocks and the fringed buckskins of backwoods hunters.

In a sudden vision, Mary Warden knew. Here lay the destiny of her country and her people.

Adam sat under a tree near Alamance Creek; behind him, the burned forest and the ravages of battle. A guard of half a dozen militiamen were bivouacked near by, cooking supper over a campfire. Two sentries paced back and forth, keeping watch that none of their prisoners attempted to escape. The men did not relish their task. They did not want to drive old friends across the border of the Province into exile. But, a short distance away, the King's officers and men kept guard over the militia so there would be no miscarriage of his Majesty's justice as interpreted by Governor Tryon.

Marcy sat waiting on a charred stump of a tree, while Adam wrote his final instructions to Owen Tewilliger.

"My dear Owen:

"Marcy will tell you the details of the battle at Alamance Creek. I suppose my own actions were the result of months of thinking, although at the moment they seemed spontaneous. I think Tryon's theatrical display settled my mind. He rode up and down before his army on his great horse, beating his medal-covered breast with his heavy fist, shouting to his soldiers again and again: 'Fire on them, or on me. Fire on them, or on me.' It sickened me, Owen. It was too much of a show for me to stomach. I had pleaded with him to wait—to try to settle the difficulty without resorting to arms, but he would not listen. He saw a chance to make himself a great hero—and he has succeeded. Half the people in the Province are praising him, including some of our greatest Whig leaders.

"I shall not mind leaving here for a time, until people come to see with clearer eyes. I have explained to Marcy about bringing David to Annandale, and Mrs. Rutledge will not take her projected journey to visit her father, under the care of Dr. Dobden. I have made all arrangements with the Doctor to that end. If she and her father decide to go to London for a season, Mr. Marsden will take care of her monetary affairs in England. I have written him full instructions.

"I would like to write in more detail, but the time is very short. My horses are saddled and I must leave at once. I'm taking Herk with me but no other slaves. I will communicate with you from time to time about disposal of harvest and crops.

"Mr. Peyton Rutledge will probably want to stay on at Rutledge Riding or at North Plantation. I'm sending him a note to that effect, as he will look after shipments of tobacco to my London agent and continue to take full charge of the West Indies cargoes.

"Please give my respects to your good wife Gwennie. Tell her I shall see that my trappers in the Illinois country send her enough wolfskins for the bed cover which she wants.

"I pray for our unhappy country, but I see no other solution from our difficulties now than a determined stand for the rights of all the people.

"Yours,

"ADAM RUTLEDGE

"P. S. Marcy will make proper disposal of my hunters. I want Mrs. Warden to have first pick. I have suggested the pack might be sent to Mulberry Hill until my return."

When Adam finished writing he sealed the letter, pressing his signet on the wax. Marcy had brought up his horse and was waiting. His eyes were troubled, his jaw firmly set.

"I'd like to say something, Mr. Rutledge, but what good would it do? These things are without justice, but—" he finished lamely.

Adam got up and grasped his hand. "We can't waste our thoughts on small matters now, Marcy, or on individual grievances. We've a big task ahead—so big that all this will seem nothing in comparison. This battle is the beginning. Blood has been let for a just cause and men have died. We know now that we will have to fight with all our strength to keep the liberty we have gained."

Marcy's eyes met his steadily. "It may be the first blood but we'll not be forgetting that a King's Governor ordered free men to be shot like dogs. Look yonder, Mr. Rutledge; there are men waiting to say good-by and bid you fair journey."

Adam glanced up. At the edge of the wood a crowd of men had gathered—husbandmen, shepherds, yeomen, trappers and mountaineers—free men, deprived now of their land and their rights to live within the boundary of the Province.

He rode over to say a word of farewell to men whose names he did not know but whose faces had become familiar to him in the past days. Whitlock stepped forward.

"The men want me to speak for them, Mr. Rutledge," the old man said, his face strangely solemn. "They want me to tell you that they take pride to themselves that you have stood beside them in battle, and have taken their punishment. Many of these men will follow the Yadkin along the trail to the West, to the Illinois country, but if you give the word they will follow you and give battle to Tryon now."

Adam listened. He was touched by Whitlock's words, more touched by the look on the faces of the men. He leaned forward in his saddle.

"It is not wise to make another attempt now, Whitlock. We are not prepared. We would only be defeated again. We must be patient a little while longer. In the end, we will win back our land and our rights to freedom." He had no time for further words. The sentries, seeing the crowd, moved forward with bayonets fixed, to disperse them and drive the prisoners deeper into the wood.

Adam had no guard. He had given his oath to leave the Province before sunup. Marcy rode with him until they reached the border. At the last, they did not speak. The strong clasp of hands was an unspoken pledge—when the time came, they would be ready.

BOOK
THREE

BOOK
THREE

Chapter 22

THE RISING TIDE

THE free Americans of all the Colonies had taken their stand. The break with the Mother Country was imminent. In England, statesmen fought valiantly to hold the Colonies by giving them the freedom they demanded. "The Right to Tax" was the phrase on every lip, but the right would be that of the Colonies, not Britain. The northern Colonies stood firm. Virginia listened to her great men; Washington had taken his stand; Patrick Henry made his appeal for the right of every man to personal liberty.

Revolution was rolling on, sweeping into a great path of flame that burned from the northern boundary to the southern gulf. The Carolinas were seething. In Massachusetts and New York revolution spread from the lowly to those of high estate. In Virginia the fire swept from aristocrat to peasant. In North Carolina the torch of revolution was held aloft by all classes. The sturdy folk of the Back Country threw off the yoke simultaneously with their more aristocratic neighbors of the seaboard.

Josiah Martin was now the Royal Governor, having succeeded Tryon who had been transferred to New York. Martin had no sooner arrived than friends of the Regulators began to apply for pardon for their leaders. Inclined to leniency at first, the Governor changed as the months passed. By the time the Assembly met in late autumn he was as much disliked as Tryon had been.

The strong leaders of the rebels had drawn together during the years after Alamance. The advocates of liberty grew in numbers. A thousand little fires fed the coming disaster. Taxes . . . Regulators . . . Riot Acts . . . burning resentment over quitrents and Tryon's Palace—"every brick and stone paid for by the sweat and blood of slaves," in the common opinion from the mountains to the sea. The Assembly, prorogued by Royal prerogative wihout the will of the people, led to a bill of rights and a new consciousness of liberty.

The matter of taxes had grown more inflammatory as time went on. Land taxes; tonnage taxes and taxes on vessels; rum and liquor taxes; a poll tax on slaves and men and women above the age of twelve; inspection and warehouse taxes on tobacco, lumber and every commodity shipped from or into the Province.

In the summer and autumn, the people were most deeply concerned with the tax on tea. It was not to be borne. A quantity of tea had come in on the brig *Sally*. The importers did not know what to do about it. Hewes and Smith had a shipment by the *Heart of Oak*. They turned it over at once to the Collector of the Port.

Mary Warden and Penelope Dawson rode about the Albemarle district talking with the women, stirring them up to a definite protest. "Our fathers and brothers and sons are preparing for a great struggle. Are we to be less patriotic than they? Are we to fall short of the example they set?"

In October they called a meeting. The Edenton resolves were drawn. Mary read them before sixty women of the Province. Fifty women signed the protest.

The fires of patriotism were burning birghtly now. Groups and crowds of men gathered in the villages and towns and at the four corners where post road crossed post road, determined to resist unjust taxes.

Young Peyton, who was back at school at Annapolis, wrote to his father and mother of the burning of the *Peggy Stewart*. He had seen the ship burn. When the news went about that the *Peggy Stewart* was sailing up the Severn with a cargo of tea, the excitement in the town was intense. The people of Annapolis took matters into their own hands. The owner was forced to set fire to ship and cargo, and the *Peggy Stewart* burned to the water line with all Annapolis looking on.

Three years after the batle of Alamance, John Harvey came to the fore again. The Governor's secretary notified Harvey as speaker of the House that Martin had no intention of convening the Assembly. This was the same trick Tryon had used when he prorogued the Assembly and took over full authority for a period of several years. Harvey, determined that this should not happen again, answered that if the Governor did not convene the House, the people would do so themselves.

The first Mary Warden heard of this new development was when William came in to tell her that he was going to the home of Colonel Buncombe where Harvey and Johnstone and several of the Iron Men of Albemarle were meeting. Colonel Buncombe had asked him to bring her.

The moment Mary entered the spacious drawing room of Buncombe Hall she knew that the meeting was of much more import than William had indicated. Several men from the Cape Fear districts had arrived. John Harvey took the chair. He stated the grievances in a manner that left no doubt as to what his course would be. He would not subscribe to arbitrary action on the part of the Royal Governor.

William Warden called attention to the fact that the Governor had the right within the law to prorogue the Assembly and govern with a council of his own choosing. There was nothing they could do about it. John Harvey's rage grew violent. Mary had never seen him so angry. Always outspoken, he stood now like a prophet, his hand raised, his burning eyes sweeping the group of men before him.

"Nothing we can do about it?" he thundered. "There is something we can do that will bring Martin to his knees, or he will have to flee to save his hide. We will assemble in convention in spite of Martin. All the Royalists together cannot prevent us. I will issue handbills under my name announcing a meeting of the Assembly." He turned to William. "If the gentleman who said that there is nothing to be done wishes to find precedent for the act, Massachusetts resorted to this method years ago. We will have plenty of support in other districts. Albemarle will not stand alone in this bold departure. England would, if she could, grind us to the earth, load us with chains of her own forging. But we are not slaves. We are free men and free men we will be until we lie in the earth in death." Harvey paused, transfixing his audience with his compelling eyes.

Mary held her breath. It was a moment of supreme tension. Every man in the room sat as immovable as granite. Peyton Rutledge's hands gripped the arm of his chair. William shifted a little so that his eyes met Mary's but she could not read his thoughts.

Mary realized, as she had on other occasions, that John Harvey stood for the best in the Province in fearless honesty and integrity. His judgment was sound; his sense of justice, fair and unbiased. Men who did not trust the judgment of the fiery Maurice Moore would follow where John Harvey led.

He stood looking at the faces before him. For a moment, Mary thought he had finished. Then he threw back his head. His voice challenged every man present:

"Let us not forget, for one moment, or ever let our people forget: it is not the England of Pitt, or Fox, or Burke, we are rebelling against. We are rebelling against a little group of sycophants, and the rule of a half-crazy Hanoverian; a stubborn man, who thinks it more important to uphold "the divine right of kings" than to hold his American Colonies. How can a man who cannot speak the language without accent, understand a Briton's love of Liberty?"

There was no longer fire in Harvey's voice. "The Colonies are striding fast toward revolt. Under these changing conditions, unless the wrongs are righted at once, a break with the Mother Country is inevitable," he ended brokenly.

William was silent as they drove home. He had nothing to say of the meeting until they were at Queen's Gift and had gone into the library for coffee.

"What do you think, Mary?" he asked. "Do you think as these men do, that the break with England will come soon, that there will be a serious revolt?"

"I believe with Maurice Moore, William. We have been in the Age of Revolution ever since the battle of Alamance," she answered. She was astonished at the question—more astonished that he should ask her opinion on anything political. She felt that she understood him less than ever these days.

He changed the subject then and spoke of the affairs of the plantation. When they finished their coffee Mary went upstairs to bed, taking the last copy of the *Weekly Post-Boy* with her. A paragraph caught her attention.

"Our shipping has suffered a great deal of loss lately from piracy after a lull of almost a quarter of a century. Reports are coming in from the Indies about losses of ships near Mono Passage and the Leeward Island. Several war vessels have been sent out to patrol the Caribbean waters and along the Carolinas. Some reports say a woman by the name of Sarah Wilson is the owner of several vessels that are claiming salvage from ships when they go through the Passage. This may not be piracy, but it is perilously near it."

Mary read the article through, wondering if any more of Adam's or Joseph Hewes's ships had been lost. She hoped not, now when they would need all the ships they had—and could build.

The fires of revolt burned more brightly now. Hooper held at Wilmington a meeting similar to the one at Edenton. Moore, Iredell and other leaders discussed injustices in public print. A new phrase came into being, *the Sovereignty of the*

People. Caswell forsook his policy of moderation and counseled his son to take up the musket if necessary. He himself, in a speech before a great crowd at New Bern, pledged to "shed his last blood in support of the liberties of his country."

Union was the word now. Union within the Province; union between the districts; union against Martin and his Royalists. The Royal Governor came back from New York strengthened by his talk with Tryon. His first official act was to issue a proclamation in answer to John Harvey's widely circulated papers asking the people in each district to elect men loyal to the Colony to represent them in a Provincial Congress.

The proclamation did not have the effect for which the Governor hoped. Rebel meetings went on. He called the Council and told them that he had received from his Majesty orders to prevent the appointment of any delegates from the Province of North Carolina to attend the proposed Continental Congress in Philadelphia.

The leaders paid no attention to the Governor's edict. They selected Hooper, Caswell and Hewes to represent them in Philadelphia. After a violent meeting a *Declaration of Rights* was adopted:

> *"Resolved:* that his Majesty's subjects have an undoubted right at any time to meet and petition the Throne for a redress of grievances, and that such a right includes a further right of appointing delegates for such a purpose, and therefore the Governor's proclamation issued to forbid this meeting and his proclamation afterward to disperse it are illegal and an infringement on our just rights, and ought to be disregarded as wanton and arbitrary exertions of power."

The excitement was intense. Men from every part of the Province, whether members of the Assembly or not, gathered in New Bern to await the outcome.

Mary Warden accompanied William when he went to the meetings of the Council. Peyton was not a member of the Assembly but he had come to consult with the merchants to see what could be done about the King's ruling that the Colonies could no longer trade with England or the West Indies. North Carolina and New York were the two Colonies excepted through the efforts of Tryon. He still professed to be friendly toward North Carolina so that he was able to persuade the Crown to make a trade exception of that Colony as well as of his new Province.

Some of the merchants were jubilant over this exception but the wiser pointed out that it was only a trick to use New York and North Carolina as bases for troops and the navy in case of war. The old military trick of "Divide and Rule." A look at the maps convinced the merchants that such a plan would divide the North and South in two, separating the Colonies, cutting off communications if war really came. At a meeting in Wilmington the merchants declared that they would not be a party to such a division. They announced themselves in favor of the new idea that was fast taking hold throughout America: to unite all the Colonies. Hewes, who had large interests in the Indies as well as in North Carolina, was a moving figure. His protégé, John Paul, who had taken the name of Jones, was still talking to the leaders, trying to persuade them to build ships for trade that could be used for defense later on. Hooper, who had come from Boston and was, through his family, deeply concerned about the situation in the North, carried people by his logic and wisdom.

John Harvey came to see Mary one evening shortly after she returned to Queen's Gift. She was shocked at his appearance. He was thin and white, and he trembled so that she had to assist him to a chair. She sent a servant for a decanter of brandy. He had been ill again, he told her, but he must keep himself upright until the business of the Assembly was finished. Too many people looked to him for leadership for him to give up. He could not fail them now. Mary poured out the brandy and handed the glass to him. After a few moments, the color came to his cheeks and his hands steadied.

"William has gone out," she told him. "He is very much worried over the quarreling in the Assembly."

"It is just as well, Mary. It is you I came to see. I want to show you letters that have come by one of Hewes's ships."

He handed her a small packet. She read the letters through without comment. They were from men in the northern Colonies who had given much thought to the present situation. She noticed one was from Hooper to Johnstone of the Albemarle district.

"Do we not play a game where slavery or liberty is at stake? Must we not have Brigadier Generals in districts and superior officers over the whole? Must not very large bodies of militia be placed along the sea coast? Were I to advise, the whole force of the Colony should be collected ready for immediate action when called for. Bid adieu to the plowshare and the pruning hook until the sword can find its scabbard with safety and honor for its owner. My first wish then is to be free; my second to be reconciled to Great Britain, if that may be done with honor. God grant, erelong when the troops of the enemy will be in our country, that we stand forth like men and fight for the cause of liberty, the cause of the living God."

Mary felt her hand shake as she folded the paper. "It is not far off," she said in a whisper.

"Not far. I suppose you have heard from William that Maurice Moore told the Governor today that his next meeting of the Assembly on the fourth would be the last."

"Yes, William told me. Do you think that is true, Mr. Harvey?"

"I think it is the truth. Perhaps Maurice was a little premature in saying it. But no matter. After this meeting all of us will be branded as rebels to the Crown. The next step will be to take away our lands. Unless we present a united front, I do not know what will happen to our poor country." He turned his somber eyes to Mary. "See that William remains firmly on our side, Mary. Sometimes I am not quite sure but that at heart William is a Loyalist."

Mary felt herself go cold at his words. "Oh, no! no! I'm sure that ever since he was in England the last time William has been heart and soul on the side of the Colonies. Do not worry about William, John Harvey."

Harvey got up. "If everyone were as loyal as you, Mary, we would have no cause to worry." He clasped her hand in a firm grip.

Mary walked to the door with him. "I wish we could laugh again wholeheartedly as we used to. Nothing seems to matter now but the fate of our poor country. I can't even get enjoyment out of hunting."

"That is too bad, Mary. It was always so refreshing to see you and Adam Rutledge riding to the hounds and to hear you laugh. You laughed easily in those days. By the way, have you heard anything from Rutledge?"

Mary shook her head. "No. Not since he left. Someone told me he had gone out to the Mississippi on a mission for the Committee of Safety."

Harvey looked at her thoughtfully. "There are men to whom responsibility is given which is outside themselves or their own will. It has come at different times in the history of the world—at great crises. I think that Rutledge is one of these men. He will find himself moved forward by the sweep of a destiny too strong to stand against. I wish he were here. God knows we need young men of his kind. He may be lost to North Carolina now that the West has roused his interest."

Mary did not answer. Every word that Harvey uttered was a death knell to her. She had thought Adam would come home now that the period of his banishment was almost over. But perhaps Harvey was right. His devotion might be a new land, not the old.

She had a feeling that there was no longer any hope. She had had no word from Adam directly. Surely he must have written her—unless— She did not want to face that alternative. He must have known she was overwrought when they quarreled; he must have made excuses for her, realizing it was a time when nerves were stretched and frayed. Surely he could forgive her words.

Mary could not understand how she had allowed her mood to betray her that day—the day she had quarreled with him. She remembered the look in his eyes—his words: "Mary, we aren't quarreling, are we?" He must have been deeply hurt. She had not explained that she had been arguing for days with William, with Samuel Johnstone, with Harvey, even with the Doctor. How could he have known how raw, how close to the surface her nerves were?

Now she realized the depth of her thought of him. . . . Adam would never know the strength of her love, but she must fight for his friendship. Once she had it again, she would never let it go.

She watched Harvey walk down the path. His tall, thin figure was bent as if he were unable to stand erect against the rising wind. She watched him pass out of sight with a sinking heart. He was a sick man. If anything happened to him, who would take his place? What other man would have the courage and the fearlessness?

When the Assembly met, the fight between the Royalists and the Whigs was the bitterest ever heard in the Hall. Martin's efforts at conciliation were futile. The room was a scene of unparalleled disorder. Men shouted and cursed, shaking fists under opponents' faces and hurling invectives. Any hope of a peaceful settlement of the long list of memorialized grievances faded as the day drew to a close.

"Liberty and Prosperity," someone cried from the gallery. The floor took it up. "Liberty and Prosperity." People were stirred as never before.

At the last, Martin prorogued the Assembly. Everyone expected it, but it roused the Whigs more bitterly than ever against him. They hated him for resorting to Tryon's tactics.

"Is Tryon to rule the Colony from New York?" they asked the next day. The burgesses disbanded and went to their homes. The split between the Governor and the Assembly had gone too far to leave any further hope of reconciliation.

Peyton and Lavinia were dining at Queen's Gift on Christmas Eve. Mary had no heart for celebration that year although things had quieted somewhat after the stormy session of the Assembly. But she knew that only the unthinking were fooled into a sense of security. She had asked the Doctor and Owen and Gwennie also. Perhaps they could, by an effort, keep away from talk of revolution for one evening. Parson Earl would come in later, after he had made his parish calls.

When she had dressed, she went down to the dining room to see if Cissie had remembered Roger's punch bowl which always came out of the ebony chest on Christmas Eve. Ebon and Cissie had mixed the rum punch earlier in the day by a rule Roger had brought with him when he came to Carolina from St. Kitts.

Year after year they had kept up the old custom Roger had inaugurated the first Christmas after he had built Queen's Gift, and Mary hadn't the heart to skip the little ceremony this year. "Ask your people to come up at twelve o'clock," she told Ebon, after she had finished her inspection. "Tell cook to have the cakes ready."

Lavinia and Peyton entered the hall as Mary came out of the dining room, the Doctor behind them. Lavinia threw her arms around Mary's neck, kissing her cheek. Peyton behind Lavinia, waiting his turn. He held a sprig of mistletoe above Mary's head and kissed her full on the lips.

"Christmas gift, Christmas gift," he cried.

"You're hours too soon, Peyton. You can't say it until after twelve," Mary replied.

Peyton kissed her again, this time without the aid of mistletoe. "I don't believe in waiting. Gather your roses while you may," he answered, laughing. His gaiety was infectious. Even William, coming in from his office, smiled. He kissed Lavinia's hand gallantly.

Owen and Gwennie arrived a moment later, Gwennie's pink cheeks half hidden by a rabbit-skin tippet and hood.

William introduced the subject of the Highlanders into the conversation while Ebon was carrying in the burning plum pudding at the end of the dinner. "I had word recently from England that eight hundred Highlanders and their clan leaders are coming out to settle in the Province. General Macdonald has petitioned the King for forty-five thousand acres

351

of land. They have asked for land suitable for raising cattle and sheep, with good soil and plenty of water, near the coast."

"Forty-five thousand acres!" Armitage exclaimed. "That's a great deal of land in one piece."

"Is there much vacant land of that description?" Owen asked.

William hesitated. "I'm not sure. I only got the inquiry today. I have not had time to check our maps. There may be that much near Campbelltown."

Owen nodded. "Of course they will want to be somewhere near the other Highland people."

Peyton made a face. "We're overrun with Scots already. I don't see why we allow any more of them with their dour looks and their laments. We ought to have more Frenchmen —we need gaiety, not sadness here."

Everyone ignored Peyton's tactless remark.

William glanced across the table at Mary. "You will be interested to know, my dear," he said, "what my London correspondent tells me—that Flora Macdonald and her husband Allan will be in the party."

Mary said, "Flora Macdonald! How very exciting! I've always admired Flora Macdonald. She is a woman of great courage and spirit."

Gwennie turned her round blue eyes on William. "Surely you don't mean the great Flora Macdonald is coming here, Mr. Warden?"

William smiled. Mary thought he seemed rather to enjoy the little stir his announcement had made.

"Indeed, yes. Flora herself—the woman who saved Bonnie Prince Charlie."

"Well, I never," Gwennie said. "How can it be she? Why would the Macdonalds be coming to the Carolinas, Owen?"

"If you remember your history, my dear, Donald Macdonald was a hero at Culloden, a hero of a lost cause. He fought for the Stuarts until all hope was gone."

"I was trying to remember what happened then," Mary said. "Do tell us, Owen. You always know your history."

"I've taught it long enough, I should remember. The General chose the lesser of the evils. He foreswore the Stuarts and took oath to George II. I think that will answer your questions."

"You mean the Scots would not forgive that?"

Owen asserted. "Peyton has just complained that the Scots are dour folk. That is true; they are not as communicative as

352

the French, let us say. But they are strong in their loyalties. They would not like a turncoat and they probably made it unpleasant for the General."

"But Flora—surely they like her?" Mary asked.

"Ah, that is different. They worship Flora Macdonald. She is their heroine. They like Allan, her husband, but the General—"

The Doctor was listening to Owen, a frown between his eyebrows, his smooth shaven face serious. He turned to William. "You say the King has granted the Highlanders forty-five thousand acres?"

"No, I said General Macdonald had asked for it. If the King refuses, Governor Martin will arrange for the land through the Granville Grant. He told me so last week."

Armitage drummed on the table with his long bony fingers. "Ah, I see. Martin wants them here. Eight hundred Highlanders added to those already here would bring the clan up to around three thousand—all fighters, all sworn to defend the Hanoverians. No wonder Martin is anxious to give them land for settlement. Can't you see how much strength they will add to the Royalists?"

A look of annoyance passed over William's face, but he did not answer.

Mary said, "They can't all be Royalists. There must be some among them who are still loyal to the House of Stuart."

Armitage shrugged. "You heard what Owen just said. These are the Highlanders who foreswore their allegiance to the Stuarts. They are in like case to the Regulars who took oath to support the King. Don't you see?"

Mary nodded. She understood now. It would mean a strong support to the Governor and the Royalists to have the clansmen come over. "Perhaps they won't come," she said.

"Perhaps not," William answered. "My letter said the plans were vague, very vague."

They went into the drawing room and played at loo and écarté until almost twelve, when Ebon entered to tell Mary that the slaves were coming to the plantation house. She got up and went to the window, followed by Lavinia and Owen. Through the dark forest and down the dark slope that led to the slaves' quarters, they saw moving lights.

"What is it?" Lavinia exclaimed. "Look! There are hundreds of lights. Why are they coming this way?"

The others laid down their cards and looked to Mary for an explanation, all except the Doctor.

"Didn't you know? Haven't you ever heard of Christmas at Queen's Gift?" he said, continuing to deal the cards.

"No, never," Lavinia replied, looking at Mary.

"My grandfather, Roger Mainwaring, instituted the custom," Mary explained. "Once a year, on Christmas, the Negroes come to pay their one penny each for their land rent. Perhaps you don't know, but many of the Negroes at Queen's Gift are free men. They have been free since my grandfather's time. They continue to live here, to plant their little pieces of ground and raise their crops. But every Christmas Eve they come to the plantation house to pay their ground rent." She smiled a little wistfully. "I wish I could have known 'Duke Roger,' as his contemporaries called him. He must have been a grand person."

"And you carry on the custom?" Owen asked.

She saw by his face that he was interested. "Yes, always. If I'm not here, they wait until I return from my journey and make an arbitrary Christmas Day so that they can pay their rent."

"One penny a year," Armitage said slowly. "I remember Roger distinctly. You are right, Mary. He was a man—a damn fine man."

"If anyone would care to come with me," Mary said, almost shyly. "It takes quite a time."

The Doctor looked up from his game of patience.

"Better go, Peyton and Lavinia. You too, Owen, and Gwennie would enjoy it. It's unique—loyal subjects come to pay homage to their Queen."

"Doctor! how can you be so foolish? You know it isn't like that." Mary was a little annoyed.

Armitage shuffled the cards expertly. "Well, they don't kiss her hand, but—"

Lavinia and Peyton went with Mary. A moment later, the others followed. In the hall they met Parson Earl.

"Am I in time, Mary?" he asked, as he slipped off his coat.

"Just in time, Mr. Earl. I'm about to go out on the gallery."

Ebon and the house servants were already there. A table had been set up. On it were Duke Roger's silver punch bowl and great piles of anise cakes and little tarts. They saw a long procession coming up the driveway. No figures were visible in the darkness but the lights bobbed up and down at different angles and heights. The approaching crowd consisted of men, women and children, three or four hundred perhaps.

Mary stood on the steps to welcome them. The dark red of her satin gown shimmered from the lights in the hall behind her. She was smiling when the first small pickaninny reached up his hands to her as the clock in the hall chimed twelve.

"Christmas gift, mistress! Christmas gift!" A hundred voices took up the cry. Mary called back, "Christmas gift, Christmas gift," as the slaves crowded up to the steps.

After the others had left, Dr. Armitage went to the door and stood in the shadows. He saw Mary step forward to greet the Negroes, her slim body bent, her farthingales swaying her satin skirts. He noticed that she greeted each man or woman by name. The old ones received more words and larger gifts, especially one old man who had been on the plantation in Roger's time and who was carried up in a chair. The Doctor watched them a moment, then went back to the warmth of the yellow drawing room.

Back in the darkness voices rose—a low solemn chant, wordless, strangely moving. Parson Earl and William came to Mary's side and helped her give out the small packages, tied with braided strands and decorated with small bunches of red holly, to every man, woman and child.

After they had greeted their mistress, the Negroes passed on. Each slave had his own gourd ladle which was filled from Duke Roger's silver bowl by Cissie and Ebon. Chaney hurried back and forth from the kitchen to the gallery, watching to see that the bowl was refilled at the proper time. After receiving the punch, the Negroes disappeared into the darkness, down the winding path that led to the quarters, their torches and lanterns a thin streamer of light.

At the cabins the real revelry began. The sound of drums and singing came across the still night air.

"I suppose some pagan ceremony is taking place at this moment." Parson Earl laughed as they went into the house. "But hang me if I care! I've been visiting the fisher folk along the lower village, taking them parish gifts, and I'm ready for your comfortable fire and a warm drink, William."

The punch bowl was brought in and they filled the silver mugs and passed the cups. William proposed the first toast, to "his Majesty, King George III." There was a moment's pause before they drank. Mary wondered how many times she had drunk the toast without a thought. Now she wondered how many times more it would be drunk before . . . but she turned resolutely away from the thought and lifted the cup to her lips. "To Adam," was her secret thought, "to Adam— may he return soon!" Even the thought of him made her blood race. She must watch herself and not allow her heart to give her away.

She went upstairs with Lavinia to get her wrap.

"Have you heard anything about Lady Caroline?" Lavinia asked suddenly.

Mary shook her head.

"Some say she is in Norfolk or Williamsburg, but Penelope Dawson has heard she is back in the West Indies again." Lavinia paused, looking at Mary. "You haven't heard anything?"

Mary looked directly at her. "No, nothing, nothing whatever."

"Strange how mysteriously she disappeared the night of the opening of the Palace," Lavinia said thoughtfully. "She might almost have been swallowed up by the storm."

"Lady Caroline was always a little mysterious, don't you think?" Mary answered to divert her.

"Adam said—" Lavinia began. But Mary was already in the hall. She didn't want to speak of Adam tonight. For some strange reason she felt his nearness, almost his presence in the house. She could close her eyes and see him moving about. They went down the stairs without words.

Mary stood at the door and waved farewell, and then went back to the Doctor who was staying over Christmas at Queen's Gift. William excused himself and, taking up his candle, went up to his room. Mary sat down on the sofa while the Doctor stood in front of the fire, his hands in his coattail pockets.

They talked a moment of Parson Earl and the problems he faced in his parish. The Parson was determined that the church would remain in the church of England in spite of the impending struggle. For that he was baited by people who said he was a Loyalist, a traitor to the Province.

"As loyal a Whig as ever lived," Armitage mumbled crossly. "I would like to skin some of these gossips with their lying tongues!"

Mary smiled a little at his words. She thought he looked very tired. "Is Crit taking proper care of you?" she asked.

The Doctor grunted. "Too good—for a fact. It's just that I dread the holiday season."

Mary said nothing. She knew his young wife had died on Christmas Day many, many years ago—yet he still grieved for her. She glanced at the clock. It was past two. "I think you had better go upstairs if we are going to Edenton for early service in the morning."

The Doctor made a face. "You go, Mary, and do my praying. I've done all my church going for the year. I think I'll spend the morning in bed for a change."

They walked up the stairs together. At the door of his room, he said, "Wait a minute. I have a little Christmas gift for you. I've been waiting to give it to you when we were alone." He went into his room and came out a moment later with a small package and a letter in his hand.

Mary caught her breath. She knew without a word that they were from Adam.

"I saw Adam in Virginia last week when I went to Williamsburg. He asked me to give you these on Christmas." The Doctor put the package and letter into her hand and went quickly into his room.

Mary put the candle on the night table by her bed, with the letter and the box beside it. She undressed slowly, methodically, and got into bed before she broke the seal on the letter.

"Dearest Mary:

"Tonight, after I talked to Armitage, I sat for a long time thinking of you and the things that are happening all about us. I wish so much that I could talk them over with you, but that is not possible now. Sometime, before too long, I hope to sit quietly beside you and tell you the things that I have seen on my journeys. Not that I have an Odyssey to unfold, but there will be some significance to the tale.

"Sara is very happy in New York with her father, among her Royalist friends. I have not the heart to disturb her, or to try to influence her way of thinking.

"Dear Mary, I would like your understanding. I'm much in need of it tonight.

"Always,
"ADAM"

She sat very quiet, without moving, the letter in her hand. After a long time she opened the box and found two jade bangles backed with gold. She slipped them on her wrist. The restless mood which had disturbed her throughout the day and evening left her. She felt strangely happy. A sudden understanding came to her then. She knew she must not push against Fate or try to force her will. She must learn to wait patiently for fulfillment.

Chapter 23

BLUE
BONNETS

FROM her bedroom window Mary watched the majestic approach of a sailing ship up the Sound. It was the middle of February, but spring was early and Cissie had thrown the casement window wide open when she brought Mary's chocolate.

"Mr. Hewes's ship she sail in dis mornin'," the serving woman announced. "Mister William, he got on he horse and ride to de village to fotch de London mail. He says to tell you he likely to bring gentlemen home for breakfast off dat ship—maybe someone come to stay a spell wid us."

Mary watched the ship swing slowly around to anchor in the bay. William had told her the night before that a Hewes ship had been sighted off the Heads. If it were a ship from London, it would bring a heavy post since they had not had one for two months.

"You had better air some bedrooms, Cissie," she said, as she poured her chocolate.

"I got young Ivory doing dat right now. I opened up de south room and de room with de flowered paper. I have a little fire built to take off de winter chill."

Mary set her cup down on the lap-tray and reached for her robe.

"You want we should sit up de quiltin' frames in de sewing room?" Cissie asked. "Martha and Ivory finished piecing dat Whig pattern quilt yesterday and Mis' Tewillinger she send over to ask if our girls could do some quilting for she next week."

Mary nodded her assent. She found it hard to concentrate on matters of the household. Cissie stood at the foot of the bed, her hands akimbo, an accusing look in her eyes.

"Seems lak you' mind hit wool-gatherin' all de time nowadays. What for you go around looking lak yo' head in de clouds? Most ladies dey think about der house dis time a yer." She leaned over to emphasize her words. "Don' you know hits spring cleaning time and you ain' had one little window washed in dis whole house?"

Mary laughed spontaneously. "We'll remedy that right away, Cissie. You can have Ebon get the housemen at window-washing today."

"Can't do dat, wid London guest coming for breakfast." She looked disapprovingly at Mary. "I think nice mornin' lak dis, with all the little birds singing and snowdrops bustin' into bloom in de grass, you'd be up laughing and singing lak you used to. I think you done forget how to make a laugh."

Mary slipped into the wrapper and swung her slim legs over the side of the bed while Cissie held the steps for her. "You are quite right, Cissie. I've forgotten how to laugh but I'm going to do better from now on."

Cissie nodded approval. "Hit's high time," she said severely. "You getting you'self old before your time—old just lak de master, if you don't watch you'self."

Mary stood at the window gazing at the slowly moving ship. Cissie, with her unerring instinct, had hit upon the truth. She realized she had lost interest in everything. She must watch herself, as Cissie said. She smiled a little when she saw that the serving woman had laid out a silk gown that suggested spring in its gay flowered pattern.

William knocked at the door while Cissie was brushing her heavy chestnut hair. "I've brought home two guests for breakfast, Mary—Captain Faulkner of Hewes's ship and Ronald MacLeod from Argyle in Scotland." He paused, glancing at her wrapper. "Will you be down soon? I should like you to meet MacLeod. He has come over on the emigration business."

Mary raised her eyebrows. "Emigration?" she asked.

"You remember. I told you at Christmas time. Eight hundred Highlanders led by the Macdonalds. They have already sailed from Glasgow. The ships should be in Cape Fear by the end of the month."

Mary remembered then. Flora Macdonald—

"Why does the man want to see you?" she asked, as she wound the long braids in a coronet around her small head.

"They're settling on part of the Granville Grant near Campbelltown. I've made all the arrangements. Will you come down as soon as you are ready?"

"I'm ready now—or I will be as soon as Cissie laces my gown."

Mary sat behind the coffee urn and listened to the conversation. Captain Faulkner she knew and liked. Colonel MacLeod was a sandy-haired young Scot with merry blue eyes.

She remembered she had seen him at the Palace when Tryon was Governor. He was bursting with enthusiasm over the coming of the Highlanders.

"Just think, Mrs. Warden," he said, his eyes shining. "Think of it, Flora Macdonald will be here in a month's time. I can scarcely wait to see her."

Captain Faulkner said, "You'll see a rare fine woman, me lad, with the figure of a girl and fire in her blue eyes, for all her hair is streaked with white."

"She must be a woman of forty-five or so," William observed. "It's been twenty-six or seven years since she took the Prince from Oisk to Skye dressed as her serving woman."

Ronald MacLeod laughed aloud. "It was my father Malcolm that went with her and a fine mess they got themselves into."

Mary said, "Wasn't he arrested, too, and put in the Tower?"

"Indeed, yes. Ha' ye never heard what my father said about that? He said, 'I went to London to be hanged, but I rode back to Scotland in a chaise and four with Flora Macdonald.' "

Faulkner laughed. "I'd forgotten, 'twas a famous saying in Scotland when I was a lad." He turned his somber eyes on Mary. "If the Prince had had the courage of Flora, there'd have been a Stuart on the throne today instead of a German." He stopped suddenly.

MacLeod reddened. "Some of us Highlanders feel the same, sir."

The usually taciturn Faulkner continued with his enthusiastic praise of Flora, but William changed the subject by asking about affairs in London.

"The Londoners don't believe there's going to be a war," Faulkner said scornfully. "They think it is a small affair that will either be smothered out in a little time or will never catch fire."

"You mean no one takes it seriously?" Mary asked.

Faulkner shrugged his heavy shoulders. "A few perhaps—statesmen and the merchants who are losing money since trading slackened."

Ebon came into the room with a plate of waffles and the men fell to eating—doing full justice to Chaney's cooking.

Later, as they were leaving, Faulkner handed Mary a letter.

"I almost forgot this. Mistress Patience Wright brought it down to the ship the day we sailed and asked me to give it

360

into your hands." His eyes twinkled at the corners as he smiled. "I hope it contains nothing treasonable—else I might swing at the end of a gibbet on Tyburn Hill."

In the afternoon Mary took the chaise and drove into the village to get the cotton bat that Cissie wanted for the Whig pattern quilt. She drove through the village, seeing few familiar faces. A company of redcoats were marching to drums down King Street. A few children and farm boys watched them, showing little interest. She went into the shop and made her purchases without seeing anyone she knew.

Crossing the lower end of the green, she met Samuel Johnstone riding leisurely along the street. Mary signaled the coachman to stop.

"I'm going to Queen's Gift," Johnstone told her. "If you'll allow me, I'll ride with you." He dismounted and gave the reins to his groom. "Follow us to Queen's Gift," he said to the Negro boy as he got into the carriage and sat down opposite Mary.

Johnstone had much to say as they drove along the muddy road, but Mary only half listened. She was watching the sunlight as it slanted down through the pines and broke into scattering golden beams over the white mass of dogwood along Queen Anne's Creek. Suddenly she was aware of words.

"He's doing excellent work," Johnstone was saying, "excellent. We have so few men we can trust to make confidential investigation of the state of the Colonies. We want to know the strength of the undercurrents—not the flow of the main stream. Yes, Adam's work satisfies the entire Committee."

Mary did not move or turn her eyes but she was intensely attentive as she waited for Johnstone's next words. She wanted to ask where Adam was, when he would come home, but she did not. She had vowed to herself Christmas that she would stop dreaming of what could never be remedied, but she was glad of this meager information. Adam was working for the Secret Committee, doing excellent work, secret work.

Johnstone turned his attention to the condition of the road as they jolted through the ruts. "We ought to petition Martin to improve it," he grumbled.

Mary nodded but did not answer. They rode on in silence. William met them at the door and, after greeting Johnstone warmly, took him to his office.

Mary found Patience Wright's letter on the hall table where she had laid it to await a more leisurely moment and took it into the drawing room to read.

"Dearest Mary:

"I don't know how much longer I'll be here in England. The situation is not too pleasant for colonials. I was talking to Dr. Franklin yesterday. He is worried, although he says not. The papers poke fun at him, call him a simpleton, gauche, a country bumpkin, especially since he lost the cipher letter with the code in the courtyard of St. James's Palace. I think he is very shrewd, but he gets on better with the French than with the British.

"I've finished the wax figure of the King but he still drops in for a glass of port every few days. He comes to argue with me about the rebellious Colonies, 'which are acting like children, and should be disciplined.' I try very hard to make him see the truth, but he is too—I was going to say pigheaded—but I won't be so crude. Instead, I'll say stubborn.

"People I meet at routs and supper parties pay little attention to American affairs—Lord George Germain excepted. Even the papers give only a meager amount of news. They are taken up with the scandalous trial of the twin brothers who conspired something or other and are likely to be executed for the crime.

"I went to see General Burgoyne's play the other afternoon. All London was there. Very dull, I thought. I ran across Lord Cornwallis in the lounge between acts. He looks worried. It is rumored that his wife, the daughter of the Duchess of Gordon, is very ill —a decline, I believe. It is also rumored that he is soon to go out to America with his regiment.

"Oh Mary, I'm deeply troubled. I do not see a single gleam of hope. I could not write so plainly, but that I'm asking Captain Faulkner to deliver this letter into your hands.

"Address me at the old number in Paris. I may have to leave here soon. When you write, give me a true picture of what is happening. I count on you for useful information.

"With love,
"PATIENCE."

Mary sat for a long time, pondering the things Patience had implied rather than put into words. She must know things she did not dare write, close as she was to Dr. Franklin. Perhaps Patience also was doing excellent work.

William asked Mary if she wanted to go with him to the public reception planned for the Highlanders by Governor Martin and the city of Wilmington. When she hesitated, he suggested instead that she meet him at Campbelltown where he was going after the Wilmington festivities were over to see that Allan Macdonald and his clansmen were settled on their land on the other side of Cross Creek. Then if she liked, they could stop over at Catawba Springs for a fortnight.

Dr. Armitage made up her mind for her. "You are tired

and run down, Mary. It's time you took the waters for a couple of weeks. It'll do you good, and William, too. If I had my way, I'd send everyone over to the Springs for two weeks in the spring—better than a sulphur and molasses tonic, and less painful."

Mary fell in with the idea. She took Ebon and Cissie with her, Ebon to drive the light coach and four, and a groom to lead the saddle horses. When she reached Cross Creek she found that the clansmen who had settled in the district years before were coming in by the hundreds from every part of the district to pay homage to the Laird of Kingsburg, but more especially to his wife Flora.

Mary arrived at Cross Creek early in the morning after driving half the night. She went at once to the little wayside inn, Cotter's Haven, where William had engaged rooms. She was delighted with the kindly Scotch woman of ample proportions who brought a pot of chocolate and a hot scone to "stay you against dinner."

From her room she could look out through the branches of sycamore trees to the village green, already thronged with people. The bluff-road along the river and the winding lanes were packed with country folk in Highland garb coming to do honor to their national heroine.

The innkeeper and his wife were proud of their name this day because the Whannels were a sept of the clan Macdonald. Their small hostel was filled to overflowing so that they were kept busy with the bar and dining room, but even so Dame Whannel had time to see that Mary was made comfortable.

Mary stood at the window. On one side, the Inn stables were plainly visible where grooms and stablemen were exercising horses, polishing carriages and coaches and rubbing harness brasses in preparation for the arrival of the celebrated Scots.

At noon William came in, bringing Colonel MacLeod for dinner. The young officer was delighted that Mary had come to Cross Creek.

"Now you'll see the clans when they gather for a celebration. Did you know that almost every clan is represented here in Carolina, and many of the septs?" he asked proudly. "I've been telling your husband that you must stay the nicht—the night, I mean—so that you'll meet Flora and Allan tomorrow."

Mary looked at William. "I thought we were starting for Catawba Springs this afternoon," she said.

"I can't get away," William replied. "I promised Allan I would go over some data about the acreage before I left. Besides, from what I hear in the village, Cross Creek will be the most exciting place in Carolina for the next two days. As Ronald has said, the clans are gathering."

"The Campbell's are coming." Ronald MacLeod whistled a bar of the old marching song. Through the window Mary saw Farquhar Campbell dismounting from his horse. He was wearing the old hunting tartan of the Campbells of Argyle, MacLeod told them. "You'll see many an ancient tartan today," he added. "The Governor won't be here and the King's officers will be blind."

"What do you mean, Colonel?" Mary asked. "Why do you say that?"

"The Highlanders haven't been allowed to wear their tartans for almost thirty years," MacLeod told her. "It's been a penal offense ever since the battle of Culloden for a Scot to wear his colors."

"You mean to say the Scots haven't been allowed to wear their tartans?"

MacLeod nodded. "I'll not be saying they haven't worn them, but it's been against the law."

William said, "I suppose old George II wanted them to forget they were Scots."

MacLeod gave a quick laugh, without mirth.

"And so all the Highlanders will wear their old colored tartans tomorrow, in honor of Flora," Mary said.

"Yes," the young man replied eagerly. "Yes, and there will be games, tests of strength and mock fighting with claymores and dirks, dance the old reels and strathspeys. I hear there are fine sword dancers among the Carolina Highlanders."

Mary turned to William. "I think I shall stay," she said.

William smiled. "I'm sure you'll be entertained, my dear. There is to be an outdoor supper and they will pipe in the haggis according to the ancient rites."

Mary laughed aloud. "That convinces me. That is something I have always wanted to see."

Campbell joined them at the dinner table. William asked him to sit down and have an ale and a bit of cheese. Campbell accepted, then turned to Mary. "I'm an emissary from my wife, Mrs. Warden. She has sent me to invite you and your husband to supper tomorrow evening. Flora and Allan will be there, and a few of our friends."

Mary thanked him for his courtesy and accepted for herself and William. "I shall be delighted by the opportunity to meet Flora Macdonald. I have admired her for a long time."

"Flora is beloved by the Scots," Campbell said simply. "We want her to like her new home and we are doing everything possible to make her and Allan comfortable here." He turned to William. "Did MacLeod tell you that we are all turning out in clan tartans tomorrow—ban or no ban?"

William smiled. "I don't suppose the penal offense act will be executed here."

Campbell glanced at Mary. She was looking at a group of crofters and herdsmen driving a flock of sheep across the green. He dropped his voice for William's ear alone. "Martin is well aware that the coming of the Macdonalds will give him staunch adherents, as most of them have sworn an oath to support the King—and you know a Scotchman's oath is his oath."

Campbell saw that Mary was listening. He changed the subject. "My wife said we would have supper around ten, after the reels and sword dancing on the green. She is expecting you also, Colonel MacLeod. She says Mimsey will be looking for a partner to fling a reel." Campbell turned to Mary. "The Colonel here is fair bowled over by Flora's dark daughter Mimsey."

Colonel MacLeod turned a fiery red. For a moment he was speechless with embarrassment. "Thank you, Mr. Campbell," he managed to say. "Thank you, I shall be delighted."

At sunset Mary had Cissie place a chair on the small balcony opening off her room to watch the gathering clans as the evening deepened. The silver ribbon of the river showed below the bluff, a swift roadway to the sea. Mockingbirds in the sycamores trilled and trilled, rivaling the pibroch moaning in the distance.

William came out on the balcony and stood at her side for a moment, watching the movement and color below.

Mary laid her hand on his arm. "I'm so glad you had me come, William. I had no idea it would be like this. Look at them down there—all the colors in the tartans, kilts, scarves, sashes and petticoats. I never realized before how many Scots had come to the Province. Are they all Royalists—all of them?"

William was looking at a group of horsemen riding along the lower end of the green. He answered her question absently. "Some of the Jacobites will never give in at heart— but most of them will remember their allegiance when the time comes."

"When the times comes—" William's words brought her

back suddenly. How often she had heard those words in the past year!

All night the noise and bustle of new arrivals at Cross Creek went on—up the river, across the Pine Barrows the Highlanders were coming. The Macdonalds would arrive in the early morning. "They will stop at the Inn for a bowl of porridge and a rasher of bacon," Dame Whannel had told Mary with pride. "The coach will stop for the relay horses before driving on to Farquhar Campbell's place."

Mary lay on her canopied bed staring into the darkness with wide-open eyes. It was not the noise of the village or the far-off wail of a lament that kept her from sleeping. It was something William had said when he kissed her good night before going to his room:

"I saw Marcy just before supper. He told me he had ridden in from the Mecklenburg plantation on his way to the coast." He paused a moment. Mary had a swift premonition of what he was going to say. She sat very quietly, braced for the words. She must show nothing of her feeling—the accelerated beating of her heart. "Marcy said he expected Adam Rutledge to be here sometime tomorrow," he finished, not looking at Mary.

Mary waited a moment. The steadiness of her voice surprised her. "I hope we may see him," she said. "It has been a long time since Adam went away." She smiled as she said good night, after she had asked some trivial questions about tomorrow's program.

When William closed the door, she sank into a chair. Her trembling knees would no longer support her. Now she lay, unable to quiet her flying thoughts.

Toward morning, she heard staccato hoof-beats along the western road. Unable to lie quietly any longer, she got out of bed. She felt her way through the darkened room and, opening the door, stepped out on the balcony. The moon was still bright. Luminous shadows dappled the flagstones of the courtyard, in the pattern cast by the young leaves of the sycamores.

The crowds had dwindled; a few voices sounded far away, down toward the river bank. The sound of hoof-beats came closer. She moved back into the shadow of the pillars. Leaning forward, she saw Herk dismount from his horse and call to a hostler. Just then Adam and Marcy rode up to the front of the Inn. Adam swung off his horse. For a moment he was plainly visible in the moonlight. Thin and lean and hard, he was dressed in a leather jerkin and hunter's fringed trousers. He raised his arms and stretched himself.

"A damn hard ride," he said to Marcy. "Did you get me a bed?"

"After battling with mine host," Marcy laughed. "But you have to be out of it by six. It's the room the landlord is saving for Flora Macdonald so she can refresh herself when she stops for breakfast."

Adam groaned. "Only three hours? It's hardly worth it."

"I'm sorry," Marcy said, "but every bed in the village is taken. Hundreds of the 'bra' Scots' are sleeping in the fields and under the trees."

"I won't look a gift horse in the mouth," Adam answered. "Come on. Tell Herk to bring up my saddlebags before he beds down the horses."

Mary heard their retreating footsteps going down the long gallery and up the stairs. She went into her room and got into bed. A few minutes later she heard the door in the room next to hers open, and the low murmur of voices—then silence. She lay quietly, staring into the darkness, her heart pounding.

Adam was home. Only the narrow wall separated them. In the morning, she would see him—speak his name—Adam. After a time, she dropped off to sleep. When she awoke, the sun was shining in her window. Outside, she heard the shouts of the clansmen, the sound of coach wheels, horses clattering into the courtyard and brakes clamping. The Macdonalds had come to Cross Creek!

She saw Adam when she entered the breakfast room. He was sitting at the table with William, his back to her. William smiled in her direction. Adam turned. When he saw her, he got up and came across the room. At the sight of his strong, bronzed face, the weary procession of empty, desolate months faded. It was as if they stood alone in the room. She had forgotten how tall he was, how easily he moved, the turn of his head, the flat planes of his cheeks. She forced a welcoming smile. Words came, perfunctory words of welcome, as they moved across the crowded room.

William held her chair. "Sit down, my dear. I've ordered your breakfast. God knows when it will be served."

Adam glanced around. "A proper crowd; the village is filled to bursting." He laughed. "The landlord got me up at daybreak. It seems that Marcy talked him into giving me the Macdonalds' room with the provision that I get out by six."

Mary lifted the glass of water to her lips. She said nothing about seeing him the night before. William caught the eye of one of the Macdonald bailiffs, excused himself, and went to an adjoining table.

Time after time, in the long months he had been gone, Mary had repeated to herself the words she would say to him when he came home. Over and over again she had pictured the scene. He would ride up to Queen's Gift. They would sit quietly in the yellow drawing room. She would tell him how proud she was of him, how proud that he had gone over to the side of the Regulators—taken his stand with humble, down-trodden people; fought their fight; taken punishment with them. Her heart beat fast at the thought but now that he was here, across the table from her, no words came to her. There was only silence between them.

The buzz of voices was in her ears, the rattle of dishes, the sound of galloping horses, the barking of dogs in the Inn yard. The excitement of the holiday pervaded the room but it did not reach her.

"You never wrote me—I did not know where you were," she said, hating herself for the words when she had spoken them.

His face changed. A look of puzzled inquiry came into his eyes. "But I wrote you—from Virginia, from New York, and again from the West." He didn't wait for her to speak. "So Tryon carried out his threat—" He broke off. She saw William crossing the room. Whatever Adam had to say must wait.

Later in the morning, William rode out with Mary to a plantation along the river where games of speed and strength were being tried out. Running and the broad jump, stone hurdles and feats with the bow and arrow took up the first hour. After that the shepherds brought in a green flock of two or three hundred lambs and ewes. Half a dozen shepherds stood at one side holding their sheep dogs in check with their long-handled crooks. The dogs barked and waved their bushy tails, looking with eager eyes at their masters, waiting for their signals. One at a time they worked, cutting out sheep, driving the flock this way and that, guided by a word or sign, finally moving them all into the fold. From the backs of their horses, William and Mary watched. In the end Jack Evans of the Chowan district, 'old Jock' as he was called, won the competition with his dog Sandy. He was very proud and came over to tell Mary how he had trained the dog from a puppy to obey the slight signs he made with his crook.

"Did you notice, Mrs. Warden," he said, "I never spoke a

word aloud? Sandy knows how to read my mind. I'm telling these young fellows that I don't hold with shouts and yells in training a sheep dog. If he's na' wise enough to know what his master is thinking he's na' wise enough to be a sheep dog."

Mary rode back to Cotter's Haven after that, while William went on up to the glen on matters concerning the water rights of Cross Creek's Mills. She hadn't seen Adam since breakfast time but she knew he had not gone on since Herk was out on the green throwing a javelin at a mark along with some young Highlanders. She went to her room for she felt the need of rest after her sleepless night. Cissie awakened her at four. She bathed and dressed and went out on the balcony to watch the parade of the Highlanders to the little church on the far side of the square.

Bluff Hector, as the parson was familiarly called, was holding a "thank service." Flora and Allan and their family were to be there and take their first communion in the new land. Mary saw Colonel MacLeod hurrying up to the Inn. She scarcely recognized him when he waved to her, he looked so young and boyish in his yellow and black plaid kilts. A few moments later, he joined her on the balcony.

"I thought we could sit here and watch the marching," he told her, pulling up a chair beside her. "We'll have plenty of time then to walk over to the church and see them present Flora with the standards. It will be a fine ceremony," he said, with visible pride. "Ye'll not see the like of it any place outside the glens of Scotland."

In the square, the people were standing in groups, ready to fall into line. Piper Tammy MacGregor came down the steps below them and piped a shrill note or two, calling his band together. Ronald MacLeod leaned over the balustrade, his eyes gleaming with excitement.

"See, there's the Macalpin over there to the left, and one of the Douglas clans. They're wearing the old colors—blue and green, with a skeleton stripe of white. The Menzies hunting plaid—a green background with a red check; and the purple, green and yellow of the Moray, very royal because of the purple background."

Mary lost track of his words. Her eyes were fixed on the kaleidoscopic color moving against the grass of the square and the young, green, tender leaves of the budding trees. The pipes were playing a spirited march—the march of the Blue Bonnets. Ronald eagerly watched the pipers as they swung into line followed by the clansmen shouting as they marched:

"On to the border,
All the Blue Bonnets
Are bound for the border—"

A hundred men, two hundred, three hundred, the groups dropped into line following the skirl of pipes, their kilts swinging as they walked, the sunshine glittering on their brass buttons and silver buckles, on their braids and the blue streamers of their jaunty bonnets. Mary caught her breath.

"It's wonderful," she said. "I know now why the Scots are fierce in battle. It's the pipes that drive them on."

Ronald jumped from his seat. "Look over there, in front of the church. There are Flora and Allan."

Mary looked. She saw Flora dressed in a bright blue velvet robe looped back over her tartan petticoat, a noble, dignified figure.

"Allan's a fine bra' fellow," MacLeod said. "They say he can throw an ox with his two bare hands. But for all his strength, it's not the Laird that leads them—it's Flora herself that the Highlanders follow."

Mary watched the crowds move by, doffing their bonnets to Flora as they passed. The pipers had taken up their positions behind them. They were playing a slow weird song of infinite sadness.

"It's the Macdonalds' lament," the Colonel told her.

A moment later, he excused himself to join the marching clansmen. Mary was so intent on watching them that she did not hear Adam's footsteps until he spoke and sat down in the chair that MacLeod had left vacant. She looked up and smiled, but remained silent.

"It's a brave sight," he said, his eyes on the square. "Do you notice how well they march? I think most of them have served their time in the Highland regiments."

She glanced at him quickly. There was a thoughtful expression on his face. He said nothing of the mass of color and life and movement. Nor did he seem to notice the haunting sound of the pibroch or the roll of the drums.

"Trained men sworn to defend the King. No wonder Martin is pleased to have the Macdonalds in Carolina," he said bitterly. "They will give his army backbone and strength."

Mary looked at him curiously. "You mean we'll have to fight these people if we go to war with England?"

"Yes, and others of their kind. There's no joy in my heart today, Mary. I cannot even look at them without thinking that we shall be at grips with them before another year is over."

Mary said nothing. The moving scene below her had lost its flavor. She looked at Adam more closely. He was the same—yet not the same. His face was stronger—it showed more character; his eyes were unreadable, as if his thoughts were on things that she did not know or understand. They were silent for a long time.

Suddenly he said, "We have come to the place where we have learned that freedom can't be held by arrangement, because people say we are free. We must realize that freedom must be fought for. Fighting is itself part of freedom."

Mary had not time to answer. William came out onto the balcony. They stood for a moment watching the crowds move off into the distance.

"Are you going directly to Edenton?" he asked Adam.

"No, I must go to New Bern to meet the Governor, to see if I can get matters straightened out about my citizenship."

"What do you mean, Adam?" Mary exclaimed.

He turned to her with a surprised expression on his face.

"Didn't you know that I lost my rights to hold property in the Province under the Act of Oblivion?"

"No, I hadn't realized," she said. "Why such a thing is unthinkable!"

"It's a fact—it was part of Tryon's punishment," he said. The new harsh note was in his voice again. "He couldn't forgive me for taking the side of the Regulators against him, but more than that, he hated me because I refused his offer of immunity. He wanted me to take the oath of allegiance and swear never to take up arms against his Majesty. That was an oath I couldn't subscribe to, even though the alternative were exile."

Mary glanced at William. He was looking out over the square as if this were all a matter of indifference to him. She could not understand why he did not voice his indignation. "William," she said quickly. "Did you hear what Adam said?"

He turned slowly. "Yes, I heard," he said quietly. "It's an unfortunate law, but it is law. Perhaps Martin can be persuaded to lift the Act of Oblivion in your case, Rutledge."

"I haven't much hope," Adam said, "but I intend to remain here as long as I wish to remain, legally or illegally. The present Governor has nothing against me, but the Province of North Carolina is ruled from New York by Tryon. Martin is his tool. He does nothing without consultation with the former Governor. A fine state of affairs," he added bitterly.

Adam left them and a few minutes later Mary watched him

371

swing onto his saddle and ride away with Marcy, Herk following. It came to her then that she had not had a chance to tell him any of the things that had crowded her mind the past months: her pride in his action at Alamance; how much she had missed him; how she had longed to see him and talk to him about the swift-moving events that were affecting their lives and the lives of all the people. She wondered as she had wondered many times, if all personal life had been taken from them—if they were to go on and on devoting themselves only to the tasks that lay ahead.

"You are looking very serious, Mary," William observed.

She managed a smile. "I was thinking of what gown to wear when we meet Flora Macdonald tonight," she said lightly, without a tremor in her voice.

William's face cleared. "That is a serious matter, indeed," he said. "Clothes should always be important to lovely women."

Half a hundred sat at Farquhar Campbell's table that night. Mary and William came late. The guests were walking out to the loggia off the ballroom where the supper was to be served. Pine and cedars from the forest and cypress from the swamps had been brought to make the canvassed space in the loggia a green bower. Branches of the rowan tree, intertwined with laurel, festooned the ceiling. Here, under the light of hundreds of candles, the guests sat down. Mary found herself seated between Farquhar Campbell and Allan Macdonald, with Flora on the other side of the host and William beyond.

Allan looked older close up; fine lines radiated from the corner of his eyes, as on the face of a seafaring man or a mountain man accustomed to looking long distances. His eyes were bold, his profile strong and gentle. He was a lion in a fight, his people said of him. He spoke warmly to Mary of William's kindness and thoughtfulness.

"It was a hard thing for my wife to leave her home," he said to Mary. "But she does not complain."

Mary glanced at Flora Macdonald. She was sitting quietly while the talk went on about her. "A proud woman," Mary thought, "so composed and tranquil she seems almost lifeless."

Bluff Hector McLain, the parson of the little Kirk of Barbecue, leaned across the table and made some remark. Flora's eyes brightened, and a smile came to her lips. Mary heard her say:

"Our people will have land aplenty now to graze their cattle and their sheep and to plant their crops—a warm pleasant land with a smiling face. It makes us welcome—but it is far, far from our ain countrie."

When she turned Mary noticed the sadness in her eyes. Allan saw the look also. He leaned forward. "A new land brings new hope, my darling. Soon you will be under your own rooftree at the end of the journey."

She smiled at him, a quiet, gentle smile. Mary had the sensation of looking at a woman who had done with life, who had spent all passion—all emotion, who was quietly waiting.

Flora sensed that her mood was dampening the spirits of those about her. She set herself resolutely to be gay. "She must always be like that," Mary thought, "giving herself freely, without reserve."

A few minutes later, after the toast to the King, they all left the table. Allan and Flora sat in two chairs at the edge of the loggia to view the dancing. Canvas had been stretched on the lawn and sprinkled with water-ground cornmeal to make it smooth for the dancing.

The moon was high, casting a light on the young leaves of the rowan trees that hedged the garden. Mary sat in the shadow of the trees that supported the canopy. The pipers, who had earlier in the evening piped in the haggis, now stood under the trees in the flickering light of torches and lanterns, the ballad singers near them. The pipes began to reel. Dancers filled the open space, gay kilts flying, the moon catching the light on silver buckles, on buttons and silver dirks.

Farquhar Campbell had made his plans well. First, a gay reel by all the dancers; then a sword dance for young men, Fletcher of Glen Orchy, Hay of Blair-Athol, Moray of the Isles, and a Campbell of Argyle. The ancient dance brought shouts of applause and cries of "Hech! hech!" when the dancers executed some difficult feat of agility and grace.

Someone cried: "MacLeod—a song!" Mary saw young Ronald talking with the tall daughter of Flora and Allan whom they called Mimsey. Reluctantly, he stepped out and, after a word to Tammy the Piper, struck a position. He looked young and strong, his gay yellow and black kilts swishing as he moved. He held his hand loosely on the gold hilt of his Shean Dhu, which was thrust into his leather belt, and began his song. In a moment, the crowd joined in, repeating the words after him like a round.

> "Come, gi'us sang, Montgom'rie cried,
> And lay your disputes a' aside:
> What signifies for folks to chide

For what was done before them?
Let Whig and Tory a' agree,
To drop their whigmigmorum;
To spend this night in mirth and glee,
 And cheerfu' sing, alang wi' me,
The reel o' Tullochgorum."

The pipes shrilled while the people sang and clapped.

Young Ronald bowed low before Mimsey Macdonald, his hand over his heart. She curtsied and he led her out. In a moment, the dance floor was filled with laughing, shouting, singing Scots.

Allan took a seat near Mary. "You see for yourself, we're not the dour folk the English say. Wait until you see them dancing the strathspey and the dance with the broad swords."

Mary spoke impulsively. "I hope you and your wife will be very happy here in Carolina."

Almost as if she had heard their words, Flora turned her head. Leaving Bluff Hector, she came over and sat down next to Allan, her hand on his arm.

"The night is so beautiful," she murmured, "the air so soft and fragrant." She looked up through the moving branches of the trees to the sky. "See, Allan, there is our star. Think, darling, it has followed us here—it will bring us happiness in this new world." She moved a little so her shoulder rested against her husband. The pipes were playing the old lament; the singers' voices seemed a part of the night.

"Is there any room at your head, Saunders?
Is there any room at your feet?
Is there any room at your side, Saunders
Where, fain, fain wad I sleep?"

Mary saw a tear glittering in the eye of the woman, and she shivered, though the night was warm.

"There's nae room at my head, Marg'ret.
There's nae room at my feet.
My bed it is fu' lonely now.
Amang the hungry worms I sleep."

Allan threw his arm across his wife's shoulder. She did not look at him—she was staring with fixed eyes at the night sky. Mary slipped away, leaving them alone. She could not stand

374

the look on Flora's face without the quick tears rising to her own eyes.

Across the lawn the guests laughed and danced, following the quick marching rhyming of the pibroch.

Mary and William left Cross Creek in the morning. Although they started shortly after sunup, the village was already deserted. The Highlanders had departed up the river and across the pine barrows to their farms along the Deep and the Haw.

William rode horseback, followed by a stable boy, leading Mary's horses. Mary sat in the back of the chaise, with Ebon on the box and Cissie beside him. She leaned back against the cushions, her mind on the events of the past two days. Adam had changed. She almost wished he had been angry with her; that he had remembered they had quarreled when he saw her last. But he didn't—he had forgotten. He was indifferent now to any emotion, save his depression over the dark future of their country. She could bear his annoyance, even his anger, but his indifference left her desolate, without hope.

Her thoughts turned to Flora Macdonald and she felt ashamed of her own weakness. Whatever Flora hid in her secret heart, the face she showed the world held the tranquillity and dignity of a great soul. Mary did not know why tears filled her eyes. She let them fall unheeded—there was comfort in tears.

They stayed in Catawba Springs more than a fortnight. Mary was rested by the quiet routine of the days—drinking the waters, walking in the quiet wood, following the little streams banked by waxen-white dogwood and the purple of the Judas trees.

The day they got back to Queen's Gift, Samuel Johnstone came over. He gave them the news that the Governor had lifted the Act of Oblivion in Adam's behalf. Mary was glad—the whole thing was so unjust—so wrong.

"Martin knows when to be diplomatic," Samuel said to William. "He prefers to be generous, rather than have the Assembly pass the pardon over his veto."

Adam Rutledge, announced by Ebon, came into the room. A few moments later, Maurice Moore and Caswell rode up. Maurice was holding court in the northern end of the Province. They fell at once to talking about provincial affairs. Ebon came in to say a messenger had come from the South. William excused himself and left the room.

"What is the situation in New York, Adam?" Caswell asked.

"Were you in the North, Rutledge?" Moore interrupted. "I thought you had been in the Illinois country."

"I came back from the Mississippi by way of Fort Pitt so that I could meet my wife in New York. I had a good chance to observe the people along the way."

"What is the talk in the West and North?" Moore asked.

" 'Unite the Colonies' is their first thought. I agree it is the only way we will have the strength to oppose England and get our demands from Parliament."

William came back into the room.

"A cup of tea, William?" Mary asked.

"I don't think I have time, Mary. I came to tell you that I'm leaving at once for Charles Town on urgent law business."

"I'll see that Ebon packs your clothes," Mary said, and left the room.

When she came back all the men, except Adam, were gone. He was sitting beside the window reading the *Post-Boy*. When she sat down, he came over, holding out his cup for more tea.

"I'm inviting myself to supper with you tonight, Mary."

"You know how welcome you are, Adam," she said. She turned as the door opened.

William came into the room, dressed in traveling clothes. As he bent over to kiss her she thought he looked worried and disturbed. "Don't get up, my dear," he said. "I must hurry. Farquhar Campbell and De Rosset are waiting for me now in the village. I'll send you a letter by courier as soon as I arrive at Charles Town. Good-by, my dear."

Mary followed her husband from the room. In the hall, she kissed him again. "I'm sorry to have you go, William. I thought you would stay here at Queen's Gift and we would give a little time to the plantation now that it is spring."

"It is impossible now, Mary," he said. His smile was almost tender. "When I come home, I'll take a week's rest, and we can settle the plantation affairs then."

She stood for a moment in the shadowy hall after he had gone before she went back in the drawing room where Adam was waiting for her.

They walked in the garden after dinner. The night was warm; a soft wind was blowing, fragrant with early flowers. Adam told her of the new country that had been his home during his banishment—the house he had built on the bluff above the spot where the great river of the West swept its yellow flood into the Mississippi. The living there was untrammeled and free, he said, not bound in or circumscribed as it was here in the Carolinas.

Mary watched his face as he talked. He seemed to be far away from the small, compact garden. Fear lay heavily upon her; she shivered a little. Adam was instantly solicitous for her comfort.

"Are you cold, Mary? Shall I get you a shawl?"

"No, but let us go inside. The nights are still chilly; the fire will be comforting."

She wanted him inside, within the four walls of the room. She wanted him sitting close to the warmth of the fire, his eyes fixed on familiar things, not looking beyond the narrow Sound, dreaming of a far river that she did not know. For a little time, she wanted him alone, encircled by her thoughts.

Ebon was laying a fire. Adam drew a chair close to the hearth. "Sit here, Mary. Have Ebon light the candles."

"No—not yet. Let us sit for a little time in the firelight," she said.

"I wonder what the Province will say to the Governor's last proclamation, accusing the Assembly of insubordination," she said, after a few moments of silence.

Adam laid his hand on hers. "Don't, please!" His voice was low. "Tonight let us forget politics. Let us forget what we must face tomorrow. Let us talk of you—of us. Tomorrow, we will throw ourselves into the torrent."

He drew his hand away and settled back. Ebon had come to light the candles. The lights flickered up, throwing shadows against the white walls. She knew he would never mention the quarrel that had lain so heavily on her heart. He had forgotten it. Men were like that—they lived actively, their minds crowded with the work of the moment. It was the women who brooded, who lived in retrospection. Suddenly, her heart was light.

When Ebon left the room, Adam turned to Mary. "Tell me about my son," he said. "How does he look? Has he grown tall? And his mother? I must confess, I've just come from New Bern. I stopped at Queen's Gift to see you before I went to the plantation."

Mary could not answer immediately. The bright moment had gone. She could never quite recapture it. She found herself speaking of the Arab woman and the boy, telling him how often she had gone to see them at the North Plantation. She told him of David sitting at Owen's feet for his lessons; of his riding about the plantation on his Arab horse, following Haskins; of his playing with Lucy's boy and with the small grandson of Cicero, who was his shadow.

"What do people say about David?" he asked.

Mary shook her head. "I do not know, Adam. I have never talked to anyone in the village. What does it matter? Azizi does not understand our conventions. She is very proud because she has your child. She sees no one but Lucy and Marcy, Owen and Gwennie and, of course, John Hawks. They talk together in their language and are good friends."

Adam got up and paced the room restlessly. "Owen wrote me that she was ill. What was the illness?"

Mary shook her head again. "Dr. Armitage did not know. He gave her a bitter tonic to give her strength. I think it is something else that ails her—she grieves for her own people and her own country."

Adam lifted a book from the table and put it back without opening it. Mary could not see his face.

"Sara has never spoken to me of Azizi or the child—yet she must know. Do you think she has ever seen the boy, Mary?"

"Not that I know of. But if she has seen him, she could have no doubt who his father is."

"Is the likeness so apparent?" he asked, not looking at her.

"Yes, in looks and actions both. He is very tall for his age. The older he grows, the more he is like you—above all when he is on a horse. He is afraid of nothing. His mother is very proud of him then. She says he rides as Arabs ride—man and horse are one."

Adam sat down again, his long sensitive fingers busy with the seals on his fob. "I have had much time to think things over while I have been gone. I've made rather a mess of my life, Mary, but there is nothing I can do about it now. I don't want David to grow up hating me—knowing. I have decided that I will take him out to the Illinois country when he is a little older. I have talked to Renault, one of the settlers there; he will have no objection to David's marrying his little Héloïse."

"Adam! Why the child is no more than seven or eight years old, and you talk of marriage!"

"I know, but I must plan ahead for him. When I was in New York, I met young Hamilton. He is—" Adam hesitated an instant, then went on—"his father and mother were not married, but no one seems to think of the circumstances of his birth. He has lived his life with courage and dignity and is already a man of importance, heart and soul with the Colonies.

I hope my son will grow to be a better man than his father," he ended bitterly.

Mary put out her hand, protesting. "Don't, Adam, don't say that. There are circumstances which we cannot control. I have come to believe that we are moved forward by our destiny in some strange unknown way." She laughed a little. "Azizi and Hawks have influenced me. I'm somewhat of a fatalist, I think. Destiny unfolds itself in its own way."

Adams smiled without replying. After a time, he said, "I have come home with my mind made up to talk to Sara. This thing stands between us like a great black wall. It grows blacker and higher as the years go on. We are so far apart we haven't a thought in common, now less than ever. Sara will always be a Royalist like her father. Shs has no use for the 'rabble.' Her friends in New York are the British officers and their wives. I have tried often to explain my point of view, but it is no use—she will not listen. She will never really forgive me for what she calls 'slipping out of my class' at Alamance."

"What does Sara intend to do when the revolution comes?" Mary asked.

Adam shrugged his shoulders. "She says she is going to London this summer and stay there until we come to our senses—and until I come back."

"You are leaving soon, Adam?" Her voice was low.

"I don't know yet. I expect Sara tomorrow. She is coming down by boat. It depends on what there is to be done here. I would like to get back to Cahokia before next harvest."

"The new land really holds you, doesn't it, Adam?"

"In a way, perhaps, but only when I think of my son. In David's lifetime, the land here will all be taken up—divided into small parcels. Already they are cutting it up into townships and sections. Mine was the last large holding under an English grant. Commerce and trade will come, but land is, and always will be, the basic source of wealth, Mary." He smiled a little. "We're quite primitive out there; we need no money. We need only produce to trade. When more settlers come, that will be changed. Money will be printed, banks established." He grew silent, looking steadily at the fire, as if seeing into the future. "These problems will belong to my son, and he must meet them as best he can." After a time, he continued: "For myself, I'm glad that I'm one of the vanguard. I'm more interested in the fight against the forces of Nature. I like the struggle against hurricanes and winds that lay waste the growing crops and uproot forest giants; heavy snows that freeze and break down the soil or the mighty force of great rivers at flood that ravage the land. It takes strength to stand against Nature, Mary, and a stout heart. There is no place for weak men in new country."

She could not take her eyes from him. All that he had just said had been written in his face. A new land was a world for strong men, not weaklings.

"Suppose the settlers come with their money and their banks in your time? What will you do then, Adam?" she asked.

Adam smiled. "I can always follow the road to the setting sun—another great river to its source. On the high plains at the headwaters of the Missouri there is room for another empire. But that is in the far future. Today, our minds are full of something else: How we can hold the little freedom we have won."

Mary watched him striding about the room as he talked. She thought, "He has gone a long way from the man who was content to cultivate a few thousand acres at Rutledge Riding —a strong man, grown to full stature."

Mary considered what Adam had said about the Illinois country far into the night, yet her dreams were not of him. She dreamed of the Highlanders—a long line of Blue Bonnets marching to war, led by Tammy the Piper.

Chapter 24

APRIL NINETEENTH

In April Mary came back to Edenton from New Bern on a small boat with John Harvey and Adam Rutledge. Two men from Virginia were on the ship. They had come up from South Carolina and they brought word that the feeling of the people was the same there as in the North. The breaking point had come. Everyone was waiting for the signal. As they talked, Mary sat near the rail watching the water. Grey-green waves moved endlessly, beating against the small ship, against the land. The pounding surf kept echoing one word: wait—wait.

They came into the Sound and sighted the Rutledge Manor House at sundown. The red brick house and the Island lay in a sea of red gold. Every windowpane caught the red gold of the setting sun—flaming and flashing with a hundred facets of fire. It was as if the whole earth were ablaze, caught in a conflagration that swept down from the very heavens.

Mary stood at the rail with Adam. "I have never seen a sunset like this in my life. The earth's a ball of fire from its center to the farthest horizon. It is so violent, it seems to catch us up and hold us. We are so puny—so helpless. Adam, I'm afraid!"

She felt him draw closer, felt the touch of his arm, the comforting strength of his shoulder.

"There is something majestic in the red fury of the sky, Mary. It has been so calm all day, now this for a home-coming." He turned. "Let us remember this day, Mary, and this evening sky." His voice was low, affectionate.

"Let us remember," she repeated after him. "What day is it, Adam? The days on the ship have been so quiet, one like the other. I have lost count."

Adam smiled down at her. "April nineteenth, seventeen hundred and seventy-five. We will remember it as a day when a golden sun turned to blood red."

"The nineteenth of April," she repeated after him. "I will remember."

Adam insisted that Mary stay overnight on the Island. In

the morning he would go as far as the North Plantation with her. Sara would want to see her and talk to her about New York and the new gowns she had from London.

Lavinia met them at the boat landing. She, too, had been impressed by the red sunset. She spoke almost the same words as Mary. "It makes me afraid somehow. It is so strange, so unreal, as if the red sky foretold a tropical storm, or is it a forecast of some terrible happening, like the old Biblical prophecies?"

She went with Mary to her room in the wing that looked out on the East Garden, and kept up a running comment on plantation news. Peyton was home; he had been in Edenton that day. Sara was improved, she thought, though some days she was very fretful, almost morose. The black woman, Judith, still watched over her with ill-humored vigilance. Her animosity toward Adam was so obvious that Lavinia wondered why Sara tolerated it.

Lavinia got up quietly and went toward the door. She opened it suddenly, looking down the hall. Satisfied that they were not overheard, she spoke to Mary about Azizi. Once she had seen Judith talking to little David. She was sure the black woman was spying. Sara had become even more religious. She read her Bible for hours at a time, yet she was bitter as ever about people. Dr. Armitage said she was improved in health but Sara would not admit it.

Mary changed her traveling dress to a dull green silk that made her skin look like ivory and brought out the warm red lights in her chestnut hair. She did not want to discuss Sara so she made no reply. Lavinia did not appear to notice her silence.

"I think Adam will have to talk to Sara about David. The child is so much like Adam that anyone who sees him will recognize him as his son. I think he had better send him off to school somewhere. He is old enough, almost eight now."

Mary pinned a stray curl into place behind her ear. "It would kill Azizi to be separated from the child," she said as she looked at her hair with the aid of a hand glass. "She is so intense—she loves the boy so much. We do not understand the nature of such women, Lavinia."

"Just the same, Adam can't evade the matter much longer. He will have to plan for the boy. It isn't fair not to. Owen thinks the same. He says the child must be sent to school. Talk to Adam, Mary. He trusts your judgment."

"I can't very well unless he asks my advice, Lavinia."

382

"He is sure to. Sara will force the issue in some way, and I don't know that I blame her very much."

Mary said nothing. She sat down on a low chair to put on her buckled shoes. Lavinia moved about the room. She reminded Mary of some graceful feline, a leopard or a panther, by the grace of her long-limbed body.

"Do you believe we will break with Great Britain?" she asked abruptly, stopping in front of the dressing table.

"Yes, I think it is inevitable."

"Do you think it will come right away?"

"I don't know, Lavinia. No one knows."

Lavinia sat down on the window seat. All the gayness was gone from her voice. Her eyes were heavy. "I'm so afraid. I can't sleep at nights. Peyton tries to put me off, but I know. He will go away with his company. They are drilling at Edenton twice a week now. They try to keep it secret, but they can't. You know what war will mean? Peyton will go at the very beginning. Oh, Mary!" She put her hands to her face trying to control the trembling of her voice. "Then it will be my son. He will follow his father, and I will be left—waiting. Why can't they make peace? What does it matter what kind of peace? Only leave me my husband and my boy. I cannot bear it, sitting day after day waiting—waiting—waiting."

Mary was silent. How could she answer? What could she say to comfort Lavinia, to strengthen her against the inevitable?

"Let them make peace with the Governor," Lavinia said passionately. "Adam, John Harvey, Judge Moore, Richard Caswell and Samuel Ashe—they could make peace. Let them give way. What does it matter? Let them think of the women and the mothers."

Mary spoke very gently. "You would not want these men to betray their people with false hopes, Lavinia. It would only be putting off the inevitable for a little while."

"You can say that. You can be strong, Mary Warden. You have no son."

Lavinia's words were a knife thrust. Mary steadied herself. When she spoke, her voice was dispassionate. "I have no son, but if I had, Lavinia, I would rather have him die than accept peace without honor."

She rose and started for the door. There was a swish of silks and Lavinia came running after her. Her soft arms held Mary close. "I'm sorry, sorry. I'm beside myself. Forgive me, dear Mary."

Mary kissed Lavinia gently. "I understand, Lavinia, I understand."

Sara came to the dining room in a wheel chair which Judith pushed into place at the table. She greeted Mary with more animation than she usually showed. Adam and Peyton hastened to kiss her and Lavinia waved her a gay greeting. Sara dismissed Judith who left the room reluctantly. Mary saw her pacing up and down in the East Garden, peering in through the windows.

There was no doubt in Mary's mind that Sara had improved. Her cheeks had color, her eyes were bright. She was pleased to be sitting at her own table again and was very gracious to everyone.

Peyton asked Adam about the effect of the Committee's report on the Assembly. Sara interrupted. She wanted to hear nothing about horrid politics. She had heard all she could bear in New York. It was only a matter of time until all the disloyal and rebellious Colonists would be whipped into line. She had heard from Sir Henry's own aide, Captain Eastbridge, that more regiments were being sent which would be stationed in Massachusetts and all the other Colonies and Provinces where there was seditious talk. She felt ashamed of the actions of some of the North Carolinians. She glanced quickly at Mary, then looked away.

"Everyone in New York laughed about the Edenton tea party," she said. "They even had cartoons in some of the London papers. Mary's name was mentioned as being one of the leaders."

Mary smiled a little. It didn't matter to her what people thought or whether she was the laughing stock in fashionable New York drawing rooms. But Adam was embarrassed and Peyton smiled at her reassuringly, as if to say, "Don't mind what Sara says."

Lavinia came to her defense. "You wouldn't say that, Sara, if you knew what it meant really. You have been away from the Province so long you have forgotten what the people here have suffered. Mary is considered a heroine among us. She is known throughout the South as the foremost Whig hostess. More great men are to be found in her drawing room than at the Governor's Palace, and I believe more plans for the good of the Colony have been formulated under her roof than in the Assembly halls."

Sara smiled, unimpressed by Lavinia's words. "I know Mary has always had a penchant for rebels, but the King's men, are they to be found in her drawing room?"

"They would come there if Mary would let them. General Macdonald told me he had never met a more intelligent woman in the Colonies, or in London, than Mary Warden." Lavinia's tone was indignant.

Mary saved the situation from becoming too serious. "That was delightful of General Macdonald. It shows he holds no grudge, for only last week I bought a hunter he coveted right out from under his nose while he was haggling over the price. I call that very decent of him, Lavinia."

Sara smiled. "Still hunting, Mary?"

"Not so much as I used to. The men were all so busy last autumn that we could get only a few together. But we had some good runs." She turned to Adam. "Did you introduce hunting into the Illinois country when you were there?"

Adam laughed. "No. Hunting out in that country does not mean riding to the hounds. It means going out to kill bears or panthers or wolves."

"How uncivilized, Adam!" Lavinia exclaimed. "I see there are none of the refinements of living in the West."

Sara broke in. "Adam has done nothing but talk about the house he has built there and the French furniture he is having brought from New Orleans. In New York, they think it unpatriotic to buy goods in France. Let us talk of something more agreeable than rebels against the Crown."

Adam rode as far as the North Plantation with Mary. He was silent, unlike himself. From time to time, she glanced at his strong profile. The lean line of his jaw and his firm chin made him look stern. She wondered what he was thinking about but did not attempt to break into his meditation. When they were fording a small creek he spoke to her.

"I'm thinking about David. I want him to be fond of me and trust me, but I do not know how to go about it, Mary."

"You will not find it hard. As I told you before, David likes the things you like. He digs in a garden Gwennie has set aside for him, and he rides all the colts. Take him riding with you around the plantation, Adam, and see if you don't become good friends quickly. He has been riding my Arab lately, which pleases Azizi."

Adam nodded. They trotted along for some distance silently. Suddenly, he turned to her, his hazel eyes troubled. "A man has many thoughts when he lives to himself as I have done much of the time during the past years. He wonders about many things. Life presents more mysteries the more he thinks. I found that when I rode through the forests in the West, cut off from the world, my mind became cleared of unnecessary influences. What I'm trying to say is that Azizi is not so important to me as she was. I feel a great affection for her but the passion that consumed me seems to have burned itself out. I wonder if you can understand what I mean? I am not so inconstant in my emotions as that would indicate, but it is the truth."

Something in Mary leaped into life. He no longer loved Azizi. He had never loved her. Passion—yes, but not a love that would endure.

They were skirting the boundaries of the North Plantation. Suddenly Mary reined her horse.

"Look, Adam!" she said, pointing with her whip. "Look, there he is."

Across the field they saw Gilsen riding a grey mare. Close behind him was a small figure on a tall horse, riding hard. The bay of hounds came to their ears.

"They are trying the young bitch pack!" Mary exclaimed. "How well David rides, Adam! A splendid seat! Look at him take that brush fence!"

Adam's eyes followed his young son. Mary watched his changing expression. She did not know what thoughts raced through his mind, but she was sure he felt proud.

Gilsen caught sight of Adam. He pulled up his horse and with a word to the boy rode over. David's face clouded. He looked from the newcomers to the milling pups. Gilsen called him, and he rode forward with reluctance. Mary engaged Gilsen's attention so that Adam could have his son to himself. They rode slowly down the road together. It was better so. Whatever relationship developed between them must come about naturally. She had a glimpse of Adam as he turned to David. The look on his face was one of intense sadness.

Mary found that Edenton buzzed with excitement. The Governor had sent for more troops. He was raising companies among the Cross Creek Highlanders and the Regulators who were still terrified for fear that he would punish them for the old rebellion. The Palace fortifications were being strengthened. A brace of cannon were now placed before the building. Ammunition and arms had come by ship from General Gage in Boston.

When Dr. Armitage rode out to Queen's Gift early one morning some time after Mary's return from New Bern, he had an air of excitement about him. He insisted that she dismiss all the slaves who were working in the hall near her morning room so he could talk with her without interruption. He had had a letter from New Bern by private courier that morning. Three leading Whigs had seized the cannon while the Governor and his council were in session in the Palace and had carried the guns away.

Martin had witnessed this act of overt defiance from the open windows of the Palace. He knew his life was at stake then. Followed by a few men, he had fled from the Palace that night by the secret passage to the river and there had boarded a sloop-of-war.

"So now we are without a Royal Governor," the Doctor said triumphantly. "Do you realize what that means?"

Mary was alarmed by Dr. Armitage's news. Her first thought was of William. He had been away for months now —his stay had been beyond his expectations. Would he be shut off, unable to come back by way of Wilmington?

Armitage hitched his chair close to her. "This is the most important thing, Mary," he told her. "I have a confidential message that Colonel Ashe is to resign his commission as Colonel of the militia. He will immediately begin collecting a body of troops among men loyal to the Colony. Any day we shall be hearing from them."

They were interrupted by slaves shouting outside the house and by the sound of galloping hoofs. Armitage went quickly to the window. A man was galloping up the driveway, leaning over the neck of his sweating foam-covered horse. When he saw Mary and Dr. Armitage, he pulled up. He was a courier from Nansemond on his way to New Bern with news.

"The British are defeated—the British are defeated!" he shouted through his cupped hands. "The battle of Lexington has been fought and won!"

"When?" shouted Armitage, putting his hand to his ears. "When?"

"On the nineteenth of April at Lexington, Massachusetts," the courier shouted back, as he wheeled his horse. "Tell all the people in your district that the colonials have got his Majesty's soldiers on the run." His voice was gay and he waved his hand as he galloped down the drive.

A thought flashed through Mary's mind. "The nineteenth of April," the courier had said. That was the night the sun had turned the whole world red. The nineteenth of April— Adam had said they must always remember that day. Now there was another reason for remembering it. The march of troops had begun. The earth would tremble under the heavy devastating tread of marching feet.

The Doctor was speaking to her. "Do you mind if I have a sip of brandy, Mary? My knees are trembling. I'm getting to be an old man—an old man, my dear."

Mary pulled the bell cord. "Then I'm old too, Doctor. My knees are wavering, my hands shake, and the pit of my stomach feels as if a giant hand had clutched it."

The slaves were gathering in the garden. A spokesman came to the door to say that the men were afraid.

"Missy," Ebon said, "better you speak to them."

Mary stepped out onto the gallery. Fifty or sixty men and a few women were standing in a group near the fountain. Their frightened faces were turned to her. She must quiet them. She had heard that the Governor had sent men out among the slaves to stir up unrest, to incite revolt by promising them freedom. She wished William were at home. He would know what to say. After a moment words came to her.

"There is no need of fear. In the North, many days' journey from Edenton, there has been a battle against the King's troops, and the King's troops have run. It will be the same here if there is a battle. The King's troops and those of the Governor will run. You must all be quiet and go about your work, and I will see that no King's soldiers come near this plantation. You understand?"

And old man stepped forward, his battered hat in his hand. "The men say to Missy that they will not let the King's soldiers hurt she."

Mary looked at the upturned faces of the faithful slaves. She was touched. "Thank you, Andrew. I will be glad to have you protect me. Now go to your work. Tonight I will have the over-looker give each man and woman an extra portion of rum."

In the drawing room Dr. Armitage had been standing behind the curtain watching her. "I was ready to come out if you needed me, Mary. But I see that you can manage by yourself. Perhaps it is as well. You women will have to run all the plantations now. The slaves must look to the women for orders when the war begins."

"The war has already begun," she answered. "The courier is riding. The news that he carries will reach New Bern in three days and Wilmington in another four or five. It will be picked up by one man after another throughout the length and breadth of the Colonies. A week, two weeks, or three— and all the people will know that the British have been defeated at Lexington, and that revolution has begun."

Armitage drained his glass. "You are right, Mary. I must be getting along. I have much riding to do before nightfall."

"And I, too," Mary said, walking toward the door.

"Will you go to Rutledge Riding, Mary? The courier will not stop there for it is off the post road. I think Adam should know this at once."

Mary came upon Adam as she rode past Chapman's Corner. First she saw Herk on the road leading three horses, and then she saw Adam and David down by the beaver dam. Adam was on his knees on the bank of the stream, David kneeling beside him. When she called to Adam, he stood up and beckoned to her. He was building a small dam in the stream to divert the water. Near the bank was a little building of stone with a water wheel, a miniature mill.

"We are making the mill pond, Aunt Mary," David called to her. "Come, see the way the water turns the little wheel."

Adam was wiping his wet hands.

"There has been a battle, Adam. At Lexington. Our men defeated the King's soldiers," Mary said.

"How did you hear this?" Adam asked, coming quickly to her side.

"From a courier on his way to New Bern."

"Look after David, Herk," he called to the Zulu. "Mrs. Warden and I will ride to Chapman's Corner. Take the boy back to the North Plantation when he is through playing." He turned to Mary. "I have been waiting, wondering when the news of the first northern battle would come."

She said impulsively, "I thought you were going back to the West, Adam. Does this make a difference?"

Adam nodded. "I can't go now. They will be calling us any day to serve in the militia under Ashe. I must stay until I have done my service."

At the Corner they came upon the courier. He was eating while his horses were being changed. Under Adam's questioning he told them that the militia was drilling all through Maryland and Virginia. The sound of martial music was echoing throughout the states. War . . . war . . . was the word on every lip. Delegates were hastening to the Congress in Philadelphia. The North Carolinians—Caswell, Hooper and Hewes—had been greeted with bands which escorted them through the streets of every city they passed on their journey North.

The courier finished his meal and mounted his horse. Mary watched him gallop down the post road through the blossoming hedgerows. War . . . war . . . He was riding past green fields with the grain showing; past blossoming gardens; following rivers and forests where waxen-white dogwood bloomed beside bushes of redbud. Riding—riding—to carry a tale of war and revolution. She put her hands to her trembling lips to keep from crying out.

At North Plantation, she parted from Adam. She would stay the night with Gwennie and return to Edenton in the morning. She did not want to talk to Sara or hear her ranting against the Colonies. Gwennie would be quiet and calm. Owen would accept the news without question. He had long believed that the destiny of the land was to be drenched with blood—watered with the blood of its defenders. The dragon's teeth had been sown long before. Armed men would spring to life from the warm, soft earth of the Carolinas to defend the land.

Along the post road a tired courier was riding—carrying the story of battle and the defeat of the King's army.

Chapter 25

MECKLENBURG RESOLVES

PUBLIC affairs were in an alarming condition. Small groups had been gathering together and meeting secretly throughout Mecklenburg County. It was time they felt to take public action. At the instigation of Dr. Brevard and the Alexander brothers, a meeting was called to select two delegates from each militia district who were to take into consideration the state of the country and adopt such measures as seemed to them best to secure life, liberty, and property from the storm which was gathering.

While they were in convention, a messenger came with the news of the battle of Lexington. Inflamed by reading this dispatch, Dr. Brevard proposed that the twenty-five men gathered set forth Resolves couched in forceful language. An awful and solemn moment had come. Men shouted and cried out: "The cause of Boston is the cause of all."

United, the Colonies would force a settlement of grievances. North Carolina would not lag behind. Her sons would stand forth as men of action, not as men who spent their days in idle talk.

"Let us act with energy as brethren leagued together," shouted Alexander, the chairman.

The Resolves were written at once. There was to be no mistaking the vigor of the people of Mecklenburg, or their opinions. They absolved themselves from all allegiance to the British Crown and abjured all political connection, contract or association with the nation who had wantonly trampled on their rights and liberties, and had inhumanly shed the blood of innocent patriots at Lexington. They declared themselves from now on to be a free and independent people—a sovereign and self-governing association under control of no power other than that of God and the general government of Congress.

Mary learned about the Resolves first in a copy of the *South Carolina Gazette* which lay unopened on her husband's desk. She turned the paper over and found it was the issue of Tuesday, June 13, 1775. How strange it was that no one had heard of the Mecklenburg Resolves in Edenton! It must be that the news had gone first to Charles Town. She knew that the traffic took a southerly direction from Charlottetown. There had been other occasions when William had known of events that transpired in the western counties from his Charles Town correspondents before the news reached the Coast.

She researched the last issue of the Cape Fear *Mercury*. The Resolves were not printed in it but another item caught her attention. It was one of Governor Martin's proclamations from his ship:

". . . . and whereas I have seen a most infamous publication in the Cape Fear *Mercury*, importing to be a set of Resolves of a set of people styling themselves a Committee for the county of Mecklenburg most traitorously declaring the entire dissolution of the laws, government and constitution of this country, and setting up a system of rule and regulation repugnant to the laws, subversive to his Majesty's government . . ."

Mary sat looking at the paper, her thoughts racing. Rebellious words had been spoken, spoken boldy without fear of consequence. Mecklenburg had done with soft words. They were the first to take their stand, to throw off the heavy yoke of the House of Hanover.

A few weeks later, when young Peyton came home from the Mecklenburg plantation, he brought the full story. He had ridden as far as Salisbury with Captain Jack. The Captain had been commissioned to carry the Mecklenburg Declaration to the Congress, then sitting in Philadelphia, and to deliver the Resolves to the North Carolina delegation.

The young boy was very much excited as he talked to his father and Adam at Mary Warden's house the afternoon of his arrival at Edenton.

"When we got to Salisbury," he said, "we stopped to change horses. One of the Committee, who lived in the town, asked Captain Jack to read the paper at a public meeting. The bold language of the Resolves incited the people of Salisbury, as it did when Dr. Brevard read them from the Courthouse steps at Charlottetown. But at Salisbury two men objected."

"What happened to them?" Peyton asked his son.

"It was very exciting, Father. There was almost a riot. The two men—they were lawyers—said the Resolves were treasonable. They tried to have Captain Jack detained. Oh! he was splendid, Father! He drew his pistols and said he would kill the first man who laid hands on him. Then he jumped on his horse and rode away at a gallop."

Mary watched the boy as he told his story. He had grown as tall and handsome as all the Rutledge men. He must be nearly sixteen. As she listened to him she thought of Lavinia. Lavinia could not keep him back any longer. He had suddenly moved out into the world of men.

"Where were you when this all happened, Peyton?" she asked.

Peyton turned to her. A slow red came to his olive skin but his eyes had the same direct glance that Lavinia's always had.

"I stood close to Captain Jack. You see, I had come with him."

"Did you draw too?" Peyton sharply demanded of his son.

"Yes, Father. Was that wrong?"

His father clapped him on the shoulder.

"Wrong, by God, no! I should have had the overlooker take the blacksnake to you if you had turned tail." He laughed.

Adam turned to Mary. "I think it is time that the Edenton district followed the example of Mecklenburg. We should declare our position, then raise our militia to the full quota."

Peyton and his son rode together to Rutledge Riding. Adam lingered.

"I am pleased with David, Mary," he said after they had discussed Peyton's story for a few moments. "I take him riding with me every day. It is extraordinary how well he manages the hunters and takes the jumps. He is a shy child with an amazing amount of unrelated knowledge. Owen pours Greek and Latin philosophy into the boy and his mother alternates between filling him full of Arabian poetry and tales of the prowess of desert Arabs in battle. That doesn't leave much to me but to teach him things that he must know about the land."

Mary took up some sewing from a small basket. "Have you ever considered sending David to King William's School, Adam? He is old enough, I should think."

"Yes, I have thought of that, but not now—not now. I want him with me as long as I can have him."

Mary turned the end of a seam, watching Adam's face from under her lashes. It seemed to her that when Adam spoke of the boy, his voice changed and grew tender, that his face softened. "How he adores the child," she thought, and was saddened by the tragedy of it. How could he carry the responsibility of fatherhood when he could not say to the world, "This is my son"? Mary knew from the little things Adam let fall that the situation was becoming intolerable. Why didn't he go to Sara and say to her, "I'm going to have my son under my roof and bring him up to live as I live." What held him back? Sometimes she was on the verge of saying to him: "Face the consequences. Don't be afraid." Sara would make a fuss and probably threaten to go to her father. But Mary didn't believe she would. It was one thing for Sara to make long visits to New York or London when she did so of her own accord, but to be forced to go because of some outside reason—that was a different matter. Sara had too much pride. She had a clever way of making all situations seem to be of her own choosing.

Adam moved restlessly about the room from the door to the window and back to the table where Mary sat. He picked up the end of the bit of linen on which she was sewing, holding it for a moment with his firm, strong fingers.

"I suppose I'm being selfish. I should think of the boy. If you only knew how I value each moment with him, you would understand my reluctance to do anything now that involves change. Change is coming so swiftly from outside ourselves that I want to hold to what I have as long as I can. Any day now we may be called. It appears quiet here in Edenton because we are in the backwash. But we will not always be. Before long we will be in the very heart of conflict. We cannot avoid it. That is why I want to keep my son near me."

He dropped into a chair, his long body sunk deep in the cushions, his head in his hands. Mary knew the things he had just said required no answer. He was talking not to her but to himself.

She looked up from her sewing from time to time. He sat without moving—lost in deep abstraction. She could not follow him into the secret depths of his soul. He was a solitary figure, remote and withdrawn from the world. As she thought back through the years he had always been solitary, absorbed in his own thoughts, carrying through his work in his own way. He was a strong man. He needed no one. His life had made him strong within himself. His habits of living, his habits of thinking were his own. Often, as he sat near her, she knew he had retreated into some deep inner recess which she could not fathom. At these times, she sat quietly, not speaking. When he wanted her he would come to her, ask for her help, her understanding. That time had not come. When it did it must come from his choosing, not from hers. She must sit quietly and wait.

A servant announced that Dr. Armitage was in the drawing room.

"Tell the Doctor to come here," Mary said.

Adam straightened his hands on the arms of the chair. "How kind you are, Mary. I think no man ever had a more perfect friend than you have been to me."

Tears came to her eyes. She dashed them away with the back of her hand. "It is dear of you to say that, Adam. I value your friendship more than you can ever know."

Armitage came into the room. His face was white and heavily lined. "John Harvey has been killed," he said abruptly. "He fell from his horse. His heart gave out. I have been warning him for months not to ride but he laughed at me. Now he is gone."

"What will we do without him?" Mary said.

"We have lost our best leader, Mary. There was no stronger or more unselfish man in the Province than John. God's peace be upon him." Armitage wiped away the tears that had gathered in his faded eyes. "Friends for thirty years," he mumbled. "I shall miss him sorely."

"I intended to ride over to his place today," Adam said to Mary. "We will have to find someone else to write the Edenton Resolves now."

The Doctor, with his hands thrust deep in the tail pockets of his coat, paced up and down the room. "He will be missed. He will be missed by everyone. I wish to God he could have been spared and the Governor and some of the Tories had been taken in his stead."

Mary smiled shakily at the Doctor's vehemence. "Samuel Johnstone will be the head of the Whig party in this district now. You will have to work out the details of Adam's idea of the adoption of an association with him."

"What association are you talking about?" the Doctor inquired. "Why haven't I been told about this?"

"I have been talking to Mary about following the example set by the people of Mecklenburg. It would be a sort of test of the patriotism of the people. Resolves to be signed by each and every freeholder in the district."

"A very good idea, Rutledge. I'm sure Johnstone will be glad to hear your suggestion. Why not see him today? I'm going that way myself. I will be glad to go with you."

Mary went back to her work—she had to keep busy to regain her composure. She was glad Adam was at home. He was a tower of strength. He would not act hastily, but he would stand firm. That was what was needed now—men who would stand firm and steady.

The months that followed were filled with intense excitement. The spirit of resistance was abroad in the land. Governor Martin was in seclusion on the sloop-of-war *Cruizer*, issuing agitated proclamations, singling out the rebel leaders for denunciation. Caswell, Hewes, Hooper, the delegates to the Continental Congress, were denounced in violent language. They replied in kind. "The powers of Government must soon be taken over by the people. . . ." The administration tried to incite the Indians on the frontier and the Negroes on the plantations but without success.

Bunker Hill and Lexington gave the people courage to resist. But the sympathies of the Province were divided. Royalists took their stand against the Whigs. The Assembly met again without the Governor. Some men tried to walk both planks. They were soon discovered and made to declare their position publicly. Friends of long years became bitter enemies. Brother turned against brother, husband against wife. What the future would bring was doubtful, but everyone knew that the day of reckoning, long postponed, was at hand. "Traitor" became a word of common usage. Committees of Safety were formed. Minute Men enrolled. Caswell's militia was up to full force, drilling daily. From the pulpit and kirk, voices were urging the people to stand on their rights. What was to happen? No one knew. Leaders must be found—men who would take on the responsibility. But who?

Out of the masses, men began to step forward. Some, already leaders, took their places naturally. Others, young and untried, frightened by the weight of responsibility thrust upon them too early, went forward tremblingly, fearful of the consequences that might come if they took the wrong way or made a wrong decision. In each village and hamlet, men took the step that placed their names among the rapidly growing group who were declared traitors to the Crown and whose lands were held confiscate.

Adam Rutledge's name was one of the first to be published. He took Mary the broadside which branded him a rebel and traitor. "At least I'm in good company," he said, as they examined the lists. "We are all in by name, Samuel Johnstone, Armitage—here I am: 'Adam Rutledge, the chief instigator in a project to hold a convention in Hillsborough on the twentieth of October that is unlawful and subversive to the Constitution.' "

"Martin's ranting like a wild man, Adam," Mary said, as she handed him the paper.

"More like a man who is afriad, I think."

Adam folded the papers and put them in his pocket. Mary watched him. She noticed again how the lines in his face had deepened. Each day seemed to age him.

"What do you think all of this amounts to? Will anyone be influenced by these words?"

"A few, I suppose. I think it is Martin's dying effort. Denouncing the Whig leaders viciously may give him satisfaction. He must have very little to do on board his Majesty's ship *Cruizer,* and after all, Mary, he is still the Royal Governor. He will be until we take over the government and run the Colony ourselves."

Adam left Queen's Gift and rode to the wharf where Marcy was waiting with a boat to take him to the Island. It was past sundown. The crimson afterglow reflected in the water as the boat put out. A light wind filled the sails. Marcy sat at the tiller, tacking the boat from side to side to catch each puff of wind. Adam sat aft, his eyes on the shore. He could see it all, the long stretch of shore line, the water boundary of North Plantation, the blazing windows of the Manor House on the wooded island, his no longer by proclamation of a Royal Governor who was still the Law. Adam Rutledge, traitor to the Crown, did not own an acre of ground in the Province of North Carolina.

"Let them take it from me," he said aloud. "Let them send their soldiers and their sloops-of-war. By God! I'll fight as long as there is life in my body."

Marcy looked up with inquiring eyes. Adam was aware that he had spoken aloud.

"Martin has issued a proclamation," he said.

Marcy laughed. "I know—named us traitors. Confiscated our land. Damn him! Let him take it if he can!"

"That's just what I was thinking," Adam said, a smile on his face. "He'll find we are not easily intimidated."

Adam returned from the Hillsborough Convention elated over the enthusiasm and determination of the people. The Convention had taken over the business of running the state. Adam told Armitage and Mary about the meeting the day he got back. Men had been sent to South Carolina to buy gunpowder. He had dispatched more men, under the leadership of Enos Dye, to the Illinois country to see what could be done about mining lead in the territory west of the Mississippi. Bounties would be offered for the manufacture of linen and woolen goods, of saltpeter, sulphur, gunpowder, common salt, and ironware. Rolling mills were being hastily built to make nails, furnaces for the manufacture of steel and a mill was going up for making paper.

"What about the military? Are the plans all made?" Armitage inquired.

"That will be in the hands of John Ashe. He has sent you a commission, Doctor. I will give it to you when my boxes come."

"Bless me! Have I a commission?" The Doctor's face was beaming.

Mary went over and sat on the arm of his chair. "Did you think that the militia of North Carolina or the Minute Men could keep in good health without you?"

"You will be Chief Surgeon of the 2nd, John Ashe's, regiment. You are to get your men together and they will be given their commissions at once."

"Serve with John Ashe? That is splendid! Where are we to get the money for supplies, Adam? I'll need instruments and medicines. Mary, your Edenton tea-party ladies can start scraping lint."

"Ashe is financing his own regiment so that the money will come from him," Adam answered.

"In that case, I'll furnish my own supplies. I can't have John Ashe take all the glory," Armitage said testily but with a twinkle in his eyes that made Mary laugh outright.

"You should have seen John at the meeting," Adam told them. "He came into the room in a state of prodigious excitement. His words rolled like the beat of martial drums. 'Let us away! Let us arm!' he shouted. Like the Athenian orator, he called, 'Let us march against Philip!' He roused the members by his passion. Men flocked to join his regiment. Next day hundreds of men were wearing printed bands on their hats— 'Who will not follow where Ashe leads?' The Minute Men, not to be outdone, got bands too—'Who will not follow where Lillington leads?' They are riding through the Province now at top speed, enlisting men from every county."

William came in while they were still talking. "What regiment am I supposed to join?" he asked, when Adam finished. Mary thought his tone was sharp, as if he did not believe what Adam was saying about the enthusiasm of the meeting.

Adam turned around when William spoke. "Your name

was brought up as a Colonel in James's regiment. But Johnstone would not give his consent. He says he wants you here, near him. He has selected you as one of the Provincial Council. He said he needed your knowledge of law and your sound advice in these troublous days."

Mary saw a shadow cross William's face. It was gone in an instant. It could not be fear. Was it disappointment? Surely he did not want to go into the militia! Adam and Armitage were both looking at him.

"How splendid of Samuel Johnstone to do that. That is the place where you will be most valuable to the Province, William," she said to cover the silence.

"It will mean I shall have to spend much time away from home, Mary. I suppose the Council will sit at New Bern."

"At different places, I believe. The December meeting will be in Johnston County at the Courthouse. You are one of thirteen men chosen to guard the destiny of our country, William. I congratulate you."

William nodded but made no direct answer to Adam. A few moments later he excused himself and left the room.

"And Adam, what of you? Are you listed to be a general?" Armitage asked, his eyes twinkling.

"Not yet. A captain in my uncle's command at the moment. I'm on special duty attached to the Edenton forces—special work under Samuel Johnstone. Peyton has been made a captain, also. He is detailed to recruit the Minute Men in Albemarle. Lillington is his commander."

Mary thought how hard this would be for Lavinia. She decided to go over to the Island to see her before the week was out. There was one comforting thought, Peyton had not been drawn for duty in Virginia or South Carolina. If there was no invasion of the Colony perhaps they would never have to fight. Martin had no troops. She said as much to Adam.

"A thousand Highlanders have landed at Cape Fear, Mary. More are arriving on every ship. Martin has asked Sir Henry Clinton for troops to be sent down from New York. Our Committee has ordered three armed ships for defense, one to be stationed at Wilmington, one at New Bern and one here at Edenton."

"You are sending an armed ship to Edenton for defense?" Mary exclaimed. "Why, Adam? We will never be invaded here. We are too far away."

"No place is too far removed to have protection in case of invasion of the Colony by land or sea. Edenton might be used by the Royalists as a base to invade Virginia or the interior of the state or as a wedge to divide the North from the South."

The Doctor stood up and wound his long woolen scarf about his thin throat. Adam picked up his heavy cape.

"I must be getting on, Mary. I'm going back to the Island tonight. I want to get to the North Plantation before dark. I promised David I would bring him a long bow. He will be waiting up for me."

Mary watched them mount their horses and ride down the long tree-lined driveway to the post road. From the window of her yellow drawing room she could see the green waters of the Sound and the Islands to the south. A few fishing boats under full sail were beating back from the banks, the rising wind billowing their sails.

The Indian summer had been long that year. Red leaves and gold still clung to the maples and gum trees. Dried leaves, caught by the wind, rustled against the windowpanes. They whirled and eddied, sweeping across the barren lawns. Slaves at the far end of the garden were raking leaves. Presently they would set a light to the pile and the air would be filled with the acrid odor of burning leaves and wood smoke.

She stood for a long time watching the changing light in the west. She shivered a little although the room was warm from the log fire. She said to herself, as she had often said before, "It will not come. Something—some miracle must happen to prevent revolution." But deep within her she knew she was not facing the truth.

That night she lay awake in her great mahogany bed. The tang of wood smoke hung in the still air. Through the open casement window she could see the embers of the leaf fire glowing in the darkness.

It crossed her mind, as she lay there in her tranquil room, that in every part of the Province men were awake—bending over maps—toiling over lists of supplies—making plans for the defense of the Province. It was like that from the northernmost boundary of America to the southern gulf. Wakeful men—drilling, marching, making ready to defend the land.

What part would the women play in the days to come? Would they sit at home waiting, always waiting; waiting and scraping lint from linen cloth? She buried her face in the soft pillow. God of Mercy, how could she bear the heavy burden of waiting?

Chapter 26

SARA
RUTLEDGE

LAVINIA, wrapped in a red cape banded with fur, waited for Mary at the landing when the ferry touched the dock. The air was sharp and cold, and a strong wind was blowing off the Sound. They hurried into the house. Lavinia took Mary to her own room in the east wing. Mary fumbled with the buttons of her furred cloak, but her fingers were numb. Lavinia came to her aid.

"I wanted to talk to you before you saw Sara. I can't quite explain what has happened but she seems even more cross and irritable than usual. One can scarcely speak of the political situation without her bursting into a violent temper."

Mary listened, her feet close to the blazing logs. "Perhaps she is ill again."

"No. She is improved if anything. It's that woman Judith. I think she has bewitched Sara!"

Mary looked at Lavinia's colorless face, her dark circled eyes. "Nonsense!" she said energetically. "Such things are old wives' tales, Lavinia. You know that."

"That's what I always thought before, but strange things happen here—uncanny things."

Mary moved out of range of sparks from the logs. After a moment she said, "For instance?"

Lavinia did not raise her eyes from the floor. "I can't say exactly. It is a feeling. No one can get near Sara. Judith always has some excuse."

"You mean no one ever sees her? No one?" Mary's tone was sharp-edged.

"Not exactly that. But we see her only when Judith chooses to wheel her chair into the drawing or dining room."

Mary's eyes moved slowly about the room. She had an uneasy feeling that there was something morbid about the atmosphere of the house.

Lavinia leaned forward. "I have seen Judith coming from the North Plantation twice within a week. I think she spies on Azizi and David. I suppose you think me absurd. Perhaps I am, but that black woman means to harm them—I cannot get the idea out of my mind, try as I will."

She got up and paced the room nervously, her fingers clasping and unclasping. Mary saw that she was greatly disturbed. She tried to calm her by speaking in a matter of fact way.

"I wouldn't think of it again, Lavinia. It is just your imagination. What could happen to Azizi or her child? They are quite safe under Owen's care."

"I hope so," Lavinia said. Her face in the subdued light was working. Her voice was unsteady. "I hope so, Mary. Perhaps I am full of imaginings now." She sat down again, as if she were very weary. "Mary, I'm going to have another child in the spring."

That accounts for her imaginings, Mary thought. She leaned forward and put her hand on Lavinia's arm. "Dear, dear Lavinia, that must make you very happy."

Lavinia made no response. She sat looking vacantly out the window.

After a time she whispered, "Pray for me, Mary. Pray it is not a boy, to march away to war. Pray that I may keep Peyton's love, Mary. He swears he never loved Lady Caroline, but I can't be sure. I started to talk to you last Christmas Eve but you seemed so cold, so unsympathetic that I couldn't."

Mary turned questioningly to Lavinia. "I—cold—unsympathetic? What nonsense!"

Lavinia shrugged. "Perhaps it was my imagination. What I wanted to tell you was that Peyton was going to the Indies again. They say she is down there. Oh, Mary, why do I make myself so unhappy by jealous fears?"

Mary sat down beside Lavinia and took her hand. "You must not allow your mind to create these illusions, Lavinia. You know Peyton loves you."

"Perhaps it is my condition," Lavinia said, blinking back the tears. "I'll try not to worry. It isn't good for me to worry now. But I think we all shall die of this waiting, Mary."

Mary had no words. She patted Lavinia's hand which lay on her lap. Life was beating Lavinia. A sudden sense of weariness came over her; the whole room seemed filled with shadows. Her body was tired, her head heavy.

The door opened slowly. Judith stood in the doorway. "Missy will see you now, Mis' Warden. Better you stay no longer than a few minutes. Mis' Sara she feel weary this day."

A look of understanding passed between Lavinia and Mary. Mary got up and followed the Negress down the long stairs, through the quiet, gloomy halls.

Sara sat in her chair near the window, a small table with her work at her side. She greeted Mary indifferently and began at once to talk of the utter futility of the Colonies' trying to stand against Britain. "Farquhar Campbell was with us a few nights ago," she said, "and he told me that the heart of the Province is loyal to the King."

Mary did not deny this. She did not wish to get into an argument. Sara talked on in a hurried voice. "Adam has gone to Virginia; he has been called there to settle some affairs of his father's estate with his elder brother, Paige. He will be gone a month or more.

"I might as well have stayed in New York, for all of being with Adam," she complained. "I'm going to Annapolis to be with my father the first of the year. Adam is home so little these days. A week here—a week at Mecklenburg plantation —then off to New Bern or Williamsburg. He isn't as he used to be—never off the plantation." She turned her wide eyes to Mary, a puzzled frown on her smooth brow. "I can't think what is coming over people—everyone so nervous, so distrait, so changed."

Mary looked at the fragile, almost doll-like woman. She thought, "Sara hasn't changed. She is still a child. She doesn't comprehend what is going on about her. It is incredible."

"I manage to keep busy, Sara. There are always things to be done on the plantation now that William is gone so much."

"I venture to say the Whiggish gentlemen can account for most of your time," Sara said. "People tell me that there are meetings at your house almost every day now. How can you allow it, Mary? Surely you have too much sense to be on the side of the rebels!" She took up her tapestry and was soon intent on the skeins of wool, selecting a strand from the tangle of colors.

Mary watched her, thinking, "Does she not realize that Adam is one of the leaders of the rebels? Does she have no conception of the seriousness of the situation? Or is she slyly baiting me to find out things that Adam has not confided to her?"

"Of course, I am a rebel, Sara. Haven't I always been on the side of the underdog?"

"But such impossible people, Mary! The riffraff and rabble

of the Colonies. Why should they want to revolt against a good and gracious king?"

"They don't. What they really want is not to break with England, Sara. Don't you realize how long it has been since Lexington? They are still trying to convince the British Ministry that if they make concessions, there will be no revolt. The leaders are trying by every means to get redress of their grievances without an actual break with the Mother Country."

Sara held off the skeins to match the colors, her head on one side, her attention completely absorbed. The room was silent except for the rhythmic ticking of the clock. After a time, Sara laid the tapestry on the table at her elbow. In turning she dropped her handkerchief to the floor. She made a futile gesture with her hands.

"I will have to ask you," she said. The words were a confession of her invalidism. Mary stooped to pick up the square of lace-trimmed linen. "Thank you, Mary. You have no idea what it means to be able to do things for yourself." Her voice was touched with resignation and pathos.

Mary said nothing. It flashed across her mind then that Sara had some reason for allowing her to come in alone, without Lavinia. She would be on her guard; she would not allow her to find out anything that had to do with the affairs of the Committee. Sara wrote often to her father and information of importance might easily travel through letters to the ears of men high in authority among the Royalists. But she was surprised by Sara's next words.

"You have seen the son of my slave girl, Azizi, haven't you, Mary?"

Sara had caught her off guard after all. There was no use trying to evade the direct question, for Sara knew that Mary went frequently to the North Plantation.

"Yes, I have seen David," she answered.

Sara spoke softly without meeting Mary's eyes. "I sent the girl away when I found she was with child. I could not have her here. I suppose the child belongs to one of the overlookers?"

Mary was speechless. How could Sara practice such duplicity? But of course she had no way of knowing that Lavinia had told Mary that Sara was completely aware of the whole situation.

"I'm thinking of having Azizi back here again. I have never found a slave who was so quiet about the rooms. I am ill so much that I must have quiet."

Mary made a strong effort not to show her thoughts. She wanted to ask her if she had talked to Adam, but she did not dare.

"I'm having the little brick cottage in the East Garden put into repair," Sara remarked as if the incident were closed.

"But what about the child?" Mary found herself asking.

"He can stay over at the North Plantation, or Marcy can have him sold. I can't be troubled by children of slaves around the Manor House."

Mary saw how well Sara had laid her plans. By the time Adam came home from Virginia, Azizi would be established in her old cottage in the Garden. There was no one with the authority to prevent such a move. Owen could not; Peyton was away. Perhaps Lavinia could manage to keep Sara from bringing the Arab girl back to the house as her personal servant.

"I understand from Dr. Armitage that Azizi has not been very well. Is she strong enough for housework?"

Sara turned her cold blue eyes on Mary. "I need a slave to do my work. If the girl is not healthy enough to undertake the light work she would be required to do here, I will have Haskins send her to the slave-market in Wilmington." There was a finality in her tone that gave Mary no opportunity for further words. "Do you mind pulling the bell cord? I find I am a little weary. I think I will have Judith put me to bed."

Mary crossed the room to the fireplace and pulled the bell cord with a quick jerk. Sara's tapestry slipped from the table to the floor. As Mary put it back on the table, her eyes fell on the open Bible. The page was open at the sixteenth chapter of the book of Genesis. Without conscious thought on her part, the page and chapter impressed itself on her mind.

Judith came quietly into the room with her soft stealthy walk. She leaned over the chair, lifting Sara's frail body with a sweep of her arms. "Better go now," she said to Mary, in her flat lifeless voice. "Better you go."

With a word of farewell Mary left the room. She had a glimpse of Sara's face as the Negress moved across the room to her bed. Her eyes were closed and the color had left her face. Her suffering must be intense, Mary thought, and a wave of sympathy swept over her. Day after day confined to her room, living with her own thoughts. The inevitable must happen. A warped mind would distort and twist, grow narrow and inflexible. Although Sara accepted Adam's relations with the slave girl as natural she was still incapable of forgiving him. Mary tried to see things with Sara's eyes. What would she have done? When she asked herself that question she was confused. She could not imagine what her own feelings would have been in like case.

A week later Armitage stopped at Queen's Gift on his way home from Hillsborough to beg a cup of tea. Mary insisted that he stay for supper.

"There has been great excitement over suspected spying," Armitage told her. "Persons tell me confidentially that they have had men watching Farquhar Campbell for some months. He is under suspicion of working in secret with the Governor and the leaders of the Highland clan. Outwardly, he is heart and soul with the Whigs and sits in the Assembly. This is very secret, Mary. I confess it shocked me. I like Campbell and don't want to believe that he is a traitor to our cause."

Mary did not have time to answer, for the servants came in just then and set a small table by the fire. Armitage moved to the table with alacrity.

"I confess to an appetite. I have been riding since early morning with not a bite to eat."

After the slaves had left the room, he returned to his subject. "They say Farquhar was with Martin when the Governor fled from the Palace by his secret stairs. They have a letter, purporting to be from the Governor's secretary, asking Campbell to arrange for a safe conduct for the Governor's horses and carriage so that he can come secretly to Farquhar's house in Cumberland. This may be a tale but the Committee is making every effort to investigate the truth before any accusations are made public."

"If it is true?" Mary asked.

"The people are in no mood to deal lightly with spies these days, Mary," the Doctor replied. "If treason is proved, it may cost him his life."

Mary dropped her fork with a clatter. Her frightened eyes were fixed on Armitage's thin, lined face. He was eating his food with placid satisfaction. How could he talk so lightly of death and traitors? It was all very well to speak dispassionately of an abstract case but he was talking now of what might happen to a friend if he were found guilty of being a spy.

He said, between mouthfuls, "Short shrift for spies: blindfolded and shot, or hung to the nearest tree. Good riddance, I say."

406

"How can you speak so calmly of such a frightful thing!" Mary exclaimed.

The Doctor looked at her over his spectacles. "War carries the swift punishments of war, my dear Mary. Traitors to their country are dealt with immediately as an example to others. It is right that they should be punished without delay." There was a deadly finality in Armitage's voice, quite different from the usual kindly tone or the irritability he sometimes assumed. "I advised them not to take hurried action in this instance. We want to win the Highlanders of the central part of the Province to our cause and Campbell has influence."

Mary sighed. There were so many phases to the business of rebellion that had not occurred to her. She leaned back in her chair, unable to swallow another mouthful of food. After a time, her mind turned to the conversation she had had with Sara about the slave girl Azizi. She would tell the Doctor. He might be able to convince Sara that she must not have the girl on the Island. Armitage could tell Sara that Azizi was ill, unable to work. Anything to keep her from bringing Azizi over before Adam got back.

A look of incredulity crossed Armitage's face when she told him. "That is a diabolical idea," he said. "It comes from this religious mania that has got hold of Sara. We can't let it go on. It will cause endless gossip that will harm Adam. I told him long ago to take the woman and child away but he would not listen to me. Now you see what will happen."

Mary leaned forward. "Just what will happen, Doctor?"

"Why, there'll be gossip, probably a scandal. Why can't Sara let it alone? Why should she wait all these years and then cause all this trouble? Women are the very devil, Mary!"

"The question is, how are we to stop her from bringing Azizi to the Island? She is her slave. Adam bought the girl for her to be her personal servant."

"Yes, yes. I know all of that." The Doctor was impatient. "But Azizi is no ordinary slave woman. Besides, Adam told me that he had freed her long ago. I shall go over to talk to Sara in the morning."

"I hoped you would say that, Doctor. You can do more with her than anyone."

Armitage drew his heavy brows together. "I wish Adam were here to settle this thing himself instead of getting me into it. I don't like it, I tell you, Mary. I don't like it. I've often wondered how it was that Adam Rutledge, that strong

407

and self-controlled man, got himself in this sort of mixup. Now if it had been Peyton, I could have understood."

Mary watched the old gentleman take out his gold snuff-box. She had wondered the same thing more than once.

"But the girl is a lovely creature, and I suppose—" he sneezed violently. "If only wives could learn a little more natural allure, it would be better. Husbands wouldn't go astraying," he grumbled. "However, that wouldn't apply to Adam, with Sara as she is. He must have some woman to lie with—at his age, with his vigor."

Armitage poured himself a glass of port. Mary stirred uneasily. She could not answer the Doctor's alarming frankness. If only he would stop talking about Adam. But what could she say that would not expose her to the piercing gaze of the Doctor's shrewd eyes?

He sipped the port slowly, raising the glass to the light. "It may be that Adam really cares for the Arabian girl. He did for a time. Remember I saw him when the child was born. He was like a man distraught—" he wiped his lips. "And I strongly suspect Sara knows that Adam is the father of the boy."

Mary watched the ruby liquid turn to blood-red where the light of the candle touched the glass.

"Why couldn't Adam have been like other men around here, taken the woman and let it go at that? But, no, he must get his emotions involved—wants to keep the bastard child."

Mary half rose from her chair. "Oh no! You must not say that."

"Why not? A spade is a spade. The boy will hear the word often enough. You women are too prone to ease over the truth."

Mary knew he spoke the truth, but it was a truth she did not want to acknowledge. How would Adam be able to protect David from all the tragic heartbreak? How—?

Armitage was watching her closely, his head bent forward. "You love him, Mary," he said. "It is a pity he hadn't the sense to come to you in the first place. With all his wisdom in some things, Adam is a fool when it comes to women. His father was before him, in a different way. He took whatever woman he coveted without much ado; he never allowed his emotions to become too involved. His wife managed to see that none of his little affairs lasted very long. Adam should have chosen you, Mary Warden."

Mary said nothing. What could she say in answer to his devastating frankness?

Chapter 27

THE BOY
DAVID

ADAM came back from Virginia in January. Mary did not know he had come home until Lavinia drove over from the Island to see her. Lavinia was more beautiful than ever. Her eyes had a look of sadness that somehow enhanced their beauty. Young Peyton was with her. The elder Peyton was in the South organizing the Minute Men. Something had happened between Sara and Adam, Lavinia told Mary, although she did not know what it was. Mr. Hammond was coming in the spring to take Sara with him to New York to some new doctor who had made extraordinary cures. Mary said nothing. She was wondering why Adam had not come to Queen's Gift.

A few days later he came. He had been called to New Bern to give an account of the activities in Virginia before the Council and, first of all, he had delivered Patrick Henry's report. Mary listened quietly. The sound of Adam's voice contented her so that she felt at peace. He stayed only a short time, as he was on his way to see Samuel Johnstone, but he said he would stop on the way back and stay for dinner if Mary would allow him.

He did not mention the rumor he had heard that Lady Caroline had been in the Colonies once more—in Virginia this time, as a guest of the Governor. He had tried to find out where she had gone but could discover no trace of her excepting that she had sailed south.

Mary walked across the back veranda that connected the kitchen with the dining room to talk to the cook about dinner. As she passed by the little office where William worked when he was home, she saw a light. But before she could call to William she heard him speaking to someone she could not see.

"Campbell must have these papers at once," William was saying. "He understands how they are to be sent on after he has read them and made copies. Did you see General Macdonald?"

A strange voice answered. "No, but I met Allan and his
409

wife, Flora. They were riding through the whole district. She is enthusiastically received everywhere. All the Scots are curious about her. They want to see the woman who hid the Young Pretender and saved him from capture. And they love Allan. I saw him on the banks of Deep River talking to a goodly crowd of Highlanders. He had a plaid thrown over his shoulder, and his bonnet with its knot of blue ribbons was on the side of his head. His tartan waistcoat was fastened with gold buttons and he had on a bluish filibeg and tartan hose. He made a brave show. The people shouted and hurrahed and many came to kiss his hand. He has more influence with the people than the General, Mr. Warden."

"That is not good. It should be General Macdonald, not Allan, who commands their loyalty. People soon forget their heroes and turn to those who make the most display. But I must not keep you. Go direct to Campbell with the papers. Make haste and be on the lookout. There are many ways in which a man may be robbed these days."

Mary walked slowly past the window. She was disturbed by what she had just heard. What could it mean? Was William . . . She refused to allow her mind to give birth to the thought. After giving directions to Chaney she went to her room to change her gown before dinner.

William came in when she had nearly finished dressing. He wore his heavy traveling coat and carried his hat in his hand.

"I'm sorry to leave in such hurry, Mary, but I have been called to a meeting of the Provincial Council at New Bern. I'm going at once by post-chaise." He kissed her forehead and stood for a moment as if he were debating whether to say something more. His mouth had a shadow of a smile that did not reach his heavy eyes.

"When will you be back?" she asked.

"I can't tell, Mary. In a week, I should think. Good-by, my dear."

Adam came back at dusk. The moment Mary saw him, she realized that he was greatly disturbed. As soon as they were in the drawing room and the door had closed behind the slave, he said, "Samuel Johnstone has just had word by courier from the Committee that the Loyalists are getting ready for insurrection in the Deep River district within a few days."

Her eyes caught his anxiously. She found herself saying, "Oh, Adam! not that—not a fight between our own people."

Adam went on, "I'm afraid so. The information comes from most reliable men. The Highland Loyalists and the Loy-

410

alist Regulators have made some sort of deal. General Donald Macdonald is to be in command. For days he has had his messengers out, secretly planning for all Scots loyal to the King to rally to the Royal Standard at Cross Creek."

Mary caught at the back of the chair for support. A terrible fear took the strength from her knees. William's visitor had been talking about that! What did it mean? She opened her mouth to tell Adam about the conversation she had overheard, but she hesitated. Would she be placing William in danger? Surely there must be some explanation. Perhaps William's unseen visitor was bringing the information that had been sent to Samuel Johnstone. The thought lifted the load on her heart. She wanted to believe in William—she must believe in him!

Adam was looking at her, his steady hazel eyes searching hers. How could she destroy his faith in William or her own by voicing suspicions that might be unjust? She managed to smile a little. Adam's face cleared.

"I thought you were going to faint, Mary. You turned so white."

"Did I? I'm quite all right. I suppose I must be a little tired. I rode miles today. Sit down, Adam. I want to hear more of Cross Creek. Are they going to stop it if the rumor is true?"

He began to pace the room, his habit when he was worried or thinking deeply. "I'm not sure. Johnstone's report is meager. The Committee of Safety will probably direct Caswell to call out the militia and march to Cross Creek to suppress any insurrection on the part of the Highlanders."

She spoke quickly, horrified at the thought. "But that would be Civil War! They won't—they can't—" she paused, looking at him hopelessly.

Adam's words came slowly. "I know what you are thinking, Mary. It is one thing to talk of fighting against professional soldiers sent here from England—or mercenaries—but to shoot at men you know, men who have been your friends—"

Another thought came to her, driving out the others. "Will you have to go, Adam?"

"Yes, certainly. I'm going down with Johnstone in the morning." He looked at his watch. "I should go home now."

Mary stopped him. "Don't go until after dinner, Adam. I —" Again she was on the verge of telling him of the conversation she had overheard in William's office—but something held her back. She moved across the room and sat down. The

411

color had left her face again, accenting the deep shadows under her eyes.

"What is wrong, Mary? You look ill." Adam pulled a chair up to the sofa where she was sitting.

Mary felt suddenly far away from him. Her mind was full of the problem of William. Adam's voice forced itself into her consciousness. "You must not let this news weigh so heavily on you, Mary. It is only the beginning."

She made an effort to pull herself together and picked up her knitting. She would not allow herself to worry nor to imagine things that might not be true. Adam sat quietly, his long legs stretched to the fire. He, too, seemed buried in thought. There was no sound but the sharp click of needles. What was he thinking that made him so grave? Perhaps, he knew more from Johnstone than he had told her. Her mind flew to something else. Had Sara really carried out her threat and brought Azizi back to the Manor House?

Adam seemed unmindful of the passing of time. She cast a fleeting glance his way. He had dropped his head, shielding his face from the firelight with his long thin hands. After a time he moved uneasily, as if he felt the silence. He drew himself up and his eyes met Mary's.

"I'm sorry. I'm afraid I'm not very good company this evening."

"Something troubles you, Adam?" she ventured.

"I don't understand Sara," he said suddenly. "She insists that Azizi must come back to the Island. God!" he burst out. "What a mess I have made of things! What a hopeless mess!"

Mary looked at him, her heart full of sympathy.

"What did you say to Sara?" she asked.

"As always I evaded the issue. I told her that the girl was not able to work."

"What did Sara say to that?"

"Nothing. She sat and smiled. I'm sorry to say I lost my temper."

"You defeat yourself when you lose your temper, Adam."

"I know. I said things I should not have said but there was something about her complacency that enraged me. I should not be complaining of Sara even to you. I'm ashamed, but no matter how I try, I cannot get past some barrier she has set up. If only I could have made a clean breast of the whole affair—told her everything. But Sara has a knack for making me stop short of what she considers unpleasant subjects. I used to be very upset when we had arguments. Now I'm indif-

412

ferent, or annoyed—never hurt as in the past. Mary, I no longer love Sara, nor she me. We are two people bound together who have no means of adjusting ourselves to living in peace and happiness."

Mary's needles clicked. Let Adam talk. Let him say the things that had been weighing him down.

"I suppose a man should manage to find some way of living so that he has at least an agreeable domestic life. But I have not found the way." He dropped his head into his hands.

Mary wanted to put her arms about him to comfort him, to tell him that he was not at fault. But how could she without betraying herself? She laid down her knitting and moved to the fireplace. How clear-cut his profile is and how strong the turn of his lean jaw, she thought as she looked at him.

"Sara does not mean what she says," she remarked after a moment. "She is only making a threat which she will never carry out."

"No, she is serious. She is determined to have Azizi where she can watch her, I'm sure. She has some plan—or that woman Judith has."

Mary remembered Sara's words. Should she tell Adam what Sara had said about selling Azizi and the boy? She decided not to speak of it. That was surely only a threat. Sara didn't mean it.

"Perhaps she wants the child near her," Mary said, wondering why she made such a false suggestion.

Adam shook his head. "No. She can't want that. I've already made arrangements to send him to school here at the Edenton Academy until next autumn. Then I shall send him to Annandale to go to school with my brother's boys."

Mary felt relieved. "That is a good plan, Adam."

"I should have done it before, Mary. You said so. Owen advised the same but I wanted to keep him near me. I have grown very fond of the boy." He paused, unwilling to show his emotion. The look in his eyes made Mary feel very tender toward him.

"I know, Adam. A child can wrap itself around your heart."

He did not answer but sat gazing at the fire. After a little, he took out his watch, the dangling seals clicking sharply. Mary knew what he was going to say before he spoke.

"I think I will not stay for dinner tonight after all, Mary. If I ride fast, I can get to the North Plantation before nine. I

413

want to tell Owen what is happening, and give Marcy a chance to pack so that he can go with me. And I can see David—" He did not finish the sentence.

Mary did not demur. She wanted him to stay but she could not press him.

He stood tall and broad, shutting out the light from the fire. When he took her hand, a tender smile softened his lean, kind face. "Why do I always come to you with my troubles, Mary?" Slowly the smile faded. A look of bewilderment came into his hazel eyes, changing into something deeper. His fingers closed over hers.

They stood for a moment looking into each other's eyes without speaking. Then he put his arms about her, drawing her to him, his lips against hers.

"Mary, how blind I have been," he whispered.

Chapter 28

PRELUDE
TO BATTLE

ADAM rode into Colonel Caswell's camp at nightfall. He had been on detached duty for nearly three months, traveling through the Province. He guided his horse through the maze of tents and bivouac fires to headquarters. Tossing the reins to Herk, who rode with him, he passed the sentry and lifted the flap of the Headquarters' tent.

He saw Colonel Lillington of the Minute Men bending over a rough table spread with maps. Two cots, some cuts of timber turned on end for seats and a long table of rough board furnished the tent. Lillington, in the new uniform of the militia, glanced up as Adam entered. He nodded toward a stump.

"Have a chair, Captain. Colonel Caswell will be back shortly."

Adam sat down on the hard seat. He was weary, worn out by the ride across the mountains through the driving rain. He was soaked to the skin, but he was used to that for he had been so for the past two weeks. Sometimes he wondered whether he would know how to get into dry clothes if he had them. Lillington seemed to have forgotten his presence. His brows were knit, his face grey and drawn as he worked by the light of a hurricane lantern. Presently he pushed the map aside and looked up.

"You look as if you need sleep, Captain. Let's not wait for Caswell to come. No telling how long he will be delayed. He is with General Moore of the Regulars. That may mean hours of discussion."

Adam took a packet of papers wrapped in oilskin from the pocket of his cloak. They were from Alexander—a detailed report of the western counties.

Lillington laid the packet on the table without opening it. "I won't read this now. I'd rather have you tell me yourself about Charlottetown."

Adam lighted a pipe. "Things are very quiet at the moment," he said. "I think most of the people who live between the Cape Fear and the Haw on the east, and the country

415

bounded by the Yadkin on the west, are largely on the side of the Governor and the King. This is due to the influence of the Macdonald clan. In fact, all of the Highlanders and many of the old Regulators are with Macdonald at Cross Creek now. Macdonald has a strong camp—five thousand men at least, and more arriving daily."

"You have all this on good authority, Captain Rutledge?"

Adam grinned. "The best! I came through their lines last night under cover of darkness. So I had a chance to estimate the numbers."

"Um!" Lillington grunted. "You were taking chances. I didn't know they had that many. Any other news?"

"On the fourteenth, the sloop-of-war *Cruizer* passed Brunswick. Martin was aboard. In fact, he is using the *Cruizer* as his official residence! Many people of Wilmington have fled, especially women and children. They are afraid of an attack on the city. Breastworks were thrown up by the Minute Men of Brunswick, guns mounted and fire rafts ready, but the *Cruizer* passed on up the river without firing."

Lillington made some notes on a paper. "Go on, Rutledge," he said.

Adam leaned over the map. "The *Cruizer* attempted to go up the Claredon River here. The intention evidently was to support Macdonald when he marches to Wilmington and to protect his provision boats. There wasn't enough draft for the sloop to pass so she moved back into a position behind the Island." Adam got up to stretch his cramped legs. "I stayed one night at the home of a loyal Whig. I found out while I was there that Colonel Rutherford, whom we thought loyal to our cause, has gone over to General Macdonald. A number of others have followed him. Rumors are flying around that Martin, with five thousand Regulars, would march to Campbelltown. So I went there to see for myself."

Lillington glanced up and down Adam's tall frame, a slight smile on his lips. "Aren't you a rather conspicuous person to try that sort of spying, Captain?"

Adam smiled ruefully. "I am handicapped. Once or twice I got into a tight place. They say the Macdonalds are riding up and down the rivers, the Haw, the Deep and the Yadkin, recruiting for General Macdonald's Royalists. They say too that Flora and her daughter are following the example set by the duchess of Gordon when she recruited for the Gordon Highlanders."

"What's that?"

"Offering a kiss and a gold piece to every lad who signs up

416

to follow the King's standard under General Donald Macdonald."

"We must not underestimate the influence of Allan Macdonald, and as for Flora—" Lillington paused.

"All I can say is that I wish Flora Macdonald saw eye to eye with us instead of being on the side of the King's men." Adam took a turn or two in the narrow space between the table and cots. "If Bonnie Prince Charlie had been a better man than he was, the Stuarts might have been on the throne instead of the pigheaded Hanoverian."

"No good wishing. We must put our minds on action now. God! Where's Caswell! We must make plans to stop Macdonald before he can march to Wilmington."

As Lillington spoke, Caswell came into the tent. Lillington and Adam rose to their feet, but Caswell waved them to their seats. He sat down and took up the report.

"You were right about Macdonald, Lillington," he said when he had finished reading. "He's got more men than I estimated. We will have to use our brains and ingenuity to outwit him. Adam, any news from Albemarle district?"

"Not too good, Colonel Caswell. My men report that Lord Dunmore threatens to invade from Virginia. His spies were intercepted near Edenton, trying to stir up trouble among the Negro slaves." Adam searched through his pockets and found a letter. " 'The spies came to Rutledge Riding,' my overlooker writes. 'We took two prisoners but let them go at Johnstone's advice. The slaves on the plantation gathered in a great crowd and shouted, Kill the spies! Kill them! We had all we could do to stop them.' "

Lillington laughed grimly. "They should have strung them up on the gibbet."

Caswell shook his head. "Johnstone was right. The men will go back to the people who sent them and report that the slaves in Albemarle district are loyal."

"Do you have anything definite about the King's army attacking from the north, Rutledge?" Lillington asked.

"Yes, Colonel. The plan is that the whole Royalist army under Dunmore will come down from the Virginia line to attack the northern counties. At the same time an attack by land and water will be launched from the south under General Cornwallis, who has sailed from England with a large number of ships. The middle section of the Province will be subdued by Macdonald. That is the plan of the North Carolina campaign according to my information."

Caswell turned to Lillington. "Who is in command at Edenton?"

"Colonel Robert Howe with a skeleton regiment."

"And Lord Dunmore's army? Do you know its strength, Captain?"

"I do not know the number, but it is supposed to be large. Dunmore offered freedom to the blacks and indentured men if they would join him. So the regular troops are augmented with a low order of whites and slaves."

"Did you see Howe?"

"No, I did not go north, sir. These reports came to me from one of my reliable men."

A young officer came to the door and spoke to Lillington who followed him out of the tent.

"How long since you have been home, Adam?" Caswell asked.

"Almost three months, Colonel."

A feeling of nostalgia swept over Adam. Three months of moving from one end of the Province to the other. He hadn't minded it so much until now when it was time to think of spring planting. They would be getting ready to plow for tobacco at Rutledge Riding. It seemed to him that a great wall was closing around him—a wall that he could not break through. He would never go back to his land—never.

Six or seven officers came in with Lillington and sat down at the long table.

"Captain Rutledge, gentlemen," Caswell said, by way of an introduction.

Adam saluted. Lillington made room for him on the bench.

"Captain Rutledge, will you please explain to these officers the location of Macdonald's army and the probable course he will take in his march to Wilmington?" He pushed the map across the table. "There, mark the route."

Adam bent over and pointed to a spot on the map. He continued with a detailed account of Macdonald's plan to take Wilmington and make it serve as the permanent base for naval and military forces of the Royalist army.

There was a momentary silence.

"A pretty scheme, by God!" said a man Adam recognized as Thrackston. "What do you say, Colonel?"

"First catch your hare," Caswell growled. "It is possible that we may force his hand a little. What do you think, Lillington?"

Adam said to his uncle, "If you have no further use for

418

me, Colonel Caswell, I will go on. I've orders from Johnstone to proceed to the coast at once."

Caswell walked with him to the door of his tent. "I have had word from the Continental Congress recommending that we confer with Virginia and South Carolina on plans for the defense of the South. They say Sir Henry Clinton will strike here first. If we don't defeat Macdonald, he will march troops north through Virginia. If that happens, General Washington and his northern army will all be caught in a vise between two strong British armies, and our cause will fail."

"Can you tell me why the Continental Congress does not act?" Adam asked. "Excepting for our Resolves, not one Colony has actually had the courage to declare itself free of British rule! Yet armies are in the field, soldiers drilling in every Colony, battles have been fought. Why are we waiting to take our stand as one united country?"

Caswell shook his head sorrowfully. "I can't answer that, although I've sat in the Continental Congress. There are many men in it who do not want a real break with Britain. Others are afraid to play what may be a losing game. That is the reason why it is so necessary for us to defeat Macdonald and his Royalists. If we can drive them from the Province, we will elect a governor and administer the affairs of the Province ourselves. There is no reason why we should wait for backward Colonies to declare themselves independent. We don't have to wait for the laggards." He hit his clenched fist against the tent pole. "We must defeat the Highlanders and drive the King's army from North Carolina.

"Do you think we can do it? Have we enough men?" Adam asked.

"I can't sleep nights thinking of it, Adam. Lord Cornwallis is expected to arrive with seven regiments at Charles Town any day now. Clinton has forty vessels armed and waiting for his arrival. Old Martin is still trying to stir up his Slave Rebellion. The time has come when we must face the issue boldly. Total separation is the only thing now."

Adam saw what deep feeling stirred Richard Caswell. He had stood long for the middle course of conciliation. Now he was in the front rank of revolting leaders.

"When I came through Virginia," Adam told his uncle, "I found the inhabitants eager for independence, but they are willing to submit their opinion to whatever the general Congress should determine. I believe that North Carolina far exceeds them all in determination. Tryon's arbitrary and despotic regime and the Regulator trouble at Alamance have hardened the hearts of the people against the rule of Britain. When I see gentlemen marching side by side with men lately their indentured servants—first gentlemen of the Province marching as common soldiers, I know we will win against the best that Britain can send to defeat us. We are fighting for a cause. They are fighting for pay. We must win or there is no truth in man's belief in freedom." Adam's voice trembled with the intensity of his feeling.

Caswell's hand was on his shoulder. "You are right, Adam. We have iron in our souls. We will not accept defeat." Caswell's face was haggard in the light of the lanterns but his voice was firm.

Adam continued, "I have been from one end of the Province to the other in these past months. I've heard of nothing but determination among the Whigs. In less than fifteen days I believe we can turn out fifteen thousand independent gentlemen volunteers. We must defeat the Highlanders and the Loyalists. Then the Province is ours."

Caswell shook his head. "No, Adam, we won't work that way. This is not a gentleman's war. It is the war of the people. It is not a war to be fought by one class—but by all classes, united."

Adam answered impulsively. "You are right. It isn't a gentleman's war."

Caswell patted Adam's shoulder affectionately. "Talk to the Council as you have talked to me, Adam. They will listen. They know you and trust you. Tell them what you have just told me before Johnstone and his Committee go up to Virginia to plan for common defense. Make it clear to them that when we have routed the Highlanders under Macdonald we will not have a dissenting vote against complete independence in North Carolina."

An orderly came into the tent and saluted Caswell. "A messenger from Edenton with a dispatch bag for Captain Rutledge," he said.

Caswell indicated Adam, who went back into the tent and, moving to the lantern at the other end of the table, unlocked the bag with his special key. It contained a sheaf of papers from Johnstone and a letter marked "Important and Confidential" in Mary Warden's hand. He broke the seal quickly.

"Dear Adam:

"I'm sorry to be the one to bring you bad news. Azizi has been sold at the slave market at Edenton. Lavinia discovered what was to happen and came to me. We went to the market at once. Azizi

420

was in the warehouse, crowded in with forty or fifty black slaves, waiting to go on the block.

"I talked to the auctioneer. He said there was nothing to do but wait for the bidding as it was not a private sale. Lavinia cajoled him into letting Azizi come to our coach to wait her turn. David was with her. I'm writing this in Mr. Hewes's warehouse. I have sent for William and Dr. Armitage. I have also sent to the plantation for Marcy. Azizi keeps saying that she is free, not a slave, but she has not papers to prove it. Perhaps Marcy or Owen will know. I'm terrified. Haskins brought her over with Fatima and David. The papers ordering the sale are signed *Sara Rutledge, Owner.* I saw them myself.

"Later:

"William has just come. He says nothing can be done except bid her in. However, he did get David—some technicality, because they had no papers to prove his birth or that Azizi was his mother. Adam, I'm prepared to swear he is my child—anything to keep them from selling him.

"This is a big auction, well advertised. There are numbers of strange men here to bid—buyers from Wilmington, New Bern and Virginia. It is too terrible. The black slaves are huddled together, weeping and crying.

"Later:

"We were outbid. A man from Wilmington, named Squires, got her. There was some connivance between the auctioneer and the buyer, I'm sure. She will be sold again in Wilmington, Squires told us. He refused to sell her here. We could not stop him. Everything was legal. They took her off at once on a shallop that was waiting.

"*Adam, go to Wilmington at once when you get this.*

"Marcy has come. He is going to Wilmington in a few minutes. He says Sara went there several days ago. He will take David with him and put him under John Hawks's care. I think it will be safer. I have written Hawks to watch for the ship. He may be able to get her. If we only knew where the papers were we could stop them.

"I have asked Samuel Johnstone to send this in his official bag to Caswell's camp. I pray that we reach you in time. I am determined to go to Wilmington with Marcy. I cannot be certain that this letter will reach you in time. In that case, I may be able to help Marcy.

"MARY"

Adam stood for a moment, his tired brain incapable of functioning. Then, with a hurried farewell to Caswell, he ran out and across the strip of wet ground to the tent that had been assigned to him. He shook Herk, who was sleeping.

"Get up, Herk. Saddle the horses. Hurry!"

The Negro sprang to his feet and disappeared into the

darkness. Adam stuffed his soggy clothes into the saddle bags and was ready by the time Herk brought up the horse.

"Which way we ride, master?" Herk asked.

Adam vaulted into the saddle. "To the coast—to Wilmington. Ride like the devil."

Chapter 29

THE GREEN
TURBAN

ADAM galloped hard toward Wilmington, his horse in a white lather. The road for miles was choked with people fleeing from the dreaded invasion of the British: women and children, household slaves carrying bundles and boxes, carriages, carts and road plodders—and the rain beating down upon them all.

Seen through the grey curtain of the rain, the fleeing people had strange frightened faces. They passed like vague shadows, turning their wondering, fear-whitened faces toward him as he rode forward against the tide. They made way for him—an officer riding hard, carrying dispatches.

At a wayside inn Adam changed horses and pressed on at top speed toward Wilmington, leaving Herk to follow. At the outskirts he hesitated for a moment. It was useless to go to the slave market at this hour. If Marcy had come in time, Azizi would be with the Moor by now. He cut across a meadow, following the river to the far side of town.

At last he came to the long whitewashed buildings, half hidden behind a high wall, where the Moor lived. He beat on the heavy gate with his riding crop, unable to conceal his impatience. The door swung back. Adam turned his horse into the cobbled courtyard. He dismounted, tossed the reins to a groom and crossed the terrace, entering the house through the iron gates. A long corridor, flagged in black and white marble, opened into a large room with a fountain surrounded by exotic plants in the center. A macaw screeched as he entered and whirled dizzily on its perch.

Adam looked around then and saw Hawks. The Moor wore a gold embroidered tunic covered by an aba of white wool. He waited near the fountain, one hand on a curved dagger which was thrust through his broad silk sash.

"Is she here? For God's sake, were you in time?"

The anxiety in his voice satisfied the Moor. "The Lady Azizi is under my roof," he said evenly. "I was in time."

Adam's throat was tight. "There was some mistake. She is free. She has been free ever since——" There was a silence between them. Adam had the feeling that he need not say more. How could he speak to this man of his wife's action? How explain that she had waited years for the right time?

"David is with her," Hawks said. "For two days she has been resting. It was a bitter experience—" He paused, not wanting to condemn Adam. "Will you be seated?" He motioned him to a low divan. "Before she comes she wishes me to explain to you certain things."

The Moor hesitated a moment, as if searching for the right words. Then he made an open gesture with his hands, palm upward. "Among our people we have a saying, 'A man's destiny is written on the forehead.'" He looked directly at Adam. "Within a few days, the Lady Azizi will go back to her people in Bahrein."

"What did you say?" Adam asked, surprised into harsh speech.

"Sit down, Mr. Rutledge. You will be patient, please, while I speak of what has happened."

Adam sat down. The Moor stood before the divan, tall, dark, wrapped in the white robes of his people. "When I first saw Azizi at your house, I knew she came from proud people. She did not tell me at first. Later I gained her confidence. Oh, I know you will wonder how that was done, but it is of no matter. She told me the name of her people and of her home. She had been captured from a caravan by a band of desert robbers. She was on her way back to Bahrein, after a pilgrimage to Mecca. From there they took her in an Arab dhow to the slave market of Zanzibar. You noticed the green turban that she always wears? To a Mohammedan that is the sign that the wearer has made the Holy Pilgrimage." The Moor paused, then went on. "I wrote letters to Cairo, to Damascus and Bagdad. It takes time, Mr. Rutledge, many, many months, even years. But now I have my answer. Her father, whom she thought killed in the desert, is alive. He wishes her to return. The Lady Azizi must now return to her land and to her own people."

Adam sat very still, the Moor's words pounding in his ears: "Azizi must return to her people." Azizi belonged to another world—a world he would never know or understand. The mystery which had always surrounded her would remain. His face was expressionless. Already he had accepted the thing he always felt would come.

"The boy?" he asked, after a time.

The Moor glanced at him, then away. "We have a rule among our people that says the man is master," he said. "The

424

boy is yours. She has taught him the rich heritage of freedom of the desert people. Her work is done. But all the years of her life her tears will flood her heart."

Adam got up and strode the length of the long room and back before he could speak. The Moor's eyes rested on him compassionately.

"One thing more I must say. The Lady Azizi comes of people who have ruled their desert for a thousand years. Great rulers who owned a thousand Arabian horses and as many camels, and who had many thousands of slaves. She has no thought of evil that she has borne you a son. Her father has many wives. She has said to me that never is it the custom of an old wife who is barren to be angry with a young wife when she bears a son to her master. For the son of her husband is also her son, to love and to protect."

"Will she see me?" Adam asked humbly.

Hawks lifted his eyes. Adam saw Azizi walking slowly down the long corridor, David by her side. He rose, waiting. Here was a new world, unknown to him—strange, unreal. Against this background the slender, swaying figure of Azizi in her shimmering satin underdress half covered by long floating veils seemed more exotic than ever. Two long braids of black hair, twisted in pearls, hung over her shoulders. On her head was the green turban. She held an end of the veil before her face but her great eyes, darkened with kohl, seemed to burn with some deep emotion. This woman was not the one he had known. The woman he had once loved passionately was a transplanted being on alien soil. Here she glowed like a jewel in its proper setting. Here she was at home. He felt for the moment strangely unsure of himself. But the child by her side was his son.

She stood in front of him, her head bent, her hands across her soft breast. The green veil dropped to one side. Adam felt his blood race at the beauty of her. Hawks broke the silence.

"You find the Lady Azizi strange? You see her now as she would be in her own land under the roof of her father."

Adam could not speak. He could only look at the woman who had borne his son. "I do not know you," he said.

She moved delicately. "I knew not myself before. Now I'm at home." She smiled up at Hawks.

Jealousy swept over him, but he was instantly ashamed. This man had harbored Azizi.

"How can I repay you?" he asked Hawks.

The Moor lifted his hands as if putting the thought aside. "It is nothing. The Lady comes to me speaking the age-old word of our race, asking shelter. I'm bound in honor to protect her."

Adam felt humble before the Eastern Law. The Moor had given her sanctuary. What of himself? Had he given protection to the lonely woman? Instead, he had taken her body. He was ashamed before these quiet people.

Azizi turned her dark eyes to him. He felt his blood leap at the deep look in them.

"I pray Allah the Compassionate to keep you, my lord." Her voice vibrated against his heart. She turned to the boy and kissed him. "David, you must go now to your rest."

David bowed over his folded arms as his mother had done. "The peace of Allah upon you," he said in his boyish voice and left the room.

A wave of strong feeling shook Adam. David Rutledge. By God, his son would bear the name. He would see to that. Let Sara weep. Let her protest.

Hawks, who had insisted Adam spend the night in his home, walked to the door with him at dawn the next morning. Outside in the court Herk held the restive horses. Adam wanted to say something of his deep feeling, but no words came. Here under the roof of a foreigner he had found understanding. He had tasted salt, drunk the ceremonial coffee and observed the strange customs of an unknown people. He leaned over his horse's neck.

"It is best that they remain under your protection until time for her to sail. If anything should happen to me—if I should not come back—send the boy to Owen Tewilliger at the North Plantation. He knows my wishes regarding my son."

"You have a premonition of death, Mr. Rutledge?"

"No, not that. But there will be a battle before long. I want you to know that David will be provided for. My land on the Mississippi is for him."

The Moor did not say farewell. He touched his forehead and his heart. "With my eyes, my lips and my heart—the blessing of Allah the Compassionate."

Chapter 30

DEATH
AT THE BRIDGE

ADAM turned in the saddle and raised his eyes to the balcony
of the house that held Azizi and David. It came to him, with
a sense of shock, that his son was marked by an alien inheritance. David and his children and his children's children
would bear the hot imprint of the desert in their blood. A
nomad people who fought for their right to live as they
chose. The heavy gates, swung open by a white-robed Arab,
clanged behind him with a deadening finality.

At the junction with the post road he drew rein. A company of militia was marching, stepping out briskly in the
crisp air of early morning. The soldiers, catching sight of
Adam's shoulder straps, saluted. Two companies marched by
before Adam saw an officer that he knew. An Edenton man
rode up.

"Colonel Caswell is seeking you, Rutledge. He has a dozen
men looking for you in Wilmington. He's back there with the
artillery."

Adam rode back. At the head of the Dragoons, he saw his
uncle mounted on a black horse.

"There you are," Caswell said. "I've been trying to find
you. Have you heard the news?"

Adam had heard no news nor received any orders. "I'm
still on leave, sir. I have two days left."

"All leaves are canceled," Caswell said shortly. "We are
marching to the bridge on Widow Moore's Creek. The clan
Macdonald has raised the Highlanders, and all the Loyalists
have joined them. Martin is issuing orders from the *Cruizer*
for all men loyal to the King to join Donald Macdonald at
Cross Creek."

Adam fell in line. "Is your brigade attacking alone?" he
asked as they rode along.

Caswell shook his head. "I'm making junction with Lillington and Moore at the bridge. Pray God that we will win
today. If we do, it will mean the clearance of all enemy armies in the Colony."

A messenger rode up. Caswell took the dispatch and read

427

it quickly. Then he put spurs to his horse and galloped ahead. Adam fell in with the Dragoons as they marched forward through the early morning mists.

After a time, Caswell came back, deep gloom on his face. He told Adam the courier was from Lillington who, unable to make the junction with them by land, would fall down river by boats. The Highlanders from Cross Creek were rallying in great numbers to follow their clan leaders. Macdonald's army would be swelled to over five thousand men, most of them seasoned fighters.

Peyton galloped up as they were talking. He had been detached from the Edenton Light Horse and was acting as aide to Caswell. He told the Colonel that a Royalist courier, carrying dispatches from Macdonald to the British Commander at the base below Wilmington, had been intercepted. The dispatches not only gave the Royalist battle plan but told a heroic story. Macdonald wrote that he was ill, but that he would be ready to fight to the death for the Royal standard entrusted to his keeping. "Many a base craven deserted in the night and went over to the Whig's camp," he wrote. On learning this he had gone to the campfire and demanded to know if there were others who wished to desert. "If there are men so vile as to desert their King on the eve of battle, they must declare themselves at once," he had shouted. Allan Macdonald and Colonel MacLeod stood beside him. Then Flora Macdonald came out of the night. Grasping the scarred battleflags, she had roused the men to pledge themselves to follow the Macdonalds to death or victory. Men came shouting to their feet, swearing allegiance to the King, to Flora Macdonald, the savior of Bonnie Prince Charlie and to Donald Macdonald, the bra' hero of Culloden Moor! "It was a grand sight," Macdonald wrote. "You can count on the Scots of Cross Creek to carry the King's standard."

Adam and Peyton fell out of the column while Caswell wrote hurried orders. Lillington was to throw breastworks along the bridgehead at Moore's Creek. If necessary, the Minute Men should cross the stream and move to Corbett's ferry. Scouts and sentries were to be posted to watch for Macdonald's approach. The success of the plan depended entirely on secrecy. The Whigs would make the Royalists attack at a point where Macdonald was not expecting to give battle.

Caswell gave the orders to Peyton who saluted and was soon lost in the mists and among the shadowy figures of marching soldiers.

Caswell ordered Adam to follow after Peyton with a second

message. This was one to General Moore. Adam went by a little traveled road and crossed Moore's creek in time to intercept the General. When he had delivered the message, he started back to his command.

Not far from Moore's camp he saw Peyton. He was sitting beside the road, his horse tied to a sapling, trying to staunch a wound in his arm that was bleeding profusely. Adam spurred his horse and hurried to him. A bullet had grazed the skin, cutting a deep furrow. Adam looked at Peyton searchingly.

"This was fired at close range," he said, as he bound up the wound with a strip from his handkerchief. "There are powdermarks on your sleeve."

Peyton turned so deadly white that Adam thought he was going to keel over. "Yes," he said faintly. "A sniper. I ran right into him in the wood yonder."

Adam made no comment. Peyton sat quietly while Adam knotted a handkerchief around his arm for a sling. "Do you think there will be a battle?" he asked.

"Without doubt," Adam answered.

Peyton leaned forward. His hand was shaking as he took up his coat. "I don't. How can we fight them? An army of country bumpkins against Macdonald's trained Scots. Why, half his men are soldiers—soldiers, I say. Every man of them has been under fire a dozen times." His voice was shrill with excitement.

Adam looked at Peyton. Uneasy thoughts raced through his mind. He didn't like Peyton's white face, his trembling hands. Perhaps he was one of those men who could not stand the sight of blood. That must be it! It could not be that Peyton himself had inflicted the wound. He would not dwell on that contingency. Peyton was a Rutledge. Rutledge men did not shoot themselves to evade responsibility. They did what was expected of them. Yet the thought kept recurring as they rode through the woods along the creek toward the bridge.

Suddenly they heard shots followed by heavier fire and after a few minutes, the roar of cannon. Adam wheeled his horse. "They are attacking at the bridgehead," he shouted to Peyton. "This way, cross the creek here! Ride like hell!"

Peyton wheeled his horse. "My orders are to go to Wilmington."

Adam caught at his bridle. "Wilmington? Are you mad? Caswell needs every man here at the bridge."

Peyton's face was lined. He jerked away and put spurs to his horse. Adam followed, cursing aloud as he rode after him. "Ride ahead of me, damn you. If you turn tail, I'll shoot."

Peyton turned. His face was white, his eyes frightened, his mouth twitching. Adam hated himself. He thought, "Peyton will be himself in a moment. It is only panic; I feel that way myself."

"Steady," he said more kindly, "steady."

Peyton did not answer. They rode close together through the woods until they came to a gap in the trees. Fighting had begun in earnest now. The rattle of muskets and the roar of cannon sounded close. The rallying cry of the Highlanders could be heard clearly in the still air. "King George and the Broadsword!" Then the long roll of drums.

Bullets were whizzing around them, spattering on the ground.

"Let me go, let me go! God damn you, let me go!" Peyton's voice was pitched high with terror.

Adam caught his arm. A ball from a siege mortar whipped over them, cutting a limb clean from a young pine tree. The limb grazed Adam's face, striking against his arm. He heard a shot—then a scream. He looked at his arm. His pistol was smoking. Peyton's horse was plunging ahead, Peyton swaying in the saddle, his hand clutching his stomach.

Terror seized Adam. Somehow the pistol had gone off. He had shot Peyton. He sped after the fleeing horse but he could not catch up. Peyton was in the stream at the bridgehead. He turned for a moment, his hand pressed close to his side.

"Adam," he cried. His anguished voice carried over the roar of battle.

Adam jumped from his horse and ran forward, but he was not quick enough. A soldier caught Peyton as he slumped from his saddle.

All about them men were shouting. The gunfire was heavy, cannons and mortars booming. Adam saw Ronald MacLeod fall at the far side of the bridge. The Macdonalds' charge had failed. Caswell's troops rushed forward, plunging deep into the stream in pursuit of the Highlanders. The battle was won. Three minutes of fighting and the Royalists were defeated.

Adam lifted Peyton in his arms and carried him to the roadside. After sending a soldier for Armitage, who was surely somewhere close by, he opened the wounded man's coat and tore away the linen shirt.

"No use, Adam," Peyton whispered faintly.

Adam caught his hand, "Peyton, Peyton, I didn't—" Words choked in his throat.

430

A thin smile crossed Peyton's lips. "No matter, Adam. I tried myself to shoot but I had not the courage." Foam gathered on his lips. "Adam—my son—watch over my son. Do not let him know—" Armitage pushed Adam aside. His hand reached for Peyton's heart.

"Too late. He is gone. Strange—very strange," he muttered to himself, his quick hands probing. He glanced at Adam, a queer look on his face. "Are you hit too?" he asked, looking at the blood streaming down Adam's face.

"No." He could not take his eyes from Peyton's broken body, his white, still face. "Can't you do something, Armitage? God! He can't be gone so soon."

Armitage's hand pressed his arm. "It's no use, Adam. He is dead. I examined the wound carefully. let's lift him over there under the tree, out of this muck. I must go back. There are others who need me." He stood for a moment, looking down on the quiet body. Then he bent over and closed the staring eyes. "It will be a comfort to Lavinia," he said slowly, "to know her husband died a hero's death."

The Doctor's words came to Adam through the daze that surrounded him, numbing body and brain. "A hero's death . . ." he had said. Then Armitage didn't know—no one knew that Peyton was running away. He, Adam, was the only one who knew—and he had killed him.

For a long time he sat beside Peyton on the rain-soaked ground. Caswell found him there and paused for a moment. His voice was kind.

"Don't grieve so much. Peyton died a man's death, for his country. I have ordered a guard. We will take him to Wilmington under the escort of his company which he so gallantly led to victory."

Adam's world was reeling about him. He wanted to cry out: "It was I who killed him, I, his cousin, who loved him as a brother." But he forced the words back. If he spoke, the world would know the truth—Lavinia—young Peyton. They must never know. He realized then that he must never break the silence as long as he lived.

A few minutes later an orderly rode up. "Colonel Caswell's compliments. Will you take a platoon and investigate the condition of the Loyalist camp, sir?"

Adam galloped down the road with his men. The deserted camp lay three-quarters of a mile beyond the bridgehead. When they neared it, he saw a tall spare figure stagger from one of the tents. Even at a distance, he recognized General Donald Macdonald. When the General saw Adam, he waved

431

a parchment in his hand. The effort almost overbalanced him so that he had to lean heavily against a charred stump to keep his knees from giving way.

When Adam dismounted and approached him, Macdonald thrust his commission as Lieutenant-General of the Royalist army into his hand.

"I surrender. I surrender," he muttered through parched lips. His glittering eyes and the bright red spots on his cheek-bones showed that fever was burning him up.

Adam called two of his men to carry the General to his tent. They laid him on his camp cot after they had routed his frightened body servant out from under it and set him to work making hot drinks.

Adam left his men on guard and galloped down the road to the spot where a group of three tents had been pitched at the edge of the wood. At the sound of a woman sobbing in-side one of the tents he swung off of his horse. While he stood hesitating, he saw another woman walking slowly down the path from the wood. He recognized the tall majestic figure of Flora Macdonald.

She lifted her tragic eyes when she approached him. He stood before her dumb, unable to speak. She held out her hand with a gracious gesture.

"There is no need of words, Mr. Rutledge. I feel your sym-pathy—it is my evil fate which will always pursue me and mine. If you will allow me, I will speak a word of comfort to my daughter. Yesterday a bride—today a widow. Then, I'll go with you to your prisoners. My husband is with them and I wish to be near him in his dark hour." She turned and lifted the flap of the tent. Adam caught a glimpse of a woman kneeling beside a lifeless body. He recognized the still white face of Ronald MacLeod.

An hour later, Adam was on his way to Wilmington, car-rying General Caswell's report of the battle of Moore's Creek to the president of the Province Council. He rode past the broken body of Peyton Rutledge as it lay by the roadside under a flag that a color sergeant had draped over the gun carriage. A long line of soldiers was marching by, each sol-dier stopping for a moment to salute a man who had given his life for his country.

The Council was in session when Adam got to Wilmington. He reported at once. President Harnett read the dispatch to the members assembled. There was instant silence; the hall was so still that the ticking of the clock sounded like musket fire. His voice was low, but it reached everyone in the room.

"Camp at Long Creek
"Sirs:
"I have the pleasure to acquaint you with the news that we had an engagement at Widow Moore's Creek bridge on the twenty-seventh. Our army was one thousand strong: New Bern's Battalion, Minute Men, militia from Craven, Dobbs, Johnstone and Wake, and a detachment of the Wilmington Battalion of Minute Men. The Tories were about three thousand. General Macdonald is a prisoner. He was not well and was not in the battle. Colonel MacLeod, one of the commanders, was slain and many other officers and soldiers were taken prisoners."

Adam listened, scarcely conscious of the words Harnett spoke.

"The list of supplies and ammunition captured:
Three hundred and fifty guns and shot bags
One hundred and fifty swords and dirks
Fifteen excellent rifles
Two medicine chests from England valued at three hundred pounds sterling
A box of Johanneses and guineas found in a stable at Cross Creek by slave named Herk, belonging to Adam Rutledge Esq., valued at 5000 pounds sterling
Thirteen wagons with complete sets of harness and horses"

There was wild cheering at the end. Men threw their cockades into the air and shouted themselves hoarse. The president rapped for order. He put into words what was in the heart and mind of every man in the room.

"Gentlemen," he said, "we have fought and won a battle. By that battle we are come to the end of British domination in North Carolina. The Governor has fled the Colony, as you know, and remains on board a sloop-of-war outside the waters of this Colony. *We are now free of the yoke.*

"Gentlemen, I salute you, a free people. From now on the welfare of the Province and its government is in our hands. God grant us wisdom to govern wisely for all the people."

Harnett paused. The people waited for his last word.

"Three minutes of battle and there is not a Royalist soldier left in all the Province of North Carolina!"

And then the cheers and excitement overflowed into the streets. People in little groups of great crowds waited for reports of the battle. Presently Harnett appeared on the balcony. Adam pushed his way through the crowds. Rumors of defeat travel fast—of victory even more swiftly. . . .

Adam opened the door of the drawing room of their old house in Princess Street, uncertain whether or not Sara would be there. She was seated near the window, winding a ball of wool. Mary Warden, holding the skein over her extended hands, saw him first. Sara glanced up and stopped winding the ball. A strange look, almost of fear, crossed her face.

"Adam, I hope you have not taken out papers for that child," she said.

"There has been a battle, Sara," he said, not answering her question.

Mary slipped the wool over the back of the chair. Her lips were trembling, her expressive eyes questioning.

"We won the battle," he said. "Macdonald's Highlanders and all the Loyalists have either fled or been taken prisoners."

The ball of bright wool rolled to the floor unnoticed. "I do not believe it," Sara cried. "I do not believe that the King's troops would run from yokels. It is not the truth!" Her voice rose shrilly. "How could they be defeated with the hero of Culloden to lead them?"

"General Macdonald was ill. Colonel MacLeod was killed," Adam said wearily, wondering how he could tell them of Peyton.

Sara turned to Mary. "That was the reason," she said triumphantly. Adam would not let her say more.

Mary leaned forward, searching his face. "Where is Peyton?" she asked, her voice sunk to a whisper.

Adam went over to Sara and took her hand. "I wish I knew some kind way to tell you," he began.

Mary ran to Sara and knelt beside her. "He is trying to tell you that Peyton—" She turned to Adam for confirmation.

"He died at the head of his men," he said slowly, forcing the words that seemed to stick in his throat. He thought Mary would see into his heart and read the truth for her eyes never left his face.

"At the head of his men," she repeated. "Peyton—"

For a moment Sara did not seem to comprehend. Then she suddenly began to sob, her thin white hands covering her face.

"Peyton, dear Peyton, you will never come again."

Adam's voice was harsh with the intensity of his emotion. "Don't, for God's sake, don't, Sara."

She did not hear him. "He was so gay, so gay, and now he is dead."

Adam strode about the room. Would it always be like this, this terrible weight on his heart and on his soul? He heard Mary say, "Don't, Sara, please. Can't you see you are killing Adam?" But Sara's sobs did not cease.

Adam looked out the window. The willows were budding. New life was stirring—the eternal promise of another spring. They would take Peyton and go home, back to the plantation. The young wheat would be pushing its way through the black earth. Peyton would become part of the spring—of the rich black earth. He sat down suddenly as he thought of Lavinia. What of Lavinia and the child she was carrying?

Judith and Mary took Sara to her bedroom. In a short time, Mary came back. She stood beside Adam as he sat looking blankly out the window. Then she put her arms about him, drawing his head against her breast. After a moment, she sat down in a chair facing him. Her voice was very low when she spoke.

"Adam, you must tell me the truth about Peyton."

He looked up quickly. His heart seemed to stop beating. Had she divined?

"Why do you ask, Mary? It was as I said, at the head of his company. I don't think he suffered—" his voice broke. He covered his face with his hands.

"I will tell you why I asked, Adam. I saw Peyton just before he left here. He was in a strange, highly excited state. He told me that he would not go into battle—he was going away to the Indies. I knew he was afraid. Now you tell me he died leading his men." Her clear, straightforward eyes were searching his.

"Amitage saw him; Caswell also," he said. "They will tell you he died a hero's death." She must not know nor suspect, not even Mary.

"Thank God for that, Adam. Lavinia will have that to comfort her. Oh, Adam, I can never forgive myself. I sent him—I told him he must be strong and unafraid for his son, for Lavinia. Now, he is dead." Tears came to her eyes. Adam wiped them away with his handkerchief.

"Don't feel so self-reproachful, Mary. You had no part in this, no matter what you advised. Peyton fulfilled his destiny. Think only of this. Tonight his body lies on a gun carriage on the battlefield with a guard of soldiers. Soldiers salute him as

435

they pass. Tomorrow they will bring his body to Wilmington. The people will mourn for him—tears will be shed by people who never saw him. Don't you see, Mary, Peyton has become a symbol of a man who died for Freedom?" He got up and stood looking out the window again. After a long silence, he turned to her. "I will take him back to Edenton tomorrow, Mary. But you must go ahead. You will have the hard task."

"Tell Lavinia?" Mary's voice trembled.

Adam nodded. "There is no one else to do it. I don't trust Sara. You will know the kindest way." Suddenly his voice broke. "What am I saying? I talk as if there were an easy way to tell a woman that the husband she loves is dead."

"But she has him now, Adam," Mary whispered. "Perhaps I should not say it, but we both know how she has suffered. Now he is hers—all hers as long as she lives."

"I know, Mary—we both know. After a little while she will have the consolation of remembering that he died a brave man's death." Adam's voice was low and not quite steady. He knew that the burden of Peyton's death would always be on his heart . . . by day and by night . . . to the very end. . . .

Chapter 31

HERO'S
RETURN

EARLY the next morning a committee of men from the Provincial Council waited on Adam: James Hooper, Samuel Johnstone and Maurice Moore. A second dispatch had come from Colonel Caswell. It reported the heroism of Peyton Rutledge who had died leading his men to victory. Dr. Armitage and Colonel Caswell had both been witnesses to his heroic action, as had a dozen men of his own company. The Council thought it proper to have his body removed to New Bern, there to lie in state at the Palace.

Adam felt the blood in his veins congeal. This was something he had not anticipated. The men were looking at him with grave, sympathetic faces. He knew they thought he hesitated because of his grief for Peyton. What would their thoughts be if they knew the truth? He had an impulse then to speak—to speak for once the stark, devastating truth. But he knew he could not. James Hooper was saying:

"I know it will be hard, Adam, but Peyton Rutledge belongs to the people of the Province now. His name is on the lips of every loyal man, woman and child, and in their hearts. You must forget private grief now."

Adam inclined his head. "After that, I will take him home to Edenton—to his wife and his son."

He got through the ordeal of New Bern somehow, strengthened by the sincere grief of the crowds who came to view Peyton's lifeless body. Rugged men passed by the bier with moist eyes; work roughened hands of women touched the banner that lay across the still body. At last soldiers lifted the coffin to the gun-carriage and the long journey homeward began.

For hours Adam rode behind the caisson. Toward night it began to rain and he got into the coach with Dr. Armitage and David. At the last he had decided to take the boy with him and had sent Herk for him. The child sat still and straight on the seat opposite. Armitage, wrapped in his greatcoat, was huddled in the corner, asleep. Adam watched the boy as they rolled through the pine woods. What would he say to this child with large eyes like his own when he grew old enough to ask? Ahead of them rolled the gun-carriage with an escort of Edenton Light Horse. What would he say to Peyton's son when he asked about his father? He closed his eyes wearily.

Along the country roads people came to watch the cortège go by. In honor of the first man to die for their freedom the men stood silently with bared heads and women tossed flowers onto the bier as it passed. Adam's mind was numb; he could not think beyond his own act. What if Peyton had got away—deserted? What would his going home have been then?

David leaned forward. "Was he a hero? The people in the village said that he was. What did he do to be a hero?"

Adam said, "He fought a brave fight, David."

"Did he fight the redcoats?"

"Yes, he fought the redcoats and he fought himself."

The child looked at him with wide eyes. "How can a man fight himself, sir?"

"I cannot tell you now, David. When you are older, perhaps."

The boy settled back. "My people fought bravely," he said. "They fought the Rashid. Every brother fought until all six lay dead on the sands of the desert."

Armitage woke up. "God bless my soul! What is the child talking about?" he asked.

"My mother told me, Dr. Armitage. Her own brothers—every man was a warrior. They had a blood-feud with the Rashid for a hundred years because the Rashid had stolen the mare, Karin, from her father's father's father, the great sheik of the Red Desert."

Armitage turned his startled eyes to Adam. "What have we here?" he asked.

Adam was looking at his son. "What about the mare, Karin?" he asked David.

"She was the most beautiful mare in all Arabia, sir. The Rashid came and took her when the mare was in foal. For that five hundred men have died, and six brothers of my mother. When I am old enough, I will ride to the desert and the men of the Rashid will die by my sword." The child's tone was quiet, his eyes clear and straightforward. "The blood-feud of our people will not end until all the people of the Rashid lie dead in the desert."

Armitage groaned. "A pretty sentiment, damme if it isn't!

438

What will you do to counteract all this teaching, Adam Rutledge?"

Adam gazed at David. "I don't know . . . I don't know," he said, and his voice was troubled.

"A bloodthirsty race, the Arabs, but strong and fearless . . ."

The boy finished the doctor's sentence, ". . . and free."

"How old are you, David?" Armitage asked, wiping his glasses so that he could see the boy's face better.

"Almost nine, sir."

Armitage shook his head. "The heritage of Freedom will make or mar, Adam. I think your responsibility is just beginning. I don't envy you the task ahead. It's a pity you can't clap him into Eton. They would know what to do to turn all this teaching to good account."

"I'm going to send him to Edenton Academy until the autumn. Then to Annandale to school with Paige's boys." He leaned over and put his hand on the child's shoulder. "You will like to go to school at Edenton?"

David considered a moment. "Yes, sir. If I can see Aunt Gwennie and Uncle Owen and ride Gilsen's horses."

Adam nodded. "Of course, you can. When you are through school, you may come with me to the country of the Illinois."

David said nothing. He sat quietly with his hands folded, his caped coat buttoned close under his firm chin, his cocked hat tilted a little over his oval face. Adam turned his eyes from the direct gaze of the child. "Heritage of Freedom," Armitage had said. Was that what he had given to this sturdy child?

He gazed out the windows of the coach with unseeing eyes. He felt weary, his secret thoughts weighing down upon him. There was no answer—no way out. It would always be the same.

At Chapman's Corner, Armitage got down from the carriage. A coach awaited him there to take him to the North Plantation to deliver David into Gwennie's keeping. Adam watched the coach drive off, the small face of the child peering through the back window. Then he mounted his horse and rode up behind the gun-carriage.

The village waited for the return of Peyton Rutledge! Negroes from the plantation and fishermen of the Sound as well as old friends with sad and serious faces. The cortège moved through the streets to the little church. Adam saw the spire of St. Paul's rising above the budding trees. Strange that the end for stormy, impetuous Peyton should be like this. People would soon forget. They would remember only the gay and laughing Peyton, the brave and heroic Peyton. He had come home to the sound of the funeral march and muffled drums—muffled drums that beat from one end of the Province to the other.

In the church Lavinia waited, swathed in flowing black robes. Beside her, tall and straight, bearing himself proudly, stood young Peyton. Lavinia wore no widow's veil to keep the people from seeing her tears. Her head was high, her bearing proud. Her hero husband had come home for the last time.

Adam had a glimpse of Mary Warden standing behind Lavinia with William beside her.

As soldiers carried the flag-draped box to the foot of the chancel, Parson Pettigrew, surpliced, sad-visaged, walked down the aisle to meet them, his hand raised to make the shadow of the cross. His full-toned voice faltered for a moment, then grew strong, filling the chapel with its warm resonance.

"I am the Resurrection and the Life—"

Adam waited a few days after Peyton's burial before he went to Sara. He dreaded the meeting, for he had decided to have a frank talk with her about David. His first hot anger had subsided but, knowing she would not give way without a struggle, he was doubly determined not to weaken this time, as he had always done in the past, at the sight of tears.

Judith barred his way with her monotonous sly song, "Miss Sara, she sleeps; better she rest—" He did not answer but walked into the room. The woman had lied. Sara was not asleep; she was sitting in her cushioned chair near the window. It came to Adam then that Judith must have lied to him many times before when he wanted to see Sara. The thought stiffened his resolve to go through the scene that faced him, no matter what happened.

Sara looked up when he came in, startled by his abrupt entrance. Something in his face alarmed her. Her expression changed quickly as she dropped back against the cushions. "Get me my smelling salts," she said to Judith. "I feel quite faint."

Judith hurried across the room. "Better you go now. Miss Sara, she feeble this mornin'."

Adam took the crystal bottle from her hand. "Leave the room," he said sharply.

She hesitated, looking from Adam to Sara. Sara glanced at Adam. There was no relenting in his stern face. "You may go, Judith. Wait outside in the hall," she said in a small, weak voice.

"Not too near the door," Adam said, as the slave left the room hastily. "I'll call you if I want you."

Sara began to cry, dabbing at her eyes with a small hand-kerchief. "I can't get over Peyton," she said, her voice trembling. "It doesn't seem possible that he'll never come into this room again."

Adam watched her silently. He knew that she was holding him off. She wasn't grieving for Peyton . . . she was alarmed at what he was going to say. She sensed why he had come—to accuse her of selling Azizi and his son, of putting his son up at public auction at a slave market. But he had made up his mind he would not speak of this. There was nothing to be done about it now. He knew that the suggestion had come from Judith. He had no way of knowing how long she had worked on Sara's emotions before she had persuaded her to give the order. He didn't want to know—he would pass over that part without words.

It seemed to Adam that he was seeing his wife for the first time. He remembered a hundred similar scenes when she had won her way through tears, through her small, sad voice. His heart had filled with pity for the tragedy of her helplessness. She knew his weakness and she had used it to her own ends.

He waited a moment before he spoke. His voice was quiet, dispassionate. "I do not like to bring this matter up at this time, Sara, when you are upset over Peyton's death, but I must. I must talk with you now, to tell you what arrangements I have made for my son."

She stopped crying and stiffened herself perceptibly. "I do not wish to speak to you now, Adam. I haven't the strength. Please come another time when I am stronger."

Adam did not listen to her words. He was thinking, "I must not let her influence me again. I must be firm." He leaned over and took her hand, searching for words that would make what he had to say easier for her. She did not stir; her hand lay lifeless in his strong fingers. He found himself weakening, thinking of her helplessness. It flashed through his mind that he could send David away—to Virginia—to Cahokia. He could provide for him in some other way—but even as the thought came, it disappeared.

"I have brought my son back to the North Plantation, Sara. I intend to keep him with me, and give him my name."

Sara sat up. Adam was astonished at the vigor of her sudden movement and the strength of her voice. "I will not allow it," she said fiercely, two angry spots of red glowing on her cheekbones. "I'll not have a child of a slave under my roof—I'll not endure such an indignity."

"David won't be at Rutledge Riding. He will be under the care of Owen and Gwennie Tewilliger as he has been since his birth. He is old enough now for me to think of his schooling, and Gwennie, with her warm kind heart, will do what she can to make up to him for the loss of his—" He was going to say "mother," but Sara interrupted.

"I will not have it," she said, her lips drawn to a thin, hard line. "I'll not be the laughing stock of the plantation people and the villagers."

Adam looked away. He waited for her to finish and then went on quietly: "It has been very lonely here, Sara. I want the companionship of my son. I want to watch him grow—to teach him to ride, to love the soil, to get joy out of spring planting and the harvest." He stopped suddenly under her scornful eyes.

"Are you taunting me because I did not give you a son?" she asked, her voice shrill.

"No, Sara," he said gently. "I could not do that but every man looks forward to the day he will have a son."

She turned her head away. Adam's heart went out to her then. His hand tightened on hers. "It hurts me to say this to you, dear, but I want you to realize what it means to me— what it might mean to you."

She turned suddenly. "The barren woman," she said in white fury. "That is what you are saying to me—Sara, the barren woman. You want her to take Hagar's child to her heart. Well, I won't. I won't, no matter what the Bible says." She fairly screamed the words.

A sudden rage rose in him. "So you did know," he said harshly. "You knew and planned. You put the girl in my way —you sent her to my rooms at night—made her attractive— knowing that one day the physical want of her would carry me out of myself." His anger died as quickly as it had come. "Why did you?" he asked lifelessly.

"You ask me that?" she cried. "I'll tell you! I wanted to keep you away from Mary Warden—that's why. I hate her! She has always tried to take you from me. I didn't mind a slave girl—" Something of his anger must have shown in his face. "I have more to say," she went on. "Think of me a moment—your invalid wife, chained to a bed day after day. You hunt, you dance, you sail your boat, you visit great ladies and listen to their flattery—while I—" Tears of anger and humiliation ran down her cheeks.

Adam's anger gave way to sympathy. "Sara, you must believe me. Mary Warden is my friend—she never has been more, nor does she want more."

"She loves you," she answered. "You are a fool if you don't know it."

Adam sat for a moment without speaking. Sara glanced at him quickly, then put her hand over his. "Adam," she said pitifully, "please don't bring the boy here."

Adam's expression changed. He said firmly, "David is here and here he will remain. I've told you that before."

"I won't have it—I won't—I won't," she cried hysterically. "You can't ask this of me!"

"There is no use crying about it, Sara. I have made up my mind." He stood up, as if to close the subject.

"I won't have it," she repeated dully. "I'll not stay here to be insulted by the presence of your illegitimate child. I'll go to my father—I—"

"Perhaps that would be the wisest thing, Sara. You are unhappy here," he found himself saying. "I'll make a more suitable provision for you—" He stopped. He could not say more. Sara was trembling violently. She made an effort to stifle her sobs. He had the feeling that she was no longer playing a part.

For a long time neither spoke. He lifted his eyes from her slight, frail body. It was too cruel; he could not say what had been in his mind to say. He could not send her away; he must make an effort to arrange some pattern of living that would include her—unless she wanted to go.

"What do you want me to do, Adam? Do you want me to go?"

"You must make the decision," he said.

"And if I want to stay here with you at Rutledge Riding?"

"Then you must stay and I'll do my best to make you happy." He was beaten—he knew it. But on one issue he remained firm. "David will be at North Plantation. You need not see him—you can forget he is here."

Tears were streaming down her face now—real tears. "I will make no further objection," she said in a smothered voice.

He touched her forehead with cold lips. "I'm sending Judith away," he said slowly, steeled against an outburst. "I'll have Lavinia lend you one of her slaves until I can buy a woman who will suit you."

Sara was visibly frightened. "What are you going to do with Judith?" she whispered. "Adam, I—"

Adam spoke quickly, before he yielded to her entreaties. "I'll have her sent to Wilmington to be sold to the Jamaica trade." He waited for her protest but she said nothing.

Events crowded swiftly now. The seaports were armed and vessels were built to defend the Colony. New men came forward to take responsibility. Leaders met and argued. How could the western counties be held in line? The plowshare of radicalism must run lightly over the ground. It was not yet time to plow deep—to overturn the fallow ground and plant the seeds of revolt. "Wait," said Caswell. "Wait a little longer. We have not the troops—we have no money. To declare ourselves now is to invite defeat and disaster—wait."

On his way back from a visit to Wilmington, Dr. Armitage stopped at the Swan in New Bern to talk with Adam. Adam sent Herk for a decanter of brandy.

The Doctor lifted his glass to the light. "The next meeting of the Assembly will bring forth important things, Adam," he said. "There is sure to be a vote declaring independence. The Continental Congress is too slow. It has been almost a year since the Mecklenburg Resolves were made and sent to the Congress for consideration. Not a thing has come from it, although Caswell gave the Resolves to Tom Jefferson at that time."

"They are probably waiting for all the Colonies to unite and take some concerted action," Adam said.

"We are thinking of acting as a separate state," Armitage told him.

Adam lighted his pipe. "It can't be done that way, Armitage," he said slowly. "We can't win from Britain unless the Colonies all fight as one. I'm convinced of that." He got up and rummaged among the papers on the desk. "Here is a letter from London, brought to me by a captain of a Dutch merchantman, that tells of Cornwallis' departure with a fleet of twenty ships, his object being to subdue the southern Colonies."

Adam looked through the letter until he came to the last page from which he read a paragraph aloud.

"I tell you this, Rutledge, so that you will know that the

Ministers in power, who guide the destinies of Great Britain, have full knowledge that a concerted action by the Colonies will mean a long and bitter fight. . . ."

Adam laid the letter down.

Armitage turned his grave face to him. "This astonishes me. Lord Cornwallis was our friend during the whole of the trouble over the Stamp Act."

Adam nodded his head but remained silent.

"Cornwallis is a soldier. He must obey orders. If I remember rightly, he defended the Massachusetts bill and the Boston Port bill," Armitage continued thoughtfully. "They say that Cornwallis is a temporizer. The ways of these temporizers are beyond me. Do you know that we have them among us, Adam?"

"What do you mean?" Adam asked, alert at the Doctor's tone.

"Your friend and mine—William Warden, who else?"

Adam felt as if a cold hand had clutched him. "You can't think that, Doctor. William was slow to make up his mind to break with England, but so was my uncle—so was I."

"I hope you are right, Adam, for Mary's sake. It would kill her. I'm a doddering old idiot but I think I see people more closely than most. I get to them at their low moments. I haven't great faith. There are men in Edenton who will make money out of the misfortunes of others. When we are at war they will charge high prices, sell goods above their worth, speculate in foodstuffs. Already they are planning to do that if we do not stop it by law."

"You must have had a bad night, Doctor," Adam chided him. "I don't believe there is a man in Edenton who would gain money at the expense of his country."

The Doctor sniffed. "You have faith in people, Adam, but you don't know them. Perhaps you are happier for that but, mind my words, we will have trouble. I know who the scoundrels are. I will be watching." The Doctor's lined face twisted itself into a look of shrewd determination. "If I find anyone overcharging or hoarding, I shall give his name to the Committee of Safety."

He changed the subject abruptly. "I've seen Sara. She is in the best of health, aside from her paralysis I mean. Lavinia, poor child, is standing up bravely. She has true courage. Strange about Peyton—very strange. I should never have imagined Peyton dying a hero!" He looked at Adam curiously. "Somehow I think there was something behind all this."

Adam had no intention of allowing the Doctor to question him about Peyton. He busied himself pouring a glass of brandy from the decanter and the moment passed without further comment.

Late in May Lavinia's second son was born. Lavinia was close to death then. For three days Dr. Armitage stayed with her day and night, not knowing whether she would come through. On the fourth day, she rallied. From then on things improved. The boy was strong and sturdy from the start.

Adam was impatient to be back on the plantation, but was kept busy at New Bern with the reorganization work. When he finally returned to Rutledge Riding, weary with the haggling and bickering of men over new laws and political appointments, he was glad to be home. For a few happy days he roamed over the plantation, looking at new lands freshly planted that year to tobacco and grain. Marcy and Owen rode with him, proud of their stewardship. The slaves sang as they worked in the field and sang as they lifted hoe and shovel. It was a tranquil, pastoral scene. David rode with him, sitting strong and firm astride a tall horse. The child listened to Adam and Marcy as they talked of problems of the plantation.

One morning when they had finished riding over a piece of woodland, Adam took David to Queen's Gift to visit Mary Warden. Mary, in a dark blue riding habit, came down the garden path to meet them, her face alight with excitement.

"Adam, Adam!" she cried when she got within speaking distance, "have you heard the news? The Continental Congress has signed the Declaration at last! They have declared us free and independent of Great Britain."

Adam dismounted quickly. "When did this happen? When did you get word?" he asked, catching her excitement.

"They signed on the fourth. Sam Johnstone had a message from Hewes late last night. William had word this morning, but no details. I was about to ride in to the village to see if there is any further news."

A slave led her horse around from the stables. Adam helped her mount and they trotted down the road toward Edenton, David keeping pace.

A great crowd had gathered in the village and packed the Commons in front of the Courthouse. They were waiting to hear an official public announcement that would confirm the rumor. Many of the men had been waiting since early morning, standing patiently. Adam and Mary rode to the north side of the green. David slid from his horse and tied the reins to a hitching post. He ran over to the Courthouse and up the steps. Adam and Mary followed more slowly, weaving their way through the crowd.

Ruffles from drums broke through the clatter of voices and silenced the waiting multitude. Bugles sounded. Six companies of militia marched down the street. In the distance a band was playing a triumphal march. A man, whom Adam could not recognize, mounted the steps and read the Declaration in a clear voice that carried into the crowd. Strong, solemn words rolled out over the silent multitude. Men and women—free man and slave standing shoulder to shoulder—went wild with rejoicing. Shouts and huzzas reached the heavens—cannon boomed a salute for each Colony in turn. Tears ran down rugged cheeks. At last, there was a united land to fight a common cause.

Adam turned to look for David. He had disappeared, lost in the rush of the surging crowd that was moving toward the Courthouse. Mary was pressed against Adam, unable to stir. He lifted her from her feet and carried her forward, waiting for a chance to get out of the crowd. After a time, he edged his way to the outskirts. He left Mary and went to search for David. The crowd was breaking up and surging down the street, talking and laughing and singing, headed for the wharf where a barbecue was in progress.

Adam walked the length of the street before he found David with five or six boys near the churchyard. David was standing apart, facing the others. His hat was gone, his jacket torn and covered with dirt. His face was cut and bruised. One eye was rapidly closing. He stood, back to the wall, his feet wide apart. When Adam came closer, he saw a boy lying on the ground. The boy started to rise but David knocked him down, shouting, "It's not true—it's a lie."

"David, what does this mean?" Adam called out. The town boys, hearing his voice, took to their heels and disappeared into the pine grove back of the churchyard.

Mary came swiftly around the corner of the wall. "Oh, David," she cried, running forward. "David, what has happened?" He drew away and stood looking up at Adam.

"It's not true what he says." Adam had a premonition of what was coming.

"What isn't true, darling?" Mary said, wiping the dirt from his face with his handkerchief.

"He said I was a bastard—a dirty bastard. He said my father was Mr. No-man and my mother was a slave. I hit him. It's not true." Suddenly the fight left him. He leaned against Mary's shoulder, the tears making white marks down his grimy cheeks.

"Of course not, course not," Mary said soothingly, tightening her arms about the child. Adam turned away. He did not want to see the boy's bruised face or listen to his accusing words.

They rode home silently, David in front of Adam on the saddle. Mary took them to Queen's Gift with her. She doctored the child's eye with soothing lotion and set his clothes right. David had not cried out again. Mary walked into the garden with him while Adam paced the floor of the drawing room.

A little later, leaving David in the garden, she returned to Adam. "The child does not realize what the word means," she said, laying her hand on his arm to halt his restless pacing. "He can't understand."

Adam looked down at her. She was smiling a little, but her eyes were sad.

"Of course not—not today, but some other day he will understand and what am I to say to him then?"

He fell silent again. It was all so sordid . . . he had wanted to protect David, to build up a wall about the boy that would hold the curious world away from him. He knew now that was impossible. He should have liked his son to remember today of all days—to remember a man reading a Declaration of Independence. The child would not remember strong, brave words that made men free. He would remember other words—words he could not understand—and a crowd of jeering boys.

"Don't, Adam, don't look like that. You break my heart," Mary exclaimed. "Don't feel so badly. Look at him now in the garden."

Adam went to the window. David was standing on a chair. Around him a dozen dogs were yelping as he held a piece of cake just out of their reach. His fresh young voice came clearly through the open window. "Jump for it, Rover! Jump for it! Up—up—up—that's it!"

"He has already forgotten," Mary said. "A few spice cakes were all he needed to comfort him."

The sadness did not leave Adam's face. "For today—yes,

448

but it will not always be like this, Mary. When the day comes that he understands he will turn from me, and nothing I can do will prevent it. I must take him away from here, into a new land, a new country where he can grow to manhood without this background of fear."

In common with many women in the Province, Mary Warden thought the Carolinians were finished with the Revolution after the victory of the militia at the Widow Moore's Bridge. Since that time the Royalists had either fled the Province, been disarmed or retreated to their plantations under bond against taking up arms.

Mary and William Warden dined one night at Buncombe Hall as guests of Colonel Buncombe. Mary smiled to herself as they drove under the great sign swinging from the entrance gate, "Welcome All to Buncombe Hall." No one but a man as generous as the Colonel would think of such a thing. The Albemarle folk had laughed when he first came from St. Kitts and built the great palace on his Tyrell plantation. But they no longer laughed. They realized his generosity was genuine and took him to their hearts.

Mary sat at the long table, covered with crystal and gold plate, and listened to the talk. Samuel Johnstone, who sat at Mary's right, spoke of a new levy of troops.

"But why?" Mary asked, suddenly aroused. "Why do we need more troops? We have beaten the Royalists. We are at peace—free from England forever."

Iredell leaned forward, his thin face serious. "You must remember we are a union now, Mary, united in a common cause."

"Just what does that mean?" she asked quickly, alarmed by the implication.

"It means that we have a common cause, a common fight. It means more than driving the British out of one Province."

Johnstone said, "It means, Mary, that we will have to send soldiers to help other Provinces who have not had our good fortune in getting rid of Royalist armies. South Carolina is calling for help now. In a short time, we must raise troops for a Continental army."

"You are saying that our men must fight in the North— and the South?" Mary could not keep her voice steady.

Iredell answered, "Yes, and in the West also. We've heard that Martin is sending men to rouse the Indians in the western countries against the mountain people. There is trouble in Tennessee and Kentucky."

449

Mary sank back in her chair. She was depressed by their words. She had hoped after the Whig victory that the soldiers would come back to their plantations to take up their old work on the land—that there would be peace once more, a long peace.

Colonel Buncombe turned to Ann Blount, who sat on his right.

"I suppose all of you women had these same thoughts. You want your men at home."

Ann's face flushed. Her voice trembled with emotion. "Why should our men fight outside our own Province?" she asked passionately. "Let the other Colonies fight their own battles as we have fought ours."

"I'm afraid it isn't as simple as that, Ann," Iredell said, quietly patting her hand. "You will have to learn to be brave and wait."

Mary looked about the table. Fine honorable men, she thought, these Iron Men of Albemarle! The women must not lag behind the men. They would have to face this new situation with some semblance of courage. She turned suddenly to Samuel Johnstone. "Samuel, how long will this war last?"

He looked down at her affectionately, wishing he could spare her. "How long? Only God knows, Mary, but I think it will be years—many years before we can hope to break the power of Britain in our country."

"How can we win?" she asked, her voice unsteady.

"Only by the courage and endurance of all our people, Mary, men and women alike. But here comes Hewes to talk to you. Ask him what you asked me. He knows more than anyone of us about what is going on since he has been in Philadelphia at the Congress."

Mary listened to Hewes with a sinking heart. For the first time she faced what she must have known since Alamance—that this was not a war to be won by a battle that had lasted but three minutes. It would be a long struggle that would rend the very souls of the people and the land.

After dinner Mary saw William signaling her from the doorway. She knew he dreaded the long drive home. Colonel Buncombe walked with them to their coach and raised Mary's hand to his lips.

"Good night, Mary, good night. I'm sorry the talk at the table was so serious. Dinner talk should be light, gay—I wonder if it will ever be that way again?"

As they drove through the pine forest, the moon came up —a great yellow globe on the dark waters of the Sound.

After some time, William spoke. "I wanted to leave early, Mary. I didn't want to stay for the discussion of the new constitution."

Mary turned her head. The light from the coach lanterns was too dim for her to see her husband's expression. "Is there something wrong?" she asked quickly.

"No, not yet, but there may be. There is a radical element that is hard to hold down. I told Sam Johnstone that he would be wise not to take any part in it but he informed me tonight that he is determined to put forth his views at the conventions and in the next Assembly."

Mary wondered at the tone of his voice but she expressed no opinion. William had been distant and silent of late, refusing to discuss the Whig victory or the "Insurrection," as he persisted in calling it.

"I think Joseph Hewes has lost his mind," he said bitterly. "All this talk of shipbuilding. He's letting that John Paul—Jones, as he calls himself now—lead him around by the nose. Seven ships—I heard him say. He'll wreck his business if he's not careful." He continued after a moment, "Maybe it's all right for Hewes. He hasn't any family to think of but a man might easily carry his patriotism too far."

Mary was too surprised at her husband's words to answer. They drove through the dark woods in silence.

Adam had a letter from George Rogers Clark late in August, asking him to join him on the secret mission to the Mississippi. This fitted in well with his plans. Sara could go to visit her father in New York. He would take David to Virginia and leave him at Annandale on his way to Williamsburg, where he would meet Clark. They would start from Fort Pitt, then follow the Ohio to the Mississippi. He would still be in time for the harvest in the Cahokia country. He wanted to get away from Rutledge Riding. Seeing Lavinia every day was a constant reminder of Peyton, and he wanted desperately to forget.

When he told his plans to Mary Warden she turned white and caught at the back of a chair for support.

"Do you think you are no longer needed here, Adam?" she asked sharply.

Adam looked at her, surprised at her intensity. "The country is quiet, now. The other Colonies will soon follow our example and run the Royalists out. Clark has a plan for the western territories and he wants my assistance. After I have talked with Patrick Henry, we will go directly to Kentucky."

"What is this plan?" Mary asked, her voice husky.

"It is still confidential, but there is a project to take the western country from the British before they realize we are in revolt."

"I think I understand, Adam. Revolution, once started, will have many angles we do not realize now. I hope you will not forget us here."

That was foolish, she thought, not looking at him. How could he forget? "Revolution changes us, Adam. It seems that I can never laugh again without its hurting me inside, in my heart. The long wait—the long silent nights of waiting. Oh, Adam, what will happen to our unhappy country?" Tears came to her eyes and fell on her cheek. She made no effort to conceal her feeling or to wipe away the tears. Adam took out his handkerchief and touched it to her cheeks. "Thank you," she said, absently. "I'm silly to cry. It isn't just the country— you are going away. How can I stand this long agony of waiting when you are not here to help me?"

Adam put his arms about her shoulders, but he was not thinking of her. "We will win," he said slowly. "We must win. We must think of every way to break through their defenses. After a while, we will have to take the offensive."

As he rode down the driveway he turned once. She was standing in the door, a small, lonely figure. Smiling tearfully, she waved her hand. From a long time, he could think of nothing but the despair on her lovely triangular face.

BOOK
FOUR

Chapter 32

WAR
LETTERS

MARY missed Adam more this time than she had ever before during his many other absences. Perhaps it was because of the pall that hung over the land, she reasoned with herself, or because of her foreboding of disaster. Try as she might, she could put little heart into the activities with which she filled her days. It worried her too that she had seen Lavinia so few times in the year since Peyton's death. On several occasions she had gone to Rutledge Riding only to be told that Mrs. Rutledge was seeing no one. Mary spoke to Dr. Armitage about it.

He tamped the tobacco in his pipe before he answered her. "I'm worried about Lavinia—she's taking Peyton's death very hard. I confess, I'm a little surprised."

"Lavinia loved Peyton in spite of the anxiety he caused her," Mary told him.

"I suppose so. Women are strange—already she has forgotten everything but her love for him. In a little time she will convince herself that she was the only woman he ever loved."

Mary smiled a little sadly. "That's the way we are, Doctor. We don't want to face the truth."

The Doctor mumbled something she could not understand. Then he said, "Go over to see her. Perhaps you can get her out of the mood she's in. I hate to ask you, Mary—I'm always asking you to help me—" He peered over the rims of his spectacles. "You are too young to take on everyone's troubles, much too young."

So Mary rode over one Sunday after morning service at St. Paul's. She dreaded meeting Lavinia, especially since she had talked to the Doctor. What could she say to comfort her, to arouse in her a natural joy in her sturdy young baby? She opened the door and went into the silent living room. Lavinia, seated near the fire, glanced up from her needlework to greet her. She allowed Mary to kiss her, then sank back listlessly in the chair. The heavy black of her widowhood seemed to blot the life from her face; her eyes were darkly circled, as if she had not slept.

The room seemed cold and dismal in spite of the crackling fire. Mary suddenly felt very young and inexperienced. She racked her mind for something to say to break through the uncomfortable silence. In her anxiety to offer solace she inadvertently chose the wrong subject.

"I saw young Peyton in the village not long ago. What a handsome, manly boy he is, Lavinia—and so thoughtful of you! How old is he now?"

"Old enough to share his father's fate," Lavinia said bitterly. "He wants to join the Edenton Light Horse but I won't let him, Mary, I won't—I've sacrificed enough!" She put her hands to her face, her body shaking.

Mary tried to quiet her as best she could, shocked by the display of emotion that her well-intentioned words had aroused. After a time Lavinia grew calm again and spoke in a toneless voice.

"You must have heard that Adam did not go west as he had planned. From Virginia he was sent on some secret missions again. Marcy told me some time ago that he was in Charles Town."

Mary hid her surprise by asking about Sara. "Have you heard from her, Lavinia?"

Lavinia gave a short, mirthless laugh. "Why would I hear from her? She goaded me all the time she was here—saying small, sly things to break my composure, to anger me—trying to force me back to my plantation when she knew I couldn't bear to step into that house again. Well, I hope she's satisfied among her Royalists now."

She stiffened her black-clad body. "I hate Royalists," she went on fiercely. "They have widowed me and made my sons fatherless. I hate them all—more than any, I hate the Macdonald clan!"

"Don't agitate yourself so, Lavinia," Mary spoke gently. "The Macdonalds were our enemies but Flora Macdonald is a tragic figure and a courageous woman."

Lavinia stared at Mary as if she were insane. "How dare you speak of the Macdonalds to me?" she asked. Her voice was shrill, her eyes burned with anger. After a moment she got up and left the room.

Mary rode homeward, lost in reflection. She was much distressed by the anguish she had just witnessed and upset by her own inability to soothe Lavinia's frayed nerves. How could a gracious, lovely woman like Lavinia have changed so much?

In the driveway at Queen's Gift she saw several saddle horses tied to the hitching rack. Without changing her habit she went into the drawing room where she found William with Colonel Buncombe and Samuel Johnstone. Johnstone had an open letter in his hand, as if he had been reading aloud. The men put down their brandy glasses and greeted Mary warmly.

"I was just starting to read a letter from Joseph Hewes," Johnstone said. "He asked me to let you see it, Mary, so that you would know what was going on at the Philadelphia Convention."

"From what I hear, there is a wide difference of opinion," Mary said.

Colonel Buncombe nodded. He was a red-faced, choleric man with a quantity of unruly brown hair tied in a club, now guiltless of powder.

"I can see what's holding them back. In God's name, why can't they stand for independence without all this arguing and backbiting? Their actions in this convention are a disgrace. No wonder they are laughing at us in England—saying on the floor of Parliament that we will never be able to weld the Colonies together."

Johnstone said, "It takes time, Edward, but it will be done."

"I doubt it." William's words came slowly. "I doubt whether other Colonies will stand out against the King much longer. After all, it's only a question of taxes. Why can't that be settled? Suppose the Colonies have to pay for the maintenance of the Colonial army and for extra food? It will not hurt us."

Johnstone did not take his shrewd appraising eyes from William. He spoke deliberately, almost, Mary thought, with premeditation. "You don't believe we should break with England, William?"

"No, no," William answered. "I'm sure we are better off as we are. Look at the trouble we are having here now—radicals against conservatives, each fighting to get his way in framing our own constitution. You should know, Johnstone. You're having trouble enough with Penn and the Halifax group. Doesn't that show what will happen here? We can't have a government strong enough to rule without the King and Parliament."

Buncombe stirred uneasily, looking at Mary, trying to signal Johnstone.

"What does Hewes say?" Mary asked quickly.

Johnstone picked up the letter once more, but there was something in his manner that troubled Mary. He seemed to be striving not to show his antagonism toward William. While he read Mary rested her head against the back of the chair. The visit to Rutledge Riding had wearied her bodily and mentally. Now all this talk of arguments and quarrels among the Colonies themselves . . .

"Philadelphia
"Feb. 14, 1776

". . . I'm sending a pamphlet called Common Sense. It is a curiosity. We have not put up any to go by the wagon for general distribution, not knowing how you would relish the idea of total independence. The author is not known. Some say Dr. Franklin had a hand in it, but he denies it. It is the first cry for complete independence since Mecklenburg raised her voice in May of last year—and of that, Tom Jefferson swears he never saw the Mecklenburg Resolves, but Hooper and I know that to be a lie since the paper was delivered into his hands. At the time he said it was ill-advised to allow one voice to declare until all the Colonies spoke together. We saw the wisdom of that, but now he 'forgets' he has ever seen the Mecklenburg papers—but that's Wily Tom all over!

"All accounts from England seem to agree that we shall have a dreadful storm bursting on our heads through all America this spring. We must not shrink from it; we ought not show any symptoms of fear; the nearer it approaches and the greater the sound, the more fortitude, calm and steady firmness we ought to possess. If we mean to defend our liberties, our dearest rights and privileges against the power of Britain to the last extremity, we ought to bring ourselves to such temper of mind as to stand unmoved at the bursting of an earthquake, although the storm thickens. I, myself, feel quite composed—resigned to the inevitable.

"I'm glad that North Carolina has taken its stand; other Colonies are more backward. The talk in the Convention is still for conciliation. Only yesterday, a delegate got up on the floor of the Convention Hall and said, 'My first wish is that America may be free; my second, that we may be restored to peace and harmony with Great Britain on just and proper terms.'

"So you see how it goes here. I'm weary of all this talking and no action. We may go on for weeks—even months. I see no prospect of reconciliation. Nothing is left but to fight it out, now that we are unanimous in our councils. Jealousies, ill-natured bickerings and backbiting take the place of reason and argument. Some of us urge strongly for independence and eternal separation; others wish to wait a little longer and have the opinion of their constituents on that subject. You must write us your opinions. Hooper and Penn concur with my views."

458

Mary waited for William to speak first, but he remained silent, his eyes fixed on the floor.

In a little time, Johnstone and Colonel Buncombe rose to go. Mary walked to the gallery with them. They stood talking while the horses were being brought around.

"Rutledge should bring us a comprehensive report of the situation in South Carolina," Johnstone said. "We sent him to find out how many regiments would be needed there. I've been nominated to head the Committee of Secrecy, Mary. All intelligence that comes in must be sifted by us before we submit it to the Continental Congress."

"When will Rutledge be home?" Buncombe asked.

"In a few weeks, unless he decides to sail direct from Charles Town to the Chesapeake," Johnstone replied.

Mary watched them ride away, her mind in a turmoil. She went slowly through the hall toward the stairway. William was waiting for her, standing at the open door of his book room.

"Will you come in a moment, Mary?" he asked. "There are a few matters I would like to take up with you."

She wondered what he wanted to talk about and hoped it was nothing serious. She felt that she couldn't listen to anything more without screaming, but she went in as he asked and took the chair he indicated.

He walked about the room for a few moments, pulling at his ear, a trick he had when he was troubled.

"I didn't continue the discussion because I was afraid I would say more than I should at this time. I don't agree with Johnstone—I don't like his views. I was about to say, I no longer like him."

Mary glanced up quickly. "He is your neighbor, William, and an old friend."

"Old friendships won't stand the strain of what is happening now, Mary, or what is to come. Every man must serve his country in the way he thinks best." He paused in his restless walk to lay a hand on her shoulder. "You are very young, my dear. You must not let events distress you any more than you can help. Learn to trust no one—keep your own council."

"Why, William! What do you mean?"

"I mean, my dear, that we have come to a time when neighbor will fight neighbor—and old friendships break under the weight of new beliefs; families will break faith within the family group—" He broke off and sat down, gloomily studying the pattern on the Turkey carpet.

Mary did not speak for a moment. Then she said, "That is a very discouraging outlook, William."

He didn't seem to hear her words. He was intent on his own thoughts. "I shall have to be away much of the time now, Mary," he said. "My comings and goings should not be made the subject of comment in the village."

The sensation of uneasiness increased in her mind. Why should there be secrecy and mysteries? Why should he go away on secret journeys? Why should Adam Rutledge be sent to Charles Town to get reports on conditions in the South? And why should Hooper and others be touring Virginia and the Province on the same task?

William answered the words she did not speak. "The preparations for war are as important as the battles that are fought, my dear. I wish I could think of some way to protect you—to keep you from experiencing the dread days that are sure to come. You are so young, Mary, so very young," he repeated. After a moment, he added, "But the men who fight this war will be young. Only a few of us are old enough to know what lies ahead."

"William!" she cried. "Why do you talk like this? Are you going into danger? You must tell me. Surely, you trust me, your wife."

"Danger will be the daily companion of all of us," he said, paying no heed to her question. "Soon we will lose all individuality; personal things will no longer matter—home or family—or life." He took up some loose papers on his desk. Mary knew the interview was over. She left the room and walked slowly upstairs. The gloom of the dark days ahead lay heavily on her heart.

The days that followed were filled with anxiety for Mary. She looked forward to Adam's home-coming, yet in her heart she knew he would not come back to Rutledge Riding before he went north.

The spring passed and summer came, with no word from him. Then one day, while she was in the dispensary for the weekly distribution of medicine to the slaves, Samuel Johnstone rode in with William. He had a letter for her from Adam. They stayed for a moment, watching her give out Peru bark and blue mass, before they went to William's office.

Mary watched them walking across the grass toward the house, glad that the breech between them seemed to have lessened. She sat quietly, asking questions of her ailing slaves, while Cissie and Ebon gave out the medicines.

It was an hour before she finished and went to the house. She heard William's voice and Johnstone's as she went up the stairs to her room. It was a long time before she broke the seal of the letter in her hand. She wondered at her instinctive restraint. Something had happened to her these past months. She remembered a time, not so long ago, when she had deliberately delayed reading a letter from Adam so that her pleasure in it would be heightened. Now she dreaded to read what she knew he must say. She sat thinking back over the days before this horrible conflict had stricken the whole country—of riding with Adam across the fields in the brisk October sunshine—of the scent of jasmine and honeysuckle in the East Garden—and of the sound of his voice. Sometimes she could scarcely remember that vibrant sound or the look on his lean strong face. Now other things intruded themselves into her thoughts: the village, as she had seen it this morning; its quiet streets; people scarcely speaking to old friends—the outbreak of feuds between the Tories and Whigs; gaols overflowing; stocks and whipping posts in constant use; the death of young men, and those of middle years. The armies had levied their toll, yet every night old Jeremiah Nixon, the watchman, walked his weary stumbling way among the deserted streets and closed shops, carrying his lantern and shouting, "All's well—nine o'clock—all's well." What a travesty! Nothing was well anywhere. She brought herself back with an effort and turned to the letter.

> "Headquarters Camp Stanton
> near Germantown
> "August 27th, 1777

"Mary dear:

"You see by the above that I have not gone west as I had hoped. When the North Carolina Brigades were sent to help General Washington I joined my regiment at Williamsburg. Tomorrow we march to Philadelphia.

"I have just come in from an assembly of the troops where General Washington's orders were read. Not an official or a soldier may leave the camp tonight. In the morning at four o'clock (if it doesn't rain) we march. We stop outside of Philadelphia so that the officers can see that the soldiers are in proper position and the lines straight and soldierly. General Nathaniel Greene's division marches first, then Stevens' and Lord Stirling's.

"Our army makes a brave show on parade, Mary. It is the General's desire that we make the people of Philadelphia, and the members of Congress, aware that we are an army.

"I have been working on the plan for three days and am full of it. I should be writing about events in Virginia and the talk I had with Patrick Henry, but that must wait for another letter. One thing I must tell you, however. I left David with Paige at Annandale. His children and the boy are great friends. It is better this way. He will attend school with Paige's boys and will be happy and content.

"Just now an officer came into our tent. He is going about the encampment, among the other officers, instructing them about their conduct tomorrow. They are to give great attention that the men carry their arms well and appear as decent as circumstances will permit. No officer may leave his post during the march through the city. If any soldier leaves the ranks, he is to receive thirty-nine lashes at the first halting place afterward. People must not be permitted to press in on the troops. There shall be no greater space between divisions and brigades than is necessary to distinguish them. The wagon trains, baggage and field pieces are to be sent to the right to avoid the city entirely. They will wait at the middle ferry for the troops.

"Not a woman belonging to the army (camp followers, etc.) is to be seen with the troops in their march through the city.

"The officers will have their hands full. We must make a good appearance in Philadelphia where the Chief has many enemies who are making it hard for him. Tonight the camp has extra patrols. The men are sitting by the fires shining arms and equipment, rubbing down horses and doing their best to freshen their tired uniforms—almost an impossible task.

"These are the orders General Washington issued today:

" 'The drum and fife of each Brigade are to be collected in the center of it, and a tune for the quickstep played, but in such a manner that the men may step with ease, and without *dancing* along or totally disregarding the music, as has been too often the case. The men are excused from carrying their camp kettles tomorrow.'

"From what we hear, Sir William Howe has his eyes on Philadelphia. If he attacks by land and sends troops by sea, we have no hope of holding him off. Thank heaven, he moves at a snail's pace!

"You must have heard that our leaders are discouraged. Congress is in confusion and does not give the Chief the support he needs. He has the worry of suspecting that some of his officers are not loyal. One Irish soldier of fortune is working to get the General out and Gates in as commander-in-chief. I do not think he will succeed, but it is depressing for General Washington not to have full loyalty or authority.

"I could not write this much, except that I'm sending it by Reading Blunt, paymaster of the North Carolina troops. It will be put into his dispatch bag and not opened until Samuel Johnstone has it.

"Mary, I have come to believe it will be a long time before we beat the British. It isn't a question of months, but of years. For the present, I will be with this army, though I feel that my real place is in the West. There is much I would like to tell you but it is not wise to write. I'm glad that there is no war in North Carolina and that our Colony is at peace—at least for the present.

"Notwithstanding the General's strict orders, there are many complaints about the conduct of the army—repeated complaints of pillaging and plundering, burning fences, stealing horses and cattle. These things are taken care of by payment of money, and the marauders lashed if caught. Other atrocities are more dire. Even with many women camp followers, some terrible crimes are committed. A man was hanged yesterday in front of the entire army for the crime of rape.

"And now, my dear, it is almost four in the morning, the hour set for the march. I want you to know that you are often in my thoughts.

"ADAM."

The next letter she had from him was dated Valley Forge, December 1777. The paper was soiled and torn, as if it had passed through many hands before it finally reached Queen's Gift. Mary found it lying on the hall table when she came in from taking baskets to the fishermen's families in the lower village. She carried it upstairs to her room.

"Dear Mary:

"We post notices telling of the success of our troops in the North, laying stress because of our own defeats and inaction here. Burgoyne has been defeated by Gates, but here we have not been blessed by Providence with any major victory.

"At Brandywine due, most of us believe, to the rank cowardice of Anthony Wayne, we lost the day. However, we retreated in fair order. Wayne will come up for court-martial soon. Some say, however, it was Hampton who mistook orders. . . . Whoever is to blame, we were the losers.

"My tent-mate, Colonel Irvine of the First Pennsylvania, was captured by the enemy when he attacked the British camp on Chestnut Hill near White Marsh early this month. We feel badly about this for his men fled and left him on the field severely wounded. He was sent to prison in Philadelphia. We have sent fifty dollars through the exchange agent, Thomas Franklin, so that he can buy a few small comforts. The depreciation of our currency is so great that it will be of small help, but we had no hard money to send.

"I have two new tent-mates: one, a charming Frenchman,

463

Count deFluery, who came with the French volunteers; the other, Captain Andrew Inglis of the First Massachusetts, a member of General Washington's family. He is a puritanical person, very reserved while deFluery is gay and full of life. They are so different that it is always amusing to watch them.

"I suppose you have heard that the British are in Philadelphia. Sara is there with her father. They came down from New York. I wish she had not come, but her father supplies the British army with foodstuffs, so he follows the troops. It would be better for her to be in New York or London. She is in the midst of the gaiety that pervades Howe's army. Strangely enough, from all reports he likes it. There are great tales about the orgies of his officers—drinking, gambling and worse. But one cannot be sure of the truth of these things.

"We are in bad case here. We have not enough food or clothing, and the winter quarters are wretched. The poor fellows are deserting by the hundreds. I don't know what we would do if it were not for Baron Steuben. He is drilling the men daily.

"The fourth man to share our tent is Lieutenant Walker who acts as interpreter for Steuben. Yesterday, the soldiers were so low-spirited and made so many mistakes that the Baron flew into a rage. He turned the troops over to Walker, saying in fury: 'Come take over, Walker—I can curse them no longer!'

"It would make your heart ache to see these poor discouraged fellows walking through the snow, feet bound in rags, shivering in their thin, ragged clothes. But I must not discourage you with my story. There will be a way out, I'm sure. The General is desperate, but determined. Orders are stricter. Officers who desert will be shot down; soldiers given three hundred lashes. The Chief keeps up his courage outwardly. God knows what his deep thoughts are when he is alone in his cheerless, comfortless tent night after night.

"You will see the spirit of the man in these general orders he posted today. In a way, they show you not only the man himself, but the fear that pervades the army and the country.

" 'For two years we have maintained the war and struggled with difficulties innumerable, but the prospect has brightened.

" 'If we behave like men, the third campaign will be our last. Ours is the main army. The country looks to us for protection. The General assures his countrymen and fellow soldiers that he believes the critical, the important moment is at hand, which demands their most spirited exertions in the field. There glory awaits to crown the brave. Peace, freedom and happiness will be the rewards of victory.

" 'Animated by motives like these, soldiers fighting the cause of innocence, humanity and justice will never give way, but with undaunted resolution press on to conquest.'

464

"Brave words, Mary, bravely spoken to hearten the discouraged. As always, I bring my worries to you. But I really should not burden you with the worries of the whole Continental army!

"It is inaction that kills us; that, and the lack of money. Some of the officers are talking about a huge lottery to raise money. So far the Chief has not given his consent. It would have to be done quietly, but through the Paymaster's Department, so there could be no criticism in the handling of the money.

"I wish I could put my foot on Carolina soil again. Its rich warmth is far away from the frozen earth that makes the floor of our tent. Do not worry about me, my dear. I'm comfortable enough.

"I heard today that I may be detached from the army and sent to the Treasury service. I hope not. The task of raising money is overwhelming.

"ADAM"

A long silence followed with little news of the armies and the Carolinian troops. In Raleigh's Eden it was hard for people to realize that a war was being fought, that somewhere in the North the great struggle for freedom was in the balance. Edenton was quiet, too quiet. There was little shipping. The trade to the Indies was cut off by Sir Peter Parker's ships. South Carolina was calling for help—draining North Carolina of militia. Leaders protested. What would happen if North Carolina were invaded? But the long peace made people forget. They protested against taxes under the new government almost as violently as they had under the Royal Government or the Lords Proprietors. A letter from Adam made Mary sharply aware that they, in Raleigh's Eden, were far from bearing the burden of war.

"I have been sent to the Treasury. It is work I do not like but it must be done by someone. My task is to stand between the Paymaster and Congress and try to help raise money for the army.

"It is terrible—beyond words. We juggle the small amounts that come in, sending a little to this brigade and to that, spreading it thin . . . all the time knowing how badly the troops need clothing and food.

"I cannot sleep at night thinking of it. If we could only have the yield of our plantation! But that is the trouble—there are no men to work the farms. Only young boys and women. The armies sweep the country bare. If we had hard money, we could buy from France, or Germany, or Spain. We have ships now, but you can understand why those countries will not take our paper.

"Bullock, Sharpe Delancy and I have been working for weeks on a plan for a government lottery. This will be very secret, for

465

his Excellency will have to have the money set aside for a particular purpose. We hope to raise a very large fund from this lottery, but I do not know just when it will be put into effect. You know how hard pressed we are when we resort to a government lottery!

"Please write me about things at Rutledge Riding—and at Raleigh's Eden. I hear little home news. I saw Joseph Hewes a few days ago. He is still talking ships and will have a place in the government. He said John Paul (you remember him at Queen's Gift?) was making great headway building ships.

"The North Carolina troops with Washington's army are homesick, but they are not in as bad mental state as the Pennsylvania Brigades. Nathaniel Greene is General Washington's 'right arm.' There is a rumor that he will be sent south. Our spies in New York report that the British are planning a southern campaign. This is General Cornwallis' idea. He is at grips with Howe and Clinton—he is a better officer than either, the General thinks. The British can thank him for their success at Brandywine, and the command of the Delaware.

"A letter *may* reach me sent to the Treasury Department at Lancaster where Congress is now sitting.

"I'm sending this with the official mail, hoping it will reach you sometime. We are in very bad position, but we may strike a blow before long that will change everything. Pray for us, Mary.

"ADAM"

That was the last letter Mary received from Adam for many months. She spent anxious days wondering what had happened. She went about the plantation listlessly, driving herself, trying to think of the tasks of every day living.

"You must get hold of yourself," Dr. Armitage said to her one day when he stopped by the plantation. "I can't have you sick on my hands—I'm too busy."

"Is there so much sickness?" Mary asked.

"No, as a whole the district is doing very well—it isn't that. I'm working day and night to get medical supplies ready."

Mary realized by the length of the silence that she was supposed to ask questions.

"Medical supplies—? Why—?" she asked.

He leaned forward. "It is the opinion of our Secret Committee that we can't hope for peace in our borders for long, Mary. If South Carolina doesn't stop the enemy—" He paused significantly.

"You mean we may be invaded from the south?"

"Yes—or from the north—or we may be bombarded from the Sound. At least, that's what Sam tells me."

466

Mary leaned forward, her eyes fixed on his. "We must do something to help you, Doctor. I'll go into Edenton tomorrow and get the women together. They had better start scraping lint and tearing bandages again. In earnest this time."

"That would be a great help," Armitage said. "I'll give you instructions if you come to my office tomorrow." He rose to go. "Besides, I think it a good thing for the women to be working; then they don't have so much time to worry about their menfolk."

"Have you heard from Adam?" Mary asked as they stood on the gallery steps waiting for his coach to be brought up.

Armitage shook his head. "No, I haven't heard a word. Neither has Owen or Johnstone." He looked at her sharply. "If it's Adam you're grieving over, Mary, I wouldn't. It's going to be a long war, and there's no time for you to be fretting yourself to a shadow about Adam Rutledge. He's married—and so are you. You've got too much sense to let anything like that get the best of you. You'll have to put your personal affairs aside now and give your mind and your heart to your country." His words were harsh, but his eyes were full of sympathy.

Mary managed a smile. "I know," she said. "I understand —don't think I'm not trying."

A few days later, a letter from Adam reached her at Queen's Gift. It was only a page long, undated and unsigned, as if he had been interrupted while he was writing.

"Fort Pitt

"Dear Mary:

"I came here last week from Philadelphia on work for the Treasury Department. The day after I came, the Commandant had word that I had been loaned to the Governor of Virginia, for a special mission with General Clark. I'm to go west as soon as he arrives.

"I found Fort Pitt in sad distress—the soldiers almost at the point of mutiny.

"Money, money, money—that is all I hear. But where are we to get it? You cannot blame the soldiers who came into the war fired with patriotic zeal to fight for liberty. If they weaken now it is because they have nothing to send home to starving wives and children, for they have not been paid their meager wage.

"Mary, I have written thus far without a word of what is heavy on my heart. The week before I left for Fort Pitt, I heard that Sara, who was in Philadelphia with her father, was desperately ill with black fever. I tried every way to get into the city—under a

467

flag of truce, or exchange. I even tried to get through the British lines in disguise, but it was impossible. I left without knowing whether she lives, or has died.

"This morning, I had a note by courier from deFleury. You remember he was my tent-mate at Valley Forge? He and Andrew Inglis will search for her as soon as our troops get into Philadelphia.

"I have had much time alone these past months. I have thought often of Rutledge Riding and the old life in Albemarle, and of my own affairs. Mary, I have never understood Sara, and have not done so much as I should have done to give her the happiness she deserved. I think of the years she has spent chained to a bed or a chair—a living death. If she lives, I will spend all my life trying to make her happy. . . ."

Mary handed the letter to William when she had finished. He put on his reading spectacles and went through it carefully.

"I was wondering how I would tell you—" he began. "I heard today that Sara Rutledge's body was being sent to Rutledge Riding for burial. I met Lavinia in the village. She said Owen had had official notification only yesterday." He stood for a moment looking out the window. Then he crossed the room and laid his hand on her arm. "One can't help thinking it is for the best, my dear, but it is always sad to lose a friend."

After a short time, he left the room. Mary sat without moving, unaware of the passing time. The memory of the early days of their friendship came to her. There was so much that she did not understand in Sara—traits of character not accounted for by her illness. Sara had been deeply religious yet she had wanted to hurt, to annoy, to be cruel to those nearest to her. Mary remembered a comment of Lady Caroline's after a visit when Sara had been unusually trying. "Weak people always get the better of the strong," she had said. "They have the tenacity to hang on about small matters that other people will not trouble about. That's Sara Rutledge —she'll always have her way with Adam through the strength of weakness."

Mary's mind turned to Lady Caroline then. She wondered what had happened to her. Hewes had told her some time ago that one of his captains had seen her in Charlotte Amalie, riding in a fine coach drawn by four black horses. The people there said she was fabulously wealthy, that strange things happened at her great stone house on St. Johns' Island, and that strange ships put into the little bay that lay hidden by the coco palms of her great estate. Mary wondered if Adam had heard of her or seen her during his long mysterious journeys in the South.

She got up and walked to the window but she did not see the beauty of the garden and of the wood and water. Her mind was filled with anxiety when she thought of the swift changes of her little world. They were rushing forward to disaster with incredible swiftness . . .

Chapter 33

CORNWALLIS
IS COMING

THE swift passage of time was measured now in events, not days or months or years—events that would forever lay their imprint on a country and on the lives of men. The tide of war moved southward. The Carolinas became the testing ground, and death and destruction visited the land.

Lord Cornwallis was ordered south. With him ships-of-the-line and the best troops England boasted: well-mounted hunters and hounds to chase the foxes to earth; troops in Virginia to move southward; troops at Charles Town to move north.

"Squeeze the Carolinas in a scissors grip! Ravage and terrorize! End the war quickly, no matter what the cost. Sweep the land like the Scourge of God, free it of rebels and rebellion!"

So Sir Henry Clinton ordered, and Lord Cornwallis concurred, for it had long been his plan. Now Clinton, jealous and afraid of the better general, let him have his way. "He will hang himself," Clinton said to his aide, "and we will be free of him. The Carolinas will be his undoing."

With Cornwallis rode Banastre Tarleton, an Adonis with waving hair and bold black eyes that could flash with lightning rage or soften with quick pity. Tarleton galloped at the head of his terrible dragoons with lifted sword, the flame of the sword that would set fire to the land.

Like a holocaust, the British swept through South Carolina from the sea to the northern border. Charles Town fell, battled from sea and land. North Carolina troops, lent to defend their southern neighbors, retreated in disorder. Their commander, Gates, ran faster than his soldiers to ignominious defeat. Augusta fell, followed by Ninety-Six. Cornwallis now tasted the fruits of a well-planned victory. The American generals, Caswell and Buford, separated near Camden in disordered retreat; Tarleton and his heavy dragoons followed in fast pursuit. Tarleton caught up with Buford and gave battle disastrous to the American, pushing him and his ragged army over the border into North Carolina. After three years of peace, the invasion of North Carolina had begun.

From North to South, from the sea to the western mountains, the word spread: *Buford has been defeated and no quarter given. No-Quarter Tarleton is sweeping all beneath the iron hoofs of his dragoons.*

A flame of wild terror spread before him, despair and death in his wake. Tarleton and his legions were but the prelude to something more terrible—Cornwallis and his iron army!

A cry went up the length and breadth of the state: *Cornwallis is coming—Cornwallis is coming!*—a cry to bring cold terror to women and children, and send the straggling, untrained soldiers to hide in the mountains and the deep swamps. *Cornwallis is coming!* The heel of the invaders was on the land!

The gentle land of the Carolinas was gashed and torn under the advancing armies. March and fight—retreat and run—rally and strike again. Blood of King's rebels and King's men watered the earth. The tide of war moved north, a mighty force of destruction.

The young untrained army of the Carolinas fought doggedly but without hope. Fought and held—fought and lost. Ran—ran—ran. Turned to struggle forward again, always without hope. They had forgotten what they were fighting for. Freedom—the word was forgotten in the stark terror of invasion.

They thought of homes at stake; of land that they had snatched from forest and swamp, raw land that had never felt the weight of plow until they had claimed it from the wilderness.

Days, weeks and months found them facing defeat that felled them to earth. Rising stubbornly to face another sun, they sank to earth again at nightfall. Then somewhere out of the long procession of time, an old battle cry rose again to the leaden skies—a cry that had served others in older days and far-off lands.

"God defend the right!" was whispered through set lips, through jaws locked in death on bloody fields of battle.

It was a struggle of raw troops, of unbearded boys, standing against men trained to the business of arms and war—raw troops, hungry, half frozen, in tattered shreds of uniforms, their bare feet bound in sacking or bark, leaving a bloody trail as they marched; boys who whimpered in the night for home and mothers—a ragamuffin army on the march over frozen ground, plunging through icy streams, hiding in the slime of swamps. The gnawing disgrace of generals who ran cut into their sick souls. "God defend the right!" The despairing cry of beaten men reached up to the ear of God.

Then Nathaniel Greene took over.

The heavy boom of cannon wakened Mary Warden from a deep sleep. She knew instantly that the dreaded invasion had begun. Enemy ships had come up Albemarle Sound to bombard Edenton and lay waste the land. The thing they had feared for so long had come at last.

She heard the sudden terrified wailing from the slave quarters, "Aiye—aiye—aiye," followed by the overlooker's rough voice cursing, shouting orders, commanding silence. Then the sharp incisive voice of William giving hurried instruction.

The fire had died to a few glowing embers and the room was cold. Mary reached for her wrapper. Thrusting her feet into furred shoes, she got out of bed. She was at the window as the second dull roar came reverberating over the water. The ships must be far off—near the entrance of the Sound.

She pulled the heavy curtains aside. It was just daylight. Below, she saw the slaves crowding around Saunders, the overlooker. Men were questioning, shouting and gesticulating. Women were kneeling on the ground, their hands lifted in prayer. Cissie was with the women, swaying from side to side, her voice raised, "Death and destruction, O Lord, death and destruction. Deliver us, O Lord God. Forgive us our sins." She was rapidly working herself into a state of frenzy.

Mary opened the casement. "Whatever are you shouting about, Cissie?" she called out. "Come up here and get my clothes. Tell Ebon to mend the fire at once."

The sound of her mistress' voice, ordering her to be about the everyday duties, brought the black woman back to reality. "For the Lord, I done forgot, Mis' Mary!"

The other slaves stopped keening.

"All of you women get about your work," Mary called. "Quickly now. Nothing is going to happen to you." She shut the window. The black women got up and moved off to their quarters, quieted for the moment. Saunders herded the men toward the woods where they were building a road for the charcoal gatherers.

Mary went back to bed to wait for the fire to take the chill off the room. A moment later, William came in. He looked

472

worried. His face was white and there were shadows under his eyes. Mary was surprised to see that he was fully dressed in his riding clothes, his greatcoat over his arm.

"Get up and dress, Mary," he said without preamble. "The privateers are coming up the Sound, shelling and destroying the plantations along the way. The Safety Committee has ordered women and children out of Edenton into the Back Country."

"I'm not going," Mary said flatly. "Why should we run like cowards because a few guns have been fired? It's absurd!"

"Don't be silly, Mary; we're not running. I have to go to Charlottetown. I want you to go with me."

"I don't want to go, William. If there is any trouble, I want to be at Queen's Gift."

"Get your clothes on," William said, as if she had not spoken, "warm clothes. I have ordered the coach. Cissie is packing your box. The whole village is moving out. I want to get started at once."

"Which way are you going?" Mary inquired.

"The interior of the Province, by the Catawba Springs road."

"What about the slaves, this house, all our belongings?"

"Damn the house! The slaves are taken care of. The overlooker has his orders. Hurry, we've very little time, I tell you. I must get away before the privateers reach here. After that, it would be too late."

"I'll stay here," Mary insisted, though she knew she was only saying words. William's exigence had enveloped her. She dressed swiftly, putting on a heavy cloth habit, laying out a cloth cape lined with squirrel and a pair of high, furred carriage boots.

Cissie came in with a canvas carryall strapped and ready. "I've got everything here, Mis' Mary, your blue silk dress and the new red wool. I put in the blue in case you go to a party. Mr. William says you travels light." She was crying.

"What's the matter, Cissie? Get your cloak and go down to the carriage."

William stopped her. "You're not taking the woman," he said shortly.

"But how can I get along without someone to dress me?"

"You can dress yourself for a day or two, I think." He turned to the weeping slave. "Stop that sniveling! Go tell Ebon to put my luggage in the coach."

Mary called after her, "Tell the groom to saddle Black Douglas."

William protested, then gave way to Mary's insistence. Mary thought it must be some work for the Colony that made him so anxious. Perhaps he was carrying papers and documents that the Safety Committee did not want to fall into enemy hands. The thought comforted her.

Mounted on her horse, she followed the coach down the long drive, turning to look back at the broad façade of the old house. She felt despondent. What they had long feared had come at last—privateersmen and galleys, frigates and sloops-of-war were sailing up Albemarle Sound. They would lay waste the beautiful land of Raleigh's Eden. Cornwallis was already at the southern border. Up and down the four rivers the hosts of war would come, trampling the rich fertile earth. The British would destroy, like a locust horde eating up the land. Edenton had no defense. The Edenton Light Horse was somewhere defending the long southern border.

Mary had heard horrible tales of brutality that came from Virginia and from South Carolina. Rumors had spread of invading ships and armies. The reports grew in volume and terror, although the Committee of Safety tried by every means to calm the frightened people. Two thousand Negroes had been sent ahead of the invading army for forage. They pillaged and looted—death, rape and violation.

The traitor, Benedict Arnold, had sailed south with a great army against the Virginia and Carolina coast. What if the British would occupy Albemarle Sound? Edenton would be the natural base for the invasion of southern Virginia. Cornwallis and his conquering army would advance from the south. North Carolina would be caught in the steel jaws of land and sea forces. They had not the defense to hold against such numbers. It would be the end forever of freedom.

These thoughts went through Mary Warden's mind as she galloped down the post road. In spite of William's protest, she cut across the woods to Adam Rutledge's North Plantation.

"I'll meet you at Chapman's Corner," she called over her shoulder as she turned. She must stop at the plantation and warn Owen and Gwennie. Lavinia was there with her youngest boy and David, who had been at North Plantation for several weeks.

Adam had been in constant motion for more than two years now. He had sent no word to her or to his friends in Edenton. She did not know, nor did anyone except the Secret Council of Safety, that he was doing the work of the Colonies in other ways than fighting. There was money to raise; meetings to be held by men of the North and South to devise means of holding the newly freed Colonies together as a unit. There were secret internal enemies—organized groups who were trying to break down the morale of Washington's armies; to oust Washington from command; to keep Congress from giving him support and money. With these men, Adam was a familiar figure, appearing from nowhere in Philadelphia, New York or Boston, at Fort Pitt or Fort Chartres.

If Mary had understood, it would have eased her heart. But she thought he had gone west to take up new land—that his old passion to acquire vast acreage had deadened him to responsibility to his country. It hurt her so deeply that she tried to put all thought of him from her mind. But she could not put him out of her heart, try as she would. In his remote detachment he was blind to so many things.

She thought of David. Mary loved Adam's son, loved him because he was Adam, a new Adam, brought strangely, almost furtively into the world—Ishmael, whose voice would be heard in the wilderness. Tears came to her eyes. Why could not David have been her child—hers and Adam's?

The North Plantation came into view. Owen Tewilliger, muffled in a heavy plaid shawl, was walking up and down the long gallery in the sun. He looked very frail and ill.

"Where is Lavinia?" Mary asked, as she dismounted, "and Gwennie and David? You must all get ready quickly and ride with us to Mecklenburg."

Owen turned his thin face toward her. She saw he did not know of the invasion.

"The privateers have come. They are shelling the plantations and villages along the Sound," she cried. "All the women and children are ordered out of Edenton. Please hurry, Owen! Call the slaves to get the horses harnessed to a coach."

Owen held the door for her to enter his book room. "Sit down, Mary. I'll call Lavinia and Gwennie."

Ths excitement suddenly left her. She laughed a little. "I needed you to quiet me, Owen," she said. "I've let Edenton's wild alarm catch me up."

Owen came back after sending a slave for the women. "We have known this was coming for three years, Mary. Why should we be alarmed now it is here? It was inevitable. You know that. Where is William?"

"I'm to meet him at Chapman's Corner," Mary answered.

"I came through the woods. I made better time that way. The roads are choked with frightened women and crying children fleeing to safety. It is all too terrible."

"Where is William taking you?" Owen asked, his self-control unchanged.

"To Catawba Springs. He has to see the Safety Committee at Charlottetown."

Owen nodded. Mary knew she was explaining William. She hated herself for even thinking that she must explain his actions. She got up impatiently. "Where are they? Where is David? We must get started at once, Owen."

Owen went to the door. At the threshold he paused. "Have you forgotten that I have been on parole ever since the first battle in South Carolina? I cannot leave North Plantation, Mary."

Mary had forgotten. "Does that matter?" she cried, "They are doing terrible things, horrible killings, not quick death, but slow torturing death. Why should you keep faith? You must come with us, Owen."

Owen shook his head. "I haven't long to live, Mary. I like to think that I have never broken my word."

"But it is a wrong oath, Owen, made under duress. Surely you—" Her voice trailed off. "I know you cannot go, Owen. I had forgotten the parole." She knew he would not leave, nor Gwennie. But Lavinia and her young child and David must go. "Please, Owen, tell them to hurry, hurry," she pleaded.

The door opened and Lavinia walked into the room. Mary had not seen her for months. She was as beautiful as ever but there was still nothing of the old gaiety.

"Hurry, Lavinia," she said. "Pack warm clothes for yourself and the boy. We must make haste."

Lavinia said to Owen, "Are you running, Owen?"

Owen shook his head.

Lavinia turned back to Mary. "I'll stay here, Mary. Gwennie won't go if Owen stays. Young Peyton will expect me to be here when he comes back with the Light Horse next month. I told him I would be waiting."

"But Lavinia, we aren't running away! You know I wouldn't do that! How could Peyton know this was going to happen? That privateers would come up the Sound? How do you know when he will be back, now that Cornwallis is at the border?"

A ghost of a smile came to Lavinia's lips. "I'll wait for him here," she said.

476

Mary made one more attempt to influence her. Taking her hands, she said, "Lavinia darling, you don't understand what this means. It will be war at its worst. The reports of the atrocities that have taken place in South Carolina are horrible. Plantations have been laid waste, houses ruthlessly destroyed, women ravaged in the most brutal manner by common hired soldiers and Negroes who follow the armies."

Owen knocked the ashes from his pipe. "The Greeks made similar charges against the Romans; the Egyptians against Philip's army; Philip made them against his enemies . . ."

Mary laughed suddenly. "And what of the Trojans?"

Owen shrugged his shoulders. "After Helen, they had reason to protest."

But his words had cleared the air. Mary turned again to Lavinia. "This much is true, Lavinia. Banastre Tarleton ordered three of his own dragoons hanged in sight of their comrades because they had committed atrocities. So the rumors must have some truth to them if he admits that. They say he has given orders that no quarter should be given and his men are not to bring in any prisoners. You know what that means?"

Lavinia nodded but she did not lose her calm determination. "Suppose Tarleton comes through here," she said. "What then?" She had a far-off look in her eyes. "I remember how divinely he danced, Mary. One night at Dorchester House, when the moon was full, we walked on the terrace. The music is still in my ears. I don't think he can have changed so much in a few years."

Mary was silenced. Lavinia started up and leaned forward, listening. "I think I hear my son calling," she said. "You will pardon me, Mary. I must go to him." She left the room with quick, light steps.

Mary stood for a moment looking after her. She said to Owen, "Has there been any word?"

Owen divined her meaning. "Nothing. We heard the rumor that General Clark has taken Vincennes."

"I know, but that was last year, and how do you know that Adam was with General Clark?"

Owen shook his head. "I don't know for certain, but I think he was."

Mary looked out to the garden. It was dreary, deserted, the sky grey and overcast. She voiced the thought that had been in her mind so long. "Owen, Owen, you don't think he is—" She stopped. She could not bring herself to say the word.

"I don't believe Adam is dead," Owen said with unbroken

calm. "Surely you know that there has been very little communication with the Illinois country in the past two years. No settlers going out—very few coming back."

"Adam should be here," Mary whispered, her voice breaking in a sudden rush of anguish. "Surely he has heard of our need. North Carolina is his country—not Illinois. He should be here now when we need all our men."

Owen drew deeply on his pipe. "Have you ever thought that Adam may be defending a new land?"

Something cold seemed to clutch at her heart, weighing her down. She turned away so that Owen could not see her face.

There was a sound of running feet in the hall. David burst into the room, his hazel eyes shining with excitement. Mary's hand flew to her throat, he was so like Adam. In the time he had been with his uncle in Virginia he had grown tall.

"Uncle Owen," he cried, his voice high with excitement. "The British are here. The ships are shelling Edenton. Listen, don't you hear the cannon?"

The dull boom of guns sounded from the north.

"We must hurry, David," Mary said.

The child turned quickly. "Oh, Aunt Mary, I didn't see you."

She kissed his smooth cheek.

Gwennie came in. Her round blue eyes were clouded and she was breathing heavily. "You have come for David?" she asked Mary.

Owen took her hand. "He must go with them, Gwennie," he told her. "It is better, my dear." His voice was very gentle.

Gwennie did not answer. Two tears rolled down her cheeks. "I will get his saddlebags," she said. "I'll pack at once." She left the room quickly.

David went to Owen's side. "Are you going, Uncle Owen?"

Owen shook his head. "We are staying here."

The boy stood, his sturdy legs apart, looking at Owen. Mary thought, "How tall he is for thirteen. His hazel eyes and his straight high-bridged nose are like Adam's, and he has Adam's wide mouth and its mobile firmness."

"I will not run from British soldiers. That would be cowardly," he exclaimed suddenly.

Owen patted his shoulder. "You're not running away, David. You are going with Mrs. Warden to the Mecklenburg plantation. Marcy is there, and Gilsen with all the horses and hounds."

478

"But why don't you and Gwennie come? I would like it better if you came."

Owen said, "I must stay here. I signed a parole to stay in my home until the end of the war. I have given my word to a British colonel. You understand what that means, David."

David nodded solemnly. "Yes, Uncle Owen. I understand. A man must keep his word."

Mary put her hand on the boy's arm. "Come, David. I see that your horse is ready. We must hurry or we'll miss Mr. Warden at Chapman's Corner."

On the gallery Gwennie was waiting. David put his arms around her neck. "I'll be back in a fortnight," he said. "Will you make Cicero feed Red Rowan? She's getting too old to hunt for herself."

Gwennie nodded. Tears were running down her plump cheeks. David shook hands with Owen. "Good-by, sir."

Mary mounted at the block. As David swung onto his horse, Owen slipped a Latin grammar into the saddlebags. "Read a little every day, David, and work on your declensions."

"Yes, I will, sir."

"Good-by, darling," Gwennie called. She added as a last admonition, "Say your prayers every night and keep your hands and face clean. Good-by—good-by, darling."

"Maybe I should have brought my sling so I could catch old Cornwallis as David caught Goliath," David said as they galloped down the drive.

Mary smiled. "I'm afraid Lord Cornwallis is too good a soldier to be caught, David."

"That's the trouble, Aunt Mary. He's a better officer than that old blacksmith Greene."

"David! You must not say such a thing! General Greene is a splendid officer."

David considered for a moment, a frown between his brows. "Then why did everybody in Virginia say he was a blacksmith? How can a blacksmith be a good general, Aunt Mary?"

Mary did not want to answer that question. She knew that many people in the Carolinas were asking the same thing. She touched Black Douglas with her heel. With a laugh David gave chase. They raced up the long slope. At the top, Mary drew rein.

"If your horse were a little faster I'm sure you could win, David."

The boy's face brightened. "Do you think so? I tried to get

479

Ceph to let me have another horse, a fine showy gelding, very fast, but he wasn't properly shod for a long trip." His voice was scornful. "This is an old draft horse, not a gentleman's mount."

Mary laughed. It was good to have something to laugh about. It had been a long time since she had laughed spontaneously.

The coach was waiting at the Inn at Chapman's Corner, a groom watering the horses. When William saw David, he scowled.

"I told you not to bring that bas . . ."

Mary leaned inside the coach window. "Please, William, he will hear you."

"I don't care if he does. Send him back to the plantation. We can't be hampered with a child. I'm in too much of a hurry."

"I'm going to take him as far as Mecklenburg plantation," Mary said quietly.

She turned to David. "Run into the tavern, David, and ask Mr. Bascombe if the hamper of food is ready."

William followed the child with his eyes. "No one would mistake the Rutledge blood," he said, anger in his voice.

"A nephew of Paige Rutledge, who had come down from Virginia for a visit," Mary said firmly.

There was a sneer on William's thin lips. "Oh, I see. You are still protecting Adam Rutledge."

Mary's face reddened, but she made no reply. A moment later she said, "Please be kind to the boy, William. He will have a hard enough time when he grows up. Won't you let him ride in the coach with you? I'm sending his horse back from here."

William looked speculatively at David who was standing at the door of the Inn. "Very well, let him ride with us. Perhaps it is as well, Mary; he may prove useful."

"What do you mean?" Mary asked, vaguely alarmed by her husband's tone and the curious look in his eyes.

William was silent. His acute nervousness expressed itself in impatience. "Damn it, can't we get started? The roads will be choked with refugees if we don't get off!" He leaned out the window and shouted to the coachman, "Tell that landlord to hurry . . ."

Mary did not know what to think of her husband's voice and agitated manner.

Suddenly he said, "You and the child take the coach and I'll ride horseback. I'll meet you at Tower Hill." Without waiting for Mary to reply, he jumped out of the coach, mounted Black Douglas and started at a gallop down the road. Mary watched him out of sight. A strange feeling took possession of her, a thought that she sternly put from her mind.

All day they rode along the crowded roads, making small headway. The panic of the early morning had grown with each hour. Terrified people, carrying cherished possessions, were flying before the horror of invasion. Carts, wagons, coaches and horses had been commandeered by the wealthy. The poor walked, but a common thought held rich and poor alike: the terror of bombardment.

At dusk, Isaiah turned in at the plantation of Meredith Chapman. Mary knew it had been closed ever since he and Willie Davenport had gone to the Illinois country two years before. The Negro caretaker ran out, glad to see a familiar person in the face of this overwhelming disaster. His wife roused herself from a deep sleep in a rocking chair close to the fireplace and automatically began to make fresh pone in the hearth ashes.

"Nothing fit fo' white folks to eat," she grumbled.

Mary assured her that they were glad to get anything hot. The Negroes told her they had not heard from Mr. Meredith for "mont's and mont's." They had been running the plantation ever since the overlooker had joined Marions' Fox-swampers in South Carolina some time ago.

The bedroom was cold, the sheets clammy and damp. Mary slept little. She called David early and sent him to rouse Isaiah. They were ready to start shortly after dawn. It was cold, a slight drizzle had set in, making the roads slippery, without traction for the coach wheels. Isaiah grumbled constantly, talking to himself as the carriage swayed and skidded along the streets. The roads were more congested now with a frightened, panic-struck mob, which made driving even more difficult.

William met them at Tower Hill. He had stopped to see a member of the Council at Tarboro, he told Mary. He would ride on ahead. He might have to go to Deep River. He would meet them at Ramseur's Mill that night. If he didn't, they were to drive straight on to Catawba Springs.

She saw he was impatient to be gone, striding up and down the room, his hands behind him, his head down. He was waiting for his body servant whom he had sent to get a carriage for him. He did not want to ride horseback if it rained.

"Is there any news from Edenton?" Mary asked. She re-

481

peated the question before William was aware that she was talking to him.

"No, no. I've heard nothing from the North. Gates is moving toward Charlottetown with all the troops and militia he can muster—cavalry, infantry and light dragoons. You must get through to the Springs before the roads are taken over for military purposes."

"Where is Cornwallis' army?" Mary asked.

William stopped in his stride. He looked at her searchingly. "I can't find out. No one seems to know. It is rumored that Tarletons' cavalry has been raiding on the Deep River. But you can't believe rumors, Mary. Still I want you to get on with all speed."

"Is the road free from here on?" she asked.

"From all I can hear, yes. Greene is somewhere around, probably near Charlottetown. They say his troops are in frightful condition, without food or proper clothing. I have just heard the Assembly at New Bern has been dispersed and a Council Extraordinary is in power. Caswell has been made major-general of the militia." His tone was bitter, his mouth drawn thin.

"Doesn't that please you, William?" she asked.

He turned away abruptly, so she could not see his eyes. "Why do you ask that?" he countered.

Mary went over and stood beside him. Her voice was gentle. "William, what is wrong? Why are you so worried? Are things so much worse than you tell me?"

After a moment, he said, "The Assembly has decided to offer a bounty of two thousand pounds to raise a new battalion. They are promising every man who enlists and serves a year one prime slave and six hundred and forty acres of land. Do you understand what that means?"

Mary nodded assent. "We're getting low on men. Oh, William, why did they loan our soldiers to South Carolina and to Washington's army? Now, when we are invaded, we have no men."

"They will have to draft for the Continental Army, not for state troops." His voice had an accusing ring in it. "That will mean another tax! God almighty! That is what the Colonists are fighting against: too much taxation by Parliament. Now they impose more taxes of their own." There was a long silence. Then he said abruptly, "Iredell has been appointed to the bench."

That was it! Mary knew how much William had counted on that appointment. He had worked for it. He deserved it.

Caswell must have been the one to throw the appointment to Iredell. She put her arm through his.

"Don't feel badly, William. There are other, much better positions than the judgeship to be had in the reorganization of the Colony."

"They think I'm too old, damn them," he muttered, his face stormy.

"Old? How stupid." She laughed. "Wisdom doesn't go with youth. It goes with experience. You have more knowledge of the law than any man in the Colony," she said with decision. Yet she knew he spoke the truth. Lately he seemed old to her, older than the twenty years difference in their ages.

"Do you really think that, Mary?" He spoke with a humility rare in him. Mary was touched to the quick. She put her lips to his cheek.

"Don't, William, don't. I can't bear to see you like this." She had no time to say more, for just then David ran into the room.

"Your coach is ready, Mr. Warden. It is driving up in front of the Inn now!"

William took up his greatcoat. Mary buttoned it and twisted his scarf about his throat. "Don't get cold, William. You know how easily you take quinsy."

He held her in his arms for a moment, then kissed her forehead. "You are very kind, Mary, very, very kind. I'll try to meet you at Ramseur's Mill. If I don't . . ."

"I'm to drive on to the Springs and wait?"

"Yes. I have sent a messenger on ahead to the tavern to have your rooms ready. It may be crowded now with the movement of troops in that vicinity."

"Thank you, William. You are so thoughtful."

He hesitated a moment at the door, his hand on the knob. "The boy will be company for you, Mary. I'm glad you brought him with you, and, Mary, if I have seemed cross and impatient the past few months, I have had much to worry me." He kissed her again. "Good-by, my dear, good-by."

Mary watched him go, moved by his unexpected gentleness. It was not like William to explain. She waved to him as he leaned out the coach window and watched him as he was driven up the long hill.

The sun came out during the morning. Driving was easier. There were not so many people on the road now. Mary noticed how few men there were on the plantations and the small farms. Women and young boys, mostly under eighteen, were plowing fields.

All day they rode, seeing scarcely anyone. The sky was blue but the air was crisp and cold. A few buzzards planed in the sky. The distant hills lay in a purple mist. It was deserted country, swept clean of people. They saw only abandoned cabins fallen into ruin and a few starved cattle and pigs grazing. From time to time they heard the sound of a cow bell in the distance.

At Wake Court House they halted. A mob of excited people were gathered on the Commons before the buildings. Mary got out of the coach and walked with David to the edge of the crowd. A burly farmer, dressed in a heavy sheepskin coat over his blue smock, stood next to her, looking over the heads of the crowd.

"What is happening?" Mary asked him.

The yeoman turned at the sound of her voice and pulled at his cap. "There be stories afloat, mistress, that the redcoats have crossed over and be driving hard toward Charlottetown. The notice up there says that all men who will enlist in the Continental army will have a slave given them and a grant of land. Six hundred and forty acres is a fair parcel of land. I don't know but I'll be thinkin' of goin' myself."

"Six hundred and forty acres of land and a slave to bribe men to fight for their country. It must be worse than I imagined," Mary thought.

The crowd opened a little. Mary saw two officers, dressed in the buff and blue of the Continental Army, sitting at a small table on the portico of the Courthouse. They were writing names in a book.

"They're enlisting soldiers, Aunt Mary," David said. He had wriggled through the crowd to the front.

"Come, we must be going on, David."

"Where you be goin', mistress?" the yeoman asked her. "Ther' roads ben't safe for a fine lady after ye cross the river at Ramseur's Mill. Ben' riding alone?"

"No, my husband is joining me." Mary moved quickly out of the crowd to the coach. "Drive quickly, Isaiah," she called. "We must make time today before it starts to rain again."

They were halted by soldiers moving into the main road from a northern crossroad. The men streamed by on foot, in wet, ragged clothes. Many had bare feet, cracked and bleeding from the frozen ground. Some had wrapped sacking about their feet; others had sandals made from peeled bark lashed in place by strips of rawhide. The carriage stopped at a ford. The soldiers were plunging into the icy water with bare feet.

484

"Why don't they wear their boots?" David asked Mary, as they watched the line wading through the swollen stream.

"They have no boots, David," she answered, her eyes on the weary men. A few men sat down by the ford to dry their clothes by a freshly lighted fire. Mary spoke to Isaiah. He gave them food from the hamper. The soldiers ate ravenously, like animals. Her heart was heavy when she looked at their drawn faces.

"In Virginia the soldiers had nice uniforms with shiny buttons," David commented as they drove along. "Are the soldiers saving their other uniforms?"

"They have no other uniforms, David."

"Then how can they fight the redcoats when they have no uniforms or boots, and are so hungry?" he asked suddenly.

Tears came to Mary's eyes. How could they? How could they hold off Cornwallis' invading hosts? They had not the strength—no courage, only despair in their tired eyes.

"Did you notice that they had no guns?" David persisted. "Only a few. I asked a man to let me see his powder horn. He said he had thrown it away because he had no powder. He said he wanted to go home so that he could rest a while. Why can't they all go home? Would there be trouble if the King had the country again?"

"Oh, David, David! Don't ask such questions!"

"I didn't know men could fight in bare feet with no powder and no guns," he said. "What are they fighting for?"

"They are fighting for Liberty, David."

The boy settled back in his corner of the coach, his eyes following the marching men.

"Is my father fighting?" he asked, after a long silence.

Startled, Mary did not answer for a moment. Then she said, "I don't know, David."

"I shall know all about my father the day I'm eighteen. Gwennie told me so."

"The day you are eighteen," Mary repeated after him. In her heart she wondered whether David would ever see Adam Rutledge again. But she must not dwell on that—not now.

William did not meet them at Ramseur's Mill so they drove on to the Springs. They were climbing now and the air was colder. They changed horses at a small relay station near Beatie's Ford. The road was clear of soldiers. The water was high, but they crossed the ford without mishap. A wild turkey flew from the ground and perched on a denuded limb of a tall tree. Grouse rustled around the dried leaves as they whirred away into the deep woods. It was silent in the forest. A few Indians slipped by like shadows.

The coach drew up at the Inn, opposite the Rock, at nightfall. Lights gleamed in the windows. Mary could see many people in the great common room. Coaches and horses stood in the courtyard. Soldiers were stabling their officers' mounts. Slaves in livery ran out as Mary Warden's coach drove up with a flourish and stopped at the steps. Two Negroes sprang to the horses' heads; two ran to unstrap the boxes at the back; others opened the doors to help the occupants of the coach alight. The wide door of the Inn swung open, a broad square of light falling on the gallery floor and the long flight of steps. The host came out, and with him two servants carrying ship's lanterns. Recognizing Mary Warden, he hurriedly pushed the slaves to one side, and came down the steps to help her from her coach.

It was warm and inviting and very gay inside the great room. Logs, fully six feet in length, blazed and crackled in the fireplace, sending off a pleasant woodsy fragrance. Women in gay silk dresses laughed and talked with officers in uniforms of the Continental Army. High officers, Mary saw from their shoulder straps. Candles in wall sconces and candles on tables and mantelboards lighted the room. Beyond the fireplace, through open doors, she saw the dining room set with many tables. Slaves, carrying jugs and great silver dishes, moved about the room. How pleasant it was! How festive!

The host, Judson, led her to a seat near the fire and loosened the silver clasp on her heavy furred cape. "Rest here until you get the chill out of your bones before you go to your rooms, Mrs. Warden."

Mary sat down. "Has my husband come yet?"

"Not yet, Mrs. Warden. Were you expecting him?"

"Yes."

Judson turned to David. "And who may you be, my little man?"

"My name is David Rutledge."

The host looked more closely, his eyebrows raised. "Ummm. . . ."

"David has come down from Virginia for a visit at Rutledge Riding," Mary said, anticipating a question.

Judson's face cleared. "Oh, one of Paige Rutledge's children. I used to know—" Judson was called away then, saving further explanation.

A slave came bearing a tray with a hot brandy toddy for

Mary and a cup of chocolate for the boy. David, his fingers stiff with cold, was struggling to unwind his muffler. A small Negro boy hurried forward to help him. Seeing David's blue fingers, he ran away, returning at once with a bowl of cold water.

"Rest you' fingers in de cold water, little master, lessen you hab de chilblains out on you' hands."

David thrust his hands into the icy water.

Mary said, "Have the boy show you to our rooms, David. Isaiah will unpack and lay out your clothes for dinner."

David went up the stairs. Mary followed him as soon as she had finished the toddy. A group of officers stood aside as she passed, staring at her curiously. They were all strangers to her: Continentals who had come from Virginia and Pennsylvania. She walked slowly up the mahogany-railed stairs to the second floor.

Before the bedroom door had closed, Mary heard the clatter of horses' hoofs, and the shouts of stableboys as a coach rolled up in the courtyard below. She looked out the window. Slaves with flaring pine knots lighted the way. A man descended stiffly from his coach. It was William. Her husband's voice carried upward.

"Get fresh horses ready, Judson," he said to the landlord. "Is my wife here?"

"She arrived about an hour ago, Mr. Warden."

"Good, take me to her room. No, not through the hall. Isn't there a side door?"

Mary heard no more for the wind banged the shutter. She went quickly into the adjoining bedroom, carrying a lighted candle. David, fully dressed, had thrown himself on a couch and was sleeping soundly. She drew a carriage robe over him and left his room quietly. William opened her door after a quick knock but, before he greeted her, he turned his head to give instructions to an unseen servant.

"Have the carriage ready in fifteen minutes. Never mind my horses. They can be stabled here until I return." He closed the door and came into the room. "Can you be ready to leave in five minutes, Mary?" he asked without preliminaries. "I must go on to Charlottetown at once."

"But, William, we have only just come. I'm exhausted by the drive."

"You can rest in the coach," he answered.

"My horses can't possibly go any farther," she said with finality.

William's hand was heavy on her shoulder.

"Mary, I must get to Charlottetown. I have to see Mac-Cullough. There's been trouble in the King's Mountain district. Don't you understand that we must get on at once?"

She did not understand. Why should this news agitate William?

"Cornwallis is marching toward Charlottetown," he added, dropping his voice. "I have messages to get through."

So that was it. She felt sudden exultation. "Call David, William. He is asleep in the next room," she said, as she began gathering her things together. William did not move.

"I don't want the boy along," he said gruffly. "Leave him here with Isaiah until you get back. It'll only be a few days."

Mary dropped her hat on the bed. "I will not go without David," she said firmly.

William looked at her. She felt that he was struggling to control himself, to keep from flying into a rage. After a moment, he opened the door of David's room and went in. They came out together, almost immediately, David rubbing his sleepy eyes and carrying his little brown leather dressing bag in his hand.

"I'm all ready, Aunt Mary," he said.

As they left the room, Mary turned toward the main stairway. William grasped her arm so hard that she cried out.

"No, this way. Make no noise."

He led the way out through the dark halls to the upper gallery. As they crept down the outside stairway, Mary could see into the brightly lighted room where the officers were dining. They went out through a side door near the stable. The coach was waiting in the shadows. A white driver stood by the door.

William said, "I have engaged this man to drive us. He knows the road. Isaiah can stay here until we get back."

Mary hesitated. There was something about this stealthiness, this almost furtive departure that she resented. She did not want to go off leaving her servant behind.

"Get in." William's voice was harsh. "Please get in, Mary."

She got into the coach. David sat down beside her. William, in the seat opposite, leaned out the window to give final instructions to the driver.

"Take the little traveled road, Barns. Tell me if you see soldiers coming. I'll watch the rear."

They drove for a long time in silence. It was very dark for the half-moon made little light in the forest. For a time David sat stiffly erect. Then sleep got the better of him and his head drooped. Mary drew the rug over him, tucking it about his legs. She moved closer so that his head lay against her shoulder. In the shadowy light cast by the small carriage lanterns William's face was a white blur. The coach rolled and swayed, bumping over hard ruts. William swore softly as a lurch threw him against the side.

"Where are we going, William?" she asked, after they had ridden miles. "Surely, you can tell me now why we are making this flight?"

"Flight? Who said we were flying?" His voice was sharp.

"I don't know what you may call it but that is how it appears to me," she answered. "Can't you trust me enough to tell me why we had to sneak out of the Inn, and where we are going?"

William's voice was quieter, almost soothing. "I have told you we're going to Charlottetown. I want to get there before Cornwallis' army comes. We cannot have another King's Mountain."

"King's Mountain? Why, we won King's Mountain. What are you saying?"

There was a momentary silence. "We didn't win, Mary. That is, our militia did not win. It is rather a sore point with them."

"I'm sure I don't understand. Our troops won the battle of King's Mountain."

"Only by the aid of the Back Countrymen, my dear. Our militia would never have won if men from Kentucky and Tennessee had not come over the mountain to help. It was their victory, not that of our militia."

The men of the Back Country! Mary thrilled to the words. Men from over the mountain who had come to the defense of old North when they were needed. Where was Adam Rutledge when the men from Kentucky and Tennessee came to win battles? The thought gave her anxiety, the old, deep-buried anxiety.

"Cornwallis will penetrate into North Carolina. He will sweep the Colony before him."

What was it William was saying? Sweep the Colony? Cornwallis and Banastre Tarleton would put the Colonials to rout? Fear came over her . . . and a new thought.

"Have you been sent to negotiate a peace, William?" She was afraid of his answer, but she must know. Suppose their leaders had given up hope! Suppose they saw defeat ahead of them and were giving way? It was too dark to see William's face closely.

"No, I'm not sent to negotiate peace," his tone was curt.

"Thank God!" she exclaimed. "Thank God!"

"The fools would be better off to . . ." William began, but he was cut short. The carriage stopped with a jerk that sent David rolling against Mary.

"Damn you, can't you drive more carefully?" William shouted.

A sharp voice rang out: "Halt! Who goes there?"

"Madam Warden's coach on the way to Charlottetown," the driver answered.

"Damn him for a fool!" William muttered. "Why did he give your name?"

Mary heard a crisp rustle of papers.

"Put these in the front of your habit," William whispered.

Mary felt the papers being thrust into her hand. She did as she was told, wondering if they were papers that he did not want the British to find.

"Answer no questions, Mary," he said in a low voice. "You are going to Charlottetown to consult Dr. Brevard."

The coach door opened with a jerk. A rough voice came from the darkness. "Get out, lady."

William leaned forward. His tone was sharp. "What does this mean?"

"Oh, a gentleman, too! All of you, out quick."

William said, without moving, "By whose authority do you order a gentleman from his coach?"

A second man came up. "Have done, Griggs, can't you see it's a gentleman?" He addressed William politely. "We're Caswell's Minute Men, sir. We have orders to bring everyone traveling this road to the officer of the day."

"Oh," said Mary, leaning forward so that she could be seen by the men. "You're Caswell's men? I thought you might be the Hessians!"

"Come, now," said the first man roughly. "Step out briskly. You can leave the child in the coach."

Mary felt David's hand tighten on hers. He was awake. "I'll take the boy with me," she said firmly.

"Step briskly, step briskly," the first soldier repeated.

They picked their way through the ruts and mud. Finally, they came to a fire where a dozen men were huddled, covered with soggy blankets.

Mary turned to speak to William. He had wrapped his coat closely about him so that the collar half hid his face. His hands were trembling. She stepped in front of him. She must give him time to pull himself together before the officers noticed his terror.

490

Chapter 34

NIGHT ENCAMPMENT

A CAMP was visible in the shadows of the trees near the roadside. Small fires burned in the center of the cleared space among the trees. Mary caught the glint of steel as the firelight flickered on stacked bayonets. The sentry disappeared into the dark. Two men rose from a fire and came forward. One of the young officers addressed William.

"Will you kindly let me see your pass, sir?" William fumbled among some papers he took from his dressing case and handed the officer a paper. The man examined it by the carriage lights. "It seems all right, Mr. Warden, but I shall have to detain you until morning."

William took a step forward. Mary felt his anger. She hoped he wouldn't lose control of himself when diplomacy was most needed.

"I can't possibly stay here. It is imperative for me to go on to Charlottetown with all speed." His voice rasped.

"Sorry, sir, but those are our orders."

"Who is the ranking officer here?" William demanded.

"Colonel Lawson, but he is away at present. He is expected before morning."

"Second in command?"

"Captain Whitney."

William's voice was commanding. "Will you please say to Captain Whitney that William Warden of Edenton, member of the Provincial Council, asks permission to drive through the lines to Charlottetown. Tell him that I'm taking my wife to Dr. Brevard for consultation."

Mary made a slight movement. William caught at her arm to silence her.

"I'll tell Captain Whitney at once, sir."

The young officer crossed the open space to a dark blur that Mary saw was the outline of a house. It was cold. David moved near the fire to warm his hands. A group of mounted officers appeared out of the darkness—ghostly shapes in the still grey light that comes before dawn. After a time the young officer returned.

"Colonel Lawson has just arrived, Mr. Warden. Will you please step over to Headquarters?"

A tall man detached himself from the gloom and approached them.

"Mr. Warden? I'm Colonel Lawson. I'm very sorry you and Mrs. Warden have been detained out here in the cold. Will you come with me?" He bowed to Mary. "I can't promise much in the way of comfort, Mrs. Warden, but I think there'll be a fire."

They walked through a dimly lighted hall into a large bare room. An orderly sprang to open the door when he saw Colonel Lawson. He placed a chair by the fireplace for Mary. David kept close to her. The officer struck a flint and, lighting two candles, stuck them into a piece of split wood on the mantel. Colonel Lawson was a man of middle years, with slightly greying hair. His lean face was stern, his eyes were a piercing grey. His uniform was not of the North Carolina militia. He was a Virginian with the Continental troops.

"What can I do for you, Mr. Warden?" he asked after he had examined the pass William handed him.

"I should like your permission to ride through the lines into Charlottetown, Colonel," William said. "I'm taking my wife to Dr. Brevard for consultation."

The officer's face cleared. "Dr. Brevard? I'm afraid you will be disappointed, madam. Dr. Brevard is at present with General Greene's army."

Mary started to speak. William interrupted her. "That is bad news, Colonel, but I think I had better go on as we planned. I will take my wife to the home of John Alexander until I can find Dr. Brevard."

Colonel Lawson searched among the papers that lay on the rough table. "Why not wait until later in the day, Mr. Warden," he said, without looking up. "We'll be moving men and can give you an escort."

Mary saw William's hand fold and unfold nervously. She must divert Colonel Lawson's attention from him. "That is very kind of you, Colonel. I assure you driving at night is not pleasant."

The Virginian turned to her. She saw how haggard his face was, how weary. "I have a room upstairs, Mrs. Warden," he said. "It is very crude, but there are two cots. You may be able to get a little rest." He called an orderly and gave him instructions which Mary did not hear.

William came over and stood with his back to the fire. "I

do not like this delay," he said in a low tone to Mary. "I must get on somehow."

Another orderly came into the room and spoke to Lawson. "A messenger from General Greene has arrived, Colonel."

Mary glanced through the open door. A young officer stood outside in the hall, his heavy cloak and his boots splattered with mud. He looked as if he had been riding hard.

Colonel Lawson murmured an excuse and stepped into the hall. "You come direct from General Greene?" Mary heard him say.

"Yes, Colonel. General Greene asked me to give you these; also, to tell you that he had received two communications from Lord Cornwallis protesting the treatment of his officers and men taken at King's Mountain. Lord Cornwallis says that his soldiers were inhumanly treated. General Greene requests that you investigate these charges; also, the conduct of our men at Gilbert's Town."

Colonel Lawson exploded. Mary heard him curse. "What about Cornwallis' treatment of our men? And what does he have to say about that butcher, Tarleton?"

"Lord Cornwallis claims our men showed less humanity than the Indians. These atrocities he lays to the Back Mountain men who marched to our aid at King's Mountain." The officer was repeating formal charges.

"Damn Cornwallis and his impudence! I know his game. He sends protests to counteract our protest about the conduct of Tarleton's men."

"That is General Greene's opinion, sir. He asked me to convey this to you by word of mouth."

Mary caught a few more words: Whittel's Mill; Pickens and Wade Hampton—names of officers in South Carolina. It was evident to her that a campaign was being planned that involved the border country. Were they caught between the two armies? She felt no fear for herself, only a strange exhilaration. At least they were making plans to hold off Cornwallis.

"Any other message?" she heard Lawson ask the messenger.

"The General says he will be here before daybreak. He asks you to get your men on the march toward Guilford. The state troops are to camp there until they are needed; also, the Virginia and Maryland Continentals."

She heard the sound of retreating footsteps. Lawson had walked down the hall with the officer. William, who had been standing by the window, came over to Mary. "Give me those papers," he said, "quick, before Lawson comes back."

Mary unbuttoned the front of her habit and took out the papers he had given her when they were stopped by the sentry. He almost snatched them from her hand, then leaned forward as if he were turning a log on the andirons. As he did so, he thrust the papers into the cuff of his riding boot.

"I'm going to try to get away before daylight, Mary," he said in a low voice. "Lawson must not suspect my intentions."

Mary glanced quickly toward the door. Lawson was coming down the hall talking to two officers who had joined him.

"Why don't you wait, William?" she whispered. "What difference can a few hours mean?"

"The difference between life and death—that is all, Mary. Be careful." Mary stood up as if she had been waiting for Lawson's return to go to her room.

"I'm sorry to keep you, Mrs. Warden. I know you are tired. Will you go to your room now?"

Mary glanced at her husband.

"I'll come later, Mary," he said. "I want to have a few minutes with Colonel Lawson."

Mary woke David and followed the orderly out into the hall and up a narrow staircase to a room directly above the one where they had been. It was a barren attic. Two cots had been set up in the middle of the room. Muddy boots and equipment were scattered over the floor; uniforms hung from nails. The orderly gathered up the clothes and boots hastily, apologizing for the condition of the room. Mary imagined Colonel Lawson's aides had made way for her.

David threw himself on one of the cots. He was asleep as his head touched the pillow. Mary wrapped herself in her heavy fur-lined cape and lay down. Through a double window that reached the floor she could see the rain-curtained hills in the grey distance touched by the first light of false dawn.

Near the house a few soldiers were moving about. Others were lying on the ground, their heads covered with their coats. She had almost dropped off to sleep when she heard the pounding of galloping horses and the clatter of spurs and sabers. A troop of cavalry was riding swiftly up the long mountain road. Far down the valley she could see soldiers marching, moving toward the hillside road, like lines of ants. Men about Headquarters' camp were stirring the cooking fires. The camp took on the restless activity of early morning.

A lean, bronzed man sat on a log beneath the window, cleaning his musket, dragging a thin strip of frayed cloth through the long barrel. He wore brown, homespun clothes, a furred cap pushed back from his lean, weatherscarred face. A long knife was thrust through his leather belt.

A dragoon reined his horse. "Hello, Josh, gettin' ready to shoot some more snipe?"

The man on the log looked up at the trooper. "Shouldn't wonder," he drawled.

"Think we'll be on the move again?"

The bronzed man looked down the valley toward the marching troops. "Don't know nothing, John."

The dragoon eased himself in the saddle, one leg hanging over the pommel. "They say Cornwallis has a power of men over the border and more marching down from Virginia. Looks like trouble ahead for somebody."

The bronzed man took a squint through the long barrel of his musket. "Don't know—maybe there be."

Mary turned in her cot restlessly. It must be that the troops were being brought together for a battle, but perhaps it meant only that the men were needed for the defense of Charlottetown. Her mind turned back to her husband. She wished he had more confidence in her, but she knew it was useless to ask him about the plans of the Provincial Committee. Why was he so nervous now? She wondered if he had been sent with secret orders to General Greene. But if so, why wouldn't he have been willing to wait until the General arrived? After a time she dropped off into a troubled sleep.

William's hand hard against her shoulder wakened her suddenly. She struggled to a sitting position. He laid his fingers across her mouth to silence her, and sat down on the cot beside her, his lips close to her ear.

"Colonel Lawson will not give me permission for us to go on ahead but I'm going to try to get away. I must get to Charlottetown before Greene's troops come. Cornwallis' men are already within thirty miles—Greene may have to fall back."

"There'll be a battle?" Mary questioned.

"I think so—I don't know." He leaned over and kissed her forehead. He stood for a moment looking down at her. "Mary, one thing I want you to remember—I have always loved you, even when you thought me unfeeling and hard."

Mary felt herself turn cold. "William," she said, clinging to him, "William, don't try to get away without Colonel Lawson's permission—please. It is too dangerous."

He shook his head. "I must do what seems wise for me to do, Mary. If you are questioned, you must say you haven't seen me since you left me with Colonel Lawson. Do you understand?"

Mary nodded. She did not understand, but she must do as he asked her. He kissed her once more, then left the room silently. She got up and went to the window. She saw William's thin figure weaving in and out through the groups of men about the fire. Why hadn't he told her what his mission was? She might have helped him. She could have talked with Colonel Lawson. William, with his austere reticence, would not be at his best when he was asking a favor from a man whom he did not know and who did not know him. The rain beat down on the roof steadily with a dull, monotonous sound. She went back to the cot. After a time, her concern for William lay less heavily on her heart.

She must have fallen into a heavy sleep for when she woke it was broad daylight. She woke to the rumbling of heavy wheels and the trampling of horses' hoofs, loud voices shouting orders, the stir and confusion of men coming and going, mixed with the clanking of chains and the creak of heavy wheels.

There was a knock at her door. The orderly said, "The Colonel's compliments, Mrs. Warden. Will you have breakfast with him?"

"Tell Colonel Lawson that I shall be pleased to have breakfast with him. I'll be down in a few moments."

She closed the door and stood for a moment looking out of the window at the rain-drenched hills. William, what of William? Had he been able to get away? Had he had time? She must try not to show her worry. She opened her dressing case and arranged her hair before the small mirror from which her face stared out at her, unnaturally white. She must be careful when they questioned her. If it could only have been some officer she knew, or who knew her, instead of this Virginian Lawson.

Three men in field uniform were standing near the fireplace when she and David entered the room. They stopped talking when she opened the door, but she had already heard a few sentences—enough to let her know that a skirmish had been fought, disastrous to their men.

"Tarleton's dragoons played havoc. They ran our fellows until they dropped from exhaustion. But he made one fatal blunder—he mistook a company of Loyalists for our fellows and fired on his own men!"

496

The tall officer said, "How the devil do you suppose the British found out that Morgan was going to raid? If they had not known that, and had not sent Tarleton to Broad River, we would have had a sweeping victory."

The first speaker, whose back was to the fire, said, "There is a leak somewhere, Colonel. Cornwallis must have had information about Morgan's attack almost as soon as I had it."

Mary closed the door behind her. She advanced a step and stood waiting—a half-smile on her red lips. Colonel Lawson came forward, bowing over her hand.

"Mrs. Warden, good morning." He turned to include the other man. "May I present General Greene and his aide, Captain Blount?" Mary bowed to the commander of the Colonial forces. She felt his dark eyes envelop her, a swift look of appraisal.

"It is a pleasure to meet you, Mary Warden. I have been told that you are one of the most loyal women in the Province." Mary had the feeling that his penetrating glance was not done with her. She put her hand on David's arm to steady herself.

"And this, General Greene, is a young Rutledge, down from Annandale for a visit at Adam Rutledge's plantation." David put his heels together and bowed stiffly as he had been taught at school.

Colonel Lawson moved toward the table. "If you don't mind we will sit down to breakfast. I have a cook who has me terrorized. Your husband will join us later?"

"Don't wait, please don't wait," Mary said, trying to make her voice sound natural. Two orderlies served bacon and eggs; a bowl of gruel for David. Mary made a pretense of eating. She could scarcely swallow a mouthful of food. Every time she looked up she found General Greene's penetrating eyes on her.

"Mr. Warden is delayed?" he asked, after he had finished his eggs.

Mary thought quickly. She would not lie, she could not. She would tell the truth, withholding the reasons. Turning to Colonel Lawson she asked a question instead of answering one. "My husband went on to Charlottetown, I suppose, Colonel?"

"What the devil!" Lawson's chair scraped as he half rose from the table.

Greene held up his hand. "Wait, Lawson, let us see what Mrs. Warden has to say." Lawson sat down again. The heavy lines between his grey eyes deepened.

"Perhaps, Mrs. Warden will explain her husband's flight," Greene said.

"Flight, General Greene? I don't understand what you mean."

"We will drop the word since it seems to annoy you, Mrs. Warden. Do you mind telling Colonel Lawson and me why William Warden left here without a pass?"

"I did not know my husband had left without a pass, General."

"No passes have been issued during the past twenty-four hours. He left without Colonel Lawson's permission. Do you know where he was going, Mrs. Warden?"

"We were going to Charlottetown when Colonel Lawson's men stopped us," she answered, not taking her eyes from his.

Greene turned to his aide. "Find out which direction Mr. Warden took, Captain Blount, and report back to me."

The young officer left the room. David stopped eating his porridge and watched the officers with curious eyes. Mary sat quietly, waiting. She hoped they did not know how fast her heart was pounding. Greene moved his chair so that he faced her without turning his head. His voice was heavy, uncultured, but his manner was courteous.

"Mrs. Warden, I must ask you to answer my questions truthfully."

Mary half rose from her chair, then sank back again. "I shall answer whatever questions you care to ask, General Greene."

"Do you know Colonel Tarleton?"

"I have met Colonel Tarleton on several occasions in England."

"Have you seen him recently?"

Mary was surprised at the turn of the questions. She expected questions concerning her husband, not British officers.

"No, not recently."

"Before you answer, think carefully. How recently?"

Mary's mind went back. "I'm not sure of the year I last saw Colonel Tarleton—Major he was at that time. It was in London nine or ten years ago."

Greene was watching her closely. Lawson stood at the window, his back to her, but Mary knew he was listening to the questions and the answers.

"Have you had any communication with him in any way —letters, notes—since then?"

Her color was rising and her anger too. "I don't know why you are questioning me in this manner, General Greene," she

498

said coldly. "I have had no communication with Colonel Tarleton or any officer who is an enemy to my country since the war began."

Greene got up heavily from his chair. He was a powerful man, broad of shoulder. Mary could understand why he was called the "Blacksmith". His face was lined, his dark eyes had the look of a man who carries a heavy weight on his mind. "I have your word for that, Mrs. Warden? Your woman's word of honor?"

Mary stood up and faced him. Her voice was firm and her glance unwavering. "You have my word, General Greene."

"Thank you, Mrs. Warden." He turned toward the window, looking out on the steady movement of troops marching along the road north of the farmhouse. She noticed his shoulders sagged; his coat was threadbare—the buff facings, once gay, were faded by wind and stained by rain. There was no sound in the room save the scraping of the spoon against the bowl. David had gone back to his porridge.

After a time Greene turned around. "Please sit down, Mrs. Warden. Believe me when I say I'm sorry to question you— but in time of war many unhappy things become the duty of a man who has the responsibility of thousands of soldiers."

Mary said nothing. She knew Greene had taken over the command when other generals had failed. He walked to the fireplace and kicked a blackened log into the fire.

"I must ask you a few more questions. Do you know Lord Cornwallis?"

"I met Cornwallis in London about the time I last saw Colonel Tarleton. He was a Colonel of the 33rd and Constable of the Tower." She moved a step closer and looked up at Greene. "Please be frank with me, General. You can trust me. Will you not tell me why you are questioning me in this way?"

Greene did not meet her eyes. "We question many people these days, Mrs. Warden," he said vaguely.

Mary persisted. "If you will tell me, I give my word that whatever you say will be confidential."

Greene set down a brass poker he had in his hand. "I may be wrong, but I believe you. I'm going to ask you one more question. Please don't be upset by it. Have you ever had any occasion to doubt William Warden's loyalty to our cause?" His tired eyes held hers, demanding truth. In spite of herself Mary's knees shook. She caught at the back of a chair for support.

"William?" she whispered, "William?"

Greene saved her from answering. His voice was kinder. He pushed a chair forward so that she could sit down. "I can see by your face you haven't suspected him, Mrs. Warden. I'm sorry to be the one to put such a thought into your mind, but did you not think it strange when he went away from here without a pass from Colonel Lawson?"

Mary shook her head. "My husband has never told me anything of his affairs, General Greene. In this instance, I thought he was to see some of the officers of the state militia and—"

Greene nodded. "You knew there was ill feeling between the Continentals and our state militia?"

"Yes, General."

"You are quite right, I'm sorry to say. There is much jealousy and bad feeling between the two."

"Surely that is why William went out without permission. It must be the reason." Mary spoke with deep feeling. Was she trying by the force of her words to convince herself?

Greene was not looking at her. His eyes were fixed on the fire. His expression was so sad, so heavy with trouble, that Mary turned away. She felt as if she had seen through the outside into the despairing heart of the man.

"I don't know whom to trust, Mrs. Warden," he said after a time. "All I know is that army information is in the hands of Cornwallis and his officers almost as soon as my officers get it. We have reluctantly come to believe that the most confidential information comes from someone high in trust in the Colony."

Mary could not answer. A lump rose in her throat. Tears came to her eyes, not for William, but for the man who was carrying the load of the army—a load that had bent his broad shoulders, taken hope from him.

"Let us hope that your explanation is the real one," he said after a long silence. "I don't care to be the man to bring sorrow or trouble to a woman so patriotic as Mary Warden."

"Thank you," she said in a muffled voice. She reached into the pocket of her habit for a handkerchief. David came to her and handed her his handkerchief, folded in a square.

"Don't cry, Aunt Mary, don't cry. Mr. Warden will come back soon."

"Let us hope so," the General said. "I'm afraid I think only of all the army, not of an individual. I'm sorry, Mrs. Warden, deeply sorry."

Colonel Lawson came back into the room. Mary had not

noticed when he had gone out. "A messenger has come with dispatches, General."

"Send him in, Colonel," the General said.

A soldier followed Lawson into the room. He was young, little more than a boy, but already the war had laid a heavy mark on his face. It had erased all joy and quick laughter and all signs of bright carefree youth. His uniform was worn and ragged, one sleeve split. His hands were cracked and bleeding, and there were great holes in his boots. The room was silent. Mary felt the weariness in the voices of the men, in their lined faces. Their tired eyes showed the long devastating strain of inaction.

Greene reached for the dispatch bag. Heavy-eyed, the boy was trembling so that he had difficulty lifting his hand. His face was drawn with fatigue and as he tried to salute, his arm dropped to his side. Mary saw that the upper part of his sleeve was soaked with blood and that a thin stream of blood was flowing down his hand. She rose quickly, stifling a cry. The soldier was swaying, his face livid, his lips bloodless.

Greene looked up from his papers as if he saw the boy for the first time. "Steady, lad, steady," he said. "Bring a chair!" he called to the orderly.

A man sprang forward in time to catch the boy as he fell.

"He's wounded, General—in his arm," Mary cried. The orderly had placed him in a chair and was holding him. Mary moved forward quickly. "Let me help," she said.

The orderly cut away the blood-soaked sleeve. A bullet had gone through the upper part of the arm. Someone brought a basin of water, bandages and lint. Mary looked at the packet. Lint—this was the lint that women scraped from fine linen. This is what it meant, not what she had thought—tired women bending over strips of fine linen scraping—and waiting—scraping and waiting. It was something different—it meant staunching the wounds of weary boys with white faces and blue lips. It meant easing broken bodies—inert young bodies of wounded boys.

The boy stirred and smiled a little. "I did try—I did try—" he whispered over and over.

She laid her hand on his forehead. "Of course you tried," she said to comfort him.

"They were hot after the dispatch bag. I ran through the woods. They could not find me in the dark." His voice trailed off, his eyes closed.

Frightened, Mary looked up at the orderly. "Is he—dead?" she asked.

"No, ma'am. He's asleep—dead asleep, ma'am. I'll carry him to the bed in the next room."

He picked up the boy in his strong arms and strode out of the room. David ran with him, holding up the injured arm. Mary walked to the window and looked out into the grey rain with unseeing eyes.

"They wanted the dispatch bag," he had said.

Suddenly she was intensely weary. The weight of war pressed down on her. War—revolution—lint; women scraping lint; broken bodies of boys; men fighting—dying.

Chapter 35

THE GREAT RETREAT

MARY WARDEN, caught up in the great retreat of Greene's army, had no way of knowing what was happening outside or the extent to which the war had engulfed the Carolinas. From November to December, when Greene took command, the tide of war had swept over the border. Tarleton raided; Morgan retaliated and exacted reprisals. Morgan's victory at Cowpens helped salve the bitter defeat of Camden. King's Mountain bolstered the Colony's waning courage. But that was a victory of Back Mountain men from Tennessee and Kentucky, who fought as Indians fought, not like militia or Continentals. Cornwallis, smarting under the defeat of Cowpens, leveled his wrath on the high-held head of his dashing commander Tarleton. He gave his energy to the business of following Morgan, MacDowell and Greene. The whole southern army of redcoats was on the move.

Trusting that Sir Henry Clinton would see that the fate of the war rested in the southern campaign, Cornwallis sent messengers and dispatches unceasingly. "Send men and ships. Men and more men. Back me up by ships-of-the-line at Charles Town. Put terror on the land."

Four rivers held Cornwallis' attention. "Cut off the bluff and blue at the Cape Fear; at the Catawba; at the Deep; at Boone's Yadkin. Keep the rebels on the run. Give them no time to breathe, eat or sleep." That was the tenor of his plea to his commander-in-chief. Clinton promised and delayed; promised and delayed, until it was too late.

When Charlottetown was besieged by Cornwallis twenty rebels, hidden behind the Courthouse, kept the British army in check. "The Hornet's Nest" Cornwallis called the town. Tarleton, thirty miles away, met the American, Buford. He demanded Buford's surrender.

"If you are rash enough to reject my terms, the blood shall be on your head."

"I reject your proposals. I shall defend myself to the last extremity. No surrender," swore Buford.

White flags of truce were being exchanged, Tarleton prepared to charge. On the instant the last flag was returned, the British commander and his men charged with fury on the Colonials. Buford had given no orders to engage. Wild with fear and confusion, his soldiers ran, offering no resistance. They threw down their arms; they begged for quarter. But Tarleton gave no quarter. Tarleton, the gay, dashing favorite of London women, had a new title to defend: "No-Quarter Tarleton." A hundred men were killed on the spot; two hundred more lay wounded on the field. "The Butcher of Waxhaw" became the maddened cry of the despairing Colonials.

The British swept forward, battle after battle. Then the battle of neighbors began—friend against friend. Neighbor saw neighbor through smoke of musket and cannon, grey ghosts of a dead past. Friends were distinguished from foes by green pine twigs on the hats of the Tories, white paper slips on the hats of the Whigs.

Cornwallis was increasingly confident that North Carolina would be subdued. He had the confidence of victory. Had not Gates run? Had not Stevens' Virginians run? Had not Caswell's North Carolina militia, unsupported, followed suit?

The Continentals indeed had put up tough resistance. The North Carolinians, under Dekalb, had made a last stand until Dekalb fell, pierced by a dozen wounds, bayonetted along with his aide who would not leave his side.

The ignominy of Camden was black on men's souls.

Down the main road to Charlottetown the army advanced. Over the border the British swarmed by the thousands. Tarleton's heavy dragoons riding furiously with swords aloft; the way covered with the blood of fleeing men, baggage and food trains; men and mules and cannon deserted; sick and wounded dragged into the deep woods. Make way for Tarleton and his Legion! In Charlottetown Hall, the Presbyterian preacher, in three-cornered hat and long sword, shouted in vain for men to stand and fight. . . . Charlottetown was choked by the retreat—choked with wounded and dying. *Cornwallis is coming, Cornwallis is coming!* Cornwallis and his victorious army. Our men are running—our defenders. Run from Charlottetown—Charlottetown is defenseless! *Cornwallis is coming— Butcher Tarleton is upon us.* Run to the swamps, to the woods, to the mountains. . . .

New troops came—green as the young spring grass of the gentle valleys. They lay down their guns, broke and ran. They hid behind fence posts, behind pine trees, took refuge behind hedges, ran in terror before Cornwallis' victorious army. Cowpens and King's Mountain victories were forgotten. Dull despair overcame the Carolinians. They had no food, no powder. The rains came, drenching weary men, beating on their tortured bodies. But Greene drove them with his iron will.

"Retreat in good order!" was the cry from every officer to the rank and file.

British troops now faced despairing men—somber-faced men who had given up hope. But there was good stock among these men who would not admit defeat: Scots, stolid Germans, Huguenots, used to the lash of oppression.

Greene moved his army swiftly now, skirting villages, traveling through forests by night, hiding in swamps. Morgan eluded Tarleton's raiding cavalry and heavy dragoons. Cornwallis cursed and fumed at delays.

"Sweep the Colony from the South Carolina border to the Virginia line!" was the British rallying cry.

They reached the Catawba only two hours after Morgan had fled. Heavy rains continued. Greene's army, fleeing, crossed the Catawba, Cornwallis and the Guards following. Davidson's men stayed long enough to put him under fire at the ford.

"Strike before the enemy reaches the Dan!" ordered Cornwallis. "Erect the King's standard at Hillsborough. Rally men to the cause of the King!" was the next proclamation.

Then the elements came with added vigor to the defense of the land. Never was there such a campaign! Rains beat down day after day. Greene threw his men into the torrent. Streams were at flood. The Americans crossed the ford and the Catawba rose in the night, making Cornwallis' crossing impossible. The British General strode up and down the banks cursing. Next the Dan. The stream rose to a torrent after Greene's and Morgan's men passed over. As in the Biblical passage of the Red Sea, Pharaoh Cornwallis and his hosts paced the banks waiting for the swollen waters to subside.

For two hundred miles Cornwallis and his army marched in the footsteps of the fleeing Continentals. The Yadkin, Daniel Boone's Yadkin, rose in mighty flood. The fords became walls of angry water. Cornwallis stood on the banks of the Yadkin and thundered curses at his officers, at his men, at the very skies that poured down walls of water to keep him from his quarry.

Four rivers were at flood. The torrential rains beat into the rich earth. Four rivers, with overflowing banks, held his Majesty's army in check. Was God on the side of the fleeing rebels?

Cornwallis, defeated by flood, filed back and took up a position on Deep River to wait. A trained soldier, he knew how to wait. He knew rains would stop, floods subside. His troops faced a new force of strengthened men. He felt the change, but did not know from where it came. Greene had become a formidable adversary. Cornwallis waited, drawing his army close about him.

The Guards came up. Colonel Webster, with the baggage, camped at Beatie's Ford. Cornwallis moved to the forks of Deep River. A brigade of Guards, a regiment of Bose, the 23rd cavalry, camped near the Swamp. Cornwallis detached Colonel Tarleton and sent him to Alamance Creek to cover the country from there to Deep River. He hoped, as soon as the rains stopped, to force Greene to a decisive battle.

Greene's numbers were less but a new vigor had come to the Colonials. Cornwallis' past victories had taught Greene a new strategy. He avoided battle, keeping his men in motion. Every night, every day they changed location, waiting for reinforcements from Virginia and Pennsylvania. They were on their own land, which gave them an advantage. Their own land they would defend with body and blood.

Greene was determined that he would choose the time for battle—he would choose the battleground, not Cornwallis. The place of his choice was Guilford Courthouse.

The steady stream of men marching in the grey rain beat into Mary Warden's brain with a despairing rhythm. The sound pounded against her ears, against her body with physical pain. She felt each dragging step of the war-weary soldiers marching through mud and slime and frozen earth—exhausted men, despairing, half frozen, enveloped by the beating grey streamers of rain.

The crackle of stiff paper made her turn quickly, conscious of the officers now seated at the long table. Strained, anxious men bent over maps—men bowed with the weight of war. Greene's face was as grey as the men who marched in the driving rain. His body sagged in the chair; his heavy shoulders were bent with fatigue and the despair of a losing fight.

"Are the Cornwallis dispatches decoded, Lawson?" Mary heard him ask. She moved to the fireplace and sat on a stool, her cape close around her slim body. Lawson's voice carried clearly across the room. She thought, "I must let them know that I can hear what they are saying," but she was too weary to make the effort.

"The first dispatch is from Cornwallis' camp at Wynnesborough, December 30, 1780. A confidential letter to Lord Rawdon—shall I read it all, General, or just the part that concerns us?" the officer asked.

"Every word that Cornwallis writes concerns us, Lawson. Read the entire letter."

"My dear Lord:

"I cannot express my feeling at the generosity and friendliness of your letter. If it had been possible to raise my esteem for you, it would have been done.

"From everything I hear of Greene's force, I don't think it possible for him to strike any blow that would materially affect my movements. I'm frightened by the report of the French at Cape Fear. That would greatly embarrass our operations and engage us in a naval expedition which I fear we are ill prepared for. A few days must ascertain the facts. Leslie is slow. Sir Henry wants me to employ Indians. I wish I knew what was going on in New York . . . whether there have been any embarkations. From private sources, I hear Phillips is now going up the Chesapeake and Albemarle Sound. If there are 1,000 French at Cape Fear, I am apprehensive. I have no communication except through private sources—very uncertain. If there are no French, and Phillips is successful on the Sound, we may make a great change in the Colonies in these next few months."

"The second letter, Colonel," Greene said without comment.

Lawson said, "This letter is to Sir Henry Clinton. It is dated January sixth, at the same camp."

"Sir:

"The difficulties I have had to struggle with have not been occasioned by the opposite army. They have always kept at a considerable distance and retire at our approach, but the constant incursions of refugee North Carolinians, the Black Mountain men, keep the whole country in constant alarm.

"I have put Lord Rawdon in command of the frontiers of South Carolina. I shall begin my march tomorrow, having been delayed a few days by a diversion made by the enemy toward Ninety-Six, and propose keeping west of the Catawba for a considerable distance.

"I shall then proceed to pass that river and the Yadkin—events alone can decide future steps. I shall take every opportunity of communication with Brigadier-General Arnold.

"I have the pleasure to assure your Excellency that the army here is perfectly healthy and in good order.

"I am, etc.,
"CORNWALLIS"

The silence that followed the reading of the second letter lasted so long that Mary turned in her chair so that she could see the faces of officers seated at the table. General Greene sat with his hands on the table looking steadily at the blank wall. MacDowell's head was lowered, his shoulders hunched, his attitude that of a charging bull. Lawson's face was grim. He was watching his commander. The young officers stood in a little group waiting for Greene to speak.

The moments dragged on. The sound of hoof-beats, the clank of chains, and the rumble of heavy gun carriages filled the room. Finally Greene raised his voice. His clenched fist banged down on the table.

"Reverse your orders, Colonel," he said to Lawson. "Order the troops to march toward Charlottetown instead of camping at Guilford. Send messengers to Butler, to Eaton and to Davidson. Draw in all troops with Charlottetown as their objective. Morgan will be the vanguard. He is to draw Tarleton as far away from Cornwallis' main army as possible—over the border into South Carolina, if necessary—engage their attention, divert them, give us time to reach Charlottetown before Cornwallis!"

Lawson leaned forward. "But, General, our men are worn out from the long march. We haven't sufficient food; we haven't guns or ammunition; and our supply trains are on the way to Guilford."

Greene again brought his clenched fist down on the table. "God damn the supply train. We'll get on without them. Reverse your men, Lawson! March them toward Charlottetown! March! March! Double quick! For once, Cornwallis will see the advance, not the rear guard of Nathaniel Greene's army."

Mary Warden's coach rolled from side to side in the deep ruts. The rain beat down, cutting into the earth. The half-frozen mud was heavy. It clung to the horses' hoofs. From time to time the soldier-driver Colonel Lawson had sent with her got down to gouge out the mud that caked the wheels.

Mary, wrapped in her fur-lined cape, sat in the back seat, David beside her. On the opposite seat was Captain Blount. Greene had sent his aide as her escort. For three weeks, caught in the changing tide of war, she had moved with Greene's army. Every courtesy had been extended her but she had not been allowed to stay behind or to move forward. She had heard nothing in all that time from William. Day by day

508

she grew more apprehensive of his welfare. She knew little of what was going on, catching only fugitive words and half-finished sentences. The Royalists under Dr. Pyle had had an uprising, quickly put down by Lee's dragoons. The Tories had expected Tarleton instead of Lee. Ninety men were killed—this happened when Tarleton's dragoons were only a mile away.

A thousand Continentals were with Greene now. It was rumored that he would get several thousand more militia from Virginia. Lillington and Butler were camped a mile away.

Mary said little but she knew she was being held so that she could not communicate with her husband. That fact made it clear to her that he had not come back to Greene's command. She worried day and night, not knowing what to think. She realized how much a part she was of the Revolution.

The land and the people had become the warp and the woof of the mighty spread of Revolt. What happened to her or to any individual was unimportant. They were all being swept on by the torrent into the great matrix of Revolution and War. Nothing mattered. In the long hours when she was alone, she found herself trying to think what her other life had been. It was so far away, so distant. The quality of the old life no longer held. Something new had come—vivid, keen and accompanied by the thunder of cannon.

She had learned now to sit silent, her body tense, watching the passing troops weaving this pattern of War and Revolt: weary men walking with flagging steps, swooning with fatigue and exhaustion; prostrate bodies, fallen into the slimy mud of swamps; men tired of striving, with no hope for the day or the day to follow. That was what was written on every face, young and old. Splashed with mud and slime, the troops marched, lifting heavy feet slowly, not fighting gloriously for Liberty, but marching endlessly, each dawning day bringing deeper despair.

It came to Mary that she had given no thought to anything but this pattern that lay before her eyes. Adam Rutledge! She had not thought of him for days on days. How far away the old gay life, too far ever to return. Had she ever laughed or known the keen exhilaration of following the hounds? What did it all mean? Was it some gigantic plan to batter people to earth and then make them rise again to strength?

She glanced at David. He smiled back at her quietly. He had so little to say, this child of Adam's—so few words—yet

509

she felt his awareness. She worried because he was seeing so much sordidness at his age, but there was nothing she could do to prevent it.

Marching men moved ghostlike through grey obscurity. Mists of rain clouded the shadowy figures, breaking them into fragments. Even when she closed her tired eyes she saw men moving soundlessly with white faces and hollow eyes. Infantry gave way to cavalry. Colonel William Washington's cavalry was moving forward. The Edenton Light Horse— young Peyton Rutledge riding swiftly by. "Peyton," she called, "Peyton," but he had already passed.

"Where are they going?" David whispered. "They were riding so swiftly!"

Mary could not answer his question. Captain Blount leaned forward. "They are riding to Guilford, to the place where four crossroads meet," he said impulsively.

Mary turned surprised eyes on him. The young officer showed signs of embarrassment. The coach dragged slowly up rising ground.

"When will we see the redcoats?" David asked.

"I don't know," Blount answered. "Cornwallis rests at the Yadkin, some say, but others say he is hiding at a ford on Deep River. Cornwallis wants battle, but General Greene is not ready—not yet. The Great Retreat is not finished." He sank back in the coach. No one spoke.

After a time the carriage stopped. The driver pulled to one side. Light artillery was passing, creaking gun carriages and tramping horses, shouting, cursing men, urging the tired horses to pull against the clinging mud.

At daybreak they met soldiers coming from the opposite direction. What had happened? Was Greene again to retreat? Would it never end? "Mary, Mother of God, protect these tired men!" she prayed wordlessly. Shoes worn; one blanket for four men; the cold nights; the beating rain; no powder. "How can we win?" Mary whispered to herself a hundred times as the day dragged endlessly by.

The rain stopped but the cold wind was penetrating. The marching soldiers tracked the ground with bloody feet. Would they have courage to go forward—courage to fight . . . ?

"What do we fight for?" David's voice was far away. "What do we fight for?"

She did not answer. She could not think. What did they fight for? She tried to bring her weary brain into action. She remembered: the right of every man to be free. She spoke the words aloud. Her dull, lifeless tone made David look at her with wide, curious eyes. Captain Blount repeated the words. Tears forced themselves from her tired eyes—tears that burned into her soul.

Forage carts were passing, piled high with supplies. There would be food at the end of the march! At nightfall the soldier-driver came to the crest of a long hill. A hoarse challenge rang out: "Stop your horses!" The coach stopped with a jerk. The door was wrenched open before Blount could reach it. Two officers in Continental uniforms stood at either side of the coach. Seeing Mary, they touched their caps.

"Who are you and where are you going?" one of them said curtly to Captain Blount.

"Mrs. Warden's coach; Blount, A. D. C. to General Greene, traveling under safe conduct." The officer glanced at the papers Blount handed him. He scrutinized the passes carefully and handed them back.

"They appear to be all right," he said to his companion. "Pass on, sir." The door slammed shut, to open again almost immediately. "See anything of a grey-haired man riding a big black horse?" the officer asked, thrusting his head inside the coach.

"No," Blount answered. "We've seen no one on horseback except a platoon of Colonel William Washington's cavalry."

The door banged again.

"Greene picks his women beautiful," Mary heard the officer say. "Did you get a look at her?" Blount's face grew fiery red. He gave her a sidewise glance to see if she had overheard the soldier. Mary kept her face expressionless, her eyes closed. He settled back, satisfied she had not heard. They rode on in silence. What was it the man had said? "A grey-haired man on a black horse." Suddenly her heart pounded. Suppose—suppose—but that was foolish. It couldn't be William they were talking about. There must be hundreds of grey-haired men riding black horses with Greene's army.

Later that night it began to rain again. Gusts of wind hit against the sides of the coach. Water dripped through the roof. Mary moved to the middle of the seat. Her feet were numb with cold. David was asleep, leaning back against the cushions. Blount spread a rug over her knees and tried to stop the leak around the window with his woolen scarf.

Mary smiled wanly. She was tired, so tired that it seemed to her that every bone, every muscle ached, but she made no complaint. She had only to look out the window, to see the marching men bent almost double to keep the stinging sleet from beating against their faces, to forget her own discomfort. Blount spoke her thought.

"I'm a swine to sit here while my men are marching in that storm."

"Your men?" Mary asked in surprise.

"Yes, Mrs. Warden, I command those men you saw at the ford."

"Command a company? Why, you are a child!"

"I'm twenty. I've been in the army for four years now."

"Mother of God, protect these boys!" she said aloud. The lad bowed his head.

"Thank you, madam."

They drove on in silence. . . .

"You are a Virginian," Mary said, after a time.

"Yes, my father has a plantation near the North Carolina line. His brother owns Mulberry Hill plantation at Edenton."

"Of course, I should have known. You are William Blount's nephew. We must be connections then—second cousins. My mother was a Blount. I like the idea of our being related."

"So do I, Mrs. Warden. Do you mind if I tell you I think you are a wonderful woman—the way you have taken all this discomfort, this annoyance, without a complaint?"

Mary smiled a rather weary smile. "You came into the army at sixteen?"

"Yes, madam. My two brothers were killed, my father injured so he had to stay at home—and I came."

Mary wrapped her hands tightly in the folds of her cape. Sixteen! War at sixteen! It came to her that all through the Colonies it was like that: boys, young, untried—buckling on swords.

"I'm afraid you are cold, Mrs. Warden," Blount said, leaning forward. "Let me tuck this rug in better."

By an effort she kept her teeth from chattering. "Thank you, I'm quite warm. Quite."

Blount opened the window and leaned out. "How much farther have we to go, Charley?" he asked the driver.

"We'll make it before long," the man answered.

"We're to camp at Troublesome Creek near the bridgehead," Blount said as he shut the window. "We could make it faster, but this glare ice is bad on the horses. They've no foothold."

"It doesn't matter, not in the least," she answered. "Nothing matters—only those men—those poor, wretched men, marching in the wind and the rain."

They were held up at the ford. Hundreds of soldiers lay on the wet banks of the stream, waiting to cross over. Fires burned in the dusk. It had stopped raining, but a blanket of mist hung above the water. Forage wagons mired in the stream. Drivers, cursing and swearing, used their whips on the jaded horses. A troop of Light Horse plunged through the stream and splashed the soldiers who stood waist-deep in the water, struggling to release the heavy wagons. The icy water drenched the wretched men, adding to their misery.

"We may be delayed here for hours," Blount said to Mary. "I'll see if I can get some food."

A moment later, she saw him join a group of officers who were standing by the banks of the stream. The mist settled down, partially obscuring the soldiers, making everything— men, trees and stream—seem without substance or form. The mist swallowed up sound; blurred figures moved noiselessly with a strange unearthly look of shadows floating in a grey world. Mary lowered a window. The air was sharply cold but it revived her. Two woodsmen, with fringed clothes and fur caps, had stopped to rest beside the coach.

"Got a flint, soldier?" one of them asked the driver. There was a scraping sound and a small gleam of light in the greyness.

"Want a pipe, Enoch?" a voice said.

"No, not me."

"Warm ya up. . . ."

"Nothing would warm me up. Eph, exceptin' corn likker!"

"Mayhap, Greene'll give you that after the battle."

"Mayhap, I won't need none then."

A silence followed. The rain-drenched trees dripped water that fell on the earth and on the soggy leaves with a desolate sound. Puddles of water lay in deep ruts. Leafless trees swayed, bare black limbs silhouetted grotesquely against the grey mist.

"Wish we'd stayed in the Territory, Enoch."

"So do I. Indians' war parties're no worse than this."

"Thinking of going back?"

"Yes, if I come outa this battle alive. Want to get back to the Mississippi River this time, as far as the Cahokia Settlement."

They were talking about Cahokia. That was Adam's country. She leaned forward to catch the man's reply.

"They say 'tis good land. Some of the boys in the company were saying a man can make a fortune on three hundred acres."

"That so?"

"Yes. Our Colonel came from there. They tell me he owns half the Illinois country."

"If I owned all that land I'd stay there, not get into this kind of a stinking mess."

"The Colonel stay there? Why, he's the feller that talked us all into coming back to defend old No'th State!"

"Pardon, may I get past to the coach?" Blount's voice called out.

"Sure you can, sonny, want that we throw our coats over the puddle for you to walk on?" the woodsman asked in a bit of good-natured raillery.

"Don't bother, you may need them to keep you warm when you run after the redcoats." Blount's voice was gay. Mary heard the sound of laughter.

"You're all right, me lad. We thought you were one of Washington's la-la Continentals."

Blount, with a word to the coachman, got in and banged the door shut. The horses started to pull, straining at the traces. The earth clung, as if unwilling to let the wheels move. The two woodsmen put their shoulders against the back. The coach moved forward slowly.

"We're going through the ford," Blount told Mary. "The cavalry will wait. They were happy to give place to General Greene's guest."

"Prisoner, you mean." The word left Mary's lips almost without her will. She was glad it was out.

"Guest," Blount repeated firmly, "honored guest, under safe conduct."

"Have done with this travesty, Captain Blount," Mary returned sharply. Her nerves were frayed by what she had seen and heard. "General Greene considers me of more importance than I am. Important enough, perhaps I should say menace enough, to set a captain of a company to watch over my welfare." Her tone was bitter. Blount said nothing. "But I thank you for performing a disagreeable task with diplomacy, Captain Blount."

"I wish I knew what it all means, Mrs. Warden," the young officer burst out. "I'm as much at sea as you are about the whole affair."

"I'm sure you are." Mary shrugged her shoulders. "Anyway there is nothing that can be done about it."

514

The coach jerked. David sat up, rubbing his eyes. "Where are we, Aunt Mary?"

"Ask Captain Blount, David. I don't know."

"Crossing Deep River, David. We are on the post road to Guilford Courthouse. You will stay tonight at Colonel Lawson's headquarters."

The coach moved slowly, horses straining at traces and buckles. The coachman shouted. The water came up to the hubs of the coach wheels. Mary saw the driver lash at the leading horses with his whip. One horse stumbled and fell into the stream, dragging down its mate. There was cursing and the screams of a frightened horse. David started toward the door, his hand on the knob.

"Sit still, David," Blount said sharply. "Don't be alarmed, Mrs. Warden." He opened the door. The water splashed into the bottom of the coach. He got out, over his boot-tops in water. A moment later he came to the door and took his pistols from a case on the seat.

"What is it?" Mary asked quickly.

"The leading horse has broken its leg," Blount said, his face white.

"What will he do with the pistols?" David asked when Blount had disappeared.

"Captain Blount will shoot the horse."

"What a bad man!" David cried.

Mary shook her head. "No, David, he is a good man. He can't let the horse suffer."

Horsemen appeared out of the grey mist and Mary heard shouts and curses followed by brief orders from a mounted officer. The coach began to move slowly through the ford, up the bank. A pale moon came out, shining through the silvered mist. Dark figures of mounted men passed them by; a group of officers were talking near her. She recognized one of the men as the officer who had questioned them earlier that night.

"Find the man you were looking for?" she heard Blount ask.

"Find the man? Rather! But he was a slick one, he gave us a three-day chase."

"What did you do with him? Turn him over to the General?"

The men laughed. "Look over there," one of them said.

Mary saw him jerk his thumb over his shoulder. She looked in the direction he indicated. Her heart stood still. For a moment she could not get her breath—she was turned to stone.

On the opposite bank, suspended from the naked limb of a tree, a grotesque figure swayed, fluttering coattails, long legs and arms dangling, black against the grey sky.

"What is it?" she asked, scarcely able to make her stiff lips form the words. "What is it?"

Blount pulled the window shade quickly.

"Aunt Mary! It was a man hanging by a rope!" David shivered. "Who was it, Captain Blount?"

Blount leaned forward. His usually kind voice was stern. "I don't know his name. The man was a traitor to his country. He is not worth your tears, Mrs. Warden."

Mary sank back against the padded cushions. She closed her eyes but she could not shut out the gaunt, grotesque figure that rocked and swayed in the cold night wind.

Chapter 36

ONE STEP
MORE

WHEN Mary Warden's carriage reached Torrence's Tavern it
was almost nine o'clock. Here they found the main body of
General Greene's troops encamped, waiting for daylight to
cross Shallow Ford. The tavern was six miles off Salisbury
Road and set in a thick wood. Mary waited in the coach,
while Captain Blount went in to arrange for her accommodation.

David was awake. He sat with his face pressed against the
window watching the soldiers about campfires and the movement of men and horses, provision wagons and gun-carriages.
Officers on horseback were converging from every direction.
Messengers with dispatch bags hurried up the steps of the
long gallery to General Greene's headquarters in the east
wing of the Inn. If Mary had not already heard from Blount
that a battle was imminent, she would have known it now.

"Greene has drawn Cornwallis more than two hundred
miles from his base," a young officer told her. "He is almost
ready to give battle."

Mary said nothing, but she wondered what would happen.
During these long weeks she had seen Greene's ragamuffin
army in its desperation. How could they fight? From where
would they draw courage and strength? Exhausted, raw
troops—young boys who had never seen a battle. What
would they do under the raking fire of the King's soldiers?

Captain Blount came back.

"Your rooms are ready, Mrs. Warden." She walked into
the Inn, David on one side, Captain Blount on the other. The
main room was filled with officers, booted and spurred, their
long capes flung over chairs and table. There was an odor of
wet, steaming woolen cloth from the drying capes and coats
before the great log fire. Colonel Lawson crossed the room
and came toward her, his face grave. Mary thought he had
aged visibly in the few weeks since she had seen him. He
bowed over her hand.

"The General asks for the pleasure of your company at
supper, Mrs. Warden."

Mary glanced down at her damp skirt. "I have no proper clothes," she said apologetically.

Lawson laughed. "It doesn't matter; we are all in the same sad condition. Captain Blount will show you the way. We will dine in an hour."

Lawson went back to the group of officers at the fireplace. Mary felt their curious glances as she passed and went up the stairs to her room, followed by David carrying the dressing cases.

A fire was burning on the hearth, taking the chill from the room. A slave brought a large brass ewer of boiling water for her bath. Mary ordered food for David and then decided to rest a moment before she bathed. She threw herself on the bed and fell into a troubled sleep.

She was wakened by a servant who told her that Captain Blount was waiting for her downstairs. She hurriedly took down her hair, wrapping the long braid about her small head in a coronet, and shook out her rumpled green habit, brushing the coat vigorously. When she glanced for a moment into the cracked mirror, great staring eyes set in a white face looked back at her. What did it matter how she looked? They were at war. In a day, two days, a battle would be fought that might mean the defeat of all their high hopes, and she was thinking of her appearance!

"How can you?" she said aloud, staring back at the white face in the mirror.

She heard voices in the hall; officers' spurs jingling against the floor.

"Cornwallis is a brilliant soldier," someone said. "No one has more courage. Did you see him at Whitsel's Mill?"

"No, I was at the Yadkin camp that day."

"He rode up and down in front of the lines on a black horse, while bullets rained all about him. You would have thought he was parading at the King's birthday celebration for all the attention he paid to our rifle fire."

"I suppose Cornwallis is brave, but he is safe enough from the bullets of these riflemen of ours. God in Heaven, Butler, I don't see how the General can expect to win against Cornwallis' troops. He's got the pick of the English army to throw against us, if we ever stop running long enough for him to catch up."

"But there's one thing in our favor." Another voice broke in. "Clinton isn't backing up Cornwallis. He isn't sending any reinforcements from New York."

518

The men moved off. Mary heard no more. She tucked a straying lock of chestnut hair into place and rubbed her white cheeks to give them color. She looked into David's room. He was eating the dinner that had been laid on a small table.

"You'd better get some sleep, David. We will be leaving before sunup in the morning."

"Yes, Aunt Mary." He raised his eyes, Adam's eyes, to her.

"Will they fight tomorrow?" he asked.

"I don't know, David, I don't know."

"A soldier told me that the redcoats were hot on our tails, but Greene wouldn't fight. He just runs and runs and runs. The soldiers are tired of running. They want sleep and rest."

"They are resting now, David."

"No, they just stopped to eat hot cornmeal porridge, and then they will go on. It will take them all night to cross the Shallow Ford."

Mary turned back at the door.

"Go to bed as soon as you finish dinner, David, and put your clothes on a chair near the fire so they may dry out before morning."

In the hall she stood for a moment, her eyes sweeping the room below. She could see forty or fifty officers in buff and blue, faded and worn. They were the militia and Minute Men, and Colonel Washington's Regulars, a few of Lawson's Virginians and officers of the Maryland and Pennsylvania Line. Near the window, she saw Colonel Lee talking earnestly with General Eaton. There was a great deal of stir and bustle in the room: slaves and servants carried hot toddies on big trays; messengers, their tired bodies covered with muddy cloaks dripping with rain, came in and departed quickly; orderlies moved from one group to another. A steady stream of soldiers passed by the windows. She saw that there was another downpour, heavier, more torrential than the day before.

She walked slowly down the stairs, the long skirt of her green habit dragging behind her. Men turned to look at her as she moved down the stairway. She held her head high, indifferent to staring eyes and curious glances. Captain Blount crossed the room and met her at the foot of the stairs. She smiled at him. Officers made way for her, bowing as she walked with Blount across the room.

They went down a long ill-lighted hall to the east wing where General Green's staff was quartered. Sentries paced back and forth at the entrance. Blount spoke a word; the soldiers stood at salute. They found Colonel Lawson alone, seated at a table looking through a pile of papers. He rose when they came in, greeting Mary with great cordiality.

"General Greene has been delayed, Mrs. Warden. He sent an orderly to say that he would be here in a short time. Will you be seated?"

Mary sat down near the fire. Lawson went back to his work. "Will you pardon me if I finish this?" he asked.

Mary smiled, but did not speak.

Lawson spoke to Blount. "Here, Lawrence, see if you can find several papers clipped together, marked, 'Cornwallis' Plans and Letters.' I seem to have mislaid them."

Mary looked about the room. It was bare: a few chairs near the large fireplace, two small tables. A long table at the far end of the room was set for supper. She counted six places. Evidently General Greene expected other guests. She leaned back in the chair. It was soft and warm. The firelight flickered; the wood crackled cheerily. She heard Colonel Lawson say to Blount:

"Men are guarding all roads into Guilford. We do not know just where Cornwallis' army is. Tarleton may be sent to cover their advance. We think he must have taken a position somewhere near Alamance Creek. The whole Province is in confusion, Blount. Our people are fast losing confidence. The situation is acutely serious. We have reports that Fanning has rallied a large number of Loyalists and is marching to join Cornwallis' force. General Greene must stop and give fight, or we'll soon be chased into Virginia." Lawson's voice was weary and dispirited.

"We have one thing in our favor, Colonel," Mary heard Blount say. "We know the country. They have some bad roads, high creeks and rivers to cross, but they don't know the fords as well as we do."

"That may be, but how are our troops going to conduct themselves when they meet the Queen's Guards, or such seasoned soldiers as the Royal Welch Fusiliers, or the Fighting 71st Highlanders?"

"I know it's bad, Colonel."

"Bad! Damn it, it's worse than that. It's suicide, Blount!"

"Our only hope is in Preston and his men getting here."

"Preston?"

"Yes, he and Colonel Rutledge are bringing the Back Mountain men. If they only get here in time!"

Mary's pulse quickened. Did he say Rutledge? It couldn't be Adam. He must have meant Peyton, young Peyton. But young Peyton was not a Colonel, nor would he be leading men from the Back Country. Her mind flashed back to the two woodsmen who stood beside the coach door. They had talked of their commander who owned land at Cahokia. She sat very still, afraid to move, clutching her hands tightly in her lap. Adam was coming! Adam would come! He would be here in time to help defend old North State. She smiled a little as she sat by the glowing fire. What matter wind and rain, sleet and glare ice? What matter the heavy roads and heavy travel? Adam would come in time!

The door opened and General Greene entered the room. His orderly took his rain-soaked cloak from his shoulders. He walked quickly toward Mary, took her hand and sat down at her side.

"It is good of you to come for a bite of supper with us. It was criminal to ask you, but we are selfish, we soldiers. We think of our own pleasure."

"I'm so happy to come, General. I'm not really tired. I've ridden comfortably—too comfortably," she added, thinking of the long line of grey men wearily plodding along the storm-drenched roads.

An orderly came in with a dispatch. Greene tore it open. "Cornwallis has been seen near the Five Mile Road," he read aloud. He turned to Lawson. "Order a detachment to capture and destroy all boats. If we can keep him on the other side of the river for a few days, it will give us a chance to rest the men at Guilford."

The Virginian left the room immediately. The door had no sooner closed after him than it was opened again, this time by a young officer who announced, "Generals Butler and Eaton."

General Greene introduced the officers to Mary. "I have kept you as a surprise, Mrs. Warden," he said, a quizzical smile on his lips. "My officers have seen so few women that the sight of a lovely one makes them forget their manners." Mary laughed and extended her hand. The officers bowed, Eaton raising her hand to his lips. Lawson came back, went to the table stacked with papers and began searching through the pile.

"I have not much to offer in the way of food. My officers complain of cornbread every day," General Greene said, as they walked to the table. "Will you sit here, Mrs. Warden?" He held the chair. Mary sat down between Greene and Lawson. Butler, Eaton and Captain Blount were opposite.

The dinner was half through before the campaign was mentioned. Butler spoke of the loss of a supply wagon in the ford. General Greene asked a question or two. Mary scarcely listened. Let them talk of Cornwallis' baggage trains, supplies and cannon. It meant little to her. *Adam was coming.* She could think of nothing else.

She sat at the table, eating mechanically. She answered questions, talked when necessary. She was two persons, one sitting quietly, half listening; the other, thinking out beyond, wondering, afraid to hope. *Adam was coming home.* She was conscious suddenly of words instead of blurred sounds.

"General Morgan's report," someone said, "with information about the location of Davidson's militia at Catawba Ford was in Cornwallis' hands in time for the General to turn his troops and take Beatie's Ford. Instead, Morgan found the leak and trapped the spy."

"I have heard nothing of this," Greene spoke sharply. "What did he do with the spy?"

"Hanged him forthwith without even waiting for a drumhead court!" Eaton answered.

"By God! Morgan will have something to explain to me," Greene said to Lawson. "Did you know of this?"

"No, General, this is the first I've heard of Morgan catching a spy."

"A man high up in the Council—I think his name was Ward—Warden—that was it," Butler said.

The glass Mary held in her hand slipped through her fingers. She had no will, no power to move. She heard the sound of shattering glass somewhere a long way off. She sank back against the chair, her nerveless hands falling to her sides. She heard voices. They were far off. Greene's voice:

"Quick, she's fainted! Damn you for a fool, Butler. The spy Morgan hanged was her husband."

"My God! How was I to know?"

"Carry her to the couch. Get water!" Lawson cried.

Mary felt herself being lifted. She was light, disembodied. A picture came to her mind, at first distant, then rushing toward her with increasing velocity. A tree with naked branches; the bleak, grotesque figure swaying in the wind . . .

Greene had laid his plans well. Weeks before, when he had gone through the country on his way to Virginia, he had selected Guilford Courthouse as a place to give battle to Cornwallis' army. The major part of the terrain was still in virgin forest. He would post his men on a great hill surrounded by lesser hills. The front line under Eaton would be on the right. On the left, Butler's men. Davidson would have field guns at the edge of the forest; beyond that lay open field surrounded by a fence running parallel to the woods. The rail fence was overgrown with bushes and vines of wild grapes and briar, ideal for sharpshooters and snipers.

He moved his ragamuffin army into these lines of battle. Lawson's Virginians were posted on the second line; two brigades of militia. The third line was placed at the Courthouse. These were seasoned Continentals from Virginia and Maryland, and Colonel Washington's dragoons. The light infantry and riflemen were placed on a hill. From there they could move quickly to protect the flank of the main line. A similar detachment occupied a hill to the left. Colonel Lee, Greene reserved to send forward when necessary to draw the enemy.

Greene was not counting on numbers but on an outside force to aid him to victory. He must show not only Cornwallis, but his own men, that he could do something more than retreat. The two hundred and fifty miles from Camden in South Carolina to their present situation had been like six hundred miles to his weary men. They had covered the distance with dragging feet, despairing hearts, defeats that ate into their very souls. Now the time had come when they must turn to give battle.

Mary, in her tent at the fringe of the forest above the Guilford post road, heard the sound of marching men all night. Physically exhausted as she was, she could not sleep. War had her in its clutching grip—war and guns and men, men who saw no farther than the next step. "One step more . . . one step more . . . we must take one step more," was their voiceless cry.

She got up from the cot quietly, so as not to wake David, and went outside. The soldier sentry was stooping over a fire, heating milk in a small pannikin. He straightened up when he saw her and offered to divide the milk. She took a swallow. It burned her mouth, but the warmth was comforting. She drew her cape more closely about her and walked a few steps to an open space among the trees. The sentry followed her.

"Don't go far, ma'am," he said. "My orders are to watch that you don't come to danger."

"I won't go any farther," she assured him. They talked together a little. The sentry walked back and seated himself on a log by the fire to finish his drink. Mary stood for a long time looking out into the night. Beyond her, across the edge of the field, fires shone dimly. She could not see the hills clearly, only the heavy massed shadows.

Somewhere, between the spot where she stood and the rise

of the hill that bulked against the starred sky, an army lay resting—an army of seven thousand men—"Greene's raga-muffins" resting for the morrow's battle. Did they sleep uneasily on the sodden earth? Or did they lie in heavy, dreamless sleep? How many of them would see the next dawn, or the one that followed? She shivered, as if an icy hand had been laid upon her. Young men, aged by war, beardless boys with trembling lips. If she could only reach out to comfort them!

A twig snapped. She turned quickly. In the darkness, she distinguished a moving shadow. A few moments later, an officer leading a horse came into the rays cast by the fire. She recognized Colonel Lawson.

"Mrs. Warden! You awake? You should be resting, sound asleep at this hour."

She made a gesture toward the slope of the long hill. "Are they resting? All of that army of exhausted men?"

"I hope to God they are," he said slowly. "I hope so."

The sentry moved from the fire toward them. He saluted when he saw Colonel Lawson.

"Bring Colonel Lawson a cup of hot milk, Grieves," Mary said. The man went back to the fire. "There will be a battle?" she asked after a time. Lawson turned from looking into the darkness.

"I don't know. We have heard that Cornwallis is camped eight miles away. My men have not yet verified this, but I assume it to be true. In that case, it will be today, or tomorrow at the latest."

The sentry came toward him with a pannikin in his hand. Mary moved toward the fire. "Let us sit here," she said to Lawson.

The Virginian gave the reins to the sentry who tied the horse to a small tree. Mary sat on the log nearest to the fire. Lawson drank the hot milk with slow relish. "It may be the last I have today. I may as well enjoy it," he said with an attempted lightness.

"I have many boxes of lint and bandages in my tent," Mary said after a silence. "I had the young surgeon, Magill, show me how to bandage and apply splints."

"You bandage and tie up broken bones?" Lawson glanced at Mary's slight figure, her delicate, fragile hands.

"I have more strength than you imagine, Colonel. I had to do something these terrible days of waiting, something, anything to keep from thinking—from thinking back, or thinking forward. I'm sorry," she said after a moment. "That was beastly of me."

Lawson's eyes held hers. "Damn it all, you shouldn't be here, Mary Warden. I told Greene weeks ago that he should send you through the lines to Edenton, but he said it wouldn't be safe. He didn't know where Tarleton was. He said the whole Albemarle section was in a state of alarm over Leslie's continued occupation of Norfolk." He drained the last swallow of milk. "The privateers have shelled the whole Sound. Did Greene tell you that the Manor House at Rutledge Riding has been half demolished by Phillips' privateers? The wharves and warehouses at Edenton, also. Your house is safe according to reports."

Mary clasped her hands tightly. "No, he didn't tell me that." She sat looking into the fire. The wood snapped and blazed. The horse pawed the ground impatiently. Beyond the first row of trees reached by the firelight, the forest thickened into gloom and deep shadows. How still it was—how tranquil. She tried to think of the words the Virginian had just spoken: "The Manor House at Rutledge Riding has been demolished." The Manor House—brick falling from brick—shells over the East Garden plowing into the earth, bursting into fragments.

"The North Plantation?" she asked.

"Safe, I believe. Rutledge will be upset by this."

"I don't understand why they would do such a thing. Sara Rutledge was an ardent Royalist, you would have thought—"

"You can think nothing in war, Mary—nothing!" He poured some more milk from a bucket into the pannikin and held it over the fire.

"Colonel Lawson—about my husband. I'm positive that he was not a spy. There has been some terrible mistake."

Lawson put his hand over hers. "There are many fine men who have remained loyal to the Mother Country, Mary." She did not answer. "General Greene should have sent you home long ago," he repeated. "It is brutal to allow a woman like you to feel the horror of war that a soldier must endure."

Mary stopped him. "He keeps me because he is afraid that I'm a spy, too. He is afraid that I will in some way convey my knowledge of his position to the enemy." All the bitterness that she had felt through the long weeks came rushing to her lips. "He has been thoughtful of my comfort, but I have known. It has humiliated me." Tears came to her eyes. She brushed them away impatiently.

Lawson watched her with kind, understanding eyes, but he did not deny her charge.

"General Greene does not know me," she continued. "He

525

doesn't know that I'm loyal. I have written to my friends, to Hewes, Hooper, even to the Governor, but I have had no reply. I have come to believe that the letters were never sent."

Lawson turned away. She saw that he knew this was true but that in loyalty to his commander he could not speak. Lawson leaned toward her, taking her hand again. "I'll send you home as soon as this battle is over, Mary, if I live."

Mary tightened her clasp on his strong fingers. She realized that she had grown very fond of this tall Virginian. "I think you are my friend," she said.

He started to say something, then withheld his words. Instead, he looked out into the darkness. Where the heavy bulk of distant hills massed into deep shadows, a thin line of light was showing.

"My men are camped just below," he said. "The second line. God grant that they stand under fire today."

Mary looked up quickly. "You think that . . ."

"I think nothing beyond the moment, Mary. Greene's plan is a good one if the men hold. But we are pitifully, tragically unready to meet Cornwallis' army. We have had a few skirmishes, quickly over, then we've turned and run, hid in bushes, run. . . . That is not war! That is no way to train men to fight." His tone was contemptuous now. "We haven't the rifles or the ammunition. We haven't the courage," he added.

The chill of fear came over her. "Do men never fight strongly out of sheer desperation? Can't they win out of crushing defeat?"

Lawson shook his head. "A small chance perhaps." He turned again to the hills. "I'm waiting for daylight," he said to her. "My scouts should be back by then. That swaggering devil, Tarleton! I'd like nothing so much as to clip his strong wings. Cornwallis is sure to send him scouting with his dragoons."

"Is Tarleton really so bad?"

Lawson laughed. "The redcoats and the Loyalists say that we are the ones who are constantly committing atrocities—unspeakable atrocities. We say the same about Tarleton. War is war. Rumors run ahead; that is part of the terror."

"Has Cornwallis many men?"

"Yes, but I don't know how many: the Hessians of Bose; the Welsh Fusiliers; the Prince of Wales's Regiment commanded by Colonel Webster, a splendid soldier; the Guards;

526

the Queen's Own; the Grenadier Guards; Yagers and light infantry, besides Tarleton's legions. A formidable lot for our green country boys to encounter at the end of three months of heartbreaking retreat."

He paced nervously about the fire, his hands behind his back, his shoulders sagging. It seemed to Mary that she had seen many men walk that way these past years. Sagging shoulders, bowed, lined faces, eyes that held the agony of fear —not fear for their own bodies, but fear for the land they fought over, the blood-watered land of the Carolinas.

Lawson came back from the clearing where he had gone to look down the valley. "It is growing light. I must go in a few minutes. Sentries have been placed near here. I trust you will be safe and out of the range of fire. Go deeper into the woods in case—" He paused, looking at her. A slow smile came to his firm, generous mouth. "Why do I say this to you, Mary Warden? The medical division is down the slope of this hill near the road." He laid his two hands on her shoulders. "Take as good care of yourself as you can, my dear." Leaning forward, he touched his lips to her forehead. "A small tribute to a courageous woman," he said lightly.

He had gone only a few yards when he came back. "If things should go badly for us, it won't be the end. We will rally and retreat. We can always do that. Remember this, Mary: in spite of all rumors, Lord Cornwallis is the same person you knew in London. Tarleton is the same charming man you met there."

She watched him go down the gentle incline to the raod.

Morning came, cold, the sky a dull, heavy grey. David hurried out of the tent, roused by the odor of frying bacon. Colonel Lawson had sent up his cook and a helper, just after daybreak, with supplies. The man made himself at home, hanging up his pots and kettles in a tree, placing boxes of provisions in neat order near a spring. He scraped a small section of ground clear of pine needles and dried leaves. Digging a hole, he lined it with stones. Mary saw he was making an oven.

Below them, on the flat, a steady stream of soldiers was passing by. They were coming from all directions, converging at the Courthouse. Light artillery, heavy artillery, foot-soldiers and cavalry. These were the Continentals, veterans of many battles. David stood beside her.

"They are brave, aren't they, Aunt Mary?"

"Very brave, David. They have come from Maryland and

Virginia and the North where they fought battles under General Washington."

"Are they braver than our men from North Carolina?"

"No braver, dear, but they know more about war."

The cook was ready for them. They sat on a log and ate from metal plates: bacon and cornbread, hot gruel to drink. The forest was silent except for the trees dripping from recent rains. A canvas had been spread for a floor, extending from the tent to the backlog of the fire. With her heavy furred boots and her fur-lined cape, Mary knew she should not be cold, but she was. It seemed as if the blood in her veins had congealed. It came to her that it was not physical cold, but fear—fear for what the day would bring. What would it bring to these desolate, despairing men?

"Why are you crying?" David asked, looking at her curiously. "Are we lost? Are we going to be captured by the redcoats? Will the Butcher Tarleton get us and hack us into bits?"

"David! How terrible!"

"That is what the sentry told me. He said Bloody Tarleton would get us."

Mary faced the boy. He was looking at her with Adam's hazel eyes.

"If they should come, David, they will do us no harm. They may take us prisoners, nothing more."

"What would happen then?"

"I don't know, but I think we should probably be sent home on parole like Owen Tewilliger."

"Well, that's better than Greene has done for us."

Mary was startled. How much more the boy understood than she had imagined.

"General Greene has been kind, David." David did not answer. For a moment she was on the point of talking to him, of explaining why General Greene had kept them moving with the army. But she refrained. She could see that he had been observant. He doubtless knew as much as she.

She walked to the edge of the clearing. Below her were Lawson's Virginians, busy with breakfast fires. "Fight on a full stomach," Lawson had said. He had managed to forage for his men. Nine miles away he had found food. His men were eating. This heartened her. There was reality in the sight. It broke through the terror of uncertainty that came with waiting. She went back to her tent to lie down. Perhaps she could snatch a little rest.

The snap of cracking ice woke Mary from sleep. On the road below, troops were marching in steady clocklike precision. Continentals in marching order. No straggling in twos and threes, or singly. With swinging steps they crashed through the ice that had formed on puddles. The layers of glare ice broke and snapped under their feet.

"They march grand, don't they?"

Mary turned. The sentry, Grieves, stood to one side, his eyes on the Continentals.

"March grand, and they've got muskets. They saw that Cornwallis has been held up by high water again. This looks like the Lord sort of remembered us and sent his servants to help us."

"What do you mean, Grieves?" David asked the old trooper.

"I mean just what I say, young master. The Lord has servants of his own. He uses them when he wills: plague and famine, storms, winds and floods. He punishes us with these servants of his, but sometimes he is kind. Didn't he swell up the Catawba? Didn't he swell up the Dan and Yadkin? Now he swells up the Deep with a wall of water." Grieves drew his grizzled brows together and looked at David. "Remember that, little gentleman; remember that when you grow up to be a man. You can't run away from the Lord's servants no matter what you do."

"Did the swollen river run after Cornwallis?" David asked, impressed by Grieves' solemn face.

"No, but the flood kept the redcoats on 'tother side of the stream and gave our men a breathing space. You will see things with your eyes and will hear things with your ears this day, little master, that you will remember as long as you live."

David turned his wondering eyes to Mary. She realized that Grieves must be diverted.

"Better go back to the fire, Grieves, it needs logs," she said. "Ask Cook to fill the kettles with water from the spring and put them on the fire. We may need hot water before long."

All morning troops marched by. David and Mary sat on the hillside watching. From time to time Grieves came and pointed out Colonel Washington's cavalry and the Maryland Continentals.

"A battle! This will be a battle," he said exultantly. "A battle like Monmouth. I was at Monmouth, too, madam, and the long winter at Valley Forge. And I marched into Philadelphia—but this will be greater. They will kill and kill and kill, today. It may be the last battle of all!"

Mary put up her hand in protest. "Please!" she said, her eyes looking significantly at David.

Grieves shook his head stubbornly. "He's old enough! Old enough! At his age, I was a drummer boy in the Irish Fusiliers."

David, who had been watching the Maryland line come into position, turned quickly. "A drummer boy when you were thirteen? How splendid! I'm old enough to fight, Aunt Mary."

"David! Do not say such things."

"I am. My mother told me. Her brothers went into battle when they were no older. They rode beside their father, the Sherif Ibn Daud, on swift-racing Hajeem. They fought their enemy, the Rashid, with sword and lance and banners flying."

"God love us! What is the lad saying?" Grieves muttered, staring at David in bewilderment.

Mary looked at the child. She seemed to see him with new eyes. Until now she thought of him only as the son of Adam. Something in what he had just said made her suddenly aware that in David was the blood of another race, his mother's people—a strong race, who fought for their heritage of freedom, "with sword and lance and banners flying."

She put her arm over David's shoulder. "You must stay close to me, David. You must take care of me."

Grieves nodded solemnly. "Yes, little master, you must take care of the mistress."

David looked from one to the other. "I would rather ride beside my father," he said quietly.

Mary turned her eyes to the flat field below. She could see no soldiers. They had been swallowed up—in the forest, behind the fences. But in the distance, along the roads, they were still moving forward: grey and white figures moving slowly at a snail's pace.

The sky was leaden. Rain would come—rain and cold icy winds would sweep over the dead. She shivered. She must keep such thoughts out of her head. Waiting, waiting, the deadly waiting! What must they be thinking, the men down below the hill, lying on the cold, wet earth, waiting?

The hours dragged by until midday. Suddenly Grieves, who was standing behind them, dropped to his haunches and extended his arm, pointing.

"Tarleton's dragoons!" he cried excitedly.

Mary looked in the direction he pointed. Down the road horsemen were galloping. Tarleton was coming. Tarleton and his butchers! Her eyes swept the length of the road that led straight to Guilford Courthouse. The road was clear. No troops were visible. Tarleton's legion came swiftly, riding straight forward into Greene's ambush.

Chapter 37

GUILFORD COURTHOUSE

DAVID caught at Mary's arm. "What is that?" he whispered.

At the bottom of the hill, drifting across the valley, lay three puffs of smoke, like small cumulous clouds. A moment later, the sound reached them, the dull boom of cannon. Cannon! They had opened fire with cannon. The surprise of Green's three-pounders, hidden in a clump of bushes, had halted Tarleton's dragoons. They checked, wheeled and scattered. Colonel Lee's cavalry took advantage of the confusion. They charged, cutting down Tarleton's troops and officers. Then they disappeared up the road, both pursuers and the pursued.

Mary looked in the opposite direction. More troops were coming, marching to the staccato beat of drums. She heard the wild skirl of pipes. The Highlanders! It was the Black Watch, the fighting 71st, advancing toward the open field. She had seen them many times in London on parade. But not like this, marching at double quick, kilts swirling, pipes skirling—not piping parade now, but piping men to battle. A solid rank they came, row on row, spreading out into battle line. How splendid they were! How brave! "Oh, Scots, do you not know that behind the fences men are waiting to kill?" Her teeth clamped down on her lips to keep from screaming the words aloud. It was too late. In a few moments rifle fire would strike them down! "God in Heaven, defend the Right," she prayed, tears rolling unheeded down her white cheeks.

Across the field other troops were running forward to close the broken ranks.

"The're mobbing the Queen's Guard," Grieves told her, pointing to a position to the west. Field pieces rumbled up; trotting horses reared and plunged; soldiers made way; guns were unlimbered, charges rammed; there was the sudden flash of a fusee. Then came the answering fire to Greene's three-pounders.

The British column advanced with fixed bayonets along the split rail fence. Mary could not see the Americans, only a few puffs of smoke from the trees that told of the presence of hidden sharpshooters. The Highlanders still advanced in formation. Mary realized that they did not know that Lawson's Virginians lay concealed along the zigzag fence.

Suddenly, they knew. The sharp fire of rifles—men falling, screaming and cursing. The front line of the British lay on the ground—one out of every ten wounded or dying. The rest took to cover, behind trees, bushes, stones. Bent over, they ran, dodging the deadly fire that came from behind the fence. Officers shouted, rallying them. Then they charged the fence, sweeping forward. Havoc—dreadful, tragic havoc before her eyes.

Grieves called out, "The Americans are giving way. God damn them all for yellow-livered cowards." He seized his musket and ran through the leafless trees down the hill.

David sprang to his feet and started to follow. Mary caught at his arm. "Stay here, David, don't leave me," she cried.

The boy tore himself loose from her grasp and ran down the hill toward the road, Mary after him calling to him to wait.

The roar of cannon came with startling regularity now. Mary saw David through the trees, far below. He was running at full speed. She stumbled after him, the skirt of her habit unhooked, catching on brambles and thorns, delaying her. At the bottom of the hill, she stopped for breath and leaned against the trunk of a pine tree. David had gone, she knew not where, caught in the wild hysteria of battle.

Then she saw him. Two soldiers held the struggling boy by the arms, keeping him back. She hurried forward. At the turn of the road she came to the big hospital tent. Dr. Armitage stood in front, directing stretcher-bearers. He was bareheaded, his white hair flying. "The British are rallying," she heard him cry. Mary pressed her face against the rough bark of the tree to shut out the sight of men charging with fixed bayonets.

Armitage, turning around, saw her. "God in Heaven, Mary, what are you doing here? Get back! Get back! Have you lost your senses?"

His voice calmed her. She walked across the open space. "I've come to help," she said quietly.

Armitage nodded. "There'll be work aplenty. The field is already black with British dead. As long as you're here, you may as well be of some use."

"Where are the Carolinians and Lawson's Virginians?" she asked.

He was sweeping the open country with his glass. "I can't see their position; they are in the woods behind that knoll," he said briefly. Then he turned to the south. "God! Look down the road! More British! The Welsh Fusiliers—the Guards. Look, Mary, take the glass, it's Cornwallis—Cornwallis himself."

Mary took the glasses. She saw a soldierly man on a big horse. There was the man who had put fear and terror into the hearts of the Carolinians. He was riding in advance of the Guards, indifferent of danger, a target for any sniper behind tree or fence. He was close enough for her to see his proudly held head, his strong aquiline nose.

"He is not without courage," Armitage said grudgingly. "The officer with him is Webster. He is a splendid officer, Mary. I don't know how our men can hold out against such troops as these!"

"God defend the Right." Mary did not know whether or not she spoke the words aloud. Beyond the hospital tent she saw David. He was standing still, white and bewildered. When he saw her he ran to her and caught her hand, but his eyes shone with wild excitement.

"It's a battle, Aunt Mary, a real battle," he cried.

Armitage saw him. "God's death! You here, David?"

The awful ear-splitting skirl of pipes! Would it never stop? The Black Watch advanced—the sturdy, grim-faced men running, their plaid skirts flying, waving from side to side. A snatch of song came from the smoke-covered field:

"March, March, Ettrick and Teviotdale,
Why the deil dinna ye march forward in order?"

The words of the old rallying song of the Scots were blurred under the boom of mortars. When the roar stopped the song rose again.

"March, march, Eshdale and Liddensdale,
All the Blue Bonnets are bound for the Border."

The shrill pipes—the steady roll of drums. "Stop! stop! stop!" Mary cried out in agony.

Armitage turned quickly, his glasses falling on the strap. He grasped her shoulder, shaking her violently. "Quiet, quiet, woman!" he said sternly.

Mary pulled herself together.

534

David was tired of watching. "If I only had Black Douglas and my grandfather's lance, I would go into battle."

"David, don't say such things," she cried.

She saw Lawson galloping up. He shouted to Armitage. "Send out the stretcher-bearers to the left flank under a white flag. Have them bring in the wounded—British and Americans, all of them." He scarcely paused to give the orders. Nor did he seem to see Mary. He turned his horse and galloped back to the line. She saw him riding up and down at the head of his men, shouting encouragement. Armitage caught at her elbow.

"Look! Lawson's men are breaking. They have thrown down their rifles! They are running—running—God! Don't they do anything but run?"

The Maryland militia gave way first. Eaton's men, then Butler's. They broke under the savage charge of the 71st. Bayonets gleamed in the light; drums beat, funeral drums, not drums of war. No longer able to bear the shrill lament of the pipes, Mary went into the tent. Her people were running. "God of Battles, save them." Her lips moved soundlessly. Soldiers were running past the hospital station, choking the road in their mad rush. Fear-stricken men with glazed, staring eyes; boys with drawn, white faces, livid with anguish and horror. She saw Lawson on his foamed-flecked horse, riding along the road, shouting above the tumult, "Rally, rally and charge—turn and charge!" But they did not hear him. They kept on running away. They were already beaten men, and the battle scarce begun.

Bloody and fierce was the battle that raged all about them. Colonel Washington's cavalry came up. They charged once, but they too were caught in the panic of fear. What was happening? Were all men in all the world running? Was Greene's army falling to pieces before they were tried and tempered by fire? Mother of Mercy! Were these strong, free men, who fought to protect their land?

Suddenly she was conscious of a new sound. It seemed to flow through her body, beat against her ears. It came out of the earth, vibrating through the air. Men were marching—the steady unfaltering pulsation of marching feet. Armitage heard it, too. He swung around, facing the west. Mary followed his fixed gaze.

Along the western road, horsemen galloped—a long line of men coming forward at double quick.

"The Back Country men have come at last," Armitage

535

shouted, his voice high. "They are coming again, just as they did at King's Mountain." Tears ran down his shrunken cheeks. "Thank God!" he whispered. "I thought they would come."

Mary stood at the tent door, her hands held tightly together. The fleeing soldiers hesitated, half turned. What were the words they heard to give them courage? Kneeling men caught up rifles. An order rang out, sharp, staccato. It passed down rank after rank of soldiers, growing in volume. *Stand and defend, men, stand and defend!* They caught up the cry. . . .

Mary heard a voice above the roar of battle and the mad skirling of Highland pipes. Was it Adam's voice carrying above the shouts and cries? The wavering lines stiffened. More men turned, caught up their rifles. Then she saw him. He was riding a great bay horse, his naked sword in his hand. He rode at a gallop down the line.

"Stand and defend!" he shouted, over and over. "God damn you for cowards!"

Words of courage passed from lip to lip down the breaking line, behind hedge fences and into woods and swamps. A new battle cry that filled the hearts of defeated men with new courage. *"Stand and Defend!"* The lines turned, hesitated, then stood as if suddenly reinvigorated.

The British column wavered. A moment before Americans had been running, now they were spreading fanwise across the battle field. The rifle fire was sharp, steady. What had happened? The British did not know, but the Carolinians and the Virginians knew. The men of the Back Country had come! Marching swiftly—the rugged, hawk-eyed men advanced. Behind every beardless, frightened boy a strong man stood. Bronzed woodsmen stood shoulder to shoulder with unseasoned boys, giving them the strength of the far-flung forests, of the deep rivers. Sturdy, weather-beaten men, with steady eyes, trained to the cunning of Indian fighting.

Greene galloped down the road, rallying his troops. Lawson whirled among his men, his chestnut horse in a white lather. He took up the cry of the Back Country men—*"Freemen . . . stand and defend!"*

Mary ran through the bushes to the edge of the road and waited. Presently he came in sight.

"Adam, Adam Rutledge," she screamed, her voice high and shrill.

Adam pulled up his horse with a jerk. "Mary," he cried. He jumped to the ground catching both her hands. "What are

536

you doing here? Get out quickly! God knows what's going to happen."

David found her then and she pushed him forward. "Here's David," she said. There was so little time for them.

Adam and David looked into each other's eyes a moment. "Go back to the tent, David. It is not safe here." Adam spoke gently.

"I will ride with you into battle," the boy said.

"No, no, stay with me, David," Mary cried shrilly. "Don't let him go, Adam, he is so young, so young."

Adam looked at the boy. "You are tall, my boy. Can you use a musket?"

A dull red came to David's cheeks, his lips quivered. "As well as any," he answered.

Adam signaled to Herk. "Give him your horse, Herk. Find another on the battlefield for yourself. David shall ride with me today." The boy swung into the saddle without touching a stirrup, his face alive with excitement.

Mary stood alone by the roadside. They did not turn to wave farewell or speak a last word to her before they rode forward into battle. She moved wearily to the dressing tent. Stretcher-bearers were coming in, carrying groaning, cursing men. She threw her cap over a bush and rolled back the cuffs of her riding habit. Bandages and packets of lint lay on a long table outside the tent—packets of lint waiting to be unrolled. Dully she carried them into the tent, stripped the covers from a box and laid out the shining steel instruments on a fresh piece of cotton cloth. After a time, she forgot father and son—even the battle ceased to exist.

Wounded men were placed in front of her. Faces passed in the line of her vision—bodies of men, broken, drowned in their own blood and the blood of their enemies. Lint, staunching wounds; bright red blood of youth; grey figures passing in quick succession; the swift sharp orders of surgeons; stretcher-bearers moving rapidly, laying down one burden, taking up another. . . .

"Get out into the air, Mary Warden." A sharp order—Armitage with sleeves rolled back, his hands and arms red to the elbow with blood. "Get out into the air!"

She walked to the opening of the tent. The roar of cannon broke on her ears. Before her, lines of men straggled by, enveloped in grey smoke. The glint of gold and red—blue—faded buff. The strong, heavy odor of powder choked her. Clouds of smoke obscured the field. Leaden clouds overhead were heavy with rain.

Greene rode up the road below the dressing station. His corpulent figure had shrunk, his cheeks sagged, hanging loosely. His dark, agonized eyes looked across the field. Lawson galloped up, his right arm hanging limply at his side.

"I have to report, sir, the Virginian line broke. My men are in complete disorder."

Greene turned to an orderly. "My compliments to Colonel Rutledge. Tell him to throw his Back Country men behind the Virginians," he shouted over his shoulder. "Go to the dressing tent and get your arm fixed up, Lawson, then return to your men. If we must retreat, let it be in good order." There was discouragement in his voice as he rode off.

Lawson swung from his saddle. He swayed, grasping his horse's mane for support. Mary ran to him and led him to the tent. Blood was streaming from a saber cut over his eye, dripping from the corners of his mouth. He wiped it away impatiently with the back of his hand.

"Webster of the Highlanders is dead," he mumbled. "I saw him fall from his horse, and Stuart of the Queen's Own. Gallant officers, both of them. God damn all War!" He talked between set teeth while Armitage worked on the shattered arm.

Greene rode up to the dressing tent. The Doctor went out but came back in a moment. "The General wants to see you, Mary," he said.

Mary went out. Greene sat on his tall horse, scribbling a line on a piece of paper. "In case we have to retreat, give this to Tarleton or Cornwallis. I have asked for your protection and safe conduct to Edenton." He handed the paper to her. "I'm sorry, more sorry than I can ever say, about your husband, Mrs. Warden. If he had been brought to me, it might have been different." He stopped abruptly. Messengers were riding toward him. Captain Blount saluted.

"Our men are retreating in good order, General. They are no longer running but are making a stand all along the three battle lines. When they are forced to give way, they give way slowly. The British loss is heavier than ours, I think."

Mary went back to her work, washing blood-caked wounds, preparing broken bodies for the swift, keen knife of the surgeon. She laid her hand gently on the smooth forehead of young boys. Enemies, wounded and dying, came under the quiet touch of her fingers.

A young Highlander of the Black Watch held tight to her hand, while Armitage cut away the flesh of his thigh to remove a bullet. The lad's sandy hair fell over his white face. Mary pushed it back from his fast glazing eyes.

"Take the pin from my plaid, lassie," the boy whispered. Mary undid the great silver pin set with a Cairngorm and Scotch pebbles. "Wear it for a lad who died far from Glen Orchy."

Hot tears came to her eyes. "You will get well," she said, smoothing his hair.

He shook his head feebly. "I ha' seen the Doctor look at ye. There was death in his look, lassie."

She knelt beside him.

"Dinna forget, Mither, dinna forget . . ." he said clearly. His fingers loosened.

She closed his eyes, laid her cheek against his. So young—so very young.

The stream of wounded men brought to the station seemed unending. Men, fainting from loss of blood, leaned against the trees or lay on the ground waiting. There was no room inside. Mary worked on mechanically, her hands moving rapidly, binding, washing wounds, making preparations for the surgeons. Adam, where was he? What was happening out on the dark and bloody field? Someone brought her a cup of hot rum. She drank eagerly. The scalding liquid brought warmth to her cold body. Then she looked up. She saw it was Colonel Lawson.

"Drink it all, every drop!"

"But your arm! You must be careful."

"They have bound it up. Mary, listen. We are going to lose the battle. In a little while Cornwallis' men will be here."

Mary clung to him. "But the Back Country men—I thought they had turned the tide."

"They did, but they could not hold forever. They have given us the chance to retreat in good order. Already our men are moving swiftly toward Reedy Ford, but Cornwallis has thrown in the second battalion of Guards near Guilford Courthouse. The Hessians and the Black Watch have recovered. Tarleton, damn him, has managed to keep his dragoons intact. Cornwallis will win this battle, but I think it will break his army to pieces." He took her hand. "You will be quite safe, Mary. You have Greene's paper?"

"Yes, I have it." She hesitated a moment, then said, "Have you seen Adam Rutledge?"

Lawson shook his head. "Not since noon. He was in command of the right wing across the field from my men. He is probably throwing his men in to protect the ford and cover the retreat. I must go, Mary. Good-by and God bless you for a brave woman. I will never forget you."

He rode off into the night, lost in the heavy shadows. As she watched him go, she had the feeling that she would never see him again. A great weariness came over her. It had begun to rain. Night hid the dark and bloody ground. The sound of pipes came from the field—a dirge, piping a last call to dead men, a lament to brave warriors dead on foreign soil.

She held the arm of a wounded man. Suddenly, she saw it was a red-coated surgeon bending over the soldier, probe in hand. The British had taken over the hospital tent. More men were carried in; some screaming, moaning; some silent, with set jaws. Mary worked on, aware neither of time nor place. The British had come without her knowing. The tents filled rapidly with Guards and Highlanders, Hessians and men of Tarleton's dragoons. She went on working. The new doctors accepted her presence without question. The stream of wounded flowed swiftly.

Then there was a lull. She was conscious that the heavy boom of cannon had ceased. An officer came into the tent. He paused abruptly at the sight of Mary. "What are you doing here?" he asked gruffly.

"That is obvious, isn't it, Captain?"

The surgeon looked up from his work for a moment. "This lady's helping me," he said.

"We've orders to clear the country of rebels. What is your name?"

"Warden, Mary Warden from Edenton."

"You will have to go to the Colonel, Mrs. Warden."

"Damn you, Captain, leave her alone. Can't you see I need her?" The surgeon spoke angrily.

Mary rolled down her cuffs and smoothed her hair into place. She followed the officer out of the tent in spite of the doctor's vigorous protest. They walked through the darkness to a great tent that had been pitched beside the road.

"Who is in command?" Mary asked, as they neared the campfire.

"Colonel Tarleton," the officer said.

Mary felt in her pocket. The letter General Greene had given her was still there. She gave it to the officer.

"Please give this to Colonel Tarleton."

The officer held it in his hand a moment, puzzled.

"Will you please be quick about it, officer? I do not like

standing in the rain." Her voice took on a commanding tone. The officer looked up quickly. He started to speak, then thought better of it and disappeared into the tent. After a time, he came back.

"Please step this way, Mrs. Warden," he said, his manner deferential now.

Mary followed him into the tent. An officer in a stained uniform and muddy boots sat with his back toward her, bending over a table spread with maps. He looked up when she entered. It was Banastre Tarleton.

"Sit down, madam," he said, indicating a camp stool.

Mary sat down. While he was reading she watched him. The years had ravaged his long oval face. It was deeply lined but he was still handsome, still dashing, even though his full dark eyes were heavy-lidded with fatigue. He glanced at her several times while he was reading the letter.

"Haven't I seen you before somewhere? Your face is very familiar."

"In London, Colonel."

His face cleared.

"I remember now. Lady Carstairs brought you to London."

"Yes."

"And I stayed with your grandmother in Northampton-shire and we rode with the Quorn. I remember how you as-tonished us all with your riding. But that was a long time ago." His voice was reminiscent. "A long time ago," he re-peated. "Strange I should remember that though I know I've seen you in London more recently."

Mary nodded, her attention on his hand which was bound up with a blood-soaked cloth. "You are wounded. Let me change the bandage, Colonel," she said impulsively. "I have been working at the hospital tent—"

Tarleton glanced down at his hand. "I had forgotten. It does not bother me now."

Mary had noted a box of surgical supplies at the far end of the tent. She went over to it and, searching through the box, found what she needed. "Please have your man bring me a kettle of hot water, Colonel," she said.

Tarleton protested for a moment, then gave the order. In a few minutes the orderly came in with a steaming kettle and Mary unbound the handkerchiefs that Tarleton had hastily wrapped around his hand and took a small silver basin from the field box that stood open on a folding table.

"The bullet is still there," she said, after a brief examination. "I think you had better send for a surgeon, Colonel Tarleton. You may have trouble if you neglect such a wound."

Tarleton moved impatiently. "Please bind it up. I will see a medical officer later. About this letter, I have sent word to General Cornwallis that you are here, Mrs. Warden. He wishes to see you."

"Why should Lord Cornwallis wish to see me?" Mary asked.

"I don't know, but I will take you to him."

Tarleton walked with Mary to Lord Cornwallis' tent, which was a few paces down the road, and left her. Mary entered the tent. General Cornwallis had not heard her approach. He sat at a table, his head in his hands, his shoulders stooped. She stood for a moment waiting for him to look up. Was this the man who had won a great battle? Was this the victorious leader?

After a short time, he lifted his bowed head from his hands and saw her. "Mrs. Warden," he said, rising to his feet. He lifted her hand to his lips. "I wanted to see you, to express the deep sorrow I feel at the loss of your husband. Madam, you must be very proud of him. William Warden died a hero, sacrificed for his country. He was as great a hero as John André, if the truth of his work were known."

Mary drew a quick breath. His words took her by surprise. She had heard William called a traitor—a spy. Now Cornwallis had called him a hero. The change was too great. Tears came, hot blinding tears. William, her poor William. Somehow the image of the grotesque, dangling figure grew faint in her mind, retreated into greyness. Another image took its place. William, stately, dying heroically for his King —dying for his beliefs and his loyalty.

Cornwallis was writing on a pad. "I will send you home to Edenton under escort, Mrs. Warden."

Mary took a step forward. She must tell him the truth. She could not let him think her loyalties were the same as William's.

"I must tell you, Lord Cornwallis, that I do not believe as my husband believed. In your eyes, I'm a rebel."

Cornwallis smiled a little sadly. "I know. One hears a great deal of Mary Warden's loyalty to the cause of the Colonies, but even though I know that, if you will permit me, I will have my own coach brought here for you."

"I couldn't think of that, Lord Cornwallis!" Mary protested. "You might need it on the march."

Cornwallis' face was tragic. "I'm not marching tonight, Mrs. Warden," he said in a lifeless voice. "My army must rest. I'm the victor of a battle today, but I'm defeated. Greene retreats, but he leaves me with my army broken to pieces, without the strength to pursue him." He turned to his table and picked up his quill.

Mary said, "I'm not alone. I have young Rutledge traveling with me, Lord Cornwallis."

"Young Rutledge? Who is he?"

"A young lad from Virginia who has been visiting at Edenton," she said hastily, hoping she sounded convincing.

"I'll include Rutledge in the pass," he said. He wrote for a moment and handed the paper to Mary.

She noticed that he had scribbled in the name Rutledge. She thanked him, then said impulsively, "You were always a friend of the Colonies before this war, Lord Cornwallis. We don't forget that."

He looked up. She was startled by the black despair in his eyes.

"This is an evil day for me, Mrs. Warden. We have won a battle but we lost the flower of the British army." He looked moodily at the ground, his strong sensitive fingers holding his quill pen. "My men were glowing with impatience to signalize themselves. They charged too quickly. We lost heavily— we have no forage, none at all. The country has been desolated by the marching troops. Today's battle has rung the death knell of our hold on the American Colonies. Tomorrow, I begin my retreat toward Wilmington."

He turned his head. Mary could not see his face, but she knew he had spoken to her out of the black despair of his soul. She left the tent and walked swiftly through the beating rain to the dressing station.

Near the hospital tent, a heavy shadow detached itself from under the trees and moved toward her. Mary stood still, her heart pounding. Then she saw that it was Herk.

"The master says he is waiting—come quickly."

Terror held her transfixed. What had happened?

"The donna must walk swiftly," Herk said to her. "Swiftly."

Mary followed Herk down the dark road, guided by the small lantern he carried. She walked blindly, stumbling over dark logs, her feet sinking in the mud and slime. They made their way across shell-broken battleground, her mind numb to impressions. She stumbled and her outspread hands touched a log. But it was not a log. It was the body of a dead soldier, lying sprawled on the ground—his stiff upturned face a blur of luminous white in the heavy darkness. She caught her breath sharply, stifling a scream. Where was Herk leading her? Where was Adam? Where was David? She thought of him with rising fear. What had happened? The boy must have lived an eternity this day. She was afraid to think—afraid to face reality. But nothing was real. The charging horses, foam-flecked mouths stained with blood, trampling over prostrate bodies of men—even that was not real. It was some horrible, grotesque nightmare. Cornwallis, the victor, tragic in his victory, was not real. . . .

They had come to a stream. Without words, Herk picked her up. Wading to his knees in the rushing water, he carried her to the opposite side. She heard groans all about her. How could she live when men were dying on the deserted battlefield?

They came at last to Adam. He lay in a clump of trees at the edge of a plowed field. David was with him, holding his head in his lap. The boy's face was white, frightened. Mary sank on her knees beside them.

"I knew you would come, Mary," Adam whispered, recognizing her.

"Adam!" she said. "Adam!" All her terror, her fear, her love, was in his name. "We must get you to the dressing station—surgeons are there—"

"No use, Mary, I think this is the end. I want to ask you to take David. It will be hard for him—" His voice weakened. Mary tightened her clasp on his hand.

"Adam, you must not give up. I will not let you go! Do you hear me, Adam?" She took the lantern from Herk's hand and put it on the ground so that it illumined Adam's face. She wiped the thin stream of blood from his earth-caked mouth.

"No use, Mary. It is no use. The earth belongs to me now."

What was he saying? In her terror she cried out to him.

"Adam, do not leave me alone. . . ."

He did not answer. She put her ear to his chest. His heart beat faintly. Suddenly her head cleared, her faculties came alive. She tore open his coat, groping in the dark with her fingers. His blood flowed heavily over her hands.

"Quick, Herk, the lantern," she said. "We must stop the bleeding."

Herk caught up the lantern. David eased the body of the unconscious man. Lint, lint from the pocket of her habit,

544

where she had put it earlier to be handy for the doctor's use. Bandages she had not used. She unwound the silk scarf from her throat. Stuffing the wound in his chest with lint, she bound the scarf around his body to hold the dressing in place, as she had watched the doctors do a hundred times that day.

"We must get him to the dressing station at once," she said to Herk. "Do you think you can carry him?"

"Yes, Donna. I will carry the master," Herk said confidently.

"Lift him gently so the bleeding won't start again. David, you take his feet. Easy—easy." She caught up the lantern in one hand. Her fingers closed on Adam's wrist. The slow beating of his pulse gave her courage.

He spoke only once on the long journey across the terrible battlefield. "Mary," he said weakly. She leaned down to hear what he was saying. "Dear Mary." She put her lips to his damp forehead. Tears fell down her cheeks onto his face.

"My dear, my very dear," she whispered.

She found Armitage working in the dressing tent beside the British doctors and beckoned to him. He stepped outside. "Come quickly," she whispered. "Adam is desperately wounded. You must come to him at once."

Armitage asked no questions. He went swiftly to the tent. In a moment he was back, stuffing instruments and dressings into a bag as he ran.

"I think the bullet is near the heart," she said, as they hurried along the path that led to the camp where she had been in the early morning.

Armitage said nothing. He followed her in silence through the woods. At last they came to the campfire where Adam rested.

"A mercy he is unconscious," Armitage said to himself, as he knelt. "I must probe, Mary. You'll have to help me."

"I can't, I can't," she said wildly. She could not bear the ordeal of feeling Adam's blood flow over her hands again. She was trembling from head to foot, as in a heavy chill. The Doctor's bony fingers buried themselves in her shoulders.

"Behave yourself, woman," he said sharply. "Hot water," he called to Herk, who was at the fire. The Zulu lifted one of the kettles that Grieves had filled and set it deep into the fire. Mary helped ease Adam's inert body. "Keep the fire going, David. I must have light," the Doctor said, as he cut away Adam's torn, blood-drenched coat. His skillful fingers moved swiftly and surely. "Delicate, delicate, so near the heart—"

he was saying as he probed. "So close—I don't know." He took out the packing Mary had put in. A fresh spurt of blood drenched his fingers. "Quick, the lint!"

Mary handed him lint and lancet—lint and bandages. Armitage worked for a long time, Mary kneeling beside him.

"Hold his pulse, Mary. He may go out. We must watch. Herk, the brandy bottle in my case. Force his lips. Some of it will go down his throat. His pulse, Mary, have a care—"

It seemed to Mary that time stood still. She was not alive. She stood apart, watching the long procession of their lives spread out before her. All the long past—then sharply she came to the present. How could they get Adam away? Could he be moved? She knew if the British found him, it would be the end. He would be made a prisoner and shot. Tarleton would make short work of him. "No quarter and no prisoners."

Almost in answer to her thoughts, Armitage said, "We must think of a way to get him through the lines."

"Can't we hide him here?" She knew they couldn't do that even when she spoke. There was too much danger. Armitage didn't even answer.

"If we could get him out the northern road, there are loyal friends who would hide him by day and we could travel by night to Edenton."

"I have Lord Cornwallis' carriage waiting for me near the hospital tent, and a pass for myself and David," she said.

Armitage straightened himself and held his hand for a moment across the small of his aching back. "I've done all I can." He turned to Mary. "What was it you said? Cornwallis' coach? A pass for yourself and David? By Gad, Mary, that may be the solution. How does the pass read? Let me see it."

She took the paper from the bosom of her habit. A thin smile came over the Doctor's tired face as he read.

"It is Providence," he said, his voice dropping to a whisper. "The pass is for Mrs. William Warden and Rutledge—no name, just Rutledge. Free pass through all British lines, by order of Cornwallis, commanding. The Gods are with us, Mary!"

"I don't see what you mean, Doctor?"

"Where are your wits? This pass does not name David Rutledge, just Rutledge. But we must be quick. I've given him an opiate. He will sleep for hours. When he wakes, if he is in much pain, you can give him this." He handed her a small packet. "One every four hours. Pray God that you get him through alive."

"But David? What about David?"

"He can go with me. I'll follow as close as I can. I cannot tell whether they will let me through or not. Herk will help, but the burden of Adam's life rests on you." He clasped her hand firmly and started away, David with him. After a few moments, he came back and thrust a bottle into her hand. "Feed him a little of this brandy every now and then. It may help."

Armitage's words rang in Mary's ears all through the long night. Cornwallis' coach was roomy. Herk had arranged the leather seat cushions so that they made a bed and put the riding lamp inside in order that Mary might watch Adam's face to see that all went well. In the flickering light Adam looked ghastly, as if he were already dead. Time after time, she leaned forward, her face pressed close to his body to catch the slow heart beat. Time after time, she changed the blood-soaked bandages, packed the wound with fresh lint, forced brandy through his set jaws.

But her anxiety had passed the peak when the Doctor had taken out the bullet. Now she was numb to all feeling. Emotion could go so far and no further. After a time, one ceased to feel, to have the power to suffer. She was bereft of all emotion but her mind functioned clearly, tempered to pure steel. "He must live, he must live," an inner voice repeated endlessly. She was no longer Mary Warden, fighting for the life of the man she loved. She was disembodied, separate, but determined. "The will to live"—she must give him the will to live.

Chapter 38

FLAME OF THE SWORD

IT WAS many months before Mary got over the effect of the fear and anxiety of the long journey from Guilford to Edenton. Three times they were stopped by Cornwallis' sentries but the pass carried them through—the pass and Herk's knowledge of little known roads.

Hours on end she sat, her fingers on Adam's pulse, praying for strength. Once she thought life had gone. She cried for Herk. He stopped the coach and ran to her aid. Together, they worked over Adam, rewinding bandages, getting warmth into him by forcing hot brandy through his clenched teeth. He opened his eyes then and called her name before he drifted off into unconsciousness.

The day before they got to Edenton, Dr. Armitage and David overtook them. Tears streamed down her cheeks when the Doctor climbed into the coach and took over.

"He's doing well enough," the Doctor mumbled, his fingers busy with the bandages. "It's all right, Mary. Settle back in the corner and get some sleep. You need it."

But he kept waking her when she dozed to tell her of things that had happened at Guilford. Cornwallis had come near being captured as he rested alone under a tree, his horse grazing near by. But the American officers had been too surprised to take advantage. Cornwallis jumped on his horse and galloped to safety. Greene was marching south, his army intact. There had been many men killed and wounded, but the morale of the troops was excellent. The Back Country men were teaching them to fight. Cornwallis' army had been cut to pieces, was retreating toward the coast, hoping for reinforcement and supplies from Sir Henry Clinton.

Mary listened. The dry, thin voice was far off—as far off as war and bloodshed. Presently she slept, her head against the side of the coach. The Doctor glanced at her from time to time, noticing the heavy black lashes sweeping her colorless cheeks. He shook his head as he pulled a rug over her knees. War takes its greatest toll, not in broken and maimed bodies of men, but in the spirit and souls of women. His gaze rested on Adam—on the long angry scar across his cheek. What stood between them now, he wondered. Surely with Sara dead and William . . . His thoughts were interrupted. Adam was turning painfully, muttering unintelligible words. The Doctor rolled a cloak into a ball to ease Adam's shoulder. He would be thankful when they reached North Plantation. There he could get Adam into a decent bed and see that gangrene did not set in.

Mary slept on when the coach stopped and the Negroes, supervised by the Doctor and Owen, lifted Adam and carried him into the room Gwennie had prepared for him. She opened her eyes only when she drove up the avenue at Queen's Gift.

Her slaves were waiting for her, their solemn, anxious faces turned toward the coach coming rapidly up the drive. Cissie ran down the broad steps, followed by Ebon. Tears were streaming down Cissie's broad black face. She lifted Mary from the coach and carried her into the house as she used to do when Mary was a little child.

They made a bedroom of William's old office. Bathed, in a fresh nightdress fragrant with the clear, clean odor of verbena, Mary lay in the linen sheets, her tired eyes resting on the soft green of the walls. She smiled at Cissie's anxious face, but she could not make the effort to speak. It was good to be home. She slipped gently into a long, untroubled sleep, dreaming an old dream of her childhood: that Queen's Gift opened welcoming arms to cradle her and keep her secure— safe from all harm.

At first the Tories reveled over their so-called victory, but not Cornwallis. As he had told Mary, he knew only too well that Guilford Courthouse was his undoing. His army was cut to pieces. He had lost too many men to complete his victory by pursuing Greene's retreating army. He could not stay where he was, for the country for miles around was swept clean of foodstuff to support either his men or his horses. He had to have supplies, so he turned his army back to Wilmington.

News from the South began to trickle into Edenton. Greene and his army had been victorious at last. He had defeated Lord Rawdon; he was besieging Ninety-Six. Everywhere spirits ran high. A new life had come to the people, bringing hope. The battle at Guilford Courthouse took on new importance. It had turned the tide for Greene. His was no longer a retreating army, but an attacking army.

Adam Rutledge made a slow recovery. He lay in bed at his North Plantation for weeks, with Gwennie Tewilliger and Lavinia to care for him. Dr. Armitage, visiting him daily, did not know what the outcome would be. The wound in his side mortified and fever followed. Delirium persisted day after day. He kept mumbling "in time for spring planting—in time for spring planting" over and over and once he spoke Mary's name quite clearly.

By early April Adam was able to sit in the garden. Mary rode over often. Owen and Lavinia and she would sit with him. Adam spoke seldom. He was very thin, the long scar an angry red on his white face. He seemed content to watch David jumping the young hunters, or Lavinia's youngest boy playing with some puppies.

"Adam has no will to get well," Dr. Armitage said to Mary as they rode home one evening at sunset. She turned quickly. The fear that had been in her for days brought panic now.

"Could it be Sara's death?" she asked, trying to keep her voice steady.

"Nonsense," the Doctor said. "You know it isn't that, nor the destruction of the Manor House. Something has happened to him, some shock that has gone very deep. I wish I knew." He looked at her with keen, shrewd eyes. "Don't you know what it is, Mary?"

Mary shook her head. "No, Doctor, I don't. But I haven't talked with him alone for months."

They rode in silence. The water was gold with the sunset and water birds flew low, uttering wild mournful cries. Biting loneliness swept over Mary. She had no hope now. She was unable to bring herself to contemplate what might be ahead of her if Adam—

"By God! I'm going to have him up on the back of a horse next week," the Doctor said suddenly. Mary made no answer. They rode without further words to the gates of Queen's Gift.

But it was several weeks before Adam rode again, and then it was not to hunt.

The day after her talk with the Doctor Mary went to Wilmington on plantation affairs. When she came home, Adam rode over to see her. The garden was fresh with spring blooming. They walked to the bench under the magnolia tree. It was very quiet; bees droned; the wind was soft and fragrant with honeysuckle.

Mary spoke of the news of the war she had heard in Wilmington; of Greene's victories in South Carolina; of Washington's army holding Clinton in New York; of the Virginia campaign with Lafayette in command.

"They are all hopeful down there," Mary said.

Adam nodded. "It is the same here," he said.

After a pause he spoke of Rutledge Riding for the first time since his return. "I do not regret anything, Mary," he said. "The Manor House belongs to another life, one that is gone forever, the easy, happy living that we shall never again know in the Carolinas."

She looked at him quickly. A sense of fear swept over her.

"Living will be hard now," he went on. "The long rebuilding, the reconstruction that comes after wars." He laughed a little. "Tubal Cain may beat his sword into a plowshare but cutting the long furrow will not be easy in this devastated land of ours." Then suddenly, he said, "I'm going away, Mary." Her eyes alone showed the pain she felt. He hurried on, as if he wanted to have the words out and done with. "It's not what you think, Mary. I'm not going to the Illinois country—not yet."

"But why are you going?" the words came in spite of her effort to suppress them. "You're not strong yet. Then the plantation—" She stopped. Words wouldn't help.

"Young Peyton will take over the plantation. It will be his land eventually—I have arranged that—his and Lavinia's." There was a dead look in his eyes. His words had a dread finality that left Mary trembling. He was going away. He wanted to break with the old life. Adam was done with the past, with the old living. She was part of that old living. She was helpless in the agony of realization.

He got to his feet slowly. She rose, also. He took her hands in his, looking at her. For a long time they stood without speaking. Then he said, "I'm going to Virginia. I shall take David to Annandale. After that—" He stopped. "Perhaps, I shall go north," he said after a moment. "They want me back in the Treasury. But I'm not sure. I may go west after a time. I seem to have lost my usefulness as a soldier." His voice was unsteady. "If I could only talk to you, to tell you, so that you would understand—" he broke off—"but I can't, not now, or ever, Mary. That is the tragedy."

Mary was too shaken to speak. In her effort to hold back the tears she averted her face, looking toward the house. James Iredell and Samuel Johnstone were coming toward them, deep in conversation. When Johnstone saw Adam was with Mary, he hastened across the intervening lawn.

"Well, this is splendid, Adam. I did not know you were

able to ride." He shook hands quietly, his face showing his pleasure in Adam's recovery.

"I was just about to leave," Adam said.

Mary had regained her composure. "Don't go yet," she pleaded. "Ebon will serve drinks in a moment."

Johnstone said, "Finding you here is very opportune, Rutledge. We've just come from a meeting of the Albemarle Secret Committee. I want to talk to you—"

Mary started to get up but Johnstone put out a detaining hand.

"Mary, don't go. You'll be interested in this. One of our men intercepted Cornwallis' courier. We have his dispatch bag."

"Anything important?" Adam asked.

"We think so. A letter to Sir Henry Clinton, written last week. It is dated the twenty-third of April, place not given, but I think it must be from Wilmington."

"Suppose you read it, Sam," Iredell suggested, cutting Johnstone's explanation short.

Johnstone took the letter from the pocket of his blue coat. "I'll read only the part that concerns us." He unfolded the letter, scanning the page. He began:

"—neither my cavalry nor infantry are in readiness to move. The former are in want of everything; the latter of every necessity but shoes. I must, however, begin my march tomorrow. The undertaking sits heavy on my mind. I have experienced the distress and dangers of marching hundreds of miles in a country chiefly hostile, without active friends or useful intelligence; and without communications with any part of the country . . . yet I'm under the necessity of adopting this hazardous enterprise hastily with the appearance of precipitation, as I find there is no hope now of speeding reinforcement from the north, or from Europe. The return of General Greene to North Carolina would put a juncture with General Phillips in Virginia out of my power."

Johnstone looked at Adam. He was staring across the garden toward the water.

"How does this affect us?" Mary asked, stirred by Johnstone's serious tone.

"If the British march through Albemarle, it will mean desolation after the army passes. Every plantation will be raided for horses and cattle; houses will be burned and towns pil-

laged as they were in South Carolina. Cornwallis will terrorize the people into submission. That's his only hope now."

Adam said nothing. He sat slumped in the garden chair,
his face unreadable. Mary glanced at him, wondering what
his thoughts were. Johnstone, also, was looking at him.

"Where is General Phillips' army, now?" Adam asked.

Johnstone shook his head. "I've had no intelligence from
Virginia the past week. He was somewhere around Williamsburg the last I heard. That bloody traitor Benedict Arnold is
in Virginia to strengthen Phillips' force. Pardon me, Mary; I
forget myself when I think of that man."

There was a painful silence. Everyone at once thought of
William Warden. Mary spoke to relieve the tension.

"Who will defend Albemarle if Cornwallis passes through
here on his way to Virginia?" she asked.

"General Gregory, I suppose," Iredell said. "I understand
the Edenton Horse is being sent back also."

"Have you sent this information about Cornwallis' letter
north?" Adam asked, looking at Johnstone.

"No, it just came through." He got up and moved about
nervously. "The trouble is," he continued, "that I haven't a
man that I would trust to take it through. General Washington must get it as soon as possible. Whoever goes must go by
way of Virginia, through the British lines." He looked at
Adam speculatively. "I wish to God that you were in better
shape, Rutledge."

There was a long silence. Mary looked from one to the
other. Adam's face was impassive. After a long time, he said,
"I had planned to go to Virginia. I intended to go to Annandale." He stopped suddenly.

Johnstone took one or two quick strides across the lawn,
then back, stopping in front of Adam.

"You are the only man I would trust with this letter," he
said. "You can see why it is of vital importance."

Adam did not answer. His eyes were fixed on the ground
in front of him. Iredell was watching him; so was Johnstone.
But neither of them pressed him too urgently to undertake
the task.

Iredell said, "If General Washington knew Cornwallis' condition, the weakness of his army, he could trap him in Virginia."

Adam nodded. "I was thinking the same thing."

Johnstone said abruptly, "You can't go unless Armitage
says you are fit."

Adam looked up, smiling a little. Mary thought, "He's more like himself than he has been since Guilford."

"There are always ways to get around Armitage," he said. "It was something else that I was thinking of—how to get across the James if Phillips and Arnold are that far down. But that's something to worry about when we come to it."

Iredell set down his empty glass and got to his feet. "We had better be going. I think we can catch Armitage at his office if we ride now."

Johnstone spoke to Adam in a low voice as they crossed the lawn to the house.

Mary did not listen to Iredell as he told her of the importance of the undertaking. Adam would ride away with them. There would be no chance to speak to him again. She could not force words of farewell to her lips when he kissed her hand. She did not trust her voice, afraid that he would know the agony of her heart.

After they had gone, she went to the drawing room and sat down on the yellow sofa. Outside in the garden, a mockingbird was singing a full-throated song. The voices of slaves, laughing and shouting, came from the lower garden. She sat for a moment with her hands clasped tightly in her lap. Suddenly, she gave way; dry, hard sobs shook her body. She did not know how long she lay, leaning against the cushions.

She sat up suddenly, surprised to hear swift footsteps. Someone was walking across the gallery. In a moment Adam entered, closing the door behind him. He strode across the room to her side.

"Mary," he said, taking her hands, "Mary!"

"I thought you had gone. I thought I would never see—" she whispered.

He lifted her chin. "I had to come back," he said, hurrying over the words. "I couldn't go without—" He waited a moment to steady his voice. "Oh, Mary, if I could only tell you —so that you would understand—" He repeated the words he had spoken earlier.

She tried to speak calmly, but her voice trembled. "There is nothing in the world that you cannot tell me, Adam," she said, clinging to his hands. "Don't go away again without telling me. Whatever it is I'll understand."

The dark wall that separated them was still there. She felt it. She saw it in his eyes before he turned away. She wanted to cry out, to beat weak, futile hands against its strength, but she could only look at him without words.

"I can't tell you," he said, his voice low.

554

There was a terrible finality in what he said—in the way he walked across the room and stood looking out the window. He turned to her again.

"If I could talk to anyone in the world it would be to you, Mary. But this is something that must die with me. I don't want you to think—" He broke off.

Mary continued to gaze at him. She no longer tried to keep her composure. A sense of futility took possession of her.

"It doesn't matter," she said tonelessly. "It doesn't matter what—"

He caught her hands in his, forcing her to look at him. "It does matter, Mary. I have hurt you. That distresses me more deeply than I can say."

"Oh, no," she said, "no, I'm not hurt."

"I can see it in your eyes. I have hurt you in your heart—you, Mary." He stood looking down at her, his eyes deep, unfathomable.

The room was silent. The low sun sent broken shafts of light through the mullioned windows onto the dark polished floor. Only one thought persisted in her mind. If he must go, let it be now—now in the quietness of the Ave Maria hour—now while she still had strength to endure. . . .

He put his hands on her shoulders and drew her to him.

"This is good-by, Mary," he said, his voice unsteady. He leaned down and kissed her parted lips with hard, devastating insistence. She clung to him in the passion of renunciation.

She watched him go away with tearless eyes. He rode swiftly into the shadows of the magnolia trees, never looking back. She turned slowly from the window and sank back on the yellow sofa.

By September a subtle change had taken place among the people in Albemarle district. Cornwallis' army had marched north by another route, leaving them free from war by land. But the threat by sea continued. The British fleet, based in the Indies, made frequent raids along the Carolina coast, capturing merchantmen, trading with the French and Danish West Indies. Privateers were untied in inlets and sounds, scuttling small fishing craft. Private ships hovered off the coast islands, flying first one flag, then another, like evil birds of prey, waiting to swoop on carrion. Hewes and Smith lost two vessels to privateers or pirates, they knew not which. Adam's shallop *Golden Orchid II* was long overdue.

A French fleet under Count d'Estaing proved no help at

all. Only the great victories on the sea of Joseph Hewes's protégé, Captain John Paul Jones, kept hope alive in the hearts of the coast people.

Soldiers began to go through the village, marching north. No one knew their destination. There were new regiments, as well as old regiments, with young, untrained boys replacing veterans who had been killed or wounded in the long southern campaign under Greene.

As they marched past North Plantation, Gwennie and Marcy's Lucy, with the young children, stood at the roadside, Gwennie giving out food, pastries, little cakes and gourds of rich milk while Lucy distributed packets that contained socks and long scarves she had been knitting through the years. So Mary found them one day when she rode over from Queen's Gift late in the afternoon. It was near the equinox, and the sky had been overcast for several days. Her groom left the jellies and preserves she had brought for Gwennie's canteen while she rode up to the house to see Lavinia.

She found her in the garden with her child and Meredith Chapman. He had returned recently from the Illinois country, full of tales of Cahokia and the great Mississippi Valley.

"A hundred families are going out from Hillsborough when this fighting is over," he told them. "They have already selected their land—not far from Adam Rutledge's and my own acreage on the Mississippi. They will call the new village Hillsborough, after their old home."

Mary felt her heart sink as she listened to Meredith and saw the light of enthusiasm in his clear grey eyes and his strong, homely face. His tall frame was sinewy and muscular. Already he had the look of the frontiersman in his eyes—fine-lined at the corners from looking long distances. He spoke of Adam and of his land along the banks of the Mississippi.

"Owen will go out after the war is over," he said confidently. "The new settlements must have schools, and who is better able to supply that need than Owen?" he laughed and turned to Owen, who had just come out from the house.

"I have already planned to go out with the Hillsborough caravan," Owen responded.

"David will go out with Marcy and Lucy when they go in the spring. Marcy will be through with his army service by then," Meredith added.

Mary looked from one to the other. She felt bewildered, dazed by the words they were speaking and the implication behind what they said. They were all looking forward to a new country, a new life. Who would stay behind and rebuild the old? Her thoughts were bitter as she galloped down the post road toward Queen's Gift. The sky was blood red, with great dark clouds gathering in the east. Fishing boats were scudding before the wind to safe anchorage at the mouth of Queen Anne's Creek. In the village, storm-shutters were being closed as she passed through.

By hard galloping she reached home before the storm. As she dismounted from her horse and gave the reins to the groom, the first great drops of rain fell.

Cissie was waiting for her. Through the open door Mary saw the logs burning in the yellow drawing room. She stood for a moment looking around her. The old house seemed to open its arms to welcome her. Cissie, arms akimbo, stood looking at her, a disapproving frown between her eyes.

"Look lak you always run home jes' befo' a storm ketch you," she said sternly. "Now you go upstair and get you'self you' bath and a nice fresh dress on. Look lak that riding habit be gluded to you' body these days. I lay out a dress to mak you look lak a lady for once." Mary laughed. Cissie continued, "You kin laugh, but tha's the word with the bark on it. It's time you mak you'self look lak a lady. Cook's goin' to fix a nice little duck for you' supper," she added, as Mary went up the stairs to her room.

Cissie had laid out a yellow brocade gown. Lace flounces finished the square neck and elbowed sleeves. A tin tub with warm water had been placed before the hearth where logs crackled. Two copper jugs, with hot water, were inside the chimney where they would keep hot.

Mary dressed slowly after her bath. When she had finished she looked at herself in the mirror. Cissie was right. It had been a long time since she had worn anything but a riding habit—a long time.

As she came downstairs, she saw that Ebon had laid a small table in front of the drawing-room fire. White linen, silver and crystal shone in the firelight. Ebon was lighting the candles in the great crystal chandeliers. Standing on a stool at the far end of the room, Cissie was lighting the candles in the wall sconces with a long taper.

Mary watched them, her throat tightening. How kind they were, how thoughtful of her comfort, of her welfare—trying to push aside the loneliness that engulfed her. She noticed then that the table was set for two. Cissie enlightened her.

"The Doctor he send he boy to say he would do heself the honor of havin' supper with Miss Mary."

Mary said, "This is very nice, Ebon. I'm sure the Doctor will be delighted to have supper here in front of the fire. Did you remember that the Doctor likes madeira instead of port afterward?"

Ebon's broad smile gave his answer. He indicated the decanters on the Chippendale table.

"Yes, Miss Mary, I remember. Cook she say she aim to fix a twelve-minute mallard, jes' like the Doctor wants hit."

Mary walked the length of the room to the French windows that led to the garden. She stopped suddenly, her hand on the rain-splashed window. A dull boom seemed to rock the room. Thunder? Or was it thunder?

"What's that?" Cissie called to Ebon, the whites of her eyes showing.

"Sounds lak somfin' beside thunder," he answered. "Sounds lak a big gun booming."

"It must be thunder," Mary said. But the second vibration was not thunder.

"Lawsee, lawsee, we's bombarded again," Cissie cried. She caught Mary's arm. "Come, we's going to the apple cellar right now."

Mary wrenched her arm free. "Don't be silly. Ebon, tell one of the grooms to ride to Edenton and find out what is happening."

Ebon left the room hurriedly. Cissie stood near the fire, her hands up to her ears. A third boom broke the silence, followed by three or four lighter explosions. Mary pressed her face to the window. The rain was heavy now. She could see nothing but blackness and thin cutting streams of white when the rain hit the ground and splashed high from the impact. She listened for a while but there was no other sound. Whatever it was, was far away to the east, down the Sound.

The Doctor came during a lull in the storm. Ebon helped him off with his wet coat and hat, and gave orders for his coachman to have supper in the kitchen.

"Did you hear the guns?" Armitage asked Mary, as he stood before the fire warming his thin shanks.

"They were guns then?" Mary asked.

"Yes, some kind of a battle offshore. They've sent men from the village down the Sound road to see if they can find out what it is." He paused. His thin, tired face was serious.

"What do you think?" she asked, a sudden fear assailing her.

"I don't know. It could be a number of things: a battle between one of the British ships-of-the-line and our defense fleet; privateers raiding; pirates—well anything."

"It couldn't be a land battle?" she asked.

The Doctor shook his head. "No, I don't think—" He stopped, the sentence incomplete. A heavy reverberation seemed to rock the room, followed quickly by lighter shocks. "It's a battle between a ship with heavy guns and one with lighter ordnance." He glanced at the table, then at Mary. "Well, we can't do anything about it, Mary," he said, philosophically. "If we're going to be raided by privateers again, I can't help it. Do you mind if we eat? I must confess, I'm hungry."

They had finished supper and Ebon was pouring the second glass of madeira when another bombardment started. This time it was closer. The vibration rattled dishes and a small pane of window-glass clattered to the floor. The Negroes, howling and screaming, ran from the kitchen to the drawing room. Mary raised her voice, trying to quiet them.

"Go back to your work," she cried. "There is no danger." Her words were cut short. A great burst of light illuminated the room, followed by the roar of guns and the sound of shattered glass. "Go to the cellar," she screamed above the roar.

The slaves fled, not waiting for a second order. Cissie and Ebon remained. Ebon went about the task of clearing the table. Cissie, ashen and shaking, refused to leave as long as Mary remained upstairs. Dr. Armitage went out onto the terrace. Mary joined him. Down the Sound they could now see flashes of light, preceding by several seconds the heavy roar of cannon.

"A sharp battle," he cried, his voice raised. "A sharp battle, between a big ship and a smaller one. I wonder what it means."

Toward midnight, the groom Mary had sent to the village returned. He had no definite news, but he was frightened. "Two ships are coming up the Sound," he told them, his eyes wide with alarm. "A big one is chasing a smaller craft." No one would know before morning what was happening. All Edenton was alarmed. People were packing up, preparing to leave the village again. Guns had been mounted and sandbags put up as a barricade along the wharf and in front of the Commons. The soldiers were in readiness at the barriers; some companies were patrolling the roads along the shore.

"They say better you hide away you' fine silver and you' jewels, Miss Mary," the frightened slave told her.

Dr. Armitage nodded. "That's good advice, Mary. Have you a good place to put your plate?"

"The strongroom, behind the books in William's library," she said. "Ebon, you and Cissie gather up the plate. Quickly now! I'd hate to lose Duke Roger's treasures to the British."

The Doctor followed her into William's library. It had been closed since his death. Mary shut the door and drew the curtains to shut out prying eyes before she opened the door concealed by the bookshelves. The strongroom was between the drawing room and the library, the extra space concealed by the chimney of the two rooms. Mary and the Doctor took the Queen Anne silver that Cissie and Ebon brought and put it on the wide shelves of the room. The Doctor examined the room by the light of a candle.

"It has ventilation and room enough to conceal two or three men," he said, surprised by what he found.

Mary smiled. "My grandfather hid some of the Culpepper rebels in there," she said, as she closed the door and slid the books back into place. "You know he was one of the leaders of that rebellion.

The Doctor nodded. "Yes, I knew, but I never heard of this hiding place before. Almost every old house around here has a secret room, but we know all about them, or have seen them. Strange—"

"My father showed it to me when I was a little girl—before I went to England," she said. "Once I locked myself in and had a horrible hour or two inside the dark room. After my father released me, I never wanted to go in again!"

"Who knows about it?" the Doctor inquired.

"Ebon and Cissie. No one else. Even they do not know the trick of opening the door. But I'm going to show you and Cissie now." She went to the door and beckoned to the slave. Cissie, wide-eyed, watched Mary manipulate the panel.

When they returned to the drawing room, nothing was said of going to bed. By common consent, Mary and the Doctor sat down by the fire to wait. The rain had stopped. At times the moon came out, only to be hidden in a few moments by heavy clouds.

Mary found herself clutching the arms of her chair, bending forward to listen—waiting for something, she knew not what. Not the boom of cannon, for they were sounding at frequent intervals now, but something more menacing. . . .

Chapter 39

STORMY PETREL

THE LITTLE French clock on the mantel struck three. Mary glanced at the Doctor. He had fallen asleep, his head against the back of the fireside chair. She got up quietly, put the afghan over his knees and went to the window. The rain had stopped, but the heavy wind bent the trees in the garden. She tried to see through the blackness to the Sound, but it was no use.

Noticing that the candles were almost burned out, she replaced them and, for no reason, carried the candelabrum to a small table near the long window which opened on the terrace. The feeble light fell on the steppingstones that led across the lawn to the boat-landing but the garden itself was lost in heavy darkness.

The restlessness that had weighed on her all evening kept her moving about. In the hall she found Cissie asleep on the couch under the turn of the stairs. Ebon had drawn a chair in front of the library door. He too slept, his grey head dropped forward on his chest, a useless old musket across the arms of the chair.

She opened the great door and stood for a moment looking into the gloom of the magnolia-bordered avenue. There was no sound but that of the wind beating against the trees of the swamp—a warning voice, deeper and more insistent than the muffled boom of cannon earlier in the night. Unable to stand the inaction, Mary caught up a dark shawl from the rack and went out.

As she crossed the terrace to the avenue, a bird uttered a low, mournful cry. A shiver passed over her. Was it really a bittern—or a signal from some marauder hiding in the swamp?

She was near the low iron fence that enclosed the burial place of all the Mainwarings who had died in the Carolinas. Flat slabs of marble, faintly luminous in the dark earth, marked their resting places. She could distinguish the graves of her father and mother and the long layer of flat stone that

561

bore the name of Duke Roger, although his restless body lay deep in the waters of Mono Passage.

How long she stood looking into the darkness she did not know. Suddenly she heard a twig snap followed by a faint rustling sound in the direction of the wooded point. She pressed her body against the wet trunk of a great magnolia tree. It might be an animal prowling in search of prey or—her mind went quickly to the rumors which had kept the village alarmed for the past month. Words from Lavinia's letter of the day before stood out clearly: "Mrs. Dawson has had an express from the North. Two ships have come in from Cadiz with clothing for our army. The French fleet has blocked the harbors of Tobago and St. Lucie in the West Indies but the danger lies nearer home. Cornwallis is in Suffolk, other officers and troops are on Roanoke and Mr. Smith's schooner was lost at the Bar . . . it is enough to alarm all Albemarle. But the most terrible rumor is that Cornwallis has released two thousand Negroes to terrorize the country, to plunder and pillage under the guise of obtaining supplies. They are supposed to be hiding in the Dismal. This last I don't believe. . . . Cornwallis would never put women and children in jeopardy."

These ominous words raced through her mind. Then, her eyes accustomed to the darkness, she saw a shadow detach itself from the heavy blackness of the dense forest and move stealthily across the lawn toward the window where she had put the candelabrum. It moved between her and the light for an instant, then vanished into the deeper shadows of the gallery.

Mary did not wait. She had no thought except for the defenseless people in the house, the Doctor sleeping in his chair, her faithful servants. Shs ran swiftly through the gloom of the avenue to the side entrance. Crossing the gallery silently, she came to the open front door. In the hall stood a man covered by a long coat, a black tricorne pulled down over his head. His back was toward the door but she saw the gleam of the pistol in his hand.

She spoke almost before she thought. "What are you doing here?" she demanded. When he saw her he lowered his pistol. In the dim light Mary saw that one arm was held by a rude sling made from a bright India scarf. He thrust his pistol into his belt and swept his hat from his head. Heavy masses of dark red hair tumbled down. Mary stepped back, her hands pressed against the door.

"Lady Caroline," she whispered. "Lady Caroline!"

Lady Caroline closed the door swiftly. Mary saw her face was livid.

"You must hide me," she said, grasping Mary's shoulder. "Quick! They are at my heels, damn them for fiends!"

"Who?" Mary asked, but Lady Caroline did not allow her to go on.

"The pirates. Didn't you hear the guns when they attacked Smith's ship? Quick, there is no time for explanation. You must hide me. The attic?" She glanced up the stairs.

"No, not there," Mary said, her mind working swiftly. "That would be the first place they would look." Her eyes fell on Ebon. He was sitting up in his chair, his gnarled black hands clutching the musket, the whites of his eyes shining, his body shaking with fright.

"Not a word, Ebon! Go to the pantry and get some wine; bring anything you can find to eat." Suddenly Mary thought of the strongroom. She caught up the candle from the hall table. "Come," she said to Lady Caroline. "This way."

Lady Caroline staggered a little and Mary put out her hand to steady her. They stood for a moment, listening. Men were shouting. Mary reached up and touched the spring behind the bookshelves. The panel slid back.

"In here," she said briefly. "I'm sorry you can't have a light. You must be quiet. I don't know whether a sound would reach the library or the drawing room on the other side of the chimney."

There was a loud knock at the front door. Lady Caroline went into the room and sank down on the one chair, her head against the stone wall. Mary slid the shelves into place and ran into the hall, closing the book-room door. Ebon was coming out of the dining room with a tray in his hand. "It will never do to have her pursuers see the food," she thought, and motioned him to go to the drawing room. Her hand on the door, she glanced over her shoulder and saw Ebon pouring a glass of wine for Dr. Armitage. The Doctor was rubbing his eyes, mild astonishment on his face.

Mary opened the door at the second insistent knock. A half-dozen roughly-dressed men stood on the gallery, dark-faced men, with heads bound in colored handkerchiefs. Daggers and pistols bristled from their belts of studded leather. A young man, less villainous-looking than the others, stepped forward. He was fair-skinned, a mop of blond hair falling over his forehead. He held a long pistol in his hand; two others were thrust through his wound belt of striped silk. He hesitated a moment when he saw Mary.

"We're looking for Sarah Wilson, madam," he said. "Have you seen aught of a woman dressed in man's clothes?"

Mary hoped she showed the surprise she felt at his inquiry. "No, I've seen no woman by the name of Sarah Wilson."

The men looked at one another, then began talking and gesticulating. The language they spoke was unknown to her.

"She must have come this way," the leader insisted. "She escaped from the ship before midnight."

"The ship?" Mary asked.

The man looked at her sharply a cold light in his small eyes. "Didn't you hear the cannon?" he asked.

"Certainly we heard cannon. Do you think we are deaf?" Dr. Armitage had come into the hall and was standing behind Mary.

"Did you see Sarah Wilson?" the sailor demanded.

The Doctor turned to Mary. "What are they talking about?" he asked her, his face showing his astonishment.

Mary shrugged her shoulders. "This man says they are searching for a woman named Sarah Wilson who escaped from their ship. One of the ships responsible for the cannonading we heard last night."

The man pushed his way farther into the hall, his sailors following. "We got one of Smith's brigs and sank another. That woman made the master believe she knew the channel in the dark. She ran us aground below the Neck, and him making trips up the Sound a dozen times with his slavers." He glanced knowingly at the Doctor. "He'd never have had no suspicion at all if she hadn't put off from the ship in the night with a couple of her Jamaica slaves. Then he went wild." The sailor laughed. "He's threatenin' to hang her to the yardarm when he gets her."

Mary gave the Doctor a quick, frightened look. His eyes flashed a warning.

"Now we'll search the house, lady," the seaman said harshly, suddenly mindful of his duties.

Mary made no demur. Instead she said, "Ebon will lead your men over the house. Won't you have a glass of wine before you follow?"

At the Doctor's indignant glance she shook her head imperceptibly. The seaman looked from one to the other. Satisfied, he followed Mary into the drawing room, hat in hand. Ebon took it from him and, holding it as if it were poisonous, carried it into the hall.

"Mind ye don't touch anything, ye scum," the leader shouted as his followers started up the stairs. "If ye do, ye'll

564

get three hundred on the bare of y'r backs." He turned to Mary apologetically. "Ye can't be too easy with Lascars and Madagascari, mistress. The captain would have given me a decent landing party, but he's got all hands working to get the ship off the spit." He sat down and helped himself to the dish of cold meats Ebon had brought for Lady Caroline.

Cissie came into the room, her eyes shining with indignation. "That Ebon, he lead that riffraff right up de stairs to our best bedrooms," she said to Mary. "That fella got no sense."

The sailor looked up from the cold duck he was cramming into his mouth. "Don't worry, black woman, they don't touch nothin'. I give them orders."

Cissie looked over his head. "I scratch they eyes if they tech one little thing," she said angrily. "Howfor they come hyer lookin' for woman dress' in man's britches? We got no such on dis plantation. Tell 'em take theyselve away from hyer."

"I've given them permission to search the house," Mary said. "Perhaps you had better tell Ebon not to forget the attic and the buttery and those little rooms in the stable."

Cissie did not answer. She left the room muttering to herself, her great body expressing her indignation.

The seaman watched her go, a thin smile on his lips. "She's a rum one! Most of them is afeered of my Lascars. People take to their heels when we sack a town."

He wiped his mouth with a napkin to show his manners and addressed himself to the Doctor, who continued to stand near the fire, a grim, stony look on his face.

"Yes, she fooled the captain, with that high way of hers. She claimed to know where two shiploads of cargo were buried up Chowan River."

The Doctor pushed the decanter of madeira across the table. "He wants to make him talk," thought Mary.

Ignoring the wineglass, the seaman poured his wine into a tumbler. He smacked his lips as the wine warmed his gullet. "We had bad luck ever since we left St. Thomas. First we ran into six ships-of-the-line off Windward Passage, and then a privateer lurking behind Roanoke watchin' the Inlet. We didn't aim to overhaul any sail this trip but when we saw three brigs without convoy the captain gives chase. The woman fooled him there, too. She said they belonged to Smith and Hewes, and they'd have no cannon. 'We'll take them between Harvey's Neck and Queen Anne's Creek,' she told him."

He swallowed another mouthful of meat. "God's death, the

brigs carried three-pounders. But we let them have a broadside. The *Golden Orchid* got it full. She sank right up to the cross-arm."

Mary glanced quickly at the Doctor. His eyes flickered a warning. Adam's shallop and one of Smith's!

The man got to his feet and went to the hall door. "Seems like they be gone a long spell," he said, his small eyes looking from the Doctor to Mary suspiciously.

"It's a large house," the Doctor remarked noncommittally.

There was a long silence. Mary thought the clock was ticking more loudly than usual. She heard a faint sound like the scraping of a chair but by an effort of will did not turn her head. She wondered whether Lady Caroline could hear the loud voice of the sailor.

In her mind she was recalling long-forgotten things: Lady Caroline at Pembroke; strange ships that put into Edenton; the sack of unset jewels; Lady Caroline at Wilmington; at New Bern; her trips to the Indies; her jewels; the Baron's interest in the fact that she always lived in a house by the shore. Was this the missing key to the mystery that surrounded Lady Caroline Mathilde? Suddenly, she thought of Peyton Rutledge. Had he been mixed up in sea-raiding, so common during those years before the war? The raiding was as prevalent now, only the pirate ships were called privateers. Under that name many a lawless vessel roamed the seas. She was aware that the sailor was looking at her. Suspicion burned deep in his shrewd little eyes.

"You say you never heard of Sarah Wilson round these parts, mistress?"

"Never," she answered truthfully, "never."

There were footsteps and the shuffling of bare feet on the hall floor. Ebon stood at the doorway, the Lascar crew behind him. One of the men spoke to the leader. After a few questions, he turned to Mary. "My man says they don't see anything suspicious, or find no woman. We'd best go back to the ship now and wait for light. The captain'll have to be satisfied. Thank you, mistress, and you also." He made an awkward bow first to Mary, then to the Doctor. "If you should set eyes on the woman, send the black man down shore until he sights our ship, the *Oriflamme.*"

"The *Oriflamme!*" the words burst from the Doctor's lips.

"Yes, the *Oriflamme*, LaTruchy, captain. Know her?"

"There was a slaver by that name, but that was a long time ago," the Doctor said cautiously.

"The first mate's name is Nicholas. He's a greasy Levantine." There was distaste in the man's voice. "I'm Crane, the third. I'm a Kentish man myself. Thank you, ma'am. I'll be taking these swine out of your sight."

At the drawing-room door, he paused, raising his voice. "If you should see Miss Sarah Wilson, ye can say that Allan Crane was pleased that she got away from that stinking ship." He walked quickly down the hall and out of the door, driving his men ahead of him with kicks and sharp words.

Mary glanced at the Doctor. "He suspects something," she whispered.

"Good God, you haven't hidden the woman, have you?" Mary nodded. The Doctor groaned. Before Mary could explain Cissie came into the room. She was carrying a pan of coals from which was rising the mingled odor of burning coffee and sassafras. She marched through the hall and the drawing room and into the library, waving the pan in front of her. Mary looked at the Doctor and laughed.

"I don't know whether it is an exorcising rite or a cleansing one," he said. Then his face sobered. "Who is Sarah Wilson?" he asked suddenly.

"Lady Caroline Mathilde," Mary told him. "She is in the strongroom. Perhaps you had better see her. I think her arm is broken."

"God's life, Mary!" Armitage followed her into the library. "When did she come?"

"While you were asleep. I got her into the room just in time."

They found Lady Caroline leaning back in the chair when they opened the door. Her face was drawn, her lips bloodless. Armitage got her onto a couch and gave rapid orders for water, brandy and bandages while his firm skillful fingers moved carefully over her shoulder and collarbone. Mary sent Ebon for hot water. She was obliged then to bring Cissie into the room to help. Even as they worked on the suffering woman, Mary's thoughts centered on one thing. This woman had fooled and tricked them all; over and over she had taken advantage of the generosity of people.

"I deserve nothing from either of you," Lady Caroline said almost in answer to Mary's thoughts. "Nothing." She set her jaw to keep from crying out as Armitage gave the quick wrench that threw her arm into place.

"That's all," the Doctor said, straightening up. He turned to Mary. "Go to your room and get to bed. Cissie and I will take care of this. Tell Ebon to double-bar the doors and keep the other servants away. Go on, get some sleep."

"You know the worst of me now," Lady Caroline said suddenly. "I heard all Crane had to say. My name is Sarah Wilson. I was a lady-in-waiting to the Queen—I stole her jewels, but I swear to God I did not know what I was doing. I was a dupe, a silly dupe in the hands of an unscrupulous man whom I trusted. You would not care to hear the whole sordid story." She paused, exhausted by the effort of talking.

"Go to bed, Mary," the Doctor said crossly. "I won't have this woman talking any more. I don't care what she is or what she has been. At the moment she is my patient."

Mary walked toward the door. Sarah Wilson opened her eyes. "One thing more. I did not bring the *Oriflamme* here. That was LaTruchy's own idea. I thought we were sailing for Pamlico Sound, not Albemarle." Her voice dwindled off. Armitage went quickly to her side and thrust the ammonia under her nose.

"Go away, Mary, go away. Can't you see the woman's sick with pain?"

Mary went upstairs to her room and undressed but she could not sleep. For a long time she sat at her window looking out into the blackness. Somewhere hidden in the darkness men on ships were waiting for the dawn.

When she walked into the breakfast room some hours later the Doctor was eating his porridge. "I've been down to the Point. The *Oriflamme* is still on the spit but they'll have it off before long," he told her. "Your overlooker says that Mr. Johnstone's long canoe, Mr. Pollock's canoe and the Caswell barge have put out from Edenton. The Caswell barge has a swivel, besides the muskets of the men. A pitiful showing," he said between mouthfuls. "The rumor is that there are two privateers at the Bar waiting for plunder. They may be war vessels or they may run up the Jolly Roger as the *Oriflamme* did."

Mary sat down. Her hand trembled as she poured her coffee. "It will be as it was when reports of invasion sent us all rushing out of Edenton at the time before Guilford Courthouse."

"Much worse, much worse," the Doctor answered. "But that's no reason not to eat your breakfast." He looked at her keenly over his spectacles. "Or do you intend running like the rest of Edenton?"

"No, no. I will remain at Queen's Gift. It is as safe here as anywhere else. I don't care whether Cornwallis comes down from Virginia, or whether his ship or any others bombard us

568

from the Sound. I can no longer be tossed about, running here and there. I am determined to stay."

The Doctor laughed at her expression and at her clenched fists beating against the table. "Good! I agree with Sam Johnstone. It is too bad that the people are in such haste to run from Edenton. I would rather see them think about defense. I don't think Cornwallis can spare men to invade North Carolina. The Marquis is keeping him too busy in Virginia, if my sources are correct."

Mary sat quietly, thinking of what he was saying. Suddenly she remembered the woman. "How is Sarah Wilson?"

"Sleeping. I gave her an opium pill. She has suffered enough, God knows." The Doctor watched Mary for a few minutes, his face showing nothing of his thoughts. "I asked her questions. Things that have been bothering me the past few years. Peyton Rutledge was mixed up with freebooters. They were using the Chowan River above Eden House as a hiding place, just as Teach did in Sir Charles's time."

He paused and took a piece of cornbread from a silver dish. "Peyton was a fool, a wayward, pigheaded fool. I suppose we should not speak of the dead, but it's God's mercy he died when he did."

Mary did not reply. She poured herself a second cup of coffee and noticed then that the pot was china, not silver.

"One thing she told me," the Doctor went on: "Peyton did not get that necklace from her. He bought it, just as he said he did, from a lapidary in St. Kitt's or St. Croix, I forget which. She had sold it and another necklace to the lapidary with the understanding that they would be broken up and the stones taken from the settings. But the man was greedy. He sold one necklace to Peyton and the other found its way into the hands of the Levantine, Nicholas. So that settles the matter of the necklaces."

"I never want to hear them mentioned again," Mary said fiercely. "They have brought misfortune to everyone who touched them."

The Doctor cut his ham, carefully removing the fat. He chuckled. "That's what Sarah Wilson said! 'They bear a curse,' were her words. It makes me laugh when I think how we were all taken in. Lady Caroline Mathilde, a lady of quality, giving harbor to pirates all the time she lived at Pembroke. But we weren't the only ones. In Maryland and Virginia it was the same. The higher the men, the easier they fell; the more eager they were to buy political preferment."

His thin body shook with silent laughter. "The Governor too." He laughed again.

Mary did not laugh. She was thinking of the night on the *Jupiter* and of Lady Tryon's tears, of Lavinia's sorrow and constant worry and her own anxiety when Adam fought the duel. She remembered too the young man who killed himself in the garden at Lady Caroline's house in New Bern.

The Doctor was watching her closely. "What's wrong with you, Mary? You seem agitated."

"The woman is evil, evil! She has brought nothing but trouble and sorrow," she said hotly.

"She is a stormy petrel, in the wake of a storm—or ahead of one." The Doctor spoke reflectively.

"I don't want her here, Doctor, I don't want to play the good Samaritan to an evil woman."

"She can't be moved now," he answered sternly. "No matter what she is, she's a sick woman now. Common decency—"

The sentence remained unfinished. There was a sound of shouting down near the landing. A moment later they heard the dull boom of a cannon. Ebon ran into the room followed by one of the younger grooms.

"Hit's the Edenton battery," he cried, stammering in excitement. "They dragged de big gun right down off our Point. They's tryin' to throw shot on dat big ship!"

The Doctor got up hastily and went to the terrace. Mary followed him. The Negroes were already halfway across the lawn, running down to the shore. But they could see nothing nor hear any cannonading. In a moment they returned to the house.

"I've put a cot and some food in the strongroom in case of emergency," the Doctor said, "but I think for the present she is safe in the library. I've given Cissie instructions to get her into hiding if any strange men come on the place. She understands."

Mary wished the Doctor would not go. Suppose the sailors came again to look for Sarah Wilson? Suppose she was tempted to turn her over to them? What would they do with her—shoot her—drag her through the water, as they sometimes did to punish offenders?

"You've let the woman in," Armitage was saying. "You've no alternative but to see it through. She's guilty enough, God knows, but I'd be sorry to see her in the hands of some of our
570

village fishermen or sailors if there are any lives lost on those ships. Piracy is a high crime to a seaman."

Mary looked into the library once after Dr. Armitage went away. Sarah Wilson was asleep. A braid of dark red hair lay against her white cheek. She looked sick and tired and defenseless. Mary put her finger to her lips when Cissie opened her mouth to speak. A moment later she left the room. In her heart she felt pity. What a force the woman might have been for good instead of evil! But she was determined not to weaken. She would not shield Sarah Wilson from the law—only from her own companions. Since she had come to Queen's Gift for protection . . . Mary turned her mind resolutely from the problem which had been thrust upon her with the coming of Sarah Wilson.

There was no cannonading during the day. Her overlooker told her that they had no more balls and must send to Perquimans to borrow some before the Edenton battery could be used against the *Oriflamme*.

Late in the afternoon, Mary went down to the stables and ordered a horse saddled. In spite of the stableman's remonstrances that the roads were filled with riffraff and were not safe for her to ride on, she mounted Queenie, her Arab mare, and started off through the woods. She would ride as far as possible on her own land, then cross before the creek and follow the wood road toward Mulberry Hill. From what they said, The *Oriflamme* must be aground somewhere near Blount's Landing.

When she came to an opening with a clear view through the trees to the Sound, she saw that the *Oriflamme* was still aground, a number of longboats close beside her trying to shove her off. Her deck guns were trained on the shore, and on Caswell's barge and two small ships which were maneuvering for position to shell her.

Suddenly a battery on shore opened fire but the shots fell short of the target, splashing the water high over the longboats. The *Oriflamme* slipped further into the water. She was almost afloat now, creaking and groaning as the sailors, with curses and shouts, prodded at her stern, using logs as a fulcrum.

Mary watched from behind a tree, quieting the restless mare. Suddenly she saw a flash from the *Oriflamme*. The men on the deck barefooted and stripped to the waist, swung the heavy tenpounders, leveling them on the ships. Then the

571

battery fired. The firing from ship and shore was almost si-
multaneous. The foremast of the small Edenton ship crashed
to the deck, its sheets tangled with the mainmast, cutting off
the wind from the mainsail.

An exultant shout went up from the pirates. The *Oriflamme* was afloat. Men were scrambling up the ropes to the
decks, running to take their places at the batteries. Cold fear
numbed Mary. Her hands were icy, her mouth dry. With the
land battery silenced, what could save the two small ships
from the devastating gunfire of the *Oriflamme*? What could
save Edenton from shot and shell, or Queen's Gift?

She thought: "I must ride to Queen's Gift," but she could
not bring herself to lift rein. She did not hear men moving
swiftly through the forest until they were almost upon her.
They passed by without noticing her, so occupied were they
with their heavy burden. She recognized them as village men.
They carried poles lashed together, piled high with dried
leaves and small twigs. Then she knew they were going to use
fire rafts. She urged her horse closer. Below, along the shore,
she saw men wearing the high boots of fishermen wading out
into the water, pushing a smoking raft in front of them.
Along the banks were others, hidden by the reeds. The rafts
would float down stream; they would surround the *Oriflamme*. . . .

It was almost dusk now. Guns were pounding from the *Oriflamme*, battering the two small ships that stood between the
raider and Edenton. Suddenly a shout went up. The pirates
had seen the fire rafts. There were shouts and loud orders on
the deck of the *Oriflamme*. Guns were turned on swivels and
aimed low but they could not reach down to the fire rafts. A
longboat put out carrying men armed with pikes and poles
to turn the rafts aside, but the shore battery opened fire again,
sending the longboats to shelter.

Mary turned her horse quickly and galloped through the
darkening woods toward Queen's Gift, her hand in front of
her eyes to shut out the carnage. She found Queen's Gift in
confusion. Plantation Negroes from the fields and the stables
had gathered at the back of the house. Women were crying
and men shouting that Edenton was taken by the pirates and
that every man, woman and child would be killed. She went
out on the porch and spoke to them.

"You are quite safe," she told them. "There's nothing to be
frightened about. In a little time the pirate ship will be in the
hands of the Edenton soldiers and sailors."

Satisfied by her voice and assurance, the slaves wandered

off to their quarters, talking and laughing, carefree as children. Mary hoped her words had some foundation in truth. When she entered the hall she thought of Sarah Wilson, whom she had quite forgotten in the excitement of watching the ships. Cissie, coming down the stair, had a long face. Mary knew at once that something was wrong.

"Where is the key to the library?" she asked when she was close enough to Cissie not to be overheard.

Cissie made no move to get it from her pocket. "It ain't no good to look in ther' for she," she said glumly. "She gone since one or six hours ago."

"Cissie, what are you talking about? I told you not to let anyone go in there," Mary exclaimed.

"You said not to let no strangers go in, and I didn't let they for they didn't come."

Mary caught her shoulder. "Tell me, did the Doctor let her out?"

"No, ma'am, hit warn't the Doctor. Hit was Mr. Peyton Rutledge and some sailor men off that Edenton ship that was blowed up last night. They wanted she, so I go get she. I knew it would be all right as long as Mr. Peyton wanted she." Cissie waited for Mary to speak, her eyes wide with fright.

Ebon came up and stood beside Cissie. "Mr. Peyton said it would be all right. He taken charge of everything now." Ebon looked at her hopefully. "He's a captain, Mr. Peyton, is with gold braid on he coat."

Mary sat down on a chair, suddenly feeling very tired. She could not tell these anxious people what they had done. "Bring me a cloak," she said to Cissie, "and tell Lugu to saddle another horse. I'll have to go into Edenton right away."

Mary crossed the hall, only half listening to Cissie's violent protests that the road wasn't safe for a lady, or no one. Soldiers were walking down the road, carrying guns. "They is mad, all of they. The overlooker, he closed the gates and put a guard around de house and stables lak it were a castle," Cissie cried. "You can't go now."

Mary unloosed the black hands clinging to her arm. Over Cissie's shoulder, she saw a square packet lying on the mahogany table at the end of the hall. Before she was close enough to see the writing, she knew it was from Adam. "When did this come?" she asked sharply.

"Mr. Peyton brought it out. He say it come yesterday or last week one day."

The letter was sealed with Adam's crest. She could almost

see him pressing his seal against the warm wax. She stood in the hallway reading by the fading light, unmindful of the roll of guns or the burning ship that flamed the sky. It was written from Annandale but it was not dated.

"Dear Mary:

"I have tried to write you before but something always comes between me and my desire to talk to you.

"I'm sending David to the North Plantation under the care of two faithful slaves for, since Cornwallis came, Virginia is no longer a safe place.

"I have just had a letter from De Fleury, the first I have had since Sara's death. He says that Sara did not want to die. Up to the end she clung tenaciously to life, not wanting to go. She called my name over and over at the last. All this upsets me, Mary. I feel that I should have given her more of myself. Her life was tragic for such a young woman.

"I'm leaving here almost at once for Williamsburg. De Fleury will be there early in October. So will Andrew Inglis, my old friend. They want me to join them. They are on leave and will have a sort of reunion at Raleigh's Tavern. They say our old Chief will be there, not the one at the Treasury but the one before that. I am eager to see him.

"I've sent David and his party by the 'Backdoor,' that is, down the valley through Hillsborough. The coast road is very crowded these days—both north and south.

"I shall be very happy to see my old friends, particularly our Chief, who will no doubt have much to tell us. Can you understand how eager I am to join them and drink a toast to old times?

"I wonder if you will understand all this. Perhaps not, but I'm sure Dr. Armitage will when you tell him about meeting my old friends at Williamsburg early in October. I think it will be a good celebration—perhaps in the Apollo Room—but perhaps at a plantation on the coast, Yancey's or Groton's. Armitage will know where they are. Let him see this letter as I have no time to write to him. Take care of yourself, Mary. I know how careless you are of your own comfort. But you are very precious to the Colony—and to your friends.

"My devotion, as always,
"ADAM"

Mary read the letter with varying emotions, curiosity predominating. Why should Adam be so eager to see old friends? So eager that he devoted the whole letter to it—not a word about himself, or his plans—just trivial talk about a reunion. Somewhat exasperated, she thrust the letter into the bosom of her habit and went out on the gallery.

The eastern sky was red. A dark moving column of smoke rose above the trees.

"I think the ship she burn," Ebon said, waving his arm toward the forest. "Careful of de roads, Miss Mary. Plenty of bad men walking around dese days. Cain't I ride with you?"

Mary mounted her horse. "No, Ebon, I need you here. Put up the storm-shutters and bar the doors. Don't let any strangers come into the house."

"Yes'm," Ebon said meekly, "yes'm."

Hoag, her overlooker, was waiting for her, behind him a groom and two stableboys mounted on powerful horses. He repeated what Cissie and Ebon had told her.

"The roads are full of refugees running in every direction. There's deserters from Virginia and strange Negroes around. Don't you want that I should ride with ye now that night's coming on?"

Mary shook her head. "I'll be safe riding this horse. He won't let anyone overtake me and I see you have given me a guard."

She trotted out through the iron gates and turned into the wooded road that led to the village before he could protest further. The groom and stableboys followed. She lifted the rein, a signal to the horse. He broke into a swift trot. As much as she disliked Sarah Wilson, she must find her and see that she did not get into the hands of angry, resentful men. Dr. Armitage's words still rang in her ears, "Piracy is a high crime to a seaman." What if they would not wait for the slow process of law?

Chapter 40

"...AT ITS OWN HOUR"

CANNONADING started when they were halfway to the village. Mary sent the two stableboys back to Queen's Gift with instructions to the overlooker to send the slaves to the swamps if shells from the *Oriflamme* fell near the house. She hesitated a moment, wondering if she should go back, but decided against it. She must tell the Doctor what had happened. After that she had no plan—only Sarah Wilson must not fall into the hands of the sailors from the *Golden Orchid* and Smith's brig.

She took a short cut through the wood road that skirted the swamp. It would save half a mile. When she reached the Long Point, she looked over her shoulder. The moon was up. The outline of the *Oriflamme* rose high. In the flashes of light from bursting shells, three small ships were visible between the raider and Edenton. These were feeble defense—surely there must be other ships that she had not seen. There was no wind. That was in their favor. She urged her horse over the familiar path.

At the ford she was stopped by a man in uniform who carried a musket. Behind him a second soldier held a lantern high above his head so the light would fall on Mary's face. She recognized the first soldier, one of the Worley boys from Suffolk Road.

"We've got orders not to let anyone pass, Miss Warden," he said dubiously. "I don't know how I can disobey orders."

"I had better call the Captain, hadn't I?" the other man said. "I saw him riding along the bank a minute ago." He went off. After a time he came back with Meredith Chapman.

"Mary Warden, what are you doing here? Don't you know that we are about to be bombarded?" He spoke rapidly, a worried look on his homely face.

"Please tell this young man to let me through, Meredith."

"I'll ride with you. We've other sentries posted along this road." He reined his horse to her side.

"What is happening?" Mary asked. "Is all this excitement because one ship is in the Sound?"

"Isn't that enough, when we have only two or three cannon and scarcely any shot? Half the village is on the road to Windsor now, the other half in their cellars. We've sent out scouts to find out what ship it is. Some sailors off the *Orchid* say it's one of Cornwallis' ships—others say a pirate."

"It's the *Oriflamme*," Mary said quietly.

"LaTruchy's slaver? Why the devil did she open up on Smith's brig?"

"I don't think the *Oriflamme* is a slaver any longer," Mary told him dryly. Meredith didn't answer. A horseman was galloping toward them, plainly visible in the moonlight. He stopped when he recognized Meredith and saluted.

"The Colonel sent me to find you, sir. The woman escaped from Rutledge's men just as they were taking her to the jail. Some of the *Orchid* men identified her. She's the one all right. They say she ordered the guns fired that sank Rutledge's ship. The Colonel wants you to come to Town Hall." He stopped, suddenly conscious of Mary's presence.

"How the devil did she get away?" Meredith exclaimed.

"I don't know, sir, the Colonel didn't say. He was in a proper rage when I saw him."

Mary said nothing. She, too, wondered how Sarah Wilson got way—but she did not dare ask a question. They rode on briskly to the head of the Common. A crowd had gathered in front of Town Hall, everyone talking excitedly.

Meredith said, "I'm sorry I can't ride to Cupola House with you, Mary, but you will be safe with your groom. Stay indoors for there's likely to be trouble here tonight. We're arming every man we can lay hands on."

Mary saw an officer with white hair step out of the door.

"There's the Colonel now," Meredith said. "I'll have to leave you. Most of the women are at Penelope Dawson's. Why don't you go there until we know what is going to happen?"

"Perhaps I will," Mary agreed. But she rode directly down past the Common and along the waterfront to the Doctor's. The quay was crowded with men looking toward the Point below Hayes. The rumble of cannon was fainter in the village but occasional flashes of shells shone over the trees. At the old Smith-Hewes docks men were fitting out long-boats and a galley.

Mary thought, "If Joe Hewes were here, this would all have been done without confusion, in good order. No one seems to know what they are about."

She dismounted at the carriage-block. "Keep the horses in

the stable yard," she told her groom. "I may want you in a hurry."

Crit opened the door an inch after she had knocked several times. His hand that held the candle was trembling, the whites of his eyes gleaming in the darkness of the hall. "Oh, Miss Mary, hit's you! I thought it was them raiders coming to get us."

"Is the Doctor here?" Mary asked.

"No'm. He's gone afightin', all they men gone afightin'. They raiders goin' to blow this place right into de water."

"Nonsense," Mary said. "Nothing of the sort."

"Dey say hit's old Cornwallis's ship, and he got plenty more waitin' outside."

Mary went into the drawing room. "I'm going to wait for the Doctor. I think I'd like coffee, if you'll make some fresh."

"Yes'm, I'll go right now."

Mary didn't want coffee, but she knew Crit would get over his terror if he had something to do. She went to the window and pulled the heavy damask curtains. The men at the wharf were working feverishly at the boats. They now had a dozen dugout canoes and flat-bottom boats to augment the defenders. Each carried three or four men with muskets, besides the men at the oars and paddles. One by one they shoved off on the dark waters. The muffled oars made no sound. For the first time, Mary felt something of terror creep over her. What if they did bombard the village!

She let the curtains fall into place and sat down by the fire.

The knocker banged loudly. Mary jumped to her feet, her heart pounding. She drew a sharp breath, then went out of the room into the hall. A woman's voice called:

"Crit, is the Doctor in?"

Mary opened the door and found Ann Blount and Stacey Chapman standing there; coming up the brick walk, she saw Ann Davenport and the two Medlock girls from Belvedere.

They rushed in with little cries and wordless sounds of alarm, silken petticoats swaying.

"Oh, Mrs. Warden, is it true that Cornwallis' fleet has shelled Queen's Gift and Mulberry Hill?" . . . "Mary Warden, do you think our men can capture a great fleet?" . . . "Did you know everyone is leaving town? Everyone—the Blairs are in Windsor and the Carrubuses have left Pembroke and gone to Hillsborough!" . . . "Cornwallis' army is at Suffolk— they're marching this way." . . . "Have you heard that a thousand slaves are hiding in the Dismal, waiting word from Banastre Tarleton to attack us?" They surrounded her, talking, half weeping.

Mary said, "It's one ship, the *Oriflamme*, the old slaver; just one ship."

There was a sudden hushed silence; then Stacey Chapman, Meredith's young sister, asked, "How do you know?"

"I saw it," Mary told her.

Suddenly Ann Blount cried, "Why not go upstairs in the cupola and see the battle?" At that they all swept out of the door into the paneled hall, calling to Crit to bring candles as they mounted the stairs.

Mary sat down. She realized that she was tired, desperately tired.

A few minutes later they all came down again. They could see nothing but a red glow in the sky, they said. Did Mary think the ships were burning? They must go back to Penelope Dawson's—would Mary come? They did not wait for her answer but trooped out the door and down the walk into the darkness.

When Crit brought the coffee, Mary drank it gratefully. Some time later she was awakened by a step in the hall, Crit's voice welcoming the Doctor. She must have slept, her head resting against the chair back.

"Did they sink she?" Crit asked anxiously.

"No, not yet." The Doctor's voice voice sounded weary. "But our ships are all around her. I don't think she'll escape this time."

He came into the room and saw Mary. "I suppose you know that Sarah Wilson got away," he said, sinking into a chair. "Yes, she gave them the slip."

"How did she do it?" Mary asked.

"I'm not sure, but I think your friend the third mate must have managed it. The soldiers who had her in charge were vague. They said a blond sailor and three Negroes came on them from behind, trussed them up and took the woman away. Young Peyton had charge of the detachment." The Doctor looked at her a moment without speaking. "Fate is a trickster," he added.

Mary remained silent, pondering over his words. Then she thought of Adam's letter. She took it out of the pocket of her habit and handed it to the Doctor without comment.

"God's life," he muttered when he was halfway through. "So soon?" When he finished reading, he looked up. His tiredness had vanished. "Back in a moment," he said and hastened to the door. Mary heard him calling Crit as he went down the hall. Wondering what the letter contained to affect the Doctor this way, she began to read it through again and stopped at the words, "The Doctor will understand."

After a little time Dr. Armitage came back into the room. When he saw her bewilderment, a smile came to his thin lips, but quickly disappeared. He sat down beside her and took up the letter again.

"Adam couldn't write more openly for fear the letter might be taken by the enemy," he explained. "It's come earlier than I thought. Listen to what he has told us. He says a reunion of old friends—Captain Inglis and Count de Fleury. Do you see what he means? That his old regiment will be in Williamsburg early in the month. Then he speaks of his chief, of the man who was his Chief before he went to the Treasury. Don't you understand that he is trying to tell us that the northern army under General Washington will be in Williamsburg early in the month? Why? To join with Lafayette and route Cornwallis. Wait." He spread the paper on the table. "There's one thing I don't make out—what does he mean by a plantation on the coast, Yancey's or Groton's?" He puzzled a few moments. Then he banged the table with his fist.

"I've got it. Yancey's and Groton's—Y and G—he means Yorktown and Gloucester. Cornwallis' army is in Yorktown and Gloucester." He got up and paced the floor, thinking hard. "It must be that they are going to put Admiral de Grasse's old plan into action; De Grasse's ships will attempt to hold off the British fleet and bottle Cornwallis up in the Chesapeake. Then Washington's northern army will march into Virginia. God in Heaven, Mary! Don't you see it's as plain as day? It's the great battle at last." He jumped up. "You'll have to help me pack supplies right now," he said energetically. "At once; there isn't a moment to lose. They may be there now." He fumbled with the letter. "No date," he said with disgust.

Mary sat without moving, her hands clutching the arms of the chair. Then she spoke as though pleading a cause. "I'll go with you, Doctor. They'll need women nurses. You remember how it was at Guilford Courthouse?"

The Doctor shook his head. "You can't go now. I'll send for you. I'll have to leave at once. If we are bombarded here I may not be able to get away. Dr. Simmons can look after the office. Come, help me pack now." Mary did not answer. She followed him to the dispensary and began putting bandages into bundles, rolling instruments into clean cotton squares. The Doctor, coat off, went from the dispensary to his office, carrying bottles and boxes of medicine. Crit came down the stairs with the Doctor's dressing cases and boxes. He opened the shutters and blew out the sputtering candles. The first streak of yellow flared in the east as the Doctor's coach drew up in front of Cupola House.

"I'll send for you as soon as I see what the situation in Williamsburg really is," he promised.

After the Doctor had gone, people began to come, women and men, a constant stream, wanting to look at the ships from the cupola. Now that it was light they could see the *Oriflamme*. The vessel lay opposite the second point near the middle of the channel. The breeze was light, still blowing from the east. If it increased, the pirate ship would soon be opposite the Bay, unless the small fleet stopped her.

The excitement on the quay continued to increase. Men were working feverishly, piling up a barricade of sandbags and barrels.

Crit roused the cook, who made coffee and hot scones to serve to the people who came. The men, who had been working all night, were grateful for food and an opportunity to snatch a moment's rest. When Meredith Chapman stepped in Mary had a chance to ask him about the woman who had escaped.

"No trace yet, but we'll find her," he said confidently. "But it won't be easy. The roads are full of people fleeing to safety. It's worse this morning, since they can see the ships." He finished the coffee and got up. "I must get back to my men. We'll get the quay and the wharves barricaded before the raider can get here, if the wind doesn't come up."

At the door he turned. "I'm worried about Lavinia," he said. "She is at their plantation alone except for the slaves. If I could find Peyton, I'd send him after her."

"Won't she be safer where she is?"

Meredith shook his head. "I don't think so. I believe the *Oriflamme* is headed for the river, not Edenton Bay—but I may be wrong."

It wasn't long after Meredith left that Peyton came in. Mary heard him ask Crit for the Doctor. When he saw Mary his tired face lighted. "Mother's ill," he said, "and here the Doctor's gone. Won't you come out, please, Aunt Mary? I don't dare leave her alone. It's her heart."

Mary hesitated only a moment. She was on the point of upbraiding him for taking Sarah Wilson from Queen's Gift in her absence, but she decided against it. "I'll go," she said. "Call my groom and tell him to bring my horse around."

"Oh, thank you, Aunt Mary. You've no idea how worried I've been."

The sun came up when they reached the edge of the village. Mary said, "You needn't come any farther."

"I'm going this way. I've got six men patrolling the road between here and Eden House." He stopped a moment, then continued: "We're trying to find that woman. I wouldn't have taken her from Queen's Gift," he burst out, "but I had to. It was my duty."

"I understand, Peyton," Mary said quietly. "How did she get away from your men?"

"I can't see how it happened. I put her in charge of good men," he added miserably. "They had her right at the door of the gaol when the pirates, who must have been hiding in the woods, leaped on them from behind. One of the men said there were a dozen pirates, but I doubt that. I think more likely half that number, or even less." He was silent a moment. "It was my fault. I was in charge, although I had gone to report to the Colonel at Town Hall. It'll be worse when they find out that she is Lady Caroline."

Mary turned. "How did you know?" she asked in surprise.

"I remember her. I wasn't too young to know about—" he gulped—"about Lady Caroline and—" He couldn't bring himself to say "my father."

"Did she know you?" It was a foolish question. Peyton was the image of his father.

He apparently had not heard her for he continued as if thinking aloud: "I don't know whether she's a pirate or not. The sailors from the *Orchid* swear she is. But I'll capture that woman and get her into the gaol." His young, unlined face was grim.

Mary said nothing. She understood his emotion only too well.

As they rode past Pembroke Mary's mind flashed back to the time when Lady Caroline was living there in almost regal state. Another thought came to her. For the first time she noticed the strategic position of the estate at the head of the Sound, separated as it was from the broad Chowan River by only a narrow neck of land, mostly deep swamp. How easily ships could sail up the Chowan, keeping near the Tyrrell side! The old story of Eden House came to her mind. What fools they all were never to have suspected!

They came to the Chowan and found that the ferry was on the opposite side. Peyton cupped his hands to his mouth, shouting. Dishon, the ferry-keeper, came out of his small house on the bank, and got into the ferry, followed by his oarsmen.

Two men in uniform rode up and saluted Peyton. Mary heard one of them say, "We've been watching the ferry since midnight, questioning everybody that passed."

"Keep close watch. There is still a chance they will try to fool us by slipping away with the refugees. Watch the ferry and the river for boats."

Lavinia, lying on a couch on the gallery, greeted Mary warmly and kissed Peyton. "There's been no cannonading since last night," she said. She sat up suddenly. "Look! There they are. The big ship has canvas up. Peyton, get the spyglass. It's on the hall table."

Peyton looked through the glass for some time. "I think you two had better go over to Eden House," he suggested.

"They've all gone to Hillsborough," Lavinia said.

"Pembroke, then. I don't think the drive will hurt you, Mother."

"Pembroke is closed. The family left yesterday and took the slaves along."

"I saw a light there last night," Peyton told her. "Perhaps you are mistaken."

"No, I'm not. Janie stopped here. They went to Bath."

"Bath! Why, Bath is as exposed to raiders or Cornwallis' fleet as we are in Albemarle," Peyton exclaimed.

Lavinia leaned back. "I'll stay here," she said calmly.

Peyton handed Mary the glass without comment. Mary saw the reason for his anxiety. If the *Oriflamme* steered straight for Chowan River, it would pass their landing.

She handed the glass back to Peyton and a look of understanding passed between them. "We can always ride out to Bandon," she said lightly. "Don't worry, Peyton, we'll be quite all right."

They moved toward the steps. Peyton lowered his voice. "I hope she doesn't find out about Lady Caroline."

Mary had no time to answer. Lavinia had heard the name. "What did you say, Peyton?" she demanded.

When Peyton remained silent she turned to Mary. "I heard him say 'Lady Caroline.' You may as well admit—"

Mary hesitated. Lavinia sat up, her face white. "You're hiding something from me, Peyton."

Mary saw it was no use to try to conceal the truth. "The woman called Sarah Wilson whom Peyton is searching for is—"

"Lady Caroline," Lavinia interrupted. She caught Peyton's arm. "You cannot go after her; I won't let you. She's evil—evil." Her voice rose in her excitement.

"Now, Mother, don't get yourself wrought up. Please."

Mary interrupted. "Peyton has his duty to perform."

"Let someone else go after her. I don't want her near Peyton, I tell you." She dropped back on the pillow, her hands covering her face.

"I'll take care of her," Mary said. Peyton nodded, glad to escape. He loathed scenes. Mary did too but, to her surprise, Lavinia sat up after a few minutes.

"I won't let her get Peyton into her clutches," she said faintly.

"You need not worry about that, Lavinia," Mary assured her, wondering where the hunted woman had gone. Where could she hide with half a hundred men looking for her?

She got up and walked to the rail of the gallery and stood looking down the river. She could see the chimney of Pembroke rising above the trees, and the long neck of swampland that jutted into the Chowan. Her eyes followed the course of the river where it flowed into the Sound. She realized then that she could no longer see the *Oriflamme* or the other boats. Turning to speak to Lavinia, she found her also looking out over the river, a complacent smile on her lips.

"Meredith wants me to marry him," Lavinia said abruptly, turning to Mary. "He says I'm too young to stay a widow forever."

Mary, watching Lavinia's expression, made no reply. Surely this was the old Lavinia, not the one who had so tragically mourned Peyton's death. What had happened to her?

"Sometimes I think I am too young—" she paused, looking at Mary questioningly—"but how can I give up the Rutledge name when my beloved husband died a hero's death?"

She sat looking at her hands clasped in her lap. Again Mary did not answer. It seemed to her more natural that Lavinia should want to go on with her life than to grieve forever for Peyton.

But Lavinia did not expect an answer. In a moment she spoke of Adam. Owen had had letters from Virginia. They

584

were expecting David any time now. She had sometimes thought she would go out to the new country with them. Perhaps when Adam went again. She looked up at Mary and said abruptly, "Are you going to marry Dr. Armitage?"

Mary sat up stiffly, her eyes opening wide in surprise. "Dr. Armitage? Why, he is like my father!"

Lavinia did not meet her eyes. "Yes, I know," she said, "but you always liked older men, Mary. This isn't my idea, my dear. I've heard it often in Edenton; it's common gossip at parties."

Mary was speechless. Lavinia got up and walked slowly across the gallery. "Surely you aren't in love with Adam Rutledge any longer," she said suddenly.

Mary felt her anger rising. Why should Lavinia say such things to her? "Was I ever in love with Adam?" she found herself asking.

Lavinia smiled a little and shrugged her shoulders. "I'm glad you got over it, Mary. You're too fine a woman to throw yourself at any man's head. Of course, Adam will marry again," she added, as if it were just occurring to her. "Why, of course he will marry."

Mary was too outraged to speak.

A slave came to announce dinner.

While they were at dinner, Peyton rode up the driveway, followed by five or six soldiers. He ran up the steps and into the hall, his spurred boots clattering on the bare floor.

"The *Oriflamme*'s sunk," he called out from the doorway. "The Edenton Battery and the culverins in the Caswell barge were too much for the pirates." He stopped a moment for breath. "They've got the pirates in Edenton now. They're chained and in the stocks."

"The stocks!" Mary exclaimed. "Why, the stocks are for petty thieves and runaway slaves." Remembering what Dr. Armitage had said, she added, "Piracy is a high crime, a matter for the Admiralty Court."

"I know, but they're going to keep them in the stocks so the people can see them, before—" His words dwindled off. He was running up the stairs, two at a time.

A moment later he came down again, buttoning his tunic. Mary saw that he had strapped a holster with a second pistol under his arm.

"Come to dinner," his mother said. "Cook has kept it in the oven."

"Sorry, I can't stop, I've work to do." He gave Mary a

585

warning glance. She got up from the table and followed him to the gallery.

"You know I told you I saw lights at Pembroke last night. I didn't think of it again till Mother mentioned that all the family and slaves had gone. When I went over to the house just now I saw someone had been there last night. There were the remains of a meal on the dining table; a bed had been slept in and there were footprints from the house to the boat-landing. I've sent men in boats to search both banks of the river but I'm afraid we're too late."

Mary watched him ride swiftly down the drive, his soldiers following. She stood a moment looking across toward Pembroke. It was sundown, the river golden in the fading light. Great cypress trees grew deep in the turgid stream, the spreading trunks half submerged. Black roots pierced the slime of the swamp, like grotesque monsters; an evil place. . . . She shuddered and went hurriedly into the bright warmth of the house.

Mary told Lavinia good-by early the following morning. Lavinia tried to persuade her to stay. Peyton had not come home, she said, a strained look in her eyes. But Mary wanted to go. She was suddenly anxious to go home to Queen's Gift.

When she crossed the ferry, Dishon, looking furtively over his shoulder, thrust a letter into her hand.

"She was kind to my sick wife when she lived at Pembroke," he whispered. "I couldn't betray her now." He ran back to the ferry before she could question him.

Mary rode on almost to Pembroke before she pulled up her horse and opened the letter.

"Mary Warden:

"I am at Pembroke. I found its doors open and inviting. While I am waiting for Crane to join me, I am writing to you. He will get me away, of that I am sure, for only I know the hiding place up the Chowan where Teach stored his treasure.

"If he doesn't come by moonrise, my slaves will row me across the river. I know a hiding place on the Eden land and a secret way through the swamps that leads to the forest roads. I have a rendezvous at Bath with one of my ships, or up the Chesapeake, or at the Inlet. There are many ways of escape open. I left the emeralds. You will find them in the Japan box in your strong-room. It amuses me to think you will give the stones to your Treasury and that the money they will fetch will be used against the King. I always loathed him.

586

"No use giving this letter to my pursuers. I will have plenty of time to get away before it is in your hands.

"Crane, the mate, thinks he will force me to give him the map Teach left. I have no map. I have already taken the treasure. You held some of the jewels in your hand at Pembroke. Remember?"

The letter was signed with the bold, scrawly cipher she used when she was Lady Caroline Mathilde.

Mary crushed the paper in her hand. The insolence of the woman! She started to throw it into the river, then changed her mind and slipped it into her saddlebag. She gave her horse free rein and, a short time later, was at the outskirts of the village.

She met Peyton and Meredith Chapman at the corner of Broad Street, near St. Paul's. Peyton shook his head.

"She got away," he said disspiritedly.

Meredith clapped his hand on his shoulder. "No matter, we've got the ringleaders. The Colonel doesn't want the woman. We'll be saved the expense of a trial before the Admiralty Court. Forget her."

Mary breathed more freely. She would not have to turn the letter over to Meredith or to anyone else. She started to cross the street, back of King's Arms Inn, but Meredith swung his horse in front of hers.

"Don't. Don't go that way, Mary. Take the upper road."

"Why?" she asked, but the word died on her lips. She saw why. Three figures dangled from the gibbets in the gaol yard back of Town Hall. She saw the purple, bloated faces of LaTruchy and the Levantine.

She turned her horse and rode swiftly along the wood road toward Queen's Gift.

A few days later two charcoal-burners came across the body of Sarah Wilson. She lay half submerged in the dark waters of the swamp, a few hundred yards from Pembroke. She still wore man's clothes and boots, but her coat was gone, her white silk shirt stained with blood from a gaping knife wound in her back. There was no boat near, and no one could guess by whom she had been killed.

When Mary heard this she thought of the woman's letter. She went to the tack room at the stable, took the paper from her saddlebag and carried it into the house. Once in her room she spread the crumpled sheet of paper on a table and reread

587

it, this time without anger. When she had finished she knew the key to the tragedy lay in the sentences: "Crane thinks he will force me to give him the map. . . . I have no map."

Mary went to the fireplace and held the letter to the flame. Whatever she had done, the woman had challenged life boldly. But her destiny had overtaken her.

The Arab saying that John Hawks had told her entered Mary's mind: "A star never rises or falls, save at its own hour."

Chapter 41

THE WORLD TURNED UPSIDE DOWN

THE WEEK that followed was the quiet after the storm. One by one the people who had fled returned to Edenton, a little shamefaced at their alarm.

But wild rumors continued to come in from the north which almost negated the good fortune of Greene's army in the south. Virginia was close: the great army of Cornwallis seemed at their doorstep.

The Edenton Volunteers marched north. Some men, the same who had fled to Windsor, complained that the town was left without protection from land or sea. They were fitting out more boats to safeguard the banks along the marshes.

Then news came that Washington's men had taken possession of Long Island and King's Bridge and that the second French fleet was on the way.

Mary could not help wondering whether Dr. Armitage had interpreted Adam's cryptic letter correctly. Was Washington really going to Virginia to trap Cornwallis? Restless and disturbed, she quieted her overwrought nerves by working on the plantation and helping Edenton women to scrape lint—anything to forget the nightmare of the past few days and the anxiety of the days ahead.

Then one morning the messenger came from Dr. Armitage. He wanted her to come to Williamsburg at once and bring all the medical supplies she could get together. A great battle was imminent and they would need all the help they could get. That was the eighteenth of October. She started on the twentieth, her birthday.

Mary took Cornwallis' coach, which had remained all these months in the coach house at Queen's Gift, and had it packed to capacity with supplies the Edenton women had prepared. Ebon drove, Cissie on the box beside him. The whole country knew that a great battle would be fought soon —perhaps the greatest of the war. Everywhere along the road they saw only anxious faces.

They drove steadily, changing horses often to facilitate the journey. When they were nearing the ferry at the James,

Ebon began to shout, pulling up his horses. Another coach was driving down the road from the opposite direction. Mary slid the window open and looked out. She saw that it was Dr. Armitage. He stopped his coach and came over to her.

"I've been looking for you, Mary. It's all over," he said, his eyes blazing in his white, tired face. "It's all over."

Before she could speak, he cried out to a group of men standing at the roadside, "Cornwallis surrendered on October nineteenth at Yorktown."

Mary grasped the window frame of the coach with both hands. "Cornwallis has surrendered," she whispered. "Surrendered!"

"Yes, and we're going home. Adam has already gone. He's carrying important dispatches they wouldn't trust to regular couriers. He'll be at Edenton ahead of us."

Mary couldn't speak. It was over—the war was over.

Armitage answered her thoughts: "No, this is not the end of the war. It will drag on, but the back is broken. The main army surrendered, Cornwallis' army, while our regimental bands played *The World Turned Upside Down*. The rest is only a matter of time. Come, get into my coach, Mary. I'll tell you all I know. Ebon can follow."

Dr. Armitage's coach rolled into Edenton shortly after sunup. Mary Warden woke up when the wheels bumped over the rough cobbles of Broad Street. They had made a fast journey, although they had been stopped time after time all along the way by people in the villages and along the country roads. Everyone was hungry for news of Yorktown. The guns had been heard for a long distance along the James, and anxious-faced men and women waited by the roadside to intercept anyone from the north who could give them more news of the battle.

The Doctor had repeated the words: *"Cornwallis has surrendered,"* so often that his voice had failed him. Then Mary took up the task. With her head out the coach window, she cried the words as they galloped through hamlet and village: *"Cornwallis has surrendered. Cornwallis has surrendered. Washington is victorious at Yorktown."*

The last stretch of the journey she slept, only to awaken when they reached Queen Anne's Creek at the edge of their village. When the coach turned into King Street, she saw that the Commons green was thronged with people. It was Market day. The booths at the lower end of the green were crowded with yeomen, with blue-smocked shepherds and their women-

590

folk. The fishing fleet lay anchored close in; the wharf was piled with nets and seafood.

In the courtyard of King's Arms Inn, she caught sight of pink-coated riders. It must be a cub-hunt or a drag, she thought. Tears filled her eyes at the familiar scene, for she noticed, among the yeomen and shepherds, armless men, men walking with the aid of crutches, and men with battle-scarred faces.

"The same, but not the same," the Doctor muttered, awakened by the jolting of the coach. "Plenty of work for me for years to come," he continued, his eyes on the group of crippled men seated on a bench facing the green.

The coach drew up at the steps of the Inn. The Doctor got out with agility remarkable for his age, and Mary followed. They were at once surrounded by friends—the riders pushing their horses close to the steps to hear the story Dr. Armitage had to tell.

Mary glanced around. Some old riders were missing; new ones had come to take their place. She realized what war had done to the village. Young Peyton, wearing his uniform of captain of the Edenton Light Horse, dismounted and came quickly to her side.

"Mother is riding today, the first time for years. I insisted, and she gave in. There is no reason for her to spend her whole life on the plantation," he said, with new masculine firmness. "There she is now, over by the pump with Meredith Chapman."

Mary looked in the direction Peyton indicated. She saw Lavinia seated on a beautiful bay horse, her face turned toward Meredith. Peyton was watching Mary. He leaned down and whispered:

"He admires Mother so much; perhaps, after a time—" He left the sentence unfinished.

Mary squeezed his arm. "It would be splendid," she said quickly, "splendid."

Peyton's face darkened. "But Mother won't listen to him. She thinks she should never give up Father's name. Oh, Aunt Mary, sometimes I wish Father hadn't been a hero. It makes everything so complicated."

He said nothing of Sarah Wilson. Apparently the whole thing had made little impression on him. She knew that episode was now a closed book in Edenton.

When Dr. Armitage came over to speak to her, Peyton mounted his horse and rode to join his mother and Meredith.

"I'm going over to Town Hall, Mary," the Doctor said. "The Council is meeting now to hear Adam's dispatches. After that, there will be a public reading so the people will know everything that has happened. Do you hear what I say, Mary? 'So the people will know'—that means that we are through with secrecy and hidden power."

He started away, then returned hurriedly. "Go down to Cupola House, Mary. I've sent word to Crit to have breakfast ready. I'll bring Adam with me when I come."

Mary sent the coach on and walked down to the street along the edge of the Commons. The crowd was swelling in numbers. She saw farmers from up the Chowan, from Perquimans and from Tyrrell across the Sound. Rumors had flown swiftly and the people of Albemarle were gathering to hear of the great victory of Washington's army.

Time after time, as she walked along, she heard the same words: "This is the end of the war. The Hanoverian's power is broken now." "We are free—free," one old yeoman shouted. "God bless General Washington and our armies."

Halfway down the green, she heard a great shout go up from the crowd, followed by a fanfare of trumpets. She turned around to see what had happened.

A company of Edenton Light Horse was riding down King Street up to the steps of the Courthouse. A sergeant dismounted and made his way to a board hanging beside the door where official bulletins were posted. He was followed by a corporal carrying a paper which he unrolled and tacked onto the board. The crowd on the green surged forward.

Men who were close craned their necks to read the message. A murmur went through the crowd. "The terms of surrender, the terms of surrender," ran from lip to lip. The news spread from the Town Hall down the length of the Commons green to the wharves on Albemarle Sound.

"Read it aloud so we can all know," someone shouted from the middle of the crowd.

"Be quiet, man," a yeoman shouted back. "Bide your time. We'll know the whole matter when the Council's through their meeting. Do ye mind the time we was afeard to be seen reading from the board?"

The crowd had not long to wait. The wide double doors were thrown open. Half a dozen men came out of the hall and stood at the top of the steps facing the Commons. Mary saw Adam in his buff and blue uniform standing behind the Mayor. The Chairman of the Council held up his hand for silence. Raising his voice, he addressed the people on the Commons.

"You all know that a battle has been fought at Yorktown and that General Washington has been victorious—" He was stopped by the roar of the crowd. Once or twice he tried to restore silence, but without success.

He motioned to Adam, handing him the papers. The villagers recognized Adam. They knew he had been with the army; he would have something to tell them. The Chairman said: "I have asked Colonel Rutledge, who was at the Battle of Yorktown, to read the terms of surrender, which you have just seen posted on the board."

Adam took a step forward. Papers in hand, his eyes swept the crowd. In an instant there was silence. His voice carried out to the eager, excited people.

"Do you remember the time, not so long ago, that you were all afraid to walk up to Town Hall, to look at notices posted on the board? You came secretly, furtively looking over your shoulder. You were afraid to read for fear one more tax had been levied, one more tax to increase your already heavy burden. Today when a notice is posted, you crowd forward openly, without fear of being seen. You know that from now on every man has equal share and equal responsibility in the government of his village, of his colony, of his nation."

The cheers from hundreds of throats interrupted Adam. He let them shout themselves out, then turned to his paper.

"These are the terms of surrender," he said in a quieter voice:

> "'Yorktown, Virginia
> October 17, 1781

"'Sir:

"'I propose a cessation of hostilities for twenty-four hours and that two officers may be appointed by each side to meet at Mr. Moore's house to settle terms for the surrender of the posts of York and Gloucester.

> "'I have the honor to be, etc.,

> "'CORNWALLIS.'

> "'Camp before York
> October 17, 1781

"'My Lord:

"'I have the honor of receiving Your Lordship's letter of this date. An ardent desire to spare the further effusion of blood will readily incline me to listen to such terms for the surrender of your posts and garrisons at York and Gloucester as are admissible.

" 'I wish, previous to the meeting of commissioners, that your Lordship's proposals, in writing, may be sent to the American lines for which purpose a suspension of hostilities during two hours for the delivery of this letter will be granted.

" 'I have the honor to be, etc.,

" 'GEORGE WASHINGTON.'

" 'York, Virginia
October 17, 1781
4½ P.M.

" 'Sir:

" 'I have this moment been honored with your Excellency's letter dated this day.

" 'The time limited for sending my answers will not permit of entering into detail of articles, but the basis of my proposals will be: That the garrisons of York and Gloucester shall be prisoners of war with the customary honors. And for the convenience of the individuals which I have the honor to command, that the British shall be sent to Britain, and the Germans to Germany, under engagements not to serve against France, America, or their allies until released or regularly exchanged. That all arms and public stores will be delivered to you, but that the usual indulgence of side-arms of officers and of retaining private property shall be granted officers and soldiers, and that the interest of several individuals in civil capacities and connected with us shall be attended to.

" 'If your Excellency thinks that a continuance of the suspension of hostilities will be necessary to hasten your answer, I shall have no objection to the hour you may propose.

" 'I have the honor to be, etc.,

" 'CORNWALLIS.' "

Adam stood quietly until the crowd had shouted itself hoarse.

"Two days later, a document containing fourteen paragraphs was written. Six men put their names to the paper. Two signed at Yorktown: Cornwallis and Thomas Symonds. Four men put their hand and seal in the trenches before Yorktown: General Washington, the Comte de Rochambeau, the Comte de Barras and the Comte de Grasse."

"That is all," Adam said. He waited a moment, holding the paper above his head. "Only two pages of writing, and the Colonies are free forever from a foreign king and a small body of men seeking to force their will on a free people."

Mary turned away, choked with emotion. Making her way through the crowds, she crossed the lower end of the Commons green and walked quickly down the quay toward Broad Street and Cupola House.

The frenzied shouts of the crowd followed her. "It is the voice of the people I am hearing," she thought. "Pray God they may always hold the freedom they have won today!"

They sat a long time at breakfast. Crit carried away the dishes but left the coffee. Adam and Armitage talked of Yorktown; of the conduct of General Washington's army; of the surrender.

"It was the act of a careful officer," Adam said, thoughtfully. "Cornwallis might have held out a few days longer but he would have sacrificed his men. He had almost no ammunition left; he was outnumbered. One of his aides told De Fleury that General Cornwallis had finally given up hope that he would get any help from Clinton. After that there was nothing to do but surrender."

The Doctor pushed his coffee cup toward Mary. "A brave man," he said. "A good soldier. I shall always think that at heart he believed in the cause of the Colonies."

Mary remembered Cornwallis as she had seen him that night at Guilford Courthouse. He had known then the end was in sight. No shouts of victory had rung in his ears that day, or any day that followed. But she said nothing of this. She was watching Adam. They had had few words other than the first greeting. Once or twice, she felt his eyes on her, but he made no effort to talk. He seemed content to sit quietly at the table, listening to Armitage.

The Doctor finished his coffee, laid his napkin down and pushed his chair from the table so that he might move his body sidewise. He looked first at Mary, then at Adam. His eyes were searching, almost accusing. Suddenly he said, "Now will you please tell me what on God's earth stands between you two?"

Mary caught her breath at the suddenness of his attack. Adam leaned forward, a dull red showing along the thin scar that marred his face.

"Answer me, Mary," Armitage said, his eyes boring into hers.

Words forced themselves from her lips. "I don't know. You must ask Adam." She was suddenly sure of herself. She was ready to fight for him—to fight Lavinia, if necessary, and Adam himself. "I don't know. Ask Adam," she repeated, her voice clear, questioning.

Adam turned from Armitage to her. The sadness in his eyes frightened her so that she involuntarily put her hand against her throat. For a few moments the silence held. Then Adam's chair scraped the floor. He got up, walked to the window and back again. His hands grasped the ladder-back chair until the joints of his fingers whitened. His voice was low; he did not look at her but at the Doctor. A feeling of futility made its way through her consciousness. Why had they forced him to speak? It was horrible. She couldn't stand it.

"Don't, Adam, don't," she cried. "Don't speak. We have no right—"

He put out his hand and touched her shoulder. "I have sworn to myself I wouldn't speak," he said slowly. "I thought that I had not the right. Now I'm not so sure. Today young Peyton spoke of Lavinia. He said, 'She should marry again. She is too young to live alone all her life because my father died a hero!' " He looked at Mary now.

"Tell me what I am to do, to say—" The words came swiftly now, released from the dark recess of his soul. "Peyton was not a hero. He was running away. Running away, I tell you, and I forced him into battle. I shot him. Now do you understand? I shot Peyton—" He stood looking at her with tortured eyes.

His words let a flood of light into Mary's heart. She looked from his bowed head to the Doctor. Armitage had half risen, both hands on the table before him, supporting his bent body.

"You shot Peyton?" he asked, his voice tense.

"Yes, with my pistol. I couldn't see him desert under fire."

Armitage walked swiftly across the room. At the door, he said, "Wait, I'll be back. Wait where you are."

Adam did not move, nor Mary. In a few moments, Armitage returned carrying a small shagreen case, the kind he used for his spectacles. "Please look at these, Adam," he said sharply. He opened the case and took out two balls—one from a pistol, the other longer and larger.

"I took both of these from Peyton's body," he said. "The pistol ball grazed his side and was embedded in the outer skin below a rib. This other bullet went through his intestines, plowed a furrow to his heart."

Adam leaned forward, his eyes staring, his face chalk-white. "Then my pistol—?"

"Did not kill him. He was killed by a musket. So you've wasted a lot of time worrying about something that didn't happen."

Adam sat down heavily, his hands resting on the table, his

eyes on Armitage's face. The Doctor put the bullets back into the case and snapped it shut.

"Now I'm going to see a patient," he said briskly. "When I come back—" He stopped, a broad smile on his thin old face. Neither Adam nor Mary heard him leave the room.

A few weeks after they were married, Adam and Mary sailed over to North Plantation to say good-by to Owen and Marcy and their families who were starting early the following morning for the Illinois country. David was going with them, and half a dozen Edenton men under the leadership of Meredith Chapman. They would journey first to Hillsborough where they would join twenty other families that were going into the new country along the Mississippi.

Mary laughed when she saw the household goods Gwennie was having loaded into great wagons: mahogany chests and tables, china, silver, chests of linen, boxes of jams and jellies, kegs of Catawba and Scuppernong wines.

"One must not change one's way of living just because it is a wilderness country," Gwennie told her. Lucy was packing also; David was too excited at the prospect of the journey to pay much attention to Adam. Dressed in buckskins Enos Dye had brought him, he kept racing from one wagon to another, his horse in a white lather. Owen sat on the gallery, surrounded by stacks of books. Two wagons were filled with volumes. "Enough books to start an academy," he told Adam, as he went on sorting them.

Lavinia sat near, her young son playing with the dogs. She had on a dark silk dress and a small cap. A bunch of keys hung from a silver chain at her waist. Already she was the chatelaine of North Plantation.

"Meredith says he will be back in the spring," she said complacently. "We may decide—I don't know what I'll do— Peyton needs me here. Oh, Mary, it is so nice to be needed!"

Mary kissed her, her heart suddenly warm and friendly toward Lavinia.

It was almost sunset when Adam swung the tiller of his sloop around and headed straight for Queen's Gift. Far down the Sound, Mary could see the tall chimney and the broken, blackened walls of the Manor House at Rutledge Riding, a symbol of the old life—now gone forever. Adam did not glance toward Rutledge Riding. His eyes were fixed on the noble façade of Queen's Gift, and on the heavy woodland beyond. The night was still. A blue heron and two snow-white cranes were standing motionless near the bank. A triangle of ducks flew low along the water, headed for the north.

Mary's eyes were on Adam's clear-cut profile; his strong, lean face, the powerful shoulder, bent now to escape the swinging sail. For a long time they had been silent. "What is he thinking?" she wondered. Fear clutched her heart. "Is he dreaming of the great country along the Mississippi? Does he regret—" Feeling her eyes, he turned, smiled, and laid his firm, strong hand over hers.

"I was thinking that we might try flax in that north field of your plantation this spring, and the lowland would be ideal for rice. Don't you think, Mary, that you could improve the quality of your tobacco if you followed the method we tried at Rutledge—contour plowing? There will be new markets to develop after this war is over and you may as well skim the cream."

Tears of relief came to her eyes. Adam had not been thinking of the West. His mind was fixed on Queen's Gift, the problems they must face to rebuild their own country after the devastation of war. The last doubt fled from her mind. He would not go away. He would stay in the Albemarle country. He would give his strength to rebuild the power of the land she loved. Almost in answer to her thought, he said:

"I've thought it through, Mary. Our place is here—now and for some years to come. After that—" he laughed. Tilting her chin with his fingers, he kissed her red lips. "One day you must see the sunset on the Missouri—where it joins the Mississippi—one day."

Mary turned her hand in his, holding his fingers closely. The light from the low sun fell on the windows of Queen's Gift, painting them with gold.

"We must make Queen's Gift the most productive plantation in Albemarle, Mary," he said as he lowered the sail.

"The loveliest plantation in Albemarle," she repeated after him. "You and I together, Adam."

The boat touched the float. From the forest, the damp earth gave off a woodsy odor of bracken and leaves and rotting brush. A warm, dank odor, redolent of the Earth's fecundity.